Shattered Omega

Omnibus

Marie Mackay

Edited by Caity Hides
Cover design by Marie Mackay

TRIGGER WARNINGS

Trigger warnings include non-con and dub-con between love interests.

Outside of romance there is sexual violence and unwanted alpha bites as well as bullying and humiliation on page, self harm. Experimentation, and rejected mates. There is also self branding, violence, experimentation, rejected mates, and depictions of mental health struggles. In passing mentions there is drug use (via experimentation), brief suicidal ideation, and brief references to human trafficking.

Other content notes include on page sexual content. A bratty FMC, spanking, body betrayal syndrome, and somnophilia. Please note this is a non exhaustive list. Please note if sexual assault outside of romance or violence toward FMC on page is an extreme content warning, listen to the end of this content warning section.

Skip now to avoid minor spoilers for sexual assault trigger.

In Chapter 15 of book 2 there is a depiction of sexual assault on page.
There is a [*] serious content trigger note before it begins so you can skip the chapter.

Details: It depicts oral sex both unwanted, and outside of the romance. The passage includes action beats of event itself, though kept to a minimum, with the FMC focusing on her emotional state in order to maintain distance. It is most extreme in the first half of the chapter.
If you would like to skip the entirety of chapter 15, the end of the book (last page) contains a Chapter 15 Summary which includes non explicit details of important information so that you can continue the book without missing plot relevant details.

Shattered Omega

Book One

"To those who don't fit in the world like they're told they should yet deserve to find love anyway."

Marie Mackay

CHAPTER 1

Dusk

I'd come for a thief.

Instead, as I crouched upon a time-worn stone windowsill, cloaked by faded red curtains and the darkness of night, I found something entirely different. Entirely more valuable.

The omega was strange and anxious as she fiddled with her room decor and talked to herself. She was small, with summer-warm skin, and an impressive—if messy—cascade of honey-brown waves that swung to her waist. I'd been around enough omegas to maintain the conviction that our pack was broken beyond repair. We never had, and never would, be drawn to one, our normal alpha instincts long since scorched away.

Until now.

Just in time.

The price of coming to this godforsaken academy meant we would have to choose an omega tomorrow at the ball. It was a task I had been dreading before this moment.

I'd come here for… *something in particular*, I thought, though I couldn't remember what anymore. I remained frozen as I watched her work. She adjusted her suitcase on the floorboards at a peculiar angle. She moved to her wooden bed, shifting sheets, blankets, and pillows. She tugged the edges, so the corners tumbled from the middle of the bed.

Was *this* beauty? It was a word I had begun to believe society had fabricated to keep us chasing fairy tales.

It wasn't until she backed up, pretty eyes narrowed on the sheets, that I realised her intention. She'd turned all the squares or rectangles in the room on their sides, and her chest loosened as she took them all in. Then she got to work on the wall hangings, turning each to odd angles. If she couldn't balance one quite right, she'd tug it off the stone wall and tuck it under her bed.

When she finished, she grabbed a silk nightgown from the suitcase.

I only just stopped my groan as I watched her pull off her dress, revealing smooth, tanned skin beneath black lace. I was rock fucking hard when she stood before the mirror, taking a deep breath through her nose, eyes closed briefly before returning her chocolate brown gaze to her reflection.

"Tomorrow it's all going to be fixed," she told herself.

I cocked my head, a smile on my face as she tucked a misbehaving lock of honey brown hair behind her ear.

She was right.

I didn't care who she was or where she came from, nor about stolen pills—or even that she had no detectable scent right now.

I didn't care about her plans or dreams.

Tomorrow, I would select her: a gift for my brothers, because I knew in my soul that this omega, clenching her fists at her sides nervously—*she* was mine.

She took another breath. "They're your mates," she said, voice breathy and gentle. "They have the best scents *ever*, and they're *going to pick you.*"

Mates?

My heart tripped, elation crashing into a brick wall. She couldn't have caught *our* scents; we'd suppressed them since we'd arrived.

Was she matched to another pack?

I halted an unnerving growl on its way up my chest. My lips drew back in a snarl, and it was only pure shock at my own primal instinct that halted me from revealing myself right then.

And thank the heavens, because next, she reached for her eye, tilting her head, and carefully removed a coloured contact with the tip of her finger. And with that movement, she gave me everything I needed. Beneath the brown of her contacts, her eyes were golden.

She was a gold pack omega.

An omega left behind.

Vulnerable.

One the world wouldn't even punish me for dark bonding.

All rational thought fled me completely.

Rookwood Academy was my one chance at the impossible, and I was here to claim it.

The problem was, I was shit at all of this. At the rich people, the academy etiquette, and trying to navigate the sheer number of omegas and alphas I'd been around in the last few days.

I'd remained quiet the whole time. It was my best option given my social capacity: I was twenty-one years old, and four of those years, I'd spent hidden away in an Estate, made to hide my nature for how broken I was. The rest of my life before the Estate—it was gone. Memories I didn't know anything of—except that nothing in my life had lent itself to social graces.

Here, I was passed in the stone hallways by others who had everything I dreamed of. Omegas that lived free, who already had what I wanted—to just be normal. The students here had a happily ever after waiting, with friends and family, a pack to love them. It was everything I'd been told I couldn't have.

"You aren't normal, Shatter. Not your scent, not your instincts. You have to stay here now, where the world can't hurt you."

But Aunty Lauren was wrong—I'd known when I caught the scent of my mates. She'd told me I would never scent match a pack. I was too damaged…

Only I had.

Because I had *seen* them today—my mates.

The ones I'd come for.

I'd dared to get close. They were celebrities here, one of the most prestigious packs in the school. Alpha packs and omega hopefuls doted on them, and I'd been able to get near enough that I'd caught their scent once more. The first had been when they'd visited the Estate, and I'd been told I must have imagined it. Now, I knew I hadn't, and once again, I caught their scent, and they didn't catch mine.

Not *yet*.

I'd hurried through the courtyard and turned the corner around an arch draped with foliage, stopping and leaning against it as I hugged my bag to my chest. Birds chirped, and the scent of earth and flowerbeds tangled with the traces they'd left behind.

Sunflower and sesame seeds.

Passionfruit.

Coconut and plum.

Perfect. Sweet.

Normal. Soothing and calming to all the rough edges that made me wrong. It was the balance I'd never had. The balance I'd been told I would never find.

It was finally safe to let my scent blockers lapse tonight. By the time they wore off, my mates would be waiting to offer me safety for the first time in my life.

Tomorrow was the ball, where Rookwood Academy's alpha packs chose the omega they would board with for the year.

At last, they would see *me.* The whole world would right itself as I claimed my one shot at a normal life.

With a deep breath, I faced the mirror in the tiny dorm room I'd been assigned. A cleaner had been in, and she'd ruined my peace, straightening everything the way it shouldn't be straightened. I'd already tried my best to make it right again, my anxiety dialled to ten as I switched all the angles so that I'd be able to catch sleep tonight. I needed to be at my best. Living like this was hard, without alphas to soothe me or drugs to dull my urges.

The early September air warmed my skin, and I tugged off my dress, replacing it with a silken nightgown. It was new, and much nicer than the cotton nightdress I'd had back in the Aster Estate. It had been in the suitcase I'd stolen at the New Oxford Central Station from a well-off-looking beta woman. I'd thought whatever she owned would help me fit in at an elite academy. I think I'd been correct—I'd received a few stares, but I'd mostly fit in.

"Tomorrow, everything will be fixed," I told myself.

Tomorrow, I'd become theirs.

I breathed deeply, fixing my gaze on my reflection. The person who stared back still didn't seem quite right. That was why I'd come, though—to reclaim some of myself. "They're your mates. They're *going* to pick you."

Feeling better, I leaned over my vanity, carefully removing the contact from my right eye. The contacts had been given to me by Aunty Lauren (only for emergencies) and were highly illegal.

Another thing I wouldn't need, soon enough.

My mates would fall for me like I'd fallen for them. They wouldn't care about my eyes or my scent. They wouldn't care if I didn't have social graces, or didn't know where I came from.

I hated my golden eyes, but I hated sleeping with sore contacts more.

Being a gold pack omega was a choice—that's what society said. To become gold pack, an omega had to fail to turn up for the injection the Institute said omegas should get within the first year of perfuming. Without it, their eyes would turn gold at the end of the year, marking them as outcasts. Enemies. Omegas who broke the rules set in place for everyone, and were capable of birthing rogue alphas, who could risk the safety of the rest of the population.

If I had chosen not to get the injection on purpose, it wasn't a choice I remembered making. Another thing stolen by memories, and I resented these eyes, wishing instead I could be worth more to the pack I was chasing.

I was a freak, *even* with the colour of my eyes—an omega so broken, only a pack would fix me. And my strange scent had nothing to do with that at all. Gold packs, at least, could have sweet scents. They, at least, were destined for scent matches, like I was told I shouldn't have. But I was broken, even for an omega with golden eyes.

I was reaching up to remove the second contact when I heard a sound that made my heart stop.

The shuttering click of a phone camera.

My heart dropped, and I spun, wide eyes fixed on the window.

I'd left it halfway open to enjoy the warm breeze before autumn arrived. Only, someone waited on the windowsill beside the curtain, tucked away and easy to miss.

The alpha leaned forward from the drifting curtains, eyes fixed on me. His phone was out as he snapped another shot of my mismatched eyes. One of true gold—damning me—one brown, a deception surrounded by a dozen laws that would damn me all the same.

I recognised the sweep of black hair against dark skin, and my heart sank.

He planted his boots on my floorboards and straightened, still not standing as he gazed about the room unhurriedly. I opened my mouth to speak, but terror left my throat dry.

Dusk Varis.

An unbonded alpha from a pack as powerful as my mates.

Dusk and Umbra Varis were brothers, even if they didn't look it one bit, while their third pack member, Ransom, had yet to make an appearance at the academy.

I knew who he was for two reasons.

First, I'd overheard more gossip about them than I had of my mates. Cold and quiet, they received no visitors and ignored all the attention directed their way by omegas.

Second, I'd broken into his pack home only days ago. Unlike most packs and omegas who flaunted their scents, Dusk and Umbra had been scentless every time I'd passed them. I'd known what that meant. His pack's student apartment was on the third floor, conveniently close to a fire escape, and I'd snuck in through his window during dinner two nights ago. Sure enough, I'd found a bottle of scent blockers to replace the one I'd almost finished, and I'd taken it.

Now the cold, dark eyes of Dusk Varis pinned me in place. His head was cocked, as if witnessing something curious, and his scent was still as imperceptible as mine.

We stared at each other for ages. I couldn't move, as if the phone he held had me in a vice. Then he lowered it, eyes darting down as he tapped on the screen.

I stumbled toward him, desperation hot in my veins, speech finally returning. "W-wait!"

He could ruin me with that photo.

Ruin *everything*.

Dusk glanced up at me, halting briefly. "Came for a thief. Found a stowaway," he murmured. He reached over, plucking the pill bottle from my bedside table.

I drew up a few feet from him, gaze flicking between the bottle and his face. An entirely different sort of panic seized me. "It's... It's not what you think."

"So, you *didn't* steal this from me?"

"I-I would have given them back." I only needed them for a few days.

"Begs the question…" he mused, standing at last. His towering height had me taking a quick step away, no matter what desperation had to say about it. He twisted the top, examining the contents. "Why not just take a few?"

Self-preservation.

That was the answer I couldn't give him though, not with the damning picture he now had on his phone. If something went wrong—if my mates couldn't save me—and I was found to be a gold pack among the predators in this place… These eyes left me vulnerable to cruel packs and alphas who would enslave an omega without blinking an eye. The law wouldn't even punish them for it.

My voice was rough. "I would have given them back."

Dusk gave me a lazy half smile, setting the open bottle back on my bedside table. My eyes darted to it, then along the surface of the table to the knife he'd left untouched. It rested behind my glass of water, my only self-defence—and a weapon I didn't truly know how to use.

His grin widened as he followed my gaze.

Again, he said nothing.

That photo could ruin you…

I edged closer, unnerved by the cool silence between us. It was like a dare, that stare.

I couldn't help the way my eyes drifted from the knife to his phone. He didn't move as I stepped toward him.

"You have to get rid of the picture," I pleaded.

He raised an eyebrow at me, lip caught between his teeth as he watched me curiously.

I was so close to the knife.

This time, his gaze never left me, as if he knew exactly what I was doing. Instead of stopping me, he sank down to sit on the side of my bed.

I darted forward.

The second my grip closed around the handle of the weapon, his aura burst into the room, smothering the space. It shivered in the air, invisible energy that alphas had, a threat that threw my every instinct into a panic. My breath caught, my gaze darting to him as I clutched the knife.

His aura was massive.

Terrifying.

It would make him faster and stronger. Right now, he could kill me without a thought.

The knife… I swallowed.

My only hope.

I moved as fast as I could, whipping the blade in front of me and pressing it to his neck, heart in my throat, knowing this might be the last thing I ever did.

But he didn't move.

Not even with me crouching over him, the deadly blade at his throat in a victory that felt strangely empty.

"Delete the photo," I hissed.

"Can't." He flipped his phone with an incremental movement. I looked down to see a text conversation on the screen.

My chest tightened.

He'd sent the photo to a chat.

How many people were in it?

As I watched, a text popped up in reply.

> Umbra: Is this just for us, or are we putting those lovely golden eyes on blast?

His pack.

That had to be the only people he'd sent it to.

He watched me with glittering yellow eyes, the phone held loosely in his hand. "So, you're here to trick your mates?"

How long had he been there? How much had he heard of me talking to myself?

I couldn't remember all of what I'd said.

"N-no." I tried to drag my gaze from the text on the screen, blood thundering in my ears.

Not trick them.

I *would* come clean.

But I couldn't wander around this school with golden eyes. It wasn't safe.

I fought the tremble in my fist as I clutched the knife.

He could bite me into a dark bond right now, and no one would blink. I'd be at his mercy for the rest of my life. Every command from him or any of his pack would be law for me, a compulsion I couldn't fight without excruciating pain.

That was the threat I lived under with these eyes. That was the warning of Aunty Lauren, telling me to stay in the Estate, to be a maid for the rest of my life.

Stay safe. Stay hidden.

I… I couldn't. Not when I *knew* my mates were out there.

I needed that photo gone. If he sent it around the school… My scent blockers wouldn't wear off until tomorrow afternoon. My mates would never discover who I was.

He still watched me, waiting for me to say something else.

Is he angry at what I'd done? The packs here were prestigious. I knew many here might consider my presence as a gold pack an insult.

"I was going to tell them," I hissed again, trying to make him believe me.

He breathed a laugh, entirely un-threatened by the knife pressed to his throat. "Who are *they*, Gem?"

I shivered at the nickname, my hairs standing on end. My instincts told me to back up right now and flee for the way he watched me. For the way he'd said that name. Something about it was a promise.

A promise I didn't want.

"I…c-can't tell you."

He cocked his head. "I wasn't under the impression you had a choice."

"I *can't*." My teeth were gritted. This was it. Three months of my life to reach this point. There was nothing else on the other side.

"How very protective you are," he breathed.

My voice was choked. "I swear I'll kill you before I let you ruin this."

Would I, though?

His smile stretched, and he lifted his phone in a taunt. "Killing me *would* ruin this for you…" He tilted his chin slightly as if testing out the way my knife felt at his neck. "Whatever *this* is."

I swallowed. "What do you want?"

"I asked *who* these lucky alphas were."

"I…" I had to measure my breathing so panic wouldn't overtake me. "They're not a part of this. Tell me what you want from me."

I'd given up everything to get here, and I was so close. I jumped as his grip closed around my waist, dragging me against him until I was firmly on his lap. I stilled, a chill running up my spine at his touch. It was foreign, something entirely new.

"A choice, then…?" he asked. I flinched as he brushed my cheek. "That's *if* you don't want the whole school to know before the ball."

I tensed. "What choice?"

"You tell me which pack you're so *desperately* keeping secret. Or…" His thumb trailed down to my lips. "You give me first run at what will be theirs tomorrow."

"W-what?" I didn't understand.

He dragged me closer, head tilted as if truly enjoying the way the blade pressed against his neck. His free hand lifted to my chin, thumb brushing my mouth. "I want those pretty lips wrapped around my cock."

I jolted back, a snarl on my face.

His eyes sparked with delight, and his grip on my waist became vice-like. I felt his arousal beneath me, and I was caught between the urge to wriggle away, and keep the blade steady at his throat.

"What will it be, omega?"

My breathing hitched as I tried to untangle his request, my mind splitting in a million directions, clawing at solutions that didn't exist.

I *could* tell him which alphas were my mates… but the amount of power that would give him… If he got to them before I did with that picture, what would happen?

I knew what it was like, catching the trace of your scent match for the first time. It had shifted my entire world. It had led me to this place, determined and bold. But I had been the only one who'd known at the time, with my scent hidden as it was. I needed to do that for them, like they had for me.

If they found out they were scent matched to a gold pack *before* they met me, though…

My chest heaved, eyes darting between his. He seemed curious, as if he truly didn't know what I would do.

"Whatever deal I take, you'll delete the photo," I whispered.

He cocked an eyebrow. "I won't send it to anyone else."

"I'll… I'll only agree if you delete it." I shoved the blade harder against his skin, enough to draw the slightest bead of blood.

His responding rumble of a growl sounded more pleased than scared. "I'm keeping the photo, Gem. You're the sexiest thing I've seen in a long time."

I stared at him, searching for the joke.

As far as omegas went, I was a mess. Alphas didn't want me around. It was because of my past, the one I had such scant details of.

"Decision?" he asked. "Or do you want me to make it for you?"

I didn't trust him. Not one bit.

But… the second option… it would be over the moment he left. My mates would never be involved.

They would never have to know.

I drew the knife away slowly.

Silence hung between us forever, as absolute as the trap he had me in. I still gripped the knife uselessly while he remained perfectly relaxed, waiting to see what I would do.

Anxiety sent my mind into disarray—scattered beads across a wooden floor.

I almost opened my mouth to ask again—because he couldn't be serious—but I caught myself.

He was giving me an out, as foul as it was.

And he had no idea where I'd come from, what I'd done to get here. What I'd do to see it through.

I didn't know what he expected, but I had to ignore his low chuckle, my heart smashing against my rib cage, as I sank to my knees.

CHAPTER 2

Shatter

I was an omega, and Dusk was an alpha. This… should be easy, right?

I stared up at him, unsure. I was sure I'd never done anything like this before. His bright yellow eyes drank me in like a man starved, and it made me want to vanish.

"No one finds out," I whispered.

He reached out, drawing his knuckles along my cheek almost lovingly before brushing across my hair.

Was it tangled? Would he think it was a mess?

My waist-length, honey-brown hair was always a fucking mess, and I'd not made any extra effort today. I'd been planning on showering tonight, so I could be my best for tomorrow. And now I had to find a way to… to please this alpha without preparation.

As if all the preparation in the world could change your scent and make you desirable.

I blinked back the tears that threatened.

Worried more about your hair than what your mates will think if they find out what you're doing right now?

But I *was* doing this for them. He would ruin it all if he found out. The Lincoln pack was the most powerful pack in the school. If Dusk found out what I was to them, he could use that.

"I won't tell a soul." His voice was melodic as fingers sank into my hair.

Dusk's eyebrows rose as he waited, as if I should be doing something.

He wanted me to get his… oh.

I winced.

He wanted me to get his dick out.

Fucking pig.

He laughed again as I averted my eyes and fumbled at his zipper. I just had to get this over with. *It means nothing.*

Nothing compared to what my mates would bring me tomorrow.

"Tongue out, beautiful," he murmured.

I clenched my jaw, staring at him, the knife useless in my grip. I didn't want to let it go, though.

Finally, I parted my lips slightly. He drew me forward, guiding my mouth to the warm tip of his cock.

I let out a whimper of fear, unsure of what to do.

"Relax, Gem."

I searched the room wildly. Did he expect me to look at him right now? I didn't want to. But closing my eyes made it feel like he'd won.

He pressed his tip into my mouth, and my eyes snapped to him in shock.

He's going to know you have no idea what you're doing.

My heats didn't behave like they should, but I'd never spent any with alphas.

"You're so pretty, all nervous like that," he breathed.

A horrible whine rose up my chest. Traitorous, because it was equal parts anxiety and elation at the praise I wasn't used to hearing.

I hated him.

I hated him more than anything else on this stupid goddamned planet, finding me at my most vulnerable, twenty-four hours from my mates. Alone.

And here he was, delivering lies and getting a reaction from me.

He couldn't mean what he said. He wasn't my mate, and I was nobody.

Useless…

I gagged as he drove his length to the back of my throat without warning. My eyes were wide as I clutched him the best I could with the knife still in my grip. He held me there for a long time, my lips pressed against the base of his swelling knot. A pathetic sound rose in my chest, fury and grief, as he stole this from me. From my mates.

Finally, he released me and let me catch my breath.

"How is an omega as lovely as you new to this?" he asked. "There should be alphas beating down your door, getting on their knees for even a whisper of a kiss from those sweet lips of yours." He pressed his shaft in again, this time, only part way.

I looked away, unable to see the taunt in his eyes as he made fun of me like that. He *was* making fun—taking joy in how fucking worthless I was.

I *hated* him.

That thought fueled me—discordant as it was, with slick between my thighs. That was new, too. I'd never been *right* as an omega, and I'd *never* had reactions like this to anything.

I was as pathetic as he was cruel, that's all, listening to praise as easy as that. He was lying through his teeth to see my reaction. He knew the truth, like every alpha before him had. There was nothing compelling about me at all. Easily mistaken for a beta—unless an alpha caught my scent. Then they were more disgusted… or even violent.

He was preying on that.

Dusk's grip on my hair was painful as he dragged me over his cock roughly, a constant onslaught down my throat, threatening my gag reflex with each thrust. My eyes watered, fingers of my free hand grasping at his leg, as if it might help.

Survive this. Tomorrow, everything will be better.

Then I'd find scent matches who would see me for who I was—a woman I didn't even know.

It was impossible to look away from him now, at the victory in those intense yellow eyes as he used me like this, his smile cruel and bright.

I was a worthless nobody.

Easily blackmailed.

But my mates were worth all of this. Together, we might be able to claw something back from what my past had stolen from me.

"Pick it up." Dusk's growl cut off my panicked thoughts.

What? I didn't know what he was asking—no, demanding. I gagged as he choked me with his length, not letting me go.

I whimpered, unable to breathe, gripping him hopelessly, trying to process words that wouldn't untangle themselves. He inched me further over him, and tears wet my cheeks as I tried to wrench back.

"Pick up the knife, or do you want my knot too?"

With a whimper of terror, I finally understood what he wanted.

The knife…

The knife had slipped from my fingers.

I fumbled for it, ignoring a sharp pain as I gripped the wrong end and the blade sliced through my skin.

"*Don't* drop it again."

I found my hold on the handle with desperation and held it tight, hoping that would somehow make this end quicker.

He groaned, eyes flickering between the knife and me as he drew out slowly.

"You're so perfect," he growled as I gasped ragged breaths around the tip of his shaft. I shut my eyes, rejecting those words. "Eyes on me, Gem." Again, he slid his cock all the way to the back of my throat and held it there.

Breathless, I whined again, chest heaving before I forced myself to meet his gaze when he didn't let go.

"You don't like me telling you how beautiful you are?" he asked. "Because you don't want it? Or because you don't believe you're the most captivating omega I've ever met?"

I tried to ignore it, but he wasn't done. "I'm going to take you home, give you a nest, and fuck you like you're the last omega on earth," he breathed. "Your mates will be dust in the wind compared to the throne I'm going to put you on."

Real tears formed in my eyes this time.

He drew out completely, letting me gasp for breath as I tried to stifle my stupid fucking reaction to his empty words. My body bowed, my hand clamping over my mouth, needing this to be over.

Tomorrow, he would be nothing but another of the thousand obstacles I'd overcome. Meaningless.

Nothing.

"Are you leaving it to me to finish?" His voice cut off my thoughts as he tilted my chin up to him.

What?

I couldn't process the question or the rush of panic that seized me when he said it. All I knew was the furious expression twisting on my face. He loosed a silent laugh, tongue pressing against his canine as he watched the reaction I tried to contain.

If he had to finish himself, that would be fucking karma.

Not a bad thing.

Not an offence of instincts I'd never had to contend with before.

His eyes finally broke from me, sliding instead to his phone. "Shame."

No.

I couldn't risk him sending that picture out. Not when I'd come this far. Fists trembling, I parted my lips, shame finally trumping my panic.

I tried to ignore that more slick pooled between my thighs as he pressed his tip to my tongue and slid back into my mouth.

"Fuck," he groaned.

I dug my nails into his legs as he roughly choked me with his cock once more. I hated the sound I made deep in my chest as he thrust me over his length viciously, fist tight in my hair, knot threatening my lips with each thrust.

When he came at last, holding his shaft down my throat and forcing me to swallow his seed, I shoved down the faintest flicker of pride.

But I couldn't tear my eyes away as he found release, a low groan in his chest, teeth catching his lip, and a crease in his perfectly straight nose. It seemed fascinatingly vulnerable. It wasn't what I expected an alpha to be like.

Finally, he let me go, and I sagged on worn wooden panels.

Then I clamped my hand over my mouth as more hot tears streaked my cheeks. Not for what *he'd* done. For what *I* had.

I didn't know how much time had passed. I heard him shift, and the tug of his zipper, then the creak of his knees settling on the floor beside me. He tucked a lock of my hair behind my ear.

"You were such a good girl," he breathed, and I almost looked right up at him as the low purr rose in his chest.

Why was he purring?

"I'll let you tell them." He dropped the phone before my eyes onto my lap.

I stared at the screen that blurred in my vision, reading the text he'd typed out but hadn't yet sent.

Don't send it anywhere. Let's keep her all for us.

I couldn't move.

His purr stuttered out, and he drew the phone away slightly. "You... don't want that, little thief?"

I grabbed his wrist before he withdrew it completely, a terrified sound slipping from my chest.

My finger shook as I pressed it to the screen and watched the message pop up in the chat. It was supposed to be over now, but the text promised more.

I wanted him gone and to never come back—not more. Although, there was a faint scratching of curiosity as to who the others were at the end of that chat.

What did they think of the photo?

What would they think of me?

What would Dusk tell them tonight when he returned? That I was... enough? Maybe...enough that he wouldn't notice how broken I was—that I might pass for any other omega he might find in this academy?

No.

It didn't matter.

Not when I had my mates to meet tomorrow.

"What do you think?" he murmured. "Are you more angry at me, or you, for enjoying that so damn much?"

I couldn't look at him as I hugged myself.

"Leave." I squeezed my eyes shut, which meant I jumped when I felt his grip in my hair, dragging my lips to—

My eyes flew open in shock as I realised what was happening.

He was… kissing me.

With not a care in the world for the cum he'd forced me to swallow. He groaned deep in his chest as I tried to rip myself free, but he towered over me, twice my size, and even with only one hand fisted in my hair, he held me against him with ease. He drove his tongue past my lips, exploring my mouth, and something about that held a frightening truth.

When he drew away, trying to string my thoughts together was like wading through a swamp.

"Fuck your match," he breathed. "Fuck the universe and its stupid choices. I'm going to give you the world."

And with that, he left me alone with the violent claws of a panic attack that didn't even know what to do with a crazy bitch like me.

CHAPTER 3

After further study, I've discovered the subject's scent is not only aggravating to alphas, but actually repels all scent profiles it is paired with.

Shatter

"With the state of your condition, with your scent, you shouldn't risk going near alphas."

"But…but for how long? I'm…I'm an omega, I have to—"

"Your scent profile isn't like anything we've seen. I'm sorry, Little One, but we've got the results. There is no scent match out there for you. Without mates… I can't, in good conscience, allow you around alphas. Not now, not ever."

They'd told me I would never have mates, but they'd been wrong. About the scent match. About everything.

And today, it all changed.

Today, I could finally discover myself with my mates at my side.

I stepped into a grand room decorated with crystal chandeliers. It was bustling with life, and above were thousands of warm, twinkling lights illuminating the sea of extravagance below. Well-dressed staff members were already moving around the ball, serving drinks to the guests. I entered with the other omegas, all of whom were hoping to score a place with a rich pack, so their education would be guaranteed and paid for. I knew the dream for many here, like mine, was more than that—a pack for life.

The alphas ahead, the ones to be courted, were all dressed well in dark suits with styled hair. The omegas around me were in gowns that outshone mine, but I didn't look completely out of place.

My outfit was simple: I wore a black dress—the nicest one in the suitcase—and matching flats. I'd put my hair was up in a bun, so no one would realise I had no idea how to tame it. My neck remained bare and was free of visible marks, which was the most important thing when trying to gain alpha attention.

I scanned the room as I moved further into the crowd. There were more omegas and alphas in one place than I could have imagined. The aura capacity was high, so security was a must, legally speaking. There was a lot of competition, but I knew what I needed to do.

When I reached them, everything in the last three months would be behind me. Everything, including Dusk Varis.

I swallowed.

He was a permanent fixture in my mind. I'd barely slept last night, and I wasn't daring enough with the scant makeup in the suitcase I'd stolen to try covering up the bags under my eyes. Worst of all, I couldn't rid myself of the thought of him, no matter how hard I tried.

"Dusk Varis doesn't like anyone." Those were the words of the omegas around me. They were obsessed with him and his stupid pack. Those who were ready early had been waiting outside for hours now, and the gossip had been flying.

"No one knows which omega they'll choose. They've stated no preferences. It's a fair game. If you can win them over, you're sorted—but they don't like anyone, don't seem that nice, to be honest. Still, worth it."

I squeezed my eyes shut, rejecting that.

Dusk Varis was a foul monster who didn't deserve any omega.

Any omega…? Or an omega who isn't you…?

I ignored the way my stomach turned at the idea of another omega joining his pack. My instincts were off-kilter from all the scent blockers. It meant nothing, though. He'd done something last night he couldn't take back, and the primal side of my brain couldn't let it go.

"You're so perfect…" In the few moments I had found sleep, Dusk's words had crept into each dream previously reserved for my mates. Would he say that to just anyone? Or had he meant it? Something about the way he'd looked at me last night had made me feel as if I might be the only omega on the planet.

I scowled at the filthy, traitorous thoughts violating my brain.

That's exactly what he wanted you to fucking think.

It didn't matter.

I had mates waiting for me. They'd wipe him from my mind. Then Dusk could pick whomever he wanted.

Fixing the scowl on my face, I followed the entering throng of visitors, hating that a part of me searched for that sweep of dark hair and piercing yellow eyes as much as I searched for my mates.

I had to stay focused on my task. He was in this room. He'd probably even *see* me, but he couldn't stop me from getting to them anymore. Another obstacle in a million, on a journey that would soon be behind me.

My scent blockers would have faded at last. I'd planned it meticulously, as I couldn't be without scent blockers for too long, or I might find myself in trouble—especially with a crowd like this, with alphas everywhere. My mates, and the bond we would have, that would fix everything.

I couldn't catch my own scent, but usually the looks people gave me told me enough. Here, however, odd looks weren't out of the ordinary. My mates wouldn't be repulsed, though. In minutes, I would know that truth.

Anxiety sent me spiralling, and I snatched a drink that was offered by a passing tray. From here, I could see the tables at the head of the room. It was the only area of the party that had seen very little movement so far.

There would be layers and layers of political manoeuvring that happened at those tables, but I could ignore all of that. Mates could break all rules.

I was about to find safety beyond anything I'd previously known. But if my mates were going to save me, I had to go to them now, before any omega got there first. I steeled myself, downing the whole glass and weaving through the crowd toward them.

I caught sight of them the moment I stepped past the thickest parts of the crowd. The tables at the head of the room were occupied by only the most elite alpha packs.

And there they were: The Lincoln pack.

Every other thought drained from my mind. Elation rose in my chest, equal parts thrill and fear as I started toward them.

The universe began its orbit around them anew.

It had been like that the first time I'd seen them, when I'd caught their scent through the bannisters, looking down at a grand dining room in the Aster Estate. I'd hidden there for ages until I was discovered and shooed away. Even then, I'd snuck back out to stare at the alphas who were visiting.

That was where I'd heard about their plans to enrol in this academy. It was why they'd visited the Aster Estate in the first place: my uncle, the owner of the house I'd come from, was their sponsor for enrolment in this very academy, which was how I knew they'd be here. It had been a journey to reach them after I'd fled the Estate, one filled with doubt and fear.

But I'd had no choice.

Colour, scent, and sound all blurred as I began toward them, faster and faster, until I barely noticed I was running. The ballroom around me vanished, all the snow-white tablecloths, the beautiful gowns, the echoing clinks of glassware and chatter now a mere blur.

A daring smile surfaced, unfamiliar muscles flirting with the corners of my lips as I ducked through the crowd. Through the throng of omegas who not only dressed better, spoke better, acted better—and were actually able to walk in heels. I'd tried (and failed) to balance in heels while dressing in my dorm this morning.

And none of it mattered as I reached them, breathless. The hair I'd warred to tame was already tumbling from my bun, spilling around my pink cheeks in misbehaving feathers as I caught my weight on the back of the single open seat at their table.

The seat set aside for the omega they would claim tonight.

The seat set aside for me.

Their scents filled my lungs with each heaving inhale, burning and beautiful in the surrounding air. Passionfruit. Sesame seeds and sunflowers. Coconut and plum.

Mine.

My mates, with aromas fresh, sweet, and intoxicating, flooding from lungs to veins and setting nerves on edge, as if every inch of my body was pricked by a thousand fireflies.

Eric, Gareth, and Flynn looked up at me in surprise, each as captivating as I remembered them to be.

I couldn't move.

After all this time, battling through a world I didn't fit into, I'd made it to them once more. My scent blockers were gone at last. They would see me for who I was.

I could be me.

And I couldn't move as nerves scored my system, turning me to stone.

I desperately tried, and failed, to open my mouth. To say anything.

With them, I could be an omega at last, no longer having to bury my spirit under six feet of soil. I could be *their* omega, in a pack where my instincts were right for once. Where I would have a true place. Where I could claim them and be claimed, and I could take care of them. I would find myself at last—to take back what was stolen.

In a pack, where my scent was *wanted.*

It was everything I'd been told I could never have.

A strange silence stretched until, finally, Flynn spoke. "Can we help you?"

He was pack lead, with sleek black hair and an air of wealth that the other two couldn't quite match.

Something was wrong. A frown knotted his raven brow, disturbing his flawless, rich-brown skin.

For him, the world hadn't come to a halt…

I managed to open my mouth, but my throat went dry, and nothing came out.

"I thought this event was omegas only." That was Gareth, and he gave me an odd look. He was the largest of them, with a sweep of blond hair and a dazzling smile I'd seen yesterday when I'd snuck by them. He wasn't offering me that smile right now, not like I'd expected. "This isn't some beta press event."

Beta?

"I'm…not…" I tried, as if my choked words could unscramble my brain. I couldn't catch my own scent, but how… how could *they* not, either?

The sound of the same shiny, black, pointed shoes Uncle had always worn clipped upon marble behind me, and I caught a new scent in the air. Something as dangerous as it was captivating, even in the face of my mates.

Midnight opium.

It hinted at florals, of pale petals and a trace of vanilla. The more dominant shades were of deep amber and roasted coffee. And then there was the last part, the piece I couldn't place, and yet seemed all too familiar.

I knew who it was before I turned, because there was only one alpha I'd ever met who could possibly have a scent like that. And last night, he'd been masking it.

"Shatter." His voice was cool, liquid silk filling my ears, his aroma overpowering all of my mates'. A hand brushed my waist. "Wrong table."

I looked up at him, frozen in fear, lips parted in shock as I still worked to catch my breath. Dusk was everything I'd spent all night trying desperately to forget.

The few pieces of black hair tumbled down his forehead, a beautiful contrast to the amber brown of his skin. His bright yellow eyes held mine intently.

"Dusk Varis," Flynn said. Every eye was drawn to the man with his hand around my waist. "They're allowing the Kingsman pack to select a beta?"

I'd vanished to my mates.

Dusk slid into the open chair, tugging me against him. I felt the insistence of his draw, as if he wanted me to sit on his lap.

No.

Everything was wrong…

A beta?

Dusk set his phone on the table beside his glass. On it, I saw the thumbnail of that damning picture, revealing my golden eyes, in the chat to his pack.

Terror and confusion collided, leaving me at his mercy as his touch became more insistent. I sank onto his lap, still unsure of what was going on. My mates only had eyes for the *alpha* who'd sat at the table, while my universe was still in orbit around them.

"No," Dusk said mildly. "But her scent is too good to share." He tugged me closer, and my nails dug into his arms beneath the table hard enough to draw blood. "I drugged her with enough scent blockers for a small horse last night."

He lifted his glass of water, swirling it.

I blinked, my mind tumbling out of control. The glass of water from my bedside table… The one I had slammed back to rid myself of the taste of him in a confused daze before bed.

He'd drugged me?

He'd drugged me, and now my mates didn't know who I was.

And he was telling them with such blatant arrogance. A faint smile was even playing on Eric's lips at the words.

Did he think I'd purposely gone along with it? That I'd chosen to?

I could barely focus, my mind clawing for a way out and coming up blank. If I opened my mouth right now and told these alphas I was their mate, would they believe me?

How could they? My story was far-fetched enough, without adding Dusk's claim.

Even for a gold-pack omega, I'm a freak. Most alphas hate me, so I escaped to get to you—the mates I should never have had. Now, if I ever want a chance at a happily ever after, you're my only hope.

Right.

Then add Dusk *fucking* Varis, an alpha from the only pack with more power than theirs in the school, slipping into my dorm last night and drugging me, so he could claim me instead…?

There was no way…

And if I blurted all of that, and they didn't believe me, then Dusk would send that picture across campus. My golden eyes would mark me, and I would be a dark bond target for every vicious pack here.

The Lincoln packs' attention drifted to me now, but it wasn't the attention I had come for. Their interest in me was piqued purely on Dusk's claim.

He set something on the table before me—a necklace with his pack's crest upon the silver moon that hung from it.

The trophy we were to place around our necks when we accepted a pack's claim. Even still, it was bold. Some omegas wouldn't get them until the end of the first week.

Dusk wasn't only claiming me; he was making a promise that he wouldn't change his mind.

"So, Gem." The silk of his voice was a breath tickling my ear. "Why don't you show everyone who you belong to?"

This *could not* be happening.

His voice was low and just for me as he added, "They don't seem particularly interested, do they?"

He absently tapped his phone screen again, the threat clear as day: put on the necklace or fight off dark bonds long before my mates could find me.

And we both knew the conclusion I had come to last night, the one that hadn't changed. Whatever threat Dusk posed wasn't greater than a dark bond. Because it was the one thing *he* hadn't done. He hadn't even threatened it.

His grip on my waist became vice-like as I continued to stare at the necklace.

"And smile for me," he whispered.

I couldn't manage that.

As I reached for the necklace, my world crumbled. My movement became familiar and mechanical, and there was no smile on my face. I remained perfectly neutral.

I sank against Dusk as I broke inside, the cool metal of the necklace a weight on my skin. A chain.

A cage.

And I knew, as Dusk nudged me in an indication to stand, the cage was closing.

Just like before.

"You have to hide it all, girl."

"I don't want this. I want to be like you." Aunty Lauren was an omega, too, but she was poised and smelled like fresh linen. Uncle liked her scent. He couldn't take his eyes off her when she walked into the room.

"I know, Little One. But you can't be. Do you know how hard I had to work to get him to let you stay here? The Institute is calling."

I hugged myself tighter, almost splitting my lip with how hard I bit it. "Why am I like this?" I whined.

Why couldn't I remember anything from before the Institute?

I'd woken up in white-hot agony one day, and now I was here at an Estate. It was better here; I was no longer buried in the smothering silence of drugs that stole my time... my mind... my everything. But now I was ruled by instincts I was fighting to keep in check, so I could follow rules I couldn't grasp.

"I'm sorry, Little One. Stay small and don't draw attention to yourself. He's doing his best, but the Institute will take you back at any sign of trouble."

"I don't mean to be trouble." I was trying so hard. I knew nothing but the place I'd come from. Everything here was foreign, overwhelming, scents and sounds and people I didn't know.

"I know you don't, but it's your scent—your instincts. You can't go destroying the room I worked so hard to convince him to give you."

"It wasn't on purpose."

I just... I couldn't make it right. I don't know what happened. They'd given me such a nice room, but the very walls, it seemed, had come for me. When I'd come to, the room was in pieces, and my blood still burned with fury I couldn't remember.

"No nesting. No scents," Aunty Lauren was saying. "We have to keep it all down."

"What about heats?" My voice was so quiet, she almost didn't hear it.

"You tell me the moment you think you might be close. Drugs, it'll have to—"

She cut off at the low, frightened moan in my chest. "No more drugs."

"Shatter, look at me. You have to listen. If you don't make this work, we'll have to send you back. The Institute won't allow you in the world by yourself."

I'd find a way to escape Dusk, like I'd escaped the Estate. Bites were rare in first term, which meant I still had time to reveal myself to my mates.

I could wait this out.

He nudged me to stand again. I couldn't help staring at the Lincoln pack as he got to his feet at my side, arm still possessively around my waist.

I'd done this before, and I could do it again. I'd thought today was the day they would see me, but I was wrong. I could survive a little longer.

I had to.

When I'd run away, I'd risked everything. Now the walls were closing in, and I was out of options; Rookwood Academy was my last chance. It wasn't just about reaching my mates. I was broken, and if I didn't leave this academy with a bond, there was nothing waiting for me on the other side.

CHAPTER 4

Shatter

The sounds of the ball were faint echoes in my mind as Dusk led me through the room. I could get through this. I would give him and his pack what they wanted until their guards were down.

The scent of my mates faded behind me.

One step at a time.

One breath at a time.

I could do this.

I was trying so hard to keep calm that I barely noticed Dusk leading me out of the main room. Not until we were around the corner in a much quieter hallway.

He turned to me, snapping his fingers and grabbing my attention. I stared into his depraved eyes as he hooked his finger beneath my chin. "Where did you go?"

I fought my snarl, not wanting to give him even that. "You… you win," I told him.

For now.

I grasped at the satisfaction I felt when his lips pursed at my words. "Don't be so dull. You'll bore Umbra out of his skull like this."

He didn't like compliance?

Fuck him.

"You should have chosen a more interesting omega then, *Alpha*." I threw that last word in with perfect balance, watching his expression darken.

"I picked the *only* interesting omega. Don't disappoint Umbra. I promise, he's much worse to handle when he's bored."

A chill crept up my spine, but I didn't flinch.

"Less than twenty-four hours," he mused.

I watched him, not understanding what that meant but refusing to ask.

"Twenty-four hours, and I was going to find out who your perfect fated mates were, anyway. I'd almost believe you wanted my c—"

He hadn't finished when I reacted. My palm caught his cheek. A slice of pink left where my nails scraped his face.

My breathing hitched, dread crawling through my veins as he straightened. There was an unnerving smile on his face. "There she is," he purred. "That's the omega I claimed."

"This necklace isn't a claim."

He smiled, reaching for it and running his fingers along the chain. I tried to suppress a shiver, suddenly unable to look at him. "It is, Gem. It means you come home to keep us balanced, right?"

I clenched my jaw, refusing to answer that, even as he drew closer.

"You'll be so good at that, right? That perfect little body of yours is going to be so good at keeping us balanced."

I felt the blood drain from my face, and all I could manage was a shake of my head.

His laugh was low. "I'm looking forward to all the ways I'm going to play with you." His fingers lifted from my necklace, closing around my chin, trying to get me to look up at him, so I squeezed my eyes shut. "I'm going to get you so addicted to my cock that you'll never even think of them again."

I shuddered at those words but still refused to look at him.

"And…" Dusk went on. "When you come home with us tonight, you'll get to see the nest we built for you."

My eyes snapped open, and it was a cruel trick of nature that the fragile, wounded part of me lifted its head in interest.

They had a nest… for me?

Safety.

It was all my omega brain could focus on. It wasn't a given that chosen omegas would get a nest. Many packs waited until they were sure the omega was a good fit first, not wanting to risk attachment.

By the way his smile curved wider, I knew he could see my desperation. It was hard to rid myself of it. My heart was pounding, and the arid wasteland, where my omega instincts had bloomed once upon a forgotten time, stirred.

"You like that?" He leaned close, hand dropping to my neck, cupping it.

I couldn't take my eyes off him. My lips parted as I tried to unscramble my brain. His hand closed tighter around my throat as he spoke, his low voice a seductive purr. "A nest all of your own?"

A faint, traitorous half whine slipped out, stifled in an instant but impossible to miss.

He smiled. "You get it, *if* you behave for me."

"I won't be your pet." I tried to hold on to the conviction that the nest didn't matter. Not from him.

"You forget what I have on you."

"The cost of that secret is a dark bond," I spat. "I'll only listen if what you offer is better."

Dusk chuckled, and when his fingers clamped down on my neck again, my veins lit like fireworks. I squeezed my eyes shut as his lips brushed my cheek. "My offer will always be better."

He let me go, slipping his arm around mine, indicating he wanted to return to the main room. Before he took a step, I asked the question that had nagged at me all night. "W-why didn't you dark bond me?"

He *wanted* obedience?

He would have it by now, and no one would have blinked twice, once it came out that my eyes were golden.

Dusk's smile was unnervingly genuine. "I won't bond you until you *beg* for my teeth on your neck."

Beg him?

He couldn't be serious.

He began leading me back to the main ball, a smirk on his lips for the vicious expression on my face.

"I can walk by myself," I hissed, fingers gripping his arm, but not daring more.

He didn't let go as he wove through the crowd toward his table. "I'm helping. If you did something stupid to make a scene, you'd be racking up even more punishment that your uptight, little omega ass doesn't want to pay."

Punishment?

I barely had time to linger on that because we arrived at his pack's table. It was far emptier than any of the others. Only one alpha waited for us, and Umbra Varis had his gaze locked on me as I approached.

Like Dusk, he was devastatingly attractive, which was a stupid decision from the universe. He had richly tanned skin and sandy blond hair that was trimmed at the sides with a few messy strands sweeping to his brows. His eyes were a warm grey, like a desert storm, and almost matched his hair. He was big, even for an alpha. I knew he'd tower over me if he stood, and the cream-coloured T-shirt he wore did nothing to hide the muscles beneath.

Dusk slid into a seat two over, which was an obvious hint that he wanted me between them. I stepped, instead, toward the seat on the other side of Umbra—and as far from Dusk as I could get away with.

Umbra snorted. His eyes were trained on me intently. "Well, shit…"

I swallowed, peering up at him, unsure what to make of that.

"I don't like admitting when Dusk is right, but you do look even more fuckable in person."

My lips parted in shock at his words, but then I finally caught his scent, distanced as I was now from Dusk's midnight opium.

Wolfsbane and blood.

What kind of fucked-up alphas were they? Both with scents that were far from what I'd been told to expect.

You're one to talk…

"*Most* omegas hate my scent," he said, guessing as to why I'd paused. "If it makes you feel any better."

I shook my head before I could catch myself. That… wasn't my reaction. I wasn't normal, and alpha scents had more of an effect on me than the average omega, yet something about his scent was particularly comforting. More so, knowing that most people hated it. His was earthy and sharp, like that first outdoor breath of air after a spring rain, and not unpleasant.

"Where's… your third?" I asked, distracting myself from the charming smile on Umbra's face at the hint that I might not hate his scent.

Ransom Kingsman was missing. He wasn't pack lead, since that was Dusk, and yet the pack *was* named after his family.

"Doesn't much enjoy fancy events like this," Umbra said.

"It was required," I countered.

"Nothing's *required* of Ransom." Umbra chuckled. "He's a Kingsman."

I let that settle in; there was a member of this pack even less tied to the rules than Dusk.

"So, that's your scent matched pack?" Umbra shifted closer, still eyeing me with interest. "Condolences."

I shot him a sour look but didn't reply. There was something off about him—too intense, like his casual words were weighted with something else.

A front.

A lie.

I tilted my head, trying to understand what I was seeing, but then his next words tripped me up entirely.

"I'd have deep-throated Dusk, too, if it meant not having to fess up to that."

My gaze slammed to Dusk, fury twisting my face, but he didn't look smug, like I'd expected. His expression was rigid, and for a moment, I saw his eyes flick toward my mates' table, a darkness in his eyes.

Umbra was unperturbed, his voice sing-song. "I can't wait to see what scent the universe decided was enough to hand *you* over to *them*."

Despite the slander, my heart leaped with sudden hope.

They'd allow my scent blockers to wear off?

If that happened, and I could just *get* to the Lincoln pack…

He made a sound somewhere between a hum and a purr. "Don't get ahead of yourself. We're keeping that scent all to ourselves."

I gritted my teeth and tried not to, but I couldn't help glancing up at him. I despised that every single thing they did or said aroused curiosity. Despite everything, they *were* something different. Something I'd never seen before.

My stomach clenched, wondering what the coming week would be like.

I said nothing, trying to keep my anxiety in check as they ate. Dusk slowly prodded at a plate of roasted veggies and rice. Umbra was working on a variety of snacks, some of which were from shared dishes at the centre of the table.

A server stopped by and asked me what he could bring me to eat, but I shook my head, and he left.

People were staring, I realised.

The Kingsman pack had an omega so soon, and I was a spectacle. Attention snagged on me, and I tried to ignore it. Worse was how hard I struggled to keep my gaze from the Lincoln table. The one time I failed, I spotted a small crowd circling. Gareth and Eric were basking in the attention, but Flynn was leaning back in his seat, and our gazes met.

My heart leaped in my chest, and for the longest moment, I couldn't take my eyes from his. Then I jumped violently at the scrape of a chair and looked around to see Umbra getting to his feet, announcing he was getting dessert.

I still hadn't eaten, despite the snacks scattered across the table and my empty plate. More servers were arriving to take some of the plates of food away.

My mind was so far from food, though, instead stumbling over the what ifs of the week to come.

What would they expect of me?

Would they expect anything at all, or would all three of them be like Dusk, willing to take whatever they wanted, as if I didn't matter?

I hadn't seen enough of Umbra to get a read on him, but he hadn't touched me yet, which set him a mile apart from Dusk. He was odd, though, and whenever I shot him a glance, I'd catch him watching me. He wasn't leering, but his attention did make me feel like prey.

My thoughts cut off as Dusk stood, and, to my irritation, slid into Umbra's vacated seat beside me. Then he began forking food onto my plate before the remaining food could be taken away. As if I was a child.

Or maybe just... *his* omega...?

I shoved the thought back and caught his wrist as he tried to pass me a bite-sized meat pie.

"I'm *not* eating."

He snorted, tugging my grip free and continuing to dole me out food. "Don't, then. Let me take a little more from you and go to bed hungry."

"I *hate* you," I hissed.

"It's hot. Keep it up."

The childish part of me wanted to get up and move over to his previous seat, but he might just follow me again, since he'd already shown he wasn't above that.

Maybe it would be worth it, though, for the simple spectacle of the Kingsman pack playing musical chairs with their omega on the night of the choosing.

Actually...

I got to my feet, decision made.

Let them all know how much I despised these men.

But Dusk didn't follow me when I sat down in his old chair. Instead, he dug his fork into the food on my plate and began eating, entirely unperturbed.

I tried not to focus on him, but the rest of the plates on the table were gone now. It was the only food left, and I couldn't stop his irritating words from floating into my head.

"...Let me take a little more from you..."

And it was as if, with each bite, he was. I didn't even *want* the food, but then he'd made it mine, and now he was stealing it. A growl threatened to come up my throat. I shoved it down, forcing my attention away.

He was being loud about stealing my goddamned food, his fork clinking on the plate each time, grating at my fucking sanity.

Finally, unable to stand the infuriating smirk on his face, I reached over and snatched the plate back—just as Umbra arrived.

"What the fuck's going on?" Umbra slid into the empty chair beside me. He set down a plate stacked with desserts.

"Couldn't wait for them to serve it?" Dusk asked him.

"Do *you* want to stick around longer than we have to?"

"Guess not." Dusk was glancing about the room dispassionately.

I pretended to ignore them, focusing instead on angrily stuffing a Yorkshire pudding into my mouth with as few table manners as I could possibly muster.

"Did they starve you before you arrived?" Umbra asked, watching me with a startled expression.

Dusk's snort of laughter had me swallowing the pudding with painful speed, which drew tears to my eyes.

"No," I snapped, scowling.

The stress was getting to me. I was taking Dusk's bait like the child he was treating me as. I shoved the plate away, folding my arms and then unfolding them, for the bratty image it so clearly gave.

"They, uh… didn't put up much of a fight, then?" Umbra asked, peering at me as he began on his mince pies. "Are they *really* your mates?"

"Yes." My temper flared. "They don't know who I am yet."

"Ah." He cocked his head. "That's the answer, then? Once they know, they'll rescue you?"

I glared at him, but Dusk was leaning forward, clearly interested.

"I told you to smile for me, and you disobeyed." His glittering eyes scanned my face as he watched me, searching for the response I refused to give him. "Do you think you looked like you *wanted* to leave with me?"

"I don't think anyone in this room believes I want to be here," I hissed.

I *wouldn't* give them that.

They could blackmail me, but they wouldn't get me to smile so everyone else could believe I was happy. They didn't know what I'd survived—the lengths I'd gone to, so I could keep that last bastion of flickering fire alive in my soul. They didn't know how far I would go to find a place where I could rekindle that.

They didn't know that, more than anything else in the world, I wanted to be me again.

I wanted what had been stolen.

"So, your mates," Dusk mused. "Your *saviours* watched me sweep away an unwilling omega before their very eyes and didn't intervene?"

"There are rules," I spat. The necklace I'd put on marked the choice they couldn't contest. "They can't, and you know it."

"Right…" He nodded thoughtfully. "They would have intervened—*wanted* to—but couldn't. They were *torn* by guilt, knowing they should step in. Instead of banging their new omega tonight, they'll be restless with the knowledge of what they saw and couldn't prevent."

My mouth was dry as Umbra breathed a small laugh.

Panic clawed at my chest, and my eyes darted to the table that hosted my mates. There was someone seated with them.

Raven hair and porcelain skin… She was beautiful. Roxy Vasilli was one of the more *well-off* omegas attending today.

A perfect match for them…

"Do you think there's a single alpha attending tonight who doesn't know what goes on here? That aren't here *because* of it?" Dusk asked, and the question drew me back to him. "It's a place to watch desperate omegas fight over alphas. There's nowhere else you can guarantee such blind, docile compliance—as every omega in this room will be so happy to offer. And that's if there wasn't a deal struck behind closed doors." He leaned back, waving a hand in the air to the room in general. "You think you're the only one here hiding golden eyes?"

A stone dropped into the pit of my stomach as he said those words so casually. I almost lunged for him, halfway from my seat, before I could stop myself. I scanned the area quickly, but the room was buzzing with conversation, and the nearest tables were distant enough that his low voice wouldn't carry. My heart was pounding in my chest, and all thoughts of Roxy Vasilli wiped away as he went on.

"You think you're the only one with a haunted look, seated at a pack table with no flirting or courting or competition?"

Again, I looked, an icy dread settling over me as I took in the room with a different gaze.

"What your precious mates saw wasn't special," Dusk said.

But… he was right.

Some tables were quieter than others, and the dividing line didn't seem to be wealth or status. There were some, like ours, that hadn't seen much movement at all. An omega had arrived and slipped into a seat, and that was it.

"Your mates aren't here *despite* the depravity poisoning every corner of this room; they're here *because* of it."

Again, there was a twist to his darkness, dragging him from what I knew, demanding my attention and interest. He spoke about the alphas here as if he wasn't one of them.

"And you're different?" I asked, finally dropping back into my seat.

It was Umbra who replied, his low whisper brushing my ear. "We're like no one you've ever met, but don't let your guard down. We're here because of that depravity, just like they are."

CHAPTER 5

Subject is showing improvement since arrival. Scent and hormone suppressants are almost out of her system. We attempted to turn her room into a nest, however, she became so frustrated at minor imperfections that she destroyed it before completion. She showed regret after the incident and claimed no memory of her actions. She struggles to regulate emotions when her hormones are heightened.

Shatter

Neither Dusk nor Umbra wanted to linger at the party.

I did.

Despite the vicious looks of envy every omega was shooting at me, it was safer. My mind kept getting caught on Dusk's promises back in the hallway.

Worse was the thought of a nest and the twisted part of me that begged me to endure what he would do in order to claim it.

From alphas who weren't my mates…

But what would it be like?

Cold and bright and horrible and clinical. Everything I didn't want.

I was sure of it.B

They were getting to their feet, and I followed mutely, hating how I wasn't sure what to do with myself. Dusk didn't leave me hanging for long, slipping his arm into mine. The touch was innocent enough that I didn't protest, letting him lead me out of the room.

The stares were more brutal now that I was facing them head-on, and I ducked my head, hoping as few people would remember my face as possible.

It didn't matter one bit.

The Kingsman Omega.

That's what I was about to be known as across the whole school.

Before, I hadn't cared what they thought, the anticipation of the safety my mates would offer drowning everything out. Now it all mattered, right down to my reputation, because instead of protection, I had nothing.

My heart raced faster and faster the further we got from the party. They would have a place in the residences. The richer alpha packs had huge apartments, or so I'd been told. And they'd had a couple of weeks to settle in.

We crossed through covered walkways and into the residential building. With each step, feeling the warm September evening air on my skin, passing students, panic sank its claws deeper. By the time we reached the door, I had tunnel vision.

This was their territory.

Their home.

I was this freak of an omega—and they didn't even know that. As far as they were concerned, the worst thing wrong with me was my golden eyes.

What would be expected of me once I entered? What if they were relying on my instincts? Dusk was right, the whole point of the omega partnership was balancing. Young alpha packs in places like this were often hormonal and volatile, and some academies mandated an omega partnership like this to keep the peace.

Yet my instincts were off-kilter, and my scent wasn't soothing. I imagined, for a moment, the drugs wearing off tonight. That Dusk caught my scent and sent me away.

And I would be lucky if sending me away was all he did…

But by that time, would my scent matches already be too attached to Roxy Vasilli?

Tears threatened my eyes.

I didn't know if I was more scared of Roxy with my mates tonight or of being turned away for being useless.

And they might tell my scent matches anyway. I'd assumed the scent match would fix everything. My aura, my insecurity… that they would be enough to make me feel confident.

But my mates had looked right at me and not known who I was.

I tried to bury that as I stepped inside, needing to focus on what was ahead. I'd been in here once before. I'd snuck in and out quickly through what I now knew was Dusk's bedroom window.

The student apartment was large and much more modern inside than the rest of the old buildings that made up Rookwood Academy. When we entered, there was a hallway to the left, down which I could see two doors that led to what I knew were bedrooms. The other bedrooms had to be upstairs, as I could see two more doors beyond the balcony overlooking the open living area and kitchen. The whole place was fully furnished and looked modern, with a sleek spiral staircase between the upper level and main floor.

Clinical, I told myself. *Like your nest will be.*

"Rules," Dusk said, having led me to the couch, where he dropped down, peering at me expectantly.

I swallowed. "You *cannot* make me follow your rules."

Dusk leaned back, cocking his head and tapping a finger absently on his knee. "The rules were for you, Gem, but if you'd rather a free-for-all…"

"I'll…" I had to clear my throat, noting the spark of feral delight in his eyes as he spoke. "I'll hear them."

His smirk sent white-hot rage bubbling in my chest.

"Our rule: until classes officially start, the nest is your territory. No one enters unless you ask."

My mouth popped open at that statement.

"Mine…?" The word was embarrassingly vulnerable, but it slipped out before I could catch it. I'd never been given a second chance at a real nest after I'd destroyed the first, even though I dreamed of one. Everyone was too worried about how volatile I would become.

I tried to claw the pathetic shock from my face, glancing at Umbra as if he was going to tell me Dusk was joking. He'd settled on the arm of the couch, watching my reaction curiously.

"And a-after classes start?" I asked.

"We can enter." Dusk's words sent a cold stone sinking in my stomach, though I wasn't surprised. "The whole point of the omega pairing is to keep us balanced. But in the nest, no one touches you without permission."

Oh.

Okay… That wasn't what I'd been expecting, either.

"That's our gift to you," he said. "We uphold that end, if you uphold yours." The words were weighted with the obvious. Still, my weary fucking heart seized that gift like it was a life raft.

"And… my rules are?"

"Just two," he said. "You do as you're told. No hesitation, no arguments. The nest is yours, but we can ask you out of it if we need something."

An off-balanced laugh escaped my lips. "I might as well have a dark bond."

"If you believe that, then leave. You'll find out soon enough." He waved his phone at me.

I glared at him, taking a step back. "I *won't* act like your slave."

The nest wouldn't be right, anyway. Not the way I needed it. It would have colours I couldn't stomach or materials I didn't want.

Like you've ever had the option to be picky before.

Not that it mattered. It was an illusion. Nests were supposed to be safe. Nothing here was safe.

Except… that was exactly what he'd just fucking offered.

Safety.

A promise of my own space.

"You'll see the nest before deciding," he said mildly, getting to his feet.

"Seeing it won't *change* anything," I said.

It wouldn't.

I absolutely wouldn't let it.

"No harm then," Dusk said, making his way down the hall. "Don't come"—his voice floated back down the hallway—"and Umbra will carry you."

I looked at Umbra, but he shrugged with an "I definitely would" look, and I stepped after Dusk reluctantly.

I noticed the way the scents changed as I stepped further into their home, as if wolfsbane and dark opium were in the very walls. There was a trace of something else, too, but faint enough I couldn't pick it out.

Ransom.

It had to be. Ransom Kingsman was their third pack mate. The one no one had seen yet.

Did he even live here? He had to, but if he did, shouldn't he be as present as the other two?

I hugged myself as their pack's scent engulfed me entirely. It should feel like a threat, as if, with every strain of a wooden floorboard beneath my boots, I stepped into the enemy's den. Instead, my chest loosened. It was one of the curses I'd woken with. I was unstable, and the scent of alphas settled me more than anything else in the world. And yet, when they caught mine… I swallowed, shoving the thought away and trying to ignore my reaction to the apartment. Fucking biology. My body knew what he was offering. It wanted this nest, no matter how wrong it was.

Would you be getting a nest if you'd gone home with the Lincoln pack? a small voice asked.

But if they didn't have a nest ready, they would have made one the moment they'd realised who I was. Of course, they would have.

Ahead, Dusk had drawn up before a door and was turning the handle.

I heard Umbra's low hum of contentment at my side, and I realised my pace had quickened with my heart. I balled my fists, deliberately slowing myself down.

It *would* be horrible. White walls and sterile metal trays flashed in my vision. Metal straps with bright lights… At the least, it would be generic, with windows, and stretching space, and—

I froze as I reached the doorframe, staring in with wide eyes.

There was no bright open space like I'd expected.

I hated windows, but this room had none. Instead, the lights were warm, with Edison bulbs in cosy lamps or hanging from the ceiling. There was a huge bed in the far corner, and the roof sloped down above it, keeping it isolated, like a separate cave. The floor was made of wooden panels, different to the rest of the apartment, with shag rugs, each tilted…

I tilted my own head, staring at the shapes across the room, the warm tapestries that were hung strangely. Even the *bedding* was… but I *couldn't* be seeing that right…

It was a real-life nest.

One being offered to *me*.

It's too dangerous to let your instincts run wild, Shatter.

No scent. No nest. No alphas. No pack. No instincts at all—bury them deep.

But this was right. Perfect.

Too perfect.

It flew in the face of every traditional idea of a nest that I didn't want, as if it was built *for* me.

More than everything else combined, *they* weren't in it. Instead, I caught the faint trace of hollowness that scent-dampening mist left behind.

I didn't realise I'd stepped in until I felt a firm hand close around the back of my neck, halting me.

Dark opium choked the clear air of the nest, and his voice was a breath in my ear. "You want my gift, Gem. You take the terms *and* your punishment first."

I stared at him with hatred, because he knew the impossible situation he'd put me in. As if I had a choice. He tugged me back a step, then the door was closing. My breath caught as it clicked shut and the nest vanished from sight.

Safety.

That's what it was. As foul as he was, he had offered me something my instincts had latched onto. Now it was gone, my pulse was erratic and my chest tight.

"Or… you can take your chances running from every cruel alpha pack in Rookwood Academy."

My palms were damp with sweat as I clutched my fingers together. My hormones were in overdrive. Stress. Anxiety. I'd been in the presence of my mates today. That still shook me. And now the nest—all so he could bully me into being whatever he wanted.

"Are those my only options?" I asked, my voice strained.

He frowned, fixing me with a strange look. "What do you mean?"

"If you're going to use the photo at every turn, why bother with the nest? Just tell me I have to do what you say, or the picture will go out."

"Would you prefer that?"

"Yes." The answer came before I could even think about it. "You're trying to pretend this is something it's not."

He folded his arms, eyes sliding to Umbra for a moment. Umbra was resting against the wall lazily, seeming content to watch, but gave a shrug. "Lay it out, then," he said. "What's the threat for the picture?"

"You're our omega," Dusk replied instantly. "We are the only ones who get your scent."

"So…" My heart raced as I glanced between them. "I can decline your nest and your stupid rules."

Dusk snorted, rolling his eyes. "Yes. You can decline your own fucking nest, and the rules that give *you* boundaries."

My vision narrowed as I stared at him, and my voice was shrill with rage. "Getting me to do whatever you want isn't for *me*!"

"Certainly fucking is."

I lost it.

My temper had always ruined everything, and still, that meant fuck-all when the world bled crimson. I leaped for him with a snarl, fury searing away all sanity. I needed him to hurt, and I didn't care about the consequences. I easily ducked his outstretched hand as he tried to grab me, caught off guard.

"*Fuck—*" I screamed, managing to get onto his back, nails out like claws across his face, and neck, and back, anywhere I could reach. *"—you!"*

I was braced for an aura that never came.

Instead, with a wrenching pain at my temple, Dusk tore me away from him with a solid grip on my hair.

Next thing I knew, he had me slung over his shoulder and was carrying me to the kitchen. I shrieked, trying to kick him, and only succeeded in sliding further down his back, leaving me worse off.

He dropped me, and before I could dive away, he grabbed my arms and pinned them behind my back. Then I was shoved forward, my body bent over what I realised was the arm of the couch.

Fuck—

"W-wait!"

He paused, and I tried to turn or move or—anything. But he was pinning me to the couch with his hips and easily holding me down with one hand. Then he bowed over me, crushing me even harder against the couch.

"Shatter." His voice was a growl in my ear. I could feel his body against me.

Shit.

He was hard.

Like, rock-fucking-hard and crushed against me.

That pretty much wiped all thoughts—and even fury—from my brain, a whine escaping my chest.

Terrified?

Panicked?

Aroused?

I literally had no idea. I wasn't used to my body reacting this way.

There was nothing else in the world but dark opium and the feeling of his body against mine. Then his fingers slid around my neck, squeezing enough that another whine slipped out.

"*Anything* I want you to do, I can make you do," he breathed. "The rules are for *you.* They give *you* control. And you're right. You don't have to take them. But act like a brat, and you'll be treated like a brat."

All I could do was pant desperately, my mind in a million pieces with his hardness pressed against me. Consequences had never looked like this before.

It was worse when Umbra appeared, sitting down on the couch beside me, like this was the best show he'd ever seen.

"So," Dusk went on. "Would you rather I pin you to this couch while I spank you, or would you rather I let *you* hold still for *me*?"

What?

My cheeks burned.

He was going to… what?

His grip tightened on my neck. "Answer me."

Finally, I grappled back a semblance of control over my hormone-wired brain.

"L-let me go," I whispered.

"If I do, you'll behave?"

I squeezed my eyes shut, nodding quickly.

He released my arms, and I caught myself on the couch. I felt his warm touch at my hips, pushing my dress up to my waist, exposing my black lace panties.

"Lovely," he murmured, and I had to work not to lean back into his touch as he drew his knuckle along the edge of the lace.

Then he vanished. His weight on me was gone, along with his touch, and… and his hardness.

I froze, not sure what to think. I didn't want to look up at Umbra, far too humiliated.

Doesn't he want you?

A villainous sound came from my throat, but I passed it off as a deep breath.

There was a sound of a glass clinking, then running water. I looked up to Umbra at last. Without the feeling of Dusk pressed against me, the cogs in my brain began turning again.

The pupils of Umbra's desert-storm eyes were blown as his eyes met mine. There was a grin on his face, and I was close enough to make out each of the few freckles across his tanned skin.

I almost opened my mouth to beg him to tell me what was going on, but that would make a fool of me.

Then Dusk was circling the couch and sitting down, a glass of water in his hand.

I stared at him from where I was balanced, still bent over the couch like an omega in heat.

"You made me fight you, Gem. I want a drink before we start," he said, taking a slow sip. "But show me you *can* manage if I give you back some control."

I wanted to cry, but there was too much slick leaking down my thighs right now for that to even feel fucking real. *That was normal*, I told myself. It just meant I was an omega.

It didn't mean I liked *him*.

"Everything gets easier if you stop fighting him," Umbra murmured to me. "Learned that the hard way."

I grabbed the nearest pillow and buried my face in it, not willing to look at them any longer.

It took too long, and I didn't even begin examining why, during that time, I was so aroused. He was a fucking alpha, the likes of which I had never been near before. Even back on the Estate, the alphas I'd been around had been either older or bonded. I wasn't prepared for the reaction my body had to the scents of packs like this one.

Biology was a cunt, and that was all.

I'd still stab him if I had the chance, *that* I was sure of, at least.

Finally, I heard him stand, and I dared to peer from the cushion, to see him approach. Unsteady relief flooded my system that this would be over soon.

I felt the brush of his jeans against my thighs again and tensed, unsure of what to expect.

I jumped at the warmth of his touch between my thighs.

Fuck… That was way too close to—

"You're soaked, Gem." His finger trailed the sensitive inner flesh of my thighs, and I tried to wriggle away, knowing how much slick he'd feel.

His hand came down on my waist, holding me firmly in place.

So slowly, his fingers trailed down, down, down—all the way to my knee. And then his touch was gone, a low laugh in his chest.

"You can go."

That was all he said.

I paused, still bent over the couch, shivering.

It took me a long time to pull myself straight, eyes everywhere but Umbra or Dusk.

I swallowed, tugging my dress down, for all the good that did the glistening of my thighs.

"I don't u-understand."

Glancing at Dusk, I only found faint humour in his expression. My stomach dropped.

I'd disappointed him. I knew it.

This was my fault, somehow.

"Accept the nest and the rules that come with it, and I'll punish you for every bratty thing you've done. Until then, there are *no* rules—though, I'd guess, getting wet to the ankles for an alpha who isn't your mate might be punishment enough."

I couldn't take my eyes from his cold stare, shrinking beneath it. When I tried to edge from between him and the couch, he caught me.

"Where are you sleeping tonight?" he asked.

"What do you mean?"

"You rejected the nest. You sleep with me, or you sleep with Umbra." When the silence stretched, he finally gave me one of his cocky half smiles I was growing all too familiar with. "I assume it's Umbra."

I opened my mouth, argument already on my lips before scowling. Then I ripped my arm from his grip and edged around the couch, grinding my words out with difficulty. "It's the couch. I'm staying on the couch."

CHAPTER 6

Umbra

I'd dream about Shatter all fucking night. I just knew it.

She was an addiction, I could tell already, and I didn't care. I hadn't even caught her scent, but I'd seen what Dusk had. She was different. That fact was as absolute as it was impossible to explain.

She'd also been completely serious about not sleeping in either of our beds, which was a pity, but I was a patient man—unlike Dusk.

Right now, she was still in the bathroom, accompanied by her suitcase. I'd stood back and watched her haul it in, while she shot me dirty looks as I grinned at her struggle.

Things had changed in a blink of an eye. One moment, the need to choose an omega—to bring someone foreign into our home—had been an axe at our necks. Rookwood Academy rules: pick an omega or leave. Kind of stupid, but I thought the Academy was worried that, without an omega, too many alphas co-existing in a small space would cause issues. I mean… were they wrong? I don't know, but there were some pricks at the ball. I'd have happily started a brawl if Dusk wouldn't wring my neck for it.

Did Shatter make me more likely or less likely to do that?

It felt like… *more* likely.

But what if she was banging you? Or like… cuddling you and purring and shit and making you all balanced?

Hmm.

That would keep me busy.

Maybe they had a point.

Before yesterday, I wouldn't have been able to picture Dusk losing his mind and putting an omega's nest together in a frenzy, even if it had been odd, the way he'd done it with all the tilted squares and shit. He'd spent *hours* shopping this morning (I'd felt the occasional baby-rage fits through the bond). "*Too many fucking choices*", he'd told me after, dragging a dozen Nesting Needs boxes in. Then he'd carried in armfuls of hair products, more than I thought it possible to own—though, that was before I really understood how much hair Shatter had. The photo didn't do it justice.

Still, I was glad, because I wouldn't claim to be an expert on things like nests.

Ransom… Well, perhaps he would—My mood slammed into freefall at the thought of Ransom, eyes darting to the balcony that overlooked the living room. Up there were two doors. My room and… the other, quiet room.

Silent for now.

Silent was good.

I *thought* it was.

Dusk's low whistle broke that eerie quiet that settled over my mind beyond the static from the room up there. It splintered the surface tension, holding everything else at bay. A low, serene, and innocent noise.

My switchblade dug into the fist I squeezed it with. My sleeve was up, the blade pressed against the skin of my forearm.

I couldn't stop, not now. But at least I knew what was happening. That was the gift Dusk would give me.

He wouldn't tell me to stop.

Never tell me to stop.

How many?

One.

The blade cut a line. A count. Blood oozed, and I held it deep enough to scar, deep enough to slice, the pain like warm air rising up my lungs, the only time I could breathe with ease.

Two.

I cut again.

Three.

Was three enough?

It… it could be…

"She's deliberately taking ages," Dusk muttered.

A distraction.

"Is she?" I asked, trying to focus on Shatter. A little ray of light behind that door.

I didn't think she was deliberately taking ages, actually, and for a moment, I smiled.

Dusk would figure it out, eventually.

From what I could tell, she had pretty good self-preservation instincts, aside from leaping at Dusk like a feral cat. But everyone had a breaking point. And that teeny omega growl she'd loosed when she'd done it—that had been hot.

So had the follow up.

The two of them together were going to make life sweet.

We deserved a little sweet.

I blinked at that thought, nerves boiling up.

Deserve?

Nothing. You deserve nothing.

Pay again.

Four.

Again.

"Do you like her?" Dusk's voice fractured the mantra once more.

My gaze snapped to him. If it wasn't for the words stealing my attention, my aura would've split the air.

Kill him. Go again. It tried to continue, tried to ignore him, but my eyes were on him. My brother.

My voice was a rasp. "Yes." But I couldn't focus on that.

"She's for him," he said, eerily calm as he watched me.

Right.

Not for me. Not even for Dusk.

Enough, though? Could she be *enough? When no one ever had been before?*

If she wasn't, I would pay until there was no more flesh or bone or blood left. A fair exchange for a debt with no ceiling…

Dusk got to his feet, sensing how close I was to being free, knowing I needed movement.

"Shatter." He banged on the door. "How long are you going to take?" He took a step back, and there was another long silence during which, my need waned. Then his brow furrowed, and I felt a spike of worry from him through the bond.

Finally—*finally*—the trance broke completely, and I tucked the knife back into my pocket.

Dusk was worried?

That was… new.

"Shatter?" He knocked again, harder. "If you don't answer, I'm smashing the door down—"

"I'm fine!" Her high-pitched squeak came from inside. I saw a shadow shift beneath the door. "I, uh… changed my mind about that couch."

"You what?"

"I'm going to stay in here, actually."

Dusk went stiff, and I saw a flash of irritation cross his features. "You are not sleeping in the bathroom."

"You said there were no rules."

Oh, I really liked that *thing* her voice did when she started getting bratty. She better not stop with that attitude. Dusk was just not wired for that, and seeing him bend her over the couch had been hot. I wasn't wired the same as Dusk, but I'd have her all the same. It had been hard not to imagine how I was going to make her sweet little body squeeze me.

I saw—and felt—Dusk's indignation, but before he could launch his aura into the space and actually break down the door, I got to my feet, catching his attention.

"Come on, mate," I said with a laugh that was still too hollow. "We just got rid of the fucking *people.*"

This was supposed to be our home now, but for the last few days, it had been movers and fixers, bringing in the stupid couch Dusk had chosen. Sorting out our rooms to meet our needs. If he broke the fucking door, there'd be a repair man.

"Anyway, you fucking idiot." I grinned. "You didn't see it coming when she hauled her whole suitcase in?"

Dusk was still tense, but—perhaps not wanting to upset me so close to an episode, blood still dripping down my forearm—he gave in.

I wanted my space to be *mine.* Just me and my pack.

And Shatter.

I relaxed as Dusk took a step away from the door, even if his expression was tight. My smile felt more real.

I didn't mind her at all—and I *knew* her scent was going to be amazing.

CHAPTER 7

Shatter

I woke to the sounds and smell of sizzling bacon creeping through the crack under the bathroom door. I blinked sleep from my eyes in the dark room. Dragging myself out of my suitcase was rough. It had seemed like a more comfortable place to sleep than the floor or the tub, but now I wasn't so sure.

I sat up, listening to the sounds of cooking from the kitchen, fingering the necklace I still wore. The wrong necklace.

It wasn't hard to process what had happened, since my dreams had been busy with yesterday's events. Where I'd previously spent my nights imagining what would happen when I met my mates, now it was just Dusk and Umbra *goddamned* Varis. Midnight opium, wolfsbane and blood, and a third scent, still faint and indistinguishable. It was better than dreams about my mates with Roxy Vasilli all night, which haunted me now that I was awake.

Had they given her a nest?

Had she kissed them?

And here I was, captured by a pack I didn't know, so far from the protection of my mates.

I bit my lip, then jumped violently at a banging on the bathroom door.

"Umbra talked me down last night, but I *will* break the door down if you try to skip the intro session this morning."

I shrank where I sat, mind racing. The packs were supposed to attend a talk in one of the auditoriums this morning.

I *could* survive this. I just had to wait for the drugs to wear off and get to my mates.

Outside, I found Dusk setting the kitchen table and… shit.

He'd cooked?

He'd cooked a *lot.*

I don't know why that made me panic. It just wasn't supposed to happen. This was an academy for prospective elite packs; the alphas weren't supposed to cook. They certainly weren't supposed to cook every breakfast food known to man and lay it out across the counter like a feast.

Was he expecting guests?

"I didn't know what you liked," Dusk said, setting a glass of orange juice on the table beside a glass of apple.

What *I* liked?

This *wasn't* for me.

That would be insane.

"Where are the others?" I asked.

"Umbra isn't a morning person." Dusk turned and held out a hand to me. I stared at it, frowning and fighting the urge to take a step back.

He was dressed well this morning, with dark jeans and a loose cream-button up. He looked like a rich prick.

"I'd like to be civil," he said.

I fixed my eyes on his piercing gaze, almost choking a laugh at those words. He'd drugged me and stolen me from my mates. Now he wanted *civility*?

I chewed on my lip as his eyes darkened, his hand still out. He didn't like it when I rejected him. Finally, I stepped toward the table, taking his hand with a clenched jaw. I knew how fast he might turn this into a repeat of last night.

I would reject him, but maybe not so overtly. And, ideally, when he wasn't *in* the room.

His smile was irritatingly breathtaking as he tugged me toward him. Next thing I knew, he'd taken me by the waist and lifted me onto the one clear area of the table. He scanned my face and outfit, and I jumped as he brushed sleep from my eyes. The motion was… gentle.

He was far too close, taller than me, even though I was sitting on the bar table. I could see every detail of his face, the specks of warmer oranges in the yellow of his irises, the ridge of an old scar discolouring the smooth brown of his left cheekbone.

I heard him slide something across the marble top and glanced down to see him line up a pad and pen beside me. "Write down all your favourite foods and anything you don't like."

"Why?"

I don't know why I couldn't take my gaze from him. "*Tomorrow* morning, I'd like to bring you breakfast *in* your nest while finding those lovely golden eyes free of contacts."

His words drew my panic to a screeching halt. "I don't want your nest or your breakfast."

He'd told me the price of that nest, and I wouldn't be saying yes to it. Still, the words felt like lies. And I couldn't ignore that my stomach did a giddy flip.

Bring me breakfast in my own nest?

I shoved the thought away.

Dusk picked something small from the table and lifted his hand to my lips. I drew back, glancing down to see a scent blocking pill.

"No—"

"The deal for the photo," he reminded me. "Your scent is ours."

Knowing, from the curve of his lips, that my expression was bitter, I let him press the pill into my mouth. Then he handed me the orange juice to swallow it.

Orange might be my favourite, but I grabbed the apple juice, fighting a grimace at the sweetness as I swallowed it down. The faster I got it down, the faster he'd back up and stop drowning me in midnight opium.

"Open up."

"What?" I asked, startled.

"Show me you swallowed."

"I'm not a child."

"Could have fooled me, locking yourself in the bathroom like that."

He lifted my chin, ignoring my grip that bit down on his arm as I tried to shove him away. His lips were so close to mine, I could feel their warmth. The mint on his breath tangled with his scent. "Open up, Gem, or I'll go searching myself."

With difficulty, I shoved down my growl *and* my humiliation, doing what he asked and fighting the urge to kick him. He was so fucking smug too.

I refused to eat breakfast, even when it hurt not to. No one had ever cooked for me before, and he made me sit next to him with an empty plate while he enjoyed it.

I wouldn't accept his stupid breakfast, though; it felt like a betrayal. I told myself my mates would have done better. Flynn would have made me an even bigger breakfast—I'd seen the way he'd looked at me across the ball. I clutched on to that flicker of hope, that Flynn knew who I was, deep down, even without my scent.

When he finished eating, Dusk shoved the still-empty notepad toward me. I grabbed the pen viciously and scribbled one thing onto it, having spent the last few minutes coming up with a perfectly bitter response. His expression hardened as he read my words. He ripped the note off and tucked it into his pocket. "As you wish, Gem."

His eyes flashed with the same impatience I'd seen last night. Instead of reaching for me, though, he got to his feet and crossed to the main bathroom. He tugged the door open, flared his aura, and ripped the lock from it. My lips parted in shock, but I didn't even make it half a step toward him before it was done.

Fuck him.

The only fucking place in here I could find privacy.

Gone.

"All right." His smile was icy as he turned back to me. "Ready to go?"

Dusk led me across the grounds to the central academy building. His arm draped over my shoulder, so all the staring students knew that he'd claimed me. Umbra had said he was busy with another school thing, even though I'd seen the schedule and he was supposed to be coming.

Officially, classes didn't start until next week, but today were introduction lectures. It was the Academy introduction this morning, and our specialty introduction this afternoon. The Kingsman pack had selected Arkology as their primary specialty (which I would never admit my excitement about), so that was where we were heading. Arkology, broadly, was the study of Alpha-Omega dynamics. I had enrolled to find my mates, but I—like my mates—had chosen as many Arkology classes as possible. It was, I'd learned when looking up the class plans, a true passion of mine, stirring faint memories. I'd taken our shared interest as a sign, so it irritated me that the Kingsman pack shared that interest too.

Still, tucked in my satchel was a scone I'd managed to pinch when he wasn't looking. Just in case I got hungry, and *not* because it looked like he'd made them from scratch for me.

"What's the second rule?" I asked as he led us up the auditorium steps to the back. It had been bugging me—though, so had the thought of the nest waiting for me. I wasn't going to take it, but *if* I had to, for whatever reason, I needed to know.

"The rules are for you, remember," he said. "Show me you can follow the first, and maybe I'll let you in on the second."

I pursed my lips as Dusk stopped in front of a booth at the back. It was a strange setup. There were rows of seats for students leading down to the central podium for the lecturer. But at the top were booths lit with low lights. All of them, I realised, were reserved for the high-level packs.

A booth reserved for us, overlooking the whole auditorium?

"What are you thinking?" he asked, watching my expression as he slid into the booth. I realised I was staring around bitterly, my nose creased. "Too pretentious for you?"

I didn't answer, seating myself beside him while maintaining as much space from him as I could.

He was right, though. I stared down at the other students, all filtering into the rows of seats below. *That* was normal—not this elitist shit.

I frowned, considering that as I let the frustration drift in. It was like I could feel the stiffness of those chairs after sitting for too long.

A thick book balanced on one knee as notes were frantically scrawled in a notebook.

It was right…

Comfortable…

The feeling of Dusk's touch on my waist blitzed the flicker of a memory away, and I was too shocked to argue as he pulled me closer.

"I want you to behave like you're mine," he told me.

I didn't answer, mind still racing, trying to claw back anything of that feeling. Memories were precious and so rare… But it was long gone in the undercurrent of my fragmented past.

I blinked, completely off balance as a slender beta male stopped at our booth, laden with textbooks. He placed them on the table, his eyes darting between the two of us as he swept mouse-brown curls aside. "Is this all who'll be here today?" he asked.

At my side, Dusk cocked his head, assessing the beta carefully.

"I'm Bolin," he stammered, clearly thrown by Dusk's coldness. "They should have told you. I'm assigned to assist your pack. These are your textbooks, but if you need any extra help in your studies—"

"Leave them there," Dusk cut him off.

He swallowed with a quick nod, pale cheeks going pink. "O-okay… But I do have to give you my number, in case any of the pack needs anything."

Dusk looked unimpressed as Bolin typed his number into the alpha's phone.

I sat with that for a while after Bolin left, before curiosity finally got the better of me. "Help with studies?"

"Elite packs come here for prestige. Qualifications that elevate them even above other alphas. But you don't think this school turns out qualified scientists, lawyers…?" He waved his hand dismissively.

I peered up at him, confirming that truly was humour in his eyes.

"How much help?"

"I'm sure Bolin would do more than *help*, if that's what Ransom's wealth demanded."

"But… these are accelerated programs," I said. "They're sending people into important roles. They have medical and surgical classes. You can't just… cheat if you want to go on and be a surgeon."

Dusk's half smile might have been bitter, except he *was* one of the elite alphas in a position to take advantage of exactly that. He didn't say anything else though, tugging the pile of books toward us and sifting through them.

"These look dull as fuck," he noted. He flipped one open, *Arkology Studies, Vol.2*, and skimmed it with scowl. "You know, the whole academy thing sounded tolerable and shit, but now we have to do this crap?" He leaned back, but I ignored him. My eyes were caught on the textbook, darting past line after line. The clinical words were soothing to read. I'd always loved reading Uncle's textbooks, though he hadn't liked me touching his Arkology ones.

It wasn't until I caught Dusk giving me a curious look that I leaned back, averting my eyes. But as the lecture started—if it could be called that, since it was mostly an introduction to the semester—I couldn't help dropping my eyes back to the text.

In tiny sips, I drank in the whole page. Then, when Dusk excused himself to the bathroom, I dove in, scanning page after page after page, a spark of joy in my veins… until he came back.

When the lecture was over, I made to stand with everyone else, but Dusk caught me by the waist.

"We're going to wait here," he said. "Though, I'd like it if you were on my lap."

I shot him a hateful look. "I don't have to do shit that you say," I hissed.

"You don't," he said with a shrug. "No rules, remember? So, maybe it's better if you don't deny me. I'm not above forcing those perfect lips of yours back over my cock tonight. Do you think Umbra would like to watch this time?"

I stared, but there was no depth to the depravity in those glittering eyes, and I believed him.

I didn't even know why he'd chosen now—we'd be leaving soon—but I slid reluctantly closer, biting back my snarl as he tugged me onto his lap.

People filtered by, and he tucked my hair behind my ear, arm winding around my waist. He *wanted* the stares that came our way from the other packs and students. He wanted them to know I was claimed. It was why we were waiting.

At least, that's what I thought, until a familiar voice sounded to our right.

"Dusk Varis?"

My gaze snapped up in shock, heat flooding my cheeks as I found myself staring up into Eric Harrington's rich green eyes. My heart tripped, and I tried desperately to shift away from Dusk as his grip became almost painful.

"Spare us a minute?" he asked, eyes sliding between us.

Flynn was there at his side, Gareth too, and a scent of fir tree and orange, reminding me of Christmas, caught my attention. My heart lodged in my throat as I saw Roxy Vasilli's fingers woven into Flynn's.

Oh, damn.

She got a *Christmas* scent?

That seemed wildly unfair.

"I'm in no rush," Dusk replied.

Eric smiled, eyes snagging on me once more, before he glanced at Roxy. "Do you mind going on ahead? Meet us at the apartment."

Roxy smiled, and my blood turned to ice as she leaned up and pressed a kiss to Gareth's cheek. "I'll have something cooking by the time you're back."

Gareth looked charmed, but I noticed Flynn's dark eyes slide to me again, as if he couldn't help himself.

He definitely knows.

But… it wasn't enough.

They were living with Roxy now. She was so pretty, with pale skin, blood-red lips, and long, glossy black hair.

Would they fall for her?

I mean… how could they not?

So, when my mates slid into the booth, I was the only one drowning in my scent matches. The only one slightly heady with the experience as Eric began chatting to Dusk.

Proposed alliance. Something about being good for the image…

I couldn't keep track.

Roxy was ahead of me, but I realised I'd been going about this all wrong. *She* was probably doing this all right. I'd been focused on my mates because I needed them, but what if she was getting to know them? Finding out what they were really like, what they enjoyed—the kinds of things *they* liked to eat.

I needed them, and my ask, when I finally showed them who I was? It was going to be massive.

If I expected them to take care of me, I needed to have a plan to take care of them too. It shouldn't be hard.

We were destined for each other.

Stupid and socially clumsy I might be, but we were supposed to be compatible.

Still, I wanted to melt into the floor. I kept feeling their gazes drift to me like magnets. But my cheeks were flushed, and I couldn't maintain eye contact with any of them, not trusting myself not to blurt out something stupid.

They were really good looking. Flynn's mid-length black hair was messier today than I remembered. It looked a little harder to tame.

That was one thing we had in common.

Dusk shifted behind me, and I realised how rigid he was. He had been since the moment my pack had arrived, even when his words were smooth and perfect. His grip around my waist was tight, as if he was as uncomfortable as me—except that didn't make sense.

I tugged at my nail anxiously, trying to snag more looks without seeming creepy.

I had to do better than fucking hair if I wanted to connect with them.

Roxy's hair was glossy and perfect and tamable.

As they talked, I couldn't keep my eyes from drifting to Gareth, who was closest. He'd been playing with a pen that he'd set down as he piped into the conversation. It was all I could focus on. It was heavy, expensive looking, with marble patterns in purple and white.

Gareth's pen, with his sesame and sunflowers scent. My hand shifted to the table, still only half focused on the conversation.

It was a visceral need, something that ached right down to my bones.

My hand inched closer and closer as the conversation continued. I had no idea what they were on about. My mates were doing most of the talking while Dusk's responses were sporadic, each a faint vibration down my spine, pressed against me as he was.

I was an inch away from the pen, so close. Gareth had leaned forward, arms on the table, obscuring the pen from the others while he focused on Dusk.

That was it.

All I needed.

Right as I shifted, Dusk's hand closed around mine, making me jump.

He said nothing, entwining our fingers and drawing me back. I had to fight to keep my expression natural as irrational rage pricked me. I could picture the amusement on his face right now.

He drew me closer, and I froze as I felt his touch on my leg.

"Sorted, then?" Eric asked. "I think we have a few of the same classes. And you never know, Roxy and…" He blinked, his eyes narrowed as he looked at me with those bright green eyes. "Your… omega might get along—"

"Shatter," I whispered before I could stop myself.

They stared at me, as if surprised I could talk.

"My name," I said, clearing my throat so my voice was louder.

Something low rumbled in Dusk's chest. Humour, perhaps? His touch crept higher beneath my skirt. I grabbed his wrist beneath the table, for all the good it would do.

They were staring at me with frowns, but I could barely focus on it as Dusk's fingers slipped beneath the lace of my panties. I gripped him harder but dared not move.

"*My* omega's name is Shatter," Dusk said coolly as he pressed his fingers up against my slick entrance. Heat blossomed on my cheeks and in my core. His touch was insistent, and one of his legs pinned my knee against the table leg and his hand bit down on my other thigh, dragging my legs apart. Right now, it would be easy for him to plunge his finger right in.

My heart was in my throat. He *wouldn't.*

Not now, with them here.

"Shatter?" Eric asked. He sounded confused, and yet the word rolled from his tongue almost reverently.

With the sound of my name on my mate's tongue, Dusk slid a finger inside me. I fought with my expression, teeth biting down on my lip hard enough to draw blood.

My grip was white knuckled on the edge of the table and his wrist. "A beautiful name for a beautiful omega," Dusk murmured.

I was trembling with fury as he began to work his finger in and out of me, but I couldn't shift away any further, not with his hand clamped on my leg so tightly. Not without a scene.

Should I make a scene?

They would help me, right? If I did?

They'd have to.

Yet, I was frozen.

Eric was glancing between us, clearly oblivious. "The omega with a secret scent."

I could almost hear the smile on Dusk's face as he replied. "That's my girl."

I was shaking as he worked in and out of my core, curling his finger to a perfect spot that made the world spin. I warred to keep a straight face, trying to untangle exactly what he was doing to me.

"That's nice," Dusk noted, and Gareth glanced down at the pen I'd been trying to snatch with a smile.

"Bought it from the artist. The resin is custom, but I have a few—if you'd like it?" He set it before Dusk, who nodded in thanks, then switched to two fingers. I bit back a whine. It was so much worse with their scents here, sending my hormones out of control.

And despite my goosebumps and nerves, it felt good.

"One question before you leave," Dusk said as Eric got to his feet.

I ducked my head, letting my hair fall in my face as I began losing the war against the rising heat in my body.

This wasn't like anything I'd ever felt before.

"Yes?" Eric asked.

"How's Roxy settling in?"

I couldn't help glancing up at that question to see Eric's startled expression. "She's… fine."

"It's just…" Dusk said, working me deeper still. I was shivering with a rising sensation I hadn't felt before, eyes downcast again. "Shatter's having a bit of trouble. Wondering if it was just us."

What?

"Trouble?" Eric asked.

"You are, aren't you, Gem?" he asked. He released my leg, lifting his hand to my chin, tilting it up to face them as he continued to curl two fingers into me. I tried to close my legs, but his hand wasn't going anywhere. "I built her a nest," he said. "Chose everything for her, set it all up. But she doesn't want it."

Shock collided with heat. My lips parted, but my mind was blank.

What would they think? That I was the kind of spoiled omega who would reject something like that.

"You built a nest?" Gareth asked. He looked surprised. "That's early."

"I… do want a… nest," I managed to whisper, trying to meet Gareth's eyes.

"You slept in the bathtub last night."

Every eyebrow shot up.

"I wasn't *in* the bathtub… I was… nervous," I said, scrabbling for any excuse, my mind still half blank from Dusk's fingers that continued working me. "I want a nest. *I do.*"

Just not his.

I wanted theirs.

Couldn't they see that?

"Oh…" Dusk sounded genuinely surprised. "Well, you should have said that, Gem. It's sorted then."

It wasn't fucking *sorted.*

I wouldn't take anything from him.

But none of that mattered right now. Tilting my head back down I let my hair cover my face completely as Dusk continued sliding his fingers into me as he picked the conversation up.

Finally, they made to leave. I never thought I'd *want* to see them go, but I was trembling, clutching the table as I fought off a rising wave of heat that was sending me into a spiral.

"What about Ransom?" Gareth was saying. "Will he show his face?"

"Ransom does what he likes," Dusk replied.

When they stepped away at last, I buried my face in my arms, releasing desperate breaths. Then Dusk's free hand clamped around my neck, and he dragged my back against his chest, fingers still curling into that sensitive spot.

I let out a gasp, unable to help looking around the huge room. The auditorium was almost empty, a few loiterers at the doors, and my mates had their backs to me as they left.

"D-Dusk…" My voice was a rasp.

"What?" he asked, nipping my ear, his voice a low growl.

Shit. "Y-you have to stop."

"And why is that?"

"I don't…" Fuck. *Fuck.* His fingers drove into me quicker, and I was seeing stars. "I don't know what's happening." I hated how pathetic I sounded.

I hated that it was half a lie, because I knew exactly what was happening, but I was just… I was terrified of it.

Dusk finally halted. The sensation was something akin to being shoved to the edge of a cliff, then wrenched back.

I let out a pitiful sob, not sure if I was relieved or furious, but then he gripped my chin, dragging me to face him.

"What did you say?" he asked, blinking down at me with those piercing yellow eyes.

"I…" I trailed off, years of shame collapsing in over my head. My voice wasn't working right. "I haven't… I don't…"

"You've never had an orgasm?" It was the first time I'd seen him stunned.

I opened my mouth to reply, then shut it.

Never.

Not that I could remember, anyway—and by the way I'd panicked, I don't think before I'd lost my memories, either.

But he didn't understand. It wasn't like I'd been able to go on dates.

Too risky.

Always too risky.

And I'd been so scared of being more of an imposition than I'd already been at the Aster Estate. They hadn't wanted me from the start, but they couldn't get rid of me.

My hormones hadn't been such a problem until I'd come here and been surrounded by alphas.

"Oh, Shatter…" Dusk breathed. "You get sweeter and sweeter, don't you?"

He pressed his fingers between my lips, the same fingers he'd been dipping into me. I jerked back, but his grip laced into my hair.

"I'm going to be your first… *everything*, then?" he asked, delight dancing in his eyes.

Nerves collided with frightening anticipation at those words.

My firsts were for my mates—something I truly had to offer.

But I could see in his eyes that I might not be getting to the Lincoln pack before Dusk stole those too.

No… I couldn't let him take more.

"The sweeter you are," he said, his breath brushing my ear, "the more there is for me to ruin."

CHAPTER 8

Dusk

On the way back to the apartment, I received an email telling me the Dean needed an urgent meeting.

My delightful little omega was going to have to wait.

"No couch. Tonight it's me, Umbra, or the nest—if you accept it," I told her as we got back. She shot me a filthy glare. I dragged her suitcase from the bathroom, and she chose to sit beside it on the couch, huddling next to it anxiously, as if it was the only source of comfort.

She was being stubborn.

She would take my nest.

Shatter was ours, and my heart sang every time I caught a glimpse of our crest around her neck. Besides, I'd seen her sneak my scone into her bag this morning.

It took every piece of my self-control to not linger on the fact that the universe had paired her with those alphas.

We were close. Too fucking close to fall apart, now. During the last class, Umbra bugged the Lincoln pack's apartment. Answers were finally on the horizon. I was sick of chasing them down, always behind. Always in the dark while we suffered.

Not for much longer.

Shatter was an unexpected twist, but I would manage it like I'd managed everything else.

She wasn't *just* a twist.

"You want to claim her for revenge?" That's what Umbra had asked as we'd watched her rush across the ball, hair wild as she stumbled before her mates, eyes so bright.

But I was on my feet in a second, adrenaline scoring my veins, urgency a fist around my throat as I realised who she was scent matched to.

Revenge?

I'd glanced back at Umbra, uncomprehending.

But he hadn't met her. He didn't know what she was.

Ours.

More than that. She was one *of us. I couldn't explain it, but I knew it, bone deep.*

And what would that pack do if they discovered their mate was an omega like her?

No.

This claim wasn't about revenge at all.

It was about her.

Before I left to meet with the Dean, I checked all the windows in the apartment, knowing full well that since she'd broken in once to steal from me, she was just as capable of getting out that way. Before I realised the intruder was nothing more than a desperate gold pack omega, I'd had locks put on every window, inside and out. There were things in this apartment that couldn't be discovered.

Shatter had followed me around the apartment, watching me lock each one with folded arms and fury in her eyes. That alone was almost enough to give me a hard-on.

The fact was, I'd just found out that *my* omega had never had an orgasm in her life. There was no way in *hell* I was letting her near another alpha.

Especially not her mates.

"I'll be back in"—I checked my phone as I made for the front door, satisfied she wasn't going anywhere. "—a few hours at least."

A lie, but I had a theory I wanted to test.

"What about Umbra?" she'd asked, looking hopeful.

"Won't be back until the evening." That, at least, was the truth.

Yup. That was definite relief in her eyes.

Good.

Let her settle in.

"I have bad news for you, Varis." The Dean was peering at me uncomfortably from behind his desk.

I wasn't familiar with him, and I'd hated every one of these stupid meetings I was forced to attend. Ransom was the recent inheritor of the entire Kingsman estate, and as such, we were the most powerful pack in the school. Despite the fact our pack lead was *me*—an unknown. I could see the discomfort in the eyes of everyone forced to deal with me.

Unbeknownst to the Dean, I was also the reason Ransom held the power he did. For a moment, I was tugged away with memories of exactly how Ransom—my pack brother—had found himself the sole inheritor of one of the most powerful estates in the city…

"…Yes, well…" the Dean went on, but his words were dull and insignificant, as always.

I could have used a blade or a knife. I could have tied him down.

I'd done neither.

Instead, I'd let him run. The sound of his footfalls and ragged breaths had been music to my ears…

"…No need to dance around the issue…" the Dean was saying.

There was a rigid smile on my face as I tuned him out almost entirely.

My soft footfalls echoed about the dark hallways of the mansion, the static of my aura shivering in the air as I hunted. It wavered and sparked and danced around me.

"The omega you selected is a fraud."

At those words, my imaginings vanished. My gaze snapped to the Dean.

Not so insignificant, after all.

"We, uh…" He looked unnerved now he had all of my attention. "When we tried to process her in the system, her paperwork came back as illegitimate. Please give Mr. Kingsman our deepest apologies. We do *try* to be—"

He cut off as I held up a hand.

"*If* her application was fraudulent, I wouldn't give the first fuck. But I happen to be certain it's not." An outright and thrilling lie.

Of course, Shatter had applied fraudulently; it suited her entirely.

"I'll review the files and resubmit them."

The Dean watched me anxiously. "I assure you, we triple checked. Some of her application tests were flawless—suspiciously so. I can't explain how she got ahold of those, but her documentation… Well, if I didn't know better, I'd say she was unr—"

"I *said*," I cut him off. "I'll review the files for resubmission."

The Dean licked his lips nervously, but I continued before he could speak.

"I encouraged her to apply. If there was an error with her submission, I am *fully* responsible."

He nodded, eyes darting between mine. "I-I'm sorry, Mr. Varis. Didn't mean to offend—"

"Shatter was chosen by our pack. It wasn't an accident," I said, the words slow and cold.

Again, he nodded, finally grasping what I was saying. This academy dealt almost exclusively in arrogant alpha packs, and if there was one thing rich alphas did best, it was staking claims without a care in the world for paperwork and process.

I got to my feet and left without dismissal, already drafting the email I needed to send on my phone outside of the Dean's office.

To: K@EProblems.com

Need these redone. Have to be good enough for Rookwood Academy. She's gold pack, but I don't want that showing yet. Find out if she's registered. If she isn't, sort it.

That would be enough.

I headed back to our quarters beneath a light, late-summer rain that lifted petrichor from the nearby flowerbeds. What might that conversation have looked like if Shatter's mates had been called by the Dean instead of me?

Could they have managed it like I would—and what might it have cost her?

I tapped my phone on and off, waiting at the doors to the housing building, not used to the anxiety bubbling in my chest.

I was used to managing this shit, but Shatter hadn't known us when this paperwork was done. If she had, it would have been perfect the first time around.

No more than three minutes passed before an email popped up in my notifications.

Sender: K@EProblems.com

Done. Not registered. Doesn't exist at all, as far as I can tell, but a more detailed face rec will take longer. Want me to go ahead with that?

The rest is sorted. Originals look like they were done by a six-year-old.

The exam results though, don't know where those came from. They're even stricter on those than the application documents. I doubt she'd have got in at all without them.

If she paid someone, fucking fire them.

I snorted, sifting quickly through the documents I'd been sent.

Then I replied to the email, giving them the go ahead to try and uncover who she really was. She didn't exist in the system at all? That didn't sound right. I needed to know more about her. I'd give them Shatter's scent, too, the moment I had it, in case it helped identify her.

It wasn't just her application. There would be documents on their way in the mail too, an omega registration card—and she wasn't listed as gold pack. Bank account. Passport. Even a forged resume with a full work history.

With my nerves finally settled, I drafted another email, this time to the Dean.

Admin@Rookwoodacademy.edu

Run the check again. There was an error with submission. Everything should be fine.

Shatter was fucking lucky.

She'd somehow found legitimate paperwork, though she'd imposed her own identity on top of it poorly. The process for applying omegas wasn't nearly as strict as it was once they got approved for a pack—then the school enrolled them officially.

No. She wasn't lucky. She'd just believed that, by now, her fated mates would have found her and cleaned up this mess.

That was... desperate. Foolish.

Insane.

But I already knew she was those things. This—this was beyond that. It was a level of vulnerability that made rage burn my throat.

No one deserved to live like that. I knew that firsthand. I'd been where she was—both me and Umbra. Something as foul as that wouldn't interrupt our pack's courting of her. I wouldn't fucking allow it.

But what I wanted to know, was where had she come from that she had so fucking little?

My meeting with the Dean had lasted twenty minutes, and the emails had taken another ten.

I stepped off the main pathway and looped around the student housing building. I scaled the fire escape on the outer wall, the view of which was mostly obscured by a large oak tree.

Once on the right floor from the fire escape, I tugged out my key, unlocking and quietly slipping through the window to my bedroom. I made sure I was perfectly silent as I crossed to my bathroom and grabbed a scent-dampening spray.

I had a nagging feeling that, if I returned early, I might find something... special.

Of course, I was right.

I was just stepping from my bathroom to hide behind the curtain, when I spotted movement. The door of my closet creaked open. I shifted back behind the door so I could watch.

I grinned as Shatter padded out.

She was snooping.

Quite thoroughly, bless. She'd even found the blue butterfly clip in my top drawer. The one she'd left behind when she'd stolen from me—the very thing that had led me right to her.

She examined it for a while, a tight expression on her face. She swore to herself and stuffed it into her pocket before rooting through more drawers.

That was good. One, because it showed self-preservation, and two, because it meant she was curious about me.

Next, I watched from the crack of my door to see her halt before the nest. She tried to open it but found it locked. She tried again, pure instinct, as a little whine escaped her chest. Then she kicked it rather violently, yelped in irritation, and clutched her foot.

I almost outed myself then with a chuckle but caught it in time.

She was *so* going to accept my nest.

Clearly having done the rounds on the rest of the house before I got back, she settled onto the couch in the living room. If I stepped out into the hallway a fraction, I could just see her. I leaned against my door frame, curious to know what was coming next.

I felt a smug smile tug at my lips as she did exactly what I hoped she would.

I watched silently, arms folded as I was serenaded by the cutest noises of frustration as she tried, and repeatedly failed, to get herself off.

I'd been prepared to intervene if needed—I would have that first—but it was unnecessary.

Finally, she staggered to her feet, honey hair a messy mane and cheeks flushed. To my surprise, she circled the coffee table to the hall—and right toward me.

I backed up, crossing my room again to stand behind the heavy curtains, waiting for the sound of her footsteps approaching. She stopped in the doorway, and I could hear her elevated breathing. I didn't have a good view yet, but I heard her enter.

Why was she back here?

I shifted enough to see her seated on the edge of my bed. There was a furious pout on her face as her gaze darted around the room. Then, to my utter surprise, she shifted back, laying down on my bedding and dropping her touch beneath her skirt.

Well. Fuck me.

I leaned against the wall, enjoying more of her whines. They were so fucking sweet that another wave of hot blood rushed to my cock. I might have been able to come just from listening.

She kept trying, bless, and it seemed to make her more and more angry every time she failed. I'd never come across an omega who was quite so primal. She was a white-hot spitfire of omega instincts, and I didn't even think she was aware of it.

Finally, when her adorable shriek of rage sounded for the fourth time, I slipped from my hiding spot.

I was *so* fucking ready to join her.

She was so focused on trying to pleasure herself that she didn't notice me at first. I stepped closer.

She jumped when she saw me, eyes wide. "N-no—"

"Stay." I barked the command, and she was completely frozen, ruddy cheeks draining of colour. She truly hadn't been around alphas much, clearly.

Before she could figure out how to get out of my command and scramble up, I hopped onto my bed and pressed my foot to her stomach, so she was fighting my weight.

"Let me go," she snarled. Her eyes were wide, face ashen as her chest heaved, perfect tits pressed against the thin fabric of her shirt. She'd removed her bra at some point during the battle for her first orgasm.

Her cheeks glistened with sweat. She clamped her legs closed and hugged herself.

"If you stay down, Gem, I won't touch," I told her.

She let out a breath of fear, turning her head so she was looking at the wall and not me, even when her cheeks blazed red.

"You're in my room?" I asked.

"I-it could have been any r-room," she stammered.

"Or maybe on the couch?" I asked with a grin.

Her eyes darted back to me, full of a fury that didn't manage to entirely hide her nerves.

"Getting off shouldn't be that hard, not unless you're thinking about the wrong alphas."

A low growl rose up her throat, and I laughed. She swallowed, turning away from me again. It was hard—really fucking hard—not to sink down and ravage her right now.

"Go again."

"No."

"Touch yourself, Shatter, and I won't touch you."

She shot a glance up at me again, and whatever she saw on my face was convincing enough.

"Unless you *do* want me to give you that first orgasm."

"Don't," she begged. "I c-can't."

There was no way I was walking away, though. Not with her lying before me, skirt barely covering the golden skin of her hips and the black lace beneath.

"Touch yourself," I commanded. "Last time I'll tell you."

Very slowly, her fingers dropped down between her legs. She shut her eyes, her trembling lip caught in her teeth.

"Give me a show, or I'll make you come when I fuck you into my sheets."

There it was. Her teeth bit down harder on her lip, and her brows bunched.

I *was* turning her on.

She loved my praise, even if she was willing to draw blood to claim otherwise. She wanted me and my scent.

"Go on, beautiful," I coaxed.

It was enough, and I was rewarded with the view of her slowly pushing her finger into her pussy. Now her eyes were shut, she relaxed a little.

"Are you thinking of them, or me?" I asked as her first breathy moan slipped out.

She tensed at the sound of my voice, though I noticed she sped up. "Them."

"Don't lie to me."

"I don't want *you.*"

"No?" I asked, watching as she switched to two fingers. "You don't want me splitting your tight body open on my cock?"

Her jaw clenched—in rage, perhaps. Or because she was fighting her own arousal. I tugged my zipper down, so I could fist my own cock. "Fuck, you're hot, Gem."

She gritted her teeth, body tense, eyes squeezed shut, and the noises coming from her were different now.

"Thinking of me yet?"

"N-no," she whined. "I want *them.*"

"You're a liar." It was hard to contain my own orgasm as I squeezed the base of my cock, knot swelling. "You're soaked at the thought of me stretching that sweet cunt over my knot."

She almost stopped, her breathing short and shallow, a noise of distress sounding from her.

"Don't you dare," I growled. "Fuck yourself with your fingers, or I *will* ruin you myself."

She dipped her dainty fingers into herself again, and I could see the goosebumps lift across her body.

"Faster."

She listened, her breaths coming quicker.

She was a work of art, glistening slick coating her fingers every time she pulled them out, nipples pressed against her shirt as her back arched, plush lips parting in pleasure.

"Are you going to come for me?"

"No."

"Shame." I grinned, watching her arch more as she got close. "I'd make you come until you begged me to stop."

Finally, she cracked her eye open, and her gaze snagged on my cock.

"I'd call you perfect." I ran my hand the length of my shaft. "And rut you until your body gives out."

I could almost feel the way her body would shake beneath me… The sounds she would make, and the way she would cry my name.

Her eyes were fixed on my fist as it slid up my shaft. Somehow, she really was new to this. All of it. My sweet, strange omega, a puzzle I intended to solve.

Then her gaze slid to mine, and her eyes squeezed shut again, as if that might shield her from the pleasure she was taking from my promises.

"Say you want me." I lost myself at that moment. I knew she never would. "Say you want me ruining you and biting you and treating you like a princess."

She tensed, a low, desperate growl sounding from her. God, it was something, seeing her crest the wave she'd been seeking for over an hour now.

Too bad she was a filthy little liar.

She let out a breath, body shivering with that last thread of tension right as my command, laced with all the weight of my aura, sliced it all into ribbons.

"Don't come."

She jolted in shock, eyes flying open, and a low whine tore from her chest. Her breaths were sharp as she shook, still burying two fingers into herself with pitiful whimpers, though all that seemed to do was make her tremble more as her body tried and failed over and over to reach the bliss that was out of reach.

I removed my foot at last, and she didn't waste time scrambling up. I leaned down at the perfect moment, my fingers digging into her hair as I held her on her knees.

"Let me show you how easy it is when you think about the right things."

It *was* easy, far easier than it ever had been before with her before me like this. It was fucking hard to stay standing, a low growl ripping from my throat as I finished. She whimpered in shock as I held her still, and my cum shot across her furious expression, her neck, and along her collarbones. Finally, when I was done, I let go of her hair.

I tucked myself back in as she dragged herself to her feet at last. My thumb brushed her chin as I admired what she looked like, rich skin glistening and covered in my seed. She was frozen in shock, wide eyes really fucking offended, which almost got me hard all over again.

"The problem, Gem…" I leaned forward, growling in her ear, caressing the sheen of my cum down her collarbone to her breast. "Is that I don't think you believe me when I tell you how fucking perfect you are."

I heard her breath hitch at that, like it did every time.

"So, you're going to walk out of my room wearing proof of it, or you can stay for another round, since you already have me ready to go again."

CHAPTER 9

The subject seeks out alphas and reports feeling soothed by their presence. Alphas do not want her around. She enjoys spending time in my office, reading textbooks. I find her scent unpleasant, but not intolerable. But if she has not taken scent blockers, her presence leaves me irritable after extended periods.

Shatter

The next day passed, and the nest called to me. It was a dull ache in my chest I couldn't shake. I'd spent all night curled up on the couch, thinking about the nest and the safety it offered. Dusk, seeming satisfied with what happened between us, had let me take the couch without arguing. I was sure that wouldn't last, though.

I felt a rush of shame every time I thought about what had happened in Dusk's room yesterday, and my body was still cranky from the denied orgasm (that I hadn't dared attempt again). I knew it was my own fault, though.

Why had I gone into his room?

I was losing my fucking mind. I just hadn't wanted him to take what was supposed to be theirs. He was stripping me of the smallest pieces of value I had to offer, *and* he was screwing up my mind.

I hated him.

I felt like I was coming apart at the seams. I didn't know what was right anymore, but I knew I was fucking up. I'd spent so long trying to get here, and then I'd gone into the room of another alpha to… Fuck.

I had to keep my sights set on the goal—my mates. No matter what Dusk made me feel or do, he wasn't my end game. But escape was looking unlikely, and I couldn't shake the inescapable worry of what would happen when Dusk and Umbra finally caught my scent.

Yesterday had proven to me how much I was living at Dusk's mercy, the echo of his alpha bark still setting my hairs on end when I thought of it. I'd shaken the command, but for a moment, when he'd told me not to move, I hadn't been able to at all.

It was more reason to find a way to reach my mates.

In the late morning, Dusk and I left the apartment to go to the academy hall and pick up our class schedules. While the schedules were released electronically (not that I had a phone or a laptop), the main hall was set up for socialising. It was a large room, with tall, arched windows and an impossibly high ceiling. The specialties had booths laid out in different places, and the air was full of the students's chatter as they loitered. The scents of alphas and omegas tangled with the room's scent of old books and aged stone.

I managed to act foolish enough to the lady at the desk that she let me rifle through the schedules myself, and I caught a glimpse of Flynn and Eric's schedule before finding my own.

Scanning the page, I committed as much to memory as I could before handing her the folder. My breath was stolen from my lungs as I backed away from the table and hit a solid *someone* behind me. Passion fruit drowned my senses, and I spun, eyes wide.

Eric.

Had he seen me looking at his schedule? Surely not… right? I'd just tell him it was an accident.

He was the tallest in his pack, and his sweep of dark brown hair was easy to spot in a crowd. He was also the quietest, though his intense green eyes seemed to pick up everything. My heart tripped over itself as that intense gaze found mine, and he lifted a hand to steady me.

He offered me a smile as I stammered out an apology, and my cheeks blazed as his scent of passion fruit scrambled my brain. I hadn't ever seen Eric smile, and it was heart-stopping, a flash of ivory that lit up his usually stony expression. But in the next moment, dark opium joined us, and Dusk's hand was slipping around my waist. Any thoughts of small talk died from my mind.

They spoke for a while about Arkology (I tucked away the tidbit that Eric was looking forward to Aura Studies, which also happened to be my favourite Arkology subclass), and I noticed how often his eyes slid down to Dusk's touch, even though they weren't talking about me at all.

Did it bother him that Dusk was touching me? The emerald green of his eyes was so impassive, it made him hard to read. Why *didn't* he smile much? Was it something I could maybe do something about when I finally got to them? If he could offer me the world, I should be able to offer him that.

It was hard not to stare dumbly. He had smooth, pale skin, a lean face, and his teeth were so straight. Dusk had irritatingly pretty teeth, but I thought Eric's were *just* a bit straighter. Perfect, actually. He must have had braces or something.

And already, he'd smiled for me.

I didn't think I'd seen him do that for Roxy.

But… how upset would he be if he knew what I'd done with Dusk yesterday?

It's something Dusk couldn't understand. There was so much more to this than just a normal scent match. I needed this Lincoln pack more than any omega had ever needed a scent match. There were chains lurking in every direction but for the one with my mates.

After we returned to the apartment, I spent the day curled up at the end of the couch, examining the classes I was going to attend and making a study plan. All the while I tried to ignore the fact that Umbra and Dusk existed, which was difficult, since the apartment was painfully open concept, and the only private spaces were the bathrooms, bedrooms, and nest.

I tried to focus on how many classes I was excited about. I'd applied for every Arkology class the school offered, and had been accepted to a good number. Dusk and Umbra, it seemed, had done the same, and aside from the two Omega Studies classes, I was with at least one of them around the clock. The good news, however, was that I knew we were also sharing many of those classes with my mates.

When dinner came around, Dusk cooked for three. I was primed to reject it when there was a knock on the front door.

"There, Gem." Dusk announced, setting the brown bag on the counter before tugging a note from his pocket and putting it on the fridge. He grabbed a sharpie and wrote at the top:

Shatter's favourite food.

Below it was my scrawl:

Anything Dusk Varis doesn't make.

I scowled as he finished serving up for him and Umbra. But I tried to plaster a pleased expression on my face as I approached the dinner table and took the bag.

Oh. It was McDonalds. I *liked* McDonalds. It had always been a treat, and it was definitely better than the stupid pot pie meal Dusk had made.

"Umbra or me?" Dusk asked when they'd finished eating. I'd remained silent, barely touching my food.

"What?" I asked.

"No couch tonight. If you won't take the nest, pick one of us."

"Umbra." The word came out of my mouth before I could think it through.

I didn't know if I regretted it.

What if I picked Dusk and let him get his stupid punishment over with and then I could have the nest?

What would the punishment even be? I'd been too afraid to ask.

But I wanted the nest. I wanted it so bad.

Not because he'd made it, but because I'd realised today that he wasn't letting me go. I couldn't get away and take a breath. I needed my space and my haphazard tilted squares. Earlier I'd even spotted Dusk dropping off a stack of the textbooks in it today, as if he'd noticed me sifting through them during the lecture…

"Well." Dusk stood, putting his dishes in the sink. "I'm turning in, then."

I glanced at Umbra, whose intense sandstorm eyes were fixed on me as he got to his feet. I jumped as he wrapped his arms around me from behind, taking a deep breath and huffing me like paint. "When will the scent blockers wear off?"

"Ask Dusk," I said, trying to keep my voice steady. "He drugged me." Still, even while I said it, dread seeped into my bones.

When he finds out what that scent is, he won't hold you like this…

Umbra's scent might be wolfsbane and blood, but as an alpha, he could weather a scent so cruel. It *even* suited him in a twisted way.

Umbra shrugged. "I just want my omega time before bed."

Omega time?

Before I could protest, he picked me off the chair with ease and tossed me over his shoulder. I let out a squeak of shock, cheeks blazing as I scrambled to push myself upright, knowing he'd exposed my butt to the room.

Umbra wasn't quite as unnerving as Dusk, but I still felt a flutter of nerves in my stomach at the sheer size of him. He easily held me and hauled my suitcase up the stairs to the balcony corridor that overlooked the rest of the apartment. Up here were two doors, and both had been locked when I'd checked yesterday.

I couldn't help peering over his shoulder and meeting Dusk's gaze as Umbra carried me to his room at the far door. As he watched, his darkness was gone, and for the first time, I thought I saw what might be softness in his eyes.

Once inside, Umbra put my suitcase down and set me gently me on my feet. Then he stood back, crossing his arms and examining me like I was a brand-new kitten he'd brought home—which, by the way this was going, wasn't far off.

I had never felt as small as I did staring up at him now. He didn't just have a broad frame, he had muscle to support it.

"Get ready for bed." He nodded toward the bathroom door. "And lose the contacts."

"What? No." I didn't sleep with them unless my circumstances were dire, but this qualified. I wasn't showing any of them anything I didn't have to.

But it wasn't just that. Why would he *want* to see the true colour of my eyes? To remind him how easy it would be for them to dark bond me? Of how little power I really had?

His brows drew down, gaze calculating.

"You have a picture," I added. "Look at that." I braced, wondering how much like Dusk he was.

Unexpectedly, he grinned, and it was quite genuine. "Alright, omega. A deal?"

I frowned. "A deal?"

"Coin toss. If I win, you do whatever I want you to."

I blew out a breath, taking a step back. I opened my mouth to say no, but caught myself. "What uh… What do I get if I win?"

Umbra's grin widened. "I'll unlock the nest for you tonight," he said. "Behind Dusk's back."

My lips opened in shock, my mind flashing to the nest—to what it had looked like. Even though I had only seen it for a few brief seconds, that had been enough.

"Okay." My throat was dry, desperation getting the better of me. "Deal."

"Heads or tails?" he asked, digging in his pocket.

"Tails."

He nodded, rummaging for a second longer before pulling out a coin. "Ready?" His eyes, fixed on me, flashed with delight.

A chill ran down my spine at that look of his, but I nodded.

The nest.

I might be able to get to the nest after all.

He tossed it, catching it on the back of his hand, then paused, gaze still assessing. Ever so slowly, he lifted his hand.

My heart was pounding, desperate dreams of safety careening through my mind. Then it sank like a rock as I stared at the carved head on the side that faced us.

Shit…

I stared at it for a long time, as if it might morph before my eyes.

Finally, I swallowed, throat dry as I looked up at him. His head was cocked, sandstorm eyes dilated as he watched my reaction.

Oh.

Damn.

He'd said if he won I had to do *whatever* he wanted?

I was dizzy with whiplash from Dusk, but now I was trapped with Umbra instead. I had to catch up.

What was Umbra Varis going to ask for tonight?

Umbra

Cuddles.

That's what I wanted. My hindbrain made that decision for me, bets and trades aside. The eyes… Well, I'd told her I wanted those golden eyes, but it was up to her.

Now she was getting ready in the bathroom.

I'd settled myself down on the edge of my bed, anticipating the omega who would walk out.

My omega. All mine, all night.

And cuddles.

Would her scent blockers wear off?

Fuck, I hoped so.

I had every intention of fucking her so good she wouldn't remember her own name, let alone *theirs*, but that wouldn't happen until I'd earned it. A coin toss didn't earn me a fuck—I'd have to get her to bet something a little more for that.

But a coin toss got me cuddles.

Dusk didn't understand this fundamental—there was no such thing as free shit. If you stole, the universe stole back. If you gave, it returned.

But the universe was unpredictable and pretty fucking petty, so I preferred living the zero-sum method.

I didn't rack up debt or payouts. I traded. That way, I always had a say.

I'd trade for Shatter, too. I'd trade a damn lot for her actually—though revealing to her my highest bid was a rookie move. That sort of knowledge cost in its own right.

I waited, still and silent, dreaming of what she'd look like when she stepped out.

Golden eyes.

Please give me the golden eyes.

Why did we vilify them? Gold was the currency of the whole world, wasn't it?

There was a buzz in my veins. Waiting to see what she would do was almost a gamble in itself.

Shatter didn't realise it, but *she* was going to be my first.

I'd never been cuddled by an omega before. I'd never been cuddled *at all* before… as far as I knew.

I frowned as my brain hiccupped violently, ripping me into a world I'd be paying debts on for the rest of my life.

A hard, sterile mattress.

My bones shook quicker than my body could keep up with. I shed sweat like I was on fire, but I was frigid, the moisture on my skin funnelling ice right into my pores. The blanket and clothes were live wires, each movement ripping along hairs like a thousand shocks of electricity.

The only part of my body that didn't ache—fire and ice, numb and electric—were the parts he touched. Where he held me against him, the whistle of a soothing song I didn't know upon his lips.

I tapped my fingers in a hopscotch along each payment on my thigh, and knee, and shin, humming to myself—a tuneless lantern leading me back home.

Back home with Dusk and Ransom.

And her.

She would come out and give me cuddles.

I needed to be home for that.

Okay. I ran it back, still tapping slowly.

I realised my error. I wouldn't make it again. I *had* been cuddled. Kind of. But Dusk didn't really count, and besides, she'd never know about that, so fuck it.

She was still my first.

The door creaked, and my head snapped up. With eyes downcast, Shatter checked around the door, like she expected me to be looming outside, waiting to pounce.

I snorted.

I was a *competent* predator, not a thug.

She'd learn.

Her honey hair was up in a bun, and she wore a pair of baggy black sweatpants with a matching long-sleeve top. Returning to her suitcase, she tucked the dress away, her gaze averted the whole time, so I couldn't see what I wanted to see.

"Is this your attempt at being as *unsexy* as possible?" I asked, cocking an eyebrow at her loose clothing.

She glanced back, smiling much too sweetly. "How's it going?"

Finally. There they were.

My heart tripped over itself.

Golden fucking eyes.

Golden eyes that were as beautiful as the rest of her.

A peace offering.

I was grinning. What had she asked? *How was it going for her trying to be unsexy?* It *wasn't.* Not even a little. She was made of unfiltered sunlight. I didn't think it was possible for her not to be hot—and that was before I'd ever caught her scent.

Fuck.

My cock throbbed at the idea of her scent. Would it be earthy, or sweet, or sharp?

I *had* to know.

"I'm still going to squeeze you until you purr for me."

She blinked, peering back at me from her suitcase with a frown. "That is the weirdest threat I've ever heard."

"Thank you." I stood and stepped toward her, wanting a closer look before I got ready for bed. Her gaze turned sharp at my footsteps. She stopped rooting and got to her feet as if I was about to jump her.

She was a frightened little bird. I didn't blame her with Dusk involved, but she'd settle once they'd prodded each other's boundaries a bit more. Dusk wasn't upfront about stuff like that—not even to himself—so she'd have to figure him out. Mine were clear as day, though all she had to do was ask.

I couldn't help my deep inhale as I neared. Sadly, she smelled like a fresh shower and nothing else, but I'd live.

Dusk had given her loads of scent blockers, and more this morning since they'd gone out to grab the schedules. I think Dusk had only taken her out so she didn't go stir crazy, since she'd been curled up on the couch all morning, jumping at every small noise and shooting Dusk foul glares. But I knew what he'd caught her doing yesterday in his room, so I wasn't buying it at all.

I knew for a fact Dusk also had a pill that would rid her of the scent blockers, but I think he wanted to keep it for the moment she accepted the nest. He was melodramatic like that.

Her gaze darted to the door, but she didn't move.

She was brave.

"Ask," I said.

She paused, suddenly more calculating, as she took me in. I liked her looking at me like that, like I was a puzzle she wanted to solve. "Are you going to… uh…?" She clasped her fingers, confidence deserting her. I waited. She'd get it back. "To make me do anything I don't want to do?" she asked quickly, her voice hoarse.

"Just the cuddles."

She wrinkled her nose.

Oh, come on. I scowled. She'd taken the coin toss. It wasn't *my* fault she hadn't checked the other side of the coin before she made the bet. I wouldn't have stopped her and then she'd be in her nest right now.

The cuddles. Were. Mine.

She was wearing *our* necklace around that dainty neck of hers.

Besides, this was nothing. If she was in Dusk's room, he'd probably be claiming her tight throat again like the lunatic he was.

Oh, the universe was coming for him.

Shit.

I hadn't really considered it until now, especially seeing her nerves. Dusk and I wanted the same stuff, and Shatter was exactly the kind of thing the universe might take away for that…

But if it wasn't for Dusk we wouldn't have found her at all.

Fuck.

I'd cover it.

I'd paid his debts before.

I blinked, something dragging me from my thoughts. Shatter was… different. She'd frozen, the blood draining from her face and leaving it ashen.

Fear.

That was the first time I'd seen her sunlight truly wane.

A low growl caught in my throat, and I was ready to tear to pieces anything that made her frightened.

She stepped back a pace, her eyes wide.

The bubble popped, and I smashed right back into reality.

My aura was out: static and chaos flickering in the room. She was staring at *me* like that. Afraid of *me.*

My blade, I realised, was clutched in my fist.

No no no. She didn't understand.

It wasn't for *her.*

I tried to put it back in my pocket, but I couldn't. Razor teeth clicked from the depths of that void dehiscing within my soul, frayed stitches straining and snapping.

Shatter took another small step back as if she dared not move any quicker.

Sunlight dimmed further.

I *had* to put the knife away.

The thought was met with something sickening, a bone deep terror pooling at the top of my mind, shivering and restless.

What if I waited, and Dusk's debt came due?

The thought was a drop breaking free, consuming everything as it tumbled silently into the abyss.

Falling

Falling

Falling

Then it shattered upon gnashing teeth with the earth-shaking sound of a gunshot.

Dusk lay face down, hair matted with crimson, staring sightlessly.

I couldn't wait.

The wound was closing above me, and I was still inside.

Another drop was in freefall.

When it shattered, Ransom was still. Still and pale. I'd stared for so long, unable to move, trying to catch the faintest movement of a breath, too afraid to close the distance and see if he had finally left me.

I *couldn't* wait.

CHAPTER 10

Shatter

I grabbed the door handle to flee Umbra's room just as I heard the bathroom door slam. I froze, still shaking from head to toe, staring back to check I was safe. He was gone.

There had been one short moment when I'd wondered if Umbra really might not be as frightening as I'd dreaded. Coerced cuddles weren't nearly as bad as what I'd been anticipating. And then he'd pulled a knife, his aura splitting the air.

How far would his aura reach?

If Dusk was in the living room, he'd know. It *had* to be large enough that he would.

Would he come?

Did I *want* him to, or want him *not* to?

Clearly not, since I was still trying to calm my breathing, my white knuckled grip on the door-knob I hadn't turned.

I wanted to stay in this room, as far from Dusk as possible. I *definitely* didn't want to run to him for help.

Instead, I'd like to run right out of here, but that wasn't an option, so it was mad alpha A or mad alpha B. *Take your fucking pick, Shatter.*

Through the door, I could still feel Umbra's aura wavering in the air. Utterly terrifying.

It was the most unstable thing I'd ever felt.

I paused, grip loosening as I turned back to the bathroom.

I could *feel* it; cracked and howling. A vicious monster and… something else. Something broken, crying for help. Wolfsbane and blood still tangled in the air, but the blood… the blood was stronger now.

Seconds ticked by as I stared at the door. I grappled with something I'd never felt. Instinct rose, more powerful than the desperate thing that just wanted a nest to curl up in. Something resilient and protective.

Something… stolen.

I was stepping toward the bathroom before I realised. I nudged it ever so slightly with my toe, taking a deep breath, then daring to peer in.

My hand jumped to my mouth, forcing me into silence as I saw what was within.

Umbra's eyes were closed as he sat against the bathroom wall. He wore only his jeans, his top tossed across the floor.

In his fist was the knife, and it shook in his grip as he held it firmly against a bleeding wound on his chest. There were three open wounds, small, vertical lines, each smaller than a matchstick, each trailing a tear of blood down his chest.

And I wasn't left to wonder what they were supposed to be, because his body was a canvas, answering that. Scars littered his chest and arms, horizontal batches of five lines.

I lowered my hand from my mouth, probing further, the insistent feeling tugging at me. I tilted my head, watching as he drew the knife away and dug it back into the first of the open wounds, dragging it down, scoring deeper.

More blood oozed out, strangely mesmerising as it slipped over the tan muscles of his chest.

His eyes remained closed, but if I had to decide, I might call him serene. I don't know when the tears came, but I felt one escape and tumble down my cheeks Sorrow twisted my heart as I watched, and I didn't exactly know why.

Broken aura. Broken mind. These wounds somehow feel like mine…

Each silent step toward him was frightening, but I took them anyway. This went beyond my mates or Umbra's pack.

This wasn't just about him. Each step was an exploration of me. Of something *I'd* never had… or something I'd lost.

I dropped to my knees, fingers outstretched.

His eyes flew open and his hand snapped out, seizing me by the neck. I grabbed onto his wrist, a whimper fleeing my lips. His grip loosened, eyes darting between mine, sudden panic in them.

"I can't…" His voice was gravel. "You can't… stop me."

It wasn't a challenge. I understood that.

It was a plea.

"I… won't," I whispered, still clinging to his forearm as though that would do me any good if he decided to squeeze. With an aura that size, he was strong enough to snap my neck with a flinch.

A fraction at a time, his hand retracted, freeing me.

We stared at each other for an age, the knife still against his chest, digging into an open wound that leaked glistening crimson drops.

He couldn't stop.

I heard that. I believed it, even. But I wanted to know more. "Why?"

Slowly, the blade shifted to the next line, digging in again, and this close I *could* see his pain. The tick on his jaw, the constriction of his pupils. His voice was rough, as if it were on the edge of breaking. "It has to hurt, or it's not a payment."

I nodded, mind prying the statement apart, trying to understand it.

He had changed. His aura had shifted, something less unstable about it. A faint thrill lit my veins. *Had I done that?*

I could do more.

I just had to understand.

I watched him drag the knife over the wounds once more, still not breaking my gaze. *That* was the change—he was watching me now, instead of closing his eyes.

He tensed, and I reached for his hand that was clenched around the knife, reckless curiosity pushing me onward. A growl sounded in his throat, but I ignored it, cupping trembling fingers around his fist, trying not to focus on how much bigger than me he was.

Then I left my hand around his, not pushing or pulling, letting him continue to work. To dig the blade into his skin over and over.

His breathing loosened, his aura getting steadier and steadier as I stayed with him.

I didn't move once. Not until something in the air changed.

Midnight opium tangled with blood, demanding my attention.

Dusk was here.

I flinched, almost breaking my gaze with Umbra, but I didn't. Because that was the whole point—*that* was what I had to offer, and this wasn't something I would let Dusk take from me.

I wasn't stopping Umbra—I didn't know how to do that—but I wouldn't leave him alone. I was tense though, unsure of what Dusk would do. It was unnatural to have my back turned to an alpha as deadly as him.

When Umbra finally stopped, there was more crimson visible on his chest than skin. That was when I dared turn. Dusk, however, was already gone.

Good.

I'd finally claimed something back from them.

I'd found a scattered fragment. Something rare. It was a fragment of what made me an omega, and I didn't want Dusk anywhere near it.

This was more soothing than the nest he'd offered me, and he'd had no say in it. They'd brought me into their home—into *their* territory—and I was carving out a slice for myself, whether they wanted me to or not.

And that slice *was* Umbra.

I didn't have to like him. Nothing like that. I wasn't *cheating* on my mates. They might even be proud of me if I told them what I'd just done.

I might even be a real omega by the time I managed to get to them.

Umbra

I wasn't going to think about what just happened.

Not only because I didn't really understand myself, but because it had been… good. And I could never hope for it again, because nothing good ever happened to me twice. It was part of the whole, living zero-sum thing.

If there were bright spots, they were nothing but a fluke. She was a damned big bright spot, though. A shooting star, sailing by.

She'd been startlingly unafraid since I'd surfaced. She'd washed the blood off and cleaned my wounds with careful focus, smacking my hand away with a growl anytime I tried to help.

She'd done a shit job, but it was worth it.

Then she'd waited, seated on my bed after I'd showered (and washed and covered the wounds again properly, since the shower undid it all anyway).

Right now, she was turning all my pillows to strange angles and tugging the blankets around my bed all wrong. Despite how fucking odd it all was, a purr threatened its way up my chest as I watched her work.

Never before had anyone slipped into that world that stole me away while I was paying my debts.

And yet, she just had.

She *was* a real life shooting star.

I'd have to take another look at payment plans if I really wanted to catch her in a net and keep her with me. But she couldn't be a part of those payments like she just had. That didn't make *sense.*

None of it made sense.

Dusk would tell me it was because my belief system was stupid. He was wrong, I just had to untangle it a bit more.

Could I pay for Shatter *with* Shatter's help?

Would she even do that again?

"You aren't sleeping with the knife." Those words of hers broke the spiralling thoughts.

I stared at her in shock. She was way too pretty to be saying such ugly things. "I can't sleep without it," I said defensively.

"Put it on the side table." She was *so* demanding right now, and I kept just… doing what she asked before thinking about it, as though she had an omega bark. There was a scowl on my face, and it was like wrenching a piece of my heart from my chest, but I dropped the knife on the side table.

"In the drawer."

I clenched my jaw, but when I didn't move, she clambered over me, ripped the drawer open and shoved it in. I stifled an unsettled whine.

Fuck.

Fine.

She'd earned that. Paid in terror and goddamned risk. I'd leave the knife in the drawer, like she'd asked. She hadn't specified for how *long.* I could get it out once she was asleep.

I got *why* she was nervous about me having it, especially since unstable alpha cuddles were in the mix—and I was kind of bleeding on her still.

But that knife would never cut anyone else's skin. Not ever. I'd rather slice my dick off than see that happen.

She settled back down beside me, much more focused on the drawer than the fact my arms were snaking around her waist and pulling her close.

If I had to say how she seemed, it might actually be… pleased.

Maybe even… *smug?*

And the way she kept looking at me was kind of intense.

And she kept ordering me about which was hot, but odd.

Oh.

Shit.

Had she… claimed me?

That wasn't how this worked. I was the alpha. I claimed her. I was giving *her* cuddles.

Only, she was wrapping her legs around my waist, holding me more tightly than I was holding her. Not fair really, since I could easily break her if I squeezed too hard. Her fingers cupped my neck, thumb trailing up and down my skin. She nuzzled closer, brushing her head beneath my chin. Then she froze, drawing back, her eyes wide.

It took me a second to realise why.

"Did you just try to… *scent mark* me?"

That made my cock so hard. Not that she would know. She was clinging to me like a koala and only to the top half of my body—and she was small enough that it worked.

But back to her wide-eyed horror that demanded instant fixing.

She couldn't scent mark me, the drugs smothering her scent meant it was impossible.

She looked furious, and it was the cutest thing I'd ever seen. But then I thought that might be genuine panic in her eyes.

Letting me go, she turned her back on me, curling up into a cute little omega roll.

I paused, trying to figure that out. She was tense. I took her wrist in my fingers. Her pulse was going a trillion miles a minute, her breaths quiet but rapid.

Uh… "What happened?"

She curled up tighter.

"I'm going to sleep." She sounded distraught, and I knew there was no way she'd be sleeping anytime soon.

"You could…" I cleared my throat. "Bite me?" That was another way omegas pissed on their territory, right? And it would open a temporary bond between us, which meant I'd get to see how her crazy mind worked a little closer.

I wanted a bite. God, I might want her bite more than I wanted to sink my teeth into *her* neck.

Her voice was muffled. "That *would* be like cheating on them."

I snorted. That was silly. "And scent marking me isn't?"

"No. I don't know. It just… seemed right." There was a tremor in her voice with the next words, as if she didn't believe them. "It's good it didn't work."

There was a sudden, loud *thump* through the walls, and she tensed in my arms. I froze, too, my pulse quickening.

Fuck…

Fuck.

"What was that?" she asked, peering back at me.

"Probably Dusk being a fucking idiot," I lied.

I waited, unsure, but then there was silence. Finally, she turned to face me. She narrowed her eyes, analysing me all over again. That determination of hers was back. "You're nervous."

"I don't get nervous."

Well, I'd never been nervous *before* now. But my knife was far away, and her eyes were liquid gold, swallowing me up entirely, still with that faint pout on her face that I didn't know how to fix.

What the fuck does she expect?

She clearly didn't believe me, because she was drawing me close. She tucked her head beneath my chin until her soft cheek was pressed against my chest, right next to the dressing of my fresh payment.

"You're going to tell me when it's gone," she said.

I almost laughed. I didn't think that was how it worked.

But then she summoned up a determined purr that *might* possibly be classified as aggressive, and clung to me tighter. My mind was wiped blank as my body relaxed around her, little vibrations shooting right down to my spine.

How long would she keep this up for? Forever, I hoped, but it took me ages to get to sleep. Always had, always…

I yawned, holding her closer, breathing slowing.

Always…

Would…

Dusk

I'd heard the loud thump, and it wasn't from Umbra's room.

I'd visited his room earlier, heart in my throat when I'd felt his aura in the air. But I'd found something I'd never expected to see.

Shatter had followed Umbra into his void.

Now I stepped up the stairs toward the other door on the balcony hallway. This part was my job, never Umbra's.

I unlocked the door and entered the room to find pitch blackness and the scent of another world. Shutting the door behind me, I waited in silence, letting my own scent saturate the space and give warning of my presence. Closing my eyes, I leaned against the wall, breathing in the smell that had soothed me since the first time I'd caught it.

Here, I was in a forest, not a room. It was damp with morning dew and white petals. Among the leaves, a tide of shadows shifted. Dark lilies and black leather.

My heart rate slowed, my breathing steady until I heard it.

I didn't turn the lights on, I following instead, the soft clinking of a heavy metal chain. The bottle of pills rattled in my pocket, the only sound I brought with me.

I was here for a job, the best of all the horrible options I had.

Maybe not forever, though.

Shatter was the first person I'd ever seen reach Umbra while he was like that. I couldn't even do that. Coming to this academy was a last, desperate chance to salvage something of what had been stolen from us. But maybe… *just* maybe, she was the answer we'd been searching for.

I would never let her go.

Shatter damned herself to us tonight. In doing so, she'd unknowingly secured her own safety.

Tomorrow she would accept the nest whether she wanted to or not. Tomorrow, I would have her scent.

It was more than a want.

I'd claim it before her mates did, like I would claim her.

Shatter, so pure and innocent, was tangled in this vile web, with or without us. She was fighting me for a fate she wasn't ready to see the truth of.

But we'd been fighting in darkness for so long, there was nothing else I could see.

Finally, there was the faintest light at the end of the tunnel.

And she was pure poetry.

The little thief that I'd stolen away from far more vicious thieves, might truly be the answer to what they'd taken.

CHAPTER 11

There was an attack. The subject was injured by an alpha in my employ. She was off suppressants, and the alpha was near a rut. We have decided to put her back on scent and hormone blockers for her own safety.

Dusk

Shatter came to me the next evening.

It was two days until classes started, and she hadn't left the apartment today. She'd clung to Umbra like a barnacle (which delighted him) and given me a sickly sweet smile when I'd handed her another bag of takeout. Umbra had burned her toast for breakfast and, irritatingly, she'd eaten it anyway, staring me dead in the eye the whole time.

I had been itching with impatience all day, but we were in a cold war, and I wouldn't crack. Umbra would, at least, tell me if she tried to turn in with him tonight. Then I would intervene. Until then, I'd give her one last chance to choose this herself. A choice from her would make it easier.

It was late, though, and I'd been about to head out to the living room and let her know her fate when I heard a faint knock on my bedroom door.

I straightened in an instant, then jumped from my bed and crossed the room.

I was met by a pair of captivating eyes framed by chaotic waves of honey brown hair. Her eyes were brown, not golden. She was wearing contacts, just for me, the little brat. She *knew* I wanted to see them gold.

Still, she looked nervous, hand clutching her arm, face ashen.

"Yes?" I asked, as if we both didn't know why she was here.

She cleared her throat, forcing herself to meet my eyes. "I would…" She trailed off, then tried again. "I want the nest."

"You're ready to accept the rules?"

"You said if I come and let you…" She averted her gaze, her delicate fists balling at her side anxiously. "Get your punishment over with, then I could have it."

"I did say that. But I need to know you can follow the rules, or it's not much of a nest, is it? We can come and go whenever. Is that what you want—?"

"No."

"So you're going to do what we say?"

Her nod was fractional, her jaw clenched. "You never told me the second rule."

I shrugged. "You already broke it." Umbra had informed me of that with a little too much delight.

She frowned, analysing me.

I grinned. "Never make a deal with Umbra."

Her lips parted for a moment, then she frowned. "Why?"

"He always wins."

"But why is it a rule?"

"I told you." I shrugged. "They're for you. I won't do anything if you break that one."

Wouldn't need to.

She looked more irritated at my answer. She was endlessly charming, and stubborn as a mule. Even if I had told her the rule ahead of time, she might have walked into it, anyway.

I stepped back from the door. "So?"

She looked around the room, clearly unsure. Then she walked in, tense as a frightened mouse, jumping as I pulled the door shut behind her.

I crossed toward my bed and sat down, beckoning her. She was reluctant, but she followed, standing a few feet away before I tugged her closer.

"Can we get it over with?" she asked.

A growl of annoyance rumbled in my chest.

Over with?

I intended to enjoy tonight. She would too, she just didn't know it yet. And at the end of it all, I got to give her the nest I'd made her.

"Lose the top and leggings."

"What?"

I tugged her closer, fuelled by the shock in her eyes. "No arguments and no hesitation," I reminded her.

"I thought this was supposed to be punishment," she whispered.

"For *you.*"

There was a long silence in which she seemed to weigh her dwindling options. Then, slowly, she tugged the top from over her head and pulled the leggings off. Beneath, she wore a black bralette and simple silk underwear. My cock was instantly hard at the sight of her rich golden skin, even though she hugged herself, trying to shield my view of her breathtaking body

"Relax," I told her. "You're beautiful."

Her lips drew into that anxious line I'd seen far too often at my praise. It wasn't anger, like some of her responses. It was something else. Even more fascinating, when her eyes slid down to my crotch, noticing my hard-on, her breathing calmed—just a little.

Perhaps that was it then. She didn't know if she could believe me. I frowned. I'd rid her of that doubt soon enough. "Take off my belt and put it on the bed."

She opened her mouth, eyes wide, but I clamped a hand over it before she could speak.

"You're here to show me obedience, not to argue with every command."

I watched the way her throat moved as she swallowed.

"I axed a good number of your punishments for what you did for Umbra last night, but you're racking them up again. Keep on, and we'll be here all night, and you'll have trouble walking tomorrow."

She would, regardless.

As I lowered my hand, she just stared at me in silence. Finally, she glanced down at my belt. I didn't stand up, and she had to sink to her knees to get a good hold. I groaned as she fumbled, and her palm brushed my crotch.

She froze again, eyes meeting mine.

God, I loved how nervous she was—and how very shocked she was going to be when I made her own body betray those furious little convictions of hers.

Tonight, I would get rid of these scent blockers of hers. I could let them wear off, but now she was in my room, I was impatient. The pill I had tucked away in my drawer would do the job for me.

Finally, she managed to get my belt free and tug it away.

"Get rid of the contacts."

She chewed on her lip for a long moment, clearly fighting another argument. Then she turned on her heel and made for the bathroom.

My cock hardened more at the sight of her strut, brown waves long enough to brush her tailbone, and her pert ass barely covered by black panties.

When she returned to standing before me, I leaned back for a moment, taking her in. She had a mane of loose hair, a luscious body, and her breasts pressed against her bra enough that I'd get a good handful. She was slender, with a faint line of abs along her stomach, sweet dips between her hips and curved thighs. Glowing golden skin that taunted me with the urge to drag her against me and sink my teeth in right now.

A sexy little fairy omega, and she was all mine.

Her brows were bunched, her cute curved nose was crinkled, and there was a furious downturn to her soft lips, enough to absolutely be a pout.

A *furious* little fairy omega—and more so by the second as she was forced to stand in silence as I drank in her gorgeous body.

I leaned forward, reaching up and tilting her chin gently, watching the way the light danced across those perfect eyes. "I don't want anything other than your real eyes on me when I fuck your tight body into the sheets tonight."

She took a step back, rich skin going ashen, but I caught her wrist.

"No." Her voice was a frightened hiss.

"'*No* is not a very obedient word."

She looked ready to run, but instead she reached out to me, almost imploring, then drew back. "*Please*." Her voice shook. She was trying to reason with me as if she were cracking a mask and stepping out of a game, and we could just turn off reality. "You never said… You never said that. I'm doing what you want." Her lip trembled. "You said you were only going to… to punish me."

"I will. And when I'm done, I'm going to take care of you."

"You said I'd get the nest."

I raised an eyebrow, getting to my feet at last and catching her before she could stagger another pace back. "Shatter," I breathed, forcing her to look at me. "You think I'd let you walk into a nest I made for you if you weren't covered in my scent? If you didn't have me dripping down your thighs?"

A whimper slipped from her, and her lip trembled.

"It's *my* nest," I said. "And you want it."

She clasped her fingers, and I saw a flash of vulnerability I hadn't before. "It's not because *you* made it that I want it."

I believed her, actually.

She was cracking. The nest was solace.

She was almost *too* wild for an omega—more than I'd even known was possible—tangled in instincts that ruled her more than she did them.

I recognised that when I saw it.

I'd seen her and claimed her as mine, consequences be damned.

Since the first night I'd seen her, I hadn't been able to rid her from my dreams. She wouldn't know how torturous it was to wait for her tonight.

I needed more of those fragments of space when I saw her crack, when I pushed her hard enough that I could see that thing she was so desperately fighting—that she wanted us.

Also, her lips around my cock… *that* I hadn't been able to shed from my hormone-riddled brain. *Fuck*, I needed her. And *she* needed her own space in our home.

I'd had her nest ready before she'd even arrived. I wouldn't feel guilty, because she'd been too stubborn to take it. This desperation was her own fault.

"What would you have done if they hadn't made you a nest?" I asked.

Her lips drew back in a snarl. "The nest they'll make me will make yours look like *nothing*."

My laugh was hollow and purely reactionary. I didn't, at that moment, think I could have hidden the sickness on my face without it.

She had no idea.

There would be no nest.

No love.

I knew the Lincoln pack's reputation though; I knew how charming of a mask they wore, and how vile the creatures beneath. But Shatter, it seemed, had been taken by it, too.

What would have happened if I hadn't found her when I did? What might alphas like them do if they discovered their scent match was an unregistered gold pack…?

Goosebumps lifted across my skin at the thought of it, and my grip on her tightened.

She wasn't ready for that truth.

"Please, Dusk." Her face was still pale. "You c-can't take that. It's th-theirs."

Theirs?

She didn't understand what bait that was. I would take everything in this world that was theirs. She may hate me for it now, but she would *see* the truth one day. It wasn't something I could tell her—not until she chose us—for those secrets, in the hands of her mates, could sow our destruction.

Again, I had to take those thoughts and bury them for the sake of the beautiful omega standing before me. *She* deserved better than to have this night tainted by her mates.

Was that the first time she'd used my name? It sounded good on her lips, especially when she was begging.

I liked that. It meant she was starting to get it.

I called the shots. It was what I did—the only one of us who could, and I kept my pack safe. Once she got that, once she stopped fighting me, she'd be happy.

"How about this? Find that first orgasm before I'm done with your punishment, and I won't make you come over my knot."

She visibly shivered, rosy lips parting slightly and her pupils dilated just enough that I noticed.

"Why are you doing this?" Her voice was pleading.

"Because I want you." It was that simple. She *was* special for far more than just her mates.

Again, I saw the little frown, the brief flicker of need in her eyes that was quickly shadowed by hurt. Again, I tried to unpack that. She *did* want her mates—or she thought she did. But she also couldn't stop reacting when I praised her, and it was the hottest thing I'd ever seen.

But was it me? Or just what I chose to say to her?

If it had her soaked for me, I wasn't sure that I cared. But that didn't stop me from wanting to know. If she was in as many pieces and Umbra and ransom, it would be my job to pick them up.And I'd do that. I'd pick them all up, put her back together and make those pieces stay in place, because she was mine, and that's what I did when someone was mine.

"Why don't you dark bond me?" she asked.

I snorted.

A dark bond was entirely unappealing. Complete control over a creature as bright as her?

Then where would we be?

Her light would fade, and I would turn to stone. Power like that wasn't a gift, it was poison. A temptation always present, wearing down who I was. If I didn't have to bleed for what I had, what would stop me from becoming the monsters I hunted?

"I won't bond you until you ask," I told her.

"I'll never ask."

I offered her a half smile. She *would* crack. "So," I said. "Shall we get started?"

Reaching out I picked up the belt, spotting the way her gaze went wide as she looked at it. I stood and tugged her gently until we were standing before the base-board of my bed, then I stepped behind her, hands dropping to her hips. I took my time, loving the way her body felt against me.

Warm, smooth flesh, a contrast to years of coldness and sharp edges.

Something precious. That's what she was.

An omega who might change everything.

She was still so tense, body hunched—afraid of me, while she chased something that would rip her apart. I shoved down the spike of fear at what *could* have happened at the gala, if I hadn't found her in time.

But I had her. She was here.

She was safe.

I smiled, drawing her closer, resting my chin on her head, feeling the way her messy waves tickled my neck, and thinking of better things. She certainly wouldn't manage an orgasm before I was done. She could try, but I'd make sure I won that bet I *needed* her, and I was going to fuck her senseless.

My cock twitched at the thought of it, and all the lurking monsters scattered like they never had before.

"Right, Gem," I murmured. "Put your hands on that footboard and don't let go until I say you can. This is your chance to show me you can listen. Let go even once, and I'll carry you straight to the nest and fuck every one of your tight holes."

Her breath caught at that, and she tried to step from my grip as she reached for the wood. I didn't let her; instead running my hand down the small of her back and feeling goosebumps light on her skin as she was forced to bend while still pressed up against me.

Shit.

She was breathtaking like that. Her honey brown hair tumbled toward the floor, the gold of her skin glowing in the dim lights I'd left on. I nudged her feet so they were shoulder-width apart, giving me a stunning view of her sweet ass hugged by black silk.

I stepped back, folding the belt in two and securing the buckle in my fist. "I'm going to punish you for lying to me."

"I d-don't know what you mean."

"You keep saying you don't want me."

"I *don't* want—" She let out a shocked whimper as, anticipating her answer, I let loose the first strike of the belt. It *cracked* against the delicate skin of her thighs, just below her ass.

Her breathing was coming in sharp pants, and I watched carefully as her skin blossomed pink, a stripe against rich skin.

While she drew deep breaths, I left her for a moment, crossing back to my bedside table and picking up the small bottle of massage oil. I poured some onto my palm, then tucked the bottle into my pocket.

Shatter jumped as I palmed the smooth curve of her ass, rubbing the oil gently into the smarting welt I'd left.

"W-what are you doing?" she asked, voice a rasp.

I didn't answer.

She was shivering, I realised, but she didn't let go of the footboard, clearly trying to keep silent, even as I massaged her sore flesh. It remained a bright pink, shining now with the thin layer of oil across it.

A perfect shade.

I continued working her tender skin, almost able to feel her confusion. "We're going to do ten…" I paused at the faintest moan of shock she let out. "But I'll stop if you admit you were lying."

She'd be crying if we reached ten, but a part of me didn't believe she'd break. She was stubborn, wild, and determined—for all the wrong things.

"Every time you defend those alphas, I will punish you and take my pleasure without you." Then I tugged at her panties, ignoring her squeak of derision as I shifted them to the side enough that they caught along the crease of her sex. I was rewarded by the sight of glistening slick. If I left them like that, they would tug just the right way every time she moved. It left me with full access, both to the sight of her pretty cunt and how wet it was getting.

"But if you're a good girl, and take your punishment without argument…" She let out a whine as I slipped a finger into her, pumping into her once, then twice with a second finger to get her warmed up. She was so fucking tight and wet that the black fabric clinging to her pussy was damp through.

We'd barely even begun.

I stepped to the side and crouched down beside her, tucking her hair behind her ear so I could see her face. Her eyes were squeezed shut.

"If you aren't lying, why are you soaked?"

"You're an alpha," she hissed. *"It's normal."*

"So you'd prefer it if it were… Eric, doing this to you?" It was dangerous, speaking one of those names, and I let a wall slam closed, keeping the fury that could come with it at bay.

She looked shocked for a moment, and I could see the way her mind tripped over that question as if she wasn't sure what to do with it. "He would never do this to me."

I stared at her, suddenly concerned I'd taken one step too far. Familiar hatred was made of vicious shadows that stretched, and bile burned my throat. *Too close to the sun…*

Only then my eyes met hers—glinting gems of gold, even distraught as they were. The world steadied, darkness fading from my vision.

"No," I said quietly. "He wouldn't. No alpha in that pack will ever give you anything I'll give you tonight."

Her brows came down, gaze shifting to something more analysing as she took me in. She was erratic, but she wasn't stupid. "I wouldn't want them to."

Ignoring her, I pressed my fingers to her lips. "Clean me off, Gem."

The look she gave me might have been enough to kill, but she didn't fight me as I pushed my fingers into her mouth, sliding in and out, enjoying the dancing hatred in her eyes as they held mine. I was still steady—more steady than I was used to. So, I took another step into dangerous territory.

"Why are you so desperate for them?" I asked, withdrawing my fingers.

"They're my mates."

"You don't know them. They've barely noticed you."

"I…" She looked surprisingly hurt when I said that. "They will. I believe in scent matches."

"Do you?" I asked.

Her expression was determined. "Yes."

"And last night with Umbra?" I stood, drinking in her beautiful shivering body again, bent over and waiting for me, however I wanted to use her.

"It didn't mean anything." Her voice became more breathless as I ran my touch along her back.

"Or how about you climbing into my bed so you could—?"

"You're an *alpha.*" She quickly cut me off, tensing as I brushed along her inner thighs. "The other rooms were locked, and you won't let me out, and I just… I needed an alpha's scent."

Is *that* what she'd told herself? I almost laughed. She was far too good at convincing herself of lies. Most omegas were deeply unsettled by my pack's scents. They wouldn't be seeking mine out, they'd be hurrying in the opposite direction—of course, until they discovered how rich we were.

"It doesn't matter if you betray them," I said instead. "They're never going to find out. They're never going to have you."

"I…" She took a breath, head tilting like she was bracing. "I'm going to get to them. You can't stop me forever."

A cold smile curved my lips. I was half taken by her determination and half irritated at her foolishness. I would keep her safe until I could show her. One day soon.

"Don't move," I told her. I'd planned where I wanted to mark her.

I tugged her panties down, finally getting a full view. She went absolutely still, breathing paused.

"You're perfect," I said. "So fucking beautiful like I knew you'd be." I wanted her to know how true those words were. I stepped closer, grinding my rock hard bulge against her cunt as I bent over, placing my own hand on the footboard, my other winding around her body, exploring her waist and hips, slipping beneath her bra to tweak her nipple.

She let out a strangled snarl as she felt my teeth graze her shoulder, the sound absolutely feral.

"There you go, Gem. Relax." I grasped her hips as I straightened, pressing my rigid cock harder into her for a second. She let out a rush of breath. "If you can get off, I won't fuck you, remember?"

I felt her shiver against me right before I stepped back, bracing the belt again and examining her. I'd barely done anything and she was panting. I cupped her pussy with my hand. "What's this?" I asked, using two fingers to scoop the pooling slick back into her ever so slowly, enjoying her unsettled moans as I did. "You're dripping at the idea of me fucking you tonight."

"You're an alpha," she said. "That's all."

So fucking loyal to them.

Such a little liar.

I held my fingertips at her entrance for a few long seconds, then drove them in without warning twice more. Her sounds were desperate, goosebumps rippled across her skin, and her back arched as she battled her own arousal. I swear she was fighting the urge to grind into my touch.

Then I stepped back, lining up the belt, measuring it up where I wanted it—right across her round ass cheeks. She tensed at the touch, clearly knowing what was coming. When it hit, she whimpered again.

Her noises were so hot. With each strike she trembled more, and by the sixth, there was slick glistening down her thighs. Between each strike, I treated her sore flesh with a massage and oil.

Her grip on the footboard was white knuckled, but still, she didn't break.

I counted out ten and she didn't stop me, admit her lie, or make any noise beyond a whimper. She didn't cry, either. *Determination, or is she not a stranger to pain?*

I tossed the belt and the bottle onto the bed and returned. She didn't jump this time as I touched her, now expecting it. I could see my work, one pink line across her ass, a perfect mark. Her skin shimmered with slick, sweat, and oil. She was mesmerising.

"You did *so* well, Gem," I told her as I dipped my thumb into her cunt.

To my delight, she groaned, so wound up from the pain I'd delivered that she couldn't hide her need anymore. Too wound up to notice when I dropped down to my knees between her legs. I would take my time, but she wouldn't make it to the orgasm she was trying so hard to reach. The pill on my bedside table would reveal her scent to me so I could have her all. At last.

My omega.

"Good girl," I praised, pumping my thumb in and out, relishing in how much slick she'd made for me.

Then I drew my thumb back, taking her thighs in both hands, and Shatter let out the cutest squeak of shock as I did what I'd been desperate to do since she'd first bent over for me.

CHAPTER 12

Shatter

Dusk was…

Fuck.

Stars shot through my veins, unwelcome visitors burning my sanity away as Dusk dragged his tongue all the way up my entrance, higher until he was… I whimpered, a shock of pleasure hitting my veins and drowning my pain as he un-ashamedly buried his face into, well, everything.

Oh my God.

Oh my God.

Heat burned my cheeks as I trembled, legs unable to give out with the way he gripped my thighs in place. I'd never felt anything like this heat rushing to my core.

I'd been fighting with my tears since the third blow, but the war I'd waged against the pain left my mind in shambles, and I'd felt things I had no explanation for. It was almost impossible to keep holding on to the bed as his tongue worked me into a puddle.

It was good. I… I needed to get off.

Then that would be it, and he would let me have the nest.

But it would be like he'd won. And I'd have less to give my mates…

He adjusted, one arm slipping between my legs and reaching up to clamp around my waist so he could draw me against him firmly. I let out a whine as, with his free hand, he pressed his thumb into me again, pumping in and out as his tongue found its way up to my backdoor.

Why was he doing that?

And why did it feel like someone had detonated an army of butterflies and glitter in my brain when he did? I couldn't think straight, and traitorous sounds were coming from my chest that I couldn't fight.

He was cheating. This wasn't *normal.* And I'd been on the edge of my first orgasm for days.

I wanted it, right?

I mean—I didn't want *him,* but I wanted him not to fuck me. Crying would be really, really fucking humiliating right now, but I could barely keep the tears at bay.

Sometimes, his grip would shift, tenderly squeezing the sore areas of my flesh with such gentleness, and it was mixing me up. He did it again, palm massaging the ache, and I let out another embarrassingly high pitched sound. I heard his rumble of a growl in response. He sounded pleased.

I tried to unscramble my brain and think about the building pleasure. If I focused on it hard enough, I could get there before he stopped me. I hated him more for making this my best option.

I struggled for the orgasm, knowing it had to be close. Finally, I felt a distant surge of warmth, like I had yesterday.

As if he was waiting for my body's reaction, his mouth and thumb vanished. This time the sound I made was visceral, containing that spark of rage I'd taught myself to stamp down to avoid punishment. But Dusk had already fucking done that part.

It took everything in me to hold on to the bed, but I managed it, hating that his hands were at my hips, holding me up because I was under threat of buckling, my breaths coming short and sharp.

It was so easy for him to lift me in his arms, and then I was being dropped onto the bed. Before I could get my bearings, he was there, and I had his entire body weight to contend with.

Fear spiked my system as I realised he was done and I hadn't… I hadn't managed to—

My thoughts cut off as his grip clamped down on my chin, and he was kissing me deeply, his huge frame crushing mine. He was groping my body as if he couldn't get enough, and he'd taken his shirt off in the time it had taken him to pin me here. The sensation of skin pressed to mine was jarring because it didn't feel bad, but I grabbed that thought by the throat and shoved it somewhere deep.

Finally, he broke for air, drawing back and looking down at me with piercing yellow eyes that were bright with lust. "Do you like how you taste, Gem?" he asked. "Because it's the best thing I've ever had."

I whimpered as his teeth found my nipple and bit down. I was still shaking from the aftershocks of the almost-orgasm. I'd had too many almosts.

I wasn't *built* for this.

"Didn't manage it?" he asked me, nipping at my breast again and getting a jolt from me. "That's too bad."

My fingers gripped his hair viciously. "*Fuck* you," I spat.

His grin was infuriatingly playful, canines flashing. "I could help you one last time—see if you can get there—before I split you open on my cock."

I blinked.

"But only if you ask nicely."

I gritted my teeth, holding back from lunging at him.

"No?" he asked, when I couldn't find my voice. "Rather we just—?"

"No!" Fuck. "Give me another chance," I begged.

He couldn't take my first time. Tears threatened my eyes again.

It was theirs.

It wasn't just something I could offer them. Was it worse if it was him? What if they ever learned that it had happened like this? Right under their noses?

Would they hate me for it?

That they knew the alpha who'd taken it from them?

Dusk sat up, dragging me with him so I was straddling his lap. Then he reached over, tugging something from the bedside drawer.

I flinched back as he lifted a piece of black cloth.

"Sit still," he said.

I bit back my nerves, still desperate for a way out as he tugged the cloth over my eyes and secured it.

Something was pressed to my lips. I felt the round edges of another pill in his hands. I snapped back, trying to turn my head, but he was insistent, pressing it to my tongue. I tried to spit it out, but it was already dissolving in my mouth. It was mild, almost powdery, and didn't taste like anything I'd had before. A low sound of panic loosed from my chest.

"It won't hurt you, Gem," he told me.

I despised that my heart rate calmed, and that the promises he made held so much weight. I no longer hesitated to trust what he told me. I struggled with trust, living in a world where I had *so* much trouble telling truth from lies. My options were either to trust broadly or to live an existence where I could never trust at all. But Dusk *was* a truth teller. He'd proved it on more than one occasion, and I despised how much safety there was in that.

But I was so close to the nest—to getting this all over with.

Now I was left in the dark, and every one of his touches set my hairs on end. Goosebumps were a constant companion despite the warmth of the room.

He took his time doing whatever it was he planned on doing, first touching me with passion—a brush along my neck, or my thigh or breast. I spiralled, overwhelmed with his scent and caress, aching right down to my core, shivering and needy until my mind wandered to the drug.

He'd been so insistent, making me take it. Not telling me what it was.

Again, his touch brushed my hips, clamping down and holding me over him before caressing my skin.

I was trembling now, my brain sluggish with lust I didn't want, but that still consumed me. Next time he shifted beneath me, a breathless sound came from my throat, unbidden and wrong.

Had he fucked with my hormones so that I wanted him? Was that what the drug had done?

I squeezed my eyes shut beneath the blindfold, fighting another needy sound that wanted to surface at his touches. He didn't stop, and I jumped as his fingers dipped below my bra and rolled along my nipple. The sound I made was low and traitorous, but I was shaking, head to toe.

Then the touch slipped between my thighs, and I let out a breath of panic, wriggling away, but his other hand held my hips in place.

"Shh," he murmured, and his fingers brushed along the slick coating my heat. "You're so wet for me."

"It's… not…" I tried to say the words, but my voice was nothing more than a whine.

I clamped my mouth shut, but he hadn't moved his fingers. I could feel them there, pressed against my entrance, but he didn't move. I was frozen, hips raised just enough that my muscles were strained.

"Go on then, Gem. Pleasure yourself, so I don't have to do it."

I still shook, desperate, needy.

Was this the drugs?

This isn't me.

I don't want this.

I needed it, though. I needed this, so he wouldn't go any further.

As he twisted my nipple, I shuddered and sank down onto him with a moan. Stars lit in my veins, and I squeezed my eyes shut, hating myself. Even though something wasn't right… it wasn't his fingers I sank onto. It was something solid and thin—about the width of a finger, but cooler.

"Good girl," he breathed, tugging on my nipple again, which made it hard to orient myself.

But he wasn't even using his fingers. I didn't know why that was so much more humiliating, but it was… impersonal, like he was playing with me.

Sometimes, the way he looked at me, I thought maybe he *did* want me. After what he'd just done it was hard to deny. But I knew any alphas who weren't my mates would hurt me with ease, and this could be a long game for him.

Would he even fuck me? Or was this about seeing how far I could be pushed?

I was afraid that this was all a game to him, when I didn't know up from down…

Still, my mind was hazy. I just knew I had to get off, as debasing at this was. It wasn't long before I sank back down with a feral relief at the feeling of the object that was filling me. My nerves were on fire. I needed release from this touch. I needed… something more.

"Beautiful," he murmured, such easy praise that shook me soul deep like the pathetic omega I was, betraying my mates like this. The heat in my core built, slower this time, a restless tide frantic to break free.

With this blindfold on, it was like he was everywhere. A whole world of midnight opium drowning me. Why was his scent so soothing?

I ground down over the rigid object, a whimper loosing from my throat. It wasn't enough. It left me feeling hollow.

He shifted, and the object was gone. I gasped as his grip clamped around my neck.

"Is it not enough, Gem?" he asked. "When you were melting on my fingers before?"

Again, I felt the thing slide inside me and I moaned. It *wasn't* enough and slick was dripping down my thighs.

I was heady with need and shame, desperate for this to be over. But he'd stopped, and my pulse was racing.

My mind still wasn't right, my body shaking as he slid the thin object into me over and over. "Tell me it's not enough," he said.

My breathing ragged, my body on fire from the orgasm left on the edge. I was moaning, frantic and pitiful. I didn't want it, yet I knew I needed it. I *had* to find a way to make it happen.

Again, he slid it in, and again I moaned with desperation at the taunt. He was holding me still so he could be the one who pressed it into me.

"All you have to do is shake your head." His words were a caress in my ear, and still he was pumping it in and out, holding me suspended over him by my neck.

"It will be," I hissed, fighting his grip to grind down on it, to find something more.

"That's okay, precious," he murmured, and the object was gone. "I can do better."

"N-no. Wait—!" But the blindfold was ripped away.

"It's okay to admit it's not enough."

"I can," I started. "I can make it work—"

That was when I caught the faintest scent of sunflowers and sesame, just as I saw what was in his hand.

Gareth's pen.

Fury rose in my chest, along with a snarl. I tried to lunge for him even close as we were, but he held me back with ease, a grin on his face as he tucked the pen behind his ear, his other hand still holding me in place by my neck.

"*I* am going to give you release."

The words were a bath of ice, stuttering out the lust high from the drugs he'd given me.

No…

But then his fingers were right where the pen had been, dipping into me just enough to make me whimper.

"That's already so much better, isn't it?"

"*Fuck*… you." I tried too hard to hold on to that hatred, but I was trembling for the release my body had been promised for too long.

"No," I grit out. I threw my whole weight against his grip. He couldn't take this from me. I didn't care what he'd drugged me with.

His laugh was low, and then he reached for his jeans.

Panic speared my system, and I tried to dive away from him. He didn't even need his aura to pin me to the bed as he tugged his jeans off. It didn't matter that I tried to claw at him with all my might. Then he dragged me back to straddle his lap.

"N-no!" All my instincts broke loose, every fear that I could have given so much, given everything, to get here, only to see him rip it away so quickly. "I hate you!" I spat. "I fucking hate you!"

"Hear this promise, Gem." His voice was a low growl, and his next words sent a chill soul deep. "I will give you everything you're too broken to ask for."

How… dare he? A furious snarl rose in my chest. My nails clawed at his flesh, furious at his words. *"Don't—"*

His hand squeezed my neck as he pressed into me, stretching me far more than anything before. The sound I made was pathetic, but the worst part was how it set fire to every nerve in my body.

He'd planned it this way. Drugging me and teasing me until there was no other response I was capable of giving. And it was overwhelming, with more stars of bliss shooting through my system as I drove my nails deeper into his flesh. None of it made a difference for how he dragged my body over his length with such ease. He barely blinked, catching my hand in his teeth as I clawed at his face and driving into me with a jarring force that made me whine.

Then he fucked me slowly, letting each thrust set my nerves on fire, getting the most horrible whimpers from my chest, half grief, half burning need.

"*Fuck*, Gem…" I swear there was a tremor in his grip as he dragged me over him the next time. "You're more than I could ever fucking dream of."

His grip tightened on my neck as he began fucking me with more speed. He was everywhere. He was everything in the world right now. Bright yellow eyes, pupils dilated with want, lip caught in his teeth as he groaned.

"You're a fragment of heaven, Shatter," he breathed. "Changing us in ways you have no right to."

I didn't know what that meant.

He lifted me, shaft still deep in my core, and positioned himself above me so my back was to the sheets. I squeezed my eyes shut.

"You're special," he told me. "No one—no omega—has ever been able to get through to Umbra before," he breathed. My eyes snapped open, and I met his gaze. "No omega has ever caught our eye."

My lips parted as I stared at him.

What?

"You're our first, Shatter," he told me.

"First?" My voice was broken with a stupid, soaring blaze of hope.

I was…?

He *could* be lying, but I didn't think he was. I could almost *feel* that conviction, midnight opium surrounding me, absolute and full of a furious want. His piercing yellow eyes were intense, contrasted against dark, rugged skin, even more shadowed by the dim room. "You are the first omega I've ever been with," he breathed. "That I've ever wanted."

I don't know why that locked my throat the way it did. I don't know why every single shift of his length within me was suddenly like shots of lightning in my veins.

It took three of his deep thrusts before my body gave in and I finally crested the wave I'd been chasing. I cried out, clutching his arm where he squeezed my breath free of my lungs, and I was unable to take my eyes from the enraptured expression on his face as he watched my body succumb to him.

My eyes rolled back with the most intense feeling of my life, drawn out with each thrust until I felt his knot press against my entrance.

I gasped, scrabbling at his arms, each sound wild. My whole body was made of bolts of electricity. The orgasm was barely over, but he was still thrusting out and in.

"I can't…" I gasped. I felt as if every nerve was on the brink of exploding.

"You'll take me, Shatter."

I jolted in shock as I felt his touch on my clit. I whined, back arching as he began circling it, driving his knot against my entrance.

"I can't." I repeated, this time more emphatically, then jolted again as he sped up on my clit. I could barely breathe, instead whining pathetically.

"That perfect cunt of yours is going to take my knot," he growled. I was trapped beneath him, overwhelmed and completely at his mercy as his knot pressed against me again.

"Dusk…" I begged. I was desperate for… For what?

For him *not* to?

It didn't matter, because he tilted his head back, groaning as he stretched me open around his knot. I cried out again, nails clawing once more as he locked my shaking body against his.

"*Fuucckk*, Gem," he groaned, and a second orgasm slammed into me, violent and overwhelming. I stopped fighting him, shuddering and going limp in his grip as the second wave wiped my mind blank. All I knew was a vicious, overwhelming bliss as he came inside me with each thrust of his knot against my walls.

He rocked into me and I shuddered, completely overwhelmed with each movement, more low whines rising in my chest with every breath.

He stroked my hair as I recovered, a trembling mess in his arms. A low vibration started. Was he…? I froze, frowning.

He was purring.

It was strange and soothing, even when nothing about him should be. "Are you ashamed?"

I hugged myself, not answering.

I… didn't know. We were locked together, and we would be until his knot released me. It was overwhelming. The wrong alpha… But I was exhausted with pleasure I'd never felt, and there was a purr rumbling against me, leaving me with something I'd never had in my life. Something I'd come here in search of.

But I shouldn't have enjoyed that, and I certainly shouldn't feel safe.

Confused—was what I was.

His fingers wove through my hair and he shifted up until he was beneath me and I was sitting on top of him again. He made me look into his eyes. "I was going to play with you anyway, Gem, just like the whole world will if you won't stop it. This time you took something back."

"No," I whispered. "You… you drugged me."

It was the only explanation for any of this.

"I did," he said with a shrug, letting me go so I had to catch myself on his chest.

"I wouldn't have done any of that if you hadn't," I said.

He chuckled, and it sent a vibration between us, sparking nerve endings right through my core. Not wanting to look at him, I curled up tighter, hating that it meant sinking further into his arms. "The drugs undid the blockers, Gem, so I could catch your beautiful scent. They didn't touch your lust."

It took a second for those words to sink in, then panic speared my heart. A sob caught in my chest, but I couldn't find my words. "Y-you're lying."

He *hadn't.*

He had to be lying.

"Shatter—" He tried to still me, but I couldn't breathe.

"You can't… You don't…" My scent. He couldn't… He didn't understand. It was dangerous. I'd been attacked by an alpha one of the few times I'd revealed my scent. *He was close to a rut,* they'd told me, *unstable.* It was why I needed my scent matches. But Dusk was locked inside of me. We were *one* right now.

What was he going to do when he found the omega he was trapped with was—?

"SHATTER!" His voice finally broke through as his fingers clamped around my chin, forcing me to look at him.

My breathing was ragged, tears streaking my cheeks. Only, of course, my terror didn't help. I knew the moment it happened. The moment my scent finally broke through the drugs.

Dusk's eyes blew wider than I'd ever seen, his whole body going rigid. He dropped his grip on my chin, though his other hand remained at my hips, holding me against him.

The way I broke this time, it was worse. Embarrassing. Shameful.

Because the tears flooding my face weren't even fear for my life. Instead, it was because, in that moment, I knew even Dusk Varis wasn't going to want me—

"Fuck!" His growl was low and vicious, his aura splitting the air and making me jump. He let go of my hip for a moment so he could straighten us where we lay, staring down at me with eyes so blown they were entirely ink black.

I couldn't move, couldn't speak.

His lips were parted in shock.

I squeezed my eyes shut, trembling.

Do it quickly.

But then I felt the brush of his touch, and his grip wove through my hair, dragging my neck into an arch. I whined in terror. He was going to make me see his hatred. But I couldn't. I wouldn't open my eyes.

Just… do it quickly.

Instead, for the second time, I felt his lips pressed to mine when they absolutely shouldn't be. My eyes snapped open as I heard the purr stutter to life in his chest again, the sound warm and… and real. He… he *couldn't* be faking that, could he?

His kiss was possessive, his tongue claiming my mouth like his body claimed me, his knot still trapping me against him.

A final tear tracked my cheeks. I was still shaking as he drew back.

He'd claimed me, body and scent, and he wasn't attacking me. His scent was thick in the air, not with hatred at all. Instead, his dark amber scent of midnight opium was a storm of reverence.

When he spoke, his voice was rough and cracked.

"How do you keep getting more perfect?"

His eyes danced with wonder, his purr still vibrating between us.

" My sweet little deadly nightshade. "

CHAPTER 13

Dusk

Shatter's scent was dangerous, both as dark as ice cold silk, and as warm as the amber of cognac. It was a threat, and set every nerve in my body on end, enough perhaps, to break me if I was any other alpha.

But I wasn't, and Shatter's scent wasn't foreign.

Quite the contrary. It was a pillar—a cornerstone of everything I was, and with it came a memory like an avalanche swallowing me whole.

The alpha below me shuddered as my fists crushed his throat. The air was thick with something vicious that melted my brain. The room was pale and bright, etched behind my lids for eternity.

I never wanted this.

I wasn't a killer.

But I didn't want to die, not when I'd made it this long.

Him or you... The whisper was desperate and absolute, sinking claws into my mind as I choked a sob.

I couldn't die.

A low growl ripped from his throat as he jerked, eyes wide, every muscle strained. He wasn't fighting me.

I was killing him, and he wasn't fighting.

That was wrong...

Fragile shards, the few remaining pieces of my mind, cracked further.

"Dusk." His croak was weak and foreign, but it seized me, dragging me back.

A name unclaimed. A name that risked blood and pain. Just like his.

No.

I felt a growl of terror rise in my chest.

I didn't know him.

He was seconds from passing out, h-he had to be. I braced to throw my weight down. Do it fast. Get it over with.

Then you'll live.

You'll be free.

He had to die. He had to, or he would kill me.

Only, he wasn't fighting. Another low, frightened noise shuddered over my vocal cords as his hand came up. Not in aggression. Instead, he cupped my face, fingers shaking as he trailed my cheek.

The haze splintered, shattered by a man so much stronger than I'd ever been. An alpha I knew. An alpha who'd claimed me as a brother in a place void of warmth.

Sandstorm eyes.

Wolfsbane and blood.

Kill him and I would live.

That day, I'd been reborn.

"I'm going to share your scent with Umbra," I breathed.

I hadn't realised what it would be like. It kept catching me off guard, how utterly incredible she was.

She tensed, frightened, finally daring to look up at me, glittering eyes still flecked with tears. "You c-can't."

I understood, at last, why she was so afraid.

"He *will* love it."

She didn't react for a long time, not until I reached over to the bedside table, picking up my phone to text Umbra.

Her delicate omega fingers closed around my wrist. "Don't." Her breathing picked up, the beautiful scent flooding the room with fear as her eyes darted between me and the phone.

I sighed, setting it down. "Alright, Gem. You did take my knot so well tonight."

She shivered against me at those words, and I wrapped my arms around her, letting my purr rumble to life again as I held her close. She was so, so perfect.

At my purr, her scent calmed by a fraction, but not completely. I held her in my arms, trapped against me, completely vulnerable when vulnerability wasn't what she'd offered. I knew that feeling, knew how it would fracture a person or make them. I'd stolen from her, taken something she'd never wanted to give, but she was strong. One day we would lie like this and it would be free of fear or worry or pain.

I knew it, because it was my dream, not just for her, but for all of my pack.

By the time my knot released her, she'd changed. All her fight had drained away. I fetched a cloth to take care of her; it was an instinct etched into every pathway in my brain. Then I gave her a bathrobe to tug around herself.

The cloth was warm against my palm, wrapped neatly as I drew it down her cheek.

When I was done, I lifted a pillow to her, and she stared at it with blank eyes. "Mark it for him."

I wouldn't keep her scent to myself, no matter how much she was afraid of Umbra catching it. Her eyes slid to me, but she didn't argue, pressing it to her neck and filling the air with her dark perfume.

When she stood, she winced. The result of the fuck, or the smarting bruise I'd left on her flesh, I wasn't sure.

"Next time, behave better and it will only be good, Gem."

She just looked at me, more hollow than ever. "Give me my nest."

I cocked my head, digesting her expression, which was much too neutral for what I'd come to expect of her. At my hesitation, she cracked.

"I did what you asked," she whispered. "You took everything." Her breathing came ragged all of a sudden and her fist closed in my shirt, fresh tears spilling down her face. "You took everything, so just give me my nest!"

Good.

That was good.

She needed to get this out now, and I would take that blame if it would soften the devastation to come. She was angry. Grief for filth that didn't deserve it, but she would have to, one way or another. Better a piece at a time now, because here, with me, she was strong even if she didn't realise it.

Ignoring her flinch, I took her hand in mine. Then I led her from the room and across the hall to the door of the nest.

I tugged my key from my pocket and unlocked the door. When I opened it she stepped inside, and her scent shifted at last with a breath of relief. Until she turned and saw me following.

"No," she snarled. "*No.* It's fucking mine. You said it was mine. You said you wouldn't come in."

"It is, but tonight I'm going to give it to you."

"What does that mean?"

I would be quick. But one more time tonight, I would cause her pain. I'd seen the level of dissonance she was capable of. If she never saw me in this nest, if there wasn't even the slightest trace of my pack, how far back could she slide, even in only a night?

I took another step, ignoring her hiss of rage, ignoring the tears that clouded her eyes once more.

"I hate you," she snarled again as I led her to the walk-in closet. I don't know why it lit a fire in my chest when she spat those words, doing the opposite that they were supposed to, but I stifled my cold smile. Instead, I opened a drawer and pulled out a nightdress before holding it out to her.

She just stared at it, then at me, and I saw the first true darkness in her eyes.

"If you would like me to leave sooner…?" I supplied.

She grabbed it and I leaned against the wall, watching her shrug off the dressing gown and pull it over her head as fast as she could manage.

Angry, sad, jealous? I didn't really care. I could stare at her forever. Especially in a pretty silk nightdress that barely covered her thighs.

It was chosen by me. Everything in here was. Would she care to unpack the clothes in that suitcase of hers? I'd already sifted through it and realised quickly that it wasn't hers at all. There was nothing, not even a few trinkets or items like most omegas might have.

She followed me to the bed, still tense with her arms crossed. She watched as I folded back the blanket, which was spread across the bed at that angle she preferred. All the bedsheets and blankets were square. I'd seen her in a strop that first night, folding the bedding so it was even before she could tilt it.

I turned to her. "Would you like to look around before you turn in?"

"No." Her voice cracked though, and her eyes darted across the room. There was a flicker of desperation in her gaze and I knew she was seeking something wrong.

She grew more rigid as she found nothing, and as she did, nightshade loosened with a reluctant comfort. A few more times she scanned the hangings across the walls, turned to their sides, to the huge bookshelf stacked with every textbook I'd been able to find on Arkology, to the broad desk beside a reading nook.

There was more to do in here, I knew that—more she must want, but for now, I didn't think I'd missed anything.

"Alright." I held a hand out to her.

She slipped by me silently, sitting on the side of the bed. She cleared her throat and her words were so perfectly even, I knew she'd done this part before. "Thank you for the nest." Her voice didn't waver. Not even a little. Her hands were folded in her lap, her chin tilted down.

I cocked my head.

A *new* mask?

One I hadn't yet seen.

I crouched before her, tugging her close and ignoring her flinch as she felt the sting of my welts against the sheets.

I nudged her chin to face me, and was met again with those blank orbs of gold.

"You're mine, sweet omega.
Your mates will never have your scent."

Tonight, I would let her place her hatred at my feet. I could live with that because she was mine, never theirs, and she wouldn't hate me forever.

CHAPTER 14

Since the attack, the subject has displayed severe self-destructive behaviours. She has connected the attack with her own failure as an omega.

She was discovered in the garden, lying in a thicket of nettles. She has expressed suicidal ideations, and we have temporarily begun twenty-four-hour monitoring for her safety. She is actively suppressing all omega tendencies by choice and is prone to panic attacks when unable to do so.

Shatter

"We have to find her a pack—"

"No pack—no alpha—could love her like that. Absolutely not."

I tensed, huddling further back under the desk. I'd snuck into uncle's office to steal his books on packs, but he and Aunty Lauren had entered, and now I was caught here, listening to them discuss me. Their scents—uncle's autumn leaves and Aunty's fresh linen—were pricked by irritation that made me uncomfortable.

"We have to try," Aunty Lauren said.

"Have to?" he spluttered. "I don't have to—"

"You are responsible—"

"Sabotage!" uncle's voice shook with fury. "What happened to her was not my fault. And now you insist on saddling me with that... that..." He took a breath, and I could almost feel him scrambling for the word. "That creature—"

"Eugene!" Aunty Lauren sounded more vicious than I could have ever imagined. I hugged myself tighter, trying to shove back tears that pricked my eyes.

"What do you want me to say?" uncle asked, sounding angry. "She's not blood—you are the one who got attached, telling her to call us—"

"She needs us. You can't truly be comfortable with the institute taking her back."

"She's not right. We both know it. Tom's been working with me for years, and now he's gone—"

"He tried to kill her!"

"Because of her scent! He's a good man, and you think we can find a pack to take her?"

"Most don't react quite that poorly. She was terrified and—if you ask me—nearing heat. I don't think we should put her back on suppressants just for this—"

"We have to." His autumn leaf scent became frustrated, like a storm had picked up in the office.

"And... you're sure..." Aunty Lauren sounded sad. "About the scent match? There's no chance—"

"None. You think I don't want this fixed? I swear, if there was any chance, I would smuggle her into the Valentine division myself. Her scent is unnatural; it repels all scent profiles I tried to pair it with. And I ran those tests myself."

I had to clamp my hand over my mouth and squeeze my eyes shut to stifle the cry that tried to escape at those words. I knew the truth, but hearing it like that...?

"We cannot keep on like this," Aunty Lauren said. "She can't even have a nest."

"She's too unstable. She is happiest when her hormones are dulled. You saw how angry she became—any little thing wrong in the room. This isn't just about keeping others from hurting her, she could hurt herself. It's not rational. There are some things that cannot be fixed without drugs."

"She is not broken—"

"Don't start."

"She is no more unstable than an alpha before a rut. For alphas, we suggest an omega. There's no reason a pack won't balance her—"

"We talked about this—" uncle sounded exasperated.

"This is not a life!" Aunty said. "What if it were me—"

"Lauren!"

"Would you allow this, if it were me?"

There was a long silence.

"I've done everything that I can," uncle hissed. "More than I needed to. More than was ever expected of me—what happened to her was not my fault."

"It was your trial. She cannot live like this. I shudder to think what the Institute will do if they take her back. But if we find her alphas to bond with. You're sure it will neutralise her scent—it has to balance her instincts, too. The Institute will allow it if we can find one. You can tolerate her, so why not—?"

"Barely!" uncle's words came through gritted teeth.

"I think if we offered enough money—" Aunty Lauren began.

"You want me to pay someone to bite her?"

I shivered.

A... pack?

A wounded, hollow part of me cracked, almost pushing me to throw myself from under the desk and beg him on my knees for it.

A pack to care for me? A nest and... love and touch... And they would know I was an omega. I would be allowed to be an omega. Properly. I shoved back my tears, drawing blood with how hard I bit my lip.

Here, I wasn't allowed to be an omega, and every day that passed on scent blockers, hiding instincts, without a nest... already missing most of my past. Now, each day, my present and future were withering.

I felt like a shell...

That's what I was in here for, to scour uncle's books on auras and packs. Aunty Lauren gave me romances, but I didn't know if they were real or not. Uncle had the real books. The books with facts and truths for me to look through and maybe find an answer—

"Find a good match," Aunty Lauren was saying. "Make sure they know ahead of time. Ensure they have the resources to keep her somewhere safe on a large estate like this one. They can care for her—"

"Even if I could, what might she offer them? She's gold pack, so there can be no children. No—"

"You have access to the Institute databases. There are packs in need of omegas for more than just children. Perhaps ones that are unbalanced—"

"You think she will balance them?" uncle spluttered. "She's more likely to destroy them."

The tears finally broke through the dam keeping them in as I trembled beneath the desk.

"Then offer them more money than they can refuse. A lifetime's worth. As if we don't have enough."

"The Institute is watching like a hawk—"

"You give them updates every week. You hold enough sway that if you were to ask them, they might allow it."

"I… I will ask. But I will make her no promises."

I woke up to diamonds and nightmares, to lights of dancing bright white kaleidoscopes blistering my vision. Only, when I blinked my eyes open, I was in a dim, windowless room with wooden floorboards.

It didn't matter how much my body ached as I shifted; comfort felt like a straitjacket, squeezing me tight, loosening my lungs instead of crushing them. It was freedom instead of a prison.

My nest.

Mine.

The first true nest I'd ever had.

Another first...

Reality clamped like an iron vice over my chest, turning warmth into terror. I tugged the blankets over my head, squeezing my eyes shut tightly, willing away reality into darkness.

Darkness, with no bites, no bright lights made of shards.

Instead, it was a nest… *my* nest, with soothing tilted photo frames across the walls—tilted squares in the blankets and bedsheets, even the bookshelves.

It was a nest I'd claimed—I'd fought for. One I hadn't had the chance to destroy before it could come to life.

Yet, Dusk was in here, too.

In the darkness, midnight opium wove into the threads of the nightdress I'd been too afraid to take off. He lingered in my senses as he'd promised he would.

I couldn't rid myself of him. Not of the way he'd held me last night or of the way my body had reacted when he'd entered me. It had been, for a few moments, bliss. A storm of bliss that had haunted my sleep and every moment since.

He'd been everywhere, the warmth of his huge muscular frame engulfing my body, his silken praise spinning webs around my soul as he claimed me; promising I would never find my mates. Promising that he was all I would ever need.

My breaths came short and sharp, another rush of heat in my core at those promises. I clamped my hand over my mouth as I screamed into the darkness.

He'd *claimed* me.

He'd claimed me, and I had come apart for him, and when he'd caught my scent at last, he hadn't attacked me or run. The purr rising in his chest had been so strong I could still feel it tingling up my bones as I remembered. It was a gift I'd been told I would never have without them. He was, somehow, another impossible, like my mates were supposed to be.

It was all my firsts, and he'd tricked my brain into believing he was a comfort he could never be. Because he didn't understand, and I could never tell him the truth, or it would seal my fate.

The lingering what if—the webs of possibility he was forcing me to consider—was nothing but a taunt, and I hated it more for that.

I *needed* my mates for more than just this curse of a scent. It wasn't as simple as Aunty Lauren had hoped that day I'd heard them arguing in Uncle's office.

There was no other option like he swore there was. And even if there was, I couldn't trust what he said.

I took a few deep breaths, and surfaced, daring to examine the room, determined to make changes so that I could blame him for *something*, but I found nothing wrong.

Tilted squares were *everywhere.*

I hugged myself, distraught at the purr that rose in my chest.

Even the pillows… Dusk had exchanged each for a square and tilted them all at the head of the bed. The blankets were the same, each one a square, each turned so a corner pointed top and bottom, brushing the floor where they tumbled from the edges.

My mind crept back to the night we met. He'd been at my window for a while, watching me for how long?

Watching and... and remembering.

Not just that... I knew my neuroticism went far beyond normal omega instincts. I'd been told that they were fuelled by hormones that were vengeful and off-balanced.

Even an alpha would think that was odd, Shatter...

My mates, I'd told myself. My *mates* wouldn't.

And now Dusk was taking that from them, too?

Fury simmered in my chest as I took it all in.

The bookshelves were the worst part in this stupid perfect nest. It wasn't until I'd turned the lights on that I finally had to face how far Dusk had taken it. The shelves were broad, and filled with dozens of textbooks. But they weren't conventional bookcases, they were angled, a stretching wall of honeycombs.

They were entrancing to look at, demanding attention no matter where I was in the room. Beside them was a study desk with a comfortable-looking chair, like the one in Uncle's office at the Estate.

I finally dared to get out of bed to examine it, wincing with every smarting step from Dusk's punishment. I ignored the flutter in my stomach as I remembered his praise as I'd taken it. I ignored the slick pooling in my thighs right now as I remembered how he'd knelt behind me while I was bent over for him and—*Fuck. No. I wont give him that.*

I found the desk equipped with everything I could ever need for studying.

Square notepads waited in the corner, angled perfectly just for me. There were sticky notes, pens, highlighters, rulers, even a set of pencils and a sketchbook, as if he'd stocked it just in case.

It was enraging.

He'd *stolen* from me.

He'd... my breaths were tight as the full weight of what he'd taken came crashing in.

The nest wasn't enough.

The shelves, the books, every little gesture. I shook, staring, then I grabbed a textbook, ripping it off the shelf and slamming it open on the floor. I would destroy it all like I'd destroyed my room in the Estate, and I would keep this moment for my mates, instead.

I tore out the first page with a scream, not expecting to feel as though I was ripping it from my soul.

My world went red.

Nothing Dusk gave me was worth that.

It couldn't be.

Another page, and another, tearing apart my own stupid instincts as I ripped apart the book. When I was done, I was a sobbing mess and my chest was still tight.

"I hate you," I choked out, the pages scattered across the floor blurring in my vision. "I hate you."

He'd ruined everything.

But it wasn't like last time, with fury turning the world red, stealing away my own sanity. His scent lingered, cool and soothing, fixing me even as I tried to hate it.

I couldn't even properly conjure my mates in my mind right now. Last night was a behemoth, a memory that cast a shadow over everything. But the flashes from it weren't from the belt, or his promise that I'd never reach my mates.

The flashes weren't what they should be.

Instead, they were moments like when he'd knotted me, trapping me against him as we'd climaxed together. The flash of desperation in his expression as he had, as if he'd truly wanted it.

Wanted to be with me.

Or it was the wonder in his piercing yellow eyes as he'd caught my scent. *"How do you keep getting more perfect?"* That's what he'd asked. And I was still struggling to suspend my disbelief of his praise. He couldn't have faked that purr after he'd caught my scent. He hadn't needed to kiss me, either.

He didn't need to do *any* of this.

And all of that...it was more than I'd even dared dream of when I'd imagined the reactions from my own mates.

Fuck him.

I would tear up every book in here. I would show him I wasn't going to stop fighting. I would get to my mates one day, and this would all be a confusing dream.

Slamming the book shut, I straightened, about to reach for the next, when I caught the title: *Aura Studies Vol.5, Seventh Edition.*

Seventh? The last I'd read from was the sixth.

How much would have changed?

I drew up at that, scrabbling frantically for where that had come from. The memory was a wisp of smoke curling up and closing its eyes, already dissolving back into the void with all the other forgotten fragments of my past.

"No... *No no no…!"* I opened the book again, eyes scanning what remained of the pages as if I could get the answer to that question at a glance.

I couldn't tell. I would need to...

"Fuck."

Stuffing down the traitorous half of my heart that breathed a sigh of relief at the realisation, I scrambled back to the desk to search the drawers for—*Yes.*

Tape.

Thank God.

That was all I needed to get to work.

It took forever, but with excruciating slowness, I taped the book up, making it whole again. Each page was perfectly fixed so that no sentence was left unfinished. Then I slumped against the bookcase, tome hugged to my chest.

Now I could read it, and maybe... just maybe I'd get another flash of that memory.

Fixing it had nothing to do with Dusk. I'd break his books all day if it was just about him.

But I *had* to read this one.

Maybe I could destroy it again once I had.

I didn't know day from night in my nest, which soothed me. I hated clocks, and time, and day turning to night. Each setting of the sun was like a promise—you'll be here again Shatter, tonight, tomorrow, and forever.

Alone. Hidden. Wrong, with no chance of being more.

So tired.

But now it was almost over.

Would it be so wrong to enjoy this nest for now, knowing my mates were so close? It was my space, after all.

I'd paid the price.

For hours upon hours, the silence in my nest was broken only by the turning of a page or scratching of pen against notebook.

Eventually, through the silence, came a knock on the door. I ignored it and it didn't come again until my stomach gurgled with desperation and I dared crack it open to find a McDonald's takeout bag waiting for me.

How long had it been there?

It didn't matter.

Stale old fries might as well have been gold when I was this starved.

CHAPTER 15

Dusk

Shatter had been in her nest all day and all night.

I didn't mind; the more she staked her claim in our territory, the better. Space was good, for the moment. Let her get comfortable with the nest, let her accept what had happened.

I had more than my wildest fantasies could ever account for. That was how beautiful she was—one night, and I had enough memories to keep me going for a lifetime.

My dreams had been a rare shade of sweet, and I kept waking, thinking she was still in my arms. A little omega lynx, purring up against my chest with a scent deadly enough to match my pack.

Unfortunately, classes officially started tomorrow, which meant I'd have to go back to hiding that unbelievable scent. I wasn't ready for her scum mates to realise what I'd taken from them.

I had, however, given her scent to Umbra. He'd been in the kitchen when I returned last night, *Breaking Bad* playing on the TV before empty couches.

The pillowcase she'd scent marked had been in my fist.

Umbra lowered a sandwich dripping with honey and gave me a *look*. He obviously knew what had happened. We didn't close the bond, not ever. And it wasn't like what I'd experienced was comparable to anything routine in this pack.

"She's in the nest," I said, keeping my voice even.

He nodded slowly, not answering.

"And pissed." Well... she would be when she recovered.

He nodded again, gaze dropping to the black fabric in my hands. "Is that...?"

"Her scent."

He narrowed his eyes, unsure. "And...?"

I just shook my head, knowing there was no possible way to explain it. Instead, I balled the pillowcase up and tossed it to him. He caught it, and for a brief instant the scent didn't catch up. Then he froze, a storm slamming in from his end of the bond, a wave of seething, clawing agony—and then it was gone.

"You're not... messing with me?" he asked, his voice rough.

"Nope."

He stared at the pillowcase in his fist, his pupils returning to normal size from full constriction.

One long moment passed, and he barked a laugh. With a grin on his face, he tucked it under his arm and went to his room, abandoning his half-finished honey sandwich.

He'd returned it to me in the morning with wolfsbane and blood woven through her nightshade. *That* was hot.

"I thought today..." He trailed off, his brows furrowed, not wanting to finish. "You know." He glanced up at the door on the balcony hallway, the one beside his room.

Oh.

Right.

My heart dropped like a rock.

"Yeah," I replied, throat dry. I peered down at the pillowcase... He was saying I should take it?

"You said..." Umbra began.

"I know. And I meant it."

I'd said she was for him. That was why I'd chosen her. And if she was, then I needed to share her scent with Ransom, too.

That evening I was ice cold with dread as I climbed the staircase. Not because her scent wasn't incredible, but because in the world we lived in, bullets shredded the tapestry of every dream we'd ever dared whisper to life. None were spared. Not ever.

A miracle was incomprehensible.

Yet, I couldn't bear that *she* might not be enough, because if she wasn't, then nothing in the universe would be.

So here I was, stepping into Ransom's room, greeted by the tide of earthy scents that made up Ransom Kingsman. His scent was, perhaps, the only thing that still put on a front of the alpha he'd once been.

At the door, I picked up the metal rod, my heart thundering in my chest, self-loathing sinking its claws in. At the end of the rod was a circular clamp, one that would fit around the neck of even the largest of alphas.

The metal was strong, a type that could withstand the power of an alpha with his aura loose.

Ransom's room was dimly lit, enough to reveal the shadow of the man I'd come for, and with him, the faintest glint sliding along the chains that held him.

He was asleep.

He could have been peaceful, the way he was curled on his side in the centre of the bed. His eyes were closed, chest rising and falling softly. Except there were manacles on his wrists, with chains long enough to give him the most freedom I could manage. He could reach the bathroom, and almost all the way to the door.

Not forever. *Too dangerous,* I'd been warned. *Once his survival instincts go, he could kill himself with those chains by accident.*

He was a prisoner. But Ransom Kingsman had been a prisoner of much worse than clinking metal cuffs for a while now.

He had moments of faint lucidity, the lamp would sometimes be on when I'd left it off. But the one time I managed to catch a glimpse of him doing it, I'd realised it meant nothing. The actions were instinct—old pathways in his brain triggering something inconsequential, lighting up and leading the way.

He was still vacant.

With the heavy rod still in my grip, I sat at his side carefully, not ready to wake him. I placed the fabric that Shatter had scented before him, air trapped in my lungs as I waited.

His breathing shifted, his brows furrowing, each inhale sharper than the last. A low, unfamiliar growl rose in his chest before cutting off.

What would happen? Would he wake in a furor worse than his usual? Or maybe…

His hand moved, clinking the chains as he reached.

His body went tense as he drew the fabric close, frown deepening. Then his eyes snapped open, a deep chocolate brown, and his pupils blew so wide there was almost no light left in his eyes. A low, loose whine rose in his chest as his fists balled the pillowcase.

My fingers clamped down on the rod, terrified of needing it.

Cold metal crushed my neck, stark against my burning skin. I writhed against it, desperate sounds tearing from my lips.

Rabid. Feral. Broken.

There were two alphas on the other end, pinning me to the ground as I grappled with it.

I couldn't breathe.

My body was on fire.

This was the consequences of fighting back. Of acting out when the drugs and pain were too much…

I waited.

Nothing. Not for a long, long time.

Ransom just curled up tighter, his breath hitching as he inhaled her scent.

Ever so slowly, I reached out to him, still tense, anticipating his madness. He'd been this calm before, but never if anyone touched him.

So very gently, my knuckle brushed his cheek.

He flinched, another wounded whine in his throat as his eyes darted up to mine. Blood roared in my ears as I waited.

Waited.

Waited...

He just stared at me, gaze as vacant as ever, but he remained still.

One by one, my muscles loosened as he still didn't react.

"Ransom." My voice was low and rough.

He flinched, eyes still fixed on me, still clutching her scent in his fists.

I tried to untangle what I was seeing.

This was… *something*, right?

I warred with disappointment from the misplaced hopes that had flourished the moment I'd realised Shatter's scent. Foolish dreams that, when he caught it, he would wake entirely.

That I would have my brother back.

That was stupid. It was only her scent on a pillowcase, for fuck's sake.

But this... this *was* something.

"I'm..." I cleared my throat, making my voice as casual as I always did for him. "I'm going to bring you to the shower, all right, mate?"

An impossible task on most days. Sometimes I needed Umbra, but I always tried to avoid it if I could.

I let Ransom keep her scent until he was under the hot stream of water.

He stood in nothing but shorts, staring at the pillowcase which I'd placed on the vanity. The steam was lifting her scent into the air.

It was everywhere, calming me as well. I kept getting flashes of last night. Of her terror when I'd told her what the pill would do. Of the way she'd curled into me with nowhere else to go. The way her tense body had relaxed when I'd begun to purr at her scent rather than… *What?*

What had she expected?

Who had convinced her to hide like she did? I would undo it all, I would make her see herself the way I saw her.

I picked up a washcloth, adding body wash and taking one of Ransom's hands, still stunned at his lack of fight. I began drawing the cloth up his forearm, the water already soaking through my shirt and sweats, but that was how this had to go.

I wouldn't leave him behind, and if he woke—*when* he woke—I would have kept every piece of his dignity intact I could manage.

He didn't react. Not even when I squeezed shampoo into my hands and began lathering it in his dark auburn hair. He was a bit taller than me, though not quite as built, and I had to reach up to do it. He hated when I did his hair—don't know why that, out of everything, triggered him.

I should shave it off to avoid issues, but he'd loved it longer. Problem was, sometimes I had to tranq him to brush it. The dark auburn waves stuck to his shoulders right now, sopping wet as it was. A good length for him. He'd like that, if he were to wake soon.

Maybe… maybe by the time that happened, he would be back.

It wasn't until I turned to grab another cloth that he moved. I spun quickly, my mind scrambling to locate the rod—but he wasn't aggressive.

Instead, he just sat down on the floor of the shower, hugging his knees with his ankles crossed. His eyes were locked on the pillowcase.

I stared for a long moment, unsure of what to make of it.

Then I joined him, sitting on the broad shower floor. It had been so long since I'd been near him like this: in peace. Two pack mates, side by side.

He was deathly still as we sat with hot water streaming over us. So, so still. It wasn't an awakening, but it was more than I'd had in a long time.

Slowly, I lifted an arm and dropped it over his shoulders. He didn't react, so I drew him against me, tugging his head to my chest.

"Fucking miss you, man," I told him through clenched teeth.

I had to keep it together. My job was to protect him.

Protect them all like they protected me.

Useless once. Never again.

The only one left.

His arm shook as he lifted it. I tensed, eyeing the iron rod that I'd left just within reach. *What was he doing?*

Nothing, for a long time, it seemed, and his hand wavered in the air between us. Then he closed it, balling it into a fist.

My heart tripped over itself.

Ransom Kingsman was our pack mate entirely by shitty circumstances. He was a man we'd barely met, joining a pack that had only recently formed. All I knew of him was panic, bravery, and a whole lot of feral alpha.

Finally, he was awake and ready to show his face. He crossed toward me first and he was a storm of nerves through the open bond.

"Hey." He lifted his arm, but instead of going for a handshake, he held out his fist.

Oh God... It wasn't even in that 'fist bump' way. It was sideways, like I was supposed to bring mine down over it.

"What is that?" I asked, eyeing the greeting with a scowl.

"Oh..." He cleared his throat, his fist wavering nervously. "Like you're supposed to—"

"I know literally what *it is." I snorted. "You know who does that shit? Tech bros and trust fund babies. Umbra!" I raised my voice. "What the fuck are we going to do with this one? He's spoiled—and I don't mean like an egg."*

"Nah mate," Umbra said with a chuckle as he walked over. "No returns. No refunds. You break it, you buy it." Umbra happily did the tacky fist-greeting with Ransom as I rolled my eyes, but it was refreshing to see Umbra grinning. "Welcome to the pack, bro. And don't mind him. He's always a grouch."

With steam in the air and scorching water cascading down his face, Ransom's eyes were finally somewhere other than the pillowcase. He was staring at the fist he'd made.

Was it... just chance?

Blood roared in my ears.

It had to be, right?

It felt like a rope was squeezing the life from my lungs as I dared raise my hand, closing my own trembling fist and bringing it down on Ransom's.

A spark lit, quick as a flash. A firework bursting to life for a moment before leaving an imprint of smoke in the air.

Him.

Fleeting, powerful, alive. The shock of joy was so violent and unfamiliar it made the world spin.

I dropped my arm from around his shoulder, reeling.

"Ransom?" I shifted into his vision.

Fuck.

Was I making it up—delusional as I climbed the corpses of a million dreams?

But… that *had* been him.

It *had* been, because the next thing I knew, the bathroom door was flung open to reveal Umbra, and through the bond from him, there was a bright flash of hope.

"You felt him?" I asked.

At the barrage of new scents and sounds, however, Ransom broke.

Too close and unprepared, I didn't react in time when his aura split the air. There was a snarl on his face, his eyes nothing but wild voids once more as he flung himself at me, a vicious sound in his chest.

No—fuck.

I grappled with him, my own aura hitting the air just in time for my body to crash into the vanity behind us.

And then the world went black.

CHAPTER 16

Shatter

I had a plan.

It was one that, if nothing else worked, would get me to my mates in the end. I'd scent marked a dozen of my scrunchies and stashed them in a little box under my bed.

I didn't know when Dusk would let me off the scent blockers again, but an item like that should hold my scent for a while. At least, I thought it should.

Now I just needed to find a way to smuggle it out. I was glad that I didn't make an attempt on day one.

Dusk was as neurotic as I'd expected.

As he served me (Umbra-made) toast, he leaned close and I noticed the faint traces of a bruise that cascaded down the side of his whole face, though it looked to be covered with makeup.

I opened my mouth to ask, then closed it, unsure. Where the hell did an *alpha* get a bruise like that?

Had he gone out last night?

When I finished eating, Dusk turned my chair to examine me like a doll again. I guess that was our morning routine, now.

He held the scent-blocking pill, but I snatched it from him so he wouldn't force feed it to me in front of Umbra.

"The uniforms fit okay?" he asked as I swallowed the pill with orange juice. I nodded, pursing my lips. Not a single item that wasn't perfect, dammit.

"Do I need to get anything to add to the nest?"

"No."

"So, it's good?"

"It's..." I swallowed, resenting the sparkle in his eyes as he gauged my reaction. *"Adequate."*

Dusk's grin was charming. "Good. Well, this is for you." He dug in his pocket and pulled out a little silver charm.

I squinted, lips parting. *"No."*

It was a star. A star beside the moon pendant on my necklace meant the pack was *officially* courting their omega. Courting wasn't mandatory; any omega selected for a pack would retain their place in the academy no matter what. But a lot of packs kept their omega purely on a contractual basis. Some even switched out their omegas between terms, as permitted.

The *star* indicated romantic interest.

Dusk's eyebrows rose. "Show me your neck, Gem." The look in his eyes promised retribution. And what kind was clear: break the rules, and he'd come into my nest.

My fists balled.

It was *my* nest. More so, now.

I wouldn't let him in.

Well, they could officially enter now, but they still weren't allowed to touch me if they were in there and I was following their rules. I could, *maybe*, live with that.

With a clenched jaw, I lifted my chin, eyes meeting Umbra's, who was watching us both with arms folded as he leaned against the door. He looked rather pleased at the sight, pupils dilating as Dusk clasped the star to the necklace.

So preoccupied with not looking at Dusk, I didn't clock what he was up to until he settled on his knees before the bar stool.

"What are you doing?" I demanded, trying to pull away again, but he grabbed my leg and held it in place so he could slip my boot onto my foot.

"I can put my own shoes on."

He ignored me. "First official day today. Be good. There's a gift waiting for you tonight."

Cheeks burning, I made a point of looking away from him as he tied my laces.

"Let me guess, I only get it if I fuck you."

"Gem..." He snorted. Then he drew me closer so that my butt was right on the edge of the seat and I had to grab him to stay balanced. It had been a few days now, but I was still sore. "I'm going to use that sweet little body of yours whenever I please. And the gift..." I felt the tickle of his breath along my thigh beneath the skirt. He grinned as I squirmed. "...is yours, no matter how badly you behave."

He didn't readjust me, clearly happy to have my fingers gripping his hair as he did up the laces of my other boot.

"I don't want your gift," I told him.

"Wrong," he said absently, "since you're rather attached to the nest, but that's irrelevant. It's from Ransom."

I paused as he stood, done with my boots. I'd asked Umbra about Ransom the other day, but he'd shrugged it off. I'd assumed he'd turn up by the first day of classes, though. "Where is he?"

"He'll show up, eventually," Dusk said. "Right. Ready to go?"

I nodded stiffly, hopping down from the bar stool.

Malicious compliance was my new best friend, I decided, as I walked along the colonnades beside Dusk and Umbra, feeling the gazes of passing students, omegas, alphas, and betas alike. I would sit with them when I had to. I would do what they asked, but I would do it with as much attitude as my foolish, needy nest-loving heart could get away with.

I would never admit it to Dusk, but the clothing he'd provided was nice. It matched the academy dress code, and it was really, *really* Shatter-proof. It didn't seem to matter what I matched with what, it all looked good together.

How long had he spent selecting it?

I supposed if he wanted me to look better for my mates, I'd let him.

Umbra

In the Arkology lecture, Shatter was enraptured.

It was absolutely adorable how much she tried to hide it, too. Originally, we'd signed up for a bunch of random subjects, since the schooling wasn't really the point of being here for us. But we'd booked our lectures together, without much concern for content, so long as some of the classes intersected with the Lincoln Pack's. Well, for *me* at least it didn't matter; Dusk *was* interested, even if he tried to hide it. Made sense, since he was smarter than he liked anyone to know—him and Shatter were the same like that.

When he'd noticed Shatter sneakily reading the Arkology books, though, Dusk had rescheduled a few of our other classes over to Lecture Hall Two, where the majority of Arkology studies were hosted.

I appreciated that. Now I got to see her all excited for classes. This morning she looked so studious it was *mesmerising*. She wore a pleated black skirt that she kept trying, unsuccessfully, to tug down whenever she caught Dusk eyeing her (every few minutes). She paired it with black leather boots, and a satchel she'd slung over her shoulder and hugged to her chest like a firstborn. Her mane of honey hair was loose, and it tumbled to her tailbone in messy waves, almost obscuring the way her beige blouse was half untucked at the back. Buttons were misaligned too, I noted, but maybe it was a style thing.

Scrappy and smart. I was into it. Suited her, really.

She was perfect for us, especially because she was fixing Ransom. He wasn't ready to see her quite yet. We'd need a few more scent tests to make sure he was stable.

I peered down at the notebook Shatter had on her lap, cracked open so she could take notes on the lecture out of Dusk's sight. She was crammed right at my side, as far away from him as she could reasonably get without sitting on my lap. Not that I would mind. I wonder how much of a prick Dusk would have to be to get her to do that?

I could just ask; she was supposed to do whatever we said. It seemed too… *free*, no matter how the thought warmed my blood.

I'd use it sparingly.

Below us, the professor asked a student near the front to come up and complete the equation. As they made an attempt, Shatter began muttering to herself—something about a five instead of an eight when a female alpha aura was concerned.

"Is that correct?" the professor asked, looking around the hall. Shatter's hand shot up like an arrow, eyes wide. Then she tore it back down to her lap, shooting Dusk a resentful look, her cheeks bright pink.

Dusk, cheeky bastard that he was, raised his own hand.

"Yes, Varis," the professor said, when no one else volunteered.

"No. The five on the first line should be an eight."

"So, the answer is?"

Dusk paused, folding his arms, but Shatter seemed unable to contain herself. "Fifty-six point two seven, and for the bottom, four-fifths to carry over," she whispered.

Dusk repeated it, a smirk twitching the edge of his lips.

"Very good. Very good. Glad to see the foundation is here. Next we're going to be…" I tuned the professor out again, eyes trailing back to Shatter. Her hands were clasped together tightly.

"Did you do that in your head?" Dusk asked.

"Uh…" Shatter glanced up at him, clearly thrown. "No…" She raised her pen in answer, then tried to close her notebook. As if I didn't already know the last two pages were strictly doodles of foxgloves and mushrooms, and none of this crazy Arkology math at all.

Shit.

She was smart.

Like *really* smart.

And I'd been so fucking right about the two of them.

They were pure entertainment. At one point, Dusk switched his pen out for another—an artsy, expensive-looking one—and Shatter went rigid. I could practically feel the rage rolling off her in waves, her eyes tracing every movement of the pen in Dusk's hand. For some reason, it was really bothering her.

"Put it away," she growled at last, and if she levelled that kind of demand at me, I'd be powerless to resist.

"Gareth gave me a gift, and you want it to go to waste?" he asked. "We're supposed to be making an alliance with them."

Finally, we went on break and Dusk leaned back, a grin on his face. "Maybe I'll ask him if he has another. I can get one for Umbra."

She lost it, letting out a precious snarl that sent blood rushing to my cock, and grabbed the pen from Dusk's hand, flinging it wildly from our booth.

We all watched it fly through the air and clip a pair of neat black dress pants.

The trace of Shatter's whine serenaded my ears as Flynn Lincoln—who looked to be halfway to the bathroom—bent down and picked up the pen, eyes finding our table. His gaze landed on Shatter, who remained halfway over the desk of the booth from the full body throw.

Well, *shit.*

Along with a low undercurrent of humour, I did feel faint concern from Dusk in the bond. We needed to upkeep the alliance their pack was trying for.

It was important, Dusk insisted. For some stupid (probably smart) reason or another. I tried not to get too caught up in the details when I didn't have to.

Dusk slipped from the booth, straightening his shirt with a sigh, and I had to grab Shatter by the back of the neck as she tried to dive under the desk entirely.

Instead of the trickle of hatred that pricked every one of my scars when I was in proximity of Lincoln Pack, I was having trouble not laughing.

"You don't get to insult your mate and hide, Little Nightshade," I told her as Dusk reached Flynn. We could hear pieces of their conversation.

"…Hope you don't take it too seriously…" Dusk was saying. Shatter was frozen, also listening in. "She's *very* possessive."

She let out a breath of fury, then wriggled from my grip, flinging herself from the booth to reach Dusk's side. With a snort—and not thinking it entirely through—I followed her.

"…The nest don't you think?" Flynn sounded amused. "Might have moved a little fast—" Flynn cut off as Shatter arrived, and his eyes slid to the star on her necklace.

His eyebrows shot up. "Oh. Well. I take it back, the possessiveness—"

"Is mutual," Dusk said with a smile that didn't reach his eyes. He slid an arm around Shatter's shoulder. She was stiff, but didn't outright fight him off.

"I'm sorry," Shatter said quickly, and I noticed her fists clenching and unclenching at her sides anxiously. "I didn't mean to be rude."

Damn. So there was a capacity for politeness when she *wanted* to.

Too bad she wanted to for this piece of shit.

I stared at him, mind wavering.

Too close…

The voices became too loud. I'd talked to Dusk about this. Sworn I was ready. Yet…

"…Dead by the morning. It's all a front. He's weak inside. He'll fail…"

And this alpha before me, was the face of that voice. A voice that haunted me. My own dignity had long since died, but Dusk?

It had destroyed Dusk.

"Tell me what they want for the next set." I was begging, now.

I had nothing left. Dr. Wren had taken pity on me, and I had to use it.

31 was dead.

He'd gone feral one day, ripping our door open. He'd shoved his way out of our room, and I'd followed long enough to see him tearing guards down like a wild animal. Then he'd drawn up as he reached a corner.

I'd heard them shouting, telling him they'd shoot if he took one more step. He'd looked back at me for a long moment, a crooked smile on his pale face, and then he placed one foot forward.

Gunshots assaulted my eardrums, and he fell, messy blond hair sticky with blood, and tired eyes sightless as that wild smile still curved his lips.

The bullet shred more than just flesh. As 31's heart stopped, they tore through our pack bond. Enough, by all laws of the universe, to destroy it.

No…

If the pack broke, I couldn't protect Dusk. We wouldn't be of use to them anymore.

I flared my aura, reaching out desperately in the dark. Somehow I found something to hold on to. Intangible and impossible, the energy was enough of an anchor that I could hold on, even though it scorched me to the soul, unnatural, agonising. I shuddered, cracks rippling through the very essence that made me an alpha; wounds that didn't feel as if they would ever heal.

Even with only two of us, the pack bond, somehow, survived.

Just me and Dusk.

He'd finally chosen a name, whispered it for my ears alone, like I'd told him he had to. Never again would he be 68. Just like I would never be a number to him.

They wouldn't break him.

So I had to be perfect. I had to be everything they needed in a test subject so it wouldn't be Dusk.

"They want the weakest." Dr. Wren's voice was low, just for me, as he drew a vial of blood. "Wounded and frail. They're testing alpha healing capacity."

I shut my eyes, nodding.

Weak…

I could do that.

Reality buzzed in my ears, a faint radio station. I flickered in and out, and then something warm brought me back. I looked down to see Shatter's hand in mine. Dusk had dropped his arm from her shoulder.

"You all right?" Flynn Lincoln asked. He lifted a hand, as if he thought he might need to catch me, but froze as I flinched. I didn't step away. It took the last of my power not to, but every instinct screamed at me to leave, a distant storm, warning that there was something wrong…

Kill him.

But *that* instinct, that was a given, a resident in every moment, as impossible as it was persistent.

With all my self-control, I levelled my expression.

For Dusk.

Do it for Dusk.

For *her*. The sooner this was over, the sooner we could get her away from this academy.

"Yeh," I forced out, finding there was already a brittle smile on my face. "Just a bit under the weather. Think I ate something bad."

Flynn nodded, seemingly satisfied.

No payments.

Not out here. I'd prepared for this.

I rolled my shoulder, feeling the ache of the ten payments I'd made last night. I'd never paid ahead of time before, but the principle was the same, wasn't it?

They ached, reminding me of my pain.

But… Shit.

Shatter was holding my hand, and it made me feel all warm and fuzzy, threatening to neutralise it all. Damn. With that comfort, what cost one, now cost three, so I tugged my hand from hers.

Flynn, luckily, had already moved on.

"…I assume you don't want it back…" he was saying, lifting the pen.

There was a long pause.

Dusk, who was a bit off-balance through the bond, clearly trying to figure me out, didn't get there before Shatter. She swiped it from his grip so fast I barely even saw it. "I should take it," she said, looking up at Dusk. "Just to prove I can be respectful and… and well behaved." Those rich brown eyes were startlingly devilish. They were better golden, without the contacts, but still beautiful all the same.

I chuckled, and all of Dusk's tension vanished. There was a bite to his smile as he nodded. "Maybe you should, Gem."

When we returned to the booth there was a strange silence, in which both Shatter and Dusk watched me oddly for a long moment. I nodded. "I'm good."

Shatter reached out for me, then withdrew, shrinking down on herself a little. I'd rejected her, I realised.

Shit.

Was she upset?

"Nice one," I said, clearing my throat and eyeing the pen in her hand. Her grin was victorious, and she stashed it in her bra, the proud intensity in her gaze akin to a deranged squirrel.

I didn't think there was anything in the world that could lift my spirits after a visit like that memory, but Shatter was here to break all the rules.

"Don't think I won't strip you bare to find it later," Dusk murmured to her, absently shuffling through the textbooks on the table for what we needed next.

The victory slid from her gaze in an instant.

She didn't respond, but later I saw her withdraw it from her bra and place it resentfully into her bag.

CHAPTER 17

Shatter

The day began looking up at lunchtime, when Dusk told us he wasn't feeling great and was going to cut the school day off early to catch up with rest.

"He's tired. Didn't sleep much last night," Umbra told me as I began on the overly large helping of mac and cheese I'd served myself. It was a relief not to have McDonald's or burnt toast.

"Is it because of what happened to his face?" I asked after a while of quiet eating. I had been wondering all morning why Dusk had a bruise like that.

Umbra grinned. "You want the truth? Let's make it a game."

I narrowed my eyes suspiciously. "What do you mean?" It was rule number two: never make a deal with Umbra.

"Trade me, Little Nightshade. Truth for truth?"

"Trade?" I chewed on my lip. That wasn't a *deal*, right? "Why?"

"Because I have some questions of my own."

"And you're not going to just… bully me into the truth, or try and command me to tell it?"

Umbra chuckled. "Me and Dusk are not the same."

I frowned, trying to parse through that one.

"Dusk pulls the trigger with the safety off." He mimed shooting himself in the head with his fork. "I balance the scales. I'll get your truths because you give them to me."

I considered him, taking my last bite of cheesy pasta. I thought Umbra might be the key to freedom. He seemed more willing to take risks, ones that might actually lead to my mates. "Okay. Deal—I mean, yes. I'll trade."

"All right. Then let's chat penalties."

"Penalties?"

"If I catch you in a lie, I get a bite."

"A bite?" My pitch leaped to an embarrassing squeak.

Umbra shrugged. "I'm not pack lead. I can mark you all I want." He looked taken by the idea. "Then when it fades, I can go again."

I wet my lips, shockingly giddy from that threat. "You *want* to bite me?" Not for a bond, either, just because he wanted to?

"I want to leave my mark all over that sweet body of yours."

I gritted my teeth, swallowing back my unreasonable omega bullshit. "You should ask for something else." He couldn't bite me—I shouldn't let him. Uncle had always warned me to be careful about alpha bites, in case they triggered violence. I wasn't totally sure what would happen if he bit me with no intention of a bond, but it couldn't be good.

"That's all I've been dreaming of," he groaned. "It's that, or no game."

I considered. If I played along, all I had to do was not lie. It wasn't like they didn't have my darkest secrets already.

"And if you lie, what do I get?" I asked.

"I won't," he said so fucking sure, but I folded my arms, and he chuckled. "*You* can bite *me*."

I wrinkled my nose, standing from my seat with my finished food tray. "Not much of a win if you're the one who wants it."

Umbra followed me, a rumble of a laugh in his chest. "Now she's getting it," he said. "Go on then, ask for something."

I set my tray down, turning to him. "Let me go to them."

Umbra laughed. "A lie isn't worth that."

I narrowed my eyes. There *was* something worth that to him? Could I figure out what it was?

I forced myself not to look around, searching for my mates in here like I did in every room I entered. It would just give him more ammo. Instead, I began toward the doors, leading us to the afternoon class. It was a bit early, but at least those booths felt private.

People had been staring at us all day, though. The omega with the untouchable alphas. The pack who'd ignored all requests and invitations from the most prestigious omegas in this place. And they were fucking about with a scentless nobody like me. I could have tolerated it, if it were my mates claiming me. That would have been a claim I could be proud of. These stares, the ones pairing me with alphas I hadn't chosen…they were like pinpricks, each one digging into my skin. I wanted to scream the truth at them all.

"All right." Umbra cocked his head. "Ask for something else."

"Fine," I said. "How about extra questions?"

"Hmm." He pondered that. "Okay. So that's the game? You lie, I get a bite, and if I lie when you ask, you get a bonus truth."

"But what if you lie with my extra truth?" I asked as if it mattered. But I wouldn't admit to him that I'd never be able to tell the difference. I was as bad at spotting lies as I was at dishonesty. I'd even left an apology note on the bench after I'd stolen that poor woman's suitcase at the train station.

"How about then you get to punish me however you like?"

My cheeks heated, eyes flicking to a group of nearby girls who were staring at us, clearly to listen in.

Punish him? My mind cycled through what that might mean.

Umbra, who'd stopped with me out in the midday air, crossed his arms, leaning against the stone wall.

"I don't know what that means," I told him.

"What do you want it to mean? You could get me to make you food all week, take you shopping, or I could be your own personal nest alpha—"

"*Nest* alpha?"

"Omegas get lonely right? What if you needed an alpha on duty in your nest to bring you snacks and drinks—and cuddle you any time?"

"I won't… need that." But my throat had gone dry.

"Then I guess you could punish me like Dusk punished you, if you'd prefer that. But you'd have to ask him for supplies. I'm not a belt kind of guy."

A strangled choking sound came up my throat, attracting a few glances from passing students. "He *told* you?"

"He tells me everything."

I wrinkled my nose.

"Also a heavy feature in my dreams. Biting you, imagining your cute sounds when Dusk punished you, imagining what sounds you'll make for me when I finally get *my* fuck—" He cut off with a laugh at the snarl that rose in my throat. "You're blushing just thinking about it, Little Nightshade."

"I'm not."

"You are."

"I'm—" Fuck. Whatever. "Just let me ask my question."

Umbra grinned. "Game on?" he asked, holding out his hand. I took it, unsettled by the delighted smile on his face. When the handshake dropped, he began down the hallway toward our next class.

"You first?" he asked me as I matched his pace.

"Yes."

"All right. Go on then."

"Why isn't Ransom here?" I asked instantly. As much as I was curious about Dusk's bruise, if we were making trades, there were more important questions.

Umbra considered that, cocking his head. "He's unwell."

I paused, taken aback by how fast he admitted that. "Unwell?" I asked. "How?"

"Is that another question?" Umbra prodded.

"Uh… Wait. Just let me think about it," I told him, my mind trying to unravel that. Ransom was sick? Did that mean he'd be back soon? He was an alpha, he likely wouldn't be down for much longer. It had been two weeks since his pack had arrived and he hadn't been seen once. "You ask yours."

"You have a scar on the back of your neck," Umbra noted, peering sideways at me. "Where is it from?"

My touch crept to my neck on instinct.

When had he noticed that?

It was a faint scar, almost entirely invisible if you weren't looking for it. Most people didn't…

"This is the best option, all right Little One? When he bites you, you accept his pack."

"But I don't know him yet." My voice shook.

"I promise, Shatter, there will not be a better option than this, okay?"

My palms were clammy as the alpha, who was talking to uncle, looked down the hall to me. He was unfamiliar. Daunting. His brows furrowed when he caught my scent, and his jaw ticked.

Uncle had paid him well to take me, I knew that, even if Aunty Lauren wouldn't say it. He was here to get me out of their hair.

He'd bite me, even if he hated my scent.

She patted my hair, sorrow in her gaze as she looked me up and down.

"What if... what if I go with him and then...?" Memories of Tom had my nails drawing blood from my palms.

"They know your scent." She cupped my cheek. "All three of them do. They didn't have any violent reactions. We're going to keep an eye on you. And heats are your call. However you want them done. Keep calm now, you know it'll be much harder for him if you're upset."

Right. My scent... it became worse for them when I was afraid or angry.

"One bite, you'll feel his offer. All you have to do is accept it. Then that's it, you're safe, and you have a pack."

Something deep in my soul quaked at her words. Taking a breath, I peeked back down the hall.

The alpha was well-dressed, hands clasped before his suit. He had a black goatee and slicked-back hair. His dark gaze pinned me in place.

"All right, Little One, are you ready?"

Despite how I trembled, I nodded.

A pack. A bite. A happily ever after.

It's what I wanted, right?

I clung to that as the alpha stepped toward me, even if the dream turned to ash, leaving something bitter on my tongue.

"It was…" I swallowed back my nerves as Umbra and I stepped into the classroom. "It was an attempted bond," I said, proud of how steady my voice was. "A normal bond."

Not a dark bond and not a princess bond reserved for mates. It was supposed to be the best I'd ever be offered…

Umbra nodded, seeming to digest that, but didn't ask anything else. I could feel him scrutinising me as we reached the booth at the back of the auditorium, his sandstorm eyes catching every part of the discomfort I was trying to hide.

The memory stuck, though, throwing me off balance.

"Why is Dusk keeping me from them?" It wasn't the question I'd planned on asking, but it came out anyway with an undercurrent of pleading. "Why does he care?"

Of course, it was Umbra too, but I knew Dusk was at the heart of it.

Umbra cocked his head, pinning me with an intense gaze. "Because he wants you."

Again, the answer was infuriatingly simple, and I couldn't argue with it. Umbra's eyes dropped to my lap where I'd balled my fists.

"You won't hate it forever—"

"I'm not staying forever, and if I do, I will."

The faintest smile quirked on the edge of his lips as he tugged a textbook from his bag, even if we were early.

"He could have chosen anyone," I hissed. "And they'd have wanted it."

"Dusk claims almost nothing in this world, but when he does, he'll splinter it to pieces before watching it be stolen away. You'll never find another man as devoted as him. Scent matches—even bites—they don't stand a chance."

I stared at Umbra who was still casually flicking through textbook pages as if he hadn't just dropped a bomb like that on me.

"He *can't* touch me if they bite me."

He just chuckled like it was the stupidest thing he'd ever heard.

"What about your next question?" I asked.

"I'm thinking about the perfect one."

I frowned. I'd thought he would ask me again about the bite—I'd braced for it.

We sat in silence until the lecture began, and it was hard for me not to get swept away by it.

"Lap, my sweet Little Nightshade," he said a few minutes after the lecture began.

"What?"

"Sit on my lap."

"No."

He looked delighted. "Is that an invitation into your nest tonight?"

I swallowed, eyes darting around the huge room before shifting toward him. Butterflies rose in my stomach as he dragged me close, fitting me between his legs. I was swallowed entirely by his crisp scent of wolfsbane and blood.

"See, that's better," he murmured as he tucked my hair behind my ear, touch trailing down my neck for a moment before it vanished. "Now you can study, and I won't die of boredom. And before you start looking, yes, they are in this class, and they'll *definitely* see you with me."

I tried to stifle my growl, but only half managed it, which got a snort from him. Tomorrow, I reminded myself, I have Omega Studies. The damned class might terrify me, but I would finally get some time away from them, and they wouldn't be able to humiliate me in front of my mates.

I could feel the faintest vibration against my back as Umbra hummed contentedly, occasionally adjusting me in his lap. Every time he did, he would take me by the thighs, each hand almost enough to circle them, and shift me.

My cheeks burned upon the third adjustment when I felt his hardness beneath me. I tensed, trying to shift away, but his hum turned into a purr at my movement, his cock getting even more rigid.

"I'm trying to focus," I hissed, glaring at the textbook as I tried to understand what the professor was saying.

"Try a bit harder, Nightshade," he breathed, his grip on my thighs becoming tighter. "Because you feel so good wriggling against my cock."

I gritted my teeth, attempting to focus on the notes I was taking.

"Do I turn you on?" he asked.

"No."

"No?" I could almost hear the grin in his voice.

I jumped as his thumb brushed up along my inner thigh, threateningly close to my panties.

"What are you doing?"

"Little Nightshade, I can feel your slick."

"It's not—"

One of his hands left my thigh, instead weaving through my hair gently before clamping down and tilting my head up.

I shivered as he shifted his head, leaning down and pressing his face to my neck, inhaling deeply, a low groan sounding from his chest with no regard for anyone else.

I went still, totally unsure what was happening, until he moved again, and I felt—*"Wait, what—?"*

Too late.

At the back of the lecture hall, where anyone could turn their head and see, Umbra Varis sank his teeth into my neck.

I clamped my hand over my mouth to stifle my gasp. A few of the students in the back row spun, and their gazes found us instantly. I heard the whispers rising like an ocean wave.

But…

Oh God.

I couldn't move, the grip of my other hand biting down on the desk as he held me in place. I'd been here before… Umbra's scent spiked in the air around me as he released his bite, but not in rage or anger. I could taste his lust.

"I could get drunk on you, Nightshade. I can't wait to find out how that sweet cunt feels when I'm buried in it."

I couldn't speak, even as his fingers loosened their grip on my hair. Nothing else happened. Nothing violent. In fact, he was still rock hard beneath me.

Finally, I managed to pick the panicked pieces of my brain off the floor. "Why did you do that?"

"You lied to me."

"It wasn't a game question."

"I never said it had to be to get a bite. I just said if you lied to me. The game's still on. Those are the rules."

Fuck.

Goosebumps still pebbled my skin, and my heart continued slamming into my ribs. But nothing had happened. He wanted me—*more* even.

"W-we're in class," I whispered, but it sounded like a half whine.

Was *nothing* sacred?

"You're here to keep me balanced, aren't you? I was feeling a bit unstable."

Of course, because he was a bastard just like Dusk, he didn't let me flee the room the moment the lecture ended like I wanted to. Instead, he waited until the Lincoln pack passed us.

Each of them—even Roxy Vasilli—was glancing our way. Those whispers I'd heard must have travelled far. But my hair was down, so they wouldn't see the bite, not unless—I let out a snarl as Umbra gripped a fistful of my hair, tilting my neck again, and dragged his tongue from my collarbone to jaw like a rabid lunatic.

The Lincoln pack stared, absolutely unable to miss the bite mark he'd left.

Eric and Gareth adjusted their eyes quickly, and I noticed a sneer curl on Eric's lips as he sped up, dragging a shocked-looking Roxy away. But Flynn couldn't rip his gaze from me. I couldn't tear mine from him either. Totally stuck, my eyes locked with his as he walked by.

It was enough to sour my mood for the whole day, leaving me spiralling with dread over what they must think. That was, until I got back to my nest and found the gift. The one Dusk had promised me from Ransom. The one I'd forgotten about entirely.

CHAPTER 18

Dusk

Weeks passed after 31 died, and Umbra was losing his mind.

I caught him in the bathroom, driving the jagged edge of a broken plastic fork into his skin until he bled. He didn't eat, and begged me to finish his so it wasn't taken from both of us.

He became ashen and frail.

We knew what was coming for us now—after 31 had been chosen. They would take one of us and run experiments until we were driven mad.

Umbra was fading, already giving up before selection. I took comfort in knowing I might be the better candidate.

But when they finally came for a test subject, it was him they took, and not me.

"Dusk!"

I woke up with a start, almost losing control of my aura.

"What?" It took a moment for the world to steady, for me to realise I wasn't back there. I was on the couch at our place at the Academy.

Umbra was safe.

We were safe—well, as safe as we'd ever been.

His bright eyes were concerned as he swam in my vision.

"She's uh… you should come," he said. "I think you broke her."

"What?" I was on my feet in a second and following him down to the nest. It must be late. I'd crashed after getting in. I'd barely slept the night before, a headache keeping me up after Ransom had caught me against the vanity.

I was fully alert, when I heard the sounds of Shatter's sobs from the nest.

What the fuck was going on?

I peeked in.

It was a bit different from how I remembered. She'd made a nest inside her nest. A corner beside the honeycomb bookshelves was stacked with Arkology books in little towers, and stuffed with blankets and a pillow. She wasn't there, though.

"Shatter?"

"I'm f-f-fine." Her voice was muffled.

Damn…

She was curled beneath her duvet, unable to contain her sobs.

"What did you do?" Umbra asked, looking hurt.

"I…" My eyes fell on her desk, where the letter I'd tucked under her door was sitting, opened.

Okay.

So she'd got the gift.

And now she was wailing.

"Shatter…" I raised my voice, and her sobbing cut off.

"I said I'm *fine.*" Her voice was far too high pitched.

Uh…

A beat passed, and then bundles of blankets were torn away aggressively as she sat up, staring at the both of us in her doorway.

I could see her lip quivering from here, and her golden eyes, free of contacts, were red-rimmed. She grasped at her hair, another sob catching in her throat. Then she stumbled from the bed and across the room, muttering something incomprehensible, expression devolving into something furious. She had me by the shirt with unexpected fierceness as she shoved me back a step. "You… c-can't…" Her face was streaked with tears and snot as she grabbed the door and tried to slam it. I stuck my foot in it.

"We're just checking you're—"

"You have to *knock*!" she wailed. She shoved it harder, and I was so taken aback that I removed my foot, letting it slam.

I looked at Umbra, but he just shrugged and lifted his hand, knocking firmly.

There was no response.

Umbra knocked again.

There was a low, incomprehensible sound from within. That was an invitation, right?

Sort of?

I cracked the door (again), peering in and doing it all over. Shatter was already back under her blankets.

"Can we come in?" Umbra asked, still looking a bit bewildered.

"I guess so." A little of the brat entered her voice.

She couldn't *really* argue. I'd told her once classes started, we could enter. We just couldn't touch her in here unless she broke the rules.

"Why did we have to knock?" I asked curiously as I headed to the ensuite and grabbed the unopened box of tissues. I had expected her to tell us to get fucked entirely.

"Because everything has to be perfect." Her voice was still muffled, and she remained a nondescript blob of duvet.

I tossed the tissue box to Umbra and sat down in her office chair, peering at the remaining untouched stack of files that had been in the envelope.

"Ransom…" She sounded choked again. "R-Ransom g-got me a registration c-card."

"What?" Umbra sounded surprised. *"Ransom?"* he mouthed at me, but I just mimed slicing my throat with my hand. He'd known we were getting registration stuff sorted for her, but I hadn't caught him up on my delivery methods—or lies. But there was no way she'd accept this easily.

Finally, the duvet pulled down just enough that her head poked out. "A card like… what real omegas have."

I contained my snort. *Real* omegas? She was more real than any omega I'd ever met. Whether she was registered with the Institute or not, that didn't change.

It offered her some stability, though, which is why I'd done it.

She reached out with her arm, hugging the blanket against herself, blue registration card clutched in her fist. "H-he doesn't even know me. Why would he do that?"

I cleared my throat as Umbra began handing her wads of tissues so she could blow her nose.

Uh… *why* had he? I hadn't actually planned this far ahead.

She gave me some breathing room. Her expression became horrified as she blew her nose and discovered how much she was dripping. I hid my humour, since she'd probably take it as an insult.

After a small mountain of tissues had accumulated at her side, she looked back at me expectantly.

"I told him you were…" I trailed off. Staying with us? I didn't want this tied to anything ongoing, courting or not. "He hired a new guy for this kind of job. Needed a test run to see how good he was."

"Oh… okay." She hugged the card closer, looking relieved. Then her eyes clouded with worry again. "So it's just… temporary or something?"

"It's all legit. Permanent."

"Can I see?" Umbra asked her. She was so emotional she burst into tears again, clambering closer to him and sitting on the edge of the bed so she could show him.

"He said my scent was poppies and elderberries." There was a quivering smile on her lips as she looked over the card again. "And he changed my last name to Kingsman…" Her brows drew down.

I froze, anticipating the storm.

Her eyes were wide as she turned the card back toward herself to double check.

"He did?" Umbra asked, also shooting me a confused look.

"Yeah…" Shatter's voice cracked. "For some reason…?"

I buried my grin. She was just so charmingly *literal.* "Sure," I said, clearing my throat. "We'll go with that."

She barely heard me, though, and I took the opportunity to pinch the papers on the bottom of the stack and tuck them in my pocket. She was so overwhelmed right now. I'd keep them for another time—perhaps when I was in the mood for a bit of omega rage.

"Can I meet him?" she asked. "Is he well enough?"

Was he well?

What did she know?

I glanced at Umbra, who just shrugged, giving me a *'no big deal'* look.

"Soon enough," I said.

Her face drained of colour. "Did you…?" She cleared her throat. "What about my scent?"

"What about it?"

"What if he doesn't like it, and—" Her voice cracked, her whole body shrinking as she hugged the card closer. "What if—?"

"He knows your scent."

"Oh." She seemed stumped by that. "And he… he liked it?" Her cheeks went pink at the question, but I answered before she could reword it.

"Even more than we do."

I saw the twitch of a smile on Umbra's face out of the corner of my eye.

Shatter stared at me, not seeming to know what to do with that. After a long silence, she glanced between me and Umbra. "Okay. I think I'm done now. You can go."

I snorted but got to my feet, feeling rather pleased.

Then I paused, spotting a flash of something that chilled my blood. "Show me your neck."

"What?" she asked, looking startled.

It took everything in me not to close the gap between us right now. Instead, I swallowed my instincts. I didn't want to ruin this. "*What* is on your neck?"

Her hand jumped to the spot I was staring at.

Their faces flashed in my mind—the men from my nightmares. Images of them biting her. Claiming her. Taking her from me so I couldn't protect her, like I wasn't able to protect Ransom.

They'd destroy her. The most beautiful woman on the planet, left hollow and—

"It's mine."

At Umbra's words, my ice cold fury vaporised.

"He bit you?" I asked, forcing normalcy into my voice. She'd spotted my demons. I could see it by the uncertainty in her eyes. I had to pull it together.

"She lost a game we played," Umbra said smugly.

"I didn't lose!" she hissed, her spark of rage smothering the momentary tenseness. "You *cheated*."

Umbra grinned. "Did not."

"I warned you, Gem," I told her as I stepped toward the door, still reeling from adrenaline. I would leave the evening as it was, not ruin it with nightmares. They just felt so close today.

They were still bickering when I reached the hall, and I had a few moments before Shatter dragged Umbra to the door and was shoving it closed right on his grinning face.

"You have no faith in me," he huffed, punching me on the shoulder, his light tone covering the concern I felt from him down the bond.

I cleared my throat as he began down the hallway. "You bit her?"

That was good. *Really* good.

It would make me happy if I wasn't so fucking on edge today.

Umbra was grinning as he turned, spreading his arms as he walked backward.

"I think I love her, mate," he said, something dazed rising from his end of the bond. I'd never felt anything like it before. A warm summer's breeze, stirring grass and lifting leaves. "I'd burn this whole place to the ground before I let them put *one* filthy tooth on her."

The smile on my face was real as he vanished down to the living room.

I was about to follow when I heard the door creak behind me.

I turned quickly and saw a golden eye peek through the barely cracked door. Shatter spotted me, then shut it again. I leaned against the wall, waiting. Sure enough, it opened again, wider this time, and she appeared, chewing on her lip and folding her arms like she meant business.

"Yes?" I asked.

She cleared her throat. "Can you tell him thank you for me?" Her voice was low, and she kept passing the card from one hand to another in trembling fingers.

I straightened, stepping closer. "Yes." She didn't flinch as I cupped her cheek and tilted her chin. Her eyes still swam with nerves. I wanted to kiss her, but somehow, despite the lie, it felt like this *was* Ransom's moment. Not mine.

"No one is going to take that away. You don't owe him—*anyone*—anything for it."

She nodded, but I could see that she hadn't truly grasped it yet.

She needed time for that.

I dropped my hand and she stepped away, her gaze meeting mine one last time before she shut the door, stunning golden orbs equal parts hopeful and unsure.

Shatter's response—her shock and tears—told me one thing that gave me hope: no matter what she claimed, she hadn't been certain her mates would do this for her at all.

CHAPTER 19

Now back on suppressants, the subject is rapidly regressing to the state she was in when she arrived. Additionally, she displays symptoms of depression, including extended periods of catatonia, and has debilitating panic attacks at any mention of her designation as an omega.

Shatter

My nails dug into my bag as I clutched it to my chest and poked my head into the classroom. It was a smaller space than the auditorium, and full of rows of desks and chairs.

But Omega Studies didn't start for another thirty minutes, and there was no one here.

Good, that was good.

This was my most unnerving class, and I wanted to give myself time to get settled.

Dusk, while forcing me to take my scent blocker this morning, had told me I didn't have to attend. "You could join us in the Genetics and Genomic Arkology class, if you want to?" he'd suggested.

"I'm fine to go," I'd replied.

The star he'd placed on my necklace was a symbol of commitment, and I could get out of Rookwood Academy's mandated Omega Studies classes if his pack agreed that they didn't mind.

"I want to," I told him.

I didn't, but that wasn't the point.

I *needed* to go.

I was good at Arkology, but this was uncharted territory. I might not remember my past before the Institute and then the Estate with Uncle and Aunty Lauren, but I was certain there had never been any omega etiquette education. Ever since I'd discovered my mates existed, I'd been filled with newfound determination to claim my omega side, even damaged and neglected as it was.

There would have to be now, though, with Roxy Vasilli competing for my mates. She held herself far too well, and I was sure she'd been to a dozen classes like this before.

I hurried down the rows and took the desk second from the back. My favourite was the back, but I didn't want to look as nervous as I was feeling.

As I sat down, I scanned the empty classroom. Two students per desk, which meant I should have a partner. My stomach did a flip as I wondered what they'd think of me.

Too preoccupied with getting ready, I hadn't even tried to smuggle out a scent marked scrunchie this morning. Dusk had ended up leaning against my doorframe, asking me why I was making them late as I fretted over putting my hair up or down for the millionth time. Indecision was its own answer, as I'd bumbled about with it to the point of no return. It was either bun, or matted mane. That also meant Umbra's bite was on display.

I poked it nervously now, trying to catch any stray pieces so it didn't look too messy. I adjusted my skirt, glancing at the clock. Twenty-three and a half minutes until class started.

Still, I was alone.

I began unpacking my bag.

Pencil case. Notebook. Spare notebook. Spare pencil case (what if someone forgets theirs?). Making friends was foreign to me, and I'd use all the help I could get.

That was another thing I could have when I reached my mates: a chance at something as normal as real friends.

My mates weren't like Dusk and Umbra, who hid from the world. With the Lincoln pack, I could maybe go out with them and meet their friends and make my own. If I got good enough in classes like this, anyway. I'd probably have to wear my contacts; I knew their reputation was important, but I was fine with that.

Cautiously, I unzipped my main pencil case and pulled out the blue registration card. I stared at it for a long moment, my throat suddenly thick. My picture was on it. My scent. A string of twelve numbers I'd spent all night memorising. My signature, which I'd practised for hours last night, before I was finally brave enough to write it. I'd made sure the Kingsman part of the name was less readable in case I had to change it when I reached my mates. Dusk had said I didn't owe Ransom anything for it. Would he understand that I couldn't stop fighting to get to them?

But the card was *perfect.*

I shoved it back inside, glancing up at the empty classroom.

I nudged the pencil case off-kilter so I could re-adjust it, foot tapping on the hardwood. After another minute of silence, I unzipped the pencil case again, and tugged out the card, placing it neatly between my pens and notebooks.

It was *Omega* Studies… this was mine now. Proof I was like them, even if Dusk forced me to hide my scent.

I returned to waiting, chewing aggressively on my lip until I tasted blood.

Shit.

Shit shit shit.

I'd forgotten tissues.

Right then, the door creaked open and the first student walked in. I didn't recognise her, but the faintest scent of cherry cheesecake wafted in. She had wavy brown hair and bright green eyes.

Would she sit next to me?

I smiled before I caught myself, then quickly covered my hand with my mouth.

Blood.

I'd look crazy.

I grabbed the collar of my cardigan, which was thankfully black, and quickly rubbed at my teeth. The tang of iron was fading.

When I looked up, the cherry cheesecake omega had already taken a seat at the front.

Okay… I didn't mind. That was a preference thing anyway.

More omegas filed in, most with charming scents: sweet desserts or elegant flowers. There was a faint misting of scent dampeners in the room so it didn't get overwhelming. I could barely contain my nerves as I watched.

Before the ball, they'd been my competition, but now… Now, especially without my mates, I needed to learn from them.

I noticed when Roxy Vasilli entered with Jasmine Lynn, and the pair took a seat at the table just behind me. I caught her orange and fir tree scent, and shrank a little. It was subtle and classy, and my mates probably loved it.

I distracted myself by keeping my gaze fixed on the newcomers.

No one had sat next to me yet, but I noticed some were entering in pairs or groups. I was already behind in socialising.

I figured out the problem pretty quickly from listening to Roxy and Jasmine chat behind me, and spotting some of the jealous looks shot their way. It wasn't until I received the same jealous looks that it clicked.

The competition hadn't ended at the ball. The other omegas had either paired with normal packs or not paired at all.

There were only seven packs on the calibre of the Kingsman and Lincoln. Packs who were both well known, rich, and endorsed by one of the speciality's governing bodies. The Lincoln and Kingsman packs, for example, were both sponsored by well known Arkologists.

Their omegas were in a different social group. *That* was why Roxy and Jasmine had entered together and why other omegas didn't want to sit with me.

If I was right, I was in luck.

Ali and Jayson Maddison were well-known, young, and married. The Barcley Pack had snagged both of them together. So there were six others. A nice even number, of which I was one.

One of them would *have* to sit next to me.

Victoria and Sienna came in together, and, of course, Ali and Jayson entered hand in hand.

That was all of them but one.

There were only four minutes until the class started, but I was feeling hopeful now I racked my brain for who remained, but then Oliver Ryder walked in, answering the question for me.

He had piercing blue eyes and a sweep of pale blond hair. He was tall for an omega, with a scent like ocean breeze. He had been picked by the Hargrave pack, who'd been sponsored by the medical program.

Right.

Okay.

He would be my partner then.

I straightened in my seat, tugging at my skirt again and trying not to stare. Oliver glanced around the room, swiftly doing the assessment that had taken me all this time. Finally, his eyes landed on me.

I held my breath, feeling a spike of pride as I realised I'd figured it out correctly, and smiled, making sure not to show my teeth, in case of lingering blood.

His gaze was so calculating that my heart began hammering in my chest. I swear his gaze flickered momentarily to the bite on my neck, and I had to fight the urge to cover it with my hand. I had their star, but I still didn't know what the other omegas would consider normal.

"Hi!" Jasmine Lynn's voice sounded from the desk behind me. "Have you met Roxy, yet? She's giving me a rundown on the new social platform OmegaGlobe is setting up. It sounds *amazing*—here, come on. You can fit."

I swallowed, trying to be subtle in how I glanced back.

Shit.

Could I say something? But Jasmine was grabbing a seat from the desk to her left, and Oliver relaxed, striding toward her and settling down at the end of their table.

I fixed my gaze back to the front of the room, cheeks burning as I battled with my urge to fiddle with my pencil cases again.

This was fine.

I was odd and scentless. And the second pencil case was a bit much.

No one else had their registration card out, either.

I tried to figure out how I might put them away without drawing too much attention to myself, but it felt like I was being pinned with stares. I checked my hair again and realised half the bun had fallen out.

Oh crap.

I must look like a mess. I should never have tried to do anything special with it–I could have just left it down. Down would have been fine. Lots of the girls in here had their hair down.

The door opened again and a middle-aged omega, introducing herself as Professor Brant entered the room. She wore a neat cream blazer and pencil skirt, and her blonde hair was tied so tightly in a bun, it must have been gelled.

I tried really hard to focus on her introduction, but it was hard.

Class had barely started, and I'd already fucked up. I was the only omega bonded to a prestigious pack who didn't have a partner, and if Roxy thought I was pathetic, it might get back to my mates.

But it was possible Oliver would sit with me next time, right?

He was only there because he wanted to talk to Roxy about whatever it was they were discussing. He also didn't know me, and a lot of the omegas had already made friends. I had to find a way to introduce myself, like Jasmine clearly had.

Professor Brant began the lecture. I tried to focus, but my notes were disjointed. It was only lesson one, so there wasn't much substance. Instead of worrying about that, I scrambled for a way to introduce myself to Oliver. I just had to say hello, or… or anything.

The opportunity came during break. Jasmine was sharing a piece of gossip in a hushed voice (I was trying and failing to listen in). Oliver burst out laughing, and I heard something hit the floor and skid beneath my chair.

Oliver muttered a curse as I glanced below me to see he'd knocked his phone from the desk. Not what I'd been hoping for, since it was hard to compliment someone on their phone. But before anyone could move, I dived to pick it up. I wouldn't give up my chance to speak to him.

Except, as my knees hit the wooden floor with embarrassing speed, the rest of my hair exploded from its fragile bun.

My face burned red hot.

Oh no.

I dragged myself upright holding his phone and fighting through a forest of honey brown tangles as I fumbled for the desk. When I finally managed it, I was looking up at three dumbstruck omegas. Roxy, Jasmine, and Oliver were staring at me in shock.

All my plans of what I would say to Oliver died on my tongue as I pressed his phone onto the desk. "It's uh…" I swallowed, grappling with a smile as I gripped handfuls of my hair, and tried to flatten them down. I couldn't even look at Roxy. In fact, better I pretended she didn't exist at all, so I didn't flee the room. "Shit." I forced a stupid laugh. "Always so hard to manage, you know?" My voice was weak.

You know?

Had I just said that to a guy with three inches of hair? One who looked like he rolled out of bed with it perfectly styled.

Oliver took his phone, giving me a curt nod.

My chest tightened.

He would never talk to me again.

And it wasn't just them. By the sudden silence around me, I knew the whole class was watching.

This was so bad.

And the damned curls were frizzy from my furious battle this morning.

I dragged myself back to my seat and shrank down, still grasping it against my head, knowing I'd have to make a whole scene to put it back in its bun. I could feel the knot from the hair tie that was still tangled up in it.

Break was almost over, too. Three and a half minutes. I didn't have time to run to the bathroom. Even if I did, I'd have to walk by *everyone* like this.

Around me, I could hear the muffled sounds of poorly stifled mirth.

A hot bubble of shame burst in my chest, visceral through my missing memories, as if I'd been here a million times before.

I barely heard the scrape of a chair.

My eyes were burning, and I winced as I bit my lip again, trying to measure my expression.

I didn't process the low words spoken behind me, or how they were almost cold. "Jasmine, Oliver. I'll catch up later."

I was so busy spiralling that I jumped when delicate fingers brushed mine, and then someone was tugging the hair tie from the huge buffle of hair that had it trapped.

They'd come to stand behind me?

"I am *so* jealous." Her voice was smooth and calm, and her scent of fir trees and oranges was as soothing as I was panicked. "I always wanted hair as thick as this."

I couldn't move, shock blitzing every other feeling as dainty hands skillfully and swiftly wrestled my impossible hair back into its bun in front of every silent stare.

Then Roxy placed her books neatly beside mine, a surprisingly shy smile on her devastatingly beautiful face as she took the seat at my desk.

I just stared, the whole English language making a mass exodus from my brain.

Oh…

Shit.

This was bad.

This was *worse* than bad.

I needed the hardwood floor to open beneath me and swallow me up right now.

Because Roxy Vasilli was not allowed to be a nice person, not when I was trying to steal her alphas.

CHAPTER 20

Shatter

That evening, Umbra summoned me away from my nest. "What's this?" I asked, noticing a full spread of snacks across the table.

I'd hidden in my nest since lunch, as there were no afternoon classes. I'd tried to read one of the Arkology books I hadn't yet opened, but instead I'd just clung to my pillows, furiously going over every moment of this morning, trying to figure out how to never look like such an idiot again.

"Movie night," Dusk told me.

"Um…"

Movie night?

I glanced around at the mountains of snack foods, and the pillows and blankets Umbra was arranging on the couch. The curtains were drawn, and the lights dim.

"All ordered in or microwaved by Umbra. I didn't make an ounce of it," Dusk said smugly, pressing a plate into my hands.

I stared over the bowls of chips, Pop Tarts, mozzarella sticks, nachos and more, my tummy rumbling.

"Why?"

"You won't tell us what you like, so we'll have to figure it out for ourselves. Plus, I heard you had a shit morning."

"How?"

Dusk tapped his nose without a word, nudging me toward the feast. I swallowed, far too tempted, but my cheeks were growing hotter at the mere memory of Omega Studies.

How much did he know?

"My morning was *fine*," I told him stubbornly.

"Really?"

"I hung out with *Roxy Vasilli*."

"Yeh?" Dusk asked, expression amused. "The omega who took your mates?"

"She's actually…" The words were harder to force out than I'd planned for. "Well. She isn't what I expected."

Dusk's eyebrows lifted.

"She… she helped me." If he had heard about this morning, I needed to set him straight. I couldn't stand the idea of him and Umbra thinking I was an idiot, too. "I'm just a bit rusty at the whole… social thing is all, and she uh… bailed me out."

"So she wants to be friends?" Umbra asked, joining us and grabbing his own plate.

I frowned, piling a few snacks onto mine. That's what I was hoping for. Well… I mean… kind of. I'd wanted *someone* to be my friend.

Just… *Roxy* hadn't been the plan.

I took a seat on the couch, knowing I needed to eat and leave and not engage in any of this movie night stuff.

"She asked if I wanted to join her for Omega Studies homework sessions after school starting next week," I said, eyeing Dusk for a reaction.

Even with Roxy there, I'd been jittery for the rest of class. Dusk had been waiting for me outside of Omega Studies after class, treatment that had drawn more attention than I'd wanted. Still, I'd said a quick goodbye to Roxy and hurried over to him, for once grateful at the way his presence grabbed attention. It was the first time I hadn't felt like the stares were following *my* every move.

"To get this straight," he said, sitting on the couch at my side as Umbra took the armchair. "You want to hang out with the Lincoln pack omega?"

I swallowed. "It'll just be in the building—downstairs. She booked a study room. No alphas allowed."

"No alphas allowed?" Dusk chuckled. "Then I don't see a problem."

"Really?" I asked.

"Sure," Dusk said, sounding far too amused.

"So… Roxy's nice?" Umbra asked, and I didn't like the grin spreading across his face. The two of them exchanged a look that put me on edge.

I eyed him, unsure about his sincerity. Sarcasm was one of those things I struggled with, like I always had a hard time telling if people were lying. But Umbra was usually quite direct, so if there was a double meaning here, it was probably on Dusk.

"I suppose so," I said cautiously.

Dusk let out a bark of laughter that made me want to stab him with my fork.

"So tell me, how is that going to fit into your grand schemes?" he asked.

I lowered my plate to my lap, glaring at them. "It doesn't *change* anything."

"No?" Fuck, he looked smug.

"*Shut* up."

"No, no," Dusk snorted. "I want to hear this. When you finally make your grand escape and get to your precious mates, how are you going to get *Saint* Roxy Vasilli out of the picture?"

"It'll be fine."

Could she stay, somehow?

It wasn't that I was against double omega packs, but the situation was delicate… If they claimed me, she would probably be dropped. Her sponsorship wouldn't be taken away, but it would look bad for her prospects.

But if they dropped her because they found their scent match…? That would be reasonable right?

People wouldn't judge her for that.

I tapped my fork on my plate, then stopped at Umbra's poorly concealed smirk.

But Roxy had fixed my hair in front of the whole class and stayed by my side. She hadn't been judgemental, like I'd expected. Instead, she'd told me we could swap notes and offered after class study invites.

It was everything I'd wanted.

Everything.

Except my mates were probably falling for her right now…

Crying wasn't an option.

I sat in irritated silence and poked at my nachos, as Umbra picked an apocalypse movie and pressed play, but when I stood to leave, Dusk's hand circled my waist. "You're staying for at least one movie."

I thought of my nest desperately, but the dream didn't hold quite the weight I wished it did. I'd been anxiously in my own head for the last few hours and I needed a distraction. I heard the dramatic intro music of the movie behind me, reminding me of the rare nights when I was invited to watch documentaries with Aunty Lauren and Uncle.

Sitting down, I made sure to put on a decently reluctant expression, so Dusk wouldn't catch on to quite how much I wished to stay.

When the second movie began, I didn't move, even though Dusk had tugged me under his arm. I heard the low rumble of a purr in his chest every time he felt me shift. Umbra had moved to the couch after the edge of jealousy in his harsh wolfsbane scent had become almost noxious. I'd caught the edge of a grin on Dusk's lips when he'd dropped down at my other side.

I spent a whole second movie caught between the two of them. A purr rumbling on one side, Umbra's fingers tapping gently along my arm on the other—anxiously, as if he couldn't quite help himself.

It would almost be possible to convince myself that *this* was... maybe what I wanted. Almost possible to believe they liked me being here—that I wasn't a nuisance or a burden.

Only... they weren't my mates.

It was hard to conjure the courage to speak when the end credits of the second movie began. "I should go to bed."

I made to stand, but Dusk didn't let me, burying his face in my neck and hair. "You were so well behaved today, I think you deserve a reward."

"A *what?"* I asked, trying to wriggle free, but instead found both of his arms sandwiching me against him.

"I could give you a reward *and* Umbra a show."

"No. No show." I tried, again, to break his grip, but he was dragging me onto his lap to face him, reminding me starkly of how he'd claimed me the other night.

When he'd knotted me... Fuck. I shivered, shoving the thought away.

"Oh, what did you just think about?" he asked, dragging me closer. "Your pupils are giving you away, Gem."

"Them," I told him quickly. "I was thinking about them."

"Right." He grinned. "Not the belt? Or the way I felt filling that sweet cunt of yours with my—" He cut off, looking delighted, catching my chin so I couldn't look away. "*There* it is. You've been dreaming of me, Shatter."

"No, I fucking *haven't*," I growled, shoving against his chest, but he only tightened his grip on my waist, shifting me over the rock-hard bulge in his pants. Midnight opium was heavy with lust.

"You're so fucking perfect, Gem," he breathed, and one of his hands dropped between my thighs, nudging aside my panties. "Now, *stay still* while I give you the reward you deserve."

The words 'stay still' were laced with a command that froze me for a moment as his thumb pressed against my clit.

I snarled. "You touching me is *not* a reward."

"I think it is."

My breathing was heavy as his command faded, and I was torn between trying to fight him and doing what he asked. At least we were out here and not in my nest.

My voice was a whine. "I'm doing what you say so that you *don't*—"

"So I don't turn your cute little ass pink."

"I won't…" I swallowed, trying to ignore the building pleasure. "I won't behave for you if it means getting something I don't want."

"Sound logic," he told me, releasing his grip on my thigh. My chest was heaving as I warred with myself.

He'd do this anyway. If I fought him, he'd make it more humiliating, or he'd drag me into the nest…

"Good girl," he told me. "Now, I want you looking at Umbra."

I swallowed, eyes darting to the side to see Umbra watching me with blown pupils. Wolfsbane and blood were sharp and wanting.

I shuddered as Dusk's thumb sped up. "I don't… I don't want your stupid orgasms."

I let out a gasp as his teeth closed around my shirt and bra, still managing to catch my nipple.

"Yes, you do," he told me. "You get snacks and cuddles."

I let out a breath of shock as he plunged one finger into me without warning.

"Good company…" he went on. "…Me worshipping that perfect body of yours, and then, when I'm done and you're high from endorphins you can stagger back to your nest and study until you pass out and dream of what it would be like to take me and Umbra at the same time."

With my gaze fixed on sandstorm eyes, I almost whined. That sounded so horribly *good* to my omega brain.

Especially when Umbra reached down to adjust himself, his teeth catching his lip as if he was itching to do more.

"I can't wait to see him ruin you," Dusk breathed, hand closing tighter on my throat as he added a second finger and picked up his speed, thumb still putting pressure on my clit. "You're going to be addicted to us, Gem. Even if you do manage to slip away, you're going to turn around and come right back."

"I w-won't."

"One day you'll beg for my bite."

He squeezed my throat and sent me over the edge. I whimpered, heat crashing through my bloodstream. Fuck, it was dizzying, and I felt slick pool around his fingers.

Umbra drank in every second of my expression as I let out noises I couldn't keep down. I sagged, shivering and curling against Dusk as he released my throat, not wanting to look at either of them. But each inhale was midnight opium and wolfsbane flooding my lungs as ecstasy dissipated in my body.

He wrapped his arms around me and nipped my ear. "I love how you get so sweet with me after I make you come."

I tensed, but didn't pull away, unable to face either of them. When he let me go, I would run to my nest and pretend it hadn't happened.

"It's all up to you, Gem. Be a good girl for us and you can keep your nest, and I'll *treat* you until you can't walk straight," he said, his touch tracing my back. "Misbehave, and I'll punish you and take *my* pleasure using your sweet holes."

He released me at last and I scrambled to my feet, not meeting either of their gazes. I hoped neither noticed how I shuddered at those words, despising that they did things to me when they had no right to. My legs were still trembling, and I stumbled before catching myself. My nerves were twinkling like Christmas lights, sending sparks of warmth through my bloodstream.

Stupid.

Fucking *stupid* and meaningless.

"Shatter?" Dusk asked when I reached the hallway.

I shot him a glance, lips pursed.

"Next time you hang out with Roxy, why don't you ask how her alphas are treating her?"

CHAPTER 21

Umbra

Dusk and Shatter settled into something of a strange normal.

The unusual routine began one morning when we caught her trying to sneak a nightshade-covered scrunchie to freedom in her pocket as we were leaving for classes.

"Couch," Dusk told her, folding his arms. "Now."

"What?" Shatter looked so perfectly stunned.

"Wait for me on the couch just like you did the first night you were here."

"For a scrunchie?" Her voice was weak, eyes darting to me desperately. But there was no way in hell I was arguing if Dusk wanted to give me a show.

"You are breaking our agreement, Gem. You should be glad I'm not dragging you back to your nest—"

"No!" Her eyes grew wide. "I… I won't do it again."

Had anyone ever told her she was a *terrible* liar? Her eyes flickered to me, all shifty-like. The lie wasn't exactly directed at me, but clearly she was worried I'd give her a bite for it anyway.

I was about to get something just as good as a bite, though, so I didn't care.

"Couch or nest?" Dusk asked. "Because if you aren't bent over that couch in the next five seconds, I'll decide for you."

Her lips popped open, her cheeks going bright red.

Like the maniac he was, Dusk raised his hand and began putting down fingers. Flustered and furious, Shatter all but ran to the couch, standing up against it. Then she looked back at me and Dusk, expression tight with rage.

Dusk raised his eyebrow, lowering his second to last finger. With a little breath of derision, Shatter lowered herself over the couch arm, giving us both a glimpse of her ass peeking from beneath her skirt.

Dusk crossed toward her, placed a hand on her waist and adjusted her slightly. I think it was so I had a better view.

I appreciated that.

"Lift up your skirt," Dusk told her.

Her protest was mostly an incomprehensible sound, and her breathing was heavy.

Dusk said nothing, waiting patiently.

Seeming resigned to her own defeat, she reached back with fumbling fingers, tugging her skirt up to reveal little black panties hugging what was, without a doubt, the cutest ass on the planet.

I cocked my head, erection raging in my pants, eyes fixed on the way she was presented to him like that.

That was it. When I fucked her the first time, it was going to be just like *that.* I almost groaned at the thought of it. I imagined looking down at her presented to me like a hot-as-fuck omega Christmas present, watching her perfect little pussy take my whole length while she made all those sexy bratty noises just for me.

I needed to find a bet worth that.

By the time Dusk's palm cracked across her ass cheek the first time, I was halfway to a Goddamned climax on pure imagination.

This was wildly unfair considering we had to go out after this. I was in a daze, staring at the blossoming pink palm print across her smooth golden skin. That was the sexiest thing I'd seen in my life.

"How many?" Dusk asked.

"What?" Her voice was high pitched.

"How many do you think you deserve? You violated our deal *and* you're avoiding punishment in your nest."

"Um..." Her voice was breathless. "I d-don't know."

Dusk slid his hand to her thighs, slipping his thumb beneath her panties and pressing it right into her sex without warning. She let out a little moan of shock and my own cock strained against my already struggling jeans.

"You're wet enough I could go for a fuck if you'd prefer—"

"No, no, no!" She whined, clutching a pillow to her face, clearly completely broken down. "Um... eight?" She threw out, sounding totally unsure.

I saw the curve of a smile on Dusk's lips as she chose a number.

He took his time, massaging her flesh between each spank, and I swear she moaned a few times while he did. When he was done, and her ass was rosy pink, he dropped onto the couch and told her to get on her knees.

Fuck me.

How the *hell* was I supposed to go to class after this?

I groaned as she positioned herself before him, face beet red now from the punishment and—based on her shifty looks in my direction—the audience.

But Dusk was not fucking around this morning, and he didn't give her time to argue.

"Fuck, you're beautiful, Gem," he breathed as he dragged her by the hair to the base of his shaft. I hadn't seen him claim her like this. Shatter's omega fury didn't let up even though her pupils were blown to the size of dinner plates. And I noticed how her eyes snapped to him every time he praised her. It was really cute, actually, like it caught her off guard and she couldn't stop her reaction.

Dusk shot me an all-too-smug smile as he fucked her throat. He could *obviously* see my raging hard-on and was taunting me for the fact I wouldn't do any of it without a trade first.

I knew what he thought of my karma stuff. I folded my arms with a scowl, leaning against the kitchen cabinet and *not* too prideful to take my eyes away—which he was also completely aware of.

Prick.

It was very, very hard to hold to that conviction when—as he finished down her throat—her eyes locked on me.

Nope. I would never get this out of my head.

And it wasn't the end of it.

Shatter wasn't following the rules perfectly, though she was very good at being obedient when she wanted to be. But her nightshade scrunchie smuggling attempts didn't stop. While I gave her points for creativity, there was just no way we could miss the faint scent of nightshade on her in the mornings.

Surprising even me, Dusk never used those opportunities to enter her nest. Instead, he exacted her punishment instantly every time. Now the image of Dusk bending her over the couch and spanking her were all that my nighttime wanks featured anymore. If I was really lucky—and the scrunchie almost made it to freedom—I'd get to watch her on her knees after again, taking his cock down her throat.

After one particularly pitiful smuggling attempt (the scrunchie was literally in her hair) I couldn't even take her furious whines of protest seriously. Especially since I doubted her misbehaving little butt had recovered from the last session, which had been the previous morning.

That time he'd used his belt (for the insult of putting it in her hair) and *fuck* did she take his cock well that day. I could have sworn she was seconds from her own orgasm by the time he was done, her pretty chocolate eyes dazed as she staggered to her feet. She didn't even protest when he kissed her.

Sure, she'd been all grouchiness and rage for the rest of the morning in Arkology class, shooting Dusk death glares, but I was onto her. It was a very smart workaround for getting Dusk's hands all over her without feeling like she was betraying her mates.

I don't think she was quite ready for *that* conversation, though.

She'd have to get over it eventually, right? She was ours. That was indisputable.

"You haven't gone into her nest yet?" I prodded Dusk one afternoon. We'd entered for the registration card meltdown, I supposed, but she'd invited us that time.

"Haven't needed to," he grunted, continuing to scan the textbook open on his lap.

Needed to?

That wasn't the point. He *could* have.

He tapped his pen on the couch arm, then caught my scrutinising gaze and rolled his eyes. "She's…" He pinched his bottom lip in his teeth, thinking. "She's more attached to it than I was expecting."

Huh.

I nodded slowly. She *was* attached to it. On the weekend, when the scent blockers had worn off, her scent was shockingly content when she appeared from her nest for breakfast (which I was getting better at cooking, now).

So Dusk didn't want to ruin it?

"Soon, perhaps. When she's a bit more settled." He glanced down the hallway to the nest, and I could see the desire in his eyes, like he wanted nothing more than to slip down there right now and join her.

Would he even want to bang her in there? Or just hold her? I'd be happy if I just got to hold her, but I hadn't gone in either. Not even just to be there, which I was allowed to do if I didn't touch her.

Neither of us had crossed the threshold.

"And Ransom?" I dared to ask.

I knew what Dusk had been doing with her scrunchies. I'd felt more flashes of life from Ransom down the bond. Each brief, but enough to give me a burst of hope each time.

Dusk wasn't confident that she could meet him, yet, and I got it. We were more resilient, but one mistake and he'd snap her in two.

"Better every time I go in," Dusk replied quietly.

My chest tightened. "We're getting him back…?"

That thought was so foreign, so impossible that I almost couldn't comprehend it. It was more than anything I could ever—

"You paid."

The world, which had been on the brink of fading away, slammed back down as Dusk grabbed me by the chin, expression tight as he caught me about to spiral.

I stared at him.

"You paid already," he repeated, dropping his hand.

Had I?

I cycled through it all again. Every moment. Every payment down to the scars along my skin.

"You destroyed yourself. You kept me safe, remember?"

I hated to remember, but the memories hurt. Sometimes if they were bad enough, the blade was unnecessary.

There was one I always returned to.

"Tell me."

"It won't help you." Dr. Wren jabbed me with another needle for another vial of blood, like I had any left in me at all.

"Tell me." My voice cracked with desperation. My body was spent from the self-inflicted torture, from the experiments they'd run. My aura was a thin thread, my nights disturbed by tremors of agony, through which Dusk would hold me.

"Next they want the healthier of the pack."

My heart dropped.

No…

It was only me and Dusk left, and I'd worked so hard to become the weakest so they'd take me. I'd starved myself. I'd bled and scarred. I'd done everything to be here in his place.

"H-how long do I have?" I wouldn't let them have him. I would never let Dusk go through this.

Dr. Wren's expression was sad, as if he didn't believe it was possible. "Two weeks."

I'd paid…?

Had I?

For Ransom, that was worth a million lifetimes of what I'd—

"Enough."

I clenched and unclenched my fists at Dusk's voice, taking a breath.

Dusk wanted hope, so if he caught it before it started, I could force myself to wait until later.

Then he could believe there would be an end to this for me.

I took a breath, sinking back on the couch and nodding.

Silence passed, in which Dusk returned to his textbook. He shared most of his classes with the Lincoln pack, a deliberate move since we wanted to get close to them, but he was surprisingly engaged with the coursework.

I was in a few of the shared classes, but the rest I'd selected on feelings alone, disgusted at the idea of sitting through dozens of Arkology lectures because our enemies happened to be stuck-up idiots. The classes I had chosen were proving a sight more interesting. Philosophy, for example. Not bad. Could give me some ammunition next time Dusk told me my karma belief was bullshit.

Well.

I hoped.

"You really okay with her going to study time with their omega?" I asked.

Tomorrow was Roxy's after-class hang out that Shatter wanted to go to.

Dusk shrugged. "She's never going to believe a bad thing *I* say about them, but maybe…" He trailed off.

I pondered that. Not a terrible plan, actually. She knew how obsessed Dusk was, and I knew how farfetched anything we had to say about the Lincoln pack was. But if she made friends with their omega… might she learn for herself?

Still, I didn't totally trust it. We both knew what her first class had looked like, Dusk had bribed an omega to give us the rundown.

The story had made me want to pack her up in a woollen bag and carry her around with me forever so she could never get hurt. Well, that would be second best, since Dusk wouldn't let me beat up omegas.

If it did go well, though? I was quite proud of her actually. Making friends and shit.

It's what she needed.

CHAPTER 22

Shatter

A really, really strange thing was happening now that I was living with the Kingsman pack.

Always, I knew where Dusk was even when I wasn't looking at him—across the room on the couch, a foot from me in our lecture hall booth, or walking behind me as we made our way to the cafeteria. Every time I sensed him moving closer, all the hair on my body would stand on end, and it would become impossible to focus on whatever I was doing (even if it was trying to read an Arkology textbook). My heart rate would shoot up and goosebumps pebbled my skin, every part of my body tense and giddy, waiting for his touch. And then it would all crumple and I'd melt into a puddle of frustration if he was just passing by to grab a drink, or reaching for a pen.

It made me want to tear my hair out, but it was the same with Umbra (if a little less intense), so it had to be an alpha-omega thing. I tried to look it up but couldn't find anything specific in my Physiology Explored: Arkology textbook.

What. Ever.

I already knew I needed alphas more than the regular omega did, and if it was like this with them, it would be one-hundred fold with my mates when I got to them.

"*What* is that?" Dusk asked. His expression was unusually shocked as I stepped into the living room, ready for the study date Roxy had invited me to.

"What?" I asked, glancing between Dusk and Umbra, who were both on the couch, and both staring at me.

"Woah…" Umbra breathed. "Are you a goddess?"

I blushed, drawing my satchel closer over the outfit, unsure of what to make of that. "Is it too much?"

I didn't know who would be there tonight. Once again, I'd had a meltdown on what to wear—though this time, my hair was down. It was the evening, and I thought people dressed up more in evenings, so I'd picked a black dress that looked least like the school uniform. There wasn't much, but the nest had a few outfits for different occasions. And when I'd put it on, it had felt kind of… magic.

They were just staring, but finally Dusk got up and stepped toward me. My skin got all tingly again as he approached, and my breath was caught in my lungs. He was eyeing my outfit, but I couldn't take my gaze from his face as he stopped only inches away.

"Shatter," he told me, knuckle brushing my chin.

I swallowed, clearing my throat. "Yes?"

He was so close, and when he was this close, anything could happen. Sometimes he kissed me, sometimes he touched me or punished me, and sometimes he told me to get on my knees and take his cock.

My heart beat like a hummingbird's wings, blood hot.

Did I do something wrong?

Was I trying to figure that out because I wished I had, or wished I hadn't?

There was no scrunchie this time, but he was always watching for any plot to get with my mates.

He took my hands and drew them to his cheeks. "Kiss me," he told me.

My throat was dry, unwanted warmth coiling in my tummy. "Y-you want a kiss I *have* to give you?"

He smiled, further loosening my sanity. "I want a kiss I know you'd be giving me if you didn't trust the universe to decide your fate."

I just stared at him, palms still pressed to his rich brown skin, thumbs brushing his sharp jaw. Those lips he wanted me to kiss, were framing a flash of white as a smile tugged at their corners. He was as breathtaking as he was vicious.

"It *was* a command," he told me.

Right. I believed him. And I was trying to keep my nest Dusk-free. When it came to plots for my mates, he'd been doling out the punishments then and there. But this wasn't a plot, which meant he might not bend me over the couch and punish me at all. He might just take me back to my nest for breaking his rules.

I wasn't sure if I was ready for that.

It felt like something we couldn't come back from. I don't know why, but *that* I was sure of.

I ignored the trickle of heat that slid down into my core at the thought of his punishments.

Gently, I leaned up and pressed my lips to his. It was a soft brush of warm skin as I chased instinct alone, not quite sure what I was supposed to do. Dusk had always kissed *me*, not the other way around.

Midnight opium spiked, sharp and wanting, and I reacted without thought, leaning up and completing the kiss. His fist tangled in my hair, a groan in his chest as he held me in place, exploring my mouth with his tongue. At the sound alone, my stomach flipped, fireflies lighting in my chest and goosebumps erupting across my skin.

His other hand dropped to my hips, then beneath the dress, grabbing my ass and dragging me against him. I let out a gasp of a breath as he squeezed the faint ache from where his belt had struck me just a few days before. I still didn't know why his punishments, of all things, made slick pool between my thighs. It made no sense at all.

"Fuck," he breathed, drawing away for just a moment, tilting my head back so he could run his kiss down my jaw and neck.

My gaze found Umbra who was pinning us both with beautiful sandstorm eyes.

"Ransom, Umbra, and I," Dusk murmured, still kissing along my neck. "We would take you out looking like that and show you off to the world—*our* Shatter Kingsman, and everyone would know the power you have." He drew back up so his lips were a breath from mine, each word a warm feather. "And then we'd come home and worship you like our queen until the sun rose."

He inhaled the whine I let out as he kissed me again, insistent for another moment. Then he drew back, catching my lip between his teeth before releasing me.

I was almost breathless as he took me in with those bright yellow eyes that seemed to see everything. That promised to keep wanting me, even when he shouldn't.

I just… didn't understand. It hadn't fallen apart yet, and that was the most confusing thing. I was waiting for him to confess that all these moments were a cruel joke.

That moment never came and it was shaking me to my foundation.

I was trying to cling to what I'd known from day one, that he was preying on my most vulnerable need with each praise he offered. But he'd done it so many times that it was starting to become difficult to keep my walls up. To remember that he'd stolen everything from me, and to convince myself that I didn't want him stealing more.

"So…" I tried to compose myself. "The dress is good?"

"The dress is stunning," he told me. "But if you go to a study session like that, Roxy may think you're going to propose to her."

"Oh. Okay." Right. I guess that wasn't what I wanted. At least I hadn't totally fucked up this time. If Dusk had seen the state of me in Omega Studies, he probably wouldn't have kissed me like that. "I'll go change—"

"Here." He unhooked his black zip-up jacket from beside the door and tossed it to me, then nudged my lace-up boots in my direction. I'd intended to wear thigh-highs.

"But… they don't match?" It was much more a question than a statement.

"They tone it down. It'll look cute."

I stared down at the jacket with narrowed eyes. I didn't have anything like it in my nest.

Dammit.

My suspicions were confirmed as I shrugged the midnight opium jacket on and caught the mischievous smirk on his face that may have well have spelled out: *and now you smell like me.*

The study room Roxy had mentioned was on the first floor of the housing building, so it didn't take me long to find it. I got there early, then hid around the corner until I saw Roxy enter. Last time I'd been early it hadn't gone right, so I waited. Since Roxy was popular, it would be better to have one of the other omegas arrive before me so she didn't think I was obsessed.

It was quiet down this hallway, which seemed dedicated to study or meeting rooms. The walls were made of rustic brick, and the floors were hardwood. There was a faint aroma of flowers from occasional vases, with a subtle hint of coffee coming from the machines in the front lobby.

No one came. Not even when the clock hanging on the brick wall said six o'clock on the dot.

I waited, suddenly anxious about being late. I didn't want to be *too* late.

I glanced back at the clock: thirty-six seconds past.

Still no one.

Damn.

I wasn't sure what to do.

Better to wait for the others, but I didn't want her to think I was rude…

Maybe just a bit longer.

At two minutes and forty-nine seconds, I cracked. That was quite enough. I hurried to the door and knocked, then cracked it open.

Inside the private study room was a spacious central wooden desk, illuminated by warm overhead lights. Surrounding the desk were six chairs with fabric upholstery in neutral browns. Roxy sat in one of the chairs, her silky black hair tied up in a high ponytail. She was still wearing her uniform from earlier in the day, which made me more anxious.

"Right on time," she said, her pretty emerald eyes looking up at me from her laptop. I didn't have one of those, though Dusk had offered. There was a whole lot of learning to be done to figure them out, and I wasn't ready for that.

Uh.

Maybe her watch was broken. I glanced at her wrist, but she didn't have one. Phone, then.

"Where are the others?" I asked, taking a seat beside her.

"It's just us."

"Oh…" I trailed off, worry finally getting the better of me. "Was it because of me?" I asked. "Because I can go, if…" I shrank. "...if it's a problem." My voice was an embarrassing whisper.

She leaned back in the seat, giving me a curious look. "I only invited you."

"Oh."

"I didn't like how catty and jealous they were getting over you."

I laughed (like an idiot) before I caught her startled expression. My laughter cut off.

Shit.

That wasn't supposed to be a joke.

"Jealous?" I asked hoarsely.

Roxy snorted. "Do you know how badly Jasmine and Oliver wanted to land the Kingsman pack?"

I stared at her, mouth dry. "No."

"They were so invested in it that other omegas were making bets on which of them would win. Nobody had a clue since your pack alphas are so quiet."

"They're not jealous of… of me."

"Oh, they are." Roxy was fighting a smile. "You've caused quite the stir."

"Have I?"

"You come barreling in—absolute unknown, get claimed by the richest pack in the school, and you have a star on your neck before classes even start. That pack is *chasing* you. I even heard that Dusk made you a nest."

Was that going around the whole school?

I slowly sank into the midnight opium jacket, cheeks heating, but Roxy seemed to find that amusing. "And you don't appear to subscribe to the rules we've all been fighting to contend with since the day we perfumed."

"Don't… subscribe?"

"You're completely unapologetic about it, too."

That sounded like a very nice way of saying I was a complete loser with no social skills. For the record, unapologetic was also inaccurate. I was *very* sorry to be like this.

"I don't know what I'm doing," I blurted before I could stop myself. And Dusk was a madman for choosing me. That was all. "They're… chasing me?" I asked, stuck on that.

She laughed, the sound loose and sweet. I hoped my laugh sounded that nice. "Umbra bit you *in* class," she said.

Right. She'd seen that.

"So? He's an alpha. They do that…" I trailed off at the look she gave me.

"You said you were *rusty* in Omega Studies," she said, folding her arms.

"Okay." I swallowed. "I've never done them."

"Ha." She looked smug. "Thought so. Okay. So you're walking around school with a star that basically means they want to bond you, and now they're biting you—but it's not a bond."

"Okay. So…?"

"Well, from the outside, it looks like you're rejecting the bond… and they're pursuing."

"Rejecting?" My voice was high. That didn't sound good for my reputation.

"It's not bad. I just mean they seem ready to bite you, but you aren't yet. Which is… unexpected."

"That would be really soon for a bond."

"The star is serious from packs of this calibre. If Oliver and Jasmine were given a star by the Kingsman pack, you could be damned sure they'd have locked in a bite within the week."

"Oh…" I considered that. There was a beat of silence while I built up the courage to ask. It was hard not to stare too hard at her. She was so pretty, and it was impossible to forget that she was the ideal omega for my mates. Would it be wrong to try and figure out what they liked by studying her?

Probably.

"Were you, uh… going for the Lincoln pack?" I asked.

"Yes, they were on my list. I'm not quite as well known as Oliver and Jasmine."

I frowned. "How is it? I mean… are they nice?"

Roxy's pretty pink lips curved up. She wore makeup, I noted, but not much. A bit of mascara, perhaps? Her hair was glossy. Did she use product? Or a straightener? There was one of those in my nest, but I didn't dare touch it. I blinked, noticing a slight stiffness to her expression.

"They're lovely," she told me after a beat.

Lovely?

What exactly did that mean? I think that was good. Like… very good, because Dusk was definitely not *lovely.*

"Would you accept a bite from the Lincoln pack if they offer?" I asked.

Roxy's eyes widened. "Oh. No. Well. I wasn't here for romance, and we spoke about that—I think it's part of why they chose me. I was optioning for the Arkology program, so the Lincoln pack was a perfect match. I'm very lucky to have been chosen by them."

My mind tried to untangle that.

That was good, right? If she wasn't interested in them long term? "So… you were going for the Kingsman pack too?" They were also in the Arkology specialty. I spoke before thinking about it, then cringed. It must sound like a brag.

"Oh, no. I didn't have them on my list," Roxy replied, seeming not to have noticed. "Your pack had an insane amount of competition especially from omegas who were interested in Arkology sponsorships. The Lincolns, slightly less. Most of my competition was within the specialty."

"I see." I nodded. "So, you said you aren't here for romance?"

"You know how it is for omegas opting in to selection."

"Uh… sure."

She shot me a grin, and thankfully explained, since I definitely wasn't sure at all. There was so much I was behind on.

"We don't always bond with the packs we are paired with, so it can give us a bad rep in certain circles. Especially if you're aiming high. Elite packs don't love the idea of an omega with another pack for years. It's better if you stick with the same pack the whole time, though. Jumping is self destruction. But if I can get out the other end with a career, I'm not that worried."

"What career?" I asked, suddenly curious.

"Pathology," she said, brightening. I cycled through what I'd read about it. *Arkologic Pathology deals with alpha-omega specific diseases, such as Persistent Heat Fever, Omega's Curse, aura sickness, or Rut-Echo syndrome.*

"That's what the Lincoln pack are going for, right?" I asked. It's why I had memorised it. Arkology was the study of alpha-omega designation, but that was broad. Dusk's course selection seemed somewhat pathology and aura focused, but I knew the Lincoln pack were doubling down on pathology. Umbra—well, I had no idea what Umbra was doing. He was in a few Arkology classes with Dusk, and the rest were all over the place. I'd seen philosophy, world history, all the way to marine biology.

"Yes. Another strike in my favour, I think," Roxy said. "But there's so much to be done in that field. Not to mention if things go well with the Lincoln pack even without a bond, they're set to go far, so the connections will be good." Her eyes were bright as she talked about it, and I felt myself relax a little more. "I assume you were going for the Kingsman pack?" she asked me.

"No… I wasn't." Shit. Should I be lying about that?

"Curiouser and curiouser," she said, poking me in the shoulder with her pen. "Who, then?"

I opened my mouth and shut it, thinking. "I wasn't." It was a lie, and not a lie. I'd come for the Lincoln pack, but aside from that, there had been no plan. No list. No other pack I wanted as seconds.

"Oh. So you were here for…?"

"Just… Arkology." *That* was a lie I could get behind.

"Just a regular enrollment?"

I nodded.

I knew it wasn't nearly as common for omegas. Competing for packs offered full rides, as well as unique opportunities in their field of study. Most were here for that. There were other places to get degrees, but in academies like this, the prospective elite packs *were* the point.

Also, despite its alpha-centric nature, there was a stronger omega culture here, which made it more comfortable for omegas who wanted to study. I had heard that most regular universities were dominated by betas and alphas.

"Wow." Roxy's eyes were fixed on me intensely. "Honestly, I hit it big on socials and got a bit of name recognition, but even then… the fees are ridiculous, and they're all about prestige here. I wouldn't have had the courage to not even plan for a pack. That's actually really cool. And… well…" She grinned. "That explains why you're a bit off balance. Imagine that. Not coming for a pack at all, and then getting picked by them. And they are *so* into you."

My smile felt forced. Okay. So it seemed like a good lie for my lack of social graces at least, but I felt guilty at her excitement. She seemed to think I was the cool one, which was definitely all wrong.

Roxy settled in, looking even more pleased. "Right. I can get you up to speed on the Omega Studies. I think it's a bunch of rubbish, but I've done classes like it before. So. If you're down…?"

"I…" I swallowed, feeling even more guilty at how badly I wanted that, and at how much I liked her. "I would like that."

Dust

Today was the first time in months that I'd heard Ransom's purr.

It was a step to healing.

All because of her.

The scrunchie scents were wearing off, but Shatter had her scent out in full force on the weekend, so I might have stolen a blanket from her nest. Shoot me. I hadn't left my scent behind and she'd never know.

I didn't care. Not if it meant this. Ransom's face was peaceful beneath his sweep of messy auburn hair as he lay curled up beneath it, a low rumble in his chest.

Shatter had wormed her way into every waking moment of my life.

I was falling so hard I wasn't sure what to do with it.

I had a flash of the last time she'd acted like a brat, the way her eyes had held mine as I dragged her sweet lips over my cock. She hadn't looked away, not even as I choked her. I'd left the scrunchie in her hair that time, fist closed around it, her incredible poison rising in the air around her. The only problem it posed was that I'd almost finished instantly. It had been a fucking task to keep my orgasm at bay long enough to savour the moment.

She was in a constant battle with contentment, living with us. There were so many more pieces I had to shift out of her way so she could see the straight path to our pack, but it was happening. I was getting there.

All I had to do was move beside her and I could see her flinch, eyes darting to see what I was doing, pupils blowing wide and giving her away.

Umbra was obsessed; I could feel his lust down the bond when he watched us. He should get over that karma shit. I wanted to see them together.

I wondered what Ransom would think of her.

I knew he would love her, but how would they be together?

Right now I was resting in his bed, listening to the low purr.

I remembered that purr. I'd heard it once when we'd taken him out to the local park, back when we thought he was getting better—that the worst had passed. Fucking idiots we'd been.

We'd all sat on a bench and watched the picnics, the children play, and the trees billow in the autumn wind. He'd been so happy that he couldn't stop his purr no matter how hard he tried, face going beet red as we roasted him for it.

There was a smile on my face but it vanished as the memory faded.

We'd been confined to keeping our identities hidden back then, not able to draw attention to him. People knew his name and face.

Regardless of little bubbles of hope, Ransom had declined every day since the moment I'd met him. We watched him lose pieces of himself before our very eyes, begging us to help him keep them. Begging us to remember when he didn't.

But I would remember it all for him so I could give it back when he returned.

There had been another flash of life from him today. We were so close. So fucking close to a breakthrough, I could feel it.

And even spending time with him like this wasn't something I'd been able to do for a while. He got vicious when around others for too long.

But for the first time, we were in rewind. Every step he'd tumbled down over months and months, they were reversing.

That was the gift Shatter offered, the breath of hope I'd never had. Because not once in the time I've known Ransom, had he climbed back up those stairs.

There were so many steps from which he'd slipped, when I hadn't known the value of what I had on each. I hadn't known that just sitting by his side even when he was silent, was something I would miss one day. At the time I'd hated it, because he hadn't spoken. At the time, I hadn't known how much more would be stolen.

I wouldn't make that mistake ever again.

There was no end to what could be stripped from me if I didn't fight back. If I let the world take and take.

It would never stop.

I'd learned the hard way, twice over. With Ransom, second.

Umbra, first.

They'd broken him.

Umbra was a shell of himself, held together by instincts and a vicious aura that kept seeping into the room like poison at unexpected moments, shaking me to my core.

He'd turned on me.

Where before, he forced me to eat his food, he now took mine, becoming violent if I argued. Then, one night when I was weak with starvation, he'd attacked me in a fit of rage, his aura out of control. I could have reached the emergency button, but I didn't even try.

I wouldn't let them take more from him.

I gritted my teeth through a scream as he'd pinned me to the bathroom floor, the blunt end of that broken plastic fork digging into my back. Even when he'd left me curled up and bleeding, my tears were silent.

I would never forsake him. Since the experiments had started, I'd had everything violated—mind, memory, body, and soul. He was my only anchor.

I had to be chosen next. It was the only peace I had. I knew what this was. He couldn't take another round of experiments.

Last time, they'd chosen Umbra for being the weakest. This time, it would be my burden to bear.

Always one step behind, even then. Because after everything, it had been Umbra they'd come for.

I'd let it happen. Not fighting hard enough.

Never again.

I opened the texts on my phone and fired one off. Decebal was our main contact. He'd been working with us since the beginning, trying to help us get to the bottom of this mess. He was the one getting the feed from the Lincoln pack apartment.

Me: Anything, yet?

Decebal: Nothing major

Decebal: They're exactly like you said. Pricks, but they haven't said anything useful.

I considered that. It was to be expected. The kind of information we needed from them probably wasn't part of everyday conversations. I would have to be patient, like I had to be patient with Ransom.

Me: How are they doing with their omega?

Decebal: She's holding her own. Doesn't seem all that impressed by them.

Me: Good.

Me: Can you keep an eye on her?

Decebal: What do you want me looking for?

Me: Anything dangerous.

Holding her own was good for Roxy's sake, but I didn't trust the Lincoln pack to take that sitting down.

Shatter had just returned from the study session glowing, and I was unexpectedly happy she'd gone. After her first class, I'd been worried. Predictable cunts had tried to tear her down, including some of the elite level omegas like Jasmine Lynn (who'd left black roses at our door every day leading up to the ball despite our utter rejection of her). But, fuck me, Roxy did actually seem nice.

The least I could do was keep an eye out.

And I didn't need to be worried about these study sessions beyond that. I didn't trust that Shatter wasn't still (probably at this very moment) conjuring more devious schemes to get back to her mates, but I'd planned for everything.

What she didn't know was that I'd placed trackers in her boots so I could find her if she decided to run off and let her blockers lapse.

CHAPTER 23

Shatter

Roxy and I were finishing off a Thursday evening study session. It had been a really good one where she'd helped clear up some of the omega etiquette questions I couldn't wrap my head around when it came to black-tie events.

Roxy was very good at picking out the most important pieces of the study material while waving away the rest. I appreciated that because otherwise it would all be far too overwhelming.

There was an upcoming ball that I knew I'd be expected to attend, and I was already having minor heart flutters at the idea. The first ball where we'd been chosen by our packs had been bad enough, but I'd been so focused on meeting my mates that I hadn't thought too hard about it. Now, I was under the scrutiny of the entire school as the Kingsman omega, all while trying not to look like a fool to my mates.

The Omega Studies textbook had outlined six different ways to eat with dignity at high-end events, including a list of foods that we were supposed to avoid. Roxy had dismissed most of them, which was good because I had been able to stay up all night researching all the pasta names I didn't understand.

We were just packing up, and I was feeling more confident about the whole situation when there was a knock on the door, and it creaked open. My eyes snapped up when I caught the trace of passion fruit in the air. Eric was leaning against the doorframe, arms folded as his eyes drifted over me and Roxy.

"Oh, did we run-over?" Roxy asked, glancing at her phone before tucking it in her pocket.

"Thought I'd come down," he said.

"We're going to study in the library after," Roxy told me. "Genetic and Genomics is proving a challenge."

"Oh," I said, scrambling for what to say to that. "N-nice–" I began, then had to grab for my book, which was sliding off the desk, as I'd missed my bag because I was staring at Eric.

His eyes flickered from Roxy, who began putting her own books away, to me. Our gazes met for a long, long time, and I couldn't move.

I couldn't pin down his expression, though. He'd smiled the first time I'd bumped into him—and still I'd never seen him offer a smile like that to anyone again. Right now, his gaze was appraising, as if he wasn't sure what to make of me.

That was abnormal, right? I shouldn't hold someone's gaze for that long.

He would think it was really odd…

Finally, he broke the stare as Roxy stood, shouldering her bag. She said goodbye, then the door closed behind them, leaving me alone with one crazy train of thought I couldn't shake.

The study session had ended on time, but would Dusk be suspicious if I didn't come back right away? I didn't usually have this kind of freedom, nor an opportunity to see my mates…

I hugged my bag closer, considering. What would he do, though? Even if he did notice, it wasn't like he'd know where I was. I could just tell him that Roxy and I went on a walk after. He seemed to be very pro-Roxy, despite wanting to keep me away from my mates.

Or… if he did find out, then he'd just punish me the way he usually did. My cheeks heated at the thought of that, and I was off in a moment, hurrying to the door and cracking it open. I peered out, but Eric and Roxy had already gone. Good. I didn't want them to see me following them.

* * *

Oh, dear.

I should not be here.

I should not be here. *I should not be here.*

I was in a back row of bookshelves, and I'd shifted a few of the books out of the way for a view down the next aisle. No one would catch me here. No one would even expect anyone to be here in the first place.

I'd been watching for a good while, listening in on their quiet conversation. They mostly spoke about Arkology, which didn't help me get any insight into Eric as a person—which is what I'd come for.

I *absolutely* hadn't intended to be spying as things got heated. Though it definitely explained why they'd picked a spot in the back of the library, where there was as much dust visible as books on some of the higher shelves.

"You really want to do this right now?" Roxy asked.

"You said…" Eric's voice became muffled, as if he was pressing his lips against her. "Of all of us, *I* was the one who needed the most attention. Tell me why?"

I heard Roxy let out a breath that sounded half exasperated, half humorous. "You like hearing me say it?"

"I do."

"You've got the least stable hormones," Roxy told him.

His laugh was low and he dragged her closer on the desk. I bit my lip.

Okay. Time to leave. Just… absolutely quietly. I could *not* get caught now.

Instead, the ridge of the shelf dug harder into my cheek as I tried to see exactly where his hands were wandering.

"Ever since you let slip *you* wouldn't mind getting caught, I haven't been able to get this out of my head." Eric's voice was low. "I want anyone to be able to walk in on us. That's what you like, right?"

I shrank, pulse racing.

Did that mean she wouldn't mind if I stayed?

Oh, pull yourself together, Shatter. Absolutely not.

Leave.

Now.

Why hadn't I left?

Why hadn't I looked away?

Instead, I was pressed up against the heavy oak bookshelves, with a vision of Eric's back as he lifted Roxy onto the table. Roxy's next words were quiet enough that I didn't hear, but then I saw Eric fumbling for her skirt, lifting it.

Okay. Okay. Enough. Really, definitely time to go.

Why was it so hard to move? I forced myself a step back, but Eric's scent of passion fruit tangled with the smell of wood and old pages, an edge of lust to it that made my chest tight.

Oh, but…

I wrung my fingers.

Mine.

He was mine.

Being around alphas as much as I had in the last few weeks had settled some of my more vicious instincts that had arisen now I was off all the suppressants, but this possessiveness was vengeant. My grip on the bookshelf was white knuckled, my eyes wide, and my body just didn't want to leave.

This was the closest I'd been able to get to him. I could stay, just a little. I mean… I couldn't *really* see Roxy.

I heard the sound of Eric pushing books from the table, a low growl in his throat.

He made that sound for someone else?

I clamped my hands over my ears as I almost loosed a whine of shame or pitiful jealousy, I wasn't sure.

Okay.

This *was* too much.

My blood was hot, though, a collision of need and coiling sickness. I'd failed. He didn't want me. He wanted her.

I took another step back at last, only to hit a solid wall that shouldn't be so close. It was then that I caught the faintest trace of midnight opium in the air.

I squeaked in shock, but a hand clamped over my mouth, muffling it.

"What on earth have I caught you doing, Gem?" Dusk breathed in my ear, voice sing-song with amusement.

I tried to shake my head, cheeks blazing.

His scent was too faint, as if he'd used a scent dampening spray to keep a low profile. But that would mean he'd *known* he wanted to keep a low profile. And how had he known to find me here?

I struggled, shock hitting my system

I was done for.

Dusk *hated* when he caught me thinking about my mates. Now he'd caught me watching Eric with Roxy?

"You're going to do exactly as I say. If you don't, I'll fuck you so good you'll be crying my name and your precious mate can watch while I make you come."

What?

I blinked, trying to process that. His hand dropped from my mouth and I tried to turn, but he moved his grip to my waist, holding me in place.

I swallowed, trying to unscramble my thoughts.

"You came here to watch him." His breath was hot against my neck. *"And you will."*

He *wanted* me to watch?

Uh… hold on. I tried to shake my head. I'd changed my mind.

This was wrong.

And what about poor Roxy?

This was horribly unfair to her, after all.

"Hands on the shelf," he told me, trailing his touch up my arms and lifting them. He pressed my fingers to the bookshelf, breath hot on my neck.

"Dusk—"

"You're going to watch your mate fuck another omega while I impale you over my cock."

No no no.

He *wouldn't.*

But I didn't dare move, his threat of exposing me was too much. They could never know. We were at least a table's length away and behind a wall of books. It was enough that the small sounds wouldn't carry, though if we spoke while they weren't moving or speaking, they might hear us. Shit. It wasn't *just* that I would die of embarrassment—what would Eric think of me if he saw Dusk fucking me? If I ever managed to tell him the truth, and he'd seen that?

"Good girl," Dusk breathed, as he then shifted my hips, nudging my legs apart with his shoe. I stifled a gasp as his fingers dipped beneath my panties. "You're dripping, Gem," he breathed. "Is this what does it for you? Watching your mate with someone else?" He drove his fingers into me and I had to grit my teeth to fight the sound in my chest. "Or was it the part where you got caught?"

I heard Eric's groan from beyond the bookshelves. I could see him adjusting Roxy's skirt.

I felt Dusk's tip at my entrance and I jumped, trying to turn. His hand fisted my hair, keeping me forward. "I said, *watch your mate fuck her.*"

Each word was laced with a command I was too disoriented to fight. My gaze snapped back through the bookshelves. I could see Eric moving as if he was lining himself up with Roxy where she sat on the table.

My heart slammed against my ribs at a million miles a minute.

Dusk wouldn't.

He would *not*—I heard Roxy's moan as Eric shifted forward. Dusk's hand clamped over my mouth as he drove into me with no warning. I let out a muffled squeak of shock as he pulled back and slammed in again.

Eric and Roxy paused. "What was that?" Roxy's voice was low.

There was a long moment of silence as Dusk inched out of me ever so slowly. My whole body was red hot with panic—and a dozen other things it shouldn't be heated about.

Roxy would never talk to me again.

I'd just made a friend, and now—

"You think we're being watched?" Eric asked, his voice humorous. The scent of passion fruit in the air was edged with lust.

"I *heard* something," Roxy said, but then I heard her low groan and saw Eric shift forward again.

"I don't really care if it gets you this wet for me, babe."

My grip was white knuckled on the shelf as I watched them, eyes wide as Dusk slid into me again, only half-way this time, teasing me.

I couldn't have taken my gaze from Eric if I'd wanted to.

My instincts were out of control.

That was *my* mate with someone else. With a beautiful omega who was making him happy. Shame collided with a shocking tide of heat that rose with every long, deliberate stroke of Dusk inside me.

Eric sped up and Roxy began letting out little pants.

"You're the hottest omega in the school," I heard Eric saying, picking up his pace. "All ours."

My heart tripped over itself. Still, a part of me wanted to shut my eyes, but I couldn't. Dusk's hand was clamped so hard over my mouth it was almost painful as his length stretched me open again. I was shaking now, trapped between the spike of pleasure every time he hit my core, and the shame of being unable to take my eyes from Eric.

"Are you this wet for me, or for him?" Dusk whispered.

I could hear Eric's low grunts as if he was nearing the edge. From my vantage, I could see the white-knuckled grip he had on Roxy's hip as he used his grip to fuck her harder.

"What do you think?" Dusk asked. "Do you think you deserve to get off if Roxy doesn't? Or should I just take my pleasure with you like your mate would?"

That wouldn't happen.

That definitely wouldn't—but Eric's low growl sounded, and Roxy didn't seem at all close to anything.

"Fuuuckk," Eric groaned, slowing his strokes, fist around the edge of the table as he finished.

"Well that was disappointing." Dusk was still fucking me with slow, deep thrusts. I was so disoriented that when his free hand found my clit, I bucked against him violently. The unexpected stimulation was like a bolt of lightning in my veins.

When I came, it was the most violent orgasm I'd ever had. My body was burning hot as I shook, crushed against Dusk's chest as he rocked his knot against my entrance and worked my clit so fast I saw stars. Wave after wave of bliss left me shaking violently in his grip, still crushed against him.

His low breath of release was just for me, and I felt him finish too, his hot seed filling me. Another moan almost slipped from my chest.

When he was done, he released me carefully and quietly. I didn't let go of the bookshelf, needing it to stay upright since my legs were shaking so violently.

I was disoriented.

Dusk tugged me to face him and drew me down onto his lap. I all but collapsed against him, ducking my head against his chest, inhaling the faintest traces of midnight opium.

"Why did you do that?" I asked, half whisper, half whine.

"*You* came to spy on him," Dusk reminded me. "Seems like a fitting punishment that you watch your own scent match fuck another omega, while his mate's tight little cunt is being railed for another alpha's pleasure." His eyes twinkled in delight. "And you feel so good when you're all confused and wound up."

My fists balled in his shirt, but I couldn't answer.

I'd climaxed watching my mate while Dusk had fucked me.

"And it can't hurt," he added, "that you see firsthand how your mates would take care of you."

Dusk

Shatter didn't meet my eyes as I relaxed on the chair, arms around her waist.

We'd go once the other two had left. I could already hear the sound of one of them picking up a bag. But I wanted to sit here a little longer. I wanted to hold her in my arms as my heart rate calmed and I came down from that.

I'd checked my tracker when Shatter hadn't returned, and I'd expected to find *something* interesting. I'd used a scent dampening spray in case I needed to keep quiet. But Shatter truly never failed to disappoint.

I wasn't angry she'd followed her mate here—there were certian instincts that I could forgive her for. But to find her pressed up against a peep hole in the library? I grinned. Beneath her sweet little omega front, she was just as filthy as I was. Besides, Eric had performed exactly as I expected. The Lincoln alphas were such prats that I didn't have to do a damned thing to convince her how worthless they were.

"You could have asked me to join you here anytime," Roxy was saying. "You didn't have to come down."

"I was craving you, babe."

There was a pause and the sound of a bag zipping up. "So it had nothing to do with her?"

I froze. On my lap, Shatter went still as a frightened mouse.

"What?" Eric asked.

"I don't know why you're all so interested in her, but I told you not to interfere with my friends."

Interested in Shatter?

I went tense, and Shatter did the same in my arms, straightening, brow furrowed as she listened. I frowned.

"Interfere?" Eric scoffed. "Come on—"

"I'm not bringing her into any of this alliance politics."

"We don't have all that much choice, do we? If it makes you feel better, I'd prefer that whole stupid Kingsman pack fail the semester and lose their sponsorship. It's going that way with a pack member who can't even be fucked to show his face. They think they're better than the rest of us."

"Eric." Roxy's voice turned cold. "I'm not making friends with her for you. I like her. I don't want her near it."

"Oh, right," Eric snorted. "You *can* be territorial? Over an omega freak, but not over the pack paying your way."

My blood turned to ice.

Fuck.

I drew Shatter against me without thinking, a pit of hatred boiling in my stomach. She was huddled in my arms, absolutely still.

"I'll be territorial the moment you earn it," Roxy said coolly.

"*Earn* it?" Eric snorted. "Did we not do that when we chose you over everyone else? You prove yourself to us, not the other way around."

There was a long silence.

"Don't… call her a freak."

Below me, Shatter lifted her head, eyes darting toward the bookshelf, even though we were too far back to still see them.

Eric laughed. "Everyone's *thinking* it. She doesn't belong here—the Kingsman pack can't be serious; she's a fucking spectacle. What was it the North Prince omega was saying? '*Doubt she even owns a hairbrush?*'"

My heart crashed into my ribs, every instinct suddenly on high alert as we heard the scrape of a bag being picked up off the table.

"*They're* the losers—"

"You won't let anyone hear you say that!" Eric snapped. "It's not your place to blow up our relationships with other packs."

Rapid footfalls indicated Roxy was exiting quickly.

"Roxy—*wait*…" Eric's voice trailed off, leaving us in silence.

I realised my fingers had clamped down on Shatter's waist punishingly tight, but she hadn't flinched.

That was… viciousness I hadn't been expecting. It wasn't right, not even for pricks like them. I may have underestimated the draw of a scent match, even one they didn't know about.

The Lincoln pack *did* watch Shatter with far more interest than I was comfortable with. They were subtle enough that I don't think she'd truly noticed, but I wasn't a fool when it came to the scent match.

Gareth was the worst, but Flynn and Eric also couldn't seem to help themselves, eyes snagging on her when she passed by. I'd seen the darkness in those looks.

The only men in the world so bent on tearing down a woman like that were men with interest they wished they didn't have.

The Lincoln alphas drawn to her, and they didn't like it.

The problem, however, was that I believed Shatter when she said she wanted to be friends with Roxy—and clearly Roxy's friendship was honest in return. But Roxy came with a pack she needed to stay away from.

I cupped Shatter's chin, but she grabbed my wrist.

"Don't." Her voice was thick.

I wouldn't have it. But what was I supposed to say?

Offer her praise she's already heard from you?

"Shatter," I said, forcing her chin up.

"I'm fine." She swallowed. Right now, she wore that mask I hated, and this time, it hosted a pursed-lip smile that held much worse at bay. Her hands were clasped in her lap, knuckles pale, her rich brown eyes fixed on my collar.

"Your mates—"

"They're well off. They have standards. I don't meet them."

A low growl rose in my throat. "If this was a competition, they're a speck on *our* shoe. You were the only one here that caught our eye."

I knew, the moment I'd said it, it was a mistake. Too much. I was pushing too hard. She didn't believe me.

There was a long silence. "They're not good men," I told her, surprised at the gentleness in my tone.

"I already know you think that."

What if I showed her everything?

I could contact Decebal right now, tell him I was coming to get the USB. The one with everything—kept in one place so we would never be found.

But she still had doubts.

She still wanted to run to them—broken as she was. And that pack could never get their hands on the truth of who we were. So I could never give it to her, not before I was absolutely certain she'd let them go.

They hadn't said anything in their home either, not that would incriminate them more than what we'd just heard.

So instead, I cupped her cheek and pressed my lips to her forehead.

"You are enough for us, just the way you are."

When we left the library, I held her hand, and I thought she might be squeezing mine just a little too hard. There was a glittering of tears in her downcast eyes.

Shatter

The straightening iron sizzled as I nudged it on the bathroom counter.

It was the next morning, and I'd been up for hours. I'd burned my ear three times, and still, my hair did *not* look like Roxy's.

I tapped my fingers on the bathroom counter anxiously.

Why cant I get it right?

It was better, but still thick, and didn't have that shine to it. With each pass of the iron over my hair, something uncomfortable twisted in my stomach. But it was better than staying curled up in bed, unable to sleep, lingering on it all. All morning, I'd jumped at every sound, afraid Dusk was going to come in and catch me.

I didn't want to see the *'I told you so'* look in his eyes. I'd cried on and off all night, and I didn't need to be made to feel more pathetic. But even after all this effort, my hair still didn't look like Roxy's.

Would it be better, though?

Still, when I hurried into the kitchen in the morning, I'd tied it up in a loose bun so they might not notice. "Going to classes early," I muttered, grabbing my scent blocker from the bottle Dusk had left on the table and taking it before he could make a fuss.

"You're leaving?" Umbra's voice caught me as I hurried to the door.

I glanced back to see he was looking at me, clearly hurt. Oh… Shit. He was fiddling with the new toaster oven he'd ordered yesterday, trying to make me a more interesting breakfast since I still wasn't eating Dusk's food.

Dusk's eyes were narrowed on me, though, and he'd frozen halfway through buttering a scone.

"What did you do?" His gaze was fixed on my hair.

I swallowed, fighting the urge to touch it. Okay. So it *was* obvious. "N-Nothing."

He got to his feet, yellow eyes dark. "Go and wash it."

"No."

"You aren't leaving until you undo it."

"What are you going to do if I don't?" I demanded. "Drag me into the shower and fuck me until I say sorry?"

Dusk scoffed. "I'd never dick you down when you've spent the morning peacocking for your mates."

My expression tightened, something angry rising in my chest. "*Good.* Guess I've found my solution." My hand was on the door.

"Shatter!" Dusk's voice was warning. "We're not finished with breakfast."

"I took my pill," I said, turning the doorknob.

"Let your mates see you like that, and I swear I'll never fuck you again."

I spun on him, eyes wide.

"For fuck's sake, mate," Umbra groaned. "You can't say things like that."

"Good!" I snapped.

Dusk's expression was bitter. "Good."

I yanked the door open and stepped through it too fast. I caught Dusk's last words as I slammed the door behind me. *"You didn't even get the back—!"*

My breaths were tight in my chest as I hunched against the closed door, hand reaching for my hair. Shit.

Even with it up I could feel the crimps of waves at the base.

Oh dear. It must look so bad.

But… this *was* good.

Dusk had just sworn he'd never fuck me again.

Fucking PRICK.

And an idiot.

He was a man of his word, too. So all I had to do was find my mates, and I was home free—even if there were still scent blockers in my system. At least Dusk would never touch me again.

I couldn't move, though. Tears pricked my eyes, something unsettled in my stomach.

This was what I wanted: for Dusk *not* to like me.

For my mates to fall for me.

It was simple, and I finally had a way to freedom.

CHAPTER 24

Based on my observation, the subject's poor hormone regulation matches that of alphas nearing rut. Her quality of life is in a rapid decline, and I wish to make a final attempt to improve it. I will need permission from the Institute, but if we can find alphas who can tolerate her scent, I believe a bond is the last option to stabilise her and give her an opportunity for a normal life.

Shatter

Don't think about Eric.

Don't think about Dusk.

Screw them both.

Just me and Roxy. And Umbra was fine too… But that's all I needed.

Panic was setting in like it used to back in the Estate. Panic that made me want to claw my own skin off, that made me want to cry and beg the universe to undo the stupid decision it made when it decided I should be an omega.

My own mate thought I was a disaster. My own mate did, while Dusk didn't.

"Dusk can never happen," I whispered as floorboards creaked underfoot in a vacant hallway. I don't know how, but I'd ended up on the top floor of the student housing building. Not class.

Dusk can never happen. Umbra can never happen. Ransom can never happen. Even when I was carrying his gift in the pencil case in my bag right now.

I wandered through old storage rooms until I found a dusty corner to settle down in by myself. I don't know why it was so comforting, surrounded by the smell of old books and dust, but my heart rate calmed as I settled in.

"I'm just going to have to figure it out with Eric…" We could work it out. We were mates. Once he knew that, it would change everything.

I cracked my book, staring at it sadly.

"It doesn't really matter what I want. I don't have a choice. Not really."

Frowning, I glanced around the room before spotting an old mop leaning against an empty bookshelf.

Okay. That would do.

I set it up at my side, sorting it out until it was right, and then cracked my textbook again.

"I'm only up here because my hair sucks and I know the other omegas will make fun of it," I told mop-Roxy. "It had *nothing* to do with Dusk."

I peered down at the page. I had the complete course curriculum, and I knew today we were studying bond etiquette, so I could do the lesson myself.

While normal bonds may be discussed between pack and omega, it is never proper etiquette for omegas who have found their scent matches to bring up a princess bond.

When making an official princess bond offer, the pack is risking much. Unlike the rejection of a normal bond, which leaves both parties in equal standing, the rejection of a princess bond offers the rejecting omega 'Duchess or Duke' status, and severs that pack's ability to form a scent match again, even after their scent match's death. This inability for another scent match has even been known to carry over into packs that have lost and added enough alphas to reform their scent match entirely.

Hmm. It wouldn't matter, right? Not for me. Not with what I knew. I considered that paragraph for a while before a clatter ripped me from my thoughts.

"Oh, shit." Mop-Roxy had fallen over. "I'm sorry." I propped her back up and looked back down at the page.

We studied for a while longer before my mood spiralled. It was bad, if studying wasn't enough to distract me.

Why wasn't it easier for me to go to my mates today?

To make Dusk live up to his word?

I *couldn't* want him.

"Right." I set my book down, clutching the back of my neck where I could feel that faint scar. "As you hide in the fucking attic."

But falling for Dusk wasn't allowed.

He didn't understand the truth.

Last night, what I'd overheard Eric say in the library to Roxy, that wasn't the real him. It couldn't be. I remembered watching them from the bannisters at the Estate. I remembered hiding there for hours until I was shooed away by another maid.

The Lincoln pack had been having dinner with Uncle, talking about the work they wanted to do in the Arkology field. Of illnesses they'd wanted to cure.

So desperate to learn about them, I'd managed to sneak past their room later, lingering enough to catch snippets of their conversation when they were alone. I hadn't heard much, but they hadn't seemed cruel.

They'd seemed… driven. Dedicated. They wanted to study Arkology to make a difference in the world—to alpha-omega illnesses.

"Roxy," I whispered. "I *know* that's not who they are."

It couldn't be.

"I swear… I know it sounds crazy, but I know what I heard."

"...Not where I thought our life was heading." That had been Gareth. I recognised his voice from dinner, low and distinct. I'd just caught his words through the door. "...is still holding out hope for a princess bond."

It was the moment I'd realised—truly realised, what they were.

"It's the only reason I risked everything to come," I said. They wanted their scent matched mate as much as I needed them. Mates didn't always offer princess bonds, but mine *wanted* to.

They were searching for love.

I knew I wasn't normal. I knew I wasn't what they'd imagined in a mate. I hugged my knees to my chest, shrinking in on myself.

What Eric had said last night hurt so badly. And Dusk had heard, and that was somehow worse, because now he knew what they thought of me, too.

Have my mates changed?

Maybe they'd been dreaming of love for so long it had made them sad.

Only, now they might discover it's you they get...

Could I have imagined it? Was I as crazy as I knew Dusk thought I was, defending Eric, still?

But I'd come this far on that belief.

If they had changed... if they would never love me truly, was that enough to give it up? When the alternatives were so much worse...?

"Do you ever get scared of..." I trailed off, not even able to imagine asking that of mop-Roxy. Even if she was the first omega friend I'd ever had—she wasn't scared of dark bonds.

She wasn't gold pack, and it was illegal to dark bond her.

Still... If I *did* ask, what would she say?

But I'd betrayed Roxy twice over. One for making friends with her in the first place when I was after her pack, and two... "Oh..."

Fuck.

I hadn't *seen* her yesterday. Not really. It was mostly Eric, and I'd been about to leave. Would she hate me if she found out?

But I'd never had another omega to talk to.

"I'm so afraid of a dark bond. It's been worse since I ran away." It felt good, saying it out loud, even if Roxy wasn't really here. "I lost everything," I whispered. My whole life before I was nineteen. I'd just woken up, and I was... no one. "I went to live with Uncle and Aunty Lauren, and I just had to figure it out." I paused, lip trembling as I tried to get it together.

It was hard, but I *needed* to say it to someone.

Umbra

Shatter wasn't in class. I'd logged onto Dusk's tracking app (mainly because I'd be really sad if he couldn't fuck her again) and discovered she'd never left the building.

Oh, thank God.

Those two were going to be the death of me.

I found her on the top floor, which seemed to mostly consist of old study rooms. I stopped before a doorway, listening, and, to my delight, I heard her talking to herself within. I presumed, anyway, since no one ever spoke back, but she left extended pauses as if coming up with imaginary answers in her head.

I stood for a while, listening in while she conducted herself in her own Omega Studies class with a fake Roxy—or so I guessed.

Eventually, I settled down, happy to sit on the hardwood and listen to what was probably a much more interesting class than real Omega Studies—whatever crap they taught in that. Sometimes she would whisper quiet enough that I couldn't hear, but then she began to talk about dark bonds, and I was left frozen.

"…And if I get dark bonded, then that's it," she was saying. "I just have this little sandwich of years when I got to be me before it's taken again. And I haven't had enough time to figure out who I am. Or what I like, or who I'd be if I got the chance."

I frowned, heart breaking at the sadness in her voice as she paused. She didn't need to worry. I knew Dusk had taken that picture of her, but he *wouldn't* dark bond her.

He'd told her that. I hadn't realised how much that fear plagued her.

A part of me just wanted to make her see how worthless her mates truly were, but there was more to it than that. Shatter was trapped. Even if I didn't really understand why, I knew it. Getting free of that, wasn't as simple as logic.

A flash of my past lit in my mind.

"Why don't you just stop?"

I cocked my head, examining those words. My own words. That hate was foreign to me now. The anger and desperation.

"Just… quit, and everything will be the way it's supposed to be."

I couldn't *see* the memory. Not really. Just a flower wilting from its own poison. Slowly fading, leaving me behind.

"You think I don't hate myself more than you hate me?"

"Impossible." It was the last thing she ever heard me say.

That word was an old wound, and it ached like something that had healed over, but healed wrong, proof of how useless and venomous that hatred had been.

I knew Dusk was frustrated. I knew what they'd both heard that piece of shit say about her last night. He needed to chill, though.

Shatter was the most important flower that had ever sprouted, and poisoning her *more* wasn't the way to stop her poisoning herself.

Best way to stop that was to just show her how much she fit with us. That no matter why she thought she needed them, it was nothing in comparison.

She'd get there.

I believed in her.

"It's stupid to worry about," she was saying, though her sniffle was contradictory. "I know that. No one's going to dark bond omegas like *us*," she added.

Right.

Roxy wasn't gold pack, and of course Shatter couldn't just go around telling anyone.

"It's just… I'm different. Please don't tell, but my scent is really strange. I need to get really good at Omega Studies because my uncle said that the only way it'll ever balance out is if I'm bonded to a pack. He said if I'm claimed, it'll settle. Like… I won't be a threat anymore. To my pack, mostly, but he hoped even to everyone else. And all my hormones will balance out, too. They're already so much more manageable since I arrived. There are so many alphas around here…" She trailed off, but my chest was puffing up.

So many alphas? Ha. What was she *on*? That was *us*, helping her out, even if she didn't want to admit it.

There was a pause.

"Well." I heard an anxious tapping like a pen on paper. "My scent makes alphas… upset. Not just alphas. Once, my blockers wore off when I was on my way to the Academy—and even betas were upset by my scent. An omega too; she kicked me out of the cafe."

Again, another pause for what I could only imagine was a fake Roxy answering.

Shatter's voice was broken. "I *really* need a pack."

I frowned. She already *had* a pack.

"No, Dusk wants me to hide my scent for his own reasons." I could almost hear the pout in her voice.

Damn.

Fake Roxy was really asking the difficult questions, huh?

"I can't afford to get behind in this class. I really appreciate you studying with me."

Luckily, it seemed Fake Roxy was on my side.

"The Kingsman pack?" Shatter asked. "Oh… I don't know." Her voice got so small again that I could barely hear it. "I'm managing, but I think Dusk exaggerates how much he likes me. I don't know… There's a catch. It doesn't make sense. It's like… I'm always waiting for the real reason they chose me, and it's all going to come crashing down."

My heart sank at those words. She really didn't think she was good enough for us.

"My scent? Oh. I mean. They don't *hate* it—"

"Liar," I snorted, cutting her off before I remembered that I wasn't supposed to be here.

Damn.

But I didn't care.

How dare she lie to fake Roxy. We *loved* her scent.

There was a long silence, then I heard the sound of her boots stomping across creaking floorboards. The door was ripped open, and I was looking up at a pink-cheeked cutie-pie with a furious expression on her face.

"What are you doing?" she demanded.

"I'm behind in Omega Studies,"

"You don't *take* Omega Studies," she snarled as I picked myself up from the floor and folded my arms.

"Exactly." How could I not be behind, then? That seemed obvious. "So. Why are you up here instead of in class?" I asked, eyes narrowing as I peered down at her.

"No… reason."

"You're hiding."

"No."

I raised an eyebrow.

"I just..." She trailed off, swallowing. "I just wasn't sure I'd got the back properly." She patted her bun anxiously. "Didn't want to go out if it wasn't right."

"All right. Well... if you want to come back with me, I still have studying to do this afternoon. I might be better company than a..." I peered into the room behind her, ignoring the way she tried to shift to block my sight, though she was too short, anyway. "A mop."

"I found it like that," she said.

With the ponytail? I nodded solemnly, like that made complete sense.

"But I guess I could come back and study," she blurted.

I side-eyed her as we made our way back to the apartment. "Do you want me to tell Dusk about this?"

Dusk had been a tense ball of aggravation down the bond all day, stubborn idiot. He thought she *had* run off to 'peacock' for her mates.

"No..." Shatter trailed off, unsure. "I mean... I don't know."

I almost laughed. She'd hidden upstairs all day at the threat of Dusk never fucking her again, much too proud to just turn around and go back to her nest. Possibly to make him suffer. It was working, too.

"All I'll say is that your mates certainly didn't see you like this. Yeah?"

She chewed on her lip, working through that, though I could see the flicker of relief in her eyes. Then she shrugged. "Sure. I guess... that's fine. I mean." She tugged at the loose strand of her straightened hair that had tumbled from the bun. "He'd be pissed at me otherwise."

"Right. You wouldn't want another punishment," I said, noting the way she scowled furiously, cheeks even redder than before.

I bit back my grin.

The two of them were the most stubborn creatures on the whole damn planet.

CHAPTER 25

Umbra

Despite intruding on her mop study party, Shatter joined me in my room for studies when we got in. I'd left afternoon Arkology class early to come and find her, so we had the place to ourselves.

Things were looking up. Ransom hadn't attacked Dusk in over a week.

I was anxious for the day she could meet him. The day I would get him back. She'd fall for him, too. How could she not?

I believed that Shatter was secretly happy—though I'd have to secure a bite from her to really confirm it. If I left a bite on her, nothing would happen at all, (except a hot as fuck mark). Since Dusk was pack lead, a role I didn't envy, he was the only one who could offer a bond bite. But if she sank her fangs into me, I'd get an omega's temporary connection. I'd be able to feel what she was like in a mini pack bond.

I wanted that so badly.

I wanted her, actually. I wasn't picky how. Being near her was good, but it was making me crave more.

Shatter had been to a bunch of study sessions with Roxy now, and she always came back glowing. She was increasingly comfortable during the evenings when Dusk asked her to join us for a movie, or to study—though she refused to help him with homework even though she'd help me if I asked.

That's what we were doing right now.

It was Friday evening, which meant no more scent blockers for the weekend. I was impatient though, and brought her one of Dusk's 'anti scent blocker' pills when I grabbed us drinks.

She narrowed her eyes at me when I placed it in her hand expectantly.

It wasn't bad for her. I'd been drugged up with all kinds of things in my life. There were hormone suppressants, which were nasty, scent blockers were a tier down but not great—though I understood why Dusk was being cautious with the Lincoln pack. We didn't know what they'd do if they found out who she was. But this pill just undid it all, which was much better, so she couldn't really complain.

She still had a pout on her face, though.

"I want your scent in my room, Nightshade." I *hoped* a few hours with her in my room would be enough to get me through the week. I could ask her to scent mark something to be sure, but then she'd be onto me.

She took a sip of her water, but then pressed the pill into her cheek. Probably told herself it was to get out of punishment, and not because she liked that we were obsessed with her scent.

She was so damned pretty. Her wild honey brown hair was loose around her shoulders, now, super fucking beautiful even half straightened with the little crimps all over it. It just framed her cute heart shaped face like a mane, and it was *perfect.*

Her contacts were gone (just for me) and the skirts Dusk had bought for her were going to be my fucking death. Every time I saw the smooth golden skin of her thighs, I just wanted to grab them and sink my teeth in. Today she'd chosen a short black skirt with matching thigh-high stockings, and she was wearing a loose white top that hung off one shoulder. The silver necklace with our crest and star hung around her delicate neck. Sometimes I just stared at it, dreaming of ripping it off and replacing it with a bond.

A princess bond—I'd give her one of those in a heartbeat.

It made omegas like… queen bee of the pack. Totally worshipped, all her wild emotions on blast so I would know right away what needed tending if she was having a bad day. And fuck, when she was horny for us, I'd been told that was a *ride.*

We couldn't, though. Princess bonds were *scent matches* only.

Dumb, since she *should* be our mate. I think the universe needed a reboot.

I could dream, though.

Those bonds glittered on an omegas skin like that necklace did. It would look so sweet on her.

She glanced up at me from beneath thick lashes, and I realised I'd started humming contentedly as I daydreamed. I should be helping her research on my laptop. It was impossible to get through an academy like this without one, but she was shit at using computers. I'd offered to help her figure it out, but she got all flustered at the idea of it. It made me wonder where she'd come from. No computer skills, no phone, even—and Dusk, notably, hadn't bought one for her, despite buying her everything else.

Probably good. She'd be finding ways to sneak texts to the Lincoln pack behind our back.

She was killing it in her classes, though, which was better than I could say, but I was doing alright in Creative Writing, which was more fun than I'd anticipated.

"You guys should let that Bolin guy know that Dusk needs extra help in Auras Quantified."

"What?" I asked. "Dusk?"

She nodded.

Nah. "*You* help him."

"Nope." She crossed her arms, expression stubborn.

"Come on, you're a mad genius at it. You'd get him on track in no time."

Her cheeks heated, but she didn't reply, reading through the article I'd pulled up for her.

"How did you get so good?" I prodded.

"I don't know. Actually…" She trailed off, looking uncomfortable.

I narrowed my eyes. "I'm calling in my truth."

"You cheated in that game," she said. "And you haven't asked me a question for weeks."

True.

I liked the idea that she couldn't lie to me without me getting a bite, so I'd just left it as it was. She'd never just told me she quit—which she could have. It made me chuckle thinking about it, especially considering she got nervous every time she caught herself in an almost-lie.

"What were you trying to avoid telling me right there?" I asked. If she was still hiding it from us after everything we knew, it must be important.

She chewed on her lip, then shrugged. "I don't remember."

I narrowed my eyes. "Are you lying to me, Nightshade? Because if you are, I get your neck."

She scowled. "No, I mean… I don't remember why I'm good at Arkology."

I frowned. "How?"

She ran her tongue along her teeth, twisting her fingers together. "I don't remember much of when I was young."

Much?

What did that mean?

"A-anything, actually. Not before I was nineteen."

My hair stood on end. "You don't remember anything before you were nineteen years old?"

She shook her head. "I woke up…" She paused. "…somewhere. And before that there was nothing."

I woke up in a straitjacket amidst darkness. I was made of nothing but feral rage.
There was endless darkness from before.
I was no one.

Was she the same?

Of course she's the same… How the fuck had we missed that?

"You never mentioned it before?"

"I don't like to think about it."

I stared at her.

I got that. Dusk and I didn't talk about it if we didn't have to.

That was probably wildly important information I should go and give Dusk right away. Instead, I couldn't tear my gaze from her.

Me, Dusk, and Shatter. We were the same. Ransom… well, Ransom was his own brand of fucked, but he had his memories. At least… I *thought* he did—or would, when he woke up.

"What?" Her voice was soft with nerves.

"We're switching the game, Nightshade," I said.

That sealed the deal.

I wanted her so badly. My cock ached like… all the time I was with her. It was getting ridiculous.

But now?

She was ours. Had to be. Like I said, there was a glitch somewhere.

Plus.

She'd love it.

She liked me already and was much more willing to show it than she was with Dusk.

"I'm not doing anymore games with you," she said. "Anyway, it was my turn to ask a question."

"You're going to want in on this one."

"Why?"

"I'll make you a bet for your mates."

She went still, golden eyes wide. She wet her lips, clearly considering. "*What?*"

"Deal is this: You get a five second head start. If you get to the front door before I catch you, you're free. Twenty-four hours to find your mates, tell them whatever you want."

Her eyes went wide as saucers. "You'd never."

"Swear it. I'll open that door and let you go."

She leaned back, clearly already hooked. "And… if you win?"

I grinned.

This was it. The bet I knew she couldn't turn down

"I get to do whatever I want to that sweet little body of yours until morning."

Her mouth dropped open in shock, but her pupils blew wide. She glanced to the door, then back to me.

"You'd… never risk it."

"I *am* risking it," I said. Dusk might wring my neck if he ever found out, but a deal was a deal and I wanted her crying my name while I fucked her so good she wouldn't walk straight for days. "Will *you* risk it, Little Nightshade?"

Again, when her eyes darted to the door, I could see her calculation. As if she was trying to figure out how much five seconds would buy her.

A lot. I knew that.

Hallway, spiral stairs, then straight through the shared kitchen and living room to the front door. It wasn't hard.

But I had my aura.

I could see in her hesitation that she was about to agree.

I should warn her, at least.

I tilted her chin up to face me. "It's all in. Bites, nest, and I promise to ruin you the way I dream of ruining you every night."

I wouldn't hurt her, not my thing, but there was nothing gentle about the way I wanted to ravage Shatter Kingsman.

Delightfully, that wasn't fear spiking her scent as she stared up at me. Her cheeks were red hot and my gaze followed the movement down her neck as she swallowed.

Would she do it?

"Okay," she whispered. "I'm in."

CHAPTER 26

Shatter

Adrenaline was pumping through my veins long before Umbra gave me the go. I stood absolutely tense, staring through the open door to his room.

I'd confirmed every rule. All I had to do was touch the front door before he caught me. Then he would open it and let me out. No scent blockers, no nothing.

Freedom.

My mates.

I was sure he'd gone mad. Maybe he'd huffed my poisonous omega scent one too many times. Uncle had never warned me that it might make alphas stupid, but then we hadn't really done many tests after Tom had attacked me. Maybe Umbra wasn't immune to it at all, it was just melting his brain a little at a time.

I took a deep breath.

Hallway, staircase, and then back across the kitchen and living room to the front doorway that was a floor below us.

I knew I could make it. I was quick, always had been, and I'd get down the spiral stairs with more ease than his huge build. He thought his aura would help him—and it would with speed, but no way Umbra could make sharp turns at speed. I'd win on the stairs no matter how strong he was. Five seconds, and I'd already be half-way across the living room on the main floor.

I dared one last glance back at him, my heart thundering in my chest. He seemed to be waiting, because that was the moment he hit the timer on his phone and said, "Go."

Stifling my curse, I launched myself into the fastest run of my life. I reached the doorway, seizing it and throwing myself down the hallway. I couldn't stumble, not once.

I'd make it.

My mates.

They were within reach.

I reached the stairs and flew down them, hair wild behind me as I took them by threes. When I reached the bottom, I hadn't even heard the first footstep on the balcony above. Then I was out in the living room.

Dusk was there.

Burying a wild laugh at what he was about to witness, I dived toward the front door. I dodged the kitchen island, hip slamming into the couch. I ignored the pain.

The front door was ahead.

Five steps away, and I still hadn't even heard Umbra.

Four steps.

Three steps.

There was a creak on the balcony.

Ha.

He'd only just started.

I'd won.

I didn't look up, even as an aura split the air.

Useless and too late.

Two steps left.

Wood groaned loudly from above.

One—

Fuck yes, I'd—! There was a blur of movement and a *CRASH!* Instead of the hardwood of the front door, I collided with flesh and bone. Wolfsbane and blood. I let out a gasp of shock as he caught me, stopping me from bouncing backwards to the floor.

What?

He'd…

Fuck.

Six-foot-seven solid alpha that had just launched over the balcony railings above and landed on the floor with a thud.

Right between me and the front door.

What…?

But…

His fists closed around my wrists, dragging them above my head as he turned us and pinned me against the wall. "I win, Little Nightshade." Sandstorm eyes were bright with delight.

My blood chilled, reality crashing right in.

"Wait." My mind was reeling.

That was cheating. Wasn't it?

He'd cheated.

He laughed, something truly delighted in the sound. "Will you be a sore loser?" he asked.

I just stared at him, mouth working as I realised what was about to happen.

"Actually," he breathed, leaning close enough to nip my ear. "I promise you will."

He lifted me in his arms, ignoring my scrambling protests as he dropped me beside the couch. Dusk was staring at us both, interest in his gaze.

Umbra pinned me over the arm of the couch the way Dusk usually had me. His fist was in my hair as he bent me forward, crushing my cheek to the pillow below.

I let out a sound of panic as he shoved my skirt up and tugged my underwear down.

My breathing was sharp. Wolfsbane and blood was thick in the air made of primal lust. I also caught the delighted edge in midnight opium.

"Wait! Please, *Umbra—*"

"Begging won't save you, Nightshade." His laugh was playful, breath brushing along my neck as he leaned close, using his weight to crush me further into the couch, trapping my legs completely. I couldn't move an inch. His hardness pressed into me, sending heat spearing through my veins. He adjusted himself, still pinning me at his mercy.

"You bet," he growled. "You lost. I get to fuck you however I want, so be a good omega and relax for me."

My mates, my mates, my mates.

I couldn't let this happen again. Worse, because this time I was closer to both of them. This time, hate was getting confused with something completely different.

I let out a breath of shock as I felt his tip press to my entrance, going absolutely still. I wasn't ready.

And… Okay. No.

He was too big.

He wasn't going to fit.

"You're soaked for me, Nightshade."

I let out a whine, but it cut off in a squeak as Umbra drove all the way into me without warning. All the air was ripped from my lungs.

Oh my God.

He *shouldn't* fit.

I whimpered again as he shifted slightly, and my fingers dug into the couch. He was so deep every movement was like an aftershock.

"Fuck," he growled. "You're so tight."

He drew back slowly, and I scrambled with the pillows, trying to lift my head, to do anything—but his grip in my hair kept me pinned. Another sound came from me when he drove in again, a feral exhale as he fucked me deeper than I thought possible.

His hand shifted from my hip, instead slipping down the small of my back beneath my shirt, making me arch further as he began thrusting into me slowly.

Heat was flooding my veins with each deep thrust, and the sounds I was making were embarrassing.

"Do you know what your scent is like right now?" Dusk's was a low sultry voice in my ear. "A fucking aphrodisiac. You're so turned on by him."

Dusk tangled fingers in my hair and arched my neck so he could look right into my eyes as Umbra fucked me.

"What did you gamble for?" Dusk asked, eyes dancing. I tried to turn my head away, but his grip made it impossible. I couldn't do anything but whine pathetically as Umbra's massive length stretched me out over and over.

"Tell him, Nightshade," Umbra said, but it was hard to get my thoughts straight. "Tell him what you gambled so I could split you open with my cock."

A snarl twisted my lips, but it was replaced with a gasp as Umbra rammed in particularly hard.

"What did you get if you won?" Dusk asked me.

"Tell him." Umbra's voice was laced with a command that seized me and I was opening my mouth before I realised it.

"Twenty-four hours to find… *ugh…!*" I grappled with the cushion as Umbra rocked his knot against my entrance, wiping my mind blank.

Dusk chuckled. "What was that? Twenty-four hours to what?"

"Go on, Nightshade." Umbra's fingers squeezed the flesh of my hips as he dragged himself out of me slowly.

"T-to—" I cut off with a gasp as Dusk reached down my top and twisted my nipple right as Umbra slammed in again. I was panting, trying to untangle my mind. "To find them," I spat out before they could do anything else.

Dusk barked a laugh, leaning back."The Lincoln pack are off campus for the weekend."

What?

A snarl tore past my lips, but Umbra began driving into me hard and my eyes rolled back, a pathetic whine loosing from my chest.

"Fuuuuck..." Umbra groaned. "You feel better than my dreams."

Dusk's gaze was too intense, making everything worse. I was going to finish before Umbra, I knew it.

"Look at you, taking him so fucking beautifully, Gem," Dusk murmured, fist tightening in my hair. *Why is everything he says so hot?*

I sobbed at that thought—it wasn't what I'd meant to think.

But the lust in Dusk's eyes made those words strike true, all the way into my lonely little omega heart.

"Keep praising her like that," Umbra growled. "She squeezes me so fucking good."

Dusk grinned, canines pointing and pupils blowing further. "Is that true, Gem? Do you like me watching him ruin you?" His voice was a whisper, hot breath tickling my ear as he twisted my nipple again. "You're our perfect pack omega, aren't you? Treating him so well with two of your alphas here."

I moaned, squeezing my eyes shut and trying to ignore him.

Dusk was getting up, though, lifting me by a solid grip on my hair while Umbra still held me in place. He was so much bigger than me, his fingers that were curled around my waist were inches from touching. I glanced up to see Dusk grinning, tongue pressing into his canine as he held me before him, my mouth an inch away from the bulge in his pants.

I trembled as I stared up at him, mind fuzzy. I could imagine him taking his cock out right now and telling me to open my mouth.

I'd done it so many times...

I dreamed of it sometimes. Of the low growl he made in that moment of bliss as I pushed him over the edge. It was wrong. So, so, wrong, but I couldn't help it.

"Do you think that sweet body of yours would be enough to take care of us both?" he asked. "I know you'd be so good at it, Shatter," he purred. "No woman in the world turned our heads until you. You're the *only* omega who will ever belong between us."

Umbra groaned, bruising fingers digging into my flesh as his tip speared a spot that made me see stars. "Fuck, you're so turned on, Little Nightshade."

Umbra found an angle to thrust deeper than before, and I grunted as his weight appeared at my back. I felt his lips brush my neck, one hand curling around it to hold me still as his knot stretched my entrance out just enough that I let out another low whine. I shook, throwing my weight uselessly away from him one last time, only because this was too much. I was right on the edge.

"Keep wriggling like that, Nightshade," Umbra breathed, then his teeth brushed my neck.

Fuck.

They have to stop.

I was going to—

Dusk dropped down before me, fingers curling around my chin and drove his tongue into my mouth as Umbra sank his teeth into the back of my neck.

My orgasm was more violent than the one in the library. A low feral sound emanating from me. Every inch of my body felt like it was coming apart, a drug flooding my brain like nothing else. I would never admit that I tried to shift back against his knot, mindlessly desperate for it to fill me.

I wanted it.

Needed it.

Primal instincts flared, sending my bloodstream to a boiling point. I trembled as Dusk released me, and Umbra picked me up and sat down on the couch, tugging me back onto his lap, facing him this time.

I was gasping for air, trying to calm my hormones.

Get it together.

Fuck fuck fuck.

Deep breaths. One at a time.

But then I felt Umbra's tip against me again. "I'm not quite done, Nightshade," he breathed, and pulled me back onto him. My eyes rolled back, a low whimper rising in the air as he filled me once more. And then his knot…

I couldn't…

A whimper slipped out, but it was too late, he stretched me over it, slowly and blissfully, a low growl of his own in the air as he locked me against him.

There was a rumble of pleasure in his chest as he rocked into me roughly. Then his grip clamped down on my hips and his sandstorm eyes squeezed shut. He shook as I felt his seed fill me, sending me over the edge completely. I *knew* the moment my scent detonated in the room like a glitter bomb.

Oh. God.

My breath caught.

Not now.

Not my stupid heats.

Not right in the middle of the living room—with two alphas who weren't my mates.

This wasn't like anything I'd gone through before. Usually I would ride them out in the huge fridge in the basement, praying no one would find me. Aunty Lauren was always so disappointed if she found out. Because my stupid fucking messed up omega heats weren't like they should be—they were short, sharp, and didn't come in cycles. Instead, they came when I was hormonal, when my omega side was riled up, or when I was too… *Fuck.* I could cry as I shook against Umbra.

My stupid heats came if I got too turned on.

It had only happened once from *that* alone—after I'd spotted my mates for the first time. And now, I'd betrayed them.

My nails dug into Umbra's back as I dragged him closer, a low whine rising in my throat.

"Damn…" Umbra's voice was rough, a low purr rising in his chest.

I reacted instantly to the sound, uncoiling like a snake, fingers grappling for his cheeks.

He was so beautiful, tanned skin, a smattering of freckles, and sweep of sandy blond hair… and shit… I'd never noticed exactly *how* hot his angled jaw was—or the thick muscles coiling down his neck and chest.

His eyes were fogged with lust, but he was holding me back just a fraction, brow creased in a frown. A growl shuddered through my body, panic tilting the world like a dizzy spell.

We were locked together.

Why is he looking at me like that?

All of this, taking me from them, stealing all my firsts, and now they didn't want me…?

"Calm down." Umbra straightened where he sat, peering at me strangely, his hand at my waist. "Dusk…!"

"I know." I could hear Dusk in the kitchen, rummaging in the drawers.

When had he left? He'd been on the couch.

Another sharp breath felt tighter in my lungs and my eyes stung.

Why did he leave?

I scrambled past the thickets of lust and panic trying to drag me down, surfacing for a moment.

"No…" I breathed.

This was wrong.

My mates would find out if I had a heat with Umbra and Dusk. That was a first they might never accept. This was too soon, moving too fast—

"Shatter." Dusk's voice ripped me from the spiral, his grip on my chin. "Look at me."

The low command in his voice didn't help. Yellow eyes pierced mine, pupils blown, and dark opium was doused in need, close to wiping away all thoughts.

Good.

He wanted me.

I could breathe only because Umbra was knotting me already. A purr battled with an unsettled growl, coming out as a rattle, fractured and confused.

"…don't want a heat with us right now, you don't have to."

What?

Dusk's words dumped a bucket of ice water over my head—if only for a second. I looked back to Umbra.

"But…?" I could barely find my words. "The game."

Umbra narrowed his eyes, clearing his throat. He looked strained, even though his voice was back to its usual lightness. "I'm going to play with you all night long," he told me, pressing a kiss to my temple. "But if you're in heat then you'll be the one playing with me. That's not what I had planned."

"You don't *want* me?"

Why was I saying that? It didn't even make sense. He literally just said he did.

But… he didn't want me in heat?

Why were tears tumbling down my cheeks?

"If you don't want it, Gem, don't take it, but decide." Dusk's voice was low. "I'm about twenty seconds away from chucking every pill like it down the sink and fucking you in to next Tuesday."

Pill?

I looked down and realised he was holding a small wrapped foil between two fingers.

To… to put my heat off, I realised much too slowly. I knew it gave most omegas a month or two. For me, it would just get rid of my heat indefinitely. Or until I was back here again with my stupid hormones.

Oh.

Okay.

They would fuck me if I *really* needed it.

At the option, rational thought flooded back, and I grabbed it from him, peeling back the wrapper, relief hitting my blood like a jet of frigid water into hot springs. So much so I didn't even have time to linger on how much I hated drugs like this, choosing the fridge over them whenever I could.

There was no fridge anymore.

My breathing eased, and for a moment, before the pill dissolved on my tongue, I thought of my mates. With blood like lava and hormones burning my brain to the ground, I thought reminding myself of them would bring me a sense of control, or drive like it usually did. What if I had everything I had right now, but with them?

Instead, I felt uncomfortable.

Because of what Eric had said?

But I'd also never had an alpha during heat before. It was a worrying idea. Of all the ways my fucked up hormones might make it weird, or off, or not like it should be.

That was probably it.

I sank against Umbra, holding him tight so I didn't have to look back at them as I waited for the pill to kick in.

CHAPTER 27

Umbra

Post heat scare, Shatter was different.

She wrapped her arms around my neck, clutching me. The only time I'd caught a spike of fear in her scent, was at the threat of heat. I didn't miss that.

Right now, she seemed nothing short of shell-shocked.

Once my knot released her, I bundled her up in my arms and carried her to her nest.

The first part—the part we'd just done–was important. The part where I shared with Dusk. But now I wanted *my* omega nest time.

"I don't understand," she whispered as I sat down on her bed.

I let out a breath, still dazed from the lingering hormones she was shedding. That heat hormone poison bomb had been something else.

If Dusk hadn't signalled absolute control down the bond the moment it happened, I would have lost myself. Deadly nightshade had turned to knives, a poison that could cut to the heart and burn a weak mind in moments.

Dusk had made the right call with the pill. She had a long way to go with us and with Ransom—even if she didn't realise that yet.

A heat with the complication of her stupid mates… I couldn't see it not breaking her.

I hadn't been lying, I *wanted* her heat, but this was our first time. It should be special. I was going to make it a night she would never forget—would never *want* to forget.

"Your heats belong to you," I murmured. "You're already giving us a dream."

That was the truth. In here, I was drowned in her nightshade. It was dangerous and familiar and freeing. An old friend.

She had no idea the beauty she held. She was the poison, beautiful only to those who were meant to see it. Deadly to anyone else.

My poison.

My freedom.

It seeped into the air of the room we'd been trapped in.

A new trial with new tricks. More ways to break me.

I wasn't prepared for this one.

As the poison sank its claws in, a paranoia whispered into my mind. Every time I looked at Dusk I knew the truth: it was him or me.

The realisation set in, slow at first, until I knew it down to my bones, until the whisper grew to a shriek, a bet, a promise, something impossible to ignore. My pulse was erratic, fingers shaking.

It was happening to him too, pupils constricting as he stared at me with those piercing yellow eyes.

An alpha. An enemy.

I shook myself.

No.

The poison…

That was Dusk before me; a man I was supposed to protect.

Even now, I had to kill him or I would die…

Dusk staggered to his feet, chest heaving, something feral in his eyes, and I tensed, all my instinct telling me to match him.

He was going to kill me.

The world spun, the white room and metal beds all swaying until he was all I could see, stepping toward me, terror etched across his face.

But… I was all he had left.

I loosed a breath as I found my peace at last.

Truth and freedom.

To die, I thought, would be okay.

Better to die than to fail again. Better to die than be the one left behind.

I wasn't strong enough for that.

Not this time…

That day, I'd reclaimed something.

Shatter's scent wasn't deadly. To me, it was beauty, and I knew to Dusk, it was the same. It was the moment we'd claimed something back—something the universe hadn't yet managed to steal. It was the moment I had truly found a pack.

A family.

I was numb to its threat. But I wasn't immune to its allure. To the way it made me want to bite her with more than marks that would fade.

Dusk was the one with the plans and the foresight, but I wanted to show her she could have us. Even right now, even with her mates.

I thought it was possible, especially since she was holding me so tightly in her own nest.

"I'm going to show you what it could be like if you let them go."

She looked up at me, eyes wide. "I *can't* let them go."

I smiled. I liked a challenge as much as I liked a game.

I turned us so she was pinned beneath me and tugged off her skirt and lace. She gripped me, but didn't fight as I pulled her to the edge of the bed.

Her low whimper rose in the air, a sweet serenade, and her attempts to get away were feeble beside my strength, though they did turn my blood warm and drive me on as I slipped a finger into her soaked entrance. Then I buried my face between her hips.

Shatter tasted like fucking heaven.

It didn't take long before she was swept away by her second orgasm. When I littered kisses along her inner thighs, I looked up to find a breathless, reproachful look in her glittering golden irises.

"We're going to do this until you're begging me for more."

"I won't," she hissed.

I tugged her closer and she tried to scramble away. But I had her number now. I knew she had to try and escape, or she didn't think her mates would take her.

I obliged in the chase, which resulted in another jarringly sexy position as I had her pinned again, face to the sheets while I cupped her heat, ignoring her squirms.

"You were so fucking beautiful, taking me like that," I told her, squeezing her ass, then I pressed my thumb into her, feeling slick pooling around the touch. She was shaking already. And we hadn't even really begun.

I hadn't ruined her yet.

I *could* go all night.

By the fifth orgasm, she was clutching me by the hair, telling me she couldn't take it anymore. By the seventh, she was begging me to stop.

I didn't, every instinct in me driving me onwards. We were competing against scent matches, and I wouldn't lose.

"Just let go, Little Nightshade," I told her. "It's not wrong to enjoy this."

"It *is*."

I grinned, adding a third finger, enjoying both the tightness and her little whine. She was still fighting the orgasm she'd been on the brink of for minutes now. The last had been intense and fast, and she was still shaking from it. I'd dragged her over my face and been rewarded with sweet, sweet juices that were still dripping down my chin and neck. I was under the impression she was shocked by that, so I was driving my fingers into her sweet cunt slower this time, letting this one build for longer. Sensitive as her precious body was, she was losing the battle she so desperately fought at my touch.

"You can't stop me." I sped up as I spoke, rolling her nipple between my fingers. "You're mine to play with all night, and I love seeing you come apart."

The movement, along with my words, undid her.

"Would you want us if they weren't your mates?"

She didn't reply, fists balled in the sheets as she shook, eyes squeezing shut.

It wasn't enough, just to see her come. She was tense and afraid and confused. To ruin her—truly ruin her—I would have to break her mind and let her put the pieces back together around me.

The most beautiful part was that she didn't seem to run out of orgasms to give me, no matter how she swore she couldn't go on.

It was a lot of work, getting a stubborn omega to climax this many times, but I had all night, and seeing her slowly crumble was worth it in its own right.

By the tenth, she was crying my name, furious, frustrated, and begging, overwhelmed tears glistening in her eyes. And by the twelfth, *finally*, by the twelfth, she cracked.

I saw the moment she let go.

The scent in the room shifted, sharp but cool now, like the first breeze at sunrise. Peaceful as everything in her world tumbled away, the nerves and fears.

Her mates.

It was just me and her.

"Good girl," I purred. "My sweet Little Nightshade."

Her pupils were so wide I couldn't see gold anymore, and they were dazed as they drifted between mine. She looked wild, chest heaving, sweat glittering across her tanned skin, long hair scattered around the bed.

"Another?" I asked, this time expecting a different response. She didn't disappoint, head nodding, lip caught between her teeth.

Good.

I tasted her again, tongue finding her clit as I pressed my fingers back in. Tasting her would never get old. She arched against me this time, grinding her hips over my fingers to give herself more pleasure.

That was hot, watching her use me like that. I flipped us so she was on shaking knees and dragged her core over my mouth again, still dipping my fingers into her. She groaned, dragging her body over my fingers and face so I could give her more, little pants coming from her.

This wasn't heat. This was better. Shatter had given in to me all by herself.

I took her to the shower afterward, holding her up since her legs were shaking. She came apart for me beneath the stream of water, head against my chest. Her dainty hands were pressed flat against the shower wall as I rolled her nipple and circled her clit until she shuddered in my arms again.

I dried her hair off and took her back to the bed where I made sure all of her blankets and pillows were at those perfect angles for her.

She was dazed, as I tucked us both in, drawing her close. "Are you tired?"

"Mmhmm."

"Close your eyes. Go to sleep."

"Are you going to stay?" she whispered. Something worried clouded her eyes as she asked it. It was like I could see her, suspended on the precipice of this safety. I could see that she suddenly realised what waited below, when the hormones were gone, when she was alone.

Not tonight. Not when I had something to say about it. "Of course I'm going to stay."

There wasn't a force in the world that could make me leave this sweet bundle of omega who was in need of cuddles all night.

She curled up closer as I held her to my chest. Her scent was heavy in the air, contented and safe exactly like I wanted it. Something stirred, tugging at my aura, loss and sorrow as I peered into this tiny glimmer of forever. A should have been. A life stolen from a shattered protector. I frowned, trying to unravel that, but the threads were slipping away, slicked with oil, impossible to cling to.

I shook it off. It had hurt, anyway, seeing that. And Shatter's pretty lashes were fluttering closed. *She* was all that mattered right now. I could feel the low hum in her body as I slid two fingers back into her, pumping in and out gently. My touch was soft enough that her breathing slowed, but I didn't stop.

She had nothing to be worried about.

I would worship her until she'd tumbled all the way into dreamland.

And, because she was so fucking perfect, she came again, even asleep, a low shudder sweeping across her body as she succumbed to my touch one last time.

It was almost impossible not to press my teeth to her neck once more as a purr rumbled to life in her chest.

CHAPTER 28

Umbra

It was Saturday evening, and I was alone, since Dusk had dragged Shatter out with him. *Strategy*, he'd told me.

Sure.

But if he wanted to spend more time with her, who was I to argue?

Unfortunately, that left me to contemplate another serious problem as I flicked through my rapidly accruing homework assignments. Apparently, I enjoyed *looking* at fish more than I liked *learning* about them.

I was coming to the sad conclusion that Marine biology wasn't my thing at all. That was fine, it just meant I could spend those classes daydreaming about Shatter.

When I'd woken this morning, she was still in my arms. She'd purred for me all night, and she'd been like a lost puppy when I led her out to breakfast this morning.

As was becoming routine for the weekends, Dusk had ordered food in so she couldn't complain. I'd led her to the table and sat her down so I could serve her myself. I would have brought it to her bed—would, in the future—but I needed her to see Dusk this morning so she could understand that he was part of the perfection that had been the night before.

She couldn't take her eyes from me as I loaded up a plate, and when I set her breakfast down she just stared up at me for ages.

It was fucking cute.

She didn't know what had happened, but I did. Shatter had let me in. And now she was confused because it didn't scare her like she believed it should.

"Thank you," she mumbled, taking the plate at last.

I smiled, then leaned down and kissed her. Her fingers wove through my hair for the briefest second before she drew away, glancing at Dusk for a flicker and then to her plate, cheeks pink. I took a seat at her side and grabbed a stack of pancakes.

Dusk looked stunned, which was a rare sight.

"So." He sat on a bar stool and began cutting up french toast. "How was the night?"

"Shatter figured out she already has everything she needs *right* here."

"I never said that." She looked at me with a pout.

"You *showed* me."

"It only happened because you're an alpha, and I'm an omega."

I'd stifled my snort. Both Dusk and I had heard the dejection in those words.

She *was* my perfect omega.

But, now they were out for the evening, and I slumped down on the edge of my bed, preparing for a dull night of studying. I wondered how her and Dusk's night would go. Might she let *him* in more, now?

I smiled at the thought, then swallowed.

Could I have her?

Was that allowed?

"You paid." Dusk's voice rang in my ears. His plea for me to slow down. To stop.

And what about her?

We were protecting her. She needed us. Needed me to convince her like I had last night. Even… even if it was good for me too.

Good?

I almost groaned as I felt the knife in my grip. My breathing was heavy. But this time, I hesitated.

"You paid already. You destroyed yourself. You kept me safe." That's what Dusk had said.

But was this what destruction looked like? If I had destroyed myself, I hadn't done a very good job.

And now I wanted happiness?

"You paid."

Dusk's yellow eyes turned golden, and Shatter was there instead, looking up at me, purring for me in her nest.

Trusting me to care for her.

Trusting *me* to care for her…

The knife shook. Faceless shadows lay still, always in the periphery, reminding me that I could never pay enough.

But could I protect her like this? With trembling knives and scarred skin? What happened when I ran out of skin to scar?

"You paid…"

I shut my eyes and for the first time in my memory, I lowered the knife.

Slowly…

Shakily…

Then—*"Fuck!"*

Agony rent me apart.

I collapsed, knees slamming against carpet as fire tore through my blood. A growl ripped from my chest, and the knife dropped from my fist.

My aura split the air uncalled, splintering into a million fragments as it did.

I felt, even through the pain, the moment it turned on me. My *own* aura, the thing that made me an alpha, began to consume me.

I fought it, even as the world began to fade.

I *had* to fight it.

I couldn't pass out. It wouldn't stop—this poison, I knew if it killed me, it would devour them next.

Ransom.

Dusk.

From where I lay I fumbled until I found my knife again, blade cutting my skin. Keeping me here. Keeping me alive.

Relief was the smallest breeze in a storm as I gripped it.

It was the only thing that would save me.

Dusk was wrong.

All my payments had come due, *right* fucking now.

CHAPTER 29

Dusk

Inviting Shatter on a date so we could meet up with the Lincoln pack was the last thing I ever imagined myself doing.

Flynn had shot me a text this afternoon, asking if I wanted to join them tonight when they arrived back from their weekend trip.

The problem was, Umbra had fallen too hard for Shatter. Now, every time the Lincoln pack passed us, I could feel him slipping into his void, barely able to control himself.

I had four options if I wanted to attend tonight: Meet them with my rabid pack mate, meet them with my murderous pack mate, meet them by myself (which would be ruder than not going at all since he'd asked to meet as a pack), or bring along their scent matched mate. The omega I'd stolen from them.

And so Shatter, somehow, was the best option.

Her eyes had gone wide when I'd told her what we were doing, and she'd been resentful while I picked out her outfit for the evening and handed her another scent blocker. She thought I was taunting her, and I let her believe it since she couldn't know the truth.

So here I was, with her on my arm as we made our way across the academy grounds. The early October air was cool, and the oak trees scattered across the grounds were turning bright reds and oranges.

The plan had seemed simple when we'd arrived at this damned place: come to the same academy the Lincoln pack had enrolled in. The necessity of rooming with a random omega had been the only part we hadn't been able to anticipate. Then bug their rooms to learn everything there was to know, and foster a relationship to get information from their own mouths.

But I was starting to realise what a fool's mission that was now that Shatter was in the picture.

It was delicate, and Umbra wasn't delicate on a good day. He was downright incapable with her in the picture. I was quite sure all he dreamed about was tearing out their throats and leaving them to bleed.

"Then she'd be ours, right?" he'd asked this afternoon as he'd joined me in the living room.

Right.

Yeah.

Just kill them so she'd never forgive us, and we might well be fucked for the rest of our lives, unstable, waning in and out of sickness.

Those flashes Umbra got, claws ripping him back to the torture we'd endured, it wasn't just trauma. We both knew it. He was sick. Stuck. His own nature, trying to burn him alive. I wasn't immune, but he got it worse than me. So much worse.

It's why it was my job to sort this out.

"You're sick, and the Lincoln pack is the last lead." Decebal's warning rang in my head. *I'd* wanted to capture and torture it out of them, but he'd shut it down. *"Only works if we can confirm they're telling the truth. You don't have enough information. And then what? Absolutely fucking not. They can't find out who you are until you have more."*

So, I was left with false alliances.

I'd considered telling Shatter everything. A thousand times today it had gone through my head, especially after I'd seen her with Umbra this morning. A part of me ached for it, to see if she would choose us.

But I couldn't risk it. If she didn't believe even one piece of the story—which was extremely likely—I'd lose her entirely, and if the Lincoln pack got a hold of what she then knew?

Not possible. Not yet, anyway.

Instead, I needed to let Umbra keep doing whatever the fuck he'd done last night until we had a chance at convincing her.

I glanced down at Shatter, who was wearing a pretty black dress, her thick hair up in a ponytail that swayed as we walked down the decorated garden lanes that led us to our destination.

There were a number of places to socialise on the Academy grounds, and we were on our way to Rookwood Club, which was open late for students.

We arrived first, and I settled into a booth with low lighting as the waitress took our order. Shatter seemed entirely blindsided by the whole ordeal, so I ordered her a cocktail with a half shot—since it would be completely on brand for her to be a lightweight.

When our drinks arrived we were left to a peaceful quiet. Music played, loud enough to be noticed but not enough to kill conversation. The lighting was all dim blues and reds, and the booths were private enough that I couldn't catch the words of other groups in the space.

I was left to mull over the *other* thing Umbra had told me this afternoon. Something that was so jarring it hadn't settled yet.

Just like us, Shatter had amnesia. She didn't remember anything prior to four years ago. That was far, far too unlikely to be a coincidence, right?

I glanced down at her, watching as she sipped her drink. She twirled the little umbrella and scanned the room nervously, as if shadows were waiting to pounce on her.

"How do you *know* they're your scent match?" I asked, tapping on my coaster.

What if…? What if she wasn't as sure as she thought she was?

"I'm not wrong," she said, glancing up at me. "I looked it up. You can't be unsure with a scent match."

"Can't you?"

"The whole world shifts when I catch their scent. It's like… there's nothing else around me. Just them. Like magnetism."

I considered her. That *was* what I'd heard.

"And it's not like that with ours?"

She shifted uncomfortably, looking up at me. "I *like* yours," she said. "I do." Umbra really had softened her last night, because her words took me by surprise.

But that was answer enough.

I let out a breath, frustration swallowing me whole.

There were, in theory, many scent match possibilities in the world at one time between packs and omegas, but it was impossible to test because once one locked in, that was it. No do overs. Scent matched for life.

Was it possible she *should* have been ours?

What she described when she looked at the Lincoln pack, I felt echoes of that when I was with her, whenever I caught her scent.

But I also couldn't deny that her nightshade had a double meaning both to me and Umbra, and my alpha instincts were long fucked. I had no way of knowing what was real.

What if she'd met us first, instead of them…?

I buried the thought deep, unable to contend with the wound that opened at what that would mean. Not when I was about to smile for them.

But what if they were dead?

That was one way to reset a scent match. I shook the thought away. Still one step behind.

More of Decebal's stupidly rational advice sounded in my head. *"I don't care how badly you want it. You cannot risk killing them when you don't know what they stole."*

It was at that moment that Gareth, Flynn, and Eric arrived.

Given how recently I'd received the invite, the thirty minute delay felt deliberate. I noticed Flynn Lincoln's eyes scanning me and Shatter, eyebrows rising as he joined us in the booth first.

"Umbra couldn't make it?"

"Not with such late notice," I said with a fake smile.

Part of why I'd brought Shatter was because I knew now, from Eric's words in the library, and the bugs, that the Lincoln pack disliked us. *This* was my last ditch effort to try and save the alliance.

I think they took Ransom's continued absence as a personal slight, which was about as ridiculous as I'd come to expect from rich prats like them. Flynn Lincoln was rich, but nowhere near Ransom's level of rich, and he was only here because his family was forcing him to make something of himself before he had access to his inheritance. Something Ransom already had.

Except, instead of dealing with Ransom, they were left with me and Umbra. Unknown pack mates that they couldn't find information on, no matter how hard they dug—and I knew they'd tried, because it was one of the conversations Decebal had transcribed and sent to me from the bug in their rooms.

As I began engaging in meaningless conversation, I noticed Shatter's anxiety. Mainly because she began fiddling, and doing things that made the Lincoln alphas stare, like chewing on the ice she fished from her drink.

I'd had to stifle my chuckle.

Keeping her in my side view only *just* made this meeting tolerable. Especially when the topic shifted to music.

Music?

Like I gave a fuck what music these leeches liked to listen to?

Did they really think this was how they'd get into Ransom's good graces? Or perhaps they just hoped he would finally turn up tonight.

He'd hate this more than I did.

Thank God it was impossible to ignore the way Shatter was now bending her miniature umbrella through the gaps in her fork. More so, when her grip slipped and the tip snapped off, flying through the air and stabbing me in the cheek.

She winced, eyes wide as Eric's ramble about R&B came to a blessed fucking halt.

Shatter dropped the fork instantly, cheeks bright red. "I'm… sorry."

The Lincoln pack were gawking at her, then their eyes slid to me, clearly waiting for my response.

I didn't react, instead brushing a loose strand of hair behind her ear like nothing had happened at all.

Shatter placed her hands on her lap, her eyes fixed on the table, expression tight, though not before she shot a panicked glance at Eric. It was *that* mask again: absolute discipline that radiated shame. I'd only ever seen it when she was truly upset, and right now she looked on the verge of tears.

So I took the lime from my drink before the waitress swept it away. Then, right as Flynn launched into a pompous tirade about politics, I set the lime on the table, fixing Flynn with an interested stare as I lined my hand up. With a perfectly precise *flick,* I sent the lime zipping right into the side of Shatter's nose.

She snapped her attention to me in shock, but I'd spared her only a glance, already fixing my gaze back on Flynn, who had trailed off.

This was probably a stupid idea if I wanted them to like me, but I felt the slightest curve of a smile on my lips. "An issue with the wrong sort of media attention?" I prodded, conjuring up the last dull thing he'd been rattling on about. "I agree. Especially since Channel Five has gone to shit."

"I…" His gaze drifted between me and Shatter again, though he seemed taken aback by my response. "Yes. Actually, I've been saying the same thing myself…"

Yup.

I knew that because Decebal had been feeding me their boring political hot takes, too.

Fucking idiots.

That, it seemed, was all it took to sweep him away into more self important drivel, the Shatter incident already forgotten.

Christ.

I hated, more than anything else in the world, that these were the lowlifes I was forced to hunt. As stupid as they were greedy. Absolute parasites.

My smile grew more and more rigid as the evening dragged on, more so as I caught their occasional lingering glances at Shatter.

Was it a *normal* amount of looks from alphas?

Gareth was droning on now, and his voice grated at my sanity. For a moment, those words whispered something different than what was spoken over a club table on a Saturday evening.

"Don't tell me it's over," Gareth groaned. "What about that drug you mentioned?"

"Atropa's poison?"

"Yes." That was Flynn. "Try it. See what happens. If they're still standing, then you can't convince us to stop."

I swallowed, forcing myself calm.

Last night I'd offered Shatter Kingsman a pill while she'd been going into heat. If I had that kind of discipline, I could do anything—including surviving tonight.

Still, in my head, I picked up Shatter's broken umbrella pieces and jammed them right into Gareth's eye sockets.

He was the worst tonight, sneaking glances at her more subtly than the others as if he knew they were wrong, eyes tracing down to the neckline of the dress *I'd* chosen…

It was good I'd chosen to wear scent blockers tonight. They'd sense the murder rolling from me in waves if I hadn't.

"What does your sponsor think of Ransom's absence?" Eric asked. "It's been weeks and not a peep? Surely he's getting antsy. Ours oversees quite a lot."

"Connolly is aware of Ransom's absence," I replied. That was the Arkologist who'd sponsored our education here as the academy required.

"Lucky," Eric snorted. "Ours is a hawk."

I shrugged. "He's more relaxed in his retirement."

"Ah. I can imagine. Still, can't expect the boost from him once you enter the field though, eh?" Flynn said.

No.

Not least because Connolly Peterson was dead.

Umbra's kill, that time.

He'd told us nothing before he died. By the time we got to him in a small cabin in the mountains, his memory was fried and half his brain with it. He hadn't been publicly tied to anything shady, but that didn't change what he knew. It hadn't changed what he'd allowed to happen.

Honestly, I was surprised he'd been left alive at all. Those hired for the cover up were ruthless. The only reason we were safe was because they believed we were dead.

Still, we'd used the fact that they'd spared him, forcing him to write the letters we needed. Letters for our sponsorship, and one for every quarter to his colleagues. He was quiet and private, and that had made this all too easy. No one would notice his absence for another year at least.

"Your sponsor is Eugene Howard?" Shatter's voice dragged me from my musings.

"That's right." Flynn glanced at her in surprise. If I'd learned one thing about Shatter, it was that no matter how much she fiddled with umbrellas, or doodled in her notebook in class, she retained *everything* around her. "One of the top leaders in Arkology Sciences right now," Flynn added, seeming pleased to be on this topic.

"He's a hard man to impress, I've heard," I said, willing to push any part of the conversation that drew Shatter's curiosity. I knew of Eugene Howard's sponsorship, like I knew everything of the pack before me. He was an Arkologist and not directly tied to those we'd been hunting.

"Oh, yes he is." Flynn straightened. "But don't feel bad if you couldn't reach him. He's almost a myth, he's so private. By pure chance I knew he was involved in some very important work for the Institute—highly classified, of course—but that was our in. Took every favour my family has, but we managed to arrange a visit at his Estate. In fact, that's where we were this weekend."

"Was a nice place, too, wasn't it?" Eric was asking. "Out in the middle of nowhere, but you don't see many buildings with that much history anymore. If you ever get the chance to visit, take it," he said with a hint of superiority that suggested he hoped I would never get the chance.

I was much more curious at the way Shatter had tensed, her eyes wider than usual as she watched them. She almost looked like she wanted to say something, but her hands balled in her lap and she shrank back down.

What, I wondered, piqued her curiosity about the Lincoln pack's sponsor?

It wasn't long after when Shatter excused herself to the bathroom, and in her absence I got my first sign of victory.

"What do you get up to outside of the Academy," Flynn asked, sipping his scotch. I couldn't help but notice Gareth's piercing blue gaze following Shatter as she stopped a waitress for directions. "If you feel the same way about how the media's going, we must share tastes—and you can be honest, we enjoy a few things outside of the… normal."

I glanced at him.

This was it.

A subtle prod to see if I would spill any incriminating hobbies. He would share if I did, I was certain. It's how the rich felt comfortable in alliances, I'd learned. Socialise, enjoy themselves, and be confident in mutually assured destruction should anything go south.

But I already knew the foul things that the Lincoln pack got up to on their own time.

"68 fights back. Won't roll while he's choked to death." Flynn barked a laugh, words slurred. "What kind of shit was that, anyway? Fucking pathetic."

I was losing my battle with the fury as Gareth actually shifted back in his seat to watch Shatter right before she turned a corner to the bathroom.

"On the topic of less than appropriate tastes we may share," I said. "What of Gareth's taste in omegas?"

It slipped out before I could stop it.

Silence rang out between us, Flynn and Eric both glancing at Gareth, who stared at me now, running his tongue along his teeth.

Fix it.

Fucking fix it right now.

They'd just given me an in. Something I could have run with, and instead… I forced a smile across my face and I lifted my glass as if it was all just a joke.

Flynn chuckled, though he was still clearly off balance.

Fuck.

"Forgive me," Gareth said with a grin. "It is hard not to stare. She's very… unconventional."

"Ah. That's what it is?"

"I'm sure she's a good match—"

"A perfect match," I corrected him.

He nodded, a sly smile creeping up his face that made me regret it instantly. "She must be… *exceptional* in other areas."

It took every ounce of my self control not to launch myself at him.

Instead, I got to my feet with painful slowness. I was at my fucking limit. "I'm turning in for the night."

I wanted to be ready to leave the moment Shatter was out. I wouldn't keep her around them for one more second.

"Well." Flynn got to his feet with a nod. "This was good. And I'm looking forward to meeting Ransom when he's around."

"Not long before he comes, I don't think," I said.

"Excellent."

Flynn clapped me on the arm.

The movement was innocent. Meaningless. Yet, for the briefest instant before his skin made contact with mine, a power surge crackled every instinct in my being.

The whole world was wrong.

It was too late to move, to back up. And I didn't even know why I should. But I braced, every muscle in my body turning to stone.

Flynn's skin upon mine was a bolt of lightning. White hot agony fried every nerve ending, turning the world into meaningless, swimming lights.

It took every ounce of self control I had; control I'd learned in a blank, white room, pretending to be well when my body was dying, to do nothing but flinch—to not let my aura split the air.

I stepped back. "Goodnight." I don't know how I made those words come out. I don't even know if I did.

I couldn't collapse. I had to get to my pack.

The pack bond crackled, an overloaded livewire, and then—for the first time in years, I felt Umbra's side of the bond slam shut.

Before it did, I felt his fleeting moment of horror. I could barely keep my thoughts straight, but I knew *everything* that was bad in this bond, was worse for Umbra.

I had to get to him.

And Shatter…

Fuck.

I could barely breathe. Every footstep rocked me, agony ricocheting through every bone in my body. I was trembling, but I forced my fists closed, forced myself onward. Still... I was losing track of where I was...

Dread dimmed my mind. It felt like a hook was lodged in my soul and was trying to rip it from my body.

Umbra...

For Umbra it would be worse.

"...Dusk...!" The most beautiful voice pulled me back from the edge of insanity. From the edge of collapse. From tumbling, mind and body, from the edge of the cliff to which my whole pack was clinging. "...What's going on...?"

She was here.

Her grip was tight. She was... Shatter was helping keep me steady. It was easier to keep my feet knowing that.

"Should I get help...?" Her words floated into my scrambled brain.

"NO!" My growl was unsteady.

No.

No one else could see us like this. It was dangerous. We could lose everything.

But she was ours.

She would...

"Umbra..." I had to tell her.

I heard how frantic she was, fear etched into every syllable of words I couldn't comprehend. I was trying to take a step with her weight beneath me. So small, yet she hadn't let me go...

Time behaved strangely. There was a mist of rain on my skin. A blur of orange leaves and grass beneath each staggering footstep. She hadn't left and she was taking us behind the buildings. The back way to keep us out of sight… Stairs blurred in my vision, and with each footfall agony threatened to steal me away.

Then we were facing a door. My hand was pressed to it, my bones still rattling in their joints. The clink of keys sent my head pounding, as if someone had rung a tower bell in my skull.

Then we were inside. Home. I knew from my pack's scents—of hers, which was here still, a salve on a burn.

Umbra.

He must be upstairs. But she couldn't help him... not yet.

I was at the counter, fumbling with drawers until I found the right one. Another key from my keychain... Shatter helped me, and then I was pressing a bottle into her hands.

She looked terrified. "D-Dusk… What's happening?" She fumbled with the pill bottle.

"Umbra..." My voice was barely working.

"He... I give them to him?" she asked.

No.

I tried to shake my head. "You... take them." She had to... to take the pills. There were two left. That was enough.

"These are...?" Her voice cracked as she realised. "I don't understand."

"Your scent..." He needed her.

Our omega.

I'd given her scent blockers only hours before, but there were two pills left. Her scent would return in minutes. The pain of my knees smashing to marble was a faint echo beneath the earth rending agony of the bond. It was on fire, crumbling to pieces. Umbra at the middle of it all.

"...Dusk...!"

Blackness edged in now I knew she had them.

And with it came a final moment of clarity.

I was on my knees before her, fists balled in her dress as she held the pills that would return her scent. Pills that handed her the freedom she'd been fighting for since the moment I'd taken her.

And now, she could run.

"Please...!" My voice was low and rough.

Just save him.

Please... let me be right. Let me have done one thing right with these scorched alpha instincts I was left with.

From the first moment I'd seen her, I'd known.

She was ours, not theirs.

Never theirs.

Please...

The world faded, my shoulder hitting the ground. It took all my strength to look up, but when I finally managed it, Shatter was gone.

CHAPTER 30

I am forced to accept that we have explored all possible options to improve her quality of life. My request is for her to be allowed to continue living out the rest of her life at my estate.

Shatter

My world began with metal walls, flashing red lights, and unrelenting torture.

Each breath was a knife dragged through seizing lungs, and my blood was corrosive, vicious claws trying to tear through flesh from the inside. Even my bones—the roots of my body—betrayed me, beds of white hot agony.

I didn't go back there. Not ever. It was the first moment I had memories of.

But it was over now.

Yet, Dusk was there; I'd seen that pain in his face as he pressed the bottle toward me. He'd fought like hell to get back to Umbra, battling a devil I'd never stop running from.

And now he was handing me my freedom as he collapsed.

For Umbra.

For his pack.

My lungs were made of lead as I stood, clutching the front door handle, tears streaming down my cheeks. The two pills had dissolved on my tongue and my scent would return any moment. My mates were out there right now. At the club, or walking home…

Dusk had taken me from them. I didn't… I didn't owe him anything.

But I couldn't shake his fear. I hadn't, before today, been able to even *imagine* Dusk afraid. Yet, his yellow eyes had been terrified as he'd stared up at me.

A sob caught in my throat.

My mates were waiting…

This might be my only chance.

Could I go to them after, though? I could check on Umbra, just to make sure he was safe…

I hurried upstairs, but when I opened the door to his room, I instantly knew something was wrong.

Disgust seized me, sinking into the fractured instincts that made me an omega. The air itself was off, crackling broken shards of intangible energy, surging and dying in cycles. I'd never felt anything like it.

Umbra had collapsed to the floor beside his bed. His scent of wolfsbane and blood was toxic and thick... wrong. And his aura...

Oh God.

I let out a low wail as I realised the strange thing flickering in the air... it *was* his aura.

Everything else in the world vanished.

I stumbled toward him, instincts I'd once thought didn't exist, taking control.

But *could* I fix this?

He was awake, if barely. His knife was in his grip and he was digging it into his arm. Not like I'd seen him do before. He was unsteady, and it was piercing to bone.

"Umbra..." My voice shook as I took his wrist, tears spilling onto him. *"Umbra!"*

Sandstorm eyes, dazed with agony, drifted to me. My scent was back, I knew by the way his breathing calmed with each inhale.

That was good, but not enough.

"I can't let go," he croaked. "Or I w-won't wake up."

He would.

I'd claimed him.

I wouldn't let him die.

My scent wasn't enough, not yet. I tilted his chin up and pressed my teeth to his neck. He jolted, hand seizing my hair with strength he had no right to.

"No. You might..." He sounded afraid.

A growl tore from my chest. How *dare* he tell me I couldn't. I ripped free of his grip, ignoring the pain in my scalp, and shoving his fist back. And the knife?

No.

He struggled weakly as I tried to tear the weapon from his trembling hands. He gripped it tight, letting out a wounded, broken sound, the aura in the air shuddering, becoming more unstable.

Fuck...

But the knife wasn't the answer. I knew it wasn't.

"Shatter–!"

No.

I threw my whole weight onto his forearm with my knee and his grip spasmed. I grabbed the knife and threw it across the room. He tried to get up, wolfsbane and blood flooding with panic, but I turned on him, shoving him back down, my fist in *his* hair this time to tug his head back.

"NO!"

But his protest was too late as I sank my teeth into his neck

Fuck.

I jolted with horror as Umbra rushed into my consciousness.

An omega's bite formed a connection, if only temporary, and weaker than a pack bond. Yet, in it, I felt the same viciousness in his aura that was in the air. I shuddered, clenching my jaw as it began trying to devour me, too.

What the hell...?

I'd never read anything about auras behaving this way—as if it was trying to escape him, ready to consume anything in its path.

But now, with me here, I felt it losing strength. I waited, holding onto him for a long time until I was sure.

It *was* waning, unable to consume us both. An exhale of relief rushed from my lungs. The strange effect it had on the air was fading too, the fragments in the air weakening with each second.

"You're going to be okay," I whispered. I hurried to his bathroom to grab his medical kit and got to work cleaning and wrapping his wound, jumping at every groan of agony from him. Tears burned my eyes again. I hated his pain. I hated seeing it. "We're going to get you on the bed," I told him when I was done and the bandage was secure.

With great difficulty, I helped him stand and collapse to the bed. He was dazed, and I could see him fading out of consciousness.

Good.

He needed to rest.

I could take care of him from here.

Everything was going to be okay.

I curled up in his arms, nudging my jaw along his, scent marking him. I felt the aura calm more as his breathing slowed.

Okay. That was good too.

I could do this.

Moment by agonising moment, he stabilised.

I held onto him, summoning up a purr and holding him tight. I would hold onto him until he was peaceful again.

I didn't know how long I lay there, but finally his aura vanished from the air entirely, all the crackling fragments fading to nothing. The tug in the bond, relentless teeth trying to destroy him, gone.

Finally I dared peel myself away. He didn't flinch, nor did he become more unstable.

Right.

I swallowed, muscles finally loosening. I cupped his cheek for a moment, taken by the warm tan of his skin and smattering of freckles.

He looked peaceful...

Had *I* done that?

Pride and relief swelled in my chest, and I stood up to take stock of the situation.

His legs were still dangling off the bed, and he rested at a strange angle. That was no good for tucking him in.

I frowned. I didn't want him waking up like this, not when I was the omega in charge.

I wrung my fingers. I could do better. Roxy would never be caught leaving her alpha like this, I just *knew* it.

So, I spent the next ten minutes trying to shift Umbra's huge, limp body up the bed. I tried burrowing beneath him and shoving; dragging him by his arms; tugging on the sheets (but they popped right out), and finally squatting over him and lifting him by the chest. That worked for a few inches until my grip slipped and I tumbled to the floor with a squeak.

Dammit.

Why are alphas so fucking big?

I just wanted him to wake up happy. I wanted him to know I'd had his back even when everything was going wrong, and when he opened his eyes, there was nothing to be afraid of.

That's all anyone wanted.

I was panting as I returned to hauling him by the chest, but he was almost there.

How would Roxy do this?

No way had she looked inelegant a day in her life.

I thought wildly of the Sleeping Beauty movie that Aunty Lauren chose one night, where the cartoon fairies had waved their wands and all the stuff had bobbed through the air to where it was supposed to go.

That's what Roxy would do.

She *definitely* wouldn't crab squat over her alpha, grunting like a pig in labour as she sweat to her ass cheeks—

THUNK!

Oh shit!

I let out a whine of horror, dropping Umbra instantly and diving for his poor head that had just rammed into the wall.

Okay.

Not bleeding.

Not bleeding.

What if he was bleeding inside? How would I know? I cradled his head, panic returning.

I couldn't save him and then accidentally kill him.

It would be okay.

I just had to tuck him in.

I made a proper nest around him, occasionally dragging his eyelid open and checking if his pupils had changed size. That's what people did when someone hurt their head, right?

When I was sure he was going to live, I took a step back, examining my work and fanning myself with my hand.

Umbra was now entirely bundled in blankets and cradled in pillows.

It felt right.

I think it was enough to make him happy when he—

I jumped violently at a loud *BANG!* from outside.

What was that?

Oh shit!

Dusk... He was still down there. What if his aura had become all crazy like Umbra's? I was rushing toward the door in a moment, terror constricting my chest at the idea of stepping out onto the balcony and looking down to see him dead below.

He was right where I'd left him, but... I thought he was breathing.

I hurried down the spiral staircase and kneeled beside him.

Definitely breathing. Still out cold. There was a tremor in his hand, though. I leaned down and scent marked him, running purely on instinct and trying not to think about my mates right now. Fix this first, mates later.

His breathing calmed like Umbra's had.

How long would he be out?

I should probably make sure he was comfortable too...

I glanced around.

There was no way I was getting him to the couch, so I brought the couch to him. I grabbed all the cushions and stacked them beside each other on the floor. Then with one great shove, I rolled him onto them. I bundled him up like I had Umbra, in blankets and pillows.

There was nothing else to do, right?

But Dusk was still shivering, even with the extra blankets on him, so I curled up under his arm.

Just for a bit.

Just in case.

Then I'd go.

Alpha management was a lot of work.

I lay there for a long, long time. Until his shaking had died down and I'd given him everything I'd given Umbra. Well, except the bite. But he was stable enough without it, I thought. And I didn't think I could handle a connection with Dusk. I peered up at him, my thumb brushing along the cool brown skin of his cheek. For a long second, I was unable to take my eyes from him.

I knew why a bond with him frightened me.

Umbra… I think I *got* Umbra. He was different, like me—or I thought he was. My bond should last until he woke, though I could already feel it waning, as if his vicious aura was burning through it faster than normal. But if my temporary bond with him did remain by the time he awoke, I think I trusted that the alpha on the other end of that would be exactly who I thought I knew.

But a bond with Dusk?

It would break me if I had a connection with him, and I learned the truth I'd been afraid of this whole time. That his attraction to me wasn't what he claimed—because how… how *could* it be, really?

And if—somehow—it was…? I think I was even more terrified to find out it was real.

Because what was I supposed to do then?

Both would break me, because I didn't have the option of falling in love with Dusk Varis.

Finally, when I was sure it had been long enough, and I was boiling from all the blankets—I checked him, but he was still on the cool side—I got to my feet.

Okay

I swallowed, staring at the door.

I had my scent and they were out there.

I could go to them: Eric, Gareth, and Flynn with their world stopping scents. They'd seemed interested in me tonight, even though I'd embarrassed myself. I'd kept catching Gareth's eyes on me and I could swear there had been want in his gaze.

The faintest feather of dread brushed my throat.

I tried to swallow it away.

Nerves were normal. Everything would change after this.

Again.

Things kept changing and that was scary, but this time was the last time. All the other changes had been on the path to get here. To get to my dream. My eyes flickered to Dusk.

Why was my chest so tight?

I had to go.

Now.

It's hormones, I told myself. I could feel them in my system as if in shock from what I'd just managed.

But Dusk and Umbra were both safe now, and that meant they could wake up anytime. If they did, they would stop me from leaving.

How would they react when they woke up and I wasn't here? With my nest and scent and all my pillow work… Umbra could still be happy if I wasn't there, right?

I had to bite my lip to shove back more tears, thinking of him last night. Of the way he'd held me against him all night. Of the safety I'd felt in his arms. When I'd woken up this morning, for the first time in my life, there had been the briefest heart stopping moment, when there had been nothing to be afraid of.

That's enough, Shatter, they were never an option.

Not really. It was just a fairytale.

The alpha's teeth sank into the flesh of my neck.

It was more delicate than I'd been expecting, the pain present but not overwhelming.

"When he bites you, accept his pack." Aunty Lauren's instructions rang in my head.

Accept his pack.

There would be an offer. I would feel it.

I didn't want this, but it was the best I could get, so I desperately searched for the offer, quelling my terror as I tried to ignore the heat of the alpha while his body pressed against mine.

Accept the offer.

Only...

I tried.

A trickle of hot blood slid down my neck, and teeth lingered, igniting every instinct in my body to flee, and yet I couldn't find what I searched for.

I couldn't say yes because there was no offer to accept.

"But... I wanted to accept it," I said stupidly. Weeks had passed since the bite and I'd tried to figure out what I'd done wrong. Now uncle had sat me down in his office, and shown me the final report he'd sent to the Institute.

The subject's attempt at joining a pack has failed. Further testing reveals that she is unable to form a natural bond. The subject is restricted only to artificial pack connections: either princess or dark bonds.

"Shatter, did you understand what it says?" uncle asked. "I'm sorry, but you will never host a normal bond."

I stared as that slowly began to saturate my mind... "B-but you said I would never have mates—and that a pack was the only thing left that might fix me."

"I did. And I'm sorry. These aren't side effects I've ever seen before."

If he was right, I needed a scent match. Scent matches were the only alphas who could offer princess bonds.

"And the Institute still won't let me leave without a pack?" What a stupid question. I was barely functional anymore.

Still, I'd take the Estate over the Institute. Both were cages, but here there were the gardens, and Aunty Lauren, and I had some freedom.

"Not with your scent as it is. They don't know enough about your condition. That, on top of your gold pack status, mean dark bonds are a real threat."

The thought sent a chill down my spine. The idea of a dark bond with this scent, one that could send alphas into a rage...

No. Far too dangerous. Uncle had been firm. I couldn't argue, either. I didn't want to step from one cage to another.

I just wanted a family... To be good enough for someone... For this unending emptiness to stop.

A tear splashed down onto the words, and I re-read the last line once again, a chill crawling up my spine as I did.

It was over.

In that Estate, I was trapped forever. It was a life that I could not keep living. Endless and alone, as I was buried slowly with every breath. The Lincoln pack was the impossible gift I was never supposed to have. Find them, forge a bond, and then I could live my life, never having to fear that the Institute would hunt me down.

I remembered the first time I'd caught their scent. On the suppressants, I'd become no one once more. Every day stretched into infinity.

The world turned grey.

And then the Lincoln pack had visited.

I'd stepped into the house one afternoon, Aunty Lauren at my side, as she took me on my daily walk. There had been three scents in the air. Alpha's scents. Colour had blossomed across the pages of my life like an ink stain, lighting up pathways in my brain long worn and wasted away.

I remembered that moment viscerally. It was a shard lodged in my heart.

I'd turned around and looked back through the door. The grass was yellowing from a heatwave, and there were flowers in late bloom like it was summer. But the last time I'd been… anywhere, snow had been falling.

That moment had held as much devastation as it had hope. Seeing, in a single breath of clarity, what was happening to me.

I was dying, slowly, absolutely, while breath still entered my lungs.

But I didn't think this miracle of mates could be real, so I waited until I was sure. But when I'd told Aunty Lauren who I thought the Lincoln pack were, no one believed me. They said it wasn't possible…

Imagining things…

Wishful thinking…

They'd locked me up until the Lincoln alphas were gone.

So… I ran away.

I'd managed the symptoms of my hormones, returning with vengeance in the four months it took me to get here. But I'd made it, knowing my mates were waiting on the other end. Knowing that with them, everything would be okay.

It was a simple plan. A simple plan Dusk was derailing with every day that passed.

A dark bond wasn't an option.

Was it?

That thought was jarring. Never, before now, had I even considered it a possibility. But I'd never, before now, met alphas who liked my scent. Who liked my scent and maybe wanted me?

"No." I told myself. *No no no.* Even the thought came with a flicker of fear. And certainly not when there was still the possibility of a princess bond. Perhaps Eric didn't like me right now, but we hadn't even had a chance, yet—not really. And Flynn and Gareth had been nothing but charming when I'd seen them.

I hugged myself. I didn't even remember choosing these golden eyes. Why couldn't I want more than a dark bond for my future? It was for life.

The Kingsman pack was a fragment of reality in a bubble destined to pop.

Still, I couldn't stop staring at Dusk. What if I left and reached my mates and he found a way to bring me back here?

I should… make sure I had backup. Just in case…

Numbly, I took Dusk's keys and hurried down to his room. There, I chose a corner window and unlocked it. He wouldn't notice, not if he thought they were locked. It would be there for me, anytime.

To leave, or… or come back?

I'm not coming back.

I steeled myself, returning to the front door and cracking it open, knowing my scent was leeching out into the hallway beyond. Once they knew who I was, there was no going back. My hands were sweaty and clammy as I remained at the cracked door like a coward.

This. Was. It.

I had my scent. I had my freedom, and I *knew* my mates wanted a princess bond just as much as I needed one.

Take the safe option.

Tense as I was, I jumped out of my skin at the sound of another *CRASH!* This time louder than before.

I spun, expecting to see Dusk awake, yet he wasn't. The sound hadn't come from the living room—nor had it come from Umbra's. I stared upwards, unsure what to think.

That sound had come from the door in the middle of the balcony.

The door that was always locked.

The end of part one...

To all the incredible PoisonVerse readers who love their easter eggs:

Unlike previous PoisonVerse books, which have been written in order, Shatter's story takes place roughly 3 months before the start of Havoc's....

Marie Mackay

CHAPTER 1

Shatter

Another *BANG* from the room on the balcony made me jump.

I should check on that.

I stared at the locked door above, heart pounding, mind racing a million miles a minute. I'd just spent Lord knows how much time making sure Dusk and Umbra were safe. Now they were both wrapped up in blankets, their auras stable.

That noise couldn't be either of them—Umbra was still peacefully vacant in the omega bond I had. He was sleeping, just like Dusk was resting on a bed of pillows in the kitchen before me.

I was trying to catch up with what had happened, and my pulse was still erratic.

I'd come out of the bathroom of the club to find Dusk gone. It had been so unexpected, I'd hurried out the front doors, alarm bells going off in my head. There, I'd found him doubled over on the pathway, body shaking, aura flickering in and out.

Never had I even *read* about something like this, let alone seen it. He had been dying, I'd known it in my gut. There was something so, so wrong with what had happened to both him and Umbra… It was more than sickness… It was unnatural.

If I was being honest, I had no idea how I'd fixed it.

But now, they were both asleep.

That noise could *not* have been them.

The clinical side of my brain had already done the calculation, but it was just so wildly unbelievable that I was having a hard time processing it.

Because if that wasn't Umbra or Dusk, then there was only one person it could be, and that was—

A knock sounded at the front door, making me jump.

I spun, staring at it, then scrambled to look through the peephole. My heart bottomed out of my chest.

Flynn Lincoln was standing outside.

"One… one second!" I called. I pressed my back against the door, absolutely unsure.

Flynn was here?

Everything I'd just been thinking about running to.

My mate was outside. Right. Now.

Instead of elation, I felt a sense of dread creeping up my spine.

What about the sound upstairs? I couldn't just leave, right? My mind thought wildly to the registration card in my pencil case—which reminded me I needed to grab that before I even thought of leaving.

Stupid.

Stupid and rushed and… *damn it*, I wasn't ready.

But if Flynn caught my scent and knew I was his match, I'd never be able to check on that room.

I ran to the kitchen, almost tripping over Dusk, and opened his drug drawer. In it was a bottle of scent-dampening spray. It wasn't as long-lasting as the pills, but it was enough for now.

I sprayed it all over myself and the whole kitchen, almost choking on the thick mist.

The knock sounded again.

"Be there in a minute!" I called.

I wasn't giving up on my mates. I could wash this off and go back to them. After. After I'd checked the room and made sure everyone was safe.

Finally, feeling ready, I cracked the door, peering out. Coconut and plum were the first scents I caught in the air, and sure enough, Flynn was right there.

Right in front of me.

"Hi," I said awkwardly, still holding the door mostly closed.

He frowned, gaze meeting mine for a long moment, then lifting to the kitchen beyond.

"Is your pack okay?" he asked. "Dusk left abruptly. He didn't look well."

"Yes," I said too quickly. "He's fine."

I couldn't explain the sudden sickness in my throat or the absolute need that gripped me to lie—to ensure that the alpha before me never saw Dusk lying on the kitchen floor, asleep.

Vulnerable…

Before he could say anything, I slipped out and shut the door behind me, so he couldn't see in.

I don't know why it was so imperative. It just was. Dusk had fought through hell to get back to Umbra. I might resent everything he'd ever done, but I couldn't deny the strength in that loyalty, just like I couldn't deny my instinct to protect it.

I fingered Dusk's keys in my pocket, making sure they were there. I *could* get back in.

I blinked, reality flooding back now there was a door between me and the alphas who had captured me.

Why was I worried about getting back in?

I should be throwing myself into Flynn's arms.

"I…" Flynn trailed off, looking unsure, glancing down at where I was gripping the keys in my jacket pocket. Then he looked back up at me, his pupils blown.

Oh… Oh my God. I'd had the door open for a while.

Did he catch my scent?

If he had, what would that mean?

Did he know who I was?

"I just wanted to check in," he said again. He looked intense. Too intense. "Are you sure I can't speak to him?"

"No. He's, uh… doing something important with Umbra."

"Okay." He took a step back, then paused. His eyes fell to my shoulder, and I glanced down to see a stain of red in my hair.

Umbra's blood.

Oh… *crap.*

He looked back at me, eyebrows raised. "Are *you* okay?"

"Yes. I am. Definitely."

He didn't look convinced.

"I promise."

Promise? Really, Shatter?

Still, he continued staring at me with pupils that were definitely blown wide. "I…" He trailed off. "Shatter…"

My pulse raced out of control at the sound of my name on my mate's lips… Thoughts of investigating the sound from the mysterious room faded away for the briefest second.

I was so fucking warm, and my brain just wasn't working straight. It had taken far too much out of me, sorting out Dusk and Umbra.

Flynn was still staring at me.

I heard sounds down the hall and glanced down to see that Eric and Gareth were both waiting by the stairs.

They'd all come?

"I h-have to go," I stammered.

"Wait," Flynn rasped. "Just… wait."

"What?" My voice was weak, metal digging into my palm as I gripped the keys too tightly.

"I just... fuck." He straightened, running his fingers through his hair. "Forgive me, but…" He looked pained. "You came to us at the ball, and now I see you everywhere."

My mouth dropped open, completely caught off guard by his words.

"I'm not the only one. It's Eric and Gareth too. You're… different."

I froze completely, staring at him.

"But Eric…" I trailed off, knowing I shouldn't say that.

Flynn frowned, cocking his head. "What?"

"I… I heard him…" My voice was weak. "He said I didn't belong here. He, uh… doesn't like my hair," I said, but Flynn's eyes darkened. "I d-didn't mean to over-hear—"

"Fuck." He leaned back, letting out a breath. "Eric's a fucking idiot, all right? And he doesn't… He's not used to…" He ran his fingers through his hair again, still so anxious. "We've never been interested in an omega like we're interested in you, Shatter."

Interested?

What?

This… wasn't the time.

I couldn't do this right now.

"And Eric," Flynn continued, "all of us—we see you with the Kingsman pack every goddamned day. You have no idea how it's killing us. So, he pretends he hates you because he can't handle it."

"Hates me?" I shrank down, Eric's words still replaying in my head like they had so many times.

"He *doesn't* hate you. Please, don't let him blow this chance. Not because Eric can't keep his mouth shut."

I couldn't think.

He was asking me for a chance?

At what?

"I'll get him on his knees for you. He'll beg you for forgiveness, I swear it." There was the faintest smile on his face.

But none of this made sense.

What about Roxy?

He knew I was her friend. And what he was asking…

"I know how harsh he can sound. He's not… Look. I know this isn't going to sell you on us, but he's not always the best, all right? He's spoiled, but he can be better. I've seen it."

My heart slammed into my ribs uncomfortably.

I'd heard them say they wanted a princess bond—I swear it. And I'd *almost* fallen for Dusk, after everything he'd done. Was it possible Eric wasn't that bad, either?

He wanted me.

They *all* wanted me?

Flynn's scent was too much for me to try to parse this out; I felt like it was weaving into my very soul. My fingers were clammy, sweat beading on my back.

My brain wasn't working right.

If it *was* Ransom in that room, could he possibly be as sick as the others? He might die if I didn't go to him. And he'd got me my registration card. Flynn would understand that.

Nothing made sense. I felt like I was splitting into two different people. One that couldn't understand why I wasn't throwing myself at Flynn, and the other that couldn't understand why I wasn't already back inside.

"I… I just need a bit of time… to…" I gripped my sleeve with my free hand, needing to clear my head. "To th-think." Goddammit, I couldn't think. Not with Dusk and Umbra nearly dying, and now Flynn's coconut and plum, and… oh… "My registration card is a really big deal…" That was Ransom—He'd done that for me. And what if he was dying? I couldn't let the one alpha in the world who'd gotten me a registration card die because Flynn's scent of coconut and plum was intoxicating.

God, I was warm.

Too many people.

This is too much.

Dusk and Umbra. Ransom. Now Flynn and the rest of the pack. How was I supposed to think straight with all of these alphas?

"I just need time," I squeaked, then turned, grabbing the keys from my pocket and fumbled with the lock on the door.

It took me far too long to find the right key. By the time I had, embarrassment had set my blood on fire.

I didn't breathe a sigh of relief until I'd slammed it shut behind me, not even daring to catch a glimpse of Flynn's expression.

I kept a hold of the keys in my fist as I looked up at the room again, almost expecting another sound.

None came.

What did that mean?

What would I find if I went inside?

But if I didn't go and look, I'd let my mate walk away for nothing.

CHAPTER 2

Shatter

Lily of the valley flowed through my system, smoothing every spike of anxiety and every worry. Every doubt that had been clawing at me since the moment I'd shut the door on Flynn. The scent in the room was cool and earthy, like a forest beneath autumn rain. It was an alpha's scent—dark and curious in a way it shouldn't be.

It didn't have the magnetism of my mates, but it was still strange and overpowering, clogging my throat and lungs, a poison that invaded every cell of my body, slowly drowning me.

I'd just look. Make sure he was safe.

That's what I'd told myself, but a floorboard creaked underfoot as I stepped further into a broad room, the air growing thicker with lily of the valley. I peered around, taking a moment to adjust to the light of the dim wall lamp. There was another sound from ahead, this time more muffled.

That was when I saw him.

A shadowed figure stood at the head of the bed, fists balled at his side. There were dents across the wall, and the side of the bed was in splinters. For a long moment, we stared at one another. In the darkness, I could just see the spark of light in dark eyes, a tall frame, and shaggy, shoulder-length hair.

Oh my God.

I had been right.

"Ransom?" My voice was weak.

He *was* here.

Had he been here since term started?

Ransom hadn't moved. His chest was heaving as he stood beside his bed, eyes fixed on me like I was prey.

But I wasn't afraid of him. It was a soul-deep truth that he needed me, just like they had.

His scent was odd… Not like Umbra's and Dusk's had been, yet something *was* wrong about it.

I took another step into the room, tentatively, trying to make him out. He hadn't responded to the sound of me entering, and the room dimmed as the door finally swung shut behind me.

At the sound of the latch clicking, Ransom reacted. His aura split the air, and then he made for me, and—

Fuck.

Those were chains around his wrists. Dark iron chains.

I stumbled back as he crossed the distance between us, too afraid to even turn. The violent clinking of metal drowned the sound of Dusk's keys hitting the floor.

My back slammed against the wall, hand fumbling desperately for the door handle that I couldn't find. I flinched, breath catching, but with an almighty clang of metal, Ransom came to a jarring stop, his face inches from mine. His wrists were suspended by chains in the air on either side of him.

A growl ripped from his throat, and he threw his weight against his bindings. I flattened myself against the wall further.

I was shaking.

What the hell is going on?

The iron around his wrists *had* to be made of the metal that could contain an alpha's strength—otherwise, he'd be free by now. But it was rare and expensive.

Low rumbles rolled up his chest with each deep exhale, and his eyes, a shade of deep, forest green, were wild.

A thousand fears crowded my mind. Memories of Tom when he'd caught my scent. The way the light had died from his eyes. The fury in them as he'd leaped at me.

It was happening again.

I glanced to the side and realised the door was to my right.

I jumped violently once more as Ransom fought his chains to get to me, but his wrists wouldn't budge, and this time, a low, strangled whine tore from his chest. He looked as if every breath was killing him. I examined him, trying to calm my breathing.

I took him in, truly, for the first time. Messy dark red waves of hair reached his shoulders, and his olive skin was clear and smooth over the angles of his lean face. He had a strong jaw and a straight nose, and his expression was twisted into a snarl.

Not angry or hateful at all.

Pain.

That wasn't what I'd expected…

That wasn't what Tom had been like. He hadn't been in pain. He'd been wild with fury and disgust, as if my mere existence was a threat.

But Ransom was chained in here—Dusk must have done that.

Oh.

"You're…" My whisper was rough as I realised what I was looking at.

He was *feral*? An alpha ruled by nothing but base instincts. It was rare these days, but I'd read everything there was to read on Arkology—on the history of alphas and omegas.

He hadn't spoken yet, and I didn't know if he would. Following a wild impulse, I lifted my hand and dared to press it to his cheek gently. He shifted, his whole body loosening as he leaned into my touch, eyes closing.

Okay. Maybe he didn't want to kill me after all.

Our scents tangled in the air, saturated with fear and frenzy, but now… his was changing. As in, right at this moment, he was becoming more present. More dominant. When he opened his eyes again, his pupils were so wide there was almost no green left.

This time, the growl in his chest sent goosebumps across my skin, and my chest became tight. With each inhale of the wild hormones in the air, my own—on edge and frayed as they were—began to tumble out of control. A familiar wave of blistering heat swept through my body.

Oh, bother.

Heat?

Again?

It couldn't be. That was ridiculous—my last was *yesterday.*

Is that even fucking possible?

For me and my stupid-ass heats?

Yes.

And I'd been burning through too many omega instincts with Umbra and Dusk when bundling them both into cocoons and saving them from rabid auras. Then Flynn and his stupid mate-scent. Add to that the alpha before me, with lust now literally seeping from his pores…

Fuck.

But my mates were close. Could I leave right now and get to them in time?

I felt a sharp cramp in my stomach and loosed a low whine. Ransom went absolutely still at the sound, his eyes boring into mine. Slick was already leaking down my thighs, and he let out a rumbling breath. He knew.

Flynn was long gone. *What are you going to do, Shatter? Crawl out into the hallway and hope no other alpha finds you before you can get to them?*

Wait.

My eyes had fallen to his left wrist, above where the cuff was fixed.

Were those my *scrunchies*?

Dusk has been giving him my scent?

And Ransom didn't *seem* to want to kill me. He was staring at me like he *wanted* me, his whole body tense against the chains that held him. His chest heaved, pupils dark and blown wide in the dim room. More than Flynn's had been.

Another wave of heat rolled through my blood, setting my pulse pounding. He was here and broken and… I thought I could fix him.

But my mates… *dammit.*

I couldn't keep fucking other alphas. Plus, this one was kind of on me.

I rapped my knuckles against each other anxiously, losing a battle against another little whine.

What's one more dick, really—in the grand scheme of things?

At the sound, he growled, chains clinking as he threw himself against them once more.

Fuck.

The sound struck me to the core, and I whined again, reaching up with both hands and taking his cheeks between them—so refreshingly cool beside my warm skin. I was panting, feeling the mass murder of brain cells as the tide of heat flooded my brain.

I was so fucking warm.

And he was the sexiest man I'd ever seen. He didn't even look real. Like some kind of fae-vampire-rockstar forged in the depths of an alpha hormone volcano.

The low rumble in his chest told me he wanted to give me everything my body was screaming for.

I wanted him.

Needed him.

So, I took a breath and stepped forward.

CHAPTER 3

Shatter

It was as frightening as it was freeing, stepping into Ransom's arms.

I didn't quite know what to expect.

His grip crushed my waist the moment I was within reach, and he dragged me against him. I reacted, hormones taking over as I wrapped my arms around his neck, dragging my body against his.

The cramps were duller, even from this brief touch. His breath was hot against my neck as he growled, low and desperate, then his teeth grazed my neck. I froze for a moment, panic setting in. But he wasn't pack lead. If he bit me, nothing would happen. He seemed just to want the feel of my skin beneath his teeth, because then he drew back and crossed the room, lowering us both to the bed.

This was more control than I'd expected so far—but it didn't last long.

All I knew was his touch. He pinned me down, grappling for my dress, aura out—wavering and unstable. I should be frightened, but I wasn't scared of him. We were in sync right now.

I trusted that.

The dress and panties were gone in a moment, torn away, and I arched toward him with a breath, needing him to fix the way my body burned. He had his own sweatpants removed in seconds, and he didn't wait, grip absolute on my waist as he lifted my hips and drove into me.

The desperate sound I made pushed him over the edge. Any lingering presence died, and he caged me in, breaths rough as he rutted me into the sheets.

I let go to Ransom like I'd let go to Umbra. It was easy, with the surge of heat burning through my body. Somehow, despite everything, in the face of Ransom, it all melted away. Even my mates.

The uncomfortable cramps in my stomach faded, and instead, each stroke cooled me like icy clouds sweeping past my skin.

It didn't matter how wrong this was. I lost myself to him—to his rut.

He was all I knew, and his scent shifted again in the room, to petals unfurling beneath the sun.

I was doing that.

His omega.

That thought sank its claws in, bringing with it bliss. He was everywhere, taking me how he needed, every strong thrust keeping my heat sated. He had my scent, and he wanted me still, giving me what my body craved. His hands, his mouth, his cock, his body crushed against mine as I clutched him, lost for words and breath.

Sometimes he would knot me, and my heat would stay at bay for a while. There was slick and cum dripping down my thighs, and whenever he stopped or slowed, I felt the heat returning.

This was what heat could be like?

When it wasn't kept at bay between goosebumps and sweat as my body battled with the temperature of a huge fridge, cramps cycling in vicious waves.

Consciousness drifted in and out, more sharply whenever he stopped.

A low whimper slipped from my chest, and I raised my hips to him. My aches loosened as I settled into position, sure it would be enough. He'd just finished, but I still needed more. I pressed my cheek to the blanket, tilting my head so I could look up at him, letting out a little whine.

I needed him *now.*

He was taking too long.

I heard his purr of approval as I arched my back further, adjusting my hips. I loved his purr. It eased my impatience as butterflies swam through the heat swamp in my tummy, making me giddy. I smiled as his thumb pressed into me, working me while he gripped his cock. His dark eyes were a storm of lust as I shifted back against his thumb, desperate for more.

I whined again, demanding him now. My desperation flipped a switch. He fisted my hair, crushing me against the bed, and—

"Mmm…"

I moaned contentedly once more as he stretched me out, grip bruising as he dragged my body over his length.

I fell again into the blissful throes of heat.

Dust

I woke up in a soft cocoon of deadly nightshade.

A purr rumbled to life before I could catch it, relief searing my system like a hot iron.

Umbra was alive. I could feel him in the bond. Happy. *Really* fucking happy, which not only meant Shatter had got to him—she hadn't left.

And *I* was alive.

And… *shit.* Ransom was there. Awake in the bond.

A huge ball of… *Woah!*

I sat up, rubbing my eyes and tumbling from a nest of blankets and cushions and right onto the kitchen floor.

That felt like a rut.

Ransom had never rutted while feral.

What was he rutting, though?

Still, he was here. Present. So I didn't care if a few pillows made noble sacrifices.

I was on my feet in a moment, scrambling to the stairs and taking them by twos. I reached his door, then froze. Instead of bursting in, I opened it just a crack. Then nearly choked on nightshade heat hormones.

How in the fuck…?

She'd gone into heat *yesterday.* Those pills were legit.

She *couldn't* be in it again.

But my nose didn't deceive me, nor did the instant bulge in my pants as I squinted to see what was going on within.

I could tell it was afternoon by the way the light was filtering through Ransom's windows, which meant I'd been out a long time.

I rubbed my eyes to focus on what was before me.

Sure enough, Shatter was in there with him. *Completely* unharmed as she knelt at his bedside.

Dear lord, she was cute. She was wearing one of his tops and no bottoms. Lace beneath? Or nothing? I wanted to go in and find out, but I controlled myself, needing to watch a little longer.

"We've gotta get them on you," she was saying. I frowned, then realised she was trying to tug sweatpants over his foot. "See if covering your dick up will help."

I had to press my hand to my mouth to stifle my snort.

"You can't just keep fucking me," she told him seriously. "I gotta get us food, or we're going to faint."

She was still in heat, though her hormones weren't out of control. She'd clearly passed the peak of it and had enough lucidity now that survival trumped mindless sex.

Ransom, it seemed, wasn't on board as she tried to feed his foot through the sweatpants. His fist closed in her hair, and she let out a little breath of surprise as he dragged her lips to his cock. Nightshade spiked with lust again, and she dropped the sweatpants, fingers curling around his calf as she relaxed, eyes crossing as she looked up at him. Little moans of pleasure sounded from her as he fucked her ruthlessly, barely letting her get space to breathe.

God *damn.*

When he'd finished, she gasped for air, cheeks bright pink as she fumbled for the sweatpants again.

"Okay. Now I'm putting them on, and then you can let me go for a few minutes."

I watched as she tugged the sweatpants all the way on, fighting with him when he tried to stop her.

Then she got to her feet, tucking a wild strand of her bushy hair behind her ear and catching her breath.

"Okay. I'll be back. I promise. With snacks. And I have to make sure the others are… are okay. And then we'll—"

She let out a gasp as he dragged her onto his lap, grinding up against her. "Oh… fuuckk." Her moan was breathy as she grabbed him for support. "Okay—Mmm." He'd grabbed her hair and arched her against him, then caught her nipple in his teeth. I could hear his purr of satisfaction as she melted against him.

Then she stiffened as he tried to tug the shirt from her.

"No!" Her voice was strained. But Ransom was already fumbling for his own sweatpants, a frown on his face, as if he didn't know why they were there. "No, no, no. Not again. I want food," she whined.

That tone didn't do her any favours. He dragged her closer, his grip on her shirt more insistent.

How many times had she tried to get away?

"Ransom!"

Oh. I'd never heard her voice *so* demanding, and her hand had snapped to his neck. He paused, chest heaving as he stared at her.

"Let go," she ordered him.

I grinned.

Slowly, she pried his hand from her shirt, then she pinned him down on the bed, hand still closed around his neck. "I'm going to fuck you," she told him. "If you stay here, right like this. Okay?"

He didn't reply, just watching her curiously. He still wasn't *truly* present, but he was there. Alive. With us. A big ball of feelings—even if those feelings were mostly lust right now. And pride. And happiness.

Slowly, she slid from above him. He shifted, but she jabbed a finger firmly in his direction. "Stay!"

His nose wrinkled, but he remained in place. She nodded to herself, taking a breath before padding across the hardwood like a teenager trying to sneak away for a party.

Then she froze, her eyes locking with mine. "Dusk?" she squeaked. "How long have you been there?"

Ransom was on his feet in a moment, chains clinking as he crossed to her.

What was he—? *Oh.*

He swept her behind him, eyes predatory as he took me in.

Protecting her?

Well… this just got better and better.

"It's okay," she whispered to him, her arms winding around his waist. He turned back to her, and I'd never seen passion in his eyes like I did in that moment.

Ransom's eyes slid back to me. Finally, there was something calculating in his gaze, like he was analysing me properly now.

Did he recognise me?

I didn't know. Not yet.

I folded my arms, nudging the door open further and leaning against the frame. No need to rile him up. This was already amazing.

"You like him," I said to her with a grin.

She'd stayed.

She'd saved us, and now…

Damn… she'd just banged Ransom through a heat—which *still* didn't even make sense, but I'd deal with that later.

"He seemed like he could use some… help?" she said weakly. "I went into heat. I didn't know where your pills were."

"You *like* him."

Ha.

He wasn't her mate. And she *did* fucking well like him.

Her fingers dug into the muscle of his torso, and she looked defensive. "So what?" There truly was something bratty in her voice. "*He* didn't force his dick down my throat the first time I met him."

Uh… that was such a lie?

The only thing that distanced me from Ransom was heat hormones. She looked so well fucked, she was glowing. But I drew up as I saw Ransom had gone stiff, eyes wide as he stared at me.

Had he… understood that?

"Say that again," I said.

"What?" Shatter asked. "You want me to lie to him? Tell him you asked nicely instead of blackmailing me and drugging me and—"

She cut off as Ransom took a step forward, pulling from her touch, lips drawn in a hateful expression as his gaze locked on me.

He… understood?

My heart soared, a grin spreading across my face for half a second, and then it froze as Ransom's low snarl vibrated through the room, an echo of unadulterated violence.

Ah.

Shit.

He understood.

CHAPTER 4

Umbra

So.

Banana splits were a *whole* thing. Like. Really, really important.

"Banana splits were what you ate when a family got back together."

That was what someone had said once—I didn't know who, but the words stuck, even when the memory didn't.

Anyway, problem was, we weren't *quite* there yet.

Earlier, I'd woken up feeling far more refreshed than I had any right to, given the last thing I remembered. But I'd been wrapped in an omega poison burrito with a pretty bite on my neck.

Her bite.

A connection with Shatter.

And Ransom was awake. And they were fucking.

Obviously.

Puzzle piece A: rutting. Puzzle piece B: heat.

I hadn't even needed to open his door to know, though I listened for a while because, fuck me, those were some *hot* sounds.

But that was his first time with her, and I needed to go and get us Indigo Berry Blast smoothies from a shop down the street. (They were, I decided, halfway to banana splits). A good compromise, since Ransom was still a bit feral, and Shatter still had her scent matches that she was all possessive about. So, we really needed a halfway point.

I'd had to step over a Dusk-omega-rollup on the way out, which meant she'd even softened to him. *And* I had a bandage on my wrist held together by sellotape and hair clips, so we were in *really* good shape.

Except, when I returned, tray of half-patched-family smoothies in hand, it was to find the apartment in a state of war.

It looked as if a bomb had gone off, and, in the midst of it, there was a colossal alpha brawl like no other.

Debris littered the kitchen island and couches. The balcony was basically gone, splintered wood all that remained, and the TV was cracked and hanging half off the wall, like someone had been thrown into it.

Ransom and Dusk were absolutely off the walls right now—and I didn't find Shatter cowering in a corner as two alphas brawled across our apartment.

No.

When I walked in, Shatter was joining in—or trying to, bless. Right now, she was wrapped around Dusk from behind as he backed up against the couch. Her fingers were woven through his hair, dragging his neck into an arch as Ransom sent a fist flying into his face.

Her hormones were thick in the air, and she was in a heat rage. I hadn't even really known that was a thing—but I was definitely looking at it. I could feel it through our special bond. Lust and rage. She was wielding nightshade like furious wildfire in the air.

She sure might act all small, fragile and cute, but Shatter was unbreakable.

I placed the tray in the fridge, since they wouldn't be having theirs all that soon by the look of it, then returned my attention to the scene.

"I said," Shatter snarled, "don't hurt him!"

"*He's* attacking *me!*" Dusk tried to duck another blow from Ransom's fist while also shielding Shatter.

"You deserve it!"

Ransom was in full alpha fury right now, muscles taut, face contorted in viciousness as he launched for Dusk again. Dusk, who'd just managed to shake off Shatter and drop her on the opposite side of the couch, darted in the other direction.

"Come on, mate," Dusk was saying, though there was a hint of humour in his voice. "You should go back to banging her."

Ransom rolled his shoulders, then pounced.

Definitely still in a rut. Just now, he wasn't fucking it out of his system.

I scratched my head, then winced. There was a tender lump the size of an egg on it—though none of my memories quite explained that injury.

Strange…

I brushed it off, focusing again on the fight.

The question was, *how* was Ransom in the living room? There were still cuffs on his wrists.

Odd, really.

Philosophy class would tell me that, rather than asking *how* he got free, instead ask *why* he got free.

Hmm.

No. It didn't fit, actually. The answer was pretty obvious: to beat Dusk into a pulp.

Not quite philosophy-level questions.

It *was* strange that he was out here while fully chained. Dusk had installed metal strong enough to withstand alpha auras. Though, now I was thinking about it, it wasn't as reliable as those alpha hooks that could be buried deep in the ground. This one had to be attached to the walls. I mean, in *theory*—

Aaahhhh.

I saw it now.

That *was* the wall of Ransom's room that made up the pile of debris across the living room.

I sipped on my smoothie. "Heh."

Ransom's chains, tangled like a dog's leash across the couch, kitchen island, and bannister, jammed again as he reached for Dusk. Someone should probably take them off him. Bit of a task, really, since he looked ready to kill.

Only, then I felt his aura wane, and he sagged.

He crashed to his knees, a low whine in his chest. Dusk reacted instantly, diving for Ransom and pinning him to the ground.

Shatter hissed, scrambling toward them, her fists around Dusk's neck as she tried to wrench him off.

"Get *off* him."

"Shatter," Dusk snarled. "He's going to fucking hurt you if you're not—"

Ransom's trembling growl ripped across the whole room, and he threw his weight against Dusk, eyes wild. His aura was still waning, though, so nothing happened.

Oh, wow.

Had he *understood* Dusk?

Shatter gave up trying to drag him from Ransom, instead scrambling to her feet and making for the kitchen. She hesitated for only a moment, fist around a knife handle as her eyes met mine.

Indigo Berry Blast burst to life on my taste buds as I offered her a wide grin. She paused only a moment longer, then seized the knife and darted away.

She liked knives, which was cute. She had a small switchblade she carried around in her school bag all the time. Dusk had found it the first time he'd gone scrunchie searching, and she'd had a fit at the suggestion we make her take it out.

"Let go of him." She shoved the knife against his throat. I cocked my head, erection raging as Dusk froze.

"What would your mates say if they could see you now, Gem?" he asked, voice a taunt, seeming rather unfazed considering there was a blade to his throat.

What I wouldn't give to trade places with him right now. My eyes snagged on the way her delicate fingers locked in his hair. So demanding…

"He's *mine*," she hissed. "I'm taking him to my nest."

Wait.

Ransom got an invite to her nest that quickly—after everything I'd done to get one?

That was all it took?

I was crossing the room in an instant and sitting on the ottoman beside them. "Nightshade." I tucked a lock of hair behind her ear, and her eyes darted to me defensively for a moment. "You should have just asked. I'd have done this for you on day one."

Honestly.

I sighed.

I'd beat the shit out of Dusk for free.

She stared at me for a moment, then glanced back to Dusk. "Move!"

"All right," Dusk conceded.

Slowly, she lowered the knife, climbing from his back. She watched him cautiously as he got up, a flicker of worry in her eyes as she dropped her gaze to Ransom, who was now curled up and heaving ragged breaths.

That drew me up. It was worry in her eyes. Genuine worry. It was flooding down the little omega bond we had, too, weak as it was.

For… Ransom?

I mean, he'd be fine. His aura got way more unstable than this, but she didn't know that.

The world shifted in that moment, and I might have caught the same from Dusk down the pack bond as we both watched her.

Something about her changed, her scent becoming something I'd never felt. Protective. Seductive.

So *very* omega.

I'd do anything she asked right now. I'd get on my knees and kiss her cute little toes, if that's what she wanted.

"Carry him to my nest," she said.

I was on my feet in a moment. "I'll do it," I offered, especially now I knew more nest invites were on the table.

"NO!" Her voice was shrill. "You"—she jabbed the knife in Dusk's direction—"will carry him, or I won't fix him."

I grinned. She just wanted an excuse to tell him what to do, I knew it. Also—such a little liar. Of course she'd fix him.

Dusk cocked his head, considering her for a long moment. Then, without argument, he went to the drawer and dug out Ransom's cuff keys. When he'd freed Ransom's wrists, he leaned down and dragged him to unsteady feet. Shatter hurried after them, trying to stifle her shock as Dusk began hauling Ransom down the hallway.

And she had no idea that she'd just witnessed something we'd been dreaming of for months.

"Food and… and tea," I heard her mutter once we got to the door of her nest.

"Tea?" Dusk asked, turning to her.

"Y-yes." She cleared her throat, lifting the knife again. "We need food and tea. H-he needs taking care of."

"Okay."

She glanced at me as Dusk failed to argue, as if she couldn't understand. Then I saw a little flicker of boldness in her eyes, and she flipped from nervous to brat, hedging her bets in an instant.

"Green tea. Marmalade on toast."

Dusk raised an eyebrow, a half-smile on his lips. "What?"

She narrowed her eyes, a snarl returning to her lips. "Green tea and marmalade on toast."

His grin was white teeth and crimson blood. "We don't have marmalade."

"Then fucking get some."

I was smiling like an idiot as Dusk got Ransom to the bed.

Indigo Berry Blast, turned out, was the perfect flavour for this.

Half-patched.

This *was* my family. She completed it.

"You're so fucking perfect, Shatter," Dusk murmured, drawing her close once Ransom was settled. She narrowed her eyes, fist squeezing the knife, even if it was down at her side. "Our sweet omega brat with so many things for me to punish."

I saw her shiver.

Ransom's growl rose in the air, but Dusk was already letting her go

"Just getting her ready for you, mate."

Ransom lunged for Dusk, but Shatter intercepted—which was good, because he could barely hold himself up. She turned on Dusk. "Get. Out!"

Dusk raised his hands in defeat.

Her scent had changed again. Not just soothing, but absolutely full of lust. I noticed how hot her cheeks were as she set the knife aside and began grabbing pillows from the bed to tuck around Ransom. He was still breathing heavily, and she paused to place her hand on his cheek. He relaxed, leaning into her touch.

Through the bond, I felt him surface—a flicker of something human clawing its way from his soul to reach for her.

I smiled.

I could watch this forever, but then I sipped again, only to hear the loud slurping sounds of my straw reaching the end of my drink. She spun, fire blazing in her eyes as she took me in, smoothie still in my fist.

Only mildly sad that the drink—and show—was over, I backed out after Dusk. I had to let her get to work. She was taking care of our pack mate in her nest, after all.

"Where are you going?" I asked as Dusk searched the apartment for keys before grabbing his spare set.

"To the store to get her knock-off jam. And don't"—he jammed a finger at me, looking entirely insane with a huge bruise blossoming across half his face—"even think about burning her toast. She gets my toast, or none at all."

The door slammed, but through the bond, I felt nothing from Dusk but pure joy.

CHAPTER 5

Shatter

This was just temporary. I kept telling myself that.

This pack wasn't mine, but Ransom needed me. For the first time, I felt like myself. A proper omega. As if this was something I could do.

Something I was *made* for.

I followed my instincts, for once never worried about if I was doing it right. I didn't worry about who I was or had been, or if I was too broken to fix someone else.

I wasn't.

I *was* an omega, and this was mine.

Ransom was coming back to me, tucked in pillows and blankets and curled in my arms.

After a while, I heard a polite knock on the door and dared to leave Ransom's side long enough to answer it, unsure of what to expect.

It was Dusk. He was holding a tray with steaming tea and a stack of toast. Beside it was a knife and a pot of marmalade.

I stared at it for an age, eyes catching on one thing in particular.

A teapot…? That hadn't been in their kitchen before.

Heightened omega instincts sent stars to my eyes as I fixated on it. It was beautiful, painted with a scattering of rhombuses and diamonds that almost had me snatching it from the tray and burrowing under the covers with it.

Oh *boy*, did I need to shed some hormones. Especially since Dusk was paying close attention to my reaction.

"Umbra went out to get it?" I asked, much too hopefully.

"Umbra's been watching *Breaking Bad* since you came in here," Dusk said mildly.

Oh.

My heart sank, but I felt a giddy little thrill at the same time.

Dusk had fetched me tea *and* a teapot?

That shouldn't make me pleased. I hated him, still. Even when those dark eyes of his bore right into my soul, and brainless butterflies lifted in my stomach every time he looked at me like that.

"Do you want me to bring it in?" he asked, peering into my nest.

I seized the tray from him. "No."

He grinned, and I almost stepped back, but something halted me. I blinked down at the teapot, a question trapped in my throat.

"Is Umbra okay?" I asked, suddenly guilty. He'd left earlier with Dusk. But he'd been so unwell…

"He'd say yes, but I could send him with the next tray?"

I chewed on my lip and nodded. "Best I look him over. Just to be sure…"

The smile that played on Dusk's lips made me want to kick him.

"And, just so we're clear, the answer is no," he said, leaning against the door frame, arrogance across every inch of his face.

"No, what?"

"No, me bringing tea and orange jam doesn't mean you haven't still got a punishment coming."

My gaze snapped to him, and I knew heat was crawling up my cheeks. My nest was saturated with arousal right now, which explained the wetness between my thighs as he said those words.

I stepped back before I could say anything that would get me in deeper water with him, then slammed the door in his face.

I hurried back to the bedside where Ransom was stirring, tray clutched in my grip. All my worries of Dusk slid away as Ransom's glittering green eyes found me in the dark.

He was awake and more present than I'd seen him yet.

I set the tray down on the side table and crawled over to him. Ransom wasn't my mate, but he was sweet and caring and sort of *mine.* He'd even protected me from Dusk.

It was my job right now to balance him, and mates simply had nothing to do with it. It was just what a good omega would do. I was doing my best—I'd even tied his hair in a bun with one of the scrunchies, since it was a bit tangled. But he didn't seem ready yet for me to tackle that properly. He was much more interested in holding me closer. Or sex.

Sure, a pack as rich as this could pay omegas to fall all over Ransom to keep him well—I whined at the thought, dragging him close—but I *could* be as good as any of them.

The spark in Ransom's eyes was fading, though. He wasn't all back, and even as I watched, his focus drifted, the muscles in his jaw tensing.

Dammit.

I needed to do better.

So, I sat him up and fed him my favourite snack (though he refused the tea) and purred for him until he settled once more, and then I drifted off in his arms.

Umbra

Despite my disgust at the mere idea of it, Dusk forced me to discuss what happened. And not the nice Shatter-in-heat shit, either. He wanted to chat *feelings* and all the negative shit.

"You nearly died." Dusk leaned back on the couch, pausing *Breaking Bad,* and rubbed his face.

I glanced down at the bandages around my wrist, clenching my jaw. "I don't know what happened. I think I—"

"It wasn't you," Dusk said.

Usually, talking about the Lincoln pack would drag me into memories. My imbalance—my curse—surfacing. I tensed, ready to disengage, but Shatter's lingering bite was like a fortress, walling me in and keeping those demons out.

I stared at Dusk. It *hadn't* been me?

But I'd been sure…

"How do you know?"

"Flynn touched me, and the whole bond began to collapse," Dusk said.

I froze. *What in the fuck did that mean?*

I didn't like it at all.

"I'm done with these stupid games," I growled. "We—"

"Ransom's getting better," Dusk said. "And we *still* don't know enough."

I grit my teeth as he echoed Decebal and his stupid, rational advice.

"You can't kill them until you know what they've taken."

Fuck him.

And Dusk always listened. Decebal didn't know what it was like. Having your living, breathing demons walk the same halls, un-fucking-punished for destroying everyone you loved.

I didn't care if killing them killed me. I *didn't* care. Yet still, I was trapped. If I died and our pack fragmented, Ransom might die. It was why we'd bonded him in the first place. To save him.

"If they were gone, she would be free," I growled.

Dusk tensed, a tic to his jaw. "I won't have this conversation—I won't risk it. She saved you, as well as him. She stayed when she could have left. That changes everything."

I felt a flicker of uncertainty. My aura was a shadowed threat I could never escape—and despite Dusk's determination, I knew we might never fix it. It might keep dragging me down and down until I never came back.

It almost had yesterday.

And yet, Shatter was a parting in the clouds—a light we'd never seen before. And I didn't know what to do with it.

"She's still hung up on them. But maybe, after this—"

"What she did for Ransom won't change anything for her," I said.

He cocked his head, curious at my confidence. The bond she'd left on my neck connected us, even temporarily. I could feel all her wild little omega feelings.

She felt safe here. She… damn, I think she might really… I swallowed. I think she honestly might love us. That hadn't happened overnight, and still, she was set on getting to her mates.

"There's something she's not saying," I said.

"How do you know?"

I shrugged. "I don't care what anyone says. *We* are everything she's looking for. If she hasn't let go of them yet, there's more to it."

Dusk said nothing to that, leaning back on the couch and tugging out his phone. Likely to update Decebal with everything he'd learned about her in the last few days.

He was desperate to learn where she'd come from. It could help, perhaps, but I wasn't convinced. Dusk had to know everything, and that need drove him.

For the second marmalade and toast delivery, Dusk bundled the tray into my hands and shoved me to her nest door. It was late—like super late—though I didn't think they were actively fucking right now. Dusk was confused about her heat, but I was quite clear on the matter: just like everything about Shatter, her heat wasn't behaving the way it should.

"She'll let you in," he said.

Would she?

But Dusk was already knocking and cracking it open. We both paused when we heard her voice cut off.

What I found within was the most precious thing I'd ever seen. She was curled up on Ransom's lap in the bed as she read from an Arkology textbook. It was extra sweet because, as far as I knew, Ransom still hadn't spoken a word. They both looked up at me.

"Umbra?"

"Yeah." I glanced down at the tray in my hand. More marmalade and green tea. Dusk had chopped up some apples to add, too.

"Do you need to stay?" she asked. "Are you stable?"

I palmed my neck, but Dusk answered for me.

"No," he told her, shoving me into the room.

I snorted. Stupid answer.

I was *never* stable.

Still, I didn't feel bad, because then she was lifting the covers in invitation and my worry vanished.

I crossed toward her and set the tray on the bedside table. I sat at her side, drawing her close and ignoring Ransom's little growl. I grinned. He'd have to get used to sharing sooner or later. And he was looking good, even if he hadn't said anything yet. His deep red hair was a shaggy mess, but his green eyes were bright and full of life. I couldn't believe he was back with us and out of chains.

I was getting my brother back.

He settled well enough when Shatter set the book down and took my arm—the one with the bandage—for examination. It was healing fast, but the cut had been deep.

"Is it doing okay?" she asked.

I nodded. Her bandaging skills needed work. I'd taken a photo so that, when Dusk replaced it for me, he was able to copy all the outer layers exactly as they had been—hair clip included—so she'd never know we'd touched it.

Seemingly satisfied, she patted it, then glanced to the tray I'd brought.

Right. Nesting alpha was my job tonight.

I passed it over, and she set it on her lap, smiling as she lifted one of the pieces of toast to Ransom. He took a bite without question, eyes drifting around the room.

"He doesn't seem to like the tea," she said sadly.

I cleared my throat, picking up the second mug for myself. Shatter cupped her own mug to her chest, watching for my reaction. I forced a smile as I tasted it, which was enough to make her beam.

A post-heat omega picnic?

This was better than I could have expected, even if the tea tasted like musty asshole.

When we were done, I was expecting her to tell me to leave. Instead, she settled beneath the covers, adjusting Ransom's arm around her waist before looking up at me expectantly.

Excellent.

I wrapped my arms around her, feeling the rumble of Ransom's growl as my arms brushed his chest. I couldn't help my chuckle. I could feel him waning in and out of the bond. He was confused right now, a collision of protection and happiness, as if he knew who I was, deep down.

I huddled closer. "You saved me, Little Nightshade," I breathed in her ear. She melted into my arms because, well, how could she not?

Oddly, her heat seemed mostly over, judging by the hormones in the air. "Where did your heat go?" I asked.

"My heats… they…" She cleared her throat. "They do their own thing."

"What does that mean?"

"Well… it's short. And instead of it being like… every few months or whatever, they just come when things are… intense."

"Intense?" I pondered on that, but she ducked her head, wriggling back against Ransom, who was happy to tug her further into his arms. "Like…?" Oh.

Oh.

"When you're all turned on?" I asked.

A grin spread on my face. I could feel my chest puffing up as she glared up at me. I'd put her into heat all by myself.

"Not just… *that.* If I'm stressed or like… doing too many omega things."

"Uh-huh?"

Boy, would that be a problem once she was in our pack.

Well. Not a problem for me. But if she wanted to go and be all professional, and work on her studies like she loved, *then* it would be. There was no way we weren't going to make her hot *all* the time for us.

Maybe we could work something out. She could work from home when she needed. We could have heats, and she could do her job in between.

There was something so sexy about the idea of my sweet little omega trapped on my knot while she flipped through textbooks and did all of her calculations and smart stuff.

Could I get her glasses? Just… just to see what she'd look like in them. Would she wear them for me?

She could be paid to do amazing stuff—change the world and all that—*and* get fucked *all at the same time.* And I'd feed and water her and make sure she didn't shrivel up and die when she got too lost in her work…

Yup.

The dream.

This was going to be amazing.

I frowned.

Would I make it to see that? If what Dusk said was true about the Lincoln pack—what were my odds, really?

One touch, and I'd almost died. I'd take them with me—no two ways about it—but the thought of death had never been such an inconvenience before.

Now, I *really* wanted to see Shatter in glasses.

Working on Arkology and shit.

There was a rock in my throat.

The thought vanished at her small gasp. I blinked as I realised Ransom was gone. And by gone, I meant he'd sank beneath the blankets and buried his face between her thighs, dragging her hips away from me.

I grabbed the depressing line of thought and tossed it off a cliff. I had better things to focus on. Like Ransom's jealousy, which was definitely working in her favour.

"Ransom!" Her voice was a squeak of surprise, and her cheeks were pink, which made me chuckle, because they'd just had filthy heat sex together.

I closed my hand around her mouth, dragging her back against my chest as Ransom spread her legs further, giving me a fucking beautiful view as he dragged his tongue up along her center and made her shudder.

"Let him treat you," I growled. "You deserve it after you saved us all."

Her moan was a siren's call as Ransom buried his fingers into her. Interest sparked in his gaze as he worked her, taking in every reaction so he could push her to the edge.

He was in love with her already. I could see it by the dazed look in his eyes as he watched her. I could tell from the bundle of feelings that kept surfacing in the bond.

I smiled.

My girl and my pack brother, right here.

CHAPTER 6

Dusk

Shatter might have been surprised when I turned up at her nest door with tea and toast the first time, but she was still failing to understand one crucial thing—she was ours.

I would get her anything she wanted. And today was proof that my choice was the right one.

Ransom had been to clinic after clinic, to dozens of omegas, and even experienced beta Sweethearts. We'd tried every drug known to science for alpha instability. Nothing had ever healed him.

Until her.

Now, it was the next evening, and I slipped into her nest. The lights were dim, bathing the rich browns of hardwood floors and the broad desk, side tables, and bedframe in a warm light. There were two slumbering figures on the bed.

I'd met with Bolin, our appointed support, today. He'd sat down to catch me up on the curriculum, as I'd claimed a heat break for the pack. There was no other way we would be allowed to stay on, Kingsman name or not.

I'd also booked repairs on the apartment, which I hoped would be done before Shatter finished balancing Ransom. I would allow nothing to interrupt that, however, when we were on the precipice of getting him back. So, they were only allowed in for repairs during the day, when either Umbra or I were present to make sure no one went *near* her nest.

Right now, our apartment was stranger-free, and since Umbra had stayed the night with her and Ransom, visiting her nest was all I'd dreamed about. She was no longer in full heat—Umbra had caught me up on the details—and Ransom's rut seemed mostly over. I settled onto the bed beside Shatter, careful not to disturb either of them.

She was the most beautiful creature I'd ever seen, sleeping beside Ransom, her hair draped over golden skin in waves and tangles, splayed around her in a crescent moon as she hugged his arm to her chest. She was protective of him, and that alone was the hottest thing I'd ever witnessed. Her expression was peaceful, a stuttering purr bubbling up here and there as her chest rose and fell. She wore his oversized T-shirt, and her legs were bare. The sheets were pushed down around her, as if she hadn't cooled down entirely since her heat had passed.

I'd wanted to check on them, but now I was here, my mind was derailing.

She'd definitely burned down my rulebook—even if she had saved Ransom. I wasn't beneath playing dirty, since she'd leached heat hormones into our entire apartment for days on end, and I hadn't been the one fucking her.

I ran my hand gently along her thigh, lust hitting my veins as she let out a low breath that sounded needy.

Out of heat, but still horny as fuck, clearly.

I caught my lip in my teeth as I dropped my touch between her thighs. Nightshade spiked the air with desire, and she shifted, adjusting to her front a little.

My thumb and pinky ran along the back of her thighs as I pressed my index finger between her legs. She wasn't wearing underwear, and slick glistened on her skin.

I closed my eyes to fight my groan, then curled my finger, finding her entrance too easily and pressing in.

She shifted, grinding against me, a little mewl breaking from her chest.

Damn.

My dick pressed against my jeans so hard it hurt.

Every time she broke the rules and let me punish her, I would prove to her how fucking perfect she was for us. It wouldn't be long before she knew we were better than any other pack the universe had to offer.

I added my forefinger, dipping both into her with care, loving how she squeezed them so tightly.

She shifted again, eyes still shut, stretching one hand out before her and—fuck. Me. She balled a fist into the pillow as she lifted her hips, back arched as she presented for me.

With that, I kissed sanity good-fucking-night.

I pushed the oversized T-shirt up to her shoulders, so I could see her full body on display while I dipped my fingers into her glistening cunt.

I froze as Ransom shifted, hand searching across the sheets until he felt her arm. Lily of the valley calmed as he drew closer. She wiggled her sweet ass, pressing back against my fingers with another needy sound.

I could have come right then.

But Shatter was my fucking ruin, and I was going to wake her on my cock.

I readjusted myself, undoing my jeans and freeing my length, then pressed my tip to her entrance. Her eyes fluttered, her fingers clutching the pillow harder.

I nudged into her just slightly.

It was thrilling, seeing how far I could go without waking her.

Cute eyebrows bunched and her lips parted as my girth stretched her out, but I was only in half an inch. I waited until she relaxed her grip on the pillow before filling her some more.

Fuck, she was tight.

It was so hot, watching her brows bunch up each time I inched deeper, her body shifting slightly as it adjusted to my intrusion.

She was still asleep somehow, and I managed to sink my whole length, right to my knot, without waking her. Again, I fought not to finish.

Instead, I pressed in just the slightest bit further, enjoying the feeling of my swelling knot as it stretched her unsuspecting body just enough that she moaned, long, low, and desperate. Any further, and I'd be locked into her. I didn't want that just yet.

Instead, I drew out, watching her eyelashes flutter again. I did it once more, stretching her over my knot, and she frowned deeper as she tried to adjust to me. I didn't know if her expression showed confusion or need. I rocked into her a few times with the edge of my knot, my blood on fire at her precious whimpers.

I was going to leave her body trembling for my knot before she'd even woken. I swear she was wetter than when I'd started.

Bowing over, I placed my hands on either side of her. Her cheek pressed further into the sheets, fists balling tight as I withdrew one inch at a time. I could feel her pussy seizing me as I pulled out, and a frustrated whine slipped from her chest. Ransom shifted again, starting up a low purr as he listened to her sounds.

I stifled a groan; I'd never felt her as tight as this.

I set a painfully slow pace, watching the shift in her expression each time I buried my length into her heat. Occasionally, she would tense, goosebumps lighting across her flesh, and I would slow until they were gone. I could feel the most primal frustration from her needy body as I kept her on the edge.

It was so fucking hot, and I warred against my own orgasm at the thought that I might be able to fuck her until she came in her sleep.

I *needed* that.

To see her wake, shaking, begging, and disoriented from the bliss I would wring from her body

I groaned as I slid into her again, hitting that spot that made her tense and her pink lips part in a little 'o'. Again, since I'd just pulled her back from the edge of another orgasm, I teased her with my knot. This time, her whine was more desperate as I stretched her pussy over it just enough to feel it, and then drew out. She arched further, breaths short and sharp as she tried to take my knot. Her tight walls squeezed me, desperate for what I was denying her. There was sweat glistening along her skin now, as if the tail end of heat was resurfacing with a vengeance as I denied her.

I would wake her to the most mind-blowing orgasm of her life, and then I'd fuck her some more.

Finally, I could see her nearing the edge again, her chest rising and falling, her eyelids fluttering each time I buried my cock into her—again, I pressed in the slightest bit deeper, letting her know how close my knot was.

And that was enough.

I woke to an orgasm that wiped my mind utterly blank.

The world was nothing but dizzying pleasure. A hand clamped down over my mouth, stifling my moans. I gripped the sheets, bliss soaring through my veins, pussy full of an alpha's cock, stretching me around a knot just the slightest bit before pulling out and driving in again.

I was shaking, cross-eyed, and panting before the world steadied.

Before I realised what was happening.

Before he rode my orgasm out and then kept going and I realised who was pinning me to the bed and fucking me.

Midnight opium filled the air as Ransom slept at my side.

I whimpered, a trembling wreck, but his hand, which was still over my mouth, tightened. "Shh, Gem. If he wakes angry, it'll undo all the hard work you've done."

I couldn't help looking at Ransom sleeping at my side, fear spiking through my veins.

Dusk drew out of me, then slammed back in before leaning close. "If I let go, will you stay quiet?"

I nodded desperately. They'd fight again, I knew that, and Ransom had just started to truly settle.

Dusk's hand dropped from my mouth, and I instantly tried to lunge away. His grip was bruising on my hips as he dragged me mercilessly back onto his shaft. I had to clamp my own hand over my mouth to stifle my yelp as he speared me right to the core.

"You said you wouldn't come in," I hissed.

His voice was low and humorous as he bent over me, stealing the breath from my lungs with another powerful thrust. "You said you'd do as you were told, and instead, I ended up with a knife at my neck." His breath brushed my ear. "You break a rule, I break one too."

I tried to ignore my dizzying, building pleasure as he continued driving into me. He'd got me aroused while I was sleeping, riding my attraction to Ransom.

"You have so much punishment to take," he growled. "I would spank you, but it'd be too loud."

Again, I tried to dive from him, but I barely moved, and the result was him slamming so hard into me I saw stars.

"How about we try something else instead?" he whispered. One hand clamped back over my mouth and his other found my nipple, fingers biting down just hard enough that I let out a muffled squeak. Worse, heat pooled in my stomach again as he flicked the same area he'd just bruised. Then his fingers shifted to my other nipple. I froze this time, his hand pressed over my mouth, tears pricking my eyes. Again, he delivered a shot of pain, and again, my body jolted with pleasure.

Then his touch dropped between my thighs, and he circled my clit. I squeezed my eyes shut, trying to wriggle away, hand still clutching my mouth as I realised what he was going to do.

What I wasn't expecting was the furious orgasm that hit my veins as his fingers bit down on my clit. He did it again, while I was still in the throes of my orgasm, slamming into me with a breath of pleasure.

"You're squeezing me so good, Gem," he purred, keeping up his slow rhythm, fucking me into oblivion.

CHAPTER 7

Dusk

It didn't seem to matter that she knew it was me. Shatter was so turned on. Still, she struggled, even when I felt her body tightening again, readying for her next orgasm.

"Stop fighting, beautiful," I breathed. "You have no idea how special you are."

And just like I'd known they would, those words undid her. A little whimper slipped past the hand I had over her mouth, and her body seized me like a vice as she came apart.

"Do you want my knot, precious?" I asked as I continued pumping into her and drawing out her orgasm.

She hadn't seen what I had, with her eyes squeezed tight shut, that Ransom was waking. I twisted her nipple again, rewarded with her nails scraping down my arm, another desperate moan slipping from her.

"I won't give it unless you ask."

I dropped my hand from her mouth so I could hear her breathless panting. I moved my touch from her nipple to her clit, circling it firmly. Her whole body seized over my length, and she sucked in a sharp breath as I tried for another orgasm so soon after the last had crested. But I knew her body was capable of more before she was spent.

Ransom was staring from me to her, his lips parted, clear confusion in his eyes as he tried to orient himself.

"Let me knot you, Gem. You deserve it, don't you? After what you did for him?"

The sound she made was half feral, but she wasn't fighting me anymore. She was too busy warring with herself for the answer I knew she so desperately wanted to give. I stopped as I sank deep into her, letting my knot stretch out her pussy again, just enough to tease. Her broken moan almost had me losing control and locking myself into her right then, but I held on.

I drew out, and she panted, wriggling back against me, her face screwing up in a frown, as if she didn't understand why she'd done it. She was overwhelmed and confused, with no idea that she was contending with her own body, which had been promised my knot over and over.

I chuckled, removing my hand from her clit, and instead, tangling it through her hair so I could press her into the sheets and make sure she was facing away from Ransom.

He was going to see how I treated our girl, so he could get off that high horse of his.

"Ask for it," I murmured.

Now unable to wiggle back against me, she paused, still panting. Suspended as she was, with just the tip of my cock filling her, she gripped me tight with each rapid breath. Her body was shaking from the last orgasm, and her scent was flooding the air like an aphrodisiac.

Ransom was fully alert now, pupils blown as he watched us. He was tense. I could see that, as if her answer here would seal my fate one way or another.

And I knew what it would be.

I withdrew from her entirely, and her low moan set every one of my instincts on edge, leaving them clawing at me to fix whatever made her so sad. I loved that she could do that to me. I was long broken, but Shatter made me feel like an alpha in a way no other omega could.

There was a pause as I nudged her slick entrance with my tip, and she shuddered. The ragged whisper came at last, almost impossible to hear. "Please."

A smile lit on my face. "Please what, Gem? Say it."

I heard her swallow, and there was another pause. Her golden skin glistened with sweat, lit with goosebumps as she trembled. "Please… knot me."

The rumble in my chest was involuntary as I slammed back in. Her eyes went wide as the breath rushed from her lungs. She was liquid, completely wrecked, as she gave in to me. "My poor little omega," I growled, gripping her hips and driving into her brutally. "Begging me to fill your perfect cunt." For three strokes, I fucked her so deep that she loosed little squeaks, leaving her a scrambling, desperate mess.

I felt stars light in my veins again, and I straightened, dragging her back against me by her neck so she could look Ransom right in the eyes. She let out a breath of shock as she saw him, but it was stifled by her moan as I stretched her fully over my knot.

"You feel so fucking amazing." I needed him to see she loved my praise as much as she liked my punishment. "Show him how beautiful you are when you come apart on my knot." I pinned her to my chest by her neck, and she clutched my forearm as I circled her clit with my other hand, all the while rutting her deep.

She shuddered, body seizing me as she desperately clawed at my arms.

Ransom had heard what she'd said.

"You're ours." A purr rumbled deep in my chest, and she let out another moan, still struggling against me as I rutted her and circled her clit. "Perfect and beautiful and everything we've ever dreamed of."

I thought the sound she made might have been half a sob, but then all thoughts wiped from my mind as she came over my knot, sending me into the throes of my own mind-blowing orgasm.

She curled up when I sagged onto the bed, burying her face in my arms and refusing to look at Ransom, who still watched like a lost puppy. I loved the way she squirmed when my purr rumbled to life again, and with my chest against her back, I knew it must send vibrations all the way down her spine and into her core.

She wasn't done.

We would be locked together for a while. With my purr still the only sound in the air, I dropped my fingers between her thighs and began playing with her some more.

Shatter grabbed the pillow and tugged it against her face, and Ransom looked utterly unsure.

"You made him better, Gem," I breathed in her ear, circling her clit slowly.

She wriggled against me, and I had to bite my lip at how good she felt on my cock.

"You fixed him when no one else could."

Shatter fought to stifle a low moan in her chest.

Locks of dark auburn hair swung past olive skin as Ransom's green eyes remained fixed on her. The look in his eyes broke my heart. I felt what he was feeling. A flash of sorrow for the time he'd lost.

Missing time once more.

And I think he knew he'd missed something huge.

I leaned down, nudging her hair back and tugging the pillow from her grip. I drew her neck into an arch, so she had nowhere else to hide as I sped up on her sensitive clit and pressed my teeth to her neck. Not a proper bite, but it was enough to send her over the edge—because she would deny it to the ends of the earth, but my claim was the one thing she couldn't fight.

Shatter wanted it more than she hated me, and it melted her every time.

"My gift," I breathed as Ransom watched her come apart before his eyes. I fought my groan at how fucking amazing that felt.

Shatter was a gift beyond our wildest dreams. One that might mean he wouldn't lose one more day for what he'd sacrificed.

Ransom swallowed, seeking Shatter's gaze, but she was still pressed against me, eyes squeezed closed.

"I chose her," I told him, letting him feel my conviction.

And in the process, I saved her from a fate worse than death.

She wasn't ready for that truth yet.

Ransom reached out, nudging her chin up until she was looking at him. His eyes scanned hers.

"Do you want to come again?" I asked. She shook her head, still breathing heavily. "For him?" I caught her firm nipple in my fingers, twisting it softly this time, knowing she would be sore from all my punishments. I was rewarded with a beautiful moan.

Even so, Ransom's growl was a warning.

"Sounds like a yes," I murmured, rocking into her slowly. Her nails bit into Ransom's forearm as she scrambled to dignify herself while her body betrayed her once more. "What if he helped, Gem?" I breathed in her ear. "How hard would you squeeze me if he had his tongue down your throat?"

I loved how easy it was to learn her truths with my knot buried deep within her, feeling her body tense up whenever I said *just* the right thing.

I rocked into her again, and the nails digging into Ransom's arms were more insistent. Her eyes were wide, holding his, and there was pleading in them. Not for freedom. No, right now, she wanted to be trapped between us.

"You're going to have to ask him," I breathed in her ear, rocking into her again and cupping her chin in my hands like a gift.

"W-would you kiss me?" she asked. There was something broken and vulnerable in that question.

Ransom was swallowed completely by her gaze, and I knew, in that moment, no one else existed in the world but her.

I drove my knot deeper.

She moaned, and he caved, drawing her into a kiss more gentle and caring than I'd believed Ransom capable of.

Her exhaustion just made the orgasm stronger, and I loved how she trembled against me, her body clenching once more over my cock. I groaned, spilling into her again, and this time, she was so full that I felt some of my cum drip between her thighs, my swollen knot unable to lock it all in.

I rode the orgasm out to its fullest, until she was a trembling puddle in Ransom's arms, and my knot finally released her.

CHAPTER 8

Shatter

Despite the week's events, I wasn't going to fail school for the sake of going into heat and nesting with Ransom—thank *God.*

On Friday morning, Dusk provided me with coursework, and I spent the morning with Ransom's arms around my waist in the nest while I studied.

I was interrupted in the afternoon when Dusk popped his head in, *rudely* ignoring the fact that *I* was ignoring *him,* and told me he wanted Ransom to do a trial night without me.

"The whole night?" I asked, my voice high.

"We have to know if he's stable without you, or we won't know what's going on."

Ransom remained voiceless, and I was trying not to take it as a personal failure. He was gentle and sweet, I just knew it, and he was *in* there. I thought he even understood what I was saying when I talked him through Aura Studies equations.

I fought the pout on my face as Ransom went stiff, drawing me close.

"Will you chain him up again?" I asked.

"No. Umbra will stay overnight with him—with you," Dusk amended, eyes darting to Ransom, and I saw his spark of hope again.

By four in the afternoon, I'd scent marked most of Ransom's room and tucked him in six times, despite the fact it wasn't bedtime (Umbra was setting up video games).

The apartment had been fixed while Ransom and I were down in the nest, and his bedroom had been given life, with couches and a TV and even a few posters across the walls featuring bands I didn't recognise. Not that I knew many musicians, outside of the opera singers Aunty Lauren liked to hum along to.

I'd also given him a bite on the neck in case anything drastic happened, and I had to know right away. I wasn't going to do this by halves. Ransom was getting better, and I'd see it through.

The last I saw before Dusk dragged me away was Ransom's beautiful green eyes fixed on me longingly, a video game controller in his grip as Umbra helped shoo me out.

"Just one night, Little Nightshade," he'd said before shutting the door.

Now, I'd been pulled onto Dusk's lap while he studied. I'd loitered too long in the living room, anxiously incapable of bringing myself to vanish back to the nest.

His hand trailed gently up and down my arm as he hugged me close, flipping through the pages of a Physiological Adaptations Arkology textbook.

Not my favourite, since there weren't many equations involved, and my mind drifted.

Finally, a question nagged at me, twisting my stomach and making itself impossible to ignore. I couldn't help thinking of the blue registration card in my pencil case. The one I carried everywhere I could get away with.

"Ransom, uh… didn't sort out my registration and papers, did he?" I asked quietly, tilting my head and peering up at Dusk. I don't know why that made me want to cry.

"He would have," Dusk murmured without pause, barely glancing away from the textbook, though I noticed a distinct clench to his jaw. "Ransom fights for people with nothing, no matter what it costs him," he said. "I did it because he made me what I am."

"Oh."

Okay.

"So," he said after a pause, "are we going to keep pretending?"

I looked up at him with a frown. There was a slight smile curving his lips as his eyes drifted inattentively across the page. "You begged me for my knot, you bit Umbra, and you went into heat with Ransom—even though there were pills and mates nearby."

"I didn't know where the pills were, and I couldn't get to my mates in time," I said.

His grin widened. "You could have left."

"It wasn't… I *was* going to leave."

"But you *didn't*."

I shrank in his arms, hating that he was saying exactly what I'd been trying not to think about. Especially now that Ransom wasn't a present distraction…

Dusk tilted my chin up, and I found myself swallowed by piercing yellow eyes. "Tell me what I need to do for you to let them go, Shatter. I'll do it."

I blinked, completely lost for words.

"I…" He trailed off, swallowing, and I followed the movement down his throat, suddenly needing any distraction. "I don't know how to tell you the truth without scaring you away."

What truth?

My heart was thundering in my ears.

"Why do you need them?" he asked. "Just tell me so I can fix it."

It wasn't something he could fix.

What I needed from him was impossible: trust that transcended a dark bond. The kind of forever it would be foolish to trust to anyone but mates.

"You've seen us. All of us. You know our secrets, our worst parts, and it's not…" He took a breath. "If it's not enough—"

That word splintered every concern I had. "Enough?"

That's what he thought?

How could Dusk Varis think he wasn't enough?

"That's… not the issue?" He seemed to see the shock on my face.

"I…" I couldn't think straight.

"Please tell me. Let me fix it."

I shook my head, my heart slamming into my ribs. No, no. He had it all wrong. "I'm broken. That's all."

"Who told you that?"

"The whole world," I whispered. "I don't fit."

He breathed a low laugh. "Then I'll break the world until it fits you."

"It's impossible," I told him.

"That's all this pack is—impossible fragments left behind. Just as impossible as you fixing us when no one else could." He cupped my cheek, yellow eyes a storm of momentary hope. "If there's one thing I *can* promise you, Shatter, it's the impossible."

I stared at him, and his promise lodged, like an anchor and chain crashing into the ocean bed, refusing to move; it was as foolish as it was tempting.

I'd never wanted so badly to speak my truth out loud, but I stalled, knowing it wasn't a mistake I could afford to make. If Dusk knew the only bond he could ever offer me was a dark bond, that might push him to it. No matter how much I wanted it not to be true…

"Ransom's going to wake soon, *really* wake. That changes everything. You'll love him, I know it. He'll love you—already does. I can feel it—"

He cut off as I flinched back, panic closing like a fist around my throat.

Dusk's face fell, as if he knew he'd crossed a line. A strange silence passed as I found no words to that, mind racing out of control. After a long moment, he sighed and rubbed his chin.

"Roxy wants to see you," he said quietly, glancing down at his phone on the coffee table.

"Roxy?" My heart lifted slightly at the idea of seeing her. I could really use a friend right now.

"She texted me. Said to let her know when you're free, and classes just finished."

"A study session?"

"Yup."

My hopes tumbled off a cliff, though. "But… Ransom—"

"You bit him. You'll know if there's anything wrong."

That was true. And I really could use a friend this afternoon. "Okay…"

I nodded. *Yes.*

It was a good plan. Everything was a lot right now. I needed some space to catch up and figure out what the hell was going on now the hormones were dying down.

* * *

Roxy met me in our usual study room, arriving with all the Omega Studies course material for the week.

We sifted through it for a while, and she caught me up on the coursework until I wasn't worried anymore. I made mental notes of the chapters I needed to reread to refresh what I'd missed—though I'd devoured the textbooks front to back already.

While we worked, I pondered the *other* thing. I didn't know how I was going to do it, but I had to find a way to talk to her about the Lincoln pack issue. The offer Flynn had made… it affected her.

The only issue was that I didn't know how to go about that without discussing the scent match thing. And if I didn't mention the scent match thing, would she be suspicious of why the Lincoln pack was interested in me?

I mean, it was me. Of course, she would. There was no reason for them to be interested in me outside of that—Eric's comment had made that painfully clear.

But how much could I trust her with?

"I missed you," Roxy said, after I'd finished reading through her notes.

"You did?" I glanced up at her in surprise, a burst of warmth blossoming in my chest at her words.

"Of course."

That sounded like a friendship thing, right? Real friendship...

Not just study partners?

I did like her so much, but I had a bad habit of misreading this kind of thing.

"So..." Roxy prodded. "How was your week?" I spotted something mischievous in her sapphire blue eyes as she looked me up and down. "You look... well."

I bit my lip, cheeks heating up. "It was... good."

Oh, this was confusing. How much was I supposed to say?

"I, uh..."

She giggled, elbowing me. "You don't need to tell."

Did omegas usually talk about things like this? Heats and... pack stuff?

"You're definitely going to take the school by surprise again."

Oh, dear. "What are they saying?" I asked, voice high.

"Okay. People are a little obsessed with your pack, to be honest."

"Tell me." I didn't know why I was asking. If it was bad, I'd just stew on it.

"Well, no one thinks you went to a clinic, since no one saw you leave. So... you had a..." She side-eyed me. "I'm just saying what everyone else is."

"What?"

"So, obviously it was a rut or a heat, and you chose to have it with them. But no bond—still?"

"Oh..." Shit.

Right.

I'd taken a week off school. There was clearly only one thing that could mean.

Being chosen by a pack didn't mean I had to spend heats with them—at least, that was true for omegas to which the rules applied in the first place, which I definitely wasn't.

Damn it.

We studied in silence for a while longer, and she seemed comfortable as I processed that. I couldn't keep track of what all of this meant for my reputation. Was it good or bad?

Was Roxy judging me?

She didn't *seem* to be.

"What would you do if you met your scent matches?" I asked after a while. I needed to find a way to get the conversation where I needed it.

Roxy considered that, a sly smile on her lips. "Why?"

"I don't know. I just... I wanted your opinion."

"Well..." She looked thoughtful, pen tapping her cheek. "I think if I met my scent matches, and they were... rich *and* enamoured with the same studies as me, then I don't see myself holding back." She gave me a meaningful look that was anything but meaningful to my stunned brain.

What?

"You... know?" I stared at her, chest tight.

She let out a giggle at my expression. "Come on, Shatter, it's been clear from the start." She was still smiling, which wasn't right at all.

Clear?

"They are *obsessed* with you."

My brain finally rebooted as I caught up.

The Kingsman pack.

She thought we were talking about the Kingsman pack.

I stared at her, wringing my hands, realising how completely impossible this conversation would always be.

"They built you a nest, and they keep your scent hidden like they own it—a bit possessive for me, but… I don't know." She shrugged. "It's sweet. There aren't many omegas who would have held out this long. What are you worried about?"

"I…" I didn't know why, but tears burned my eyes at her words.

Roxy reached for me. "Oh, babe… okay."

She pulled me into a huge hug, and I clutched her in surprise, still fighting not to actually cry in front of her.

But why was she saying all those nice things about the wrong alpha when I didn't know how to process it? It wasn't her fault. She didn't know—dammit. But this conversation had gone nowhere close to where I needed it.

I was such a mess.

I blinked furiously. My confidence was shot. I had no idea what to say to explain any of it. The hormones were gone, and I felt like I'd fallen into a hole.

A very confusing hole.

And now she was going to see me crying.

What would she think? That I was crying because my scent matches wanted me?

She was so kind and held me so tight. And I hadn't told her about what Flynn had offered me. Or the fact that the alphas who had sponsored her were my mates.

More tears burned my eyes.

When she drew back, I ducked my head, letting my hair fall in front of me like a curtain. I pretended to stare at the textbook.

Get it together.

I took a breath, blinking furiously, but it didn't work. I tried to rub my eyes without her noticing. I froze as I felt my contact crease in my eye.

Fuck.

I was never supposed to rub my eyes—especially not when crying. I didn't. I'd trained myself out of the habit when I'd run from the Estate. But right now, I was such a mess.

"Is this just about them?" Roxy asked me. "Or did something happen?"

She sounded so concerned, but I barely heard in my panic.

I blinked carefully. Desperately.

Flatten.

Please flatten.

Instead, I felt the contact get caught on my eyelash.

"Shatter?"

My fists balled in fear. If I looked at her now, she would see the colour of my eyes.

How could I leave without her seeing? There was no way…

I dared reach up in a last-ditch attempt, hoping I could push it back in and undo this mess.

Of course, at the nudge, it fell.

I watched it tumble from my eye, as if in slow motion, and jerked forward to catch it. But the contacts that hid golden eyes were clear, coated in a sheen that subtly shifted gold to brown. They were almost invisible to spot. One second too late, and it was gone.

My breath caught, and my gaze raked over my skirt, my knees, the floor, which was made of old hardwood, with dozens of cracks it could slip into.

Gone.

My breath caught.

"Shatter?" Roxy sounded worried. "Are you okay?"

I tried to force calm into my voice, but my knuckles were white on the edge of the table. "I have to go," I whispered.

Could I get back to the apartment with no one seeing?

I was still searching my skirt and the floor desperately. Maybe it was caught in the crease of my clothing—

"Babe." I saw her reach out in my peripheral, and then she took my hand, squeezing. "If something happened, you can tell me. I promise—"

I felt the brush of her touch too late as she swept my hair out of the way. I glanced up on pure instinct for a split second before I slammed my eyes shut.

My blood ran cold in the darkness, knowing I'd been too late.

I heard her little inhale of shock.

The sound that meant Roxy knew I was gold pack.

CHAPTER 9

Shatter

"Shatter—" Roxy cut off as I shifted my chair back.

"I have to go."

"No." She grabbed my wrist with a death grip. "Don't move. It… it fell?"

"I…" I swallowed, eyes still firmly shut. "I need to—"

"You aren't going out there like this." I could hear her moving, her fingers brushing my skirt, as if searching.

She was worried *for* me?

But I didn't understand. Why hadn't she said anything else?

"Fuck." Her voice was muffled, like she was under the table.

I dared peek out of one eye to see my assessment was correct; she was on her hands and knees with her phone flashlight on.

"I can… I can never find them once they're gone," I said weakly.

I still didn't understand.

"You have spares?" she asked, backing out and glancing up at me from her knees and poking her head out from under the huge desk. I met her eyes fully now, then panicked again.

But she knew.

She already knew.

"In my bathroom," I whispered. I couldn't carry spares with me. Having those discovered put me at far higher risk than what had just happened.

I wasn't supposed to rub my eyes.

"Tell me where." She got to her feet. "I'll be right back."

"But…"

"Oh my God, Shatter…" She trailed off. "They don't know? Is that why you're upset?"

I stared at her in shock.

I hated lying to her, but I was such a mess that I didn't know what I should say and what I shouldn't. She knew my most dangerous secret already, and she'd barely flinched. She didn't even seem to want not to be my friend anymore…

Roxy sat back down, looking at me in surprise. "Shatter, I don't think you have anything to worry about. They can't keep their eyes away from you when you're around them. I've never seen a pack as obsessed. They're in love with you."

In… *love?*

It rang of what Dusk had said earlier. The word that had already turned me into the disaster I was tonight.

"No, they… they know." I didn't know how to process this. I hated the lies between us more than ever.

"Oh." She looked relieved. "That's… that's good, right? If they don't have a problem with it?"

"I…" I winced, still scrambling between this conversation and the tail end of the terror I felt at being found.

"Are you worried about their reputation?" she asked quietly. "Even if that mattered to them, their name is big enough they don't need to worry about that sort of thing. You… you know that, right?"

I swallowed, feeling another round of tears coming on.

"First, the contacts." She got to her feet. "Tell me where they are."

Once I'd given her the details of where they were, she vanished in a hurry, and I was left in a strange silence. My shoulders were hunched, head ducked down, afraid someone might walk in.

My anxiety was still buzzing.

What just happened?

Maybe this was all a joke, and she'd never come back. Except, I didn't think it was.

I think… *Could* I tell her everything now?

I wanted to.

Even about the Lincoln pack. We could find a solution. I still didn't know what to do with that offer, but Roxy was too important to get hurt because of this mess.

She returned ten minutes later and produced my contacts case from her pocket.

I stared at it for a long, stunned second, something stuck in my throat. She'd actually got it?

I took it from her, glancing up. "He let you in?"

"I told Dusk, and he didn't ask any questions."

"Thank you." My voice was weak. I fumbled to replace the missing one, relief flooding my system as I did. But I waited for her questions, unable to fully dispel my nerves.

How was I going to answer them?

"Are you all right?" she asked.

I blinked, gaze flitting up to her again. Her dark blue eyes were full of concern, rather than judgement.

"I think so."

Kind of. As well as I could be.

There was another heavy silence, and I broke it, too anxious to wait. "I, uh… I have amnesia. I don't remember anything before I was nineteen."

She frowned. "Nothing?"

I shook my head. "So, I, uh…" I trailed off awkwardly.

Becoming gold pack—not turning up for the Institute's injection within a year of perfuming—was a choice. One that most judged harshly. "I don't know why my eyes are gold—"

"You don't owe me an explanation, Shatter."

I bit my lip, suddenly feeling like I was going to cry again.

"It's illegal," I whispered. If I was discovered to be hiding my gold pack status, I could get in a lot of trouble. Would she be in trouble if I got caught and someone found out she knew?

"Well." Roxy cleared her throat. "Last year, when my car broke down, I made seven grand from mailing scent-marked clothing to lonely alphas and betas, and I, uh…" She dropped her voice to a whisper. "I didn't declare a penny of it. So, I guess we're even."

Wait.

What?

That drew me up.

I suppose she *did* have a lovely scent. I didn't think many omegas smelled like Christmas.

"What kind of clothing?" I asked with a frown.

Her smile grew positively devilish, but before she could answer, there was a knock on the door.

I glanced up, heart pounding until I reminded myself that my contacts were secure and present.

When the door opened, I was surprised to see Eric peering in. At his scent of passion fruit, my stomach did an uncomfortable swoop.

"Oh. What's up?" Roxy asked.

"It's ten minutes later than when you said you'd be done," Eric said, frowning. "We don't have much time to study before the party"

"Right," Roxy said, glancing at me. "Actually, I might have to bail—"

"No. That's okay," I said quickly. I didn't want to be the reason Roxy looked bad in front of the Lincoln pack. Not after everything.

"I have… everything I need." I smiled awkwardly at Eric before meeting Roxy's eyes.

"Are you sure?"

"Yeah. Absolutely."

Roxy got to her feet, then looked at me curiously when I didn't join her. "I just… I need some time to figure myself out." I said the last part quietly, so Eric didn't hear.

She nodded. "Just… find me if you need anything else, okay?"

I nodded.

"And I mean *anything*," she whispered as she bent down to pick up her bag.

"Thank you."

After she left, I sat for a long time, trying to untangle everything.

I was so confused.

Was Roxy really the friend I'd dreamed of for so long?

I couldn't quite get my head around it. Even with all the proof, it just seemed too good to be true.

I hugged my bag to my chest, my mind racing through everything that had just happened.

Roxy had said it… that she thought the Kingsman pack wanted me. And it didn't matter how many times I heard what they claimed was the truth, I didn't know how to make it fit with me.

Why *would* Dusk love me as I was?

Umbra and I… I fought the little smile on my lips. Umbra was like me. Different. And for some reason, that was easier to accept.

Ransom… Well, I don't know. He was rich and good-looking, and I was worried about when he woke up properly.

But Dusk was the enigma. Completely and utterly.

I didn't fit with a person like him. Not really. Up until now, it had been easy to be angry at him. To put him into a box and say he was having fun—taunting me and taking things from me. I might not understand it, but I'd seen it before.

But now he wanted me to smash that all to pieces. To convince me he was serious?

He *couldn't* be serious.

I jumped at another knock on the door.

I frowned, then hurried over to it, cracking it open.

I was met by a set of green eyes and the sweet scent of passion fruit once more.

"Eric?" I asked, voice high. I tried to look past him, but I caught no scent of oranges and fir trees. "Where's Roxy?"

"She wasn't feeling social."

Oh.

"Why are you here?" I asked.

"Thought I'd wait for you, but you didn't come out."

Had he been outside the whole time I'd been thinking? "You said you had to study?"

He folded his arms, watching me intently. "This was more important."

"Important?"

I couldn't have another conversation like I'd had with Flynn. Not again, not when I hadn't told Roxy. And—dammit. I hadn't. I'd been distracted by the eyes, then the scent-marked clothing. She still didn't know.

"I… I should go." I was determined to push past him, no matter how good he smelled.

"Shatter. Please, would you give me a minute—"

"I can't." I edged by him and into the hallway, but he followed me.

Fuck. His scent was everywhere, and I was confused enough as it was.

"Five minutes, no more," he said as he reached the stairwell on the second floor. "You are very hard to get alone."

I glanced up at him in surprise, halting for a moment. "We…" I trailed off, averting my gaze to the floor as a pretty red-haired beta woman passed us.

I hoped she didn't notice who we were.

"We shouldn't be seen together," I told him, stepping toward the next flight of stairs.

He held out a hand to stop me, eyebrow raised, then stepped toward a door nearby, opening it.

"There. No one will see us."

I glanced inside to see a small closet, then I checked the hall. It was empty now.

"Look," I whispered. "I really can't—"

"I want to apologise," he said, voice low.

That caught me off guard. "Apologise?"

"Five minutes. I'll never live it down if I don't make every effort to say this to you."

I don't know why we needed a closet for that. "I—*oh!*" His fingers closed around my arm, and he easily tugged me in before I could protest.

Shit.

It was just me and him, alone, crammed between dusty shelves and boxes of cleaning supplies. Passion fruit smelled so fresh and sweet, overpowering the sharp scent of cleaning supplies that it tangled with.

There was nothing hostile in his scent, though I wasn't as in tune with it as I was with Dusk's, Umbra's, and Ransom's.

He was handsome—that was impossible to ignore, even with that frown as he considered me carefully. He had thick dark-brown eyebrows that were perfectly shaped and intense green eyes. His skin was pale in that porcelain way that Roxy's was, and it suited him.

I wasn't comfortable, though. Not the way I should be with my mates. Flynn said he hadn't meant it, but Eric's words in the library stuck with me, weighing me down whenever I was feeling most insecure.

"Flynn spoke to me," Eric said, as if reading my thoughts. "It seems to have got around that I said a few unsavoury things about you."

I took a breath, the torment echoing in my mind again. *"...Doesn't even own a hairbrush..."*

I shoved the memory away. "He, uh... he said you didn't mean it..." My voice was weak.

"Actually, I believe he claimed I only said it because I was infatuated with you."

"What?" My heart tripped over itself. "He... it wasn't phrased quite like that..."

"Shame. Because it's the truth."

My lips parted in surprise, but he continued before I could speak.

"I've been..." He cleared his throat. "I've been so angry since the ball."

"Angry?" I asked, startled.

He leaned back slightly, jaw ticking, and it was enough to make me shrink down. "We messed up," he said simply. "That's been clear ever since. I should have known, the moment you came to our table, how special you were."

Shit.

This was the same as when Flynn had come knocking, but worse.

"We didn't," he went on. "And then you turn up at school with their star, and I..." He wrinkled his nose, looking away from me. "I'm just angry at all of it. I even checked your entry scores. You're the most intelligent person I've ever met. It's incredibly intimidating."

"Intimidating?" My voice was high pitched. "But you have Roxy, and she's smart and really—"

"She's not *you.*" Eric cut me off, looking so intense it was hard to keep eye contact. "But I have to pretend she is when I'm... with her."

I froze, cheeks going bright pink. "You... no. That's wrong."

Guilt turned my stomach. She didn't deserve that.

"I know," Eric said. "That's why we're dropping her."

Wait. No. "You're *what?*" My voice was hoarse.

That would be terrible for Roxy's reputation.

"We don't want Roxy caught up in this, but the others... they can't take it."

"The others?" I asked. "What about you?" Could I talk Eric into not dropping her?

"I… Well…" He rubbed his chin. "I had a different idea."

"To keep her on?" I asked.

He nodded. "I'm sure you know that the Barclay pack has two omegas?"

What?

My lips parted in shock. But… if they picked two, Roxy wouldn't lose her place. "Two omegas? Like Roxy and…?"

"You."

My lungs felt too big all of a sudden, and my eyes darted to the door.

Oh dear. This was *really* bad timing.

He was offering me everything.

Actually everything, because Roxy wouldn't even get hurt. And he was offering right when it was impossible for me to say yes.

I tripped over that thought violently.

Shit.

Shit, shit, shit.

Even one week ago, everything would have been different. But now there'd been the heat, and I'd met Ransom, and I was all confused about what I was supposed to be doing with myself.

Eric smiled, flashing those perfect teeth for me, like he so rarely did. "You're very cute when you're nervous."

I realised I'd been wringing my hands together.

I dropped them.

"I…" My words were failing. He was close, far too close, with those beautiful green eyes I could get lost in. His hands were pressed to the wall on either side of me.

"You're worried about being seen with me, but did you know there are already rumours out there that you don't want the Kingsman pack?"

Uh… fuck.

"Are there?"

That wasn't good. If people thought I was disloyal—

"Well, how *could* you?" Eric asked. "When you can't take your eyes off us?"

My fists balled in my skirt as I stared at him. "I… I don't… not on purpose—"

"I hope the rumours are right."

My mind raced a million miles an hour.

"We're going to make you a formal proposal. We'll give you our star, and then you'll have a real choice."

Their star?

He had to be joking.

This was madness. "Why would you risk that?" I asked. If I said no, it would be humiliating for his pack.

"Because I think there's more to this than meets the eye." He reached out, and I jumped as his touch grazed my cheek. "I think you want us as much as we crave you, and I'd risk rejection if there's the smallest chance you say yes."

I tried to shift away from his touch without being too obvious. "But i-if I say no, and then you drop Roxy, you'll still have to take another omega."

"Yes," he replied. "And it won't be her, and she won't remind us of you every day."

He took a step back, thank God, clearly done, but before he turned the door handle, he looked back at me. "Did you go through heat with them?" he asked.

My mouth popped open. Was he *supposed* to ask something like that?

I didn't think so. It absolutely couldn't be good etiquette, no matter how out of the loop I was.

"If you had, I think I would be rather relieved."

"Why?"

"Because if you had a heat with them, and there's still no bond, then perhaps we do have a chance, after all."

When the door of the closet shut, I was left in a terrible silence. I waited a long time, mind numb. When I stepped out into the hall, for a moment, it was as if the fading scent of passion fruit was drowned in midnight opium.

It was my own imagination, forcing me to realise that my mates had fallen for me without ever having caught my scent.

And they were too late.

CHAPTER 10

Dusk

Eric: You know what I hate? How hard she wants us to work just to get some.Gareth: You're the one who picked her.

Eric: You wanted the crazy roses chick.

Gareth: Apparently, she puts out whenever. What's the point of this place if I can't get my dick sucked when I feel like it?

I was reading through the transcriptions Decebal had sent me this week. Any pieces of information that he thought might be relevant. This one, like most, turned my stomach. A part of me wanted to take them to Shatter and read them to her, so she would understand the kind of vermin her mates were. But this wasn't the worst of it, and these alphas were so foul, while she was so fucking pure, that I ran the risk of her thinking it was a trick. That I'd fabricated it to convince her to commit to us.

It's the only way I saw that conversation going right now.

Instead, I read on, committing to memory everything, as I always did.

Eric: I'm bored of this stupid school. Four years? Can't we just wait for his parents to kick the bucket? We already fixed his fucking problems.

Gareth: He was right to be paranoid. Don't tell me you wouldn't be the same if it was you.

Eric: It's not me. He wants sympathy? Then he shouldn't have blackmailed us into keeping pack lead. Fuck him. I almost hope it blows up in his face.

Gareth: Yeh. Fucking. Right. How much of his money did you spend last week?

My eyes dropped from the transcripts as another text came in.

My heart skipped a beat at the words.

Decebal: I found her.

The text stared up at me from my phone before the next popped up.

Decebal: It was the interest in Eugene Howard. Sending it with encryption. Delete it. This isn't shit you want getting around.

Decebal: There was more, but we were kicked out the moment we got into the server. Couldn't get back. This stuff is locked up tight.

I tapped it open, already walking back down to my room.

I'd print it, and the electronic files would be destroyed. There were some things that couldn't be left to hack. Some things I only trusted in my hand, able to be burned at any point.

Like the photo I'd snapped of her golden eyes. It was long gone.

After I'd printed out the information, I went to my safe in the back of my closet and unlocked it, pulling out the folder I'd been building. It was the only place I felt safe keeping this information. Anything incriminating about Shatter would end up in here. Nowhere else, just like the information I had kept on our pack. I sat down on the bed, finally finding the courage to read what Decebal had sent.

It was a photo of a handwritten report. I recognised the Institute stamp on the top, matching ones I'd seen a thousand times before. My heart skipped a beat.

Centre for Omega Enhancement.

The underbelly of our government, responsible for managing unusual aura cases. I knew of them because they were one of the groups that wanted to see us captured.

Why was it on a document about Shatter?

It was confirmation that my draw to her wasn't a fluke—she *was* one of us.

My eyes scanned the page. It was a report by Arkologist, Dr. Eugene Howard. The man Shatter had been interested in—the one who had sponsored the Lincoln pack.

Subject: Subject Number One - Failed Experiment

To: The Center for Omega Enhancement.

From: Dr. Eugene Howard - Lead Researcher

Objective: Evaluation on Omega Subject Number One's safety in society by assessing her well-being and identifying risks to her and others.

I scanned the sheet, sifting through them, and my blood chilled as I read the contents. The words blurred together, painting a picture of the true nature of what had been done to her.

Shatter was a victim of experimentation, just like we had been.

...Unforeseen incident constituting sabotage...

...Incident involving the omega subject Number One...

...Instead of the anticipated Dr. Balch serum, the subject was inadvertently injected with a substance later identified as "Atropa's Poison." A drug used in illegal experimentation of alphas in the same facility prior to repossession by the Institute...

Two words stuck: *Inadvertently injected.*

Something had gone wrong, just like with Ransom.

I re-scanned it. *Illegal experimentation of alphas?* I checked the details again, and my heart sank as I recognised the location.

It was the same facility.

The experimentations Umbra and I had been a part of, those had been illegal. Run by scum, looking to make a profit, with no ethics involved. When it was shut down, it had been repossessed by the Institute. We hadn't dug, too afraid to poke them, for fear of them discovering who we were. Whatever happened there, it was supposed to be better.

Yet, she was the same as us.

As I read on, everything fell into place. Guilt was a fist around my throat as I forced myself to continue.

...The sabotage, which resulted in the deaths of four members of staff, was a vengeful act by an alpha previously subjected to experimentation in our facility during a separate program that was shut down due to severe, illegal, and unethical practices...

The program Umbra and I had been a part of.

...He had intimate knowledge of the facility's workings, ultimately leading to the injection of Atropa's Poison into the omega subject on the day of the program's launch...

Most of those alphas—the ones like us—had died. We'd seen their bodies, but maybe a few had escaped. I had never considered what that could mean…

But one, at least, *had* escaped. They'd returned with vengeance, and Shatter was the one who had paid. She'd been injected with the same substance we believed Ransom had been injected with.

A drug that was dangerous and never designed for injection at all.

I was scanning papers from the documents I'd had before—the old papers containing details of our pack. I'd read all of them a thousand times, but I had to see it for myself. Finally, I found an old report: Blood tests from Ransom, right after he'd begun to deteriorate.

The laboratory findings reveal the presence of "Atropa's Poison" in the patient's bloodstream. Atropa's Poison is a restricted substance, toxic to alphas, inducing symptoms of paranoia, anxiety, loss of aura control, and heightened aggression toward others. Most significantly, Atropa's Poison results in delusions compelling them to harm others for self-preservation, driven by a fear of imminent death.

Atropa's Poison is conventionally administered via inhalation rather than injection.

Symptoms from injection: unknown.

Prognosis from injection: unknown

I knew the poison back to front. It was a weapon of war, not intended for use on betas or omegas. I grabbed a pen, scribbling a note and taping it to Ransom's old records.

"Did she become Ransom's cure?"

I had to keep it logged. It happened rarely, but sometimes I was swept away by the past, just like Umbra, my own instability catching up with me. When I woke up, I didn't always remember what had happened. Nothing here could be lost.

I took a picture and sent it to Decebal, then returned to Shatter's logs.

...Given recent revelations and ethical considerations regarding both staff deaths and the Institute's methods of subject acquisition, I, Dr. Eugene Howard, have decided to step back from the program. Subject One is now under ethical monitoring and resides in my home with restricted access to citizens. Presently, she is confined to the Estate for ongoing observation and care. Continued updates will be provided to assess her readiness for reintegration into society...

That must be how she'd met the Lincoln pack. They'd visited the Estate, and she'd been there. She'd caught their scent, and they'd never caught hers.

In the latest assessment, I aim to provide a comprehensive overview of Subject One's symptoms.

...Mood swings and heightened instinctual omega behaviours... Irregular and shorter heats... No memories prior to injection... Scent of deadly nightshade remains, and, significantly, is incompatible with conventional pack matching.

Another unfortunate revelation has come to light. Subject One is not able to establish a conventional pack bond. My hypothesis suggests that she can only form a princess bond or dark bond. This, combined with her inability to scent match at all, and her gold pack status, leave Subject One immensely vulnerable in society.

I froze, almost dropping the paper as I read those words.

No.

Unable to form a conventional pack bond?

I blinked, swallowed by terror that was rising in my throat, everything about Shatter's determination to reach her mates suddenly making perfect sense.

There were three types of bonds: regular bonds, princess bonds, and dark bonds.

A princess bond could only be offered by mates. If we couldn't offer her one, that meant... *All we'd be able to give her is a dark bond?*

I read and re-read the words, not processing them, scanning the rest of the page, as if it might undo the truth before me... The rest was jumbled and irrelevant in comparison.

...Barring the day of the incident itself, Subject One's symptoms pose a danger primarily to herself and not others... I request that she continue to reside under my care for life, advocating against her transfer to the Institute.

No.

Fuck.

This couldn't be right. My hands were shaking.

That's it?

Nothing else? Nothing undoing the truth that I'd just read.

"Shatter..."

I got to my feet, the world spinning.

Everything made sense. Her panic when I'd claimed her. Her desperation to paint her mates as saviours, no matter what... She thought they were her only chance.

And was she right? Now that I knew all our pack could ever offer her was a dark bond?

I would fix this. I *had* to fix this.

I got to my feet, making for my door. I had to tell Decebal I needed the thumb drive. We were careful about it, keeping the data offline.

The information on it—the vile truth of what had happened to us—didn't just incriminate the Lincoln pack. If anyone realised Umbra and I were in those records, it could get us a one-way ticket to an Institute cage—that's if we weren't killed on sight.

But Shatter wasn't holding out on us because she didn't want us. She was afraid of a dark bond. If I showed her what was on it, then I could show her these transcripts too. She'd know why we had them.

I had hoped the Lincoln pack would incriminate themselves beyond doubt from the apartment bug alone, but they hadn't yet. Not enough to outweigh the suspicion she would have when she discovered we were bugging their rooms.

But if I showed her everything... all of it, even the parts that put us at risk...?

That had to be enough.

I reached for my phone, only to realise there was another text from Decebal, along with a missed call.

Decebal: These were from today. Just got them. Urgent.

I read through the data, stomach sinking.

Gareth: What do you think about the Kingsman pack? They've been out all week. Heat?

Flynn: I don't know. Ransom still hasn't shown. What are they playing at? They can't stay here if he won't attend.

Eric: I always get the feeling their pack lead is mocking us. Just me?

Flynn: He was so fucking pissed when he caught you eyeing up his omega.

Eric: She's the one who can't stop staring at us. Fucking weirdo, if you ask me. They gave her a nest, and she still wants us.

Flynn: What pack gives an omega like that a star before term even starts? It's a fucking insult. She doesn't fit here, either.

Eric: She looks ready to burst into tears if you speak to her wrong.

Gareth: I'd still fuck her.

Eric: Think they'd drop out if we got her to give us that star?

Gareth: So… fuck with their omega and take her star?

Flynn: We'd blow up any chance of an alliance.

Eric: Fuck the alliance. They're not serious, and they're not going to last. Besides, they're obsessed with her. They might just go packing if we fuck that up. Once they're out, we're top, anyway, right?

Gareth: Or they'll come for us. Not really that bothered, though. Never even seen Ransom.

Flynn: They won't. Not if we get her to give us the star.

Eric: I think I have a way to do it. You said she overheard me talking about her? What was it she said?

Decebal: Nothing else. They left the apartment. This was at lunch today. Be careful.

Sickness turned my stomach at what I'd read. *Where is she?*

Roxy. She'd gone with Roxy.

I was already crossing to my door. I couldn't risk Shatter getting anywhere near the Lincoln pack, not if she was their target. I reached the hallway, heart pounding in my chest. I tried to keep my panic to myself, so I didn't disturb Umbra and Ransom tonight.

I just needed to know where she was, and I'd settle. Plus, they didn't know Shatter was gold pack, which kept her safer.

I knew a thousand vile truths about the Lincoln pack and what they were capable of. They had no boundaries when it came to omegas, not when pride was involved.

We'd tracked them for a while, digging into their every move, above or below board. Before the academy, they'd frequented social clubs that hosted gold packs for entertainment—places that all but owned the omegas in their "employ." All were gold packs with outcast designations—omegas who had broken the law or were deemed dangerous.

And they especially favoured establishments with the least rules possible. They were particularly competitive with other packs. One night, they'd lost a lot of money to another pack. The next, they'd paid for an evening with the omega their rival pack favoured. We couldn't find the exact details, but whatever they'd done was so bad the establishment had removed her from their roster.

I wouldn't let something like that happen to Shatter.

Scanning the hallway before me, I spotted the room she and Roxy studied in, but when I opened it, I found it empty, and my blood chilled as I caught the faintest trace of passion fruit in the air.

Eric had been in here?

Where is she?

I was left, frozen, for a long, panicked second before I ripped my phone from my pocket, opening the tracker I hadn't used since I'd caught her sneaking off to the library.

CHAPTER 11

Numbness settled over my body as I reached the Kingsman apartment.

The door was unlocked, which wasn't normal. Had Dusk left it like that so I could let myself in when I came back?

He wasn't in the living room anymore, but the TV was on, playing a show I didn't recognise. I hugged myself, eyes darting up to Ransom's room.

What am I supposed to do?

The Lincoln alphas were my mates, and they wanted me.

It was everything I had ever dreamed of. My own poisonous scent would no longer put me in danger, and I would never be under threat of a dark bond again.

The Kingsman pack... they couldn't offer me what my mates could.

The only ending with them was a dark bond.

My fingers crept to the tiniest scar on my neck. It was almost completely faded now. Tears burned my eyes.

But I stood for an age, desperately wondering why those moments with Eric paled the more I replayed them—as I understood, at last, the truth I'd been running from.

I was stepping down the hall to Dusk's room before I could think, stopping at his door.

What was my plan?

Talk to him. Tell him everything.

Tell him that I wanted his pack and hope he had an impossible answer?

But even breathing in midnight opium in the hall, I felt it.

I'd have to tell him why I was scared of a dark bond, though even admitting that put me at risk. Before, I'd been afraid that, if he found out that was the only bond he could ever give me, he would do it right then, knowing he had to keep me from my mates.

But if I told him I *chose* him… It would change everything.

Dusk could have dark bonded me by now, and he hadn't. It was the truth I couldn't let go of, the tiny daring part of me that believed everything he'd ever said. Because if it wasn't true, if this was about a claim and nothing else, he could have stolen my freedom forever.

He wants more.

He *was* the impossible, already breaking rules I'd been caged by. A new path was lighting before me, one unknown… Where, before, the only option was to run to my mates—claim a life safe and protected where my scent wouldn't put me in danger—there was now them.

I could choose *them.*

I don't know how they slipped beneath my defences. I didn't know when Dusk had become safe, but my life was made of dead ends, and Dusk broke all the rules.

Maybe… no bond? Could we make that work?

Could they protect me, anyway?

I wasn't sure. I didn't have the answer, but we would figure it out.

A brief moment of hope lit in my chest. A thrill, as I truly realised what I was about to do. Through the fear, the unknown, I had something… mine.

This pack was mine.

A family who wanted me for who I was.

Outside of fate, it was a piece I could claim back. *My* trade; I would face my fears for this choice. Give up safety for the first true freedom I had ever claimed.

Daring and terrifying, it gave me a piece of *me* for the first time since I had woken as no one.

With this choice came a thousand possibilities I'd never dared dream, not even with my mates. I'd known I wouldn't be their ideal, that I would have to beg them to accept me. But the Kingsman pack wanted me as I was—that's what Dusk had said… wasn't it?

With them, could I maybe have something more than just normal?

Pages of an old book rustled, buried beneath tomes dedicated to years of survival.

Would the Kingsman pack mind if I wanted to take a serious job in the Arkology field? And what about a library? And I'd always loved looking at Uncle's aquarium. I wanted my own angelfish one day… And then, what about…?

Hmm.

I shrank, fingers finding the star on my necklace.

That was probably too far, right?

Once, I'd collected picture after picture from magazines, building the image of another dream. One so daring for a person with eyes like mine that I ripped it up the moment I'd finished making it.

Too far, Shatter. Definitely too far.

I rapped my fists together anxiously, eyes darting back down the hallway.

But what if they also happened to want a beach wedding? Barefoot at sunset, with an archway decorated with seashells… It looked so pretty in the pictures. Even if I didn't think I'd ever been to a beach, since memories of smells didn't come when I tried to imagine it. But I needed to pull myself together. We didn't even know how bonds would work yet….

I pushed Dusk's door open, a daring smile on my lips, but the room within was empty.

My gaze dropped to the bed.

What is that…?

That warmth I felt flickered as I crossed toward the open binder and stared down at it.

I blinked, and all the daring, blinding, brilliant hope vanished at once, leaving me in the cold.

I found myself confronted with a photo of me. It was years old, and I was in a white gown—though, in this photo, I was as far from a beach wedding as it was possible to be. My hair was tied back, expression drawn, and my face gaunt. Seeing it was like a shot of memories injected into my brain.

White walls.

Machines and pain; needles and drugs.

"Subject One," I was named. I knew where that was from.

Why did Dusk have this?

I sifted through the stack, heart growing heavy, chest constricting with every second.

There were more. And not just of me. Dusk's handwriting scrawled across a file on Ransom.

"Did she become Ransom's cure?"

My blood chilled.

I picked up the file, a high-pitched ringing in my ears, and scanned a few of the pages, eyes drawn to the handwriting on top of the printed text.

There was a list of what I thought were potential cures, some crossed out. I stopped on one.

"Omega bond—potential to balance and heal."

Beside it was the note:

"Too risky. Can't justify a permanent bond unless we are certain it will work as a cure."

I read that twice, ice crystallising in my stomach. I glanced back at the first note I'd seen. The one about me being Ransom's cure.

Dusk… knew?

For how long?

Claiming me at the ball. Playing into my deepest fears. Whispering worship. And had he known where I'd come from and what I was missing?

My hand jumped to my mouth.

A fix for Ransom—was that all I'd ever been?

A cure.

A pill.

An experiment.

Not worth anything beyond what my broken body could do…

But… I'd come in here to tell him the impossible, a truth big enough to rip my world in two. Without answers, just a confession and trust that he might be able to find a solution.

I'd come to tell him that I chose *his* pack.

That I'd chosen him.

That dream was turning to stone—not at all what I believed it was. Not if he'd known. He'd pretended all this time, knowing it could only end in a dark bond.

There was more here. A whole folder of information. I had to read it. Would it have answers—

"Shatter." I jumped as I heard Dusk's voice from down the hall.

He was back.

"Shit…" I dropped the file, digging fingers into my scalp as I got to my feet, my breathing ragged. If he knew I'd read this, what would he do?

I needed… I needed help. This was all too much.

Roxy.

She'd said I could come to her with anything.

I managed to take a few steps back before I heard him calling for me again, sounding urgent.

I fixed my expression just in time to see him appear in the doorway. His eyes were wide, and he looked frantic.

"Shatter!" He stepped toward me, and it was hard not to stumble back. "I thought… *Fuck.*"

"Are you okay?" I asked, forcing my voice steady.

What should I do?

I had to make an excuse to get to Roxy.

"Yes, I…" His eyes fell on the papers on the bed, and he frowned.

"I just got in," I said quickly. "I was looking for you."

"So was I. We need to talk."

Talk…? I tried very hard not to look back at the bed. To give away what I'd just read.

"Things have changed. I…" He trailed off, eyes darting to the papers again.

Changed? What had changed for him today?

"You stayed with us when you could have left, and now Ransom…" He trailed off again, wonder in his eyes. "He's almost back. I should have let you in before now."

Ransom... That was it. He was maybe hours from being fixed...

My stomach twisted in terror as my mind wandered to the notes. He hadn't wanted a bond with an omega until he could be *sure* it would work.

And now he wanted to talk... To let me in?

A dark bond I would never see coming...

I tucked my fist behind my back, so he couldn't see me digging my nails into my palm, fear spiralling out of control. "I... I came to you about Ransom," I said.

I had to stall him. To escape and get to Roxy before anything else happened. She knew I was gold pack—I could tell her everything. She would tell me if I was overreacting or if my fears were real. She would know what to do.

Dusk frowned. "What about him?"

"He... he took a turn for the worse."

Dusk's eyes went wide. "He did?"

"Not physically. It's his aura... It's hard to explain, but I can feel it in the bond. That's why I came to find you. I think he should come back to the nest tonight."

"Oh..."

"It's urgent. I don't know what's wrong or if I'm just not... not enough."

He crossed toward me, and it took every ounce of my control not to run. He cupped my cheek and tilted my chin up. "You are enough, Shatter. Of course you're enough—you're a miracle. I'm sure it's just a setback."

I nodded.

"Once he's balanced, then we can talk. Just tell me what you need tonight."

"I think I just need to be with him alone," I said.

"Absolutely. I can go and make some tea—"

"No." I cut him off too fast, panic rising in my chest. I couldn't handle his sweetness. The reminder of what he had been to me. His brows came down. "I just mean... I think I need to be totally alone with him. No interruptions. I just... I want him to get better. Maybe... if I do a good enough job, he'll be back with us tomorrow."

Dusk's smile was devastating, and it was hard to shove the tears away.

"Okay. I'll bring him in." He pressed his lips to my hair, a purr rising in his chest as he held me against him. It vibrated through my body, soothing and beautiful. "Don't worry," he breathed. "You'll fix him. You're perfect, Shatter."

I almost cracked before I'd shut the door of my nest behind me.

Ransom was right on the brink of being healed.

A low sob sounded in my throat, but I clutched it, needing to hold it together just a little longer.

Was that the only reason I wasn't dark bonded?

He had to know I could fix his pack first. He already knew all he could ever offer me was a dark bond. A bond for life. A way to force me to stay forever.

They weren't my family. They were using me as Ransom's cure.

What would happen after—when he no longer had to pretend?

Could there be more to this?

I wanted so desperately for that to be true. There were more papers in that stack, maybe papers that had more story to tell...

But if I gambled on that truth, I might be dark bonded by tomorrow.

CHAPTER 12

Shatter

I pretended to sort out my pillows when Dusk and Ransom arrived at my room. Umbra wasn't there, thankfully. I didn't know how I'd face Umbra. He'd always been different… like me.

My heart ached, and I didn't know how much was heartbreak and how much was fear.

I tucked Ransom in, forcing back my grief, unable to help cuddling close to him once again. There was a frown creasing his brows as he looked down at me, and he lifted a hand, stroking my cheek with his knuckle. For a strange moment, I thought he was going to open his mouth to speak.

He held me tighter as I tried to pull from his arms, a low whine in his throat, as if he knew I was leaving.

"No matter what happens, you're going to be okay."

It mattered to me more than it had any right to. He wasn't my mate, but I had to make sure he was okay. I'd tell Roxy it had to be a part of the plan we made. Somehow, Ransom would wake up. He was a part of this, but not by choice.

My alpha…

The one I'd claimed. The one I'd saved. It was almost enough to change my mind.

But I had to leave now, or I might never.

"I'm not scared of a bond with you," I whispered to Ransom. "I just… I don't know if he's who…" My chin quivered. "Who I think he is."

The man I'd been about to hand everything to.

Yet, all Dusk had ever said and promised might have been a lie.

Ransom was still frowning, but I peeled his grip away. He tugged me back to him, desperation in his deep green eyes.

"I can't." There were tears in my eyes. "P-please let me go. I promise to come back for you. I just… I need Roxy to help me figure this out."

I would be safe when I was with her. That's what friends did in emergencies. They protected each other, and I think she would do it for me. I didn't know what it involved, but she was really clever and kind. Dusk would never come and dark bond me in front of her.

W-would he?

They both knew I was gold pack now.

Surprising me, Ransom pulled me closer, cupping my cheeks with both hands and drawing me into a kiss. I clung to him for a second, inhaling his scent, a cool forest after rain, lily of the valley making me feel so safe. And then, when he drew back, he let me go.

Stifling my sob, I grabbed my pencil case and hurried from the room. Dusk was down in the living room, and it wasn't hard to cross to his room without being noticed.

The folder and its contents were no longer on the bed. I didn't dare spend more than a minute looking around for it, hoping I could get the rest, but the shadows of the dim room revealed nothing. I stopped when I saw the iron safe in his closet.

Within, I knew, must be the pages. Information that could, perhaps, change what I'd seen?

But it was out of reach, and I might never get away if I didn't go now. I fumbled for the window that was still unlocked, just like I'd left it, picking up my pencil case from the sill before I climbed through.

I wiped a tear on my sleeve as I slipped into the cool night air.

The metal fire escape was just to the right of his room, and it wasn't a hard climb, even with shaking hands. I tried not to think at all as I dragged myself over the railing. It was cool out, and the early evening air was heavy with the promise of rain.

I had to wait until I got to Roxy before I panicked.

She'd told me I could come for anything.

I needed her hug. Her calm words. She had been rational and level headed, even when she'd seen my eyes. I needed her answers to all the questions that were making me dizzy with fear.

Am I better off taking my chances with mates who want a princess bond, or a deal with a dark bond for life with a pack who just wants to use me?

That shouldn't be a hard question, but I'd fallen for them…

I'd only taken a few unsteady steps around the edge of the building when I curled in on myself, hand on the stone wall beside me as I almost crumpled.

I took a shuddering breath. No tears. Not yet.

Wait until I was in Roxy's arms.

But I don't want any of this…

Despite spending so long struggling to believe it, I didn't want what Dusk offered to be a lie. For the first time, I'd finally admitted the truth I'd fled for so long.

That he mattered.

And what about Umbra?

That thought almost broke me. I thought I knew Umbra; I'd bitten him and felt him through a fleeting bond.

"*He* couldn't have been lying, right?" My whisper was to no one but the stone wall of the academy. Was… some of it real?

Is that enough?

I forced myself onward, hurrying around the building, shoving back memories that choked up my mind, forcing themselves present even as I tried to ignore them.

Dusk had held me in his arms, wanting me, even though my scent was wrong…

He'd become something so beyond my wildest imaginings that I had been willing to give up my mates. I'd been willing to step into the unknown… to risk a life with no answers.

Scrambling to shove together my broken heart, I took deep breaths, carrying on to the front doors. I shoved back thoughts of Umbra's boyish smile, of when he'd held me all night, a purr rumbling in his chest.

I reached their door on the second floor, hearing the sounds of talking and laughter spilling out from under the door, so different from the home I'd just fled.

The party. Eric had mentioned a party.

Shit. Would Roxy want to see me with that going on?

But I was out of options.

I patted my hair down aggressively, so it wasn't such a mess. I didn't want her to panic when she saw me.

Bracing, I lifted my hand and knocked.

I waited as the seconds passed, then I heard someone approaching. I jumped as the knob turned and the door before me swung open.

Eric's green-eyed gaze dropped to where I stood, and his expression brightened. "Shatter?"

I swallowed, trying to find my voice. "H-hi. I'm here for Roxy."

CHAPTER 13

Ransom

Years before…

I drove in numb silence, speeding through the pitch-black road to the city of New Oxford.

I didn't know what I was doing or where I was going. I just had to get as far away as possible. There were two alphas crammed into the single passenger seat of my Bugatti. The one with dark skin and piercing yellow eyes clutched the other in his arms, as if he'd never let go. The second was vacant, with a sightless gaze and blood smearing his face and chest.

Dead…

All the others are dead…

It was all I could think while fixated on the road as I felt that alpha's eyes weighing me down. I reached for the air conditioning, only to realise it was already on full blast. The air in here was still too hot.

I drove until we were deep into New Oxford, then parked in a back alley near a local club I frequented. Tugging out my phone, I scrolled to a number I'd thought I would never need. One of my cousins had given me this contact in case I ever got in trouble with my dad. He was a hacker who didn't work the regular channels and wouldn't be on my dad's radar.

I jumped when I heard a voice answer the call.

"Yeh?"

"I'm Ransom Kingsman. I need to hire you."

"What's the job?"

"I…" I trailed off, glancing over at the two alphas. One was still vacant, while the other watched me intently, piercing yellow eyes guarded.

"I… I need help." My heart was racing, my mind sluggish. "Or they're… they're going to die if I c-can't…" I trailed off, panic seizing me.

There was a pause, and then I heard loud typing on the other end of the phone. "All right, man. One sec. I'm pulling in my pack mate. He's going to talk you through it while I do the work."

"No one else can know." My voice cracked with desperation.

"No one but me and him. That's how this works, all right?"

I nodded, then realised he couldn't see me. "Okay."

There was a long pause, then muffled voices. Finally, a new voice appeared on the other end of the line.

"Ransom, yeh?" he asked.

"Yes."

"I'm Decebal. You're going to talk me through this, and we'll fix it. You said someone would die?"

"I'm with some alphas, b-but my dad can't know."

This was my fault…

The truth hit me.

This was *my* fault.

I'd shut the experiments down… I'd blown the whistle.

"You're at The Crimson Bullet right now?"

I froze, terror seeping through my system. "How do you know that?"

"There's a GPS tracker on your car. It's not well hidden. If you didn't know, I'm guessing it was Dad?"

"N-no…" My throat was closing. "But I went… He's going to know where I was—"

"Back it up. Where do you want him thinking you were?"

"New Oxford… here at the club. C-can you do that?"

"Yup…" There was a pause. "Already done, all right? One thing fixed. It's an old tracker, not an instant feed. Have you got any photos of you at the club from another night?"

"Um…" I fumbled with the phone, putting it on speaker as I dragged up photos with shaking fingers. "From a few weeks ago." There I was, getting piss drunk beneath the cage.

And all the while, these guys were going through hell…

"Send them over. We'll take care of the timestamps and socials. Tonight, you were getting plastered at The Crimson Bullet. No one'll know any different."

"Okay."

"Now, you said someone was in danger? They're with you?"

I glanced over once more. "I need somewhere to take them; they're sick. But they're d-dead if my dad finds them."

There was a pause, and then the voice on the other end of the line became clearer, as if he was paying more attention now. "I can sort it. How many?"

I was caught for a moment, the words stuck on my tongue. My voice cracked with tears that suddenly flooded my cheeks. "T-two."

Only two.

Out of how many?

This was my fault. My dad was connected to the place, and when I'd discovered what they were doing with it, I'd told him. He'd acted surprised—had asked me not to call the authorities, telling me he would deal with it discreetly. Safely.

I'd believed him.

"I'm getting it shut down, Son," he'd told me.

I'd believed him, yet something had itched at the back of my mind to go. To see for myself.

So, I'd gone.

Sickness turned my stomach.

The bodies of dead alphas had littered sterile rooms as barren as prison cells… All dead. Not just dead—executed.

They'd have seen it coming, staring down the barrel of the guns pointed at them. Nothing more than animals… I could barely focus on the words over the phone. "… Need access to your funds and a list of stupid shit you might buy that won't draw suspicion. It has to be expensive—like safe-house expensive, yeh?"

"I can do that…"

"You said they're sick?"

"I… don't know… They're just n-not well."

What happened to them in there?

"Do they need to get checked out?" he asked.

My voice raised with panic, still choked with tears. "I s-said *no one* can know about them."

There was a pause. "How about this, yeh? We get you booked for a long vacation in the Bahamas or something? You can stay with them here, but you won't draw suspicion from your dad? Everyone will think you're gone."

I ran clammy fingers through the locks of hair that were tumbling loose from my ponytail. "Y-yes."

"I have some medical training. I could come if you'll let me. If not, I could talk you through some checks."

"I…" My mind was fuzzy. I couldn't think straight.

"Are you all right?"

I… I was… I had to get them to a safe place…

"Ransom?" Decebal's voice was urgent but too far away. The world was spinning. "Ransom!" The phone was slipping down my cheek, but I jolted at his tone, lifting it back.

"Are you hurt?"

"I… me?"

"Yes. You. Are *you* hurt?" His voice was fading in and out. "Ransom?"

"He was injected." The low voice beside my ear was new.

I blinked, realising it was the alpha with piercing yellow eyes. He was holding me up, and my phone was in his grip. I stared at him. He was so steady, while I was shaking and falling apart…

How… How wrong is that?

When it was him I'd almost got killed.

"Who is this?" Decebal asked.

The world was still spinning, worse now, with black spots in the corner of my vision. The soothing voice of the alpha sounded again, but I couldn't see him anymore.

"He was injected by something when he saved us. I don't know what."

The low curse on the end of the phone was the last thing I heard before the world went black.

Ransom

Present

I drifted in and out of reality like a tide that couldn't quite reach shore.

I *think*… I'd banged an angel.

?

Impossible.

Probably.

Unless I'd died without realising. An angel of death, maybe—beautiful, all the same. But in flashes of reality, she was everywhere. We were one, breathtaking and entangled.

It felt like I had been absent for an eternity. Meeting Dusk and Umbra was a blur in my past. My hands shook as I introduced myself to the two strangers now bonded to me.

No other choice, I'd been told. *Too unstable. I would have died without the bond.*

I didn't resent it, though.

Instead, I felt unworthy of it.

Then came the darkness. I was plunged into a pitch-black nothingness that lasted an eternity.

Their scents—midnight opium, wolfsbane and blood—were my only connection to time and meaning, giving me threads of presence, even in the deepest void.

But now the darkness flickered as I'd found the beautiful eyes of my angel. The tunnel, finally, had an end.

I'd thought, at first, she was a reaper. An angel with poison, here to finish me at last. But instead, her poison had been vicious enough to claw through my cage of darkness.

Now, she was everything, and I was alive.

I was alive, and I could feel her with me. She resided in my mind, tied to me by the bite she'd left me with, an ache upon flesh I hadn't even felt until her teeth had sunk in.

Only… I was restless.

She was upset. So, so upset. This plane I existed in, these bonds, they were the only reality I could hold on to. I felt every shift, every echo and movement.

And then…

She was leaving us…

I didn't want her to, but she'd begged me to let her go. She'd been so afraid, but she'd promised to come back.

She'd *promised.*

She was my angel, so I knew she would, but I still felt her every step of the way as she left. She was devastated, anxious, on the verge of cracking.

I started to worry.

How… long had passed?

I fought again to surface.

Come back…

I clenched a fist, my flesh connecting with my mind again.

Real.

Controlled.

Body and mind truly finding one another for the first time.

Not enough.

How long has passed?

Her hope vanished.

It was her wash of terror, in the end, that saved me. A tide of fear and pain that shot through our connection like a lightning bolt.

My angel…

I fought to wake, fear gripping me. I *had* to wake. I had to go after her… The walls that had held me hostage for so long shattered.

I staggered to my feet, the world crashing in around me. My life was above, and one piece at a time, it was crashing through a broken ceiling, breaking across the floor, out of order and out of place.

I knew only one thing, absolutely.

She was in trouble.

Weak palms flattened against the wall as I dragged myself to the door. Then I was outside, staggering to the hallway.

I was so weak. I'd missed so much.

Again.

They were both there, both my brothers in the room beyond.

Dusk looked up first, and he was on his feet in a second, making for me, and I grabbed him by the shirt when he arrived.

She wasn't an angel at all. She was *my* omega. Claimed and bonded to me.

And she was in trouble.

An alpha's claim at her neck…

A claim she didn't want…

Her terror burned through the old cobwebs of my mind, and I finally spoke the first word my brain was able to form.

"Shatter."

CHAPTER 14

Shatter

"I need to talk to Roxy," I said.

"Roxy?" Eric peered down at me oddly. "She wanted to dodge the party tonight. She's out."

Out?

I swallowed, clutching my pencil case close to my chest. "Do you know where she is?"

"Coffee shop or the library. Here, I can text her for you—"

"No. That's okay." I was already taking a step back. I needed to find her myself. My head was pounding. I was so confused and on the verge of tears again.

"Wait." Eric caught my arm as I stepped away, and I dared a glance up at him. "I'll text her. You can wait with us."

"Really. I-I'm okay—"

"I have no intention of letting anything happen to you if you're in trouble." Those words stopped me dead.

"I'm not…" I trailed off.

How bad did I look? My eyes must still be red.

I *was* in trouble, though. That's why I needed Roxy. She would know what to do. And she'd kept my secret.

But Eric was already tapping on his phone.

"I c-can't come in." They were having a party. He was dressed differently than earlier. Instead of his white school button-up, he wore a black dress shirt with a breast pocket, the top few buttons undone, so it looked a bit more casual. "I'm not dressed right, and my hair—"

"Is perfect," Eric said, looking up at me sharply. There was something stiff in his words, and his jaw clenched. "It's always been perfect, Shatter."

I stared at him. Something caught in my throat.

"I told you, you're important to us. Please, just wait here until Roxy's back—I'll worry otherwise. She shouldn't be long."

The mention of Roxy settled my nerves.

"I've already texted her," he added, taking a step back and nodding inside. "She'll be on her way."

Oh.

Shit. Now if I went searching, I might miss her.

I could wait here for a bit, and he knew I wasn't here for the party…

Still, I took a breath before entering the party, letting Eric walk in front of me so he could take the lead. It was loud, with music playing and people in each room. Alphas, omegas, and betas chatted on couches, playing games or standing about with red cups in hand.

"Let's get you a drink," Eric said as he led me into the kitchen. "You look like you could use one."

"I…" I trailed off as I saw Oliver Ryder and Jasmine Lynn staring at me from through the door to the living room. Jasmine had frozen, a drink halfway to her lips, eyes wide. "I really shouldn't be here," I said. "I can wait for her outside."

The omegas already thought so badly of me. I didn't want them getting the wrong idea about me and the Lincoln pack.

What if Roxy came in and read it all wrong and then she wouldn't talk to me?

And I'd brought my pencil case. It had my registration card in it and was super important, but even I knew that wasn't something you were supposed to bring to a party.

Eric brushed a lock of my hair, and I looked up at him sharply. "I'm taking care of you until Roxy gets here." He turned and picked up a red cup from a stack, handing it to me, waving at the selection of glass bottles along the counter. "What do you like?"

Uhhh… I glanced at them, unsure, trying not to shoot a glance back at Jasmine and Oliver. I edged closer to the counter, trying to read the labels, as if I knew what any would mean. I'd barely ever drank at the Estate—maybe a glass of wine here or there.

"You all right?" Eric asked.

"Yes." I reached for one with golden liquid at random, trying to seem confident. He was being so nice. I needed to pretend to be normal for five minutes until Roxy arrived. I couldn't look foolish in front of Eric.

I wasn't stupid enough to believe he was the kind of man who wanted a beachfront wedding with a gold pack omega. It was unlikely he'd even want me pursuing a career. I knew that, but I might be back at square one, and my scent matches might end up becoming my only option.

No. *Don't cry.*

I was so scared of what the future held now—or the idea that the Kingsman pack might not be in it…

Don't think about it, not until you talk it out.

I looked between the bottle and the glass desperately, wishing someone else would come in and make one before me. I shouldn't fill the whole thing, definitely not, but how much should I use?

I glanced back at Eric, who was watching me curiously, a faint smile on his lips.

"I can pour it for you?"

I stared at him.

"Um…" I stammered, when too long had passed. "Sure, just… not too strong."

"Half strength," he said, almost to himself. Then he glanced back up, as if he couldn't take his eyes from me as he unscrewed the top. "Don't party that much?"

"Not really."

Would he think that was strange?

"Where did you grow up?" he asked.

"Around here," I lied.

He grabbed one of the small glasses on the counter. I watched carefully, flashes of my first meeting with Dusk coming to mind.

He drugged your drink and stole you from the alpha standing in front of you. Why are you sad about running from him?

Eric tipped the bottle, eyes sliding back to me for half a moment. I smiled nervously, trying not to seem too intense.

I crossed my arms, forcing my gaze down the hall to the rest of the party, but as soon as he turned back to the bottle, I watched again. He poured the alcohol into the glass twice over, then filled the rest of the cup with coke.

I memorised it, so I didn't look stupid in case there was a next time. Easy. Two of the little glasses, fill the rest with coke. Double it if I wanted a normal drink.

And no pills to drug me. But Eric was my mate—he'd never do something like that.

I hugged my drink and my pencil case to my chest, trying to shove Dusk from my mind again as Eric led me back to the lounge.

Roxy was coming.

We arrived at a set of couches in the far corner, where Flynn and Gareth were waiting. Flynn's eyebrows shot up when he saw me, and Gareth straightened.

"Shatter?" Flynn asked, getting to his feet, cutting off his conversation with an alpha from the Hargrave pack. He crossed toward me, eyes intense as he took me in, and I saw a little frown crease his face. He glanced at Eric, then back to me.

"Are you okay?" he asked, and I was grateful that his voice was low, so no one else would hear.

"She's waiting for Roxy. In a bit of trouble."

"It's not… not a big deal," I lied again.

"You look…" He trailed off, clearly aware of the stares we were getting. "Are you in danger?"

I opened my mouth, then shut it, glancing around. "I… really sh-shouldn't be here."

"You're waiting with us." His voice was firm, and his hand was on my waist, leading me to the couch.

I sat between him and Gareth, anxiously hoping no rumours would start before I could sort this out. I was sandwiched between the scents of sesame seed and sunflower, and coconut and plum. Each was as mind scrambling as Eric's passion fruit, which wasn't what I needed right now.

"You all right, love?" Gareth asked. He was well built, with tanned skin and blond hair. I remember how much he'd caught my eye when I'd first seen their pack. But now his bright blue eyes and sesame scent seemed wrong. So far from sandstorm irises or the dark, woody scent of wolfsbane… So far from what I knew.

I nodded, taking a large drink and blinking harshly.

It tasted horrible, and nothing like the one I'd had with Dusk at the bar the other day. I must have picked an awful-tasting alcohol. Or maybe this was how these sorts of drinks were supposed to taste when they weren't full of sugar, like the one at the bar.

"You don't like it?" Eric asked, clearly catching my poorly hidden reaction.

I glanced down at it. "It's great."

Roxy better hurry. They were being too nice. It was muddling me up.

Oliver and Jasmine entered the room, and I abandoned my dislike of the drink, hoping it would at least keep me from bursting into tears in front of other omegas before I could leave.

They took the couch on our left, where Oliver's pack was lounging. I could feel Jasmine's eyes burning into me and had trouble figuring out where I was supposed to look. Eric was watching me occasionally, perched on the arm of the couch, poorly hiding his concern.

The conversation was rowdy, and the Hargrave pack was discussing sports with Flynn and Gareth. I sipped on my drink and dug my nails into my pencil case, trying not to count the seconds.

"You're the only omega who will ever belong between us." Dusk's words sounded in my head, and I shoved them away.

I hadn't realised how deep those thorns had sunk in until they'd been ripped free. Now, breathing felt like trying to hold air within shredded lungs. I took another long drink, forcing back the heartbreak and pain.

My fault… foolish and stupid for ever listening to them, for falling for them…

Usually, I would be taking note, trying to memorise everything Flynn and Gareth were saying about what team they supported in Aura boxing, but I just couldn't.

I felt a slight buzz settle over my mind. Good. Calmer was good.

When far too long had passed, and Eric glanced at his phone again, I got to my feet and edged to him. "How long until she's back?" I whispered.

"She got delayed," he said.

Eric caught my expression. "We're worried, all right? I can tell everyone to go home if—"

"No." Oh gosh, no. My cheeks heated at the thought of it. That would be so much worse.

"Tell us what you need, Shatter," he said.

"I just…" I failed to stop my glance over at Oliver and Jasmine. "I don't want anyone thinking anything that might hurt Roxy," I said. "I really need her."

"All right. Come on." Eric got to his feet and nodded for me to follow.

"Where are we going?" I asked. When I stepped to follow him, the world spun a little.

Oh. Damn.

I shook it off, looking down at my cup and realising it was empty.

"Somewhere quieter," Eric said as we reached the next room, which was just as loud, but at least didn't have Oliver and Jasmine in it. "You said you wanted to talk to Roxy alone anyway, right?"

"Yes."

Thank God.

"I get the impression you find crowds a bit overwhelming."

I thought back to the way they stared at my stupidity at the bar last week. "Was I…?" I swallowed. "I'm probably making a fool of myself."

"Nah." He shrugged. "I don't do well in crowds either, though Gareth still insists on hosting these damn things."

"Oh…"

Either he was telling the truth, or he was making an effort to make me more comfortable.

I set my cup down on the counter as we passed the kitchen and hurried after him, down the hall where it was quieter. Eric opened a door for me, but before I stepped in, I noticed one of the Hargrave pack alphas—Jericho, I think—watching from the doorframe he was leaning against in the kitchen as he chatted to another party-goer.

That was okay. It was a relief to be away from all the watching eyes, and if anyone talked about it, Roxy would know I was just waiting for her.

"Um…" I paused as I stepped in. This was a bedroom—Eric's bedroom, I knew straight away from the scent of passion fruit. "Is this right?"

Eric just gave me a strange look.

Was I asking stupid questions? My mind was slower than usual. Calm, which was good, but slower.

"She knows to find me here, right?" I asked, glancing around again.

The large bed was neatly made, and there was a desk with an open textbook. I was in my mate's bedroom. And it was so… normal looking and straight and all lined up.

What would he think of how I nested?

Stupid.

No decisions. Not yet.

He was leaning against the closed door, watching me curiously. I think I was imagining the intensity in his gaze.

"Roxy doesn't know about what you said… earlier." I twisted my hands together anxiously. "She should know."

"Does that mean you're considering us?" he asked.

"I… no… I don't know."

I was.

I had to.

I just… didn't want to. Not anymore. Not now that Dusk had offered something better.

Something that was never real…

I dragged myself away from that train of thought. "If you want to go back to the party, I can wait here for her," I said.

"Actually, I hoped to get you alone."

"Again?" We'd *just* spoken.

I looked back to see him tucking his phone into his breast pocket, then fixing his intense eyes on me. "I… really should speak to Roxy first."

"This doesn't affect her."

"It doesn't?"

"It's about what you said, about hearing me say you didn't fit in."

I shrank, everything else tumbling out of my head as he said that. "Oh."

"Where did you hear that?" he asked.

"Just from…" I trailed off, brain working too slowly. "From rumours…"

As if I was with the in-crowd enough to know what rumours were going around. I couldn't blow this with Eric, though. Not when everything was so uncertain. And he was being so nice.

He straightened and stepped toward me. My eyes darted around the room nervously, but his knuckle brushed my chin.

Okay.

He was close. Way too close. His scent was sending my mind into a spiral—and the drink had hit harder than I thought it would. "I have only mentioned your hair one time, Omega."

My gaze snapped up, meeting intense green eyes in absolute horror, and I took a step back, only to feel the wall behind me.

Oh…

Oh no.

Eric placed his hand on the wall between me and the door, then hooked his finger under my chin, holding me in place.

Dusk did the same thing sometimes, but he did it when he was being all serious with me. Never when he was actually angry.

Is Eric angry?

"Where did you hear me say it?" he asked.

"I…" I trailed off. My chest was tight with panic, every warm drop of blood in my body hitting my cheeks at once.

He knew.

I could see it in his eyes.

"Did you follow me and Roxy to the library that night after we left?"

Again, my mouth opened, but no words came out. A long, silent second passed.

"You did, didn't you? You watched us?"

"It… it was by accident."

"Accident?" he asked. "Yet, if you heard what I said, you stayed right to the end."

My lips parted as I scrambled through my sluggish mind to find an answer to that.

"I told you, people notice how much you watch us. *I've* noticed. I've been wondering about it for a while."

"It's not what it looks like," I said, trying to untangle this all with a swamped mind. I didn't understand. Earlier, he'd said he liked that.

"Tell me why you were there."

I had to set this straight. "I… followed you."

"And?"

Fuck. But he knew, already. "I… I saw you and Roxy in the library, and then things got heated—"

"Did you leave?"

"No…" My voice was weak. But he knew that too.

"Why?"

"I…" My eyes dropped to the floor, crushing my pencil case in my grip.

Because Dusk found me before I could… You'd have stayed, anyway, Shatter.

Because you're my mate…

I couldn't say it.

Not before I'd talked to Roxy, and she'd helped me figure this all out.

But how did I make it not sound that bad? I couldn't figure him out—if he was angry, or disappointed, or what? He was changing too often, and the world was still unsteady. "I was… I was interested in you."

"Me or the whole pack?"

"Um…" Fuck. "The pack. But it doesn't mean anything, I swear."

"You stayed to watch me fucking your best friend. But it doesn't mean anything?"

My stomach dropped. I couldn't let him discover we were mates yet. "No. It… it was just… like a crush. It was stupid."

His eyebrows shot up, like he hadn't expected that.

Fuck.

"A crush?" he asked. "You have a crush on us?"

I swallowed. Not the characterization I would choose. Not great if Roxy heard, either, but I couldn't find a way to un-commit, and I didn't know how else to explain this away. "Y-yes."

"Yet we offered you a chance at our pack, and you're here to see our omega, not us?"

I stared at him, lips parted, unable to come up with an answer to that. "It's complicated."

Dammit.

I wish I could read him.

"Complicated?"

"With the Kingsman pack," I explained. They still had that photo. It put me in danger, even now. The moment Dusk realised I'd run, he could send it out.

I needed a game plan.

"You're following me around with a crush, but you're wearing their necklace and won't consider our offer—" He cut off, leaning away, all calculation falling away for understanding. "You… don't have a choice?"

"What?" Adrenaline hit my veins at those words.

"With the Kingsman pack. You don't have a choice."

"I…" *Shit.*

My mind was swimming. If he knew I was being blackmailed, would he guess what the blackmail was?

This was all happening too fast.

I needed my friend, now.

I jumped as the door beside us opened.

Relief flooded my system as I looked over. But it wasn't Roxy. Gareth and Flynn were stepping into the room.

"Where's Roxy?" I asked, trying to push the whine out of my voice. I was too panicked. I needed to calm down.

"Answer my question first," Eric said. He glanced over at Gareth and Flynn.

Flynn was looking between us curiously. Gareth's gaze was fixed on me in a way that twisted me up. It was far too intense.

"She followed me and Roxy to the library, watched the whole time."

"I swear," I whispered. "It's *not* what it looks like."

"What do you think it looks like?"

"I… don't know…"

Oh dear…

This was it.

He knew.

He'd just figured out I was their mate. What was he—? "It seems like we have a sweet little omega stalker," he said. My gaze snapped to him in a moment, but he went on. "One promised to the Kingsman pack."

"Promised?" My voice was weak.

What did that mean?

Like… betrothed?

That was crazy.

"As if you don't know the kind of circles the Kingsman family deals with," Eric said, glancing back at me. "Especially Ransom's father."

"She might not," Flynn said, glancing from me to Eric. "It explains why she's so…" His gaze fell on me for a minute, sweeping up and down appraisingly. "Different. Some of those families keep their daughters hidden, hope they perfume and trade them out like cattle for good alliances."

"One of them got a damned good deal." Eric snorted. "Trading you for a Kingsman alliance."

What?

Keeping up was so hard. One small drink shouldn't have me this slow. I was just so exhausted, and broken, and now things were spiralling quickly.

"I'm not promised to them," I stammered. They had it all wrong.

"What family did you come from?" Gareth asked, totally ignoring what I'd said.

"I don't know what you mean."

"None that'll be a threat to our name?" Eric asked, looking to Flynn.

"To a Lincoln?" Flynn snorted. "No one in my family needs to trade their daughters away like animals."

"So…?" Eric pushed.

Flynn shrugged. "If we mess it up, they'll take the blame."

Mess it up?

Gareth grinned, eyes darting to me in a way that made my skin crawl.

"I already have her confessing to stalking us," Eric said, tugging his phone from his breast pocket and tossing it to Flynn.

"W-what are you talking about?" I asked, eyes wide.

What did that mean?

Flynn was looking at the phone with a smile.

Had he been recording what I'd said?

Why?

"*That's* why they picked you so fast at the ball?" Eric asked. "And why Dusk watches you like a hawk? I bet they have something riding on it working out."

No, no. This was all wrong.

I could fix it.

All I had to do was tell them I was their mate, then they'd understand, and it would all stop. I hadn't wanted to, but then I'd made this all happen with my stupid crush lie…

I opened my mouth but froze as Flynn turned and casually flipped the lock on the door.

The world seemed to slow, and the words got stuck on my tongue as fear gripped me.

Instinct warned me to silence, adrenaline flaring in my veins as I looked between them.

"W-where's Roxy?" I asked, my voice cracking.

Eric snorted. "She's in her room. Wanted to dodge the whole evening."

In her room?

Dread crawled up my spine as I stared at him. He'd had planned this since the moment he'd opened the front door.

"W-what do you want?" I tried to keep my voice steady, but I saw the truth Dusk had been warning me about all term. He… had been right about them.

I tried to edge toward the door, but Eric shoved me back against the wall easily. The movement was almost casual, predatory.

I swallowed, glancing to Flynn and trying to hold myself steady. "I w-want to leave."

Flynn grinned. "When you've finally got us all to yourself?"

My pulse picked up as I saw the malice dancing in his eyes.

Despair rose in my chest like vomit, but I shoved back my tears.

I'd… I'd misread everything.

Again. Over and over again, I didn't know how to translate this world I'd fled to beyond the Estate.

They can't discover you're their mate. That warning was sure, despite every misdirected instinct that had led me here.

If they knew, it would be worse. I didn't mean anything to them—not really. This was a game for them. Right now, I could see that.

It *had* to stay that way.

I bit my lip so my chin didn't quiver as I glanced at last to Gareth, in hopes I might find something on his face in the way of mercy.

I found nothing. He was tense, blue eyes fixed on me with anticipation.

Masks had fallen away for monsters beneath.

My mates…

My scent had always been a secret with sharp edges, ones that had been cutting me open from the inside. And in one moment, it became something completely different. Something precious, something mine.

Something I needed to protect.

"What… what are you going to do?" I dared to ask.

Eric's voice was low and full of delight as he offered me his perfect smile that, once having tripped me up in its beauty, was now cruel. "We're going to ruin the Kingsman whore who's been stalking us all term." His voice was low and full of delight. "So that no one ever wants her again."

CHAPTER 15

[*] Beginning of serious content trigger

Shatter

I tried to close my eyes.

I'm here because I want to be.

I'm not afraid.

Fear was my enemy. My scent blockers were strong, but if I was afraid enough, my adrenaline could burn through them.

The hardwood ached beneath my knees, and I came up with a million reasons why that was okay.

It was okay. These were my mates. It was good I was here, even when Eric roughly forced his length down my throat.

I arrived at Rookwood Academy at the start of term. I found my mates. They are sweet and caring and they want me.

I'm with them right now.

Eric's fist isn't so painful in my hair.

Flynn is behind me, kneeling too, one hand at my waist, the other constricting my throat.

It's good.

He likes me.

If I closed my eyes, I could pretend that. But when I did, Eric held me deep enough I couldn't breathe, and I had to open them again. Then, I could see his cruelty. I could see Gareth leaning against the wall with his phone, filming me. My pencil case was in his grip. He'd taken it from me when Flynn had forced me on my knees.

I fixed my gaze on the lamp by the bedside as Eric dragged me over him again.

Don't cry.

I'm with my mates. I have everything I came for. They know how I am, and they love me.

"You feel so fucking good, little stalker," Eric groaned.

My world began with pain, metal walls, and silence.

I was strapped down, and one word flashed on the blaring screens. Big, red, blocky letters.

ERROR

ERROR

ERROR

The word blinked over and over into the cold silence, branded into my brain with the pain that racked me timelessly.

My beginning.

The moment my memories began.

Alone in a room—or so I'd believed, until the scents from beneath my gurney began to curdle with the sterile air.

Flynn roughly tugged at my shirt, ripping past the first few buttons.

There's no reason to be afraid.

Flynn's hand fumbled at my neck, searching for something.

What was he doing?

It didn't matter… *I'm like that blinking sign. An error. Broken. Told I will never be wanted. But now, they love me.*

I am their *omega.*

This is everything I came for—

The story I told died in an instant as Flynn tore away my necklace.

N-no!

Dusk. Umbra. Ransom.

A sob caught in my chest, panic surging in a torrent as I tried to cling to the lies.

I love them. They're my mates, and I love them—Teeth grazed my skin, and I jolted in terror.

No, no, no. My mates love me. They want to bite me. A princess bond, like I heard them dreaming of.

But I felt the flicker of a real bond, and it tore through every delusion, dragging me into a void. It was a lurking shadow. A promise like I'd never felt as Flynn's teeth broke my skin.

I went deathly still.

A dark bond.

My mind went blank, terror constricting my heart, another whine in my chest.

I want Dusk.

Eric groaned, yanking me forward and choking me harder as my body seized with fear.

I want Dusk.

I almost broke then, tears nearly flooding my cheeks.

I want Umbra's huge arms wrapping me tight.

To feel Ransom at my back, purring as he sleeps.

But I'd left them.

I'd run.

I don't know what happened or how much time had passed, but the teeth remained, the threat of a bite violently shaking me to the soul.

Incomplete.

It… it wasn't complete. I held on to that as I felt the warm trickle of blood down my back.

Then Eric pulled back, and Flynn's teeth were gone. I didn't have time to catch my breath as Eric groaned again, finishing.

I was going to throw up. With fear. Disgust. I didn't know.

A hand clamped over my mouth and nose.

"Swallow, little stalker. That's what you wanted, isn't it? A taste of us?"

Once more, I shoved back tears as I did what he asked.

It was over.

I'd done what they wanted.

[*]

"She's fucking terrified." I could hear the laughter in Gareth's voice as he dragged me to my feet. "Why?" His grip was painful on my arm. I wasn't steady. From the corner of my eye, I saw Flynn picking himself up, and I cringed away. "You didn't think he was actually going to bond a freak like you, did you?" Gareth shook me, forcing me up to look at him. I… I had to give him what he wanted, so he'd let me go. I tried to shake my head through his grip.

"Why did biting you feel *that* good?" Flynn asked, and there was a fleck of red on his lips. I hated the way his gaze was fixed on me. The way his pupils were blown.

The scents in the air were wrong now, and I had to remind myself he hadn't completed any bond. It had just been a threat…

"Because she's obsessed with us?" Gareth had me by the arm and was dragging me to the bed. "Think it makes omegas taste sweeter?"

A low whine rose from my throat. "W-wait. I did what you wanted—"

Gareth laughed as he shoved me onto the blankets.

I threw myself against his grip in terror. "You can't—"

"Get a grip, slut. You think we'd fuck you?" Gareth asked as he pinned me. "After you had a heat with them?"

My breathing was rapid as he pinned me down.

"We're going to make it so no alpha ever wants to have a heat with you again." Panicked sounds rose in my chest, but Gareth clamped a hand over my mouth. "Make a sound, and I'll take a turn, just like Eric."

It didn't matter if I tried, anyway; the music outside was loud enough, no one would hear.

I couldn't do this.

I couldn't be here.

I reached for a piece of me I'd only ever fled from as I lay on the bed. For the first time, it was a relief when time became meaningless as I was swept back into the place where I was no one.

It wasn't absolute like it had been, but it was something. My eyes traced the curve of the vase shape that made up the bottom of the lamp on Eric's side table. The pebbled texture along the surface. My pencil case rested beside it.

They were hurting me, and I didn't dare make a noise. It was Gareth above me now; he said something with a laugh, but I didn't hear it. His teeth hurt, digging into my flesh, nothing like the bite Umbra had left me. Not soft or passionate or loving…

Eric's fist was bruising on my wrist as he repositioned me. He wanted to bite me again.

Again?

I don't know how many I'd endured… Would they heal?

Alpha bites that weren't intended as bonds healed fast, but… but these were deep. Deliberate.

I clenched my teeth, battling tears through the pain, and kept silent. It would end eventually.

I focused on my pencil case. In it was my registration card.

That I could walk away with.

I clung to that, telling myself it didn't matter what they did to me here. The blinking ERROR sign had branded me since the moment I'd woken. I was broken already. Used by Dusk. Unwanted by my mates.

It didn't matter what they did.

This was my fault.

I'd been so stupid coming here, thinking it would be different.

Why? When my uncle had warned me.

My mates were matched with a broken omega, one stupid enough to want more. And I was the one who'd fled the only place that had ever offered me safety.

How much time had passed?

I hurt so badly. Even my mind ached from trying not to be here. How much of my life had I lost to silence, a nightmare of wishing I was present when I couldn't be, and now…?

They were talking. The words drifted in and out, forming meaning somewhere in my mind.

Again, the silence flickered, and tears pricked my eyes, but I shoved them back, seeking the cold room with bright lights and cold metal against my back.

The room I'd woken in, when shock had won, and I'd had no tears, despite the agony shredding me, bone to soul.

I could hear the sounds playing from a phone. My own voice, echoing back at me.

"You came to watch me fucking your best friend?" Eric asked, his voice tinny in the recording.

"It… It was just… like a crush. It was stupid."

Gareth's laugh was sharp. "No way did she say that."

They were going to send it out… to… to who?

Everyone?

Would Roxy see?

Would Dusk?

I shattered for the millionth time since I'd been left to watch that blinking ERROR sign for hours.

My gaze focused as Flynn picked up my pencil case. The quiet in my mind flickered, waning again.

That's all I have.

He searched it, pulled out a marker and tossed it to Gareth, who was above me again. I shut my eyes as I felt its cool tip upon my forehead.

He was *writing* something on me?

Why was he doing that?

This part was… different. Not just about territory, it was cruel… They were my mates. They were supposed to love me. To cherish me.

I reached up at last, trying to grab his wrist, a choked sound escaping my chest, but he laughed, and Eric pinned my arm to the bed as Gareth crushed my chin, holding me still.

I tried to calm my breathing.

He didn't take the card.

It's all that mattered. My only chance at… at anything.

Then Gareth was gone, and I tried to ignore the echoes of the Sharpie on my skin. The dark bond they'd threatened hadn't been completed. I could still get away.

Every muscle in my body remained frozen in fear.

It would be over soon.

There was a thundering knock on the door, and I jumped. I lifted my head, but Flynn was pinning me to the bed in a second, hand clamped over my mouth, dark eyes holding mine in threat as Eric crossed the room.

The knock sounded again, and I heard the lock click as Eric opened it.

"Where is she?"

Roxy?

I tried to turn, eyes wide, but Flynn's grip became painful, and his dark irises glittered with threats. He lifted a finger to his lips, tongue pressed to his canine. My blood still traced his lips.

"She left. She was looking for you," Eric replied.

"Someone said she was in here."

Roxy is looking for me?

Finally, one tear broke free. Not for them.

I… I think she was my friend for real. I had to leave after this, and I would lose her.

Eric snorted. "Nope."

"Let me see—"

"Enough." Eric's voice was cold and edged with an alpha command. "We didn't choose you, expecting you to question us at every turn. If I say you aren't welcome, then fuck off."

"Open the door." Roxy's voice was vicious. I jumped as Flynn's hand on me became painful, and I realised I'd shifted, reaching for her. I was torn between screaming for her and keeping my silence.

But if they locked the door…? She couldn't push past three of them.

Then what would they do to me?

Gareth's threat stuck in my mind. And if she saw me… what about the video? I think Eric had cut it to sound like I'd betrayed her—as if I'd come looking for them, not her.

She already knew I'd lied about my eyes.

"I don't give a shit about you and your stupid ego," Roxy snarled. "If she's not in there, then show me."

Eric laughed. "Get fucked, Roxy."

I heard the door slam and the lock turn.

I trembled as they spoke, the words not sinking in.

"…She's throwing a fit…"

"…We're almost done…"

Almost done…?

I clung to that until Gareth's voice broke through my hope. "We're really letting her go that easy?"

I blinked, surfacing fully, something about those words sinking deep into my consciousness, dragging me up.

He was on the bed at my side, fixated on me. There was something… not right in his eyes.

Don't let alphas bite you, Shatter. We don't know what will happen.

My uncle's warning rang in my ears. My mates weren't becoming violent from the bites they'd left, but that wasn't the only threat I faced from the Lincoln pack.

"Nah," Flynn said. "I'm not done."

Instincts rose at the shift in his tone. I knew it, even as I lay still, waiting for it to be over. But I could feel that possibility slipping away.

Were they realising the scent match?

They'd had a plan, but it was fading now. Even their scents were shifting. Before, I was in a room of predators, now… now they were changing.

Claim seeped into their scents.

"Dusk…" My voice was a desperate whine. It was the first time I'd spoken in what felt like an age. I don't know what seized me, but I knew what I had to do. "Dusk," I choked out.

I wanted Dusk.

All this time, he'd protected me from this.

He would never do that again now, but it didn't matter.

The frightening edge of their scents dulled, claim dying for arrogance as Gareth laughed. "You think he'll take you back? After you came crawling to us? He's going to find out you've been chasing us all term."

It… it was working. Eric dragged me up, fist back in my hair. "Are you going to run to him, little freak?"

I hugged myself, eyes closed.

"Look at me."

I shook my head. "I want… Dusk," I whispered, and in my voice was real desperation.

That was where it had all started—on the first day at the ball, when they'd only had eyes for him.

A competition.

A challenge.

And they hadn't seen *me*.

Now, I needed that.

Fury spiked, and then Eric hauled me to my feet. "Go on. Run to him, little stalker. Show us what happens when he finds out his omega's been ruined."

It was almost over.

I clung to that.

They'd done what they'd set out to. My body was marked but not claimed. I would never be wanted by another alpha again.

It was pitifully ironic. Today, I'd learned Dusk's love hadn't been real. But the Lincoln pack were the only others I could have had a chance of a future with.

It was Eric who hauled me out. I fought him at first, panic constricting my throat as I realised my pencil case was still in the room, but he just laughed as Flynn tossed it to him. Then he was dragging me out, and there were people around us. I hugged myself, but… they'd done up my shirt, I realised. No one could see what they'd done.

I felt a thousand curious eyes on me, some dropping to my neck.

The only bite they'd left there was at the back, hidden by my hair, but my necklace, it was gone.

Shock numbed me. I barely heard the laughter, the words exchanged.

"Came to our door, begging to be let in…"

What was he saying?

"…Turns out she's a little stalker freak… started crying when we wouldn't give her a bond…"

Someone laughed.

No—that wasn't true.

I hadn't cried.

Not for them.

I tried searching for Roxy, but I couldn't see her anywhere. I saw Oliver and the look of derision on his face.

Then it was quiet.

We were in the hallway, and the door shut behind Eric.

"One last bite, just for luck, since you are so in love with us."

His hand was tight around my throat. He was so much bigger than me.

I sucked a breath through clenched teeth as his teeth grazed my shoulder, pushing back the neckline of my shirt and breaking skin.

Balling my fists, I buried my whine of pain.

I want to go.

He didn't let go of my neck when he drew back.

When I glanced up at him, I regretted it, my gaze instantly falling to the floor. I'd never been more afraid of my contacts failing. Of them realising I was gold pack.

Not with the strange look in his eyes.

The cruelty kept flickering out for something else. His jaw would tick, muscles on his neck going taut, as if shoving me out of this apartment had been the plan, but he didn't want it to be the plan anymore.

It looked like madness. A monster I didn't want to provoke.

I just want to go.

He had the Sharpie in his hand again, and he was writing something across my skin, below my collarbone.

"For Dusk, if you crawl back to him." He pressed the pen into my hand and drew my chin up roughly, thumb crushing my lips. "I wonder what they'll do when they see we've defiled their precious little prize after she came begging us for attention," he murmured. "How angry will he be? Maybe he'll take you back, and the whole school will know they're nothing but worthless pricks, picking up leftovers from other alphas."

I don't know when he'd become angry, but his eyes were burning when he dragged my chin up to face him.

His lips were drawn in a sneer. "But I don't think any pack will ever want you again."

I was shaking to my bones, adrenaline scoring my system, horror and sickness drowning me.

This was wrong.

So wrong.

His scent was still cloyingly sweet. He shouldn't be able to do this to his own mate, but I… I was so broken.

He let me go at last, stepping back, that depravity shadowing his eyes for the briefest second as he took me in, gaze drawn to the bites before he ripped my shirt back over my shoulder. It was dark, I realised. The blood wouldn't be visible.

That was good.

He held out my pencil case to me. I stared at it, desperate need rising in my chest. With my registration card in there, it was the most valuable thing I owned. I reached for it, but Eric pulled it away. Then he turned it, unzipping and upending it across the floor.

I flinched with each clatter of pens and pencils upon hardwood, my breaths tight again. Eric took a step back, glancing down. I took the chance to look, seeing my blue card grazing the toe of his shiny leather shoes.

When I looked back up, he was watching me, something cruel glinting in his eyes. A dare. To watch me scramble at his feet one more time.

It wasn't dignity that stopped me; it was the pure rocketing fear still in my system. The fear that he might realise, even now, who I was. Or what I was.

My contacts had already failed once.

He was cracking, and my scent could come out at any moment, breaking through the drugs from the terror I hadn't been able to control.

So, I fled, stumbling down the hallway, side pressed to the wall, too afraid to turn my back on him. He didn't pursue, and I almost fell down the stairs as I made for the exit.

CHAPTER 16

Dusk

Ransom had just woken, made of nothing but terror in the bond, when there was a banging on the door. Umbra reached it first, ripping it open to reveal a deathly pale Roxy Vasilli.

"What?" Umbra's voice was filled with more fear than I'd ever heard.

"Th-they have her." She sounded close to tears.

"Shatter?" I demanded.

No. She was in her nest.

"I-I didn't know what else to do. They wouldn't let me in, but I know she's with them. I think she's in danger. You have to—" She cut off as Umbra shoved past her.

"Umbra!" He had to wait. He couldn't go charging in there. Not with what had happened with Flynn. Umbra had nearly died.

I paused only a heartbeat to tear a key from my keychain and shove it into Roxy's hand. "If you think they know you came to us, stay here," I told her.

She nodded numbly.

Ransom was already halfway down the hallway after Umbra, but I caught up to them by the time they were down the stairs.

"Umbra!" I snarled, reaching him as he got to the Lincoln pack door. "You can't—!"

Just… he had to wait. *He* couldn't be the one—

"Don't fucking tell me what I can't fucking do!" he hissed, spinning on me. I hadn't seen him this wild in years. "If they have her, I'll kill them."

"We will, but you need to back—"

Before I could argue, Ransom flared his aura for a brief moment, and the experience was downright unnerving. He'd ripped the front door open before we could say another word.

Shit.

I exchanged a glance with Umbra, and then I was after him.

"Where is she?" Ransom's furious growl ahead was met with a crash. Yells echoed around the apartment, and then a few betas and omegas were shoving past us, terror on their faces as we shoved into the room ahead.

Ransom was crossing the kitchen to a living room beyond.

I could see the Lincoln pack, but—where was Shatter?

"Ransom fucking Kingsman shows his face at last." I recognised Flynn's voice.

"Looking for your omega?" That was Eric. "Turns out, she's a little stalker freak. Been obsessed with us since—" He cut off.

Ransom—still not fully present, even in the bond—honed in on Eric in a moment.

Before I could stop him, he was crossing the room, shoving Flynn out of the way. I felt a flash of dread, but nothing happened. Nothing like before, when Flynn had touched me.

Ransom's aura exploded out, an invisible shockwave, as he grabbed Eric's shirt in his fist.

Eric and Gareth matched him, but both auras paled next to Ransom's, and Eric barely had a chance to flinch before Ransom slammed him into the wall, crumbling the drywall to dust.

His aura was harrowing. Broken. Leaving silence in its wake.

Eric's face was pale, his eyes wide.

"Where is she?" Ransom sounded more animal than human.

"Sh-she's gone."

"Where?"

"She r-ran out of the building."

"DUSK!" Umbra's voice from behind me sounded urgent. I spun, taking a step back to see Umbra was still at the door, picking something up from the floor.

At his feet were the scattered insides of Shatter's pencil case, and in his hand was her registration card.

She wouldn't have left that, not unless she'd been terrified.

I would kill them.

I would tear them limb from limb. Peel their skin from flesh and watch them bleed. I would listen to their screams until they died down to nothing.

But Shatter came first.

Shatter

It was a cool evening. Chilly droplets cascaded around me, shimmering in the dim light of the academy grounds. The wet pathways glistened beneath my boots.

There was nothing left for me.

Dusk had been right. I choked back my sob. He'd been right, and I still didn't know if anything had been real between me and him. Even… even if it had been, they would never take me back now.

Their necklace was gone.

I was marked by other alphas.

Alphas he hated.

There was nothing left for me here.

Could I go back to the Estate? Beg Uncle and Aunty Lauren to take me back? Would they? Or would they send me to the Institute if I showed my face there again?

I sank to my knees on a garden pathway, body trembling.

My mates.

I never… I let out a low, pained sound. *I never want to see them again.*

Or think about them.

Not ever.

This shouldn't have happened.

They never should have been able to hurt me like that…

And Uncle was their sponsor…

Would he blame me for this?

Could I try to make it on my own?

I had the set of contacts in my eyes right now, but even my registration card was gone. My teeth chattered in the cold air as the truth hit in full force.

Eric was right. Dusk, Umbra, and Ransom would never want me, even if it had been real…

I'd given up the safety of the Estate. I'd given up the Kingsman pack.

And my mates were cruel and horrible.

Footsteps thundered, and I looked up.

"There she is!"

Rough hands grabbed me, and there was a sound of laughter. An unfamiliar scent of chamomile flooded my senses. That was an alpha. I tried to pull away, but an aura hit the air.

"W-wait—"

There were two of them.

"Said you ran off into the grounds after they rejected you," one was saying. "Didn't seem to mind the idea of another pack picking up their seconds."

"Let go!"

I heard a laugh. "No one's going to believe you. We've got a video saying the Kingsman slut is looking for out-of-pack company."

They'd seen the video?

My… my mates had sent it out to everyone…

"N-no." The world was still spinning. I couldn't think straight.

I was shaking. My scent. I had to calm down.

How much stress had I been under tonight?

I'd fought so hard to keep calm, but my scent could come out at any second, adrenaline burning through the blockers.

I'd be dead.

My breath caught as a pain shot over my scalp. Someone was dragging me up. I wasn't going to make it.

Pathetic. Weak. Five minutes on my own, and—

I whined as the alpha's grip tightened, dragging my arms behind me. "Don't!"

"No one's buying it," a nasty voice said. "You're a little freak, stalking alphas who don't want you."

I whimpered as a hand clamped around my neck. Shock burned through my system, a fissure scoring deep into my sanity.

I wasn't ready.

I'd survived my mates. *Just.*

This was too much—

Another aura split the air; it was shaky static and held so much power that it drew the alpha up. He spun, searching for the source.

Umbra.

I saw him standing just up stone steps from the alphas who held me, his sandstorm eyes dark in the night as he looked down at us.

He came for me?

It was one, tiny flicker of hope in the darkness as the fragments of my shattered life tumbled down around me.

My whimper slipped out as I tried to reach for him, his storm of wolfsbane and blood in the air. But it was different—the iron tang of blood consuming it.

He was different.

His eyes were fixed on them, devoid of the tender, caring alpha I'd come to know. His low growl echoed around the space, and the alphas let me go, turning tail and fleeing.

Umbra moved faster than I thought possible, taking the steps in fours as he threw himself after them. There was nothing human left in his expression.

Then I caught sight of Dusk.

What are they doing here?

He made for me, but I took a few steps back, that flicker of hope snuffed out as panic seized me.

I gripped my shirt, terrified. He could never see the bites.

The truth.

What they'd done.

Dusk drew up, seeing my fear, holding his hand up, as if in surrender.

His aura wavered, furious, threatening.

I couldn't focus.

They were here. Not to save me… To tell me I wasn't even enough for them anymore. I knew it.

"Shatter…" Dusk's voice was broken.

Another whine rose in my throat at the sound of my name.

He closed the distance at that sound, drawing me against him. And I wanted to lean into that touch. To let it sweep me up and carry me back to my nest.

But…

"You… you can't." The words left me as hollow as they sounded. Still, he drew me closer.

I lashed out as he tried to wrap his arms around me, my nails catching his cheek.

I didn't want this. For him to pretend, only to take it away once he saw what they'd done. The fissure in my sanity cracked further, but he didn't let me go as I slammed my fists against him, a scream in my chest as I tried to get away.

I couldn't do it…

And then I caught lily of the valley, and another set of hands dragged me from Dusk.

Ransom…?

Ransom was here?

Awake.

I sobbed.

Too late…

Too late…

"Shatter?" His voice was low, melodic. As beautiful as he was. "My omega."

Finally, tears flooded my cheeks as I shook my head.

No.

Not anymore.

He was too late, and I never wanted him to see what they'd done to me. He drew me close, but his arms were like barbs, promises I'd dreamed of and could no longer have.

The fissure became a chasm, and the last of my sanity drained away.

CHAPTER 17

Ransom

There was a harrowing irony to the fact that I woke as she vanished.

From the bond she'd left on my neck.

From reality.

When she saw me, her eyes went wide, and a shadow of fear crossed her face.

Fear at… at me?

A low, wounded sound rose in her chest. I tried to reach for her, but she recoiled.

She fought me, distressed sounds rising in her chest as she tried to get away. I let go, heart beating a mile a minute, but the moment I did, she staggered, turning and trying to run.

"Shatter!" Dusk caught her arm, but at the touch she spun on him, eyes wild and empty as she lashed out.

Again, I saw what was written in black lines upon her skin. The word *'Stalker'* was written across her forehead.

A prank?

I couldn't understand. She was terrified. An angel worth the whole world twice over—and someone had tormented her?

The alphas back there… I didn't know who they were, but I hadn't done enough. I would go back—

"Enough!" Dusk's aura split the air, his word weighted with command. It was for her, not me, and it had her frozen still.

I took a step forward, but Shatter flinched from me and Umbra grabbed my arm.

When had he got back?

"Look at me," Dusk growled at her.

Her gaze darted around wildly, anywhere but him, until his fingers closed around her chin and he dragged her to face him. "We had a deal, Gem. Rule number one."

Her expression crumpled, her breaths becoming sharper, but her eyes locked on him.

I frowned, but Umbra's grip became firmer as I tried to take another step forward. Something flickered in her eyes at Dusk's words, finally, something human surfacing in our connection.

Dusk didn't take his eyes from her. "You aren't going to run from me."

She was shaking still, face ghost-like in the moonlight.

"Do you understand?" he asked. His yellow eyes were piercing in the night.

Finally, she made the slightest motion of a nod, and when Dusk let her go, she didn't move.

I stepped toward her again, but she recoiled, this time her fist closing around Dusk's sleeve as she cowered behind him.

I shoved down the aching wound at seeing terror in her beautiful eyes at the sight of me.

She was my angel. One that scattered the darkest of voids. She didn't need to be scared of me. Not ever.

Dusk didn't let go of her as he dug into his pocket, but his eyes found mine.

"Are you okay?" he asked, voice rough.

I nodded, though it was a lie. How could I be when she wasn't?

Dusk drew out his keys and tossed them to Umbra.

"We're going to the cabin."

"But—" Umbra began, and I felt the tense hatred in him through the bond.

Dusk cut him off, the full weight of pack lead in his words.

"We're. Going."

Dusk

The moment Shatter was in the car I shut the door behind her.

She needed a few moments alone—safe. Ransom was staring at the tinted windows looking lost, and I'd never felt Umbra this dark in the bond before.

I was shaking.

Everything I was terrified of had happened. They'd got ahold of her. Tormented her, humiliated her—

"They sent a video around campus." Umbra's voice was low, and he looked a second from cracking his phone.

I shoved it down. "Don't watch it."

"We don't know what happened—"

"*She's* the priority."

The cabin wasn't just for Shatter.

I needed Umbra out of here, too. His demon had surfaced, his side of the bond nothing but fury. I hadn't seen this side of him for a long time. I needed him on a different hemisphere from the Lincoln pack, or they'd both be dead by morning.

Ransom, at least, had been able to touch them without nearly fucking dying, though. I had no idea why, but I'd deal with it later.

I couldn't say I wasn't at risk of getting us both killed either. Dread was a swamp at the back of my mind, threatening to drag me in.

I would kill them.

We would.

Just… *Fuck.*

Not yet.

"Her first."

I was dialling Decebal's number, leaning against the closed door, praying he'd pick up. And she could have a few moments alone and I could figure out what the fuck to do.

My hands were shaking, her fear piercing me to my marrow.

What had they done?

How long had she been gone?

Why hadn't I noticed?

Their scents were all over her. How long had she been with them?

"Yeh?" Decebal's voice cut me off from my thoughts.

"Decebal." My voice was rough. "We need help. Shatter, she…" I trailed off, searching for words.

"She's feral, Dusk," Ransom snarled. "Fully fucking gone, alright. She vanished from the bond with me."

"Is that Ransom?" Decebal sounded stunned.

I paused for a moment, finding Ransom's eyes, the little flutter of hope in my chest lighting again before reality came slamming down. "She… woke him."

"And now she's fucking gone!" Ransom's voice was low. *"What happened?"*

"I… I fucked up. Decebal. I need you on this. We're going to the cabin. Her mates, they…"

The world tilted violently at the thought, dread had me in a stranglehold.

This was my fault.

I pushed her.

I'd sent her running.

Umbra's hand was on my arm, and Decebal's voice sounded in my ear. I blinked, realising I'd lost a few moments.

Not now.

I didn't have time for stupid fucking aura shit and disassociation while Shatter was hurt. This stupid fucking sickness could wait.

"I swear, Decebal, I won't watch this happen to her." Not again. Not when I'd just got Ransom back. "What do we do?"

"I can meet you there." Decebal was saying. "Check her over—"

He cut off as I heard another voice in the background.

"Alright, give me a few hours. We'll come up with a plan. Do you know what happened?"

"Her mates," I said. "They… they hurt her…" Again, I was almost ripped from reality as I tried to piece it together. A video around campus? And what was written across her face—*Stalker…*? They thought… Bitter relief flooded my system for a moment. If they thought that, they hadn't figured out she was their scent match. "I don't know how. Like… like it was a game."

"Yeh. I know the kind of things they think are games." There was a pause. "They're her mates, Dusk. If they hurt her, rejected her—do you know what that can do to an omega? And she's unstable already. Sounds like she's regressing to how she was back when she was at that Estate—when she was off the meds."

"I'm not giving her anything," I hissed.

"Wouldn't suggest it. Until I get there, just… just do your best—" He cut off again and I heard another voice distantly. "Ah. Shit. I can't tonight, not anymore. I got work—"

"Decebal!" I growled.

I *needed* him.

"Rain check, mate." His voice became fainter as he spoke to someone else in the room. "It's important." There was a pause. "You'll be fine. Gavin's really isn't my scene anyway—and Eliott was meeting us there, right?"

His voice got louder again as he returned to the call. "Alright. I'm on my way. You remember the protocol with Ransom. Same shit. Make sure she's safe. If there's anything that seems to trigger her further, don't push her. Anything you can do to ground her, do it, remove anything that makes it worse. I'll meet you at the cabin, alright?"

Ransom

The massive Lexus SUV we'd arrived at wasn't one I'd seen before. I used to be into cars, but the model was unrecognisable.

How many years had I missed?

I wasn't ready to ask yet.

Dusk hung up the phone, then opened the door to the back seat. Shatter was curled up in the far seat, clutching her knees to her chest, eyes wide with terror as Dusk got in.

I took the front beside Umbra even though it killed me. But I didn't want to frighten her more. Decebal had said to remove anything that made her worse, and right now, the only one she was okay with was Dusk.

"Are you hurt?" he asked.

She didn't answer.

He reached for her but she choked a sob, pressing herself against the far door, covering her face and neck with her hands, fists balled in her hair to obscure herself from view.

My heart cracked in two again as Umbra turned the engine on.

I couldn't stand it.

She was everything. She'd saved me, and I'd woken too late to protect her.

"Shatter, if you don't tell me, I will check myself," Dusk said quietly.

She shrank further against the door, tugging on her hair viciously, but shook her head.

Good.

I met Dusk's eyes and nodded. Whenever she answered like that, I felt a flicker of her in the bond.

She was hiding from us, as if she was afraid of us seeing her.

Shatter remained curled up in the back seat, silent, almost catatonic for the whole ride. Dusk was beside her, but she flinched every time he reached out, and nothing he did soothed her.

Her scent became more frightened the more we drove.

When we arrived, he took her in his arms and carried her to the cabin. He set her up in his room, but when I got a glimpse inside, she'd curled up on the bed, hugging her knees to her chest, eyes blank.

She was my angel. The reaper that had brought me life, instead of death, and I wouldn't be okay until she was.

CHAPTER 18

Shatter

I remembered, in vivid detail, what it was like to lose myself to the instincts that ruled me. Back to the time when I was taken off the meds and the world would fade, and I would return to myself, my room in ruins. Or locked in a pitch-black cellar after losing my temper.

It had happened again when I'd seen Ransom out in the dark and rain. I had felt myself fading, panic taking over.

Until Dusk's command.

It had been jarring, suspending me in a reality to which I couldn't have clung to by myself. He'd stared down at me, rain flecked hair stuck to skin that was umber in the night, a stark contrast to piercing yellow eyes that held mine.

Absolute.

Sure.

I was coming apart at the edges, and his voice had held me together.

Time passed in a blur, and there was a rumble of a car engine around me. The warmth of a car speeding along a highway. All of their scents were tangled in the small space.

Lily of the valley, wolfsbane and blood, and dark opium.

Mine rose, too. I knew the scent blockers must have failed by now, even if I didn't know exactly when.

The car ride had gone on forever.

I'd shivered in Dusk's arms, but he hadn't let me go. The affection was false, though. It would only last until he discovered the truth.

Time tripped over itself, scattering like beads across the floor. Sometimes I was with Dusk in the car.

Then I was back there.

In a room that smelled like them. It was slowly lodging into my consciousness like a great pillar, roots diving too deep to ever be dug up.

Passion fruit scented the sheets, and their teeth were on my flesh.

I knew what they were doing, even when I didn't want to. Marking me with bites deeper than umbra had ever given. With everything but a true claim.

Marking me with bites so vicious that they would scar, and every alpha who saw me would know...

Flynn's were the worst, his bites ripping me from the silence of my mind with the threat of a dark bond. His eyes danced with joy when I clutched him, terror a knife in my heart. Yet the dark bond never completed.

My body ached.

Finally, the car stopped, and Dusk picked me up in his arms. We were outside for a moment, and I inhaled the scents of trees and rain before I heard a front door opening and boots upon creaking hardwood. Everything inside here smelled of pine, and there was comfort in its unfamiliarity.

Dusk's territory.

He set me down on a large bed with faint traces of dark opium.

"Stay." His aura flickered, and his command came through, gripping me. I listened. Not because I wanted to be on the bed, but because there was a frightening safety in letting his dominance, his aura, take over.

And because I think a small part of me was terrified of finding out what his punishments might look like after he saw my body—when he realised it held no interest to him anymore.

He left me for a time, and I didn't know how long I spent in silence. When the door creaked, I growled.

I don't think I'd ever done that before. The first time it opened, I caught the scent of lily of the valley, wolfsbane and blood, but the door creaked no more and they were gone.

Safety returned with the silence as time slipped by, fading in and out.

Finally, the door creaked again, and my growls were ignored. The bed shifted as the weight of a body offset it.

I couldn't look up and see him, but dark opium could give him away from a million miles.

I curled up tighter, afraid.

Again, the bed shifted, and then his warm touch was everywhere. I reacted, fighting him, a rough wail in my throat as he held me down. Just like always, he didn't care what I wanted. Something warm was on my face. A damp cloth… He pinned me in place, washing my forehead.

I didn't understand. I fought him harder, but then the cloth was gone, and he curled up around me until I could barely breathe. I wailed louder, unable to stand his touch.

"I'm sorry." His whisper was rough.

I shuddered.

Why was he saying that?

"I failed you."

He was purring, but there was something desperate in the sound, as if, for the first time, he wasn't sure it was enough to drag me to the surface again. And like an avalanche, all my feelings came crashing down, and I was bawling my eyes out.

I couldn't take it.

I wasn't ready to feel this or face this.

Not yet. My breaths were choked, ugly tears tracking my cheeks. And he held me tighter. Even though I didn't know why.

I didn't understand.

I didn't understand why I was here with him right now.

Was it possible they hadn't seen the video? That it hadn't reached them yet?

Nothing he offered would last. He would see the marks that seared across my body, and he would vanish.

Ransom was awake, though. Would he dark bond me to ensure he would stay that way—even if I disgusted him?

I shoved Dusk away, terror blinding as sanity faded once more.

In a flicker of violence and rage and fear, he was gone.

I was left panting and alone on the bed.

I don't know how bad it got, but the midnight opium that lingered in the room was edged with fear like I'd never imagined it could be.

My mind had vanished again, tugged down into murky depths at the fear of what would happen when they saw. I still had that Sharpie in my pocket, the one Eric had pressed into my trembling fingers.

When they saw what I was, now…

I dared tug at my shirt and look down, and was met by the blossoming, angry bruises of their bites. Dried blood smeared my skin.

Marks of my own failure.

My own stupidity.

Not enough. Never enough. Not even for my mates…

I crossed toward the closet, desperate for anything that could protect me, the marker Eric had left me with clutched in my grip as reality faded completely.

Dust

I waited an hour, and then I couldn't wait any longer, my own fear of leaving her alone getting the better of me.

I'd had to leave.

She'd tumbled so far from sanity that her nails had dug into her own flesh until I pinned her by her wrists. Then she'd lost it, low, wounded wails coming from her chest. Her scent was free in the space, and it was broken.

It wasn't until I'd let her go and backed across the room that she had settled. Her body wracked with heaving sobs as she curled up in the bed, barely able to breathe.

But I couldn't leave her alone for too long.

This was her sickness, I realised. I was witnessing what those logs described. The boundless agony of the instincts she was chained to.

She was an omega, and her mates had rejected her.

They hadn't *just* rejected her…

I knew her history. I knew she'd been in states like this before, and I knew she'd been suicidal.

When I finally dared return, it was to find her huddled up in the corner of my closet. She was wearing one of my bathrobes, and it was much too big for her.

That was good—at least, I thought it was.

But their scents were still here.

She'd slipped back into stillness. Her scent had settled, a bed of deadly petals rustling only slightly in the breeze.

"Come on," I said quietly, holding out a hand.

I would get their scent off of her.

She didn't move, her fingers clutching her hair so tight, I was sure she'd pulled some out.

"Get up." I used my alpha bark again. She flinched, but then she shifted to her knees, fumbling with a shelf to stand. Her eyes were still distant, not meeting mine.

Her scent settled further, and I wasn't sure why. It was far from calm, but instead of the vile sickness that had saturated it before, it had changed.

Fear?

It felt like it.

Of me?

I frowned.

She was disobedient at every possible moment, but right here, she'd stood without argument.

"You're safe," I told her.

She didn't look at me.

I noticed her cheeks were too pink, and sweat glistened on her forehead. I pressed my palm to her cheek.

Far too hot.

It couldn't be her heat again, could it? She said they were erratic.

I don't know what we'd do if it was, but nothing in her scent gave that impression.

I slipped my hand in hers and tugged her forward a step. She came with me to the bathroom, expression still empty.

It took me a while in the bright lights of the bathroom to realise what was off. She looked wrong… her figure, even with the robe, was strangely shaped.

She fought me, but I tugged the robe open. It was then that I understood why she was so warm. And what I'd missed—even in the short time I'd been gone.

I should never have left her alone. Not for a second.

Beneath the robe, she was wearing a dozen layers of fabric, as if she'd put on every piece of clothing in the closet. There was a shirt wrapped around her neck, but when I reached for it, her breathing became desperate as she flattened herself harder against the bathroom wall.

"I'm not going anywhere," I told her. Not this time. I couldn't. She was overheating as it was, and if she'd lied and was physically injured beneath it all, I needed to treat it.

I knelt, every movement feeling like lead as I realised how terrified she truly was. How much shame she was carrying.

I'd failed her, if she was still afraid of that.

I cupped her cheek. "I'm going to take some of these clothes off."

She just shook her head, the slightest movement. A glittering tear tumbled down her cheek.

I shut my eyes for a moment, then reached out and undid the messy buttons of an outer shirt. Then the zipper of a hoodie beneath.

More tears began to leak down her cheeks, and her tremors became violent. Nightshade had lost all threat. It weighed in the air as heavily as it did on my soul, edged with fear.

I was afraid of what she was scared of me seeing.

Finally, I reached the last layer, a long-sleeve button-up and massively oversized.

She clutched the hem down, with short, sharp breaths from her nose as her eyes fixed on the ceiling. She still had the other shirt wrapped around her neck.

"Show me."

She shut her eyes at the command, her fingers trembling on the first button. She undid it but didn't open it.

Her breath caught, her eyes on the ceiling as her chin quivered.

"When I came to your room, I wanted to…" Her voice caught. "I wanted to tell you I chose…" Her voice broke beyond repair.

Relief flooded my heart as I heard her speak, even if the words broke my heart.

She'd been about to reject them.

To choose us.

"I read… some of the documents…" Her voice caught. "And I know you only wanted me because I could f-fix Ransom…"

I froze.

"And I just… I was just… I was just looking for Roxy. I was s-so confused."

I shut my eyes, fingers tangling in hers again as I held her tight.

"Shatter…" *Shit.* That's why she'd left? It all clicked. If she'd read the notes I'd just made…

"But you…" Her voice was cracked and hollow. "You won't… you won't want me. Not even to dark bond me."

No…

"I never wanted that," I whispered.

Fuck.

Why hadn't she told me she'd seen them?

But… She must have been terrified that if she told me she knew, I would bite her right then.

"I swear to you, Decebal found those files today."

There was a long, long silence as she stared at me, then a broken sob shook her whole frame. "It's too late. H-he said, no alpha is ever going t-to… to want me ever again."

I reached up, cupping her cheek. "*Nothing* has changed, Shatter," I told her. "Not since the day I met you."

"You won't…" Her words were breathless, and her eyes darted to the door. "I c-can't. You don't understand." Another whine shook her. "Y-you don't know what they've… th-they've—"

"You think I care if they've marked you?" I asked. She thought I didn't know what they were capable of.

They had, I knew that much. I knew it by her terror.

She thought I cared about that? As if the Lincoln pack wasn't already a bleeding scar across my entire fucking life.

"I told you I love you—"

I cut off as a strangled sound tore from her. Her grip became vicious, and she tried to pull away, true panic in her eyes.

Getting to my feet in an instant, I tugged the shirt from around her neck. There were no marks there, but the necklace was gone.

I wasn't expecting how much that cut, seeing the arbitrary symbol of the claim the academy handed us taken by another.

I pressed her against the wall by her neck, gently but firmly. She grappled with my arms, wild eyes losing their humanity again, but I wouldn't let her run this time. "There is nothing I love that hasn't been broken and put back together. That someone hasn't tried to take. You are mine, Shatter, and there is no bite on this planet that can change that."

Tears wet her cheeks as she shivered, each breath wracking her whole body. She just shook her head, expression so broken.

"Show me." My command was absolute, and she did what I asked, fumbling with the last of the buttons as tears dripped from her chin to the floor.

Fuck—

I saw her skin at last.

A low growl of fury tore from my chest, making her jump.

Her eyes met mine, her whole body freezing, as if ripped from a daze. She tried to pull the shirt closed in desperation, but I caught her wrists.

The Lincoln pack hadn't just left a mark on her skin; they'd brutalised her.

Each bite was clearly visible, a dozen, at least. Even through the mess of blood and blackness. They weren't dark bonds, but Shatter *herself* had—I placed my hands on the vanity, needing to steady myself.

This went beyond a claim or a prank.

Bite after bite marred her skin and torso and arms, and the wounds were angry, covered in thick lines of black ink—scribbles that covered most of her skin, all made by a Sharpie.

She'd done that, I realised. In the time I'd left her alone. I'd seen the Sharpie laying on the floor of the closet.

She'd made each dark stroke in a desperate moment of panic, trying to hide the marks beneath ink, as if that might erase what had happened.

It was denial. Self-hatred.

Hatred they'd given her.

And I had failed her.

She was fading again, and I looked back up at her, cupping her neck once more, getting myself under control.

"Nothing has changed," I whispered.

She couldn't understand me; I saw it in her eyes.

I tugged off my shirt and led us to the shower, but before we got in, I gently removed her contacts. She didn't fight me. Instead, she went deathly still as I turned the water on, waiting for a comfortable temperature. Those wounds were fresh and angry and would need healing, but I wouldn't allow another second to pass with their scents on her.

Not after what they'd done.

She shivered in my arms as the warm water streamed over us. I was gentle using the soap, trying to avoid her wounds as I freed her of their scents.

My pulse was erratic as I worked, my alpha instincts trying to rip me apart as I saw, again and again, their marks. But those instincts had been long warped, overwritten by drugs and madness, and none worked the way they should—the way the Lincoln pack wished they might.

I wiped her face again with the cloth; the word across her forehead was faint now, but I needed it gone.

I saw the other message left for me. Almost entirely scribbled over beneath her collarbone.

"Dusk's little whore"

It was the last confirmation I needed. This went beyond a vendetta. Brutalising her like this? It wasn't a calculated prank; it was the sharp edge of insanity I recognised. Obsession and hatred.

Arrogant, entitled alphas twisted by a draw they felt but could not understand.

Hating her for what she couldn't control.

Hating me.

I should have never, for one moment, doubted her. I should have shown her everything sooner.

Her eyes were distant, not feral now, but reserved, as if she didn't know what was happening as I drew the cloth along her skin. I was caring for her, and she didn't trust it.

She believed that these marks meant I couldn't still love her.

I washed her hair, fingers running through her thick locks with conditioner before I rinsed it out, then sat her on the vanity, towelling off her hair and drying her skin in patches so as not to touch her wounds.

I hadn't been able to get all the black ink off, but her beautiful, tawny skin was mostly free of it.

Then, before I did anything else, I drew my jaw along her temple, leaving my mark.

Her scent shifted, panic turning to something… desperate. Like the faintest trace of hope trying to break through—as if a part of her was daring herself to believe what I was doing.

"I didn't know," I told her. "The papers you found about your history… I only just got them. I swear it."

Her lip trembled as I said that, and she looked away.

She blamed herself for not believing.

How could she have?

I hadn't given her that space or allowance.

"I've had so much worse stolen from me, Shatter," I murmured, drawing a towel over her long hair again. "All of it, I dragged from the edge of hell itself. Carrying you back—I could do that with my eyes closed."

She was still and her eyes fixed, her body trembling as I drew on new undergarments. Umbra had made a trip to the store to stock up on food and essentials, since we hadn't had any clothes for her here.

The bralette was soft against her skin and wouldn't tug against the bites. The Sharpie had mostly washed off, but I pulled the medical kit from the cupboard and got to work cleaning the bites. They were deep, deep enough to scar, but they weren't bleeding anymore.

There were some truly deep ones across her breast and shoulder. They would need dressing, but I would do that after. Every bite or red mark, where their nails had dug in to keep her still, every bruise—they all carried her terror. All surfaced a thousand imaginings of how frightened she must have been, reflecting the moment in which she realised what her mates truly were.

As much as it frightened me, there had always been something beautiful about how much light she could see in darkness. Her faith in even them.

And now they might have stolen that from her forever.

So, I committed each mark to memory. They were for me, not her. I would deliver this back to them ten-fold.

The pain and the humiliation.

The agony.

And the earth-shattering moment in which they realised they had lost.

I loved her more than I had even known when I'd dared say it to her today.

She didn't believe me, not yet, as she was still fading in and out of reality. Still trying to run. I understood that more than most.

But running wouldn't help her heal.

I left her only for a moment, to change into a dry pair of sweatpants, before I took her in my arms and set her down on the edge of the bed.

Then I got the fireplace going, so there was a flickering, warm flame dancing in the hearth.

When I returned, she was exactly where I'd left her, her damp hair dripping down her golden skin and over her bites.

The room would warm up quickly. It was beautiful here, the whole cabin was—a slice of heaven to host what had, for the longest time, been our pack's hell. But I'd never stopped appreciating it. I think I'd come from somewhere that had taught me things like this were worth never getting used to.

The bed was set before the far wall that was barely a wall at all. Timber beams held together great windows that arched over the bed. The clouds had cleared, and the stars twinkled down from above.

I wanted her to see them, when she was ready to see beauty again.

I sat on the bed and shifted behind her. She tried to turn, but I placed my hands on her shoulders. Then I retrieved a belt from my drawer and drew her arms behind her back.

She flinched, trying to turn again, her body tense now.

"Still," I murmured.

She listened, not fighting me as I secured her hands behind her and made sure the buckle was positioned at the back, so it wouldn't dig into her skin.

Why *was* she listening with such ease?

If anything, I thought her scent was less afraid than before.

"What are you doing?" she asked, voice quiet. Her eyes were wide, golden orbs as I returned to stand before her.

"Showing you the truth."

She might listen to what I said now, but if I didn't restrain her, she'd fight me.

There was a metal poker in the fireplace. One with ridges that Umbra used to favour, to make the payments on his skin before we moved out of the cabin.

I shifted her so she was lying back against the pillows, tear-tracked face still a mask of emptiness as I leaned close, pressing my lips to her neck.

"Nothing has changed since the day I met you." I'd say it until she understood. "You are mine, Shatter. Every mark they left on your body, they're mine, too."

CHAPTER 19

Shatter

Shock blistered through every other emotion as Dusk shifted closer, his lips caressing the first bite.

The one at my shoulder.

Eric's.

Then he drew back and ran his lips along the next.

Gareth's.

There was one upon my breast.

Flynn's.

I'd been frozen as he'd given me that, the lurking promise of a dark bond chilling me to my bones.

Over and over, Dusk kissed the foul marks my mates had left. It took too long. There were far too many. He pressed his lips to each, and the memories threatened, each blow duller than the last. His grip curled around my thigh and waist, holding me in place, and yellow eyes pinned me every time he drew back.

Absolute and sure.

Safe.

Eric had sworn he couldn't, yet somehow, Dusk still wanted me. He could look at me. He could kiss me.

I didn't understand.

He pulled back at last, leaving me to stare up at him, finally a stirring of something that wasn't horror in my chest.

That was until he crossed to the fireplace and drew a metal rod from it. At the end, which glowed red, was a thin, straight line.

I tensed.

What is he doing?

He settled in front of me and, before I could open my mouth in protest, flipped the iron and pressed it to the same spot on his shoulder where Eric's bite was on mine.

His expression tensed through the pain, but he didn't waver.

"No!"

I understood, all of a sudden, why he'd restrained me. I tried to sit up but couldn't, eyes wide with shock.

"I failed you," he growled.

"You d-didn't."

"You don't trust my claim, Gem. If you did, today would never have happened."

"I…" I couldn't say it, though. That I trusted that he loved me? That he wanted me—even now? Even after everything. "It's not your fault," I choked.

He'd never wavered, but *he* wasn't the problem. How could he think he was the problem?

I'd been promised I would never have anything, while he'd promised me the world.

It wasn't that I didn't *want* to believe him—I did. I wanted it so badly, it had driven me to run at the slightest possibility of having that dream stolen.

"Please…"

He couldn't… those marks would scar forever.

Dusk gritted his teeth as he pressed it to his skin again. A hiss of hot iron upon flesh rose in the air, but he held it there.

"Stop it!" I cried, managing to struggle into a sitting position, but it was too easy for him to cup my neck and hold me in place as he branded himself again, his aura splitting the air this time as a low growl of pain rolled through his chest.

He went on for what felt like forever, his body shuddering from the agony of it.

Agony he was enduring for me.

How many bites?

Five? Ten? I didn't want to count.

When he finished, he set the iron back on the fireplace and returned to the bed. His aura lingered, not for physical strength, I realised, but for the tolerance to the wounds he'd put on his body. As an alpha, he had faster wound healing, which was increased by the presence of his aura.

I was silent, my heart racing a million miles a minute as my eyes traced the angry red wounds across his body. He drew my chin up as he settled on the bed before me and pressed his lips to mine.

The kiss was shocking, and familiar in that, too.

He had a habit of kissing me when he absolutely shouldn't. I swallowed, my eyes tracing the wounds again, now he was closer. The patches of flesh were warped and angry. So much more painful than mine. But I was swallowed by piercing yellow eyes.

"It's my job to protect you, Gem. From them, from the world. Even from yourself, if that's what you need," he murmured. "Your scars are my scars. My weight, my burden."

"It sh-shouldn't be."

There was a faint smile on his lips.

"It's no more your choice now than it was then. I claimed you, Shatter. I decided you were mine. I took you from your mates, and I never asked you. I won't abandon that claim because it costs me."

My lip trembled as he still found new words to knock me flat.

"If this is what it takes to put you back together, this is what I'll do." He tucked my damp hair behind my ear, the smallest smile playing on his lips. "And see, now you're far more concerned about my scars than yours."

At his gall to smile, I burst into full-blown tears. "B-because you *b-branded* yourself."

"Do you believe my claim now?"

I couldn't answer that, but he hadn't released my chin, and I was still drowning in his intense eyes and the comforting scent of midnight opium.

"Do you?"

With a choked sob, I nodded.

"I love you. It should never have taken you this long to be sure of that," he said, wiping my tears, since I couldn't. "I've wanted you every day, from the moment I met you. They never had the power to change that, Shatter." His hands traced my body, somehow perfectly avoiding all the wounds, as if they were already fixed to his memory.

I stared at him. He had seen it all and still hadn't wavered.

I think… I think this is what love meant.

I didn't realise until now how much I hadn't dared believe I was destined for love. Not even with my mates.

Dusk was sitting up and freeing my wrists. "Decebal's on his way. He's going to wait until tomorrow to take a look at you, but he'll flay me if I don't clean these."

"Who?"

"Ransom's contact. He helps us with… a lot of shit, actually. But he's medically trained."

"Oh. Okay."

Dusk got to his feet and headed to the bathroom. I sat up, watching him open the medical kit. After he began digging inside it, I clambered out of bed and crossed to him, nursing a little anxious ache that rose now he wasn't in the same room as me.

He glanced up when I clutched my arm, leaning against the doorframe and trying not to look too creepy as I hovered. Maybe I should act like I came here for a reason.

I peered through the huge pile of clothing on the floor as a distraction, trying not to think about what they had meant for me, even an hour ago.

"Ransom… he's awake…?"

Dusk's eyes lit up in a way I'd never seen, a smile curving his lips, as if he couldn't help it. "You saved him," he said as he pulled apart some gauze.

I tried to bury the flutter of panic in my stomach at that thought. Tomorrow, I would see Umbra and Ransom after… after everything.

I don't know why Dusk was safer.

Perhaps it was what he'd said… He'd never asked. But Umbra was different… Dusk had claimed me, but Umbra was stuck with me. And he was such a beautiful person, and I was such a mess.

And Ransom…

Oh…

I swallowed.

He'd grown up in one of the wealthiest families in New Oxford. What was he going to think of me when he met me? *Really,* really met me. I had just been an omega with a scent he didn't hate (somehow), and I was there at the right time.

"He already loves you," Dusk said, catching my expression. "He'll only fall harder when he meets you."

I said nothing, chewing on that and trying really hard to believe it.

I felt like I was teetering between this safety with Dusk and a void of darkness below. He dressed his wounds and then mine, and when he was done, he took us back to the bed and held me close, still careful around the bites.

"Now." He knelt before me on the bed. "Lie down and let me finish proving to you that you're mine."

I tensed, suddenly nervous, but he was lowering me down against the pillows. "What do you mean?"

He couldn't. Not when I was like this. Shame lingered, my own mistakes scorching me to the bone.

Fighting him with his aura out, though, was useless, and before I could gather the breath for another protest, he'd tugged the black lace of my underwear out of the way and found my clit with his tongue.

I let out a low moan, my back arching, and he dipped his finger into me.

Fuck.

I arched into the touch as his hand clamped over my stomach, trapping me so he could work me deeper, his tongue drawing a low moan from my chest.

"Relax, Gem," he breathed, drawing back for a moment. Again, I didn't fight his command, and my body unwound, succumbing to his touch.

It wasn't until that moment that I realised how wound tight with terror I'd been. Not until the shock at what he was doing hit me with such force that tears pricked my eyes.

My vision swam and I blinked, glancing up and finding myself staring into the starry night sky, pleasure building with each deep breath as Dusk pulled me more firmly against him, drawing my gaze back to piercing yellow irises shadowed by the sweep of short, raven hair.

Another low moan escaped my chest as he pumped a second finger into me, slower and deeper, drawing the sounds out with each thrust. I could feel the slick pooling between his fingers as he worked me, tongue pushing me further and further toward the edge.

Tonight, I'd tumbled lower than any point in my life. I'd made every mistake it was possible to make, and somehow, he was still here

How was he still here, when I was covered in their marks? He was an alpha.

In a flash of panic, I was back there. *The grip Eric had on me was painful, he was smiling, finding delight in my fear—*

A low growl cut off the thought, something guttural in the sound as Dusk dragged me from the memory. He'd drawn his tongue from my centre and moved in a flash, palm pressing against the mattress at my side, rich dark skin inches from mine as he held my gaze.

I reached up, hands cupping his cheeks, but he caught my wrists and pinned them above my head.

"You're mine," he breathed, leaning down, teeth grazing my ear as he drove his fingers into my core again, as if in echo of that claim. I moaned as his breath tickled my ear. "You're not theirs. You won't go back there. Do you understand?"

I nodded, teeth catching my lip with another whine as his fingers found that perfect spot. Then the dark vanilla of his midnight opium sent me into a daze as he scent marked me again, his jaw running along mine.

"Good girl," he growled, pumping into me slowly enough that goosebumps lifted across my skin, and I tried to arch against him once more. His lips trailed my neck, warm breath tickling my skin before his teeth found my nipple.

"Mmmm." I shuddered, thrown right to the edge of pleasure before he released me, drawing his fingers back, too, before pressing them back in.

I gave in to him, letting it hold me, an impossible safety as my wounded body melted beneath his touch. With each breath, my moans grew as he began working me faster.

"That's it, Gem. You're so fucking hot when you're right on the edge." He remained like that for a while, head cocked, pupils blown as he watched me writhe beneath his touch as he slid two fingers into me at an agonisingly slow pace.

Then he drew back again, tongue finding my clit once more.

I cried out, an orgasm scoring my veins as he drew it out, adding a third finger and speeding up. He didn't stop as it died down, dragging me against him more firmly as I shook, breathing heavy as I tensed, body already alight with one orgasm.

He worked me harder, fingers driving in over and over as I shuddered.

"Again, Gem. Relax for me." This time, when my muscles loosened, it threw me over the edge of the next violent orgasm, desperate whines sounding in the air.

He didn't stop, fingers still working my channel. "I can't—"

"You can. One more release, beautiful."

My eyes rolled back, heat and pleasure and hormones leaving me a trembling mess.

The world swam, and a fuzzy cocoon of warmth felt like it was encasing my mind. It was safe here. It felt good and warm and... I think I was purring.

I didn't think that would have been possible tonight.

Then he was beside me, his rich scent like another layer of that cocoon.

I... I wanted more of this safety.

I think that was a moan rising in my chest as I reached for him, needing more, needing... something. I felt something soft against my skin and realised he was tugging a T-shirt over my head. "To keep the dressings safe," he murmured, "but I'm not going anywhere."

I let out a breath of a whine, feeling the edges of the cocoon weaken, threatening to fade. I felt how hard he was against me, and I shifted back, nails digging into his arm. I didn't want any of this to be over. In here, even the aches of my wounds faded into the background.

He'd scent marked me.

He'd claimed me.

He was safe when nothing should be.

I didn't want this to end. I thought of that night with Umbra. Of a cocoon of safety just like this, wrapping me tight until I fell asleep.

"You're so perfect." Dusk's whisper was soothing, and then he drew me against him, his chest warm against my back.

I felt his touch between my thighs, rubbing my clit again. My purr rose again, warmth spreading through my body.

I shuddered with another orgasm, but I was glad when he wasn't done. I tried wriggling against him, and I thought I might have heard his chuckle.

Feeling him adjust, I let out a sigh of relief as he entered me. Bliss swept me away as his length stretched me out, sinking deep into my core.

Another claim.

My purr was louder than ever as he slid into me over and over, a lazy tide of pleasure washing in until my eyelids became heavy.

Finally, he drew me against him, and my purr cut off for a groan of need as his knot rocked against my entrance, pressing in until I shuddered with another orgasm.

Dusk hadn't left me behind.

The last thing I thought, before sleep swept me away, was that the only thing that was missing was his claim on my neck.

CHAPTER 20

Umbra

I woke in my old room.

The cabin was one we'd lived in for a long time, and its strong attachment to nature was probably one of the things that had saved me during those years.

But it carried with it a heavy weight.

Ransom's tumble into insanity painted every inch; it was in every scent or creak of hardwood. This was the place where we'd lost our brother.

Slowly.

Agonisingly.

Yet, this time when I woke, things were different. Because in my room was the scent of lily of the valley. Morning sunlight filtered in through the huge windows, as if an offer of new hope.

And he was here beside me.

Ransom had climbed into my bed, like I'd climbed into his a hundred times when he was fading.

He was sleeping like he did often—clutching a pillow to his chest. His auburn hair was tied up in a messy bun, and he was snoring loudly.

I found my own slippers tucked just beneath my bed, then glanced back at him. Ransom's long-ass limbs were sticking everywhere, and I'd been pushed to the edge of the bed.

Pretty rude, to be honest. That was what girlfriends or omegas were for—platonic pack mates were *not* supposed to be bed hogs.

I got to my feet, yawning and scratching my belly. One of the marks on my abdomen had healed into a keloid scar, and it always itched.

Right. Breakfast.

Dusk used to always make it, but I'd beat him to it this morning.

"Dude."

I glanced back to see Ransom rubbing his eyes and blinking around the room.

"What?" I asked.

There was a lot to get through today, including patching up a very wounded omega, but hearing Ransom's voice lifted my heart every time.

"You still hum when you're happy." He snorted.

Did I?

"So what?"

Ransom grinned, dragging himself into a sitting position and blinking sleep from his eyes. "It's cute."

"I'm not *cute*." What a ridiculous notion.

I'd nearly ripped the spines out of those alphas in the rain yesterday. Decebal had told me he'd been on clean-up duty and that they were both in hospital. I'd told him I was disappointed they weren't in fucking caskets. I stuffed violent flashes of that memory into a little box, refocusing on Ransom—and the fact I was happy. (And the original *point*, which was that I was perfectly vicious, thank you very much.)

"I bet she *loves* it." Ransom chuckled.

My humming?

"She's never mentioned it, actually."

"Very polite of her," he said with a grin as he crossed to the closet door and unhooked the night robe and shrugged it on.

He had stuff in his room, but I suppose he didn't know that yet.

"Pretty impressive, really," I said as I passed him and made my way into the kitchen to start the coffee.

"What is?" he asked, taking a bar stool at the kitchen island and examining the connected kitchen and living room in the morning sunlight. It was a grand place, with thick timber beams supporting huge windows that opened out into the forest beyond.

I eyed him, with his robe hanging open, showing off his lean, tanned torso. A few auburn strands had escaped his bun, swinging about his face. He hadn't lost much muscle mass being sick; he'd spent too much time fighting us. Or the bed. Or the wall.

"Four years out feral, and you still manage to look like one of those rich trust fund kids."

He grinned as I pulled out the sausages and eggs. I'd left last night with Decebal to grab some essentials, including more clothes for Shatter, since she was the only one who didn't have a stash here.

Decebal had taken the spare room in the basement, as usual, but he slept in when he visited, so I doubt we'd be seeing him for a bit.

"She'll see us today, right?"

I nodded. "Dusk is going to fix her up." He was good at that.

"Why… why did she want him and not us?"

"He's like… the Shatter whisperer. Don't let it hurt your feelings; they have a whole language."

"Language?"

"Mostly involves brattiness and spankings and shit."

Well, it *had*. Now it was something else.

"Excuse me?" Ransom froze as he grabbed orange juice from the fridge, doing a perfect "blinking guy" meme.

"Hard to explain," I said.

"Yesterday, when she was really upset. He…" Ransom trailed off, unsure how to put it to words. I knew what he was talking about. She'd been on the edge of madness, and he'd brought her back, sweeping in and giving her commands like only Dusk could.

"She didn't… *choose* us, though?" Ransom asked. "At first." Ah, yes. Ransom had apparently been a bit distressed about that. It was why he'd torn apart our living room back at the academy on the Indigo Berry Blast day.

"Not at first," I said.

Ransom tapped his fingers on the oak table, nodding slowly, eyes narrowed. "He… chose her?"

"M-hmm," I said, turning on the stove and grabbing the oil from the cupboard.

And *that's* why Dusk was still safe when no one else was. I hadn't seen it until yesterday: the truth of the strange structure he'd built between them.

She'd been faced with the ugliness of the world in a way that could break a person. Her monsters had come for her, and she wanted to hide. I understood that. But hiding from monsters didn't take their power away, and she needed support she didn't know how to ask for.

For me to push into her space, though? What was between us would have to change. I would have to speak out loud the parts she was too afraid to look at. But Dusk could step behind her defences without asking, because he'd always stepped behind them without asking. He could be what she needed without drawing attention to anything. He didn't have to change at all. When the ground was crumbling from beneath her, he was absolute.

I dumped the sausages into the pan, listening to the satisfying sizzle.

Dusk was like that for me, too, now I thought about it, if on a different axis. That was value beyond what could be put into words.

Hmm.

Was that the payout?

She'd endured what he'd done, survived it, then chosen it. In return, she got something back. I thought so, anyway.

There was balance to that, I thought, as I tossed the sausages about.

Not a balance Dusk could have predicted—he played with fire when it came to the universe, but this time…

Maybe it had worked out.

I didn't really care. Right now, all I cared about was that *someone* was with her.

I peered back at Ransom, who still looked unsure.

"It's just who he is," I supplied. "Has been ever since you saved us."

Ransom's expression darkened, and I had to remind myself that he was years behind on healing. Everything we'd all gone through at the facility, the things we'd seen… How fresh were those memories for him?

And us, too—*we* were different. I had to catch him up.

"We'd switched somewhere," I said. Last Ransom knew, the fragments left of me from that place had made up an entirely different person. "I broke. He stepped up."

Ransom knew me back when I hadn't found the person Dusk let me become. I remember the night he'd taken pack lead from me. I'd fought him and lost and woken as someone else. The first lights of dawn after an unending night.

"He was only able to do that because of what you did in that place," Ransom said quietly. "You protected him. He deserves the chance to make it up to you."

I snorted. "Doesn't matter, anyway. Turns out Dusk's a control freak. Give him power and he never gives it back."

Ransom grinned.

"Plus," I added, "we're even now. He found her, and she fixed you, so…" I shrugged.

That was it. Shatter was the best gift in the whole universe. I'd go through those experiments all over again if that was the price of having her in my life.

"She *is* ours," Ransom said quietly. He was tense, eyes drifting to Dusk's door.

Oh, good. Ransom was on board. "'Course she is."

"What's she like?"

"I don't know… she's… Shatter. She's just perfect."

Dust

I woke to sunlight streaming through the huge windows of my room in the cabin. Outside, I could hear the familiar sounds of tree branches rustling in the wind and birds singing in the late fall air.

It was impossible to escape the scent of earth and pine here; it lingered in the bones of this place, sweeping in with every open window or door. The air had a texture to it, the heavy exhales of a thousand trees—so different from the city. And all of that, I'd woken to a thousand times before.

Except, this morning was different.

Because in my arms was an omega.

My omega.

Tangled with the bark and earth were the light petals of nightshade, a balance of sweet and bitter that complemented the smooth earths of the cabin.

She was facing me. We'd come apart during the night, and I'd readjusted her shirt, making sure her dressings were safe. Even then, when I'd slipped away briefly for the bathroom, she'd been restless when I returned.

Now, her slender arms were wrapped around my waist, her cheek pressed to my chest as little purrs shuddered through her body with each exhale. I was quite sure she was drooling on me, which was oddly adorable.

Her wild, honey hair was ruffled and messily spread across the pillow behind her. The sunlight spilled past open curtains, and her golden skin looked like it glowed with the morning rays.

I felt a moment of sorrow, seeing her peace, knowing that it wouldn't be so simple when she woke.

My omega, a survivor when she never should have had to be.

I slipped a hand through her hair, unable to look away, guilt swallowing me whole. Her purr rose at the touch, and golden eyes creaked, large and beautiful, as she blinked away sleep, getting her bearings.

Her brows bunched for a moment before her eyes met mine.

Then she retreated, one arm drawing away from me as she wiped her mouth, a little warmth blooming on her cheeks as she glanced down at the small trail of drool on my chest. I grinned, taking her chin between my thumb and forefinger and pressing my lips to hers before she could get embarrassed about it.

I drew away, and there was a flash of a smile on her face. Breathtaking beauty contained in a perfect bubble.

A bubble that couldn't last.

I saw the moment it popped—when her eyes darted around the room, taking it in. It was the moment her memories came crashing back. Like a storm blowing in, a shadow crossed her eyes. Her smile dissolved, the glow of her cheeks draining away. Her purr stuttered out to nothing, and she squeezed her eyes shut for a moment, her chin quivering.

"I'm sorry," I breathed, sitting us up gently and letting her sink against me, clinging tight. She was shaking.

"If there's anything else you need to feel safe, will you tell me?"

She drew back, capturing me in those beautiful eyes once more. I could see her mind working, something desperate forming on her face. She opened her mouth, then closed it again, as if unsure.

"Tell me."

"A-anything?" she whispered.

I frowned. "Name it, Shatter."

She swallowed, that odd look lingering in her eyes as she regarded me.

"Today," I added. "I'm going to show you everything, so you know I'm telling the truth—"

"I believe you. You… and your pack. You are everything I wanted. I just didn't see it."

"We're not leaving you." That was a promise I wouldn't break.

"Would…" Her breath caught. "Would you bond me?"

A chill slithered through my spine, setting my hairs on end, and my heart turned to stone. I leaned back, taking her in.

There was only one bond I could offer her.

What?

"Shatter—"

"You… you said anything. I thought you wanted—"

"I want you in our pack," I breathed. *God,* I wanted that more than anything in the world. "But we'll find another way."

Not a dark bond.

Her expression fractured.

"There's…" Her voice trembled. "There's no princess bond. There's nothing else but that, and I d-don't want… I don't want to be afraid anymore."

"Because we can find another way. I told you, Shatter. I don't care who says it's impossible—"

"And if I get bitten while we wait?"

"I won't let that happen," I growled, chest tight.

Never.

But tonight…

That had shaken me, when Umbra had opened the door to Roxy and I realised Shatter was gone…

I finally spoke out loud the thing that lurked at the corners of my mind every moment I was with her. "What if we were supposed to be your mates? What if…?" Could I tell her I had no intention of letting the Lincoln pack survive?

"Dusk…" Her eyes clouded and she shook her head. "If th-this is what mates mean. I don't want them."

I stared at her, believing that truly. And it didn't matter. "I can't."

A dark bond?

"P-please, you said…" Her breathing was short and sharp. "You told me you would bite me if I begged—"

"Not like this."

"You d-don't want me?"

"I can't—" I began, but she cut me off.

"I lost everything. You and Umbra and Ransom, I want… I want your pack to be my choice before that's taken from me too."

My pack?

The words gave me whiplash, hearing that she wanted to choose—not just me, but Umbra and Ransom too? She would be ours forever…

"Is it a choice if you make it when you're scared—?"

"I chose you already when I came to your room. When I wasn't scared, and Eric told me they wanted to offer me a place with them and I…" Her voice became choked. "And I believed him, but I still… *I still chose you.*"

My mind raced. "You aren't in a good place tonight—"

"I hurt." Tears beaded in her eyes again. "I hurt so fucking much. Dusk, please, I don't want them to have any more power. I want you to have it—"

"You don't know what you're asking."

"Don't!" Her fingers closed around my neck, her voice suddenly harsh. "Like I haven't spent all my life afraid of this."

"I can't be your monster."

"I was wrong about what I should have been scared of. I was wrong, and I ran from you, and you were my choice, and I don't…" She choked on a sob. "I don't want that taken from me too."

Her eyes glittered, tears finally tumbling down her cheeks, a thousand wounds in golden orbs.

My fault.

And she was begging me to fix it.

I never knew, until that moment, how weak I was in the face of her pain.

"We're going back," she whispered. "And I'm going to see them again." Her voice trembled, and I could see her fear so starkly. "They're going to be so angry, and what if… if they learn who I am…" Her voice cracked. "I was wrong. They never wanted a princess bond—"

"A princess bond?" I asked.

Why had she believed they wanted that? It wasn't common, even outside of gold packs.

"I… it doesn't matter. I think I made it up. I know they don't want me, b-but I don't want to live in a world where it's possible that they bond me."

My own blood turned to ice at those words. I knew she believed that they didn't want her, but the marks across her body—they told me a different story. The Lincoln pack had brutalised her.

No. I didn't believe they didn't want her at all. I believed, down to my marrow, that the only reason Shatter had escaped today without a dark bond was because they didn't know who she was, and they didn't know she was gold pack.

"I won't let them dark bond you, Shatter. Never in a million years."

"Will you…" She swallowed. "You can make that promise real. If you—"

"No."

"P-Please, Dusk."

I realised what she was asking for.

Safety.

That's what my bite offered her.

I'd always wanted to bite her. Dreamed of it.

Just… not like this.

"I'll do anything." Her voice was thick. "You said… you said if I begged you."

I hated that she was begging now.

That, after everything she'd gone through tonight, her fear led her to this.

I stared at her, the picture of beauty. A wounded goddess, with tears trickling from pleading eyes, illuminated across the golden tan of her cheeks. Her nose was pink, and her lips blood red.

"P-please. I can't… I can't go back alone."

"You will never be alone."

"I will. You have the bond. I don't."

I'd never seen her so wholly as I did in that moment, chained by fear and begging for freedom. The centre of the whole world.

"I c-can't face them alone."

She cupped my cheeks, and I was swallowed into eyes shimmering gold.

The most beautiful omega in the world. In pain. The ebbing tide of nightshade stuck to my throat and lungs, coating my skin—a scent so beautiful and powerful and wounded.

I can't do it…

"You can keep me safe from them," she whispered.

The world slowed at those words. Dizzying in their truth. I *could* protect her, not just in this moment, but every moment from now until forever. From monsters so much eviler than even she had seen.

I *could* bite this fragment of heaven into our pack, where she would never be alone again. Where she would be safe. Where the horrors of what had just happened would never happen again.

Her lip trembled as she begged me, and each of her words was a hook, sinking into my heart, demanding action, a jarring, desperate ache building and building.

"P-please, Dusk."

CHAPTER 21

Shatter

Teeth sank into my skin once more.

Different this time: gentle, loving, and desperate.

For a long moment, I felt nothing. He drew back, his piercing eyes finding mine. I shook my head, realising he must have tried a normal bond—a last attempt to save me from what I was begging for. Just like the first time I'd been offered a normal bond, I felt nothing.

I curled my fingers around his neck, breathing growing rapid as he paused, every desperate nerve in my body alight.

I wanted this.

"If I got a princess bond with them, it would have been because I had no other option," I whispered. "But you are my choice, the only choice I've ever made because I wanted to."

There was a long beat, and midnight opium was filled with despair. He wasn't going to do it.

A sob caught in my chest, and fresh tears flooded my face.

He won't do it.

But then he growled, fingers weaving through my hair, dragging my neck into an arch, and his teeth found my skin once more.

A bond lit—stronger than anything Flynn had threatened. This was real. I collided with his pack, and for the first time in my life, I wasn't alone. For the first time in my life, I had a family.

CHAPTER 22

Umbra

One blink, an explosion of light in the pack bond, and suddenly… we were four.

Ransom straightened where he sat, eyes wide as he looked at me.

I was on my feet in an instant, instinct on high alert.

Shatter was… she was pack.

Then the realisation hit me.

"No…"

Dusk had… *No!* I was crossing the kitchen in a daze and ripping open the door to his room.

They were on the bed. Shatter was beneath him, hair scattered around her, an oversized T-shirt riding up her hips. Her golden eyes were wide as Dusk pinned her to the bed, his teeth at her neck.

My aura split the air, and Dusk looked up, bright yellow eyes finding me in a second, a glisten of her blood on his lips and trailing down his umber skin.

The world came to a halt.

I *knew* we were different, me and him—I thought, I *believed*, that he had been right for her after what had happened—but this?

I was upon him in an instant, ripping him from her and slamming him against the wall. "What have you done?"

After everything she'd gone through.

He was pack lead—I'd never once, before this moment, regretted that. Only, I wasn't met with the defiance I was expecting. Dusk's eyes were shocked, darting between mine, absolutely unsure.

"Umbra!" Shatter's voice caught me off guard, and then she was shoving her petite frame between us, her fingers gripping my shirt desperately. "W-wait!"

"Shatter…" My voice was rough. I couldn't take my gaze from the poisoned mark on her neck, leeching darkness across her skin.

"I…" She was breathing heavily, and she looked afraid. "I asked him to."

"You what?"

"I…" She trailed off, glancing back at Dusk. "I wanted…"

With me and Ransom in the room, she was getting overwhelmed again. Only, this time, I could feel her panic like it was mine. A twisted ball of darkness and self-doubt—no, no.

That was wrong.

"I wanted…" She pressed back against Dusk, spiralling viciously. But I could feel what she wanted, bundled away deep and hiding behind panic and darkness.

I sank to my knees before her. "Oh, Nightshade…"

She wanted everything I wanted.

She wanted a pack.

"Please d-don't be mad," she whispered, voice thick.

Mad that she was ours? I cupped her cheek as she stared at me, still so unsure. "Never."

But as for Dusk, *he was a goddamned—*

She stumbled into my arms, gripping me so tight that she crushed the thought to dust. I drew her against me as an uneven purr rumbled to life in her chest.

Ah… Fuck.

"I love you," I breathed.

It was done; she was ours, and even I couldn't contend with my rising tide of relief.

The Lincoln pack would never be able to touch her.

My eyes found Dusk's again as he vanished from the bond. I'd never seen him look this shocked in my life.

Shatter broke from me only when she spied Ransom in the room. Her eyes were nervous again.

"He's been dying to meet you," I told her, nudging her forward.

She blinked, swallowing, clearly trying to find words. "H-hi."

Ransom cupped the back of his neck and was doing that freakishly-still-reptilian thing he did when he was observing something he didn't quite know how to process. "A dark bond?" he asked, voice rough.

"I… I asked for it." I nudged her another step, and she moved toward him awkwardly, wringing her hands. "I, um… I guess I'm in your pack and you don't even really know me."

"What's new?" he said, a smile twitching his lips. His pupils were blown wide as he took her in, and there was nothing but a primal curiosity from him down the bond until he snapped it shut, eyes flicking to me, like he'd felt me prodding.

"You're, uh"—Shatter swallowed, her head flinching in our direction like she wanted to look at us again—"really pretty."

Ransom's grin was cocky this time.

She shouldn't be throwing compliments around like that; they went to his head quick. I grinned too, then caught Dusk's eye, which reignited the volcano of fury that had built as I'd rushed in here.

"What the fuck were you thinking?" I mouthed.

He rubbed his face, looking lost.

He replied under his breath as Shatter said something else to Ransom. "She was… very…" He trailed off with a wince. "…sad."

Oh, for fuck's sake.

"Of course she was, you fucking prat—after everything?"

I still couldn't say, truthfully, I was unhappy, but a dark bond was for life. And she was… well, even with her state of panic, she was… pleased. Really pleased.

It was *Dusk* who wasn't.

He was supposed to be the calculated one. The one who listened to Decebal and his stupid good ideas.

Right now, he looked… well, actually, he looked horrified, as he ran his fingers through his hair. "She was crying."

"Oh, *now* that's a problem for you—?" I cut off as I took a proper look at his torso. What in the fuck had he done to himself?

They'd both gone and cracked.

No fucking warning.

"Next time you need a babysitter, fucking well tell me—" I cut off at a spike of surprise from Shatter down the bond, and then a thump across the room.

We both looked over to see Ransom had pinned her against the wall. Her legs were tangled around his waist, and they were making out intensely.

We both stared for a long, long moment before what they'd been saying clicked in my head.

"Did you just command her to kiss you?" Dusk snarled, shoving past me.

Ransom broke from the kiss, looking defensive as he eyed Dusk's approach. "She was nervous."

"Five seconds with a dark bond, and you're already—"

"It's fine." Shatter looked flustered, cheeks pink, and her lip definitely wasn't trembling anymore. Her eyes were wide as she glanced up at Ransom, and I felt the little spark of—*huh.* Okay. This whole… possessive alpha-omega situation hadn't changed one bit with Ransom waking.

"Uh, guys, is everything—? Oh." Decebal cut off as a snarl ripped from Ransom's chest. He dropped Shatter instantly, spinning on the door. Her T-shirt tumbled down to cover her to mid-thigh, which settled my little spike of defensiveness. He was an out-of-pack alpha, after all, and she was ours.

Decebal took a step back, lifting his hands. "Shit. I'll be outside."

CHAPTER 23

Dusk

"A dark bond?" Decebal asked as he seated me in the kitchen chair to inspect my wounds. His tattooed arms were folded, a pierced eyebrow raised as he peered down at me with dark eyes. "And what in the fresh fucking hell did you do to your body?" He prodded one of my burns like the prick he was. I let out a growl, wrestling with my aura, though many of the coverings I'd applied last night had fallen off. "Don't you start."

I wasn't ready to hear it. My ears were still ringing with shock, and I'd left her in the bedroom with Umbra and Ransom.

I'd fucked up.

It had been a moment of weakness.

"Let me clean them," Decebal was saying. "You and Umbra are as bad as each other."

"She's the one who has wounds that need—"

"Let them fuck or celebrate or whatever else they're doing. I'll check those after."

Gritting my teeth, I allowed him to unzip his med kit and get to work while containing my flinches and growls.

His scent of cranberries and roses was obscenely settling to my frayed nerves.

How many times had he come out to this cabin for a desperate call because Ransom had taken a turn or Umbra's void had dragged him down for too long, and I was scared he would go too far, and I couldn't stop him? Not on my own.

Or the times we'd never talk about because some of those calls… they'd just been me. At the start, when Umbra was still in and out and Ransom was deteriorating, Decebal would sometimes get a call with an emergency that turned out not to be an emergency at all.

He'd never said a word about it.

He'd crack a bottle of whiskey, sit out on the porch with me with a cigarette, even if it was the dead of winter, and we'd drink in silence until my aura went away and everything seemed manageable again.

Once, he'd even brought his pack mate, the seer, who'd sat on the couch, trashing all the top scores on one of Umbra's favourite fighting games until he'd surfaced.

Umbra was still pissed he couldn't even rank, and "RedEyedBandit" still dominated the entire scoreboard.

Finally, Decebal spoke into the silence. "The two alphas in the hospital, they're no longer in critical condition. Paid off the pack. They won't say a thing."

"What?" I blinked, trying to figure out what he was saying.

"I went to the campus first to clean up after you. Thought you might need it—and I was right. Umbra nearly killed those two alphas. I assumed it was to do with the… incident."

"Oh."

That tide of burning fury rose again, and I fought to keep my aura down as the memory flashed in my vision. Panic had me in a vice, blurring the world. *It was dark and rainy, and she was beside an archway on the grounds. Two alphas had her.*

They had their hands on my omega.

She was terrified, crying.

In that moment, Umbra and I had been one. Only, he got there first.

Pure fear was the only reason they weren't dead. Umbra had returned the moment he'd felt us through the bond—that was when she'd started screaming, feral and broken.

"They should be dead," I muttered.

"Umbra had the same sentiment. But if it makes you feel better, from what I heard, they're going to wish they were," Decebal muttered. "I'm not blaming you, but that kind of shit is going to ruin your plans if it keeps happening."

I shut my eyes as he continued to work, peeling off the covering on my chest this time.

"*Why* are the brands all over your fucking chest, mate?"

"They're her…" I trailed off, still not recovered from the last wave of hatred. "The scars they gave her."

There was a long pause, and I heard him breathe a curse. "Bites?" he asked at last, as if he didn't really want the answer.

"Never…" I grit my teeth as I felt him prod at another wound. "Never seen anything like it."

"You'll get revenge."

Not soon enough.

We fell into another silence as he worked.

"Have you checked your texts?" he asked, when he was about halfway done.

"Phone's dead."

I didn't want to charge it. Not with the video I'd been sent. I didn't want to see it—I didn't even want the possibility of seeing it.

"I went into the apartment," Decebal said. "That friend—Roxy—is in there."

"I told her she could stay. She told us Shatter was gone."

"Figured. Sent an email to the Dean to get her into the apartment on your floor. Thought you'd want her close."

"The Lincoln pack—?" I began.

"Dropped her."

That meant they knew she'd ratted on them. It meant she may not be safe.

This conversation wasn't enough to keep me grounded in sanity. Not with the searing pain of each brand as Decebal cleaned them. Not knowing that this was Shatter's pain.

And I couldn't kill them.

I couldn't do *fucking* anything.

Instead, I'd fucked up—I'd goddamned dark bonded her.

Had it been fear? Had the Lincoln pack, stupid fucking idiots that they were, baited me into that?

I'd never seen her hurt like that. I didn't know how weak I would be, faced with it.

"A bond was a decent solution, given the circumstances," Decebal murmured.

"Decent solution?" I asked. "It was stupid."

"Then, why did you do it?"

I glared at him. "When *you're* faced with an omega begging you to do what you know you absolutely shouldn't, telling you they *need* you, and you can... can fucking fix everything—then tell me how you fucking do."

Decebal snorted. "I'll get back to you on that when we find ours."

We'd spent a fair amount of time with Decebal over the last few years. His pack didn't have an omega because they were waiting for a scent match. He'd admitted once, with a few drinks in him, that he was holding out for his scent match more than any of his pack brothers. A secret romantic.

"She asked," he added. "It's not... unheard of. And you have an omega who loves you. For all the goddamned plans we've come up with to fix things, she just walks on in and brings Ransom back."

"Are you jealous?"

Decebal gave me a half-smile. "Once you get it registered and a seer assesses it, everyone will know she asked," he said.

"I know."

Dark bonds were absolute. For life. But seers—alphas and omegas who had the ability to visualise auras—could determine whether the dark bond was taken or given with permission. It didn't affect the bond itself, but it did affect reputation.

As if we gave a fuck about reputation.

"Problem is..." He tore off a piece of tape to dress my last brand. "You just gave up one of your healing options."

"What does that mean?" Shatter's voice carried through the living room.

Ah *shit.*

I looked up to see her in a T-shirt, leggings, and a fluffy white dressing gown, golden eyes bright and scared as she stared between us.

Decebal glanced over, frowning, then looked back at me. "I assume you're going to tell her."

Great. "Well, now I fucking am."

She wouldn't be pleased.

She crossed toward us, her nightshade scent carrying in with her. Umbra and Ransom both entered the room behind her.

"You know that we're... sick," I said.

She looked between us. "You mean... like what happened the other week?"

As on edge as I was, flashes of that night threatened to rip me away at the mere mention of it.

Wading through agony to get to Umbra, so terrified I'd be too late, so terrified she'd leave...

One touch. One fucking touch from Flynn, and that was enough to almost kill us…

I hated it.

"Yes." I cleared my throat as I caught her giving me a funny look. "One of the possible solutions to our sickness was a… a princess bond." I winced, knowing she'd be upset.

"You mean it's happened before?" she asked.

"We'll explain everything. Decebal brought the information."

"But... you needed a princess bond?" Shatter pushed.

"Princess bonds are the only absolute cure to aura sickness," Decebal said. "It doesn't seem like a huge jump to assume—"

"Except," I interrupted, "I was never going to risk biting an omega into our pack just for that."

"They would have been a scent match... you would have wanted to...?" She looked pale all of a sudden.

"Oh no," I spluttered. "You"—I jabbed my finger at her—"don't get to seduce me into dark bonding you with *scent matches are worthless* rhetoric and then throw *that* in my face."

Shatter pouted, folding her arms, but didn't seem to have a response to that.

Umbra chuckled as he crossed to his huge pan of sausages and eggs and began serving up.

Shatter

We'd had breakfast, and Decebal had retrieved a USB from his car. "It has everything on it," Dusk had said. Umbra was printing it out right now for us.

Until then, Decebal had wanted to look at my wounds. I wasn't ready for Umbra and Ransom to see them, so Dusk, Decebel, and I were in another room in the huge cabin. It had a pool table, a home theatre, and a big cove of couches. I liked it here. Every room had huge windows, showing the trees outside, which reminded me a bit of the gardens in the Estate.

"The two on your shoulder and arm, could I check them over and make sure they're not getting infected?" Decebal asked. "I could check them all—"

He cut off, catching my expression.

"But I…" He cleared his throat. "I assumed you might not want me to, given where some are. We can just see if Dusk did a decent job."

Oh. "Okay." I nodded. "How do you know where they are?" I asked.

"Dusk informed me he matched yours." Decebal snorted.

"Right."

Decebal was tall, with deathly pale skin, a scar across his left cheek, and tattoos that crept up to his jawline. He looked super badass, though he was gentle as he peeled back the dressing that Dusk had put on.

"It's all right?" Dusk asked at my side.

"Yeh. Just want to make sure. Going to give it another clean."

I tried to settle as I felt the cool touch along the wound. It didn't hurt as much as yesterday.

"Are you okay with my scent?" I asked, hyper-aware that I was no longer on any scent blockers. He was an alpha, with a nice scent of roses and cranberries.

"I think so," he said with a shrug.

"But… it's not good?" I asked. I knew he'd read over the files, just like Dusk had. I heard Dusk's rumbling growl at my side and darted a look in his direction.

"I don't get much information from other alphas," I whispered.

I just had to live in fear. And Decebal seemed calm.

Dusk rolled his eyes.

Decebal chuckled. "I can understand why it might be… unexpected, but it's not too much." I heard him rooting around in his kit. "You were told one of the solutions was bonding a pack?"

"Yes." My voice was small.

"I can't say for sure, but I think the bond balanced it out. It's not aggravating like it was described in some of the logs I read."

"It's, like… worse for alphas if they're near a rut, right?"

Decebal chuckled. "I'm perpetually near a rut," he said. "But it's not bad, though I've never been much into the super sweet omega scents, anyway."

"What's mine like to you?"

"Floral, earthy. When we match an omega, I hope it's like that."

I smiled as he finished and moved around to my arm, where Dusk helped me tug the shoulder of my shirt down.

"You watching?" he asked Dusk.

"Yup."

"Do it properly. It'll help with the scarring."

"What about him?" I asked. "Should I learn, so I can do his?"

"He doesn't want help with the scarring."

I frowned, but Dusk folded his arms stubbornly.

I paid attention, anyway. I had to help patch Umbra up, and it was looking like there was a lot more to it than I'd thought.

"So, you're waiting for your scent match?" I prodded, interested in that.

"Yup."

"They built a nest and everything," Dusk added.

"Really?" I asked, eyes wide.

Decebal grinned. "You don't think I look the type?"

"No. I didn't mean…" I trailed off, cheeks going pink as my eyes darted across his tattoos.

He *did* look intimidating. I'd even noticed the scar down his cheek, peeking from the loose strands of wavy raven hair that had escaped his ponytail, and his piercing eyes were beetle-black and a little unnerving.

Definitely not the kind of alpha who looked like he'd built a nest for an omega he hadn't met.

Decebal didn't seem offended, though, as he covered up the bite on my arm. "Right. I think they're good. I'm having a smoke, then Umbra should be ready."

"What kind of stuff are you going to show us?" I asked.

"There are some things that you and Ransom need to know. About us. About the Lincoln pack, things I should have told you before."

The Lincoln pack?

I swallowed back my nerves, nodding as Decebal shut the patio door.

"Before that, I just… need to ask him something," I said. "Alone, if that's okay."

I didn't want Dusk hurting more, but the mention of my mates brought up lingering worries.

Dusk stiffened, his gaze darting from me to Decebal, who was settling on a chair on the porch. He nodded, though it looked difficult for him. "I'll be just in the kitchen."

I followed Decebal outside, and he looked up at me curiously as I sat opposite him. It smelled like sweet pine and day-old rain in leaves and soil. Decebal's cigarette tangled with his cranberry and rose scent pleasantly as he peered up at me, taking a drag.

"Can I ask you something?" I asked. "But you can't… can't tell them."

His scent was calm, and I couldn't help but trust him.

"Depends on if it puts them at risk. They pay me."

I shook my head. "It's nothing like that."

"Then, my lips are sealed."

I repositioned in my seat a number of times, gaze fixed on a squirrel that was scurrying up a tree trunk. Finally, I found the courage to speak.

"Some of the bites…" I chewed on my lip. "There couldn't be any… half bond or part bond, right?"

Decebal frowned. "What does that mean?"

"Well, for some of them…" I fisted my shirt tight in an attempt to keep my voice from shaking. "When it was Flynn, the pack lead… it was like I thought there was going to be a bond—a d-dark bond. But then there wasn't."

Decebal's eyes darkened. "If he didn't complete it, you're safe."

"Okay. Good." My chest loosened. "I might have just imagined it, anyway—"

"I doubt that." There was a twisted expression on Decebal's face. "That is something a pack lead can threaten—an intimidation tactic for cowards. If he was, it wasn't by accident."

I stared, unsure what my face was doing right now. I tried to fix it, and Decebal was kind enough to look away as he took another drag.

"I've worked with your pack for a long time," he murmured. "Seen some fucked-up shit—on their case and others. There are no vermin lower than alphas who abuse their power to hurt omegas." He looked sick. "Not how it's supposed to work."

The cigarette smoke rose in the air, much less sweet than Uncle's cigars had been. I didn't hate it, though.

"You're still worried?" he asked after a long pause.

I tugged my knees onto the wooden patio chair and hugged them to my chest. "What if me being in the bond hurts them?"

"It won't."

"How can you be sure?"

He looked back at me, a smile playing on his lips. "You are the only good thing that has happened to that pack in a long time."

I considered that, finding it hard to argue with. And Decebal seemed to know everything about me, Dusk, Umbra, and Ransom, which was a little unnerving. But comforting, too, when he said things like that.

"You remind me of him," I said.

"Dusk?" he asked.

I nodded.

Decebal laughed. "We couldn't be more opposite."

"Why?"

"The pack Dusk was given was broken, and he put it back together, piece by piece. I was given an amazing family, and I…" He trailed off, turning the cigarette in his hand. "You're worried you're poison, Shatter? None of you are. I'm the poison in my pack. I know it when I see it."

I frowned. "Is that why you want an omega?"

"For me?" he asked. "No—well, yes, if you ask me on a selfish day, but I don't have anything to offer, not really." He took another drag of his cigarette, nearly finishing it. "An omega might balance us, though… Bring Bane out of his shell, make them all happy—maybe soften up my pack lead. He carries a lot. He's done a lot, for all of us. He deserves that."

"And you don't?" I asked.

"I don't deserve any of my pack, let alone the omega destined for them."

I frowned, sad at the resolution in his eyes, the absolution of his scent, the edge of roses turning bitter. "You'd have to be a part of it," I said.

He grinned, seeming rather unphased. "I would be. If we got an omega, I'd spoil the shit out of them. I'd make sure they had the world. Dusk and I, we have that in common—pack is everything."

I considered that for a long moment. He'd said he was nothing like Dusk, but I didn't believe it.

Was it possible Dusk felt like this sometimes?

I was his omega now. It seemed I had to watch out for that.

CHAPTER 24

"This is everything we have."

With Ransom at my side on the couch, I stared at the pile of documents. Umbra had been concerned when Dusk sat us down, worried I wasn't ready—that I needed more time to recover—but he didn't understand.

I needed this.

I tentatively reached for the top paper, eyes scanning the sheet, my heart sinking as I read. The words before me wiped everything else away. Paper after paper outlined fragments of trials: alpha experimentation.

Illegal practice… Shut down upon discovery… No survivors…

My heart turned to stone as I understood, at last, the connection between us.

"You were…" I trailed off, looking up at them. "You were at the same facility?"

They were like me? All this time…

"Same place, different owners," Dusk said. "The Institute took over after it was shut down. That's when you arrived."

I read through everything: the snippets of logs of what had been done to Umbra and Dusk, the pain they had suffered. The information was sparse, some were accounts from Dusk and Umbra, compiled by Decebal. I drew up as I read about the death of… shit. "Your pack mate died?" I asked.

"We didn't really know him," Umbra said quietly.

"But the pack bond didn't break?" I asked.

That should be impossible. There had only been three in the bond at the time.

It *should* be, and yet, I was in that very bond right now. Dusk hadn't spun fantasies the other night. He was right. They *were* the impossible—a green sprout breaking through snow.

Umbra was sitting at my side, and I was glad for his arm around me as I read on. He'd been the most present in this new bond that occupied part of my mind. I leaned on him, needing to be reminded that, no matter what I read, he *had* come out the other side.

Ransom had the smallest list. He hadn't been a part of the experiments. He'd been injected with Atropa's Poison when they were leaving. His symptoms came on more rapidly, but they were clear-cut.

For Dusk and Umbra, that wasn't the case. The symptom list was long, even if many had been crossed off with dates beside them.

Insomnia, headaches, seizures that were unique to Dusk, and Umbra used to get phantom pain that would last for days. PTSD wasn't crossed out. Decebal had drawn an arrow toward it with the scrawl that read:

DISSOCIATIVE FLASHBACKS, SOMETIMES ENTIRELY IMPOSSIBLE TO ROUSE THEM FROM. AURAS BECOME UNSTABLE AND SHIFT TO SOMETHING UNRECOGNISABLE. SAME AURA INSTABILITY PROGRESSING OVER TIME. PATIENTS CLAIM THE AURA IS

—I frowned.

"Hostile to its own host?" I finished the line out loud, looking up. Decebal had to be the one who'd done the examinations on them.

"It's not an official diagnosis. They can't risk seeing a real doctor. I have a bit of experience, but I'm out of my depth."

"I saw the sickness," I said, glancing at Dusk. He was seated in the armchair, one leg propped up. His chin rested on his knees as he watched me and Ransom scour the notes. "When you collapsed. That's what it felt like, like it was trying to destroy you."

I looked up to Umbra.

"I manage them with the knife," he said. "Keeps me grounded. And Dusk…"

"I lose time." Dusk shrugged. "It's not as bad as Umbra. Barely happens anymore. He… he took most of the experimentations."

"Those are the symptoms," Decebal said. "The aura shit, that's the real sickness."

"It's more extreme than it's ever been," Umbra said. "It's slower usually, creeping closer."

"Like… your auras are poisoning you?"

"Tell me about the other week?" Decebal asked, glancing around. "I didn't fully understand from your message."

"It was like your auras were untethered," I whispered.

"What?" Ransom looked at me sharply. "But that's…" He swallowed. "That's deadly."

"I've never considered that," Decebal said, gaze fixed on me. "But I've also never seen it as bad as you have."

"It felt like… it wasn't his aura anymore or… or something."

When an alpha lost their pack suddenly or violently, their aura broke.

The missing pack bond left a wound that would never close without help, leaving them unstable—as if they were walking around with a wound that never stopped bleeding.

To seal the wound, they had to do one of three things: take another pack, sever their ability to join a pack completely, or do the last option of the three. The worst option. Make the choice to release their aura entirely—to untether it.

Once they'd done that, their aura would then draw energy from the alpha's own body when used. For a short time, they could gain as much strength as they wished—could become frighteningly strong and dangerous—but once that energy was gone, the aura died, and the alpha died with it.

"That's what it felt like. Like… it was burning *you* up." I frowned. That day, Umbra hadn't chosen to untether his aura—he couldn't have, since his pack was intact, even if he had lost a pack mate. "It's the closest thing I can think of, but it still doesn't quite fit."

I'd read lots about untethered auras; any time I managed to sneak from Uncle's study, I'd read an obscene amount on anything alpha-related.

"Even when untethered, the aura should only exact cost when used," I said. "Umbra's was out of control, consuming him, no matter what he did."

It was similar, but it wasn't the same.

I was staring down at the black-and-white documents, something sick in my stomach. Ransom was right. Untethering was deadly almost every time. If the sickness wasn't cured, would it… would it kill them? The truth was creeping in slowly.

I could feel numbness swallowing me whole.

I had a family at last. A family I loved. And now I might lose them?

Lose Dusk or Umbra? The thought was so charred and horrifying, I had to shove it back. Something thick stuck in my throat.

"But I balanced it…" I whispered, looking up into Umbra's sandstorm eyes. "I anchored you. It couldn't consume us both. Maybe it won't come back now?"

He drew me closer, but wolfsbane wilted, the traces of its sweetness fading. "Maybe."

He didn't sound hopeful, which wasn't like him at all. "What… what was the goal of the experiments?" I asked, my voice weak. If I could just get a better understanding of this, I could try to help fix it.

"No idea. They locked it down tight," Decebal said. "If we knew that, we might not still be here."

"What about *how* you ended up there?" I asked Umbra and Dusk. "Do you know?" Maybe that would help.

But my question was followed by an odd silence that I couldn't read.

"I just thought, if you came from somewhere…?" I swallowed. "What?"

Decebal cleared his throat, shifting uncomfortably.

After a long beat of silence, Dusk shrugged. I noticed his jaw was clenched and his gaze fixed on me. "The organisation that ran experiments, before it was shut down, got their alphas from the Cimmerian Vaults."

My blood ran cold, lips parting as I stared between him and Umbra.

"What?"

I understood his words, but they didn't make sense. The Cimmerian Vaults was a fortified prison that held the most insane and aggressive alphas. Alphas that cracked and lost their sanity entirely. Not alphas like Dusk and Umbra. They were different—I'd always known that—but they weren't insane. Not like you had to be to end up in a place like that.

"I don't like it, but the experiments did one thing right," Dusk said quietly. "Brought us back from… wherever we were."

"But why the Vaults?" It was another alpha-specific thing I'd honed in on in my Arkology textbooks. The Cimmerian Vaults had a whole chapter. It was a logistical nightmare keeping the alphas contained and safe. "Why would the people running the experiments want to deal with containment?"

"All the alphas that were taken ended up registered as dead. Not uncommon in a place like that. It was untraceable."

I nodded, mind racing a million miles a minute. "And… typically alphas like that are stronger, right?"

"Their auras?" Decebal asked.

"Yes," I said. "The auras of the alphas who end up there are typically at least twice as strong as the average."

"And you think that might be why they wanted alphas like that for the experiments?"

"If they were doing experiments on alphas specifically, I would assume auras would play a part in it."

"We just assumed they used the Vaults because no one would look into missing alphas," Dusk said. "And we'd be less likely to rat on them if we were insane to start with."

"But…" Decebal was rubbing his face. "It's not like there aren't other ways to get a hold of alphas. Probably *easier* ways. The New Oxford Trafficking ring is no stranger to alpha trafficking. I just… never thought about it like that."

"So, they didn't just need alphas," Dusk said. "They might have been looking for alphas with particularly strong auras."

"Does that change anything?" Ransom asked. I noticed he'd vanished from the bond, and his jaw was clenched. I reached out and took his hand, though I wasn't sure what he'd think of that. But he squeezed it, his rich, green eyes finding mine. I swear he settled a little.

"You know where you came from? Before, I mean?" I asked. "Before the Vaults, even. They might have your history."

"Yeah," Dusk said. "Decebal found our files."

I straightened. They had those answers? A little flicker of warmth lit in my chest. That was something I'd never had.

"We don't want it," Dusk added. "Not until all of this is over."

"You don't?" I asked. I couldn't imagine that. Not looking when the answers were right there.

"But all of this. It's not…" Dusk took a breath. "It's only half of it."

"What does that mean?" I asked.

"We both came to the academy for the same reason."

I frowned, shrinking against Umbra at the look on Dusk's face.

"The Lincoln pack."

I opened my mouth, then shut it. It took a while for me to find my voice. "My mates?"

"This part is rough, Gem," Dusk said. "If you're not ready—"

"I need to know."

I knew they were monsters. With every movement or shift, my body ached— evidence of that very fact—but all of that paled next to what he was telling me.

Dusk tugged the bottom folder from the stack and handed it to me. "This is new to Ransom too. We found out later. There's a video, but you don't need to see it. It's transcribed."

I opened the file, and ice crept up my spine as I read, horror scratching at the corners of my mind.

The last piece of the puzzle.

CHAPTER 25

Dusk

One Year Earlier

"Sit down."

I stared at Decebal, jaw tight. "Show me."

"I said, *sit.*"

What did he need me to sit for? He said he'd found the truth at last. The video paused on the screen before us held all the answers.

The truth of our nightmares.

"Insurance for the organisation who ran the trials—"

I winced, and he paused.

Trials?

He meant torture. Death. We were nothing but numbers, lab rats, lower, even, than humans. Decebal didn't press play, his beetle black eyes pinning me until, finally, I sat down on the couch, nodding that I was ready.

It was the one and only time I ever saw the video. Decebal kept it on a drive, locked away. We hadn't been recognised on it, but that didn't mean we couldn't be.

It didn't matter, though; every second had stuck with me forever.

The flickering, low-resolution video was a camera feed. It showed a lounge with upper class couches and a glass coffee table. Across the wall was a huge screen—another video feed—and on that screen was a room of white and metal.

A room I knew intimately.

"What is this?" My voice was rough.

Decebal had seen some shit. He'd grown up in the Gritch District—and he looked like it too, with tattoos to his jaw and darkness in his eyes, even in the face of the worst we'd uncovered. But right now, I could see how tense he was, his pale skin almost sickly. He just shook his head as he glanced at me.

"Whatever you thought this was, Dusk. It's worse."

On the screen, three alphas entered the room, glancing around and making themselves comfortable. One began pressing buttons on the remote, and the feed on the screen changed. Each time it flickered, it landed on another room. A black identifying number in the top corner. And each time, the occupants changed.

"What is this?"

"An observation room," Decebal said.

My heart tripped. "For… us?"

"Yes. For all the subjects."

Something was stuck in my throat.

"To fund the trials, they ran…" Decebal grimaced. "Bets."

"Bets?" I asked, voice hoarse. "They're betting on us like… racehorses?"

Decebal nodded. "Which subjects are going to live, which will die. Who will survive with enough strength to be useful for the experiments they're running."

My world shook with every word. At the horror of what he was saying.

That place had been my worst nightmare. For them, it had been a game?

"The only good news is," Decebal went on. "The packs that placed bets were also benefactors of the trials. This pack—they were the ones who bet on you and Umbra. They were the ones involved in what was taken."

"And we still don't know what they were trying to do with the experiments?"

"No. But the pack in this room—they took something. As far as I can tell, it's linked with your pack."

"You think… if we know what they took, we could figure out why we're still sick?"

Decebal looked uncertain. "It's the only lead left."

My memories had long collided with those videos, moments merged—torture with entertainment.

I felt the moment 31 died, a splintering tear through the pack bond.

He'd got free, and Umbra had followed, but I'd been too scared to take more than a step out.

I heard the gunshots in the distance.

Flynn was on his feet in the room, crossing to the pad on the wall. "No. *Don't you dare kill* him—" Flynn cut off as a gunshot rang out, audible even from the camera feed. "Fuck!"

Umbra had me by the shirt. "Get back inside."

He looked wild.

"B-but he's…" He was dead.

"Get inside!" He was shoving me through the door, despite his trembling.

31 had died. Our pack mate…

We should have splintered into a million pieces, but somehow… we didn't.

Flynn balled his fist, and the rest of the pack was on their feet. "Do you know how much I had riding on this?" he snarled into the comms. "I don't care how many people it takes to get him back in the cage. They weren't *supposed* to get out. And they weren't supposed to *fucking die*—"

"Wait—*wait!*" Eric looked down at his phone, then back up at the screen. "It's not over."

"How?"

"They said the bond didn't break."

There were only two of us left in our pack, something that should have been impossible. And in the centre of it was Umbra. My rock.

The one who kept us together.

"We just can't do that—"

"I'll double my bet," Flynn said, cutting off the voice coming from the intercom.

There was a pause. Eric and Gareth had frozen, staring at Flynn. Then the static rang out in the room again. "*Double* it?" the voice asked.

"I haven't got much choice, do I, since you killed their fucking pack member."

"We don't usually take this route until later—"

"There isn't a later. You said if they survive the poison, they stay in?" Flynn demanded.

"Yes," the voice replied. "But with only two members… I mean, it's unheard of. And the risks—"

"I don't care about the risks."

"That's a lot of money, if you lose," Eric said to Flynn, looking unsure. "And if they kill each other, it's over—"

He cut off as Flynn slammed the comms button. "Just give them the fucking poison."

Atropa's poison crept into my mind, ruining me. Turning me on my brother. My fists were tight around his throat as I shook.

"What's he doing?" Gareth demanded. "Fight back, you fucking oaf!"

"He's just going to roll over?" Eric asked.

Flynn was standing before the screen, a scowl on his face as he watched.

Umbra didn't fight me. His hand came up, brushing my cheek.

Terror and confusion collided, and then I was reeling back, letting him go. I knew who he was. He was my brother.

My pack.

And he would die before he killed me.

"Yes!" Eric was laughing. "That's it. We just killed the odds."

They were celebrating.

I clutched Umbra, bones quaking.

My brother.

And I'd nearly killed him.

"My lucky pack," Flynn was saying. "Tell them I'm in—*all* in, and bring us more drinks." The doorman bowed his head, then left.

"Damn, for a moment there…" Gareth blew out a breath.

"Flynn called it," Eric was saying. "Pack five is our golden ticket."

"At least 68 fights back. Won't roll while he's choked to death." Flynn barked a laugh, words slurred. "What kind of shit *was* that, anyway? Fucking pathetic."

The days flickered by, and the Lincoln pack returned, week after week as we suffered.

Umbra was losing it.

He pinned me to the bathroom floor, a plastic fork digging into my skin. I curled up, trying to find solace in the knowledge they wouldn't take him next time.

"You've got to be joking." Eric laughed. "Trying to get himself picked?"

"He knows, right?" Gareth asked. "He's got to know."

"I think he does," Flynn snorted. "But I don't give a shit what he does. It's fucking working."

Umbra was gone.

They'd taken him.

After everything, they'd taken him again.

I lost it, aura flaring, the world burning around me as I felt his pain and fear through the bond. I threw myself against the walls until I was black with bruises, until I hurt so much, I couldn't feel him anymore.

"He didn't see that coming this time? How fucking thick is he?"

That was the day the Lincoln alphas were brought a black suitcase. That last day they had visited.

Inside that case was what they'd stolen—the missing piece we'd been hunting. But no words were exchanged on the video feed, addressing what was inside. When it was set on the table before Flynn, Eric clapped him on the arm.

"Beat more than just the odds this time."

Present

My own mates entered this horrifying picture.

I learned, at last, what role they had to play. With every line, I read the truth.

My pain, it was the smallest piece; there was more to all of this, spanning further than I could have imagined.

"An observation room?" Ransom asked, his voice rough as he read behind me. "They were watching while they… they ran experiments on you?"

Dusk's expression was twisted. "They were betting."

"It wasn't just that," Decebal said. "They made a sport of it, but they were there for a reason. We don't know the full story, but they were there for the experiments as much as the bets."

"*Her*… mates?" Ransom asked.

"All the major players involved are dead or insane, so they're all we've got. We know they took something, we just don't know what it is. The day they left, they walked away with a suitcase. We don't know what was inside—"

"We hope whatever it is will give us answers," Dusk added, catching Ransom's expression. "Thought it was the winnings at first, but those were deposited into an offshore bank account Decebal's pack mate dug up."

"Whatever's in there will help you get better?" Ransom asked.

Decebal nodded.

"And they didn't recognise you at the academy?" I asked. If the Lincoln pack had watched…

"The feeds weren't detailed," Decebal said. "And neither Umbra nor Dusk…" He glanced between them apologetically. "They looked *different* back then. Hair was short, and they weren't… well. Their names were their own choice; the facility never had those."

I understood. Even that picture of me in a white gown with my hair up and expression drawn. I was all but unrecognisable…

"They're our last lead," Dusk said. "But we know they're close to it. What happened the other week, when I collapsed, it was because Flynn touched me."

My gaze snapped up to him, throat dry.

What had he just said?

Everything that had happened was because Flynn had *touched* him? My mind was racing in a thousand directions, a thousand puzzle pieces trying to fit together all at once.

I needed to read these files again.

"Who?" Ransom asked.

"Their pack lead. He put a hand on my arm, and—"

"And you nearly died," Decebal said.

What the hell does that mean? There was more to this… More even than Decebal's notes showed.

"Question is, how do you plan on dealing with them, if you can't touch them?" Decebal asked.

"He can," Dusk said, nodding at Ransom. "He was never a part of the experiments. He touched Flynn in the apartment too. Nothing happened."

"So, whatever happened is contained to you and Umbra?" Decebal asked. "I'll take any good news."

"Why are we fucking around with academy enrollment?" Ransom demanded. "We know where they sleep, just—"

"No," I cut him off, worry rising in my chest. "We don't know how they're connected."

"Then, grab them and make them tell us."

"Decebal shut that down," Umbra muttered.

"Why?"

"Because they're it," Decebal said, leaning back in his chair. "If they panic and lie, we have no way of knowing. We don't even know if the answers are actionable. I suggested the academy. Bugging them and getting close—"

"That turned out fucking stellar, didn't it?" Umbra asked mildly.

"Well, you can't control your temper, and I wasn't expecting an omega scrambling Dusk's brain."

"Fuck you," Dusk muttered.

"What about now, with Shatter?" Umbra asked. "She knows all about Arkology shit. She'll know if they're telling the truth."

"No—no. Not enough." My voice was weak. "I still don't… I don't understand what all of this means. I've never read anything like this before."

"Thank you." Decebal waved at me. "Plus, once they know, there's no going back, and you're on your last goddamned life."

I shivered at that statement.

"Okay. I'm with him," Ransom said quietly.

"Oh, for fuck's sake," Umbra groaned.

"So, what's the plan now?" Ransom asked. "We just go back there and wait?"

"Yes. You'll be close if anything turns up. And the moment they find out she's their scent match, it's not like they'll be going anywhere—" Decebal cut off at the growl from Dusk. Panic spiked my system, setting me on high alert.

"They only find out if Shatter wants them to."

Every eye was on me.

How did I look right now?

Not good. I nodded, trying to swallow back my terror. Instincts still warned of danger; the desperate need I'd harboured to keep that secret when I was in Flynn's room, praying my scent blockers wouldn't lapse, lingered like a bitter taste.

I took another breath, feeling Umbra's warm touch trailing gently up and down my arm. I was safe with wolfsbane and blood. Midnight opium. Lily of the valley.

I *was* safe.

Realising I'd withdrawn in the bond, curled up and afraid, I opened it up again, gently reaching out and feeling them there.

I *was* safe.

I was… but… I felt a sudden wave of nausea, and for the first time since I'd run from Eric, the first ripples of hatred. *I* was safe, but my mates weren't.

What they'd given me—their words, their actions, the pain—had made me feel so small. I wanted to turn my back on my own reflection, frightened of how weak and pathetic and worthless I was.

They'd done that to me, and they'd done it before. The very people that made up the fortress at my back, that gave me the strength not to run…

They'd tried to do it to them too—my pack.

Tried to make them nothing.

My mates had laughed as Dusk and Umbra were ripped apart. Had stood in that room, speaking as though they were less than human. Making bets and reducing them to nothing but a game. A bet.

I gripped Umbra's hand tight, looking back at the papers before us.

What they'd taken from my pack… they still had it. And my fear was nothing in the face of that.

CHAPTER 26

Ransom

The look of absolute fury on Shatter's face as Decebal had reached out to collect the stack of papers was almost enough to get a smile from me—even when I felt sick at what I'd just learned.

She went from despair to protectiveness in a split second, a growl rising in her chest, her narrowed eyes fixated on Decebal's hand.

Decebal drew back, eyebrows raised. "We have to destroy them."

"*Destroy* them?" In moments, she'd seized every piece of paper from the coffee table, clutching them to her chest like someone had threatened to steal her firstborn.

"I have the same data in my safe at home," Dusk told her. "But if the Institute gets a hold of those papers—"

"They'll... take you?" She stared at him in horror. "Like Uncle was worried about me being taken?"

"If that's all they did, we'd be lucky," Dusk said.

Again, Decebal tried to tug the papers from her, but she wouldn't let them go.

"Just wait. I'm not *finished.* There's... so much information, and I need to fix it." She pulled it back from Decebal's grip.

"Fix it?" Umbra asked.

"When I read textbooks, everything is in order. This is a disaster; nothing is together right."

"You think we're missing connections?" Decebal asked with a frown.

"Everywhere."

He glanced at Dusk, but Umbra looked unexpectedly happy. "She's a genius. You need to let her have them."

"Genius?" Decebal asked, and I echoed the surprise.

My omega was a genius?

I peered at her. Her hair was wild, eyes wide as she clutched those papers to her chest desperately.

Of course she was.

And... *could* she help, perhaps? Offer something they didn't know?

I needed something other than despair.

"You know how you said you didn't know where she got those entry exams?" Dusk asked Decebal.

"Yeh."

"She took them."

He looked taken aback. "Those numbers were hacked. There isn't even a record of scores that high."

"I *did* take them." Shatter's nose wrinkled with indignance.

"Lucky," Decebal said. "It's the only reason they overlooked the rest of your admission disaster."

"I worked really hard on my admission," she said.

"You didn't fill in a last name."

"I didn't have a last name."

"Well, *now* you do, since Dusk asked for—" Dusk coughed loudly, and I noticed him shoot a glare at Decebal.

"What did you ask him to do?" I asked.

"You can keep the papers," Dusk said to Shatter. "And if you figure something out, we can just add them to my safe back at the apartment."

Decebal frowned. "Dusk, you know it's risky to just leave them around—"

"She thinks she can figure something out," Umbra put in. "She *should* look."

So, that was that. Shatter gathered up the intel like an omega possessed and got to work.

It was comforting, feeling her determination down the bond. It was enough to distract her. And I would live through her feeling of *doing* something.

I'd barely kept up with the conversation.

All I knew was that my pack was sick—still. It was getting worse, and the foul pieces of shit who'd hurt my omega were involved with that too.

I helped that the others put lunch together while she worked, and as afternoon rolled in, Dusk clapped me on the shoulder and nodded toward the games room.

I followed him down the hallway, making sure he could feel me poking at him through the bond. He was still vacant.

Was he upset because he'd bonded her?

It was clear as day that he loved her. God, we all did. She was the only certainty since I'd woken. I mean, *sure*, it was a dark bond, but Umbra had told me it was the only option.

A technicality.

It just made it easier to keep her safe.

"You're back… fully?" Dusk asked as he lifted a pool cue from the rack on the wall and tossed it to me. The familiar weight of it in my hands was comforting. Another little piece of reality to remind me that it was over.

"I… yeh." I thought I was, anyway.

I could see already that he was afraid I might disappear again. But… I didn't think I would. Everything was different now. What she'd done didn't feel like a temporary fix.

"I haven't had a chance to slow down since you woke," he said quietly. "And you're… okay?"

"No."

Dusk paused as he pulled the coloured balls from their pockets on the table.

"I thought… I was dead, Dusk," I said quietly. It wasn't just that she had brought me back. Every moment I'd surfaced, even for a second, it had been a nightmare. "Until her."

Our perfect omega.

"I won't be okay until my pack is. You, Umbra, and her."

And she was going to save them. I just knew it. She'd been sitting on the living room floor for hours now, commandeering the entire space, having shoved the coffee table, couch, and recliner to the walls. She'd spread Decebal's intel everywhere, her side of the bond locked down tight for the first time as she frantically read and re-read every page before placing it in its own place on the floor.

She shot Decebal reproachful looks every time he so much as coughed, as if he might come and sweep them all away.

Umbra seemed content to hang out by the kitchen island to watch and feed her. He told me (rather knowingly) that he believed the pieces of paper tilted at the most extreme angles upon the floor were the ones she deemed most important. We couldn't tell, because she hissed like a cat every time one of us tried to peek, a furious tide of omega indignance surfacing violently for a second.

I could have watched her all day, too. She *was* my solace.

She changed us—the pack I remembered. Before, every new weight threatened to tug us under. *With* her, the world felt brighter, more manageable, somehow.

Even now, a room away, I could feel my dread creeping back, the trauma too fresh. That stomach-turning darkness, like a demon had me in its grip.

I hadn't just been gone; I'd been trapped in a body that wouldn't work.

There were flashes of brightness lighting up that darkness for moments. Memories lighting so briefly, like Dusk with his arm around my shoulder, holding me against him. There was a whole world out there, one that continued turning for all the seconds I'd been gone. But for me, this was it. This was my world—Umbra, Dusk, and now her.

I watched as he set up the rack, letting me work through the silence.

I just drank it in. The scent of midnight opium, an edge of bitterness spiked like strong coffee, overpowering the softer side of amber and vanilla.

He was on edge; I could see the clench to his jaw, even as he set up our game.

I loved pool.

I used to play with him and Umbra for hours in the slices of reality I'd had before sickness took me completely. This room was one of the last memories I had.

"Sometimes you would come, right? Or Umbra would spend the night?" I asked, trying to keep the desperation from my voice. He tilted his head toward me as he placed the last ball.

"You… remember?"

Relief washed over me. I hadn't imagined it, after all. "Fragments," I said.

I would never tell him it was a worse nightmare when I did wake. When I surfaced for a few brief moments to see cuffs on my wrists. Aware for just one second too long. One second was enough to know what had happened to me.

Enough to know that I was going back in any of my next breaths.

It was hard to describe that horror. Like running in a dream, but you never moved, only a thousand times worse. Every time I blinked and woke, it could have been months—Dusk looked more gaunt or Umbra's hair was a different length.

Sometimes I would linger long enough to know what it cost my brother to come and see me. His scent would douse the room until I lost it, and he'd wake to my fist around his throat…

Dusk tossed me the chalk, and I caught it just in time, nodding for him to start. I ran it over the tip of my cue, still trying to drag my mind from the darkness. To dispel the tremor from my hands.

How many times had I wished I would die, so I didn't risk hurting them again? So I wasn't more of a burden on their lives that I had already broken beyond repair.

The demon's claws had sunk deeper with every memory, making every waking moment sickening and stomach wrenching.

Until her.

I'd thought, when nightshade seeped into my senses, waking me at last, and the demon was gone, that I had died at last.

My reaper. The beautiful angel that freed me.

Dusk made the break shot and pocketed a solid. He'd feel me spiralling, but he said nothing as he sank another two.

"You got better," I said. My voice was hoarse.

He surfaced in the bond, yellow eyes meeting mine with a grin, a rare moment of the part of him I'd so rarely seen, a moment of youth and happiness. He turned back to the table and sank another, and I had to clench my jaw to fight the tears that burned my eyes. Despite everything I'd just learned, he was happy.

He might die, but he was happy because I was here.

I'd grown up with obscene wealth and total and utter isolation. I'd known nothing but connections borne of dependence… need… money… Conditional and cold.

Dusk and Umbra had been here this whole time, fighting for me when I could give them nothing. If I'd died, they would have inherited my wealth.

They'd fought for me for no other reason than because they loved me.

Despite every agonising second of darkness, it was worth waking up for that.

A stiff smile curved my lips as I watched him play, pocketing five of the solids before the cue ball scratched.

"Ah. Fuck." He leaned back. "Go on, then." He sighed, sitting on the wing of the couch.

I stared at the table for a while, tapping my finger on the cue. When I finally lined it up, I knew the shot I needed.

I sank my first striped ball. It was therapeutic, focusing on the angles, measuring the table and distance, or where to stripe the cue ball, knowing I could rely on instinct here. The only place I could.

But as each stripe hit the pockets, dread dug its claws deeper.

Finally, there were no more stripes without the hint of a foul.

It took me too long, and I almost expected it to fail. It felt like it *should* fail, but I sank the black ball easily, ending the round.

Dusk snorted. "Four fucking years to get ahead. Still not enough."

My heart sank.

I'd won. My sickness hadn't taken this from me, and all I felt was disgust. Shatter was in the next room, dealing with shit that actually mattered.

What was I good at? Sinking pool balls and getting shit-faced without a hangover? "I'm…" I trailed off. "I'm fucking useless," I muttered.

"That's a bunch of crap."

"She's going *A Beautiful Mind* on this shit, and I'm just—"

"You *just* woke up—"

"Exactly. I just woke up." My voice shook. "All this time, you were sick, and I was taking all your—"

"Ransom." Dusk's voice was sharp.

I spun on him, my voice more aggressive than I meant it to be. "What?"

"Shut the fuck up."

I opened my mouth, then shut it, blindsided.

Dusk snorted, setting his cue down and shoving me in the shoulder. "I didn't keep your spoiled ass alive for years just so you could wake and whine my goddamned ear off."

I chewed on my cheek, knowing there was a bitter expression on my face. He raised a finger and jabbed it at me. "Oh, no. No fucking sulking. You know what? We did you a favour, mate; neither of us warned her you were a spoiled little shit."

"It's true." I glanced at the door to see Umbra leaning against the frame, watching us as he popped open a bag of chips. "Sun shines out of your asshole as far as she's concerned."

"So, do us a favour and quit moaning."

I choked a laugh before I caught myself. But then Dusk had tugged me into a hug. "Bench it for five seconds and let me be happy you're back."

"All right." My voice was weak.

I held on to him too tight, and Dusk dragged me back to the ground when I was otherwise in freefall, just like he always had.

* * *

It was evening, and Shatter showed no signs of freeing the living room from crime-scene-investigation classification.

Umbra was still out there with her, watching with popcorn like it was a show. Dusk and Decebal were in the games room, watching TV.

That meant I had no excuse to avoid tackling the thing I'd been dreading dealing with since I'd woken.

"Fuck." The brush got stuck in my hair as I tried to drag it through my locks.

Dammit.

Four years without a single hair mask. Not a surprise. It wasn't like Dusk knew what good hair products were. The issue was, I had an omega now.

My hair couldn't literally be matted.

I had to talk to her at some point—properly, actually, talk to her. I'd woken in a state of panic, the tail end of a rut in my system, and every time I caught sight of her, all I wanted to do was jump her bones. By the way her scent hit the air every time she looked at me, she wanted the same.

Maybe talking was overrated.

She was mine. We were going to be fine.

I tensed with a snarl as the hairbrush snagged again.

"Dammit."

But I jumped as I caught sight of a glittering golden flash in the mirror. I spun to see her at the doorway, peering in curiously. My heart thundered out of control as her scent breezed in, white petals of nightshade, like a cool breeze on a summer's day.

She stepped toward me, her fists bunched in her T-shirt.

I tugged at the brush.

Thoroughly stuck.

Well.

Shit.

She reached me, eyes wide as her gaze flickered from my face to the brush, something nervous in her expression.

I tugged at the brush again.

Nope.

This was the first time we'd been around each other without something fucking insane going on. Literally, kind of our first actual… meeting. This was the worst romantic introduction in the history of ever. Period.

"Uh…" I trailed off, totally lost for words. I didn't get nervous around girls, but she was so fucking pretty. Her nose had a cute curve to it and wrinkled adorably when she was snarling at Decebal earlier. Her cheeks almost always had a little blush of pink, and her eyes. I could get lost in her eyes. I had. I remembered the first moments, an angel with golden eyes.

She was still staring at me, then at the brush, and her scent was getting oddly… possessive.

She lifted her hand, then drew back, rapping her knuckles against each other anxiously, like she was about to do something she wasn't sure about.

"You're… having hair trouble?" she asked. Her eyes shone—and when had her pupils blown that much? Even in the bond, I felt her tumbling far from the intensity she'd had when she was studying. If I had to name it, I'd say she was on the edge of feral.

I nodded.

Another wildly strange beat passed, and a smile wobbled on her lips for a moment. Then she leaned up and drew her jaw along my cheek so gently, I wouldn't have known what it was—until nightshade drowned me.

That was a scent mark.

Then she had me by the arm and was dragging me from the bathroom. She stopped me in front of the bed and was making me sit rather aggressively.

What was going on?

She got to work, plucking strands of my hair from the hairbrush. Even more oddly, little purrs kept rumbling in her chest.

Once she was done, she scent marked me again and began to brush my hair gently, from the ends to the roots. It was going to take a while, but she didn't seem to mind.

A number of times, I opened my mouth to speak, then shut it. I didn't need to. This was fine, even if I had no idea what was going on.

Then I felt her prodding at me through the bond. I made sure it was open for her. It was hard not to feel calm with her scent everywhere and her touch occasionally brushing my neck or cheek as she worked through my hair.

"You're done with the information, then?" I asked at last.

"Oh, no. Um… you seemed a bit stressed… in the bond."

My hair stress was that obvious?

Sure. Right, that was my problem. Not the looming threat of the death of my pack mates Decebal had just delivered.

I let her continue detangling my hair for a little longer before I dared ask. "What's the takeaway?"

There was a long pause, and when she spoke, it was in a small whisper. "It's… bad."

My heart sank.

I'd looked through the papers. I'd processed it as best I could, though I didn't have the mind she obviously did.

"Will you help me save them?" She sounded anxious. "Both of them."

I froze, and the hairbrush halted its movement.

"What do you mean?" I asked. The meeting we just had was proof enough that saving them was exactly what we were trying to do.

"Dusk is…" She trailed off, hairbrush falling away, and I shifted so I could see her. She settled on her knees before me, something pleading in her eyes. "He spends so much time thinking about you and Umbra and… and me, that anything he's planning might…"

"Leave him behind?" I asked.

She cocked her head, the look in her eyes confirming it as she examined me. Her wide eyes were a storm of nerves and ferocity the likes of which I'd never seen.

"There are other options he didn't have before—ones that could help—but he's not going to want to try them."

I narrowed my eyes. "If it helps Dusk, it helps Umbra. He'll be in. Why don't you want him to know?"

She chewed on her lip, eyes calculated. "Because they involve me."

I considered that, but I didn't think it was the full truth. Not if she was coming to me instead of him. "You mean they might hurt you?"

"No. I mean..." She tugged on a lock of hair. "Not necessarily. But my... my scent matches are involved. I think he's going to shut down anything that might make me a part of it."

"They hurt you." That fact was a hot coal, constantly present in the pit of my stomach, igniting rage at every reminder.

Her brows drew down, and the nightshade in the room turned sharp. "They're hurting Dusk and Umbra."

"But you think it might put you at risk."

"I don't know. I need to go through some of my Arkology books, but I have some ideas..."

"I don't want you in the firing line, Little Reaper. You're already more a part of this than you should be—"

I cut off as her hand snapped out, grabbing my shirt in her fist, eyes blazing. "You didn't see them the day Dusk collapsed. You didn't see how close to death they were—what Umbra was doing to stay alive." Her voice cracked, tears filling her eyes. "I think that's where they're headed, and we can't risk being too late."

I stared at her, hating, once again, how much I'd missed.

"This is it for me. I'm already a part of it. You—*they*—are my pack. My family. It's all I've dreamed of. I won't..." She took a breath, voice shaking. "I'm not going to let them die."

Warmth spread through my veins. With every corner I turned and every new thing I learned about her, she became more extraordinary.

"Okay," I said. If being her support is what I had to offer this pack, I would do that. And I would make damn sure whatever insane plan her crazy little brain came up with didn't get her hurt in the process.

"Okay?" she asked, as if she hadn't expected it.

"I'll help you protect them."

Her smile was enough to stop the world.

"Kiss me," I told her.

I'd done it before, and I'd craved it since. The command lit between us, igniting the bond that made her ours. Her palms brushed my cheeks, and her energy through the bond—anxiety, anger, fear—all drained away for peace as she melted beneath the command, submitting to it in a strange moment of freedom.

Her fingers wove through my hair as she pressed her lips to mine, and I realised she'd brushed out every last tangle.

CHAPTER 27

Umbra

Shatter had been obsessive about those files for too long. It was ten in the evening, and she'd barely stopped—ducking out only once for a short time to see Ransom, but she'd been back at it the moment she'd reemerged. The living room looked like a bomb had gone off in it.

Her anxiety had switched out for frenzy, and while I loved that she was trying to save us, it worried me.

I sat down on the couch that had been shoved backward so she could have more floor space. She was chewing on another pen, since her first had exploded all over her earlier. There was still evidence of that in her hair.

She glanced up at me, then back down at the papers, a shiver of nerves taking flight from her end of the bond. They did that every time she stopped for too long. Every time the papers in front of her stopped offering solace amidst obsession.

The bond completed my picture of her—the things I'd suspected but couldn't confirm. Shatter was someone who'd been running from her fears for as long as she had memory. With every victory came a dozen failures, until her world was made of nothing but doubt.

And now our pack was at risk of being one of those failures.

She was afraid, not just of this, but of the trauma that was chasing her, the pain from her mates that she hadn't had time to process.

"Are you… are you okay?" she asked, looking up at me while fidgeting with a stack before her. Shifting it back and forward, eyes snagging on words, like she couldn't quite look away.

"I could use some cuddles," I said.

"Oh." She reached out, beginning to gather up papers.

Oh ho ho, I didn't think so.

"In the hot tub."

She opened her mouth to argue, but I quickly added, "Hot tub cuddles are my dream."

I had a lot of dreams, but she didn't need to know that.

Her jaw clenched as she looked down at the papers, as if trying to figure out how she could make them waterproof.

"For a bit," she said.

Psh.

I'd cuddle her for as long as it took for her frenzy to die down. She'd asked for the dark bond. I wasn't going to throw around commands like Ransom, but if it was necessary to order her to keep cuddling me so her very important brain didn't melt out of her ears, then that was just life.

And *that's* how I found myself climbing into the warm tub beneath the stars with my sweet little siren nightshade.

I was right, too. She wasn't better. The frenzy had been a mask. She kept her T-shirt on, scared to show me what was beneath.

Her scars. The bites.

I knew.

Schooling and me, well, we might no longer be friends, but I wasn't totally stupid.

Yet, those scars were hers, and I didn't need to see them unless she wanted to share. I had spotted a dressing peeking from beneath her T-shirt sleeves, though.

"Can you keep them out of the water easily?" I asked, suddenly concerned.

"Oh, yeh. They're, uh… they're higher up." She got all flighty when she said it, even in the bond.

She needed to know she was safe with us, no matter what.

I could do that. One little bit at a time.

The water bubbled around us as I drew her close, savouring the feeling of her arms around me. Her body pressed to mine. Her scent tangled with the hot tub and earth and pine from the trees beyond.

We sat for a while like that, and I felt her unfurl like a flower in the bond. Frenzy fading for that fear again. It wasn't nice, but it was good. If she stayed curled up tight like that, it would eventually start tearing its way out from the inside.

"I love you," I breathed as the bubbles died down, running my thumb up and down her waist where my hand rested.

She leaned back, something so sad in her eyes that it broke my heart. "What if you and Ransom see, and you don't want me anymore?"

"That, Nightshade, is never going to happen."

I caught her wrists gently, lifting her hands and pressing her palms to my chest. I lifted them slowly, so she could feel every bump of endless scars that marked my body as the canvas it was. My payment.

And she'd never run from me.

She shut her eyes, the soft wing of a butterfly smothering gold as a tear tumbled down her cheek, glittering beneath the stars and the moon above us.

I wiped it away, cupping her face as I left her hands pressed to my chest. "You're strong, Shatter. You're going to be okay."

I know she didn't believe it, but I knew it.

"Will *you* be?" she asked.

"I've decided… yes." Dying wasn't an option anymore. "I need to see you in glasses."

Her brows bunched, all cute-like. "My eyesight is actually quite good…"

"Might not be when you're old. I'll wait."

A smile trembled on her lips for a moment, and then she settled back against me.

"You haven't used the dark bond," she whispered after a long time.

"No."

Surprisingly, I felt a trickle of worry from her.

"Would you like me to?" I asked.

There was a pause. "You didn't want it, did you?"

"I didn't want anyone taking that choice away from you," I replied.

"He didn't."

I knew that now. "I want you," I told her. "That's what matters."

"I know I was running from it before… but then…" She trailed off, as if she wasn't sure how to explain it.

That was okay.

I could see her.

Everything she'd placed on a pedestal had turned to dust. The script had flipped—and this, *this* bond was the only part she could control when the cramped world of dreams was torn from under her.

That was going to have to change. I wanted her to build her world of dreams and choices that was bigger than she could ever even imagine.

"I'm… I *am* okay with the dark bond," she whispered.

A purr rumbled to life in my chest as I drew her closer. "That's trust I don't know what to do with."

She leaned back, finally brightening a little. *Truly* brightening, and not just in a frenzy. She drew me close, pressing her lips to mine.

I slid my dripping fingers through her hair, ignoring how they tangled in her locks, and pulled her against me further, lifting her and kissing her.

She took one of my wrists, her other hand still holding me in a kiss, and ever so slowly, slid it beneath her shirt, lifting it higher, as if she perhaps wanted me to know. Wanted to risk letting me find her wounds and discovering I might push her away.

Never.

She broke the kiss, eyes holding mine, wild hair backlit by the moon, a shadow cast across her face, golden eyes glinting dimly like a dying firefly at night. She'd paused with my hand at her ribs. Her lip caught in her teeth, and her breaths came sharper.

I felt her delicate fingers shake.

"You don't have to, Nightshade. Not until you're ready. I won't love you any less."

One more beat passed, and then she curled in on herself. I dropped my hands, pulling her tight against me once more.

She was so small.

It was hard to reckon with what had happened. To imagine anyone hurting her.

I shut my eyes, violent hatred lurking between the cracks splintering across my mind. The only thing keeping me tethered was the cool petals of nightshade tangling with the hot tub chemicals, and the earth and pine in the forest beyond.

Just enough to lull to sleep that dormant beast. The half of me that had lived in the Cimmerian Vaults. It had woken once for her, already. When I'd seen those alphas with their hands on her… without a care for her fear or spirit or soul—what made someone important. Creatures like that, if they were no more, karma had no complaints.

She had to understand, though, and I don't know if she did.

"They're going to die," I said.

She was gentle, but this wasn't something I could protect her from.

"The price cannot be you," she whispered.

"I know."

"Glasses, remember?"

The fact was, I knew I was broken. But before, I'd been so broken, that I'd never cared that I was.

But now?

I cared if it meant not being enough to protect her.

There was a gift in there somewhere, the frightening fragments of a person long gone. A piece to claim back. As dangerous as it was tempting, and equally impossible to ignore.

I was a shell, left to scrounge from the rubble of a person I would never be again. There had been a monster before the experiments, a monster from the Cimmerian Vaults, but that wasn't where the rubble came from. The rubble came from destruction before that. The faintest flash of memory and life I felt when I rubbed a coin between my fingers or shuffled a deck of cards. In the moment I'd watched a young boy tumble from monkey bars when we'd brought Ransom to the park, or when I caught the sweet scents of a candy shop.

The rubble came from there. And it was in black and white on the document Decebal had dug up on my past.

Dusk used those files as motivation, a prize for the moment we were free. I would never look. I'd burn them the second Decebal handed them over.

That hadn't changed, but the reason… *Shatter* had changed the reason.

Before, I knew there was no point to knowing. Now, I didn't want to because I couldn't risk it. I couldn't risk breaking again, when I had something to heal for.

"We're going back tomorrow," she said quietly. The silence had stretched for a long time. I drew her closer.

"I promise, Nightshade. We won't rush you into anything."

When we returned to Rookwood Academy, she wouldn't face her monsters alone.

CHAPTER 28

Dusk

Decebal had got everything sorted with the Dean. Shatter was going to stay in the apartment with Ransom for the week under the guise of catching him up with course work. Well, she *would* also be doing that, since we were committed to the academy for longer now.

Beyond that, I wasn't sure. I would be damned if the Lincoln pack ruined her studies. We'd never planned on actually staying at the academy after we got what we needed, but she was our omega now, which meant if she wanted to see her classes through to the end, that's what we'd be doing.

"Dusk?" Decebal caught me in the doorway as I was making for the car. The others were in, and we were ready to leave.

"Yeh?" I asked.

"I just had a thought. You said Shatter was different from any omega, from the first time you met her?"

"Understatement," I replied.

"Now she's woken Ransom and saved you and Umbra after Flynn touched you."

"Right."

"What if it's because of what happened to her at the facility? She got injected with something she shouldn't have. The poison they were using while you were there—her scent even matches it. What if it's tied with how she's healing you?"

"What are you getting at?" I asked.

"Vandle."

I froze, staring at him. "You think her scent—?"

"She brought you back. What if she could—?"

"I *won't* take her into that place." My voice was low. "Even if we wanted to—?"

"We wouldn't have to," Decebal said. "All we'd need was her scent."

Shit. He was right.

"All right. Book a visit."

I was left to ponder that as I drove us back to the academy. Shatter was in the back with Umbra, playing cards, and Ransom was at my side. He was quiet again, but I thought he was less down. I hoped he'd heard me. I got it, feeling helpless, I really did, but he'd suffered enough.

The closer we got to the academy, the more nervous Shatter was through the bond. Umbra noticed, too, because he even let her win a game. I *knew* he had because that was a trick deck, and she literally couldn't win unless he wanted her to.

Upon her victory, they stopped playing, and she curled up under his arm, fading away in the bond, as if she didn't want us knowing how she felt.

I still hadn't surfaced, either. I should, I knew that, but I hadn't got a grip on my own feelings about dark bonding her, and she was so happy to be a part of our pack, I didn't want her getting a flicker of it.

When we pulled in, it was already starting to get dark. Shatter didn't put her contacts in, but she did tuck a scarf around her neck and pull the hood of Umbra's oversized hoodie up.

We got back to the apartment without many witnesses, which meant she was free to hide here until she was ready to leave.

When I opened the door, it was to find an omega on our couch. I'd offered to let Roxy stay, but I still hadn't turned my phone on, and I don't know why, but I assumed she would have left by now.

Roxy scrambled up, dropping the blanket she'd been curled up in on the couch, turning from the baking show playing on the TV.

"Shatter!" She looked more of a mess than I thought Roxy Vasilli could look, with hair in a messy bun and bags beneath her eyes. Her phone slipped from her hands, and she was racing across the room, throwing herself upon Shatter before she made it through the door. "I'm so sorry."

Shatter held her, eyes wide with alarm. "It's okay," she said.

"No, it's not."

"I lost you your sponsorship—"

"They can burn in hell, for all I care," she hissed, drawing back. "All that—" She cut off, her face blanching. The scarf Shatter had been wearing had tumbled off in the hug, revealing the poisoned mark across her neck.

Shatter's hand jumped up, and she looked panicked. "Uh..." She glanced at me desperately, which was when Roxy unfroze, a growl rising in her throat as she tugged Shatter away, absolutely vicious.

Shit. She was going to think—

"W-wait!" Shatter said, tugging on Roxy's sleeve.

I frowned. What *would* she think? Actually, I needed to know.

My voice was quiet as I stepped past them both. *"Shatter. Not a word. Go to your nest."*

Shatter's eyes widened at my tone and the dark bond command. She took a shaky step back before halting. I didn't feel the pain myself, but I *knew*, somehow, that it rolled through her body, an alert that she was fighting my command. Her jaw clenched, and her look was beyond hurt.

Shit.

I hadn't meant for that to happen.

"Go," I said again. This time, it wasn't a command.

"How *dare* you!" Roxy snarled.

I shot Umbra a look. He examined my expression for a long moment. "Come on, Nightshade," he said. "Give them a minute." Shatter frowned, but she let him lead her away.

"Fuck, no." Roxy was stepping after her, but I caught her by the arm.

"We need to talk."

"Don't touch me, you foul—"

"*Don't* test me."

Roxy froze, her eyes hateful, before she glanced down the hall at Shatter, clearly worried my words meant I would take it out on her. I didn't correct her. I needed to see this for myself, because it might be the other shield that protected Shatter now that we were back.

"Ransom," I growled. He'd been frozen in the doorway behind me, caught between anger and confusion. I nodded down the hall where I heard Shatter's nest door shut. She was still completely vacant from the bond. He glanced between me and Roxy one last time, but thankfully, followed the others.

The moment he was gone, Roxy turned on me. "I trusted you," she spat as I stepped into the kitchen and opened the fridge, thankful that Umbra's beer was still there.

Thank *fuck*.

I'd just hurt my omega with the dark bond I should never have given her.

It had been thoughtless.... too easy...

Roxy rounded on me. "I came to you to protect her!" she hissed. "And you do *this*—after everything she went through?"

"I need you to be aware of two things," I said, crossing my arms and tapping my finger on the edge of the beer as I leaned against the fridge. I could trust Roxy, I believed that. But I needed this from her, first.

"Shatter is scent matched to the Lincoln pack."

Roxy froze, staring up at me with wide eyes, her mouth working soundlessly for a moment. "Why—why didn't she tell me?"

"Because," I said. This was the second thing Roxy deserved to know, for Shatter's sake. "I've been drugging her every morning before school so that they would never catch her scent. The decision not to tell anyone was mine, not hers. She never had a say in the matter."

Roxy looked about as disgusted as I expected. "Why?"

"Because I think the universe made a mistake. They don't deserve her."

I could see it in her eyes—she thought I was right. Though, now she didn't think Shatter belonged with me, either.

I cracked the beer and crossed to the couch, reaching for the remote and turning to the TV to flick through channels.

Roxy was having none of it, following me and ripping the remote from my hand before throwing it back on the couch.

"You dark bonded her because of *them*?" she snarled. I could see her working through the new information, piecing it together.

"She's mine," I said quietly, cocking my head and fixing my gaze on her. Roxy leaned back, her lip curled in a snarl. Her scent was an assault in the room. I'd noticed she'd been using a dampening spray, so her scent was muted, but now it was like being smothered by an angry Christmas tree. Really quite unsettling, actually.

"That's what this is?" she demanded. "You can't stand that she's matched to them after what they did, so you had to one up them?" Her eyes were wild with fury. "You're fucking sick."

I stared at her, working through that.

"It wasn't her fault," Roxy hissed. "She must have been…" She trailed off, eyes wide. "If they're her mates?" She looked like she wanted to throw up. "It must have broken her. And you go and fucking break her some more"—she shoved me—"for the sake of some stupid alpha pissing match?"

Okay.

Right. That… that was good.

But Roxy was far from done. "You can't hide that she's gold pack. Everyone is going to know you stole her freedom. That she was just caught in the fucking middle."

I breathed a sigh of relief, running my fingers through my hair. I dropped down to the couch, all the energy draining from me as I took a swig of the beer.

Good.

"That's it?" Roxy demanded. "You'll stop me from seeing her, and—"

"You can see her." My voice was rough.

"But you—"

"I have no intention of hurting her." I shut my eyes for a second. "I just needed…" I trailed off. "Shatter asked for the bond. She was upset, and I was… I was weak."

Irrational.

Foolish.

Roxy was staring at me in shock. "Why didn't you say that at the start?"

"I just needed to know…" My voice was strained. "When the school finds out, I don't want her hurt again. I needed to know everyone will blame us, not her."

She'd gone through enough. Everyone had seen the video.

"You're worried about her image?"

"She has enough going on without having the whole academy hating her," I said. "And if everyone thinks she's the victim, then…" Well, it was the best of all the bad options.

"Shit."

"What?" I asked, glancing up again.

"The Lincoln pack," she said. "If everyone finds out they're her scent match, they're going to look…"

"Like the fucking monsters they are?"

This was about more than image. When she returned with us, they would be angry. If the whole school saw me as an enemy, the Lincoln pack would too. It would shift their attention from her.

And the fact that they would be ruined if the scent match ever became public? Silver fucking lining. It was a tiny thing in the bigger picture, but I was going to relish the looks on their faces when they realised how badly they'd screwed up.

"You're going to stop hiding her scent, then?"

"When she's ready."

I wouldn't push her on that. It was her choice.

Roxy was already backing up to go see Shatter.

"One more thing," I said, halting her in her tracks. "The Lincoln pack—"

"It's over. I got an email saying they'd dropped me for inappropriate conduct. They're claiming I sabotaged political relationships. Goes against the contract." She sounded resigned.

I had underestimated her. For some people, getting dropped would have been the end of the world. Getting chosen by a pack meant her tuition would be covered, but if they were claiming Roxy violated the contract, they could withdraw it. It would also wreck her reputation. But instead of leaving, or going to a bar and drinking, or going back to her family for the weekend to mope, she'd stayed here, waiting for Shatter. By the gaunt look in her eyes, she hadn't slept much.

"Stay here tonight. I've talked to the Dean. There's an open apartment two down, since the Rodger pack merger. It's yours."

"That's all right. I'll find a place off campus."

I narrowed my eyes. "Why?" Was she scared of the Lincoln pack?

"Getting into this school was great, but it's not cheap. I know some omegas sharing a place. I can see if they have a—"

"It's covered."

Roxy folded her arms. "I can deal with student loans like everyone else."

"I wasn't asking."

There was a long silence.

"You gave up the Lincoln pack sponsorship because of my pack," I said. "To protect *my* omega. It's covered. Plus, I'd rather you were close, in case they're a problem." It wasn't like the Lincoln pack couldn't catch her entering and leaving campus. At least, this way, I could keep an eye on her. And them.

"Shatter's probably tearing her hair out waiting for you," I added, seeing her brewing a stubborn argument. She ran her tongue along her teeth, then sighed and nodded, heading down the hall to Shatter's nest.

CHAPTER 29

Shatter

"Shatter!" Umbra grabbed me around the waist and hauled me away from the bookshelves.

"But I—"

"No."

"She's going to—"

"Think your nest is awesome. Because it is."

I glared up at him, pouting, hyper-aware of the oddly angled stacks of books on the floor beside the bookshelf. They were too perfectly positioned for Roxy not to know it was on purpose.

Umbra had been pissed about the whole "dark bond command from Dusk" thing, but I wasn't. I'd felt his spike of panic when I fought his command. I knew he hadn't meant it.

"He called the shots for years," I'd said. "He's not used to having to be careful about that."

And the pain had been… Well, it wasn't the worst thing I'd ever felt, but the bar was high for me.

But now the true issue had arisen, since—despite the dark bond command situation—we all knew Dusk had a plan, and that meant Roxy was going to be coming in here at any moment.

To my nest.

And all of its madness—

A knock sounded on the door.

"Shit." My gaze snapped up.

Ransom, who'd been watching the fight between me and Umbra from my desk chair, got to his feet and crossed to it in an instant.

Oh *dammit.*

She was here.

She was here, and my books were all—

I squeaked as Umbra (noticing me sticking my foot out to at least knock the stack over) grabbed me by the waist and tucked me under his arm like I was a misbehaving puppy. Then he walked me across the room and set me down before a rather startled looking Roxy, who was standing at the door.

"Hi…" I said, straightening my shirt and trying to fix my glare.

Roxy stifled a smile, looking between me and Umbra. "Can I come in?"

"Um…"

"Yes." Umbra spoke for me.

I wrinkled my nose. "Fine. But you have to go." I tried to shove him out the door and was about as successful as if I'd tried to move a brick wall.

Ransom, at least, had the decency to exit without rudeness, giving me a little kiss on the forehead before he left. See, *that* was sweet and not embarrassing.

"I'll go," Umbra said, "but Roxy needs to know the nest rule."

"Nest rule?" Roxy asked as she stepped in. She was looking around at it. At *all* of it.

"Nothing can be straight," he declared. "Not ever. Not even a little bit—"

"Shut *up*!" I hissed.

With a broad grin on his face, Umbra exited the room, offering me a smug little salute as I slammed the door in his face.

Oh bother.

"It's amazing," Roxy said, staring around.

"You don't have to say that to—"

"I'm not. I'm jealous. Your instincts are off the walls."

I shrank. "I know." My voice was quiet as I tugged at my hair.

"That's a good thing, Shatter," she said, looking back at me.

"Oh. But, I mean, it's not like… normal… and Omega Studies—"

"Wants to train omegas to fit into little boxes so that they all like the same things and behave the same way. Only keep the instincts if they fit. Truthfully? Most alphas don't even want that, let alone the fucking omegas." She smiled as she stepped up to the bookshelves, peering at them curiously. "I grew up learning that. It's a fucking task to undo all that work. I wish I knew who I was, like you do."

I almost laughed but caught myself because she seemed serious.

I didn't know who I was. Literally, figuratively…

"No wonder they're obsessed with you. You are what real alphas look for."

"Real alphas?"

"I don't know." She shrugged. "Any alpha worth being with."

Hmm.

Okay.

That was definitely a compliment.

"Are you okay?" she asked. Her voice turned more serious, and my stomach flipped.

"Um…" I tried to ignore the dark cloud that threatened to return as my mind scrambled for a response. I straightened and unstraightened my pencil case on the desk. "I mean… I'm going to be." Shit. The notebook wasn't quite right, either. If Umbra insisted on me leaving everything off kilter, it could at least be off kilter the *right* way. "And, uh… Dusk's sorting it all out," I said. "Ransom's behind in classes, so the Dean is letting me tutor him for the week." I frowned, adjusting my candle beside the new arrangement. Also, my words were coming out so fast, but I couldn't seem to slow them down. "Bolin's going to drop off the coursework, so I won't… I won't have to go out for a bit."

And see everyone. All the people who had seen that video.

And Roxy knew…

Oh my God, Roxy knew…

"The library, I…" Fuck. My cheeks blazed, and I ran my fingers through a tangled lock, refocusing my attention on the pencil case. It *still* wasn't right. "I swear, I didn't—"

"They're your mates," Roxy said quietly. I looked at her in shock as she sat down on my desk chair right beside me. "Dusk told me."

"It doesn't make it okay."

"Not okay, like… having sex in an open library?" she asked.

I chewed on my lip, shrinking down.

"I didn't watch it," she said quietly. "But I, uh… I got enough context before I turned off my socials."

"I was…" I chewed on my lip as Roxy examined the items on the table, then reached out and turned the pen at an angle. It fixed the puzzle, perfect unevenness, removing the tangent lines and dead space just right.

"I imagine you were quite confused," she said quietly. "That Dusk wasn't your mate, and he seems to care, and Eric was, and he's… Well, he's a vile piece of garbage, not worth the alpha title he was born with."

With nothing left on the desk to distract me, I glanced up at her. "I didn't… I didn't see that in time," I whispered. "I… I'm so… so s-stupid." My voice cracked, then Roxy was on her feet, drawing me into a hug.

"No, no, you're not, babe. I would have been so mixed up too if they were my mates."

I hadn't had a hug like this since Aunty Lauren, with slender arms that packed the same power as Umbra's.

And it was okay to cry in front of Roxy. Not that I didn't trust my pack, but they ached for this almost as much as I did. The undercurrent of rage in the bond that they had for me, it was… comforting. It made me feel so much less alone, but it curdled with their pain. Instead, I could cry to her, as she led me to the bed and held me tight.

So, I did.

I cried so hard that it was hard to breathe, and she had to rush to grab tissues from my desk before hugging me again.

It took me a long, long time to get it out of my system, and Roxy stroked my hair, something sorrowful in her cosy scent of fir trees and oranges.

When I finally looked up, I saw there were tears in her eyes. "I'm sorry, Shatter. I tried to…" Her voice wavered. "I tried to find you, the second I knew—"

"I know."

It was why I loved her voice. It was the only voice I'd heard when I was in that room. The only voice that wasn't theirs.

It was the moment I'd realised she really cared about me.

I had a friend.

And she'd blown up her contract with the Lincoln pack to get to me. She'd been here all weekend, and she'd…

I frowned.

What about all her stuff? Classes were tomorrow morning, and her things must still be in the Lincoln pack apartment.

How would she study properly?

Wait, wait, wait.

I stumbled from her arms and launched myself across the room in an instant, pulling open the drawer of my desk before I found what I was looking for. I grabbed the pencil case and rushed back, holding it out to her. "I have a spare one—i-if you need it."

Well.

Actually, I'd have to put together another one, since mine was gone. But that was okay. Umbra had saved my registration card, and that's all that really mattered.

Roxy took it from me, a smile on her face that dispelled the building nerves. "Thank you."

"And… obviously anything else you need until you can get your stuff."

"Thanks. Dusk offered to set me up in an apartment on this floor. I don't know when it'll be ready."

My heart lifted. "You'll stay over tonight?"

"They seem all right if I take the couch—"

"No, I mean like…?"

Roxy's eyes lit up. "Like a slumber party?"

A… A what?

"Yes. I mean… I-I don't know if my nest is good for that—"

"It is. I love it in here."

"Oh. Okay."

"So. Pyjamas. Gossip. And we'll need slumber party food."

My mind emptied of everything but pure alarm. "R-right. Well, my pyjamas are in the closet. Do you want to find us some, and I'll go get the slumber party food?"

Slumber party food?

As soon as I was outside and the door was shut, I panicked. I ran down the hallway so fast, I almost tripped right into the living room on my face.

"What's wrong?" Dusk looked alarmed as he crossed toward me, eyes scanning my expression. "Shatter, about earlier—"

"No, no, no, *help me!"* I hissed. "Roxy wants a slumber party, and she said there needs to be food."

"We can get food," Dusk said.

"She said *slumber party food.* What does that mean?"

It sounded like code.

I didn't know codes.

"I think it's just snacks—"

"You're *boys. Alpha* boys. What if there's a secret language, and I'm supposed to know it?"

Ransom snorted, and Dusk was grinning, but Umbra—the *only* rational one—was pulling out his phone. "I'll look it up," he said.

Thank fuck someone was taking me seriously.

Oh…

Oh dear.

"She's gonna know I've never had a slumber party before."

"No. She isn't," Dusk said. "Umbra will sort out the food, and I'll bring in the TV from my room, so you can watch chick flicks."

"That's a thing?"

"It's a thing."

"What if it's only a thing in alpha slumber parties?"

"I…" Dusk looked so stunned that Ransom beat him to answer.

"She has a point." Ransom folded his arms. "Do we *truly* know there isn't a significant divergence of features between alpha and omega slumber—*OW!*" He cut off as Umbra, who was still scrolling through his phone furiously, leaned over and flicked him in the ear hard enough that he yelped.

Dusk snorted but was already heading back to his room.

I rushed after him, my heart in my throat.

I was almost tearing my hair out by the time he was unplugging his TV. "W-wait."

He set it down on his bed, turning to me.

"What if it *is* a divergent feature? Then she'll think I'm like… an alpha or something." Would that be worse than her thinking I'd never been to a slumber party before?

My *friend* was inside my nest right now, ready to have a slumber party.

"It sounds more serious than a girls' night," I went on. "It's like… like a whole party. Do you *usually* watch movies at a party?" Snacks, sure. Pyjamas… that was a little confusing, but movies? I mean… were we supposed to watch while the music was playing? I'd never even heard of a party without music. Or was it like an interval thing? And if so, what kind of interval? Would she figure it out when I got the wrong ratio of movie to music time?

"You're going to be fine," he told me.

"Dusk." I seized him. "I *need* you to be sure. This is not a mop." That was the wrong word.

"A mop?"

Drill. "This is not a drill."

"I am absolutely completely certain that chick flicks are not an alpha-slumber-party exclusive feature, all right?" he asked.

"You didn't even look it up."

Umbra was looking things up.

I changed my mind.

I needed a phone.

"Gem." My eyes snapped to him as his grip closed around my chin. My breathing settled instantly.

"Y-yes?"

"I'm going to set up the TV. You are going to tell Roxy that you want to hear what her ideal slumber party is, what her favourite snack food is, and what movies she likes. You're going to collect the data she gives you and figure out the right move from there."

"Oh. Okay." That sounded surprisingly doable.

A plan.

I could execute a plan. Especially when data was involved.

Later, I was curled up with Roxy in my bed. The movie on the TV was far more educational than I was expecting, with really pretty blonde girls explaining social cues and complexities in a way that was easy to understand. I took mental notes. I had to watch more of these.

There was a tray of tea on the bedside table, and two huge baskets of snacks, from chocolate bars to popcorn and a variety of chips.

Roxy had all but pounced on the chocolate bars when they'd arrived, which meant Umbra had picked right, and I was starting to get the impression that music wasn't a necessary feature of a slumber party, even though it was a party—since Roxy hadn't brought it up.

Finally, Roxy got sleepy and curled up at my side, pillow in one arm, stack of chocolate bars in the other.

I buried myself between the covers and pulled the duvet over us.

"It was the perfect slumber party," she said with a yawn.

Was it?

"Oh. Good." I ducked my face into pillows so she wouldn't see my stupid smile.

"And I like your scent. It's really… calming."

"Calming?" I asked. That was new.

Maybe bonding alphas really had toned it down, like Uncle had said it might.

"It's like jasmine and earth… a little deadly. I like it."

"Thank you," I whispered.

"It's unique… different…" She yawned again, a small smile on her face. "Everything they're going to hate when they find out… When you're ready…"

I frowned.

Would I ever be ready?

I was still so scared of them.

I wasn't scared of the idea of them hating my scent, though. I thought maybe that *was* a little satisfying, actually.

"What about the ball?" she asked.

"The ball?"

"Next weekend. It's the charity event they're hosting."

Oh. Right. I'd totally forgotten.

"What about it?"

"I don't know… if you were ready by then, you could ruin them at a ball."

"Ruin them?"

"You have their secret, Shatter. One that will ruin them worse than they could ever ruin you."

"What do you mean?"

"What they did to you—publicly—when people find out they did that to their own scent match… Money won't be enough to save them. No omega will go near them again."

"You… you really think so?" I asked.

"We could go shopping, get you a revenge dress."

"A what?"

"Like… the sexiest dress in the world. And then you walk out for the first time since they saw you, looking like a goddess, scent out, and then they realise how badly they fucked up."

I mulled that over, enjoying the flash of vindictiveness in her eyes as she said it.

"If you're up for it, babe. You don't have to."

"I know."

I didn't know if I was bold enough, but the idea did make me feel a little warm inside.

"Roxy, I…I'm sorry that being friends with me meant—"

She frowned. "I'm *not* sorry I'm friends with you." Her fingers tangled in mine, and she squeezed tight. The fir trees tangling in the air around me wilted. "I stayed with them longer than I should have. My mom and sisters kept telling me what an amazing opportunity it was, and I should have been grateful to land a pack and have my tuition covered. No one ever walks away from something like that. But they weren't…" She swallowed, like she wasn't sure how to say it.

Ice slid through my veins.

But she was Roxy. She knew what she wanted and how to manage alphas. "They didn't… hurt you, did they?"

Had I missed that, somehow?

"Not like…" She swallowed. "Not like they hurt you. But they weren't very nice. They'd find little ways to punish me if I wasn't what they wanted."

"I'm sorry."

"I'm really happy it's over. My family is going to be upset—they care a lot about reputation. But Dusk said he was going to cover my tuition, anyway, so they can't be that mad."

"He did?"

"Yeh. I mean. I told him he didn't have to but, uh… he seems like the stubborn type. I also got the impression it might already be done."

I snorted before I could catch myself.

Roxy gave me a wry smile, closing her eyes and squeezing my hand again.

Her scent settled, a peaceful Christmas morning, fresh orange and fir trees out the window. "I think I would have stayed if it hadn't met you, and I think I would have changed into someone I wouldn't recognise," she said.

"I'm glad you're free."

CHAPTER 30

Ransom

I woke in Shatter's bed to the softest touch against my skin. I didn't move as she gently brushed her thumb along my cheek. Nightshade was a drug in the air, and I could feel her in the bond. She felt safe and warm and… very possessive.

I kept my eyes closed, trying not to smile. If I smiled, she'd know I was awake.

I still needed to get to know her properly.

Roxy and Shatter had spent most of the day together yesterday while Dusk and Umbra went to school. In the evening, we'd helped Roxy set up her new apartment. Maybe I was being a coward, but Umbra had let slip how important Roxy was to Shatter, so I didn't want to interfere. That, and… *maybe* I was nervous.

Shatter kept breaking all my rules. I didn't *get* nervous over women.

It didn't matter how nervous I was, today, I had her all to myself. And the best way to get insight on someone was to see what they did when they didn't know they were being watched.

Based on the dissatisfaction and boredom down the bond from Umbra and Dusk, I guessed we'd overslept the start of classes.

I watched through mostly closed eyelids as Shatter sat up in bed, rubbing her eyes. When she settled, she began tapping her finger anxiously on her thigh as she peered around.

"You have a pack now…" She trailed off, more of her internal conversation clearly happening in her head.

Oh, she *talked* to herself?

That was unexpectedly delightful.

"…Or what will they think? Or if there are visitors—?"

She cut off, and then she was out of bed like a shot, and I thought I spied alarm on her face as she hurried from the room.

I sat up, considering that.

Why had no one warned me she was this cute?

It didn't feel out of place… Flickers of memories drifted in from when I was waking up. We'd had a heat together. I remembered something about her wrestling sweatpants onto me… That was definitely a little funny, but that memory merged with the next, which was my taking a swing at Dusk before throwing him into the TV.

I grinned, getting to my feet and walking to the door, then I cracked it open and peered out.

I could see half the living room and kitchen down the hall.

What was she doing?

Scrambling around in nothing but a T-shirt, tanned legs on full display, she grabbed couch cushion after couch cushion and—oh. I chuckled.

She was drawing her chin along them.

Scent marking them.

All of them.

When she was done with the couch, she hurried to the kitchen, where she opened drawers and scent marked (seemingly) random handfuls of cutlery, bowls and plates, the toaster oven—she had to bend over the counter for that, which gave me a wonderful view of her ass hugged in lace—and whatever else she could find. Then she hurried up the steps to the balcony.

Yes.

She wasn't going to leave our rooms untouched. She vanished into Umbra's first—I could see up to her knees at this vantage—then she made for mine. I hoped she marked every pillow and blanket and item of clothing…

I backed up around the door as she came back down the hallway for Dusk's room. Once I heard the latch from across the hall click, I dared to peek back around.

She was standing in his doorway, more tentative now.

Why was she hesitating?

"…Hmmm…" She shrank a little, fists balling in the hem of her shirt and tugging at it. "On one hand, he's mad at you for convincing him to dark bond you…" She trailed off. "But he's pack lead, so… I have to, right? What if he thinks it's rude that I haven't?" She straightened at that, then charged into his room in a rush.

The smile on my face was broad as I watched her pick carefully through the pillows on his bed, as if Dusk had a preference to which she left her scent on. What a ridiculous notion. He'd want her to mark them all.

Then she vanished—into his closet, maybe?

Finally, she returned to his bed, traced a finger along the lamp shade, before leaning down and marking it. Her face fell the moment she'd done it. "Oh… he's going to think you're so weird…" She tugged at her hair.

Next thing I knew, she grabbed all the pillows she'd just scent marked and shoved them under his bed.

Then she vanished again to his closet, returning with an armful of clothing. For a moment, she seemed to second-guess herself, eyeing the doorway and forcing me to duck away.

Was she considering removing them completely?

When I dared peek back around, she'd clearly decided not to, stuffing them under his bed also—and giving me another fantastic view of her from behind. Finally, she stopped at the lamp. She stared at it for a long second. Then she grabbed a handful of her shirt and tried to rub at its surface, as if that would neutralise the scent mark.

I contained my snort with immense difficulty.

She looked so genuinely concerned. Finally, she unplugged the lamp and stuffed it under the bed with everything else.

Very subtle.

I'm sure Dusk would never notice.

When she looked like she was done, I backed up from the doorway and sat down on the edge of the bed, so it looked like I'd just woken up.

She was… well, she was… incredible. How had we managed to find an omega like this? And what was she so worried about, second-guessing everything?

The door creaked open, and I glanced up to see Shatter slip in. She froze when she saw me, cheeks going pink. "You're awake."

"I am."

As she neared, I couldn't help reaching out and tugging her closer by her hips. She was so fucking beautiful, I could stare at her all day.

"I'm sorry—it's my nest, and you didn't even wake up with—"

She cut off as I put a finger to her lips.

"I'm going to need you to stop doing that."

"What?" she asked, eyes wide.

"Doubting yourself. Your instincts make the rules, all right?"

That, and anxiously warning me that, when we got back to the school, we were going to meet "real" omegas, as if I'd catch sight of one and regret she was ours. I'd been sick for a few years, not born yesterday. Probably best not to tell her I'd spent far too many of my teen years drunkenly partying.

"My… instincts?" she asked.

"Yup."

"Well…" She looked concerned. "I'm going to have to read through my Omega Studies textbook again—"

"No." Absolutely not. "I don't want a commercially packaged omega. I want you."

"You don't understand, I'm not… I spent a lot of time hidden from alphas, and my instincts—"

"Are everything we need. No studying. No nothing. They're perfect. If you feel you need to do something, I want you to do it."

"O-okay." She glanced at the door, clearly cycling through everything she'd just done and wondering what I might think.

"Good." I tugged her closer, pressing a kiss to her stomach over her shirt. "Now. What are we going to do today?"

"I have a plan for studying—"

"I want to go shopping first."

"B-but we can't study while shopping."

"Exactly."

"But Dusk said—"

"Fuck Dusk and his rules." I snorted. "I'm years out of date. I don't even have a phone."

She shrank a little. "Won't he be upset?"

"I hear it's quite the show when Dusk is upset with you."

Her whole face went beet red. "I don't think… he's…" She trailed off, and I grinned.

"Come on. Get dressed. We're going out. We'll grab breakfast on the way."

Shatter

He'd stopped at a breakfast place on the way to the mall, and I'd had a stack of pancakes, which tasted amazing.

Now we were wandering about, and I was out in public with my alpha.

It was refreshing to be away from the academy, but it was more difficult than I'd anticipated. People kept looking at him funny, which I got, but he was kind of mine now. Or… I was his. Whatever. It should mean something.

Was it normal for people to stare at someone as much as they stared at him?

He *was* good-looking—like a magazine model—tall and lean, with tanned skin, and his brows were dark, which contrasted the rich green of his eyes. He always had a casual mess to his auburn hair that fell from his just in the right way to seem deliberate (though I'd watched very carefully as he tied it up this morning and was disappointed to find he didn't do anything special).

Everyone's eyes seemed to snap to him, to me, then to the dark bond on my neck, and then right back to him.

We entered a clothing shop, and there was a very pretty omega who was helping people pick out fashion. She reminded me of Roxy a bit, with glossy hair and a beautiful smile. Except, when she approached us, she placed a hand on Ransom's arm before spotting me. She withdrew it until she saw my dark bond, then she returned her gaze to Ransom, like I didn't exist. When her hand touched his arm the second time, I growled before I caught myself.

I cut it off in an instant, embarrassment flooding my system, though she flinched back, eyebrows shooting up.

I couldn't shake the red from my vision, the world a blur of rage that I tried really hard to manage. I did, though. Uncle had been right about one thing—the bond had balanced out my instincts a bit.

I didn't settle until Ransom led us out of the store.

"Hey, Little Reaper, look at me."

His palm cupped my cheek, and I snapped my gaze up to him. It was hard to miss the delight down the bond from him, even when he was trying to keep his expression serious.

"Why… why did she do that?" I asked.

"Some people rank bonds like that. You'd own a princess bond. We'd both own a normal bond, but the alphas own a dark bond. The direction of the claim means some people think we're open for—"

"Flirting?" I asked, my lip trembling.

"Something stupid like that."

"No." My voice was an embarrassing whine, and I glanced around to see a passing couple shooting me funny looks. "Dusk said I seduced him into the bite. That means it's mine—you're mine." Ransom had difficult hair, just like me. That ranked the same as a scent match, right?

Ransom's smile soothed my nerves. "I am," he said, leaning down and pressing his lips to my forehead.

I swallowed. "I'm sorry for embarrassing you like that."

"Please," he snorted. "Growl at omegas all you want, but know I've got eyes only for you."

"Okay." That was good, I thought, because it hadn't felt optional when I'd done it.

"And I've never been so turned on in my life."

I snapped my gaze back to him and saw the truth in his eyes. "Really?"

"Uh-huh. Just like all the scent marking I found in my room when I grabbed my jacket."

Oh… well, I hadn't expected him to find it so quickly. My heart still raced thinking about it. "That wasn't too much?"

"I loved it."

My chest warmed with pride at that. Okay. Ransom liked it. Maybe Dusk wouldn't be mad, after all. I wasn't very good at giving my alphas space.

Next, we stopped at a beauty shop, and Ransom picked out a bunch of hair products. It definitely cheered me up when he told me half were for me, though I'd have to get him to explain how to use them.

Last on the to-do list was tech, and when we entered the phone shop, Ransom looked at all the phones with a rather lost expression on his face.

"I'm behind," he said. "What model do you have?"

"Uh... I don't," I said.

"You don't have a phone? Oh, for fuck's sake. Why didn't Dusk get you one?"

"He... he thought I was going to run away. And, anyway, I don't know what I'd do with a phone."

Ransom rolled his eyes and bought each of us one based on the shop worker's recommendation. Then he bought us both laptops, despite my protests that I didn't know how to use one.

"It can help you with your investigation," he said. "Plus, the guy said this one is simple to use."

Investigation definitely meant the Dusk and Umbra stuff.

"I've got all my textbooks now."

And I had a list of things I needed to recheck. The untethering, for example, and how exactly bonds and auras interacted with a pack breaking. They'd lost their third member and stayed intact. I needed to understand the mechanisms behind that so I knew where they might have diverged from the normal.

I had Bolin's list of course work, so I wouldn't get behind, but honestly, it was a lot of stuff I was already familiar with. Instead, I planned on using my study time to do a deep dive into a few things I needed to brush up on in order to hash out some of my theories on Dusk and Umbra.

"Well," Ransom said. "With a laptop, you can find studies that aren't in the textbooks, and with a phone, you can text Decebal and ask him if he can dig up any more secret studies that the textbooks will never publish."

"Secret like... banned?" I asked.

"Doesn't the Institute have a running list of shit they don't want accessible?"

"Yes..."

"Decebal's pack mate can get into all sorts of shit like that."

"Really?"

"Yup."

Dammit. I *would* have to learn how to use the laptop. I had been watching when Umbra tried to show me my way around it; I'd just not wanted to.

But secret Arkology studies?

"Fine."

We arrived home with bags and bags of shopping. Dusk looked up at us from the couch, where he had his textbook and laptop out. "A really productive way of studying," he said.

"We... we're going to do it," I said quickly. "I swear."

I hurried Ransom down the hallway to my nest and gathered up all the right textbooks.

"Okay. So." I settled on the bed with a stack of books. "I have all the chapters that we absolutely have to go through to catch you up. Maybe I can read them out loud, and then I can ask you questions about it to make sure you've got it sorted."

"Sounds like a plan," he said, settling beside me.

We read for a while, and he focused at first, but after two chapters, he looked bored. That was okay. "The, uh... the next bit's really interesting. It outlines the connection between aura size and—" I cut off as I felt his touch trail along my waist and looked back at him.

"Keep reading, Little Reaper," he said, shifting behind me. The command settled in the bond, and I glanced back down at the words, trying to find my place. "It's really cute how much you get into it."

I opened my mouth, reading the next sentence as he readjusted my hips. "On your knees, baby, and keep reading."

What?

"Um..." I tried to stammer out the next sentence as he shifted behind me, sliding his hand down my back and pressing me into an arch as I clutched the textbook, propped up on my elbows.

"...the... the difference in aura size can alter the... the outcome, which is why precise equations are... are..." I let out a little moan as he tugged my panties aside and pressed his finger into me.

"You said the chapter was crucial."

"I-it is."

"Well, I've decided using this sweet cunt of yours is also crucial."

"But you won't learn anything—"

"*Eyes on the book.* I need my education."

The command seized me again, and I stammered out the next half of the sentence before he tugged my panties down, and I felt his tip at my entrance.

"You're doing so good, don't stop."

He slid into me, and my blood lit with lust as he filled me up. I moaned, stumbling over words that were still tumbling from my lips, beyond my control.

"Fuuckk, Little Reaper, keep going."

My blood hit a boiling point as I stammered, eyes fixed on the book as his tip slammed into that perfect spot deep in my core.

Finally, the words jumbled as bliss threatened to overtake me. I was panting.

"You're going to finish the chapter before you finish," he growled.

I whined, my body shaking from need as I searched the page for my place again.

"R-Ransom," I begged. "I can't... mmm..." I trailed off as he drove into me again and my body shuddered.

"You're almost done, and you squeeze me so fucking tight when you're right on that edge."

More words came out, finally losing their meaning as my brain turned to mush. I was trembling, desperate, and each time he sank into me, his knot would stretch me out just a bit, his tip pressing into my core.

I could hear his low panting, as if he was holding off too.

Finally, I panted out the last word of the chapter. His fingers closed in my hair as he shoved me down against the page, driving into me so hard that I saw stars.

I cried out as the orgasm that had been building surged through me. Each stroke was another jolt of pleasure, and low whines sounded from my chest as he drew it out over and over, his own release warm in my core as he filled me up.

"Fuck, you're so sexy," he growled as he pressed into me again. "Now. Next chapter?"

CHAPTER 31

Shatter

Dusk was at my side on the couch the next evening, his head buried in a textbook. For the last hour, I'd been edging closer on the couch as he studied.

Things were getting better. But I knew he was still reserved with me because of the dark bond.

"How's the week going?" I asked, peering at his Arkology: Genetic and Genomics homework. "Have you seen them?"

It was Wednesday, and I knew they had a lot of classes with the Lincoln pack.

He nodded, turning to me. "I'm doing all right, but Umbra was never good with this to start with. He's about ready to crack."

"But… he can't go near them—"

"I know. I'm thinking of requesting a transfer. We might be at this academy for a while if you want to stay, so better to find him shit he's actually interested in. Or he could drop some classes entirely if he wanted. We intended to get close to them, but that's off the table now, anyway."

"Would *you* drop them?"

"No." He glanced down at the textbook. "I'm actually not hating it."

I brightened at that. "Really?"

"Yeh."

"I could… help you study some time?" I offered.

He grinned. "Once you're done helping Ransom, maybe."

I nodded, but a blush was creeping up my neck.

"What?" Dusk prodded, but Ransom had emerged from his room and was making his way down to the kitchen.

"It's not going so well on the studying front," I whispered.

We'd tried again this morning, but it had ended in a lot of sex. Study sex. I couldn't lie and say I didn't like it, but… "I don't think he's going to catch up," I whispered.

There was a small smile curving the edge of Dusk's lips. He dropped his voice to match me. "Does he need to transfer too?"

"I'm doing my best. But, uh… we'll have to see."

He nodded. "What about the ball?" he asked. "You don't have to go, but Ransom mentioned you brought it up…"

"Roxy said something about a… a revenge dress?" I eyed him, wondering if that meant anything to him.

He cocked his head, leaning back a bit, a little twinkle of malice in his eyes. "*Did* she?"

"But if Umbra's having a hard time—"

"It's on Saturday. Decebal just texted, and we've got to follow up on a lead. He's booked it for the same night as the ball. I could ask Umbra if he wanted to join Decebal, then he won't have to sit in the same room as the Lincoln pack."

"What's the lead?" I asked. He'd put the files we'd brought back—the ones with all my notes on them—into his safe, but I had them all organised in my head like a textbook. If there was more information, I needed to figure out where to file it.

"I'll give you all the details, but it might be a dead end. I don't want to get your hopes up."

"Okay. Well, maybe that would work… Would you want to go?" He'd implied it was hard for him, too, to see them.

"Shatter, if you want to ruin that pack, I will be at your side every second. Sounds like Roxy will be too."

"Okay. I mean, I'm not totally sure yet." But I was going to emerge from here eventually, and every spare moment I'd had this week had been working on figuring out what had happened to Dusk and Umbra. It was therapeutic.

I hated them. It was new for me, to hate anyone that much, but their taunts, what they'd said about Umbra and Dusk while they were watching them being ruined. When one of their pack had died…

Vile sickness turned my stomach every time I thought of it.

Decebal had told me he'd get me secret articles as soon as he had some. I'd given him a list of topics I was most interested in.

"Only if you're up for it," he said. "You can change your mind as much as you—" He cut off at the sound of a strangled growl from Ransom in the kitchen behind us.

"Where the *fuck*—?"

I spun on the couch to see him rifling through the cutlery drawer desperately before slamming it shut. On the kitchen island was a bowl of leftovers.

"What is going on?" Dusk asked.

"The… the cutlery… there's no more… *Argh*." He looked furious.

"Umbra reorganised it last night," Dusk said.

"Umbra?" Ransom demanded. "That greedy *bastard*," he hissed under his breath, and then he was taking the stairs by threes.

We both watched him cross the landing and then bang on Umbra's door loudly.

Umbra answered, and it was hard to hear them through angry hisses, but I swear I heard Umbra say something like: "Well, you took the toaster oven."

The… toaster oven? I glanced back to see that, sure enough, it was gone from the kitchen.

"I did *not*," Ransom's voice rose with outrage.

Wait… the toaster oven?

The cutlery?

I froze, cheeks going bright pink as memories of me rifling through the kitchen and scent marking everything at random came floating back into my mind.

Oh, dear…

Dusk was craning his neck and peering into the kitchen, clearly also noticing the vacant spot where the toaster oven had been.

"Here," Umbra was saying. "Make it a deal. A coin toss. You win, you get all the shit I took, I win, I get all the shit you took."

There was a pause, then Ransom folded his arms. "All right, then."

"Oh…" I reached out from the couch, but it was too late.

"Tails."

A minute later, Ransom (now a seething demon of alpha indignation in the bond) was hauling the huge toaster oven into Umbra's room.

"Might as well bring the game consoles too," Umbra said, a smug grin on his face. "Since I assume we'll be playing in here."

"Fuck you," Ransom snarled.

"Shatter," Dusk said, making me jump. "Do you have *any* idea what is going on?"

"No." I shook my head instantly, trying to keep my voice serious. "None at all."

"So, it couldn't *possibly* have anything to do with the fact I unearthed half my wardrobe and a lamp from beneath my bed yesterday?"

"I… I don't have *any* idea how that happened."

He raised an eyebrow. "Come here."

I was shifting toward him in an instant, and he pulled me onto his lap.

"Are you lying to me?" he asked. "Because you know what happens to lying omegas in my pack?"

"I…" My lips parted as he squeezed my butt, dragging me closer. My pulse began racing as I stared into his piercing eyes, body growing hot. "I mean… I *might* have scent marked a few things around the apartment…"

"The cutlery?"

"Some of it."

Dusk raised an eyebrow. "The toaster oven?"

"Umbra bought it to make me breakfast."

And he was getting way better. Yesterday morning, he'd roasted tomatoes and had only overcooked the eggs a teensy bit.

"I just thought I should make sure the home was ours. I know you have doubts about… the bond."

His fingers wove through my hair, dragging my neck back. I froze as I felt him press his teeth to the bond.

"I love you, Shatter," he breathed. "You belong in this pack. That's the end of the conversation."

He drew back, still holding me. I bit my lip, unable to take my gaze from him. He was far too good-looking, with his gorgeous deep amber skin and bright yellow eyes.

"But we are not stable alphas. Keep scent marking kitchen appliances and cutlery, and you might drive us all back to insanity."

"Noted."

"I'm not saying you *shouldn't* do it. I'm just saying we have to be more careful. If you do feel you need to, you can, but"—his eyes twinkled with mischief as he leaned close, breathing in my ear—*"you leave it in my room when you're done."*

The command locked in place through the dark bond, surprising me.

"But the others—"

"You won't tell them about this command."

My lips parted as that locked in too. "That's cheating."

His grin was wicked as he leaned back. "I work smart, not hard, Gem."

CHAPTER 32

Shatter

"Tonight is the night," Ransom declared.

Umbra looked determined as he rubbed his hands together, waiting for the popcorn to pop in the microwave. "If we don't get RedEyedBandit off my scoreboards—"

"We'll do it." Ransom was absolutely determined.

It was Thursday evening, and Ransom and Umbra had told me they'd show me how to play the game the two of them had been obsessed with since we'd returned from the cabin.

It was full of duelling monsters and looked pretty challenging, to be honest. But they'd been battling each other almost every night since we'd arrived, and it did put a smile on my face—watching them get competitive over it.

On the other hand, Ransom's catch-up studying had been abandoned entirely. He'd taken me out for lunch today, which was great, and we'd fucked again, but he had retained nothing at all. He was smart, but it wouldn't be enough, at this rate.

Instead of pushing it, I'd happily joined Roxy this afternoon. She was still setting up her new apartment. Since it was pack-sized, she had room for a nest.

She swore blind she'd never been happier now she was enrolled without needing a pack, but I thought her week had been rough, when it came to the academy. She wouldn't go into detail, but she'd mentioned something about the other omegas, and I wondered if they were pushing her out.

I'd also prodded her to tell me what people were saying about me. I'd been so careful, even just hurrying down the hall to Roxy's place, since I didn't want to see anyone, but my time was running out. I needed to know what I might be facing. She hadn't wanted to give me the details, but I'd convinced her to give me the gist of it.

Everyone was, apparently, going with the Lincoln pack narrative, since I haven't been spotted. I'd tried not to imagine what people thought of that.

That I was the crazy stalker obsessed with them. That I'd wanted to be with them like that... I'd been seen coming into their party, even going into that room with Eric…

"You're in tonight, right?" Ransom asked Dusk, dragging me from my spiral. Dusk was standing from the couch where he'd been studying.

"Actually, I'm going to turn in." There was something odd about the smile on his face.

He'd been in and out of the bond more today, but now he was gone. I frowned as his figure departed down the hallway. I tried to refocus on what Ransom was saying. Umbra had caught my eye, though, and I realised he was a little worried about the bond.

Umbra nudged me. "You want to go?" he asked. I looked back to him and Ransom, who had settled happily under a blanket—which was definitely one I'd scent marked on my rampage. He nodded in agreement, eyes darting after Dusk too.

"We can show you another night, if you want," Ransom said, clearly noticing something was up.

I considered that, staring down the hallway after Dusk. "Maybe…" I chewed on my lip, then got to my feet. There was something off about Dusk tonight. "You sure?" I glanced back at them.

They both nodded.

"All right." I followed Dusk down the hallway. I was their omega. It was my job now to pay attention to things like this.

I stood before his door for a long time, trying to figure out what I was going to say. I'd never actually… visited him like this. Like… like I wanted to spend time with him or see him.

Would he think it was odd? Did our relationship have room for that?

I took a breath and knocked, realising I'd been there for a while. I heard movement from within, and then the door opened. There was a little spark of confusion in his eyes as he peered down at me.

"Is everything okay?" he asked, glancing back down the hall to where Umbra and Ransom were already shouting over the game.

"Everything's fine. I just thought I could see what you were doing?"

"They were going to show you how to play," he said, frowning.

Hmm. Maybe I'd read it wrong. "I mean, if you'd rather be alone—"

"Never," he said, catching me off guard, "would I rather be alone than with you."

"Oh." A whole different kind of buzz unsettled my stomach at that. "Okay."

There was a curve at the corner of his lips as his gaze dropped to where I tugged at my hair anxiously, then he stepped back in invitation. The first thing I noticed when I stepped in was the folder on the bed—the one with data on all four of us.

It was open, with pages scattered around.

His mission. Our mission.

I sat on the bed, watching as he took the spot beside me, my eyes darting to the papers with a hint of yearning.

"You looked after them for a really long time," I said.

He raised an eyebrow, analysing me. "I did."

"Did you ever get tired of it?"

He let out an amused breath. "Quite the contrary."

I tried to detangle that, looking back at the pages. "You were, uh… studying this again?" I asked, nudging the analysis on Ransom's sickness that I'd already committed to memory.

"If I read them out of order, it helps me see everything in a new light. And I'm going through your notes."

I nodded, considering that, and building up the courage for my question. "What… what would you be doing if you weren't doing this?"

Dusk barked a low laugh, fixing me with a curious gaze. "I'm a codependent shell. I don't think there is anything else."

I blinked, taken off guard by those words.

Dusk didn't talk about himself much. Actually, he never talked about himself. I'd never noticed that until those words settled over me, digging up more meaning with every second of silence that passed.

He didn't seem sad or upset, like the words might imply. He was carefully watching my reaction.

"They get on really well with each other," I said slowly, eyes drifting to the door for a second before returning to him.

He nodded. "They do."

"And they're healing each other."

A trace of humour crinkled his eyes as he drew back a little, taking me in more completely. "They are. It's good."

"And they don't need you… l-like they did before."

"No."

"You give me… balance." The word slipped out, as true as it was unexpected. Dusk had been the balance to my instincts at every turn. Ones that were supposed to be impossible to tame. "I… I need you."

There was a long beat. "It would be entirely unhealthy for that to make me feel better."

"Does it?" I asked.

A smile played on the corners of his lips, but he didn't answer.

"If they're healing each other," I said. "Who's healing you?"

"I don't know if there's anything that needs healing."

I frowned. I didn't think that was true.

He was broken in his own quiet way.

"But you don't think you have anything else outside of… this?" I glanced at the papers across the bed.

"I suppose not." He looked at the pages, too, his expression drawn. "I don't know when it happened. I just looked behind me one day and…" He trailed off, searching for words, but my whisper tumbled out.

"And it was spring, but… but the last thing you saw was snow…" I realised it might not make any sense at all, but his yellow eyes were fixed on me more intently than they ever had. "I… I'm just saying… there might be a way back from that."

It was the path I was on right now.

"I would like that."

I wanted to be theirs. And that meant it was my job to take care of him.

"But there are more important things to discuss."

"There are?" I asked. I looked to the papers on the bed. Had he made a breakthrough?

"Yes. Like the fact that you scent marked half of my clothes and shoved them under my bed—and then tried to lie to me about it yesterday."

"Um…" My gaze snapped to him, my eyes wide.

"Why did you hide them?"

I don't know what I had been thinking. It had been a haze of instincts, and then panic. "I just thought… you're annoyed at me for talking you into dark bonding me—"

"I'm not annoyed at you."

"You… you aren't?"

He cocked his head. "I'm annoyed at myself. Not you."

"You shouldn't be."

"I don't want you second-guessing those sexy instincts of yours," he growled. "Understand?"

I nodded.

"I have to punish you for that. And the lie."

Something molten trickled into my core. "Y-you do?"

"But first, we're going to discuss my command the other day."

"Oh…"

"When we came back, and Roxy was here, I need you to know I didn't mean for you to get hurt."

"I know," I replied. "You didn't know I was going to fight it."

"I should have, and I'm sorry," he said. He looked so earnest that I was getting all odd about it. I still wasn't used to Dusk's apologies. "I'm going to be more careful."

I nodded. "Thank you."

"Now." He leaned back where he sat, raising an eyebrow. "Tell me why, when Ransom commanded you to kiss him back in the cabin, you got all hot and bothered."

Oh… I swallowed, suddenly finding his gaze very hard to meet. "Well…" I tapped my finger on my thigh. "It was sexy."

"I'm going to need a little more than that, Gem."

"It was like… I don't know. He's interested in me, and I like it when…" I trailed off, embarrassment making it impossible to meet his eyes.

"When what?"

Was I really about to admit this to Dusk?

"When he takes charge."

"Just Ransom?" he asked.

My voice was small as I wrung my shirt in my fists. "No."

"So. Tell me if I'm wrong. You like praise, you like it when I'm in charge…"

Oh shit. We were really going to talk about all of this?

"What about when I don't let you finish?" he asked.

"I don't know why that's so hot," I whispered.

He grinned. "A little praise and a little degradation. You're so sexy, Shatter."

That settled my heart a bit, even though it seemed like such an odd thing to like.

"I like it when… you get off too," I added. If we were already here, I might as well admit it.

"When I tell you that you can't?"

"M-hmm." My cheeks had never been this hot before.

"So, it's a turn-on when I tell you I'm going to use your sweet little body until I'm done?"

I chewed on my lip with another nod. There was slick pooling in my panties.

"Did you like it when we were out in public and you could get caught?"

"A bit."

"Did you like the idea of getting caught, or that it wasn't allowed?"

"Um…" I frowned. "That it wasn't allowed."

"And when I woke you with my cock?"

Oh… shit. My scent shifted at those words; his grin was enough to confirm that.

He adjusted so he was sitting beside me, and I had to look up into his eyes. "You're so perfect," he breathed, curling a finger beneath my chin. "But you are going to say if I ever have a command that makes you uncomfortable—from me or the others."

"Okay."

"And I need to know if there is anything you don't want to do."

I frowned. "Like… what?"

"I need to know if there's anything you don't want, or if anything has changed."

Changed?

It took me a moment before I realised what he meant.

The Lincoln pack.

For a second, my mind flashed back to that room, but I dug my nails into my palms to ground myself. "Did you, uh… did you watch the video?" I asked, my voice quiet.

"No."

Oh.

Okay. That was… unexpected.

That was another thing I was going to have to face. A school of eyes that had seen that. Had seen Eric… Again, nails dug into palms.

"No." I shook my head. "Nothing has changed."

Not between me and Dusk. Not now he'd taken my scars. "I want… I want you to take it like you took… the scars."

I saw a flash of rare vulnerability in his eyes, as if he hadn't expected that.

"Is there anything else I should know about?"

"I…" I tapped my finger anxiously again. "About the, uh… the punishments…"

Maybe I really shouldn't tell him this.

"What about them?"

"They make me really want to…" I winced. "...To fuck you."

Something humorous twinkled in his eyes. "The first time I bent you over the couch, you were literally dripping through your panties for me."

"Yeh, but you… you pressed your dick against me, and I'd never been touched by an alpha. And then, the other times, you're always so… so I don't know… you always did other things at the same time, so I just thought—"

"Shatter, your scent gives you away if I even say the word *punishment*."

"You knew?" My voice was weak.

All this time?

I was going to die.

"You gotta quit being so fucking cute. I have a plan for the evening, and you're about to derail it."

"But it's not weird that I want you to… I don't know. That I like it?"

"No." He snorted. "And for what it's worth, I dream of turning your hot little ass pink, then fucking you until you scream my name." He leaned down and nipped my ear. "I love claiming you and ruining you—and doing it on my own terms."

Goosebumps rippled on my skin as his thumb brushed across his bite.

"Now, you're going to go into your nest and find the sexiest lingerie you can find. Then you'll go to the living room and wait for me in your usual place on the couch."

"Out there?" I asked, eyes wide.

Ransom.

Oh, fuck. He was going to see at last.

"Yes."

"Can I cover up my bites—"

"Always," he said. "Now. Go and give them a show."

I was standing before I realised it, finding it so natural to give into his commands when I was this turned on. It didn't take me long to find something to wear.

Umbra and Ransom both looked up from the TV as I made my way down the hallway in black lace and a cream shirt that cut off at my waist.

I didn't meet either of their eyes as I stood at the edge of the couch, then leaned forward, lowering my chest to the couch cushion below, my palms pressed at my sides.

The game paused, and wolfsbane and lily of the valley turned possessive.

"Little Reaper, *what* are you doing?"

"Waiting for Dusk," I said quietly.

I took a breath, relaxing in that position, relief coiling with anticipation as I waited.

Dust

I found her waiting, with perfect obedience, in the living room. Her head was turned to the side, cheek pressed against the couch, and her stunning golden eyes found mine.

"Good girl," I purred, stepping up behind her and letting her feel how hard I was for her. She shifted back just a bit. I would never get tired of looking at her. Honey hair scattered about her in waves as she waited, presented like this.

The video game had paused, and Ransom was eyeing us both with interest while Umbra had his arms crossed, watching like it was a show he'd been waiting for.

"Tell them what you did, Gem?"

"I… I scent marked your room and then hid your stuff. And then I lied about it."

"And next time?"

"I won't second-guess my instincts."

I squeezed her ass, loving the way goosebumps rippled across her skin at the faintest touch. I'd let her wait for a while, knowing the anticipation would get to her.

She loved my punishments, and hearing her admit that at last was music to my ears. Now she was buzzing with contentment and relief. I monitored that closely as I flicked the clasp of my belt. She went extra still at the sound, and there was a definite spike of anticipation from her.

I tugged it off, withdrawing the small pot of massage oil from my pocket. I could swear she lifted her hips slightly, stifling the beginnings of a purr as I rubbed oil into her skin.

"Five, Gem," I warned her.

I had plans tonight beyond just this, and I didn't want to wait long to fuck her.

She let out a little whimper at the first strike, and I watched her skin turn pink from the mark.

"Good girl," I purred as I massaged the spot again. I dropped my finger to her panties, slipping my thumb into her cunt just to hear her moan. "Prop yourself up, let them see you properly."

Umbra growled with approval as she lifted herself up. His hand cupped her neck, pupils blowing, and wolfsbane was a drug in the air. Ransom had cocked his head, staring with utter intensity as he watched. In the bond, he was a mess, half shock, half lust.

"After you take your punishment, you're going to let me use your holes without complaint, aren't you?" I asked.

"Yes," she said, breathless.

"And you won't come tonight, not until I knot you."

I felt her shiver again. "No, Alpha."

Sweet mother above. I was done for if she started to use that term in earnest. Ransom's whole body was tense, as if he wanted to pounce on Shatter and sweep her up for himself. I felt a little shudder of that feral part of him surface—the unbalanced, possessive alpha that had grown up an only child—watching his omega being touched by someone who wasn't him.

Not just touching her but turning her perfect skin pink.

I grinned, then leaned back, examining her. I shifted the shirt further up her back so I could see the way her ass tapered to her hips, and the goosebumps along her rich skin, which glistened with the oil I'd rubbed into it. The black lace was barely present, a thin thong that shaped around her butt, accentuating her curves.

I readied my belt again, stepping back. Umbra had eyes only for her as he cupped her neck. The game controllers were left forgotten, and I watched as Ransom's slipped to the floor without him noticing.

She let out another whine as the belt made contact with her flesh again.

By the time I reached the fifth, she was shivering, one hand gripping Umbra's wrist as she panted lightly. Slick was dripping down her thigh already.

I stepped back, and she straightened, turning to me. Her eyes were wide and dazed, lips parted. I cupped her chin.

"You're going to go back to my room and put on the blindfold that's on my bedside table. Then lie on the edge of my bed and play with yourself until you're about to come." Her mouth dropped open, but I wasn't done. "Then you'll switch to fingering your sweet pussy until you're close again. You'll keep doing that until I tell you to stop."

All she could do was nod, eyes wide.

"Go on."

She took a step backward, darting her gaze to Umbra and Ransom before hurrying back down the hall to my room.

Both of them turned to me, and I buried my smile at the look of utter shock on Ransom's face.

"We can watch, right?" he asked weakly.

"Absolutely not."

"But we're pack."

My grin widened. I swear, at the sound Shatter made on the third strike, I'd felt a flicker of murder from him. Lust—absolutely, but I got the impression he had been on the edge of wrestling the belt from me to take over.

"You can dream about it," I said.

"You're going to… stay in here while she…?" Ransom trailed off.

"God, no. I'm going to go and watch."

The sight that met me when I entered my room put to shame every imagining.

Shatter lay on my bed, knees up as she dipped two fingers into herself—which meant she'd come close to the edge already. Even from the doorway, I could see her body shivering.

I watched for a while, in a constant state of war with my own self-control. She was hottest when being edged. Her whines became so desperate, and then the orgasm she got at the end was beautiful.

Finally, I joined her, crouching down and pressing my finger to her entrance. She jumped, a moan sounding from her chest.

"Dusk?"

"Yes," I answered, dipping into her with a second finger, watching her arch against the sheets.

"I…" Her voice shook. "I want your knot."

"You're going to take my knot, beautiful, but I'm going to play with you first."

I stood and removed the rest of my clothes.

"You can stop touching yourself," I said. She uncurled from her position, already shaking with exhaustion.

"Stand up."

I helped guide her to her feet, so she was before me, then I pressed her hands to my chest. I paused for a moment as she ran her touch up and over the healing brands. Then one of her hands dropped to my cock and circled it as she pressed her lips to the mark I'd made for her.

I growled, almost pinning her to the bed and claiming her right there.

"I want..." Her voice was breathless. "I want it to be like when you used to punish me."

I nudged her chin up. I knew what that meant to her. I hadn't seen the video, but I knew what it contained. I knew what Eric had done.

She wanted me to take it back from him, like I'd taken the scars.

"Tell me who you belong to," I breathed.

She hesitated only a moment, brows creasing at the unfamiliar question. "You."

"And these perfect lips?" I asked, thumb pressing against them.

"Yours, Alpha." Her voice was quiet, almost sultry, and her scent had become more needy than ever before. There was a warmth to it which was new.

It read, to me, as safety.

Trust.

Something more absolute than I'd ever felt from her.

There was a low rumble in my chest.

"You're going to use them to get me off," I told her. *"You're going to keep playing with yourself, and the closer you get to your orgasm, the more you're going to choke yourself. I want to finish in your tight throat before I let you finish. Is that clear?"*

"Yes, Alpha," she replied, lip caught in her teeth, nightshade becoming an aphrodisiac.

It wasn't that I had to use commands. I knew she would do what I said, but the feeling of her submitting to me like this was a high I had never anticipated. It was more than just about how hot it was; it was her trust, and the safety she felt whenever she allowed herself to be swept away by the command.

Her scent was a storm of lust in the room as she sank to the floor, fingers not leaving my length as she did. I groaned as she took my tip between her lips and began to work my cock.

I closed my fingers in her hair and around the blindfold, so I was everywhere for her, but I let her do the work, my command driving her onwards.

It wasn't long before she was shaking as she neared her own orgasm, taking me deeper and deeper. Knowing that drew me right to my climax, and the nails of her free hand dug into my thigh as she dragged herself over my cock.

"Fuck, you're so goddamned beautiful," I groaned, tugging the blindfold from her.

This was on another level, feeling the command between us, seeing her eyes water as she desperately choked herself on my cock, shuddering with an orgasm she couldn't reach.

Her nails drew blood along my thigh as I came, my grip rough in her hair as I unloaded down her throat.

She was panting when I released her, and I had to help her to her feet before I lifted her in my arms and set her down on the bed near the headboard. She let out little moans with almost every touch, and with what strength she had left, she tried to drag me closer.

"I want you," she whined.

"You'll have me, Gem. I'm going to take care of you." I pressed kisses along her skin, careful around the healing wounds. "When you were out there, did you want them to join in?" I asked.

"Yes." She'd chosen me tonight, and I would be just a tiny bit selfish about that. I would keep her to myself, but not forever.

"You're going to take us all, aren't you? There are so many ways we're going to ruin you." I drew her closer, lifting her hips enough that I could line it up against her entrance.

There was a low, feral growl in her chest as she felt me, and her back arched, trying to take me sooner.

"I'm going to enjoy watching Ransom and Umbra take you while I claim your throat," I breathed, pressing into her all the way. I leaned forward, cupping her neck, my thumb brushing the bite I'd given her as I rocked into her. "Squeeze me, precious."

"Mmm." The sound that rose in her throat as I felt her tight cunt clench over me like a vice was so hot.

"Fuck." I almost came right then. "Would you be able to take us all?" I asked as I slid out of her slowly. "Your whole pack at once?"

She nodded, a needy whine slipping out at the words. Her fingers dug into my hair to the point of pain as I slammed back in and set a pace to leave the whole bed shaking. The sounds coming from her with each stroke were so hot, more so, knowing they'd be loud enough that Umbra and Ransom could probably hear.

"Would you like that? Letting them fill you up while I told you to fuck them however I want?"

"Yes," she whined, arching against me so she could take me deeper with each thrust. "Please," she begged. "Knot me, Dusk."

She was shaking, each exhale accompanied by a little moan.

That was enough to send me over the edge. I slammed in. She cried out, her whole body seizing over me as I pressed my knot into her.

Fuck. Me.

My grip was punishing on her waist as I rutted her with my knot buried deep, finishing violently as her whole body arched, her grip enough to tear my hair out as she was wrecked by the orgasm she'd been denied for so long.

I turned us so she was resting on my chest, and I propped myself up at the head of the bed. She curled up against me, still shivering with little aftershocks.

I wrapped my arms around her, pulling covers over us and holding her close. It was a long time before she surfaced, and still, her eyes were dazed as she peered up at me. I traced circles on her skin with my thumb ever so gently, almost touching one of her wounds. I had helped her treat them again this morning, and they were healing bit by bit.

"I want to go out with Roxy tomorrow," she whispered. "To pick out a dress."

"For the ball?" I asked.

"Yes."

"You've decided?" I asked.

"I… I need to do it. I want to."

"All right. Then, we're going." I'd already checked with Umbra, and he was good to visit Vandle with Decebal. If Shatter wanted to ruin the Lincoln pack at the ball on Saturday, I would hold her hand the whole way.

CHAPTER 33

Shatter

I gazed up at the fancy dress shop through Roxy's car window. It had that high-end look, and I always pictured Aunty Lauren shopping at places like that.

Nervous, I'd kept my contacts in and my hoodie up, hiding my bond when we left the apartment, and don't think anyone noticed me.

Dusk caught up to us when we reached Roxy's car, insisting he could drive and wait outside, but Roxy practically beat him back with her handbag, then bundled me through the passenger side door.

Ransom had given me one of the plastic money cards he used at the mall, along with the secret four-digit number. He said I could buy whatever I wanted. I thought that was a good thing, but when I told Roxy that at Starbucks, she nearly choked on her cream-topped drink.

"So. Revenge dress?" Roxy grinned, eyeing me. I nodded, ready. "I need to know I can face them. And if I'm doing it, I'll do it with all the strength I can muster. You need one too."

"A dress?" she asked.

"A revenge dress." I'd looked it up. We both qualified for one, as far as I could tell. The Lincoln pack had dumped her, right?

"Both for the same pack?" Roxy's face lit up. "That's going to be amazing."

In a huge changing room with light pink decor, we had a dozen dresses to try. The woman at the front had eyed my oversized hoodie (Umbra's), but Roxy looked like she belonged, so they let us in.

Roxy went first, pulling the curtain back every few minutes so I could see her in dress after stunning dress while she gave me a rundown on the ball politics.

"It's a charity ball," she was saying as I heard her wrestle with fabric behind the curtains. "The Lincoln pack announced they're officially open to omega applicants, and there was an announcement that they made an 'exceptional donation', so they get honorary seating."

"What does that mean?" I asked.

"Probably that they're put up at a head table. I'm sure they want to look like they rule the place. But—" Roxy cut off with a little hiss of frustration. "One sec. Zipper." She drew the curtain to reveal a pretty, sapphire blue dress that was half done up at the side. I helped her hold it together, so she could tug it closed. "The event organisers are apparently in a scramble because there was another last-minute donation. They're setting up honorary seating for another pack."

"Another pack?" I asked.

Roxy gave me a sly smile before adjusting the dress over her bra. "Your pack. Definitely."

I considered that. If she was right, we were going to be front and centre. I was going to be making a statement.

Roxy glanced at herself in the mirror. "A bit bulky, I think. I'll be sweating."

"I love the colour," I added. "Matches your eyes."

As Roxy requested a less bulky dress in the deep sapphire colour, I sat on the pink vintage couch, mulling over what she'd said.

I glanced at the rack of dresses I'd chosen, eyes falling on one in particular. The most daring one.

Could I…?

"If I arrive at the ball dark bonded, with golden eyes on display, they'll think it was Dusk, won't they? They'll think I am the victim?"

Roxy looked over at me, a frown on her face. "I think… the moment the truth comes out, people will think that you were caught in the middle."

In other words, they wouldn't know any of this was my choice—that the bond was my choice.

But the Lincoln pack already believed I was pathetic.

Roxy vanished behind the curtain to try on the dress she'd been handed, leaving me to think.

Decebal had sent me some studies at last, and I'd read some fascinating, if unfinished, studies on the correlation between aura instability and aura strength. The reason it had been cut short wasn't mentioned, but the last thing the study had listed was man-made impacts on unstable auras.

It would make sense that the Institute wouldn't want the knowledge of how to artificially destabilise auras to be public knowledge. But if they cut the study short, then it also implied they knew what the results might show.

I thought back to the trials that Umbra and Dusk had been in. Pushed to the edge. Caged up. Atropa's Poison put into the very air they breathed.

Was that knowledge already in the hands of others?

People who were using it for their own gain. For money.

It hadn't just been about bets. What they'd done to Umbra and Dusk was deliberate and calculated. Decebal and Dusk had listed extensive theories, linking the bets to the tests, believing that they were studying endurance.

Weaponising alphas wasn't a new concept; there was money in that, and wars that depended on it. It wasn't a bad theory. Ransom had helped me figure out my computer well enough now that I'd researched the history of Atropa's Poison. It was a drug developed for war. Alphas were resilient to some of the worst chemical warfare, and their primary weakness, Agritox, was a reactive compound, and thus confined to physical forms, like bullets. The compound, because of its unpredictable nature, posed challenges in large-scale production for warfare, requiring advanced facilities and expertise.

But Atropa's Poison could be used as a gas and, instead of killing alphas, turned them on each other. It was a way to take out enemy packs on the front line, not only neutralising the effects of aura-steroids banned by the Geneva Convention for front-line use—but turning those very alphas against their own.

It wasn't at all far-fetched that the tests were weapons-based and were trialling alpha resiliency to different drugs or stressors. It would also explain their desire for alphas from the Cimmerian Vaults, as those might be in line with alphas on the front line if illegal steroids had been used. Their top theory was that the Lincoln pack were, perhaps, involved in funding to get the first claim of a drug that would make their auras stronger.

It wasn't a terrible theory. And alpha auras were connected to one another when they were in a pack.

Were they trying to find a way to… to replicate that outside of a pack? To take the strength of one alpha and give it to another?

Yet, the more I considered the tests, the less sense the theories made. The testing had been erratic. Umbra had been picked over and over again. He'd convinced them to take him instead of Dusk, but his repeated selection made it an unreliable benchmark.

I didn't think that they were intending to get stable data.

It didn't seem as though their pack was being measured at all. Rather, they were the ones being tested—pushed and pulled in one way or another.

To what, though? I had no idea, but I was close to a breakthrough. I could feel it. I'd been scouring texts on omegas balancing packs and how it worked.

I wasn't there yet; I didn't have answers, but from everything I understood about omega-alpha relations, my role was important.

I was an anchor in the pack.

There was a chance, if a solution presented itself, that I may be the centre of it.

It was the part I would never say to Dusk.

Already, people thought so little of me at the academy, outside of Roxy and my pack. I'd tried over and over to fit in, to be what they wanted me to be, and I'd failed.

And I'd found love, anyway. My pack and my friend, they wanted me as I was.

Roxy settled on a stunning velvet dress in the same rich blue, and then it was my turn. I stood, crossing to the rack and lifting the daring black dress from it.

I didn't think I was going to take long.

This had to be the one.

It was the scariest thing I'd ever done, opening the curtain for Roxy to see me once I had managed to get it on, glad to find it was a perfect fit.

As I expected, her eyes went wide, face blanching. I braced for the worst, and yet as her gaze traced each mark across my chest and arm, the bites that the dress didn't hide, I realised the truth I'd been hoping for when it came to my scars—one I could never have known until this moment. It was a truth that no one else knew, not even Roxy.

These marks no longer belonged to the Lincoln pack.

Dusk had claimed every single one of them, and showing them off, that, to me, was like showing off this bond that I loved so much.

No one else had to understand.

"Is it okay?" I asked.

"Shatter, it's beautiful, but…" She trailed off, like she wasn't sure how to say what she was thinking.

"No one will believe I would choose to show these?" I asked.

I knew that.

"I don't believe in shame, Shatter. I don't, but if you don't want the narrative—"

"I do." Dusk wanted that narrative, and I knew now that I wanted it too.

"You do?"

"He… he wants to protect me with it. I agreed to that."

"They won't just think he claimed you, Shatter. They're going to think he's cruel."

I swallowed, glancing down at the smooth black fabric and the bites that were on display. "That's okay."

Dusk didn't give a shit what anyone thought of him. He never had. I envied that about him. And it was my own little claim to something powerful in a way, choosing this, and knowing everyone would read into it exactly what I wanted them to.

Everyone was wary of my alphas. Dusk was an unknown, and people thought Umbra was unstable. If the world wanted to see me as a victim, as weak and pathetic and small, I would let them.

Because there might be a time in the future when I could use that to protect them, just like they protected me.

CHAPTER 34

Umbra

It was late Saturday afternoon.

Ball day, and revenge dress day. Since I was going out with Decebal this evening, Shatter had told me she wanted me to see her before I left.

At last, I stepped into Shatter's nest as Roxy ushered me in. It was messy, the bed scattered with boxes of makeup, brushes, straighteners, and all the stuff Roxy had brought. But I noticed that for only the briefest of seconds as my eyes found my omega.

Shatter…

I lost my breath entirely.

Holy *fucking* shit.

She waited beside her desk, looking anxiously over at me.

Her dress was black, with delicately thin straps and a neckline that dipped scandalously low. It clung gently to slender curves before tumbling to the floor. It had a slit to her upper thighs, through which her smooth legs and golden heels peeked through.

I'd heard her debating with Roxy in the living room earlier over the heels; she liked them but wasn't sure she'd be able to stay upright. She'd decided to risk them when Dusk and Ransom swore they (or Roxy) would be with her the whole time, so there was no chance she'd fall.

When she turned, showing it off for me, I saw the back of the dress dipped to her tailbone. Her hair was stunning, and it was still *her*, volume tumbling over her shoulder and down her back, but the honey brown mane was a silky jumble of curls and waves. I noticed, by the way it fell right now, it was covering her chest. The place I knew the marks were.

Beneath, how much of the dress hid them?

I noticed she wore a necklace like the one she'd had before, only now it was golden. It had our pack's symbol and a new star, with Dusk's bite contrasted beneath it.

I'd crossed the room before I realised, stopping before her.

"All right, I'll leave you two alone." That was Roxy, who I'd entirely forgotten was here. I glanced over to see her grabbing an armful of the beauty supplies. "See you there."

"You're sitting with us, right?" Shatter asked Roxy as she was leaving.

"Yup. Just gotta finish getting ready—and *don't* ruin the makeup."

I dragged my gaze from Shatter to see Roxy narrowing her eyes at me.

Ruin it?

Roxy couldn't rightly assist in making Shatter look like a golden goddess and then drop *that* bomb on me.

I was going to ruin my omega.

If the makeup wasn't high quality, that wasn't my fault.

There was another long second of silence as it closed, and Shatter's cheeks went pinker than ever as she looked back at me.

"I'm really not sure about the heels." She peered down at them, and I admired their beautiful gold shine that matched her so well. "I'm not good at walking in them—"

"I love them," I said quietly.

"Do you?"

"They're perfect," I told her. "*And* it means you can't get away from me," I added.

Bonus.

"You don't think it's too… much?"

"You are going to steal the show." No doubt about it.

Dusk had made that massive donation to get them a throne tonight, but it meant he had to go to the ceremonies beforehand and get thanked a bunch and all that dull shit, while Ransom got to escort her in. So, Dusk wouldn't see Shatter until she walked into the ball when it began.

By the look of her, I thought he might faint.

Shame I'd miss it.

And it wasn't just the captivating outfit and shimmery makeup—or even the way she wore it, with adorable excitement she deserved—it was the dark bond. The way it was on full display, and she was putting that on display for the world.

It made me rock fucking hard just knowing that.

"Okay. Well. Good," she said. "Because Roxy made it so pretty."

"And no scent blockers?" I asked.

She shook her head, a flicker of determination in her eyes.

Her hands were at her chest, pressing her waterfall of curls close. I could see shimmering golden swirls across her skin, over her collarbones, and… Something got stuck in my throat as I saw the trace of a wound peeking out from where her hair fell.

The marks she'd been too afraid to show me before now

Gently, she took my hand and lifted it to her chest. "You… you can see," she whispered.

I held her gaze for a long silence, my thumb brushing her skin. Finally, I moved her locks, sweeping them back and over her shoulder, still holding her eyes.

It took every ounce of courage I had to drop my gaze.

When I did, the marks I saw across her skin sent ice through my veins.

I'd expected the worst, but I hadn't truly known what the worst might look like. I counted at least ten, and one mangled mark beside her collarbone that looked like it had been bitten twice. They were surrounded by swirls and patterns in gold, but I couldn't see that, not when each of those marks symbolised her pain.

Her fear.

Fear I hadn't protected her from.

My monster stirred, howling and ready to kill.

I would *never* have bitten her like that. Alpha bites healed differently than normal wounds. The bite I'd given her at the start of term wouldn't scar—it wasn't deep enough, and it wasn't a bonding mark. But the Lincoln pack had ensured the wounds they'd given her wouldn't heal.

Her hand came to my cheek, her scent calm in the air. There wasn't anything fearful in it like there had been in the hot tub.

"They're yours, not theirs," she said. It was the first time I felt a flicker of fear from her, as if she was making an offer she wasn't sure I would accept.

I forced myself to look back, to understand those words. The bites across her flesh—though vicious and cruel—were also beautiful. I saw the gold, now. Truly saw it. Roxy had used shimmering paint, and delicate lines had been drawn across her skin, outlining each bite like it was precious.

I looked again, following the marks, as if they were constellations, realising that it was the same pattern Dusk now had across his chest.

"They're… ours?" I asked.

"If…" She swallowed. "If you want—"

I cut her off so she could never finish that with uncertainty, pressing my lips to hers and drawing her close.

There was a spark of joy from her down the bond.

"Sit," I commanded.

I loved her, and she was everything right now, claiming those marks for us. I sank down before her and hooked my hands behind her knees.

Fuck, she was beautiful. A black and gold goddess, honey brown hair almost matching her tanned skin in the low light. She smiled, and a purr rose in my chest as her fingers tangled in my hair, forcing my head back so she could look into my eyes.

"I love you so much, Little Nightshade," I breathed.

There was shimmery makeup smudged across eyes, necklace, and bites. The distinct golden swirls reached down her arms, and there were even a few between the laces of her heels and up her thighs.

I traced my lips along the marks on her calf, easily drawing her closer as I kissed higher and higher. The dress was light and easy to push up.

I could worship her forever.

She let out a little breath of pleasure as I dragged her closer, so her butt was right on the edge of the bed.

I pressed her dress up again and tugged her panties down. Her legs tangled over my shoulders, and she let out the cutest little breath of pleasure as I found her clit with my tongue. She had to let go of my hair to catch herself on the bed, since I wasn't too concerned at all with her balance.

Nightshade flooded the room, dark and sweet.

She felt safe with me, even when I'd seen her scars.

That was all I needed.

I would never get tired of the taste of her, or the way she let out the sweetest little moans when I treated her just right, or when I slid a finger inside of her, working deep.

She was so sensitive that she was shuddering over me in less than a minute, which was good, because it meant I had time to go again. This time, I lifted us, lying down on the bed and dragging her over me.

It was easy to hold her steady and beautifully suffocating over my face, and I was in fucking heaven. She was shivering, her whines so sweet, I might lose myself entirely and say *fuck the night and the ball and the rest of the world* and just lock us in so I could keep going.

I worked my fingers deeper this time, and with a deep, shuddering moan, she came again, spilling juices over my face.

Fuck.

Yes.

When I drew away, she was panting, cheeks pink and cute.

I wished we had more time tonight. How I wanted to see her come apart for me until she broke for me again. I loved her.

I loved that, even in this dress, she was shy, anxious Shatter underneath it all. My omega.

It made it so much sexier.

Also, Roxy's makeup was perfectly fine, so she wouldn't have my head.

When I stood, she also got up, even if she was unsteady with the heels and her climax. "It's not dangerous, what you're doing tonight, is it?" she asked.

"Nothing like that." It was a long shot more than anything else, but now I had dreams of glasses and banana splits, so I'd try whatever there was to try.

I tugged a handkerchief from my pocket.

"This is the one to scent mark?" she asked.

I nodded. She knew I was trying for answers tonight.

She drew it along her jaw, her scent dousing the air. I tucked it into my pocket.

"I love you."

Warmth bloomed in my chest, hearing her whisper those words to me, and I seized her by the hair, drawing her up into a kiss, a growl in my chest.

For a moment, I forget everything else.

I forgot the weight I carried.

I needed answers from Vandle because I couldn't hide the truth from her forever. It was a truth that even Dusk hadn't noticed.

I was at the front line.

The sickness always reached me first.

I hated it, and it didn't make sense, because I knew Shatter was perfect. She'd saved Ransom—saved us all.

But when Shatter had entered the bond, it hadn't stabilised.

At first, I thought I must be imagining it, but with every day that passed, it had become impossible to ignore. My nightmares grew like stretching shadows in the evening, claws extending, a darkness getting closer and closer.

Even now, I had to check that my blade was in my pocket.

The thing that kept me safe when I had to leave her side.

Because since Shatter had joined our pack, my sickness was getting worse faster than it ever had before.

And tonight, I had to get answers.

CHAPTER 35

Dust

The ballroom was decorated similarly to how it had been the night of the choosing. Crystal chandeliers adorned the ceiling, their lights reflecting off every surface to bathe the room in a warm glow. The second floor had been opened up as the guest count went beyond just academy students.

The main floor buzzed with a low energy already. There were staff members setting things up, and early guests, which included me, the Lincoln pack, and the charity event organisers and representatives.

The Lincoln pack's setup mirrored ours: our seats were stationed on raised platforms against the wall, with lavish decor leaving them looking something like thrones. Beside the setup was a long table with four seats for us to take when we wanted to eat. Thank God, since sitting here alone made me sick of this obscene display—designed, I was sure, to encourage such donations like the ones we'd made.

The Lincoln alphas were far enough away that I could see them—which I much preferred—but couldn't catch their scents.

Good.

That meant Shatter would have more control when she arrived. They wouldn't catch her scent straight away.

It had been a dull few hours. I'd been thanked repeatedly for my donation to the New Oxford Arkologic Research Foundation. The foundation members and other donors were socialising already, drinking champagne before the main event, and—from what I'd heard—discussing things like upcoming research strategies and the impact of new studies on prevalent diseases.

The staff, who were flitting around and setting things up, were dressed in formal attire. The room smelled like the subtle muted presence of scent dampeners and flowers, which were arranged on every table.

It was about half an hour from the official opening when I spotted Roxy enter. She wore a deep blue dress, ideal for the revenge Shatter had told me she was also claiming tonight.

We were over halfway through the first term, which meant seeking partners outside of those that were originally chosen was back on the table. The politics were a bit more messy, as packs didn't often like to announce they were dropping their omegas ahead of time. And most didn't do what the Lincoln pack had, which was considered quite extreme.

Although I doubted Roxy would have trouble finding a pack, I didn't think she was looking for one. I had helped Umbra and Ransom carry some of her new furniture into her apartment over the last week, and when I entered, it was hard not to look around for the Christmas baking and gifts beneath the tree. I swear she'd left her festive scent mark on every surface. She'd thoroughly claimed the whole damn place, and I got the impression that she was very happy being pack free.

"How is she?" I asked as Roxy plucked a wine bottle from the table beside us and poured herself a tall glass.

"Nervous." She took a seat, her orange and fir tree scent present, though muted beneath scent-dampening spray. She chose the seat beside me as, with the two of us, it would look odd for her not to. I didn't mind. Shatter had extended the invite, and Roxy had proven she had nothing but Shatter's best interests at heart. "But she is going to devastate them," she added. "You just wait until you see her."

Roxy looked the picture of vengeance as her gaze slid, just briefly, to the pack across the hall. I followed her gaze to see the Lincoln pack in utter shock. They were staring, the whites of their wide eyes clear as day, even across the room. Flynn's mouth had dropped open, and Eric had frozen with a glass to his lips.

"That's a pretty sight," she said.

"I agree." The first blow of the evening, seeing Roxy join me. They'd think this was the play. That we were claiming her after they'd dropped her.

"They aren't ready for tonight," she mused.

"I don't think so." It was a pleasant thought. Before this, I'd thought I was nothing more than a hunter. It was part of who I was, chasing down those who had wronged us, who had caused the death and suffering of every alpha at that facility and making them feel that same pain before they died. But what Shatter was about to do to the Lincoln pack? It was satisfying in an entirely different way.

I would take anything, since I, quite literally, couldn't touch them.

I was still working on ways around that.

"It was a good play, out-donating them," Roxy said. "I bet they weren't happy."

I grinned. "I've been told I have a flair for the dramatic." The Lincoln pack had been giving me smug looks all week, which didn't help the constant urge I had to tear them into little pieces, but this afternoon, they'd been stiff as I collected the majority of the praise by doubling the donation they'd made in order to secure the spotlight for the day.

And they didn't yet know that it was a spotlight I'd claimed for her.

Despite the occasional tremor from Shatter through the bond, there was enough conviction to drown it out. A determination that had been building since she and Roxy had gone shopping yesterday.

Tonight was everything.

The Lincoln pack would realise what we'd taken. It was a part of the torture I needed them to carry. To know that they'd failed. That she was stronger than the pain they had given her.

They would know their own loss before I finished them. And Shatter, my omega, would be free. Free of the foul mates the universe had destined for her. Free of the torment they'd believed had been enough to leave her crushed.

This was everything I wanted for her, and I would be at her side every step of the way.

Today, she was brave enough to face her monsters.

And if Shatter wanted to claim tonight to destroy the monsters who believed they could break her, then I would make her a queen and put her on a fucking throne.

Umbra

Where Decebal and I were going tonight wasn't the sort of place I ever wanted Shatter to step foot in.

We parked before a daunting-looking building. It was out of the city and far from prying eyes, a place so isolated that everyone else could forget it existed.

That's what everyone preferred to do with things like this—things that didn't fit.

Hide them away and pretend they don't exist.

Shut the doors and close your eyes…

It was mid-afternoon when we arrived, and the weather was miserable. Huge, angry waves smashed into the rocks and beach below, and the wind howled.

Appropriately ominous, I thought, as I looked at the huge building inset just a bit on the cliff's edge. It looked like an old fortress, forest on one side, ocean on the other.

There was nowhere in that building where crashing waves couldn't be heard, or the tang of ocean salt and washed-up seaweed wasn't present in the air, strong enough to taste. Out here, it blended with the damp earth and forest that stretched behind.

I knew that, and didn't know that, all at the same time. I had no memories, just a certainty that it was so.

I also knew the darkness within. The thick walls of stone. Cages of metal designed to keep alpha auras contained.

When we stepped up to the front doors, we were met by guards. I let Decebal deal with the formalities, instead staring up at the weathered walls.

We were made to sign a waiver, show our IDs, and were given a long speech about safety and regulations that I tuned out entirely before we were accepted inside. I don't know who Decebal was pretending we were. Probably should, though, in case they asked. If nothing else, I could just act stupid and let Decebal do the talking.

Dusk had been with us when we'd come last, and he'd hated every moment. But I'd found a strange solace here.

It was cold inside. No amount of heating could truly warm up the bones of a place like this. But cold was a sanctuary after the harshest of burns…

For Dusk, this place was the face of an old enemy.

For me, it was an old friend.

Our footsteps echoed with strange familiarity as we entered a hallway with dim, flickering lights that looked out of place against the stone. Even the electricity in here struggled to contend with the atmosphere, with a building that was truly a living, breathing creature. The faint metallic smell of old metal bars and aged electrics that struggled to survive lurked in every inch of this place.

It wasn't long before I heard the faint howling from within. Screams and cries, the sweet serenade of insanity. It was an old companion, a dream always just out of reach… I'd never quite been there, I didn't think. Always yearning, yet never arriving. Not like some, whose world was washed away, and when the tide drew back, the lines in the sand were gone.

All payments.

All debts.

The immortal vice, unbound at last…

"You all right?" Decebal asked, glancing at me.

I realised I'd started humming.

"Yup."

More than.

I did quite like it here, and I'd forgotten the comfort it offered. I'd never found that again—well, not until Shatter, anyway.

I smiled at the thought of Shatter, and the guard who was leading us into the gaping mouth of my oldest companion gave me a strange look—likely, because I'd begun humming again.

He didn't recognise me. Dusk and I were completely different people than we had been when we were here before, and Decebal had checked the staff. They turned over guards far too often for that to be a concern.

He led us up some stairs and down a few more hallways, and all the while, the howls and screams of prisoners grew. As we stepped through a colonnade, I peered down at a courtyard. It was empty right now, broad, with large metal structures for exercise. And the gates on either end were barred. It was all made with the same metal. The kind that stopped even the strongest of alphas, auras and all.

What a cost it must have been, building a place like this. It's why the prison was a fortress made of stone, I was sure. So they could minimise the amount of metal they needed.

Finally, we stopped at a door, and the guard dug in his pocket, pulling out a set of keys. He unlocked it, opened it, and waved us through. A few of the howls rose louder in the air, their owners clearly now far off.

"Cell twenty-three."

Decebal thanked him, and we entered. It became warmer as we stepped in, diverted into the limited capacity they had for the living spaces.

The hallway was wide, and understandably so, as the cells were on either side. Flaking paint along the floor marked the safezone the guard had warned us about at the gates. A flailing few arms, taut as they reached from between cell bars, signalled the cost of a misstep. The auras were thick in the space, though there was a heavy mist of scent dampeners in the air, a small attempt to limit chaos. The scent of dampeners didn't hide everything, though. Not the musty dampness that lingered in every crack or the acrid tang of sweat, fear, and madness from the alphas within.

Decebal led the way, and I lingered, unable not to peer into every cell we passed, to meet the vacant eyes of the alphas within.

And each was a harrowing mirror of what I knew I'd once been.

CHAPTER 36

Ransom

"Am I going to have to carry you in there?"

Shatter was very cute to watch, stumbling up the pathways to the main building, continuing to let go of me, so she could get her practice in before the ball.

"I think I basically got it—oop!" She caught the back of her heel on her dress and stumbled. I caught her before she fell, captivated by the grin on her face.

Once we got to the entrance hall, she made me escort her to the bathroom so she could check her makeup and hair before she took off her shawl.

She might be smiling for me, but inside, she was a ball of wound-up anxiety. I peered around while she was inside, noticing a worker tugging open the entrance to the stairs, opening the balcony above. A rather cheeky idea popped into my head.

When she returned, I swept her into my arms, ignoring her squeak of surprise as I carried her up the side stairway, instead of through the main doors.

"What are you doing?"

"Detour," I told her.

She was too nervous, still.

I could fix that.

I set her down before the balcony railing that overlooked a beautiful ballroom. The party had begun below, guests mingling, drinking, and dancing while music played. The low sound of chatter rose in the air. I'd picked a spot on the balcony that was above the side of the room where the platformed seating was set up. That meant we couldn't see the Lincoln pack or Dusk.

Good, and good, since he'd denied me the opportunity to watch them the other night.

"Hands on the railings, Little Reaper," I told her. *"And don't let go."*

"Uh… why?" Her voice was suddenly nervous as I used the bond.

If she was starting to believe dark bond commands meant sex, she was dead on. I enjoyed how blindsided she was by everything, though, so I didn't say anything. "Tonight, Dusk is going to put you on a throne, so I'm going to fuck you in front of all the peasants."

She let out a breath of shock. "Ransom. That's really rude."

I chuckled, nipping her ear, cupping her neck. Fuck, I loved how she melted against me at any sign of dominance, the faintest vibration of a purr in her chest, like she couldn't help herself.

"Hold up," she said, as if trying to fight her reaction to my touch. "Aren't there people up here? And anyone can look up and see us."

She was so precious. "They can, can't they?"

"But we'll be late," she whispered, eyes still darting about for passersby.

"You know, Umbra was right. Seeing you and Dusk was quite the show. But I can't say it didn't make me a little jealous. If I delay him seeing you like this because you're—what were his words—*letting me use your holes without complaint*? I think I can live with that."

"Right now?" she asked.

I tugged at her dress. The silk was cool and thin enough that it was easy to shift the slit over her hips without revealing her to the whole ballroom.

"Arch your back for me," I breathed. The heels were perfect for this, getting her so much closer to my height.

"You can't," she pleaded as I tugged at her panties.

"You're tense, Little Reaper. I'm going to help you relax."

"Umbra already did."

I laughed, pressing a kiss against her neck, freeing my cock with a decent amount of subtlety beneath the waves of black silk. "Tell me the truth. Do you really not want me to fuck you?" I asked.

"I…" She let out a little whine of irritation at the command. "I always do, but that doesn't mean we should—" She cut off with a breath of shock as I drove my cock into her without warning. When she whined like that—it didn't matter if it was rage, or brattiness—I just needed to fucking claim her.

"You take me so good, Little Reaper," I growled.

"Wait!" Her voice was breathless.

"Yes?" I asked, pressing into her deeper as I cupped her neck and ran my teeth along her jaw.

"We're right in the middle of the party." Her voice was weak.

No one would catch us. I'd told a worker opening the balcony to close it off for another half hour before letting anyone else up.

The only view anyone was getting was from below, and they wouldn't see much. Not that I was against that at all, but she was ever so shy.

"Was Dusk lying when he told me you're wet for him when he plays with you around the academy?"

"Well…" She swallowed. "He's…" She trailed off. "He's Dusk."

"So, you're happy for someone to catch you being claimed by him, but not me?"

"That's not…" She let out a breath as I slid into her. "Not what I meant. And we weren't in the middle of a… a party."

"Well, maybe it's a bit more my thing." I'd fuck her on a stage with an audience and wouldn't blink, but I think that might make her faint. "Turn around."

I drew out of her, careful to keep track of her dress, so when I lifted her and set her on the railing, she was covered.

"What—Ransom!" Her arms wrapped around my neck, and she glanced back over the ledge.

"You think I'm going to drop you?" I asked with a grin, letting my aura flare slightly as I stepped close, nudging her knees apart. With one hand tangled in her hair and the other at her hips, I drove into her.

She let out the sweetest little moan, her slender arms still wound around my neck. I saw her glance over her shoulder again, eyes wide as she took in the crowd below.

"Do you want me to let you down?" I asked.

Her eyes snapped back to me, and I saw a flicker of a thrill in them.

Oh, she was so very into this.

I grinned, and she let out a little gasp as I dragged her back over my length roughly.

"Good girl," I breathed, driving into her again, my palms resting on the small of her back, feeling her heels dig into my back as she wrapped her legs around me, too.

She was so beautiful. Through the bond, she was a ball of nervous energy, flitting between humiliation and thrill, like she couldn't make up her mind.

"They'll kick us out—ugh!"

I drove into her roughly, cutting her off. "I've never been kicked out of an event in my life," I growled. "I'm Ransom Kingsman, and you're my omega."

I took her like that for a while, taking my time, loving the sweet little sounds she made as I fucked her. My own thrill rising every time she tilted her head, clearly trying to watch for passersby or to glance down at the ball below. Whenever she did that, she'd clench over me so tight, and I wasn't sure if it was fear or arousal.

"You know what I want to do tonight, after we go home?" I asked as I slid into her. She was shaking, and I could feel the slick dripping down her thighs.

"I want to fuck you like this with Umbra and Dusk. I want to see how you take them, Little Reaper. And I want to know if you can take us all."

She groaned again as I rocked my knot against her. I felt her clench around my length and stayed right up to my knot, enjoying her tightness.

"Do you think you would like that?" I asked.

"I…" She moaned, tensing again as I pressed my knot a fraction further.

"Wait—Ransom!" Her voice was frantic. "You can't—"

"Answer me." I drew back before feeling her stretch over me again, almost all the way.

"Yes," she breathed. "I want you."

"Together?" I drew out and pressed back in.

"Yes."

"Say it."

"I want…" She was panting as I drove into her. "I want all of you."

"Come for me, Little Reaper," I growled.

Fuck.

She seized over me, trying so hard to be quiet, the sweetest groans trapped in her chest as she came apart. I fucked her with long strokes, spilling into her. My orgasm was so blinding that I stepped back, leaning against the pillar to our left, suddenly not trusting myself to hold her steady.

It wasn't hard to hold her, though, since she was clinging to me like a koala, her lip caught in her teeth as she watched my orgasm as if she was very proud of herself.

I set her down and helped her get her bearings, tucking her hair behind her ear and almost losing myself in her dazed, golden eyes.

"I can't believe you did that," she whispered, but I could see the hint of mischief in her expression.

I grinned. "I'm going to have to be creative to keep up with Dusk and Umbra. They've had much longer to steal your heart."

Her brows drew in a frown.

"You don't have to do anything to be important to me," she whispered.

I stared at her, something suddenly caught in my throat.

"I love you already," she told me.

It warmed my blood to hear her say it.

"But was that about you making me feel better, or you?"

"You," I said indignantly.

"Sometimes when you see me with Dusk, you're sad," she said. "Are you jealous?"

I considered her. "Yes. But not… not like it sounds."

She frowned up at me, eyes imploring me to tell her. "If you're going to fuck me on the ballroom balcony so I'm less nervous about going in, then you have to tell me, too."

Ah. So, she had seen through that.

I snorted, wincing a little at the words about to come out of my mouth. "It's hard not to feel useless. To try and figure out who I am or… find my place."

"You're the centre of this pack."

"Oh no, that's you now," I said.

She considered me. "I don't…" She swallowed. "I don't know who I am, either," she whispered. "I never… never got my memories back. I don't think I ever will. It's like… I'm… no one."

"Shatter…" I stared at her. "You truly believe that?"

"I have no memories—"

"And I have all of my memories. Of school and friends who never saw me as anything beyond a bank account, of nights getting drunk at bars because I didn't know what else to do with my time or what I wanted from my life. Of a father who turned out to be a monster. I have a lifetime's worth. I have all of that, and I am stranded. But you—you are the most fascinating person I've ever met," I told her. "You know what you love, what you want, and what you love, you are good at. You fight for your dreams when a thousand others would have given up. And you aren't just caring and protective over the people you love, you're brave, choosing to face your monsters when no one would judge you for running. What more to a person is there?" I asked. "Nothing that could be found on a piece of paper."

She stared at me, and even through the bond, I felt her stunned silence.

"I intend to follow you around like a lost puppy, so I can learn some of your tricks."

A smile wobbled on her lips, though her eyes were still dazed, as if she were still trying to untangle what I'd said.

"Until then, you'll let me help you save them, so I can feel like I'm doing something. You tell me what you need, I'll do it. Anything."

"You should be studying Arkology."

"Anything but that."

Her smile widened, and I drew her into a kiss.

"Are you ready to go in now?" I asked.

When I pulled away, she looked anxious again, eyes darting down to the ball below. She nodded, still tense.

"What is it?"

"You said I was brave." She swallowed. "That's not true, I'm… I'm really scared of them."

I knew that.

I'd been in her nest nearly every night this week. She had nightmares, her breathing picking up until I tugged her into my arms and purred for her. She hadn't even woken up.

I drew her close, my voice a whisper just for her. "If you weren't, Little Reaper, then it wouldn't be called bravery."

CHAPTER 37

Shatter

Entering the ball with Ransom was one of the most unnerving experiences of my life.

I'd never felt so many eyes on me. Eyes that lingered in shock as they met mine, then widened some more when they trailed down to the bite on full display on my neck.

For one wild, brief second, I wondered if anyone had seen us on the balcony. I looked up and was horrified to see that it was really quite visible. But then a nervous giggle bubbled up my throat. Spotting Ransom fucking me on the balcony wasn't going to be anyone's takeaway from tonight.

No. It was mine. Another thing I could claim while they were all focused on the things my pack would never let define me.

My neck and eyes.

At first, there was a stunned silence. All I could hear were the musicians playing and my own heels clicking on the marble floors. Then I heard a crescendo of whispers rising through the air.

It was okay.

Ransom's arm was in mine.

I saw the Lincoln pack first, beyond the dance floor with its milling crowds and dancers, to the circular dining tables around which packs loitered and socialised. All three of them were on a raised platform, their seats like thrones.

Gareth, Eric, and Flynn were just like I remembered them at the choosing. When, to me, they'd been different people in every way possible from the monsters I now knew them to be.

They must have caught sight of me at the same moment I saw them, because I saw Flynn lean forward in his seat, lowering his glass, eyes fixed on me. Eric said something, and Gareth cut off his conversation with an omega who was perched on the arm of his chair, his head snapping in my direction.

I heard an echo of Gareth's laugh. The cold tip of a marker pressed against my skin. Eric's fist was painful in my hair with Flynn's weight at my back. Teeth threatened, a cruel prank that toyed with my freedom…

I almost stumbled, but Ransom drew me closer, his arm winding around my waist. We'd used scent-dampening spray—not enough to stifle our scents entirely, but enough to mute them, which was event etiquette. But with every deep breath, my fear was offset by lily of the valley, a cool forest with damp earth, just like the trees outside that cabin.

He was here, with me. We'd just snuck onto the balcony so he could claim me.

My eyes scanned the room momentarily, and I realised that where he'd claimed me was right above the Lincoln pack's seats.

I felt the echo of a smile on my lips.

Right over their stupid thrones, he'd given me everything they'd tried to steal.

Everything they'd sworn I'd never have.

Now he led me swiftly away from the Lincoln pack, and I felt the brush of his breath at my ear as he leaned close. "There are much sweeter things to be looking at, Little Reaper."

I glanced up at him, then followed his gaze across the ballroom. My heart tripped over itself as I saw the Kingsman pack was seated just like my mates. Roxy was waiting, and Dusk…

My smile grew at the sight of him. He was frozen, on his feet before his chair, lips parted as he stared at me. Just like Ransom, he was dressed up in a really smart outfit. With the shiny shoes and a black button-up that was cut all stupid perfect around his shoulders and figure, making him look almost as devastating as when he was wearing nothing at all.

"You've got him speechless," Ransom murmured. "I don't think I've ever seen Dusk—oh."

He cut off with a chuckle as Dusk finally unfroze himself. He took the steps from the platform by twos, eyes wide as he began toward us. I stopped, drawing Ransom up, suddenly as unable to take my gaze from Dusk as he was from me. He was weaving through the crowd, almost knocking people over, still not sparing a glance anywhere else.

Then he was before me, midnight opium a roiling storm of passion, sharp edges of amber smoothed by traces of dark vanilla. He cupped my cheek, still something dazed in his expression.

"Fuck." His growl was low. "Shatter…" He swallowed, his gaze dropping to my neck again.

To his bite.

To the scars—*our* scars.

All my fear was gone. With Ransom and Dusk, and Roxy, waiting.

"You are…" He was lost for words.

"Yours?" I whispered.

The sweetest smile curved his lips, and then he leaned down, kissing me with complete abandon for the people around us.

Then he hooked his arm in mine on my other side, and he and Ransom both led me up to our seats.

What followed was a small fight, since I wanted to sit next to Roxy, which meant I couldn't sit next to Dusk *and* Ransom. Naturally, Dusk won, pulling a pack-lead-command like I'd never heard him do before. Ransom wrinkled his nose, clearly debating whether it was worth fighting (not the end of the world, but it could contribute to pack imbalance) before slumping down on the end seat at Dusk's side.

Roxy was giggling at the whole thing, a half-finished glass of wine in her hand, her eyes sparkling and her cheeks a bit pink. She seemed so happy, it was making me smile.

"Did you *see* their faces?" she asked. "Eric looked like he was about to throw his drink. And I think they scared off all their interest."

I dared another glance, only to see that they were still staring, and Roxy was right—there were no longer any omegas nearby

They'd seen the dark bond, and they knew I was gold pack. Which was more shocking to them, I wondered?

If it was the fact I was gold pack, what would that mean?

I realised it didn't worry me.

A breath released from my lungs, something pent up, building since the moment I'd run from Eric.

They could see me. They could see my scars, my eyes, and my bond.

They had, and so had everyone else.

I wore every insecurity on display, and I was still in one piece.

The world hadn't fallen apart.

The only thing the Lincoln pack didn't yet know was that I was their scent match.

That could wait for now as I settled in. Content to watch the dancers on the floor and the many groups that flitted about, even if I could still feel a thousand gazes flickering my way. I knew the chatter would repeat my name, would paint a picture that wasn't true, and that was okay, because that was mine too.

A weapon I could use.

With the scents around me, I had nothing to hide from anymore.

I had my best friend, I had my pack, and it was everything I'd ever dreamed of.

Umbra

Vandle was a loose end that the Institute had left alive.

The clear reason for that was staring us in the face.

The alpha in the cage we'd reached was tall and slender, but right now, he was curled up in his bed, eyes staring sightlessly at the wall. I knew he was prone to violence at the slightest provocation. During our last visit, he'd nearly taken out Dusk's eye.

That time, he hadn't said a word.

He was the only alpha we knew of who'd ended up back here after being in the experimentations. The best we could tell, he was part of the early trials—which had failed, and somehow, he'd escaped.

He might never have been caught, except he'd returned to the facility after it was shut down. He'd returned when the Institute had taken over and continued a different set of experiments on omegas.

He'd sabotaged them, and now we knew that meant he was the reason for Shatter's curse.

The reason she'd been injected with Atropa's Poison.

Whatever they'd done to sedate him after that, it had been the last nail in the coffin. His sanity had cracked, and instead of killing him, they'd thrown him back in this cell.

A fate worse than death for most.

He knew things that even the Institute didn't—that was Decebal's theory. They didn't want to end his life, in case the information he had ever became crucial for them to know. But in the meantime, he posed no threat.

At least, they didn't think so.

I stepped up to the thick bars, releasing my aura into the space.

Vandle flinched, eyes snapping to me, but he didn't move.

"Careful," Decebal murmured.

I waited for a long moment. Finally, Vandle shifted. He placed his feet carefully on the ground, sitting up, head cocked as he stared at me. Every movement was slow and deliberate.

His face was gaunt, skin pale and sickly. His clothes were baggy and worn, and his eyes bloodshot.

I could see the distinctive colours. One white, one red. His hair was shaved short. That's how they *all* were in this place, and how it had been at the facility too.

Easier to manage.

From what I could see of it, it was silver.

Vandle was a seer.

He could visualise auras. In another life, he could have made good money working with the Institute and selling that skill. They were rare, though Decebal also had one in his pack (the RedEyed*fucking*Bandit that had ruined all my scoreboards while I'd been in the throes of my sickness).

Vandle watched me intently, head tilted back, a snarl forming on his lips as he bared his teeth.

That was the reaction we'd got last time. He could see my aura. Could he see how broken it was? How much we were alike?

Last time, it had made him stir, even if it was not enough to pull him back.

Decebal shifted at my back, tugging the metal cigarette case from his pocket. It was empty, since they'd made him throw the last few out at the gates. We were allowed no contraband, and no alpha scents—we'd been doused with scent-dampening spray as we entered.

And absolutely, under no circumstances, were we to bring in omega scents.

Decebal, however, flicked the bottom compartment of his cigarette case open and withdrew the small silk handkerchief that Shatter had scent marked.

Would it be enough?

I didn't *like* handing her scent to the alpha who'd ruined her life, but it could mean saving us all.

Protecting her…

I had a lot of hatred to go around recently, but it was hard to place it at Vandle's feet. He was an alpha long broken.

Seconds after Decebal handed me the piece of cloth, Vandle was on his feet, eyes wide. His aura flared… or tried to. Like so many here, his was broken and fragmented. It was nothing more than flickering shards of energy shuttering in and out, trying to cling to life. Some harrowing in their power, never lasting long.

He crossed toward me in an instant, seizing the fabric from my fist, eyes wild as he examined it.

I narrowed my eyes, watching carefully.

He was shaking, I noticed, as he turned the fabric in his grip. More, with every second that passed. Still, I almost jumped when a burst of cracked, insane laughter broke from his lips.

CHAPTER 38

Shatter

"I don't have to dance, do I?" I whispered, clutching Roxy's arm as we headed into the bathroom. I was getting better with the heels, but certainly not enough to dance.

"I hope not," she snorted. "Take me to a club, then maybe. This is much too fancy."

"Some of those packs out there are really good," I noted. There were some pretty ballroom-like dances going on.

We were about an hour in. Beautifully dressed omegas and beta women were filling the party, and for once, seeing them didn't make me worry.

I had seen the love in Dusk's eyes as he'd reached me, the stunned, absolute passion as he took me in, head to toe, despite everyone else here.

I was enough for him, Ransom, and Umbra.

That was what mattered.

I was done checking my hair and was waiting for Roxy by the exit when I heard words from around the corner that drew me up.

"What do you make of the dark bond?"

I froze. That was Oliver's voice floating from the hallway beyond.

"That was a power play," Jasmine's voice came in reply, which wasn't a surprise, since they were often together.

I shrank against the cream wallpaper, the texture of its flowery swirls pressing against my back where my dress dipped down. The last I'd seen or heard from them was that night at the party.

They were talking about me, no doubt about it.

"Showing off her eyes *and* a dark bond in one night? And if what the Lincoln pack said was true about her pining over them?" Jasmine laughed. "Here—" She cut off. "Check the back straps, will you? I don't think they're right."

I heard a muffled sound, then Jasmine continued. "If you ask me, they were toying with her, acting to the school like they're obsessed, but I think they were taunting her. When she tried to make a run for it to the Lincoln pack…" She trailed off. "They're predators. The only interesting alphas in this place."

I chewed on my lip. That was good, though. It was exactly what I wanted. What Dusk wanted.

"You think so? The way Varis was looking at her—"

"She's his prize. Of course, he was—"

The conversation halted as heeled footsteps approached. A brunette beta with a shimmery black dress and matching purse came around the corner, giving me a little smile as she passed me on her way into the bathroom.

At that moment, Roxy appeared at my side, ready to go, but I put a finger to my lips, giving her a meaningful look. She closed the last few steps with a frown, careful about keeping her heels as quiet as possible.

"You believe what they said about her asking for those bites?" Oliver asked after a moment.

"Come on." Jasmine sounded amused. "You've seen her. She's pathetic, actually admitted to following them around? And if she thought it was going to get her a bond from them? Plus, someone said her scent is god awful, so she probably is desperate."

"Yet, you want to take a run at them tonight?" Oliver asked.

"That was the plan," Jasmine replied.

Roxy's eyebrows shot up, and I frowned. *Jasmine wants to try for the Lincoln pack?* She already had a pack, a good one.

"You're not worried about how they look, after what they did?"

"Like I give a damn. Besides, I don't think that gold pack slut knows how to handle alphas, anyone can see that. Give me a run, I'll have them around my little finger. I want to show her how a real omega does it. She was a mess in that video, stammering all over the place—and she thought they might keep her?" I could hear the sneer in her voice.

The old, wounded part of me wilted, the part that was always worried about never being good enough as an omega.

"She gives us a bad name," Jasmine went on. "Plus, the North Prince alphas are so dull. I need a challenge."

"No way for you to take your shot without the whole room seeing," Oliver replied.

"That's fine." Jasmine laughed. "The North Prince pack know I'm trying for it."

"They're okay with that?" He sounded surprised.

"Told them if I failed tonight, I'd stick around for my heat. Dan hasn't got a clue I've been winding him up on purpose. He's near a rut. He told the others to shut up about it if they had a problem."

Roxy wrinkled her nose in disgust, but Oliver laughed. "*That's* how you got them so obsessed with you?"

"Piece of cake."

Their talk died down as I heard more footsteps passing.

It sounded like a group of girls who'd had a bit to drink. They were giggling, and I could hear snippets of their conversation, even from here.

"...dresses and makeup are iconic. Talk about an entrance. They both look like queens."

"I wish I had an alpha to put me on a throne," another said. "Gold pack or not, I'm jealous."

"You think they're going to match the Barclay?" That was the first female voice. "Get two omegas."

"If they have a dark bond, they can't have two."

"Some get a second by title, though, not unheard of..." The voices trailed off and there was a long silence.

"Two omegas?" Oliver repeated into the silence. "You know, I don't think it's impossible that's what they're going for."

"Let's go back in. I need another drink." Jasmine sounded bitter. "You watch. By the time I'm done, no one will even remember that gold pack shit."

We waited for the sounds of their footsteps to vanish entirely before Roxy spoke. "I bet she was planning on being queen omega tonight, securing a spot with the Lincoln pack and being the centre of it all."

I was silent.

I knew they'd taken pieces of that video and put it together all wrong. I knew that the Lincoln pack was getting attention tonight, that omegas had been approaching them for a chance to join their pack.

Yet, hearing it like that, how easy it was for Jasmine to write me off, to claim I'd *wanted* the Lincoln pack to bite me like that—

My thoughts cut off as Roxy's hand squeezed mine.

"She's delusional," she said. "And, for the record, you manage your alphas better than I ever thought was possible."

I smiled, trying to shove away the ache in my chest. "It's okay," I told her. "We knew this was going to happen."

"You still shouldn't have to hear it."

We'd waited long enough for them to be long gone and headed back. Ransom was waiting by the doors back into the ballroom, his hand slipping around my waist as he drew me from Roxy's supportive grip.

I leaned my head against him, happy to inhale his cool, earthy scent.

I took my seat between Roxy and Dusk again, tuning in to the conversation between an alpha named Percy, who I recognised as the lead of a pack that had a booth in our Arkology classes. He was talking to Dusk with enthusiasm.

"...foundation has real personal meaning to me. Thank you again, and..." His eyes slid to me, snagging on my neck before he forced them back up. He gave me an odd smile, then frowned, as if he wasn't sure he should have. "And, uh..." He returned his attention to Dusk. "Congratulations to your pack for the new bond. All of you." He made sure to nod at Ransom, too, then awkwardly gave me and Roxy a half nod. I could see the effort it took for him not to look back at my neck as he did.

"Thank you," Dusk replied.

"No one knows how to react," Roxy said with a giggle once he was gone.

I only planned on one drink tonight, and I sipped it slowly, listening to Roxy's social commentary and forcing myself to relax.

I wasn't used to being on display like this, but the rich, deep amber of midnight opium grounded me, and Dusk's fingers tangled in mine, tracing my palm soothingly as the music played on.

I'd tried so hard to ignore the Lincoln pack, but it was difficult. Their lack of attention didn't last long. There seemed to be a new omega speaking to them every time I dared glance. Every time I did, I saw, even from this distance, one of them looking at me. As if my attention drew theirs.

Once, I swear Gareth cut off mid-sentence as his eyes met mine, and the omega perched on the arm of his seat was forced to nudge his shoulder to drag his attention back to her.

My memories were still vile, recent enough that their thorns hadn't dulled. Not entirely.

But I didn't regret tonight. They had hurt me, but they hadn't broken me.

And now, they couldn't ever hurt me again.

They didn't have that power anymore.

I glanced down, finding a smile as I watched Dusk's finger trace my palm.

"Ransom's a total diva if you give him attention," Dusk chuckled. I glanced up. Ransom had gone to fetch us another bottle of red. "Literally strutting. Look at him."

I smiled, watching Ransom as he picked up a bottle from the long set of serving tables. He was getting stares as much as I was, and Dusk was right—I could practically see him puffing up at the attention. I pouted a little when I realised how much of that attention was from omegas.

"Don't be jealous." He snorted, catching my expression. "It could be a room of enraptured birds, and he'd bask in the attention the same. It's in his blood."

"I'm not jealous," I said, far too quickly.

Dusk grinned, leaning back in his chair.

Again, before I could catch myself, I saw a pretty blonde omega I didn't recognise join Eric. She was clearly enthralled by him, and he caught my eye, offering me a nasty smirk before I tore my eyes away.

I wondered when Jasmine would make her play.

She'd seemed so confident that it would work. I didn't know if I wanted it to, but I thought, perhaps, they deserved each other.

When we saw Jasmine next, however, she wasn't approaching the Lincoln pack at all.

Instead, she came sashaying up the steps toward us. At the sight of her shimmery black dress and the sway of her glossy, high-ponytail, I tensed.

What is she doing here?

I noticed more attention on us than usual as Jasmine lowered her glass to her side, stopping between Dusk and Ransom and holding her hand out delicately, fingers curled, as if they were going to reach up and kiss it.

"Jasmine Lynn," she said. "I left you flowers, but we never got a chance to speak. It's lovely to meet you, Dusk..." Her gaze slid to Ransom, as if I didn't exist. "Ransom. I saw you at the party ever so briefly. That was an... impressive show."

I was absolutely still, every hair on my body standing on end as I stared at her.

The ball fell away, the dancers, the music, the thousand watching eyes.

"We aren't open for courting," Dusk said, his voice icy enough, I'm surprised it didn't send her running.

Why is she here?

Jasmine pouted, drawing her hand back.

My lips pulled back in a snarl, fingers clenching on the rests of my chair. Blood pounded in my ears, but I remained frozen, holding on by the thinnest thread, struggling to keep at bay the rage that used to rule me. But it was lifting its ugly head, cracking the balance my pack offered me since I'd been bitten.

She wasn't here for them.

She *couldn't* be.

They were mine...

"You have a pack already, don't you?" Dusk asked. His continued coldness settled me by the slightest of fractions, but the thundering of my heart against my ribs was almost painful.

"Not one like this," she replied, voice silky smooth. "I would drop them in a heartbeat for a pack with a little extra..." Her gaze darted to me, sliding down to the dark bond on my neck. "Fun."

I saw red.

"Oh, you *little*—" Roxy began, but cut off.

I let out a primal growl and, dress and heels notwithstanding, threw myself at Jasmine with all my might.

I took us both down, and we crashed into the marble, sanity forgotten in the seat behind me.

"They're *mine*!" My voice was guttural, primal instincts sweeping me away as my nails dug into her arms hard enough to make her shriek in pain.

Not enough.

I'll kill her.

"Shatter! Let go."

I realised my fist had closed around her stupid ponytail.

It wasn't a conscious decision to fight Dusk's command, but the red of my vision only intensified with the spark of pain that tore across my body at the defiance of the dark bond. I growled again, and then Jasmine whined in terror as my teeth sank into her neck.

My body shook with thrilling instinct as I held it there, and Jasmine went limp in my grip, a terrified whine in her chest.

What I'd just offered her was nothing close to a bond.

It was a threat.

The pain drained away as Dusk released the command, and then I felt his touch on my neck. Cupping it gently.

"Shatter."

No.

I wasn't done.

Jasmine was shaking beneath me, more pathetic whines sounding with each panicked heave of her chest.

"You won, Gem. You can let her go."

I frowned, then released my bite at last, knowing there would be blood on my lips. I didn't care.

I... I had what?

Won?

Won what?

Oh... Oh *dear*...

The world flooded back in, and horror rose in my chest. We were in the middle of the ball. My gaze flicked up from the pooling blood on Jasmine's neck.

I'd bitten her.

The whole room was watching.

Dusk cupped my neck more firmly as he gently drew me back, further from Jasmine.

Jasmine scrambled back the moment she was free. "Get your filthy fucking gold pack b—"

"Finish that sentence, Omega"—Dusk's growl was more cutting than I'd ever heard it—"and I will finish what she started."

He didn't even look at her. His yellow eyes were fixed on me.

Then, before I could even catch my breath, he'd dragged me forward by my neck and pressed his lips to mine. I melted into his touch, the kiss and its iron tang of blood returning my sanity. Then he was drawing me to my feet, not a care for the watching eyes of everyone in the room. When I glanced in Jasmine's direction, she was fleeing, unsteady on her heels.

Dusk leaned forward again for another kiss, and this time, his teeth caught my lip, a rumbling purr in his chest as he held me close. When he drew back, he lifted a hand and wiped away what I knew had to be a smear of blood on my cheek. When he sat, he drew me onto his lap, his arms winding around my waist possessively.

My whole body was hot with embarrassment as I glanced at Ransom and Roxy.

To my surprise, Roxy was failing to hide a look of delight, while Ransom was staring at me with blown pupils and a feral glint in his eye.

"Gem." Dusk cupped my neck, his thumb running along my jaw as he tilted my head up, his voice a low growl in my ear. "You never have to fight to prove we're yours. That's our job. I was about to tell Jasmine to fuck off."

"Keyword—*have* to," Ransom put in. "Like I said before, it's fucking hot."

Roxy's giggle drew a nervous smile upon my own lips. "If anyone was wondering about territory," she said. "They aren't anymore."

"I don't know what happened," I whispered.

"You bit her *and* scent marked her. She'll be walking around with that beat down all evening."

"Marked her?" Why had I done that... ?

Oh, bother.

I needed to get better control of myself. Apparently, alphas were totally capable of balancing me in the bond—until they were the things my instincts were going nuts over.

"They're just going to think I'm even more crazy."

I tried not to pout.

I didn't regret it; I just couldn't fit in, no matter how hard I tried.

Roxy chuckled. "I doubt anyone here has dealt with honest-to-God territorial omega instincts in their lives. A good dose of reality, if you ask me."

CHAPTER 39

Umbra

"You're like…" Vandle's voice was charred and cracked with misuse. "Like me." He met my gaze, head cocked, Shatter's scented handkerchief balled up in his fist.

"Yes." This was it, I realised, as I stared into mismatched eyes. The first breakthrough we'd had in forever. Vandle was awake.

"I was in the experiments," I said. "Like you."

He grinned. "They put you back together, so they could break you again…"

"Tell me what you know about that?"

"Too much," he rasped. "He liked me, you know? The Doctor."

"Dr. Wren?" I asked, heart racing. "He… he helped me."

Vandle's smile stiffened, the edges of a snarl drawing at his lips. "No. He toyed with you, with the others."

"Toyed with us?"

"That was his job, too, you know? To push you. To see how far you would go to protect each other."

I felt my blood chill, but Vandle was going on, the cracks working themselves out of his voice as he used it. Now that he was, he couldn't seem to stop.

"But he cared about *me*." There was a madness and frenzy to his words. "He freed me when I should have died, kept my secret, so I could help him spy the auras and give him more data. But no matter what I did or said, they never…" He flinched, scrunching his eyes shut for a moment. "They never stopped. Not until they were forced to. And they killed everyone…" His expression twisted into something sick. "Everyone… but you?" He frowned, but then shook it off. "And then, when I went back, they opened it again."

"The facility?" I asked.

"Why?" His eyes went wide, one blank white, one red, and he ran his fingers along his scalp. I could see red marks through his buzzed-short hair, as if he did that often. "I went in. Took one of their white coats to make sure things had changed. I was going to leave forever after that. But…" His speech was getting frantic, the edge of a growl in his voice. "They had *omegas*. And I couldn't… I had to stop them. What they did to us, I couldn't…" His breathing came too quick, and I was worried he would slip back into silence.

"What did you do?" I asked. *Keep him talking.* I would know if he lied, which would be a good indicator of the usefulness of this conversation. I knew the answer already.

He was responsible for the mixed-up vial.

Shatter had been the one to pay, getting an injection that had broken her.

"I thought…" His breath caught. "I thought it would be enough to stop it. But… it didn't work." His madness broke for a moment, sorrow cresting his expression as he looked down at the handkerchief in his fist.

"You recognise her scent?"

"I was there when it changed. It was beautiful… but then… she didn't die."

"You meant to kill her?"

A low, wounded sound rose in his throat, catching on the way up like a dry, broken sob. He looked back to me. "I never wanted her to, but I knew if she did, then so many more would be saved. But Number One survived, and so did the experiments, and I was brought here…" He frowned. "How long has it been?"

He looked around the cell, at the cracked walls and bare room. I didn't answer, knowing if I told him that, we might lose him.

Instead, I digested what he'd said, sickness turning my stomach. And yet, I couldn't find hatred.

"She fought the poison, just like you did," he whispered. "A survivor. One worth a thousand of me."

"What does that mean?"

"Do you know why they gave us that poison? The Atropa abomination?"

"Why?"

He stared down at his fist, where he held Shatter's scent. "Strength testing."

"What?"

"The kind of bond that remains if a pack survives that—well, they needed that strength. Not something I survived."

"Needed it for what?" I asked.

Vandle's fist closed around the iron bar of the cage, his expression turning into something so hollow that I feared I was truly about to lose him.

"You didn't survive?" I asked instead, trying to understand that.

"I… I killed them all."

Ah.

I swallowed, remembering the way the poison had felt the first time I'd been exposed to it. The primal fear it had instilled, telling me to kill—that I had to kill, or I would die.

"Your… own pack?" I asked.

"Of *course* I did." Vandle's lips drew thin in a snarl. "And then I was useless to them. If Dr. Wren hadn't taken pity on me, I would be dead too. Not because of them. No one… no one survives once the poison gets them. Kill them… then kill me…" His breath caught. "Dr. Wren wouldn't let me end it, though… He put me to use…" He frowned. "But now… *look.*" He took a step closer, examining me properly. "You survived"—he laughed—"and you're free. You aren't supposed to be, you know?"

"Why?"

"You were *designed* for a cage. They would never have paid so much if they thought you would one day escape… If they thought you might find them."

"They?"

"Your better half. You're alive, aren't you—so you must have one."

"What does that mean?"

"You don't know?" A bark of an insane laugh slipped out. "Walking around with half a body and never even noticed?"

The words struck too close to the lurking shadow in the back of my mind. "Tell me what that means."

"You never figured out what they were doing with all of the tests?"

"They covered it up."

He grinned. "Well, it would have made locating sponsors too easy. It would have put their whole illegal operation at risk."

"What were they doing?"

"What do the rich hate more than anything?" he asked, his voice taunting. "What they can't control—what their money cannot fix. A sickness like a plague among them, and yet there is no cure outside… not outside of a scent-matched omega."

Ice seeped into my blood as I stared at him. "A scent match?"

"Nature punishes alphas who dare defy her," Vandle whispered. "So, they turn on her, warping and butchering her and forcing her to break."

I grabbed him by the shirt, trying to quell my panic.

Shatter was the Lincoln pack's mate.

What is he talking about?

But Vandle was in a frenzy, lips drawn as he spat the words with madness. "They don't want to wait for the cure that might never come—a scent-matched omega—a princess bond? That is a dice roll without the power they so dearly crave."

My mind was racing.

"The experiments were for a *cure*?" I asked.

"You," Vandle hissed. "You are the cure."

"For what?"

How serious was this sickness? How far would the Lincoln pack go to fix it?

Enough for them to gamble on an illegal fix…

There was a wide smile on Vandle's face as he stared at me, but he said nothing.

"Tell. Me!" My pulse was erratic, panic choking me.

Something only a princess bond with a mate could fix…?

Shatter was about to reveal her scent to the Lincoln pack *tonight*.

It might be too late already.

It was Decebal, in the end, who answered from behind me, his voice low and stunned.

"They were trying to cure aura sickness."

CHAPTER 40

Aura Sickness: A phenomenon where an alpha's aura begins to deteriorate until it vanishes entirely. An alpha without an aura loses the ability to forge pack bonds or omega bonds, leaving them strongly resembling betas. Traditional or dark bonds with a scent-matched omega have been known to cure aura sickness, with unreliable degrees of success. The only absolute cure for aura sickness is a princess bond with a scent-matched omega.

Shatter

We almost went the whole ball without an interaction with the Lincoln pack.

I finally began to enjoy the evening. I people-watched with Roxy, letting her explain gossip and politics to me.

Ransom, to Dusk's amusement, tuned in for Roxy's explanations with more attention than he'd had for any of our studies this week, claiming he needed to catch up on politics.

I think I could face my classes after tonight.

Actually, I was sure I could.

"Are you still going to take Omega Studies?" I asked Roxy as we reached the snack table with napkins in hand.

Now she was pack-free, it wasn't mandatory, though it was encouraged.

"I think I'll keep one of them. Otherwise, I thought of transferring into another Arkology class."

"Really?" I asked, eyeing a few pieces on a plate full of pretty cheese.

That sounded exciting. I knew Dusk attended an Arkology class on Tuesday and Thursday morning. Maybe we could take that class together too?

I opened my mouth, about to ask if she would mind that, when a familiar, snide voice behind me drew me up.

"I had *no* idea." Eric's voice was obnoxiously loud. "If I had known it was a gold pack bitch at the time, I might have been a bit rougher."

I tensed, my breath catching in my lungs.

It took all my courage, but I forced myself to turn.

Eric stood further down the snack table with the same blonde omega I'd seen earlier. Roxy was stiff, fury blazing in her blue eyes as she stared at him.

Then Dusk was there, stepping in front of me before I could do anything.

I caught the scent of midnight opium and lily of the valley, and my heart settled, if only a little. I still didn't want Dusk getting too close.

Eric grinned. "Did you see the video?" he asked, gaze shifting to Dusk. "I made it just for you—and Ransom Kingsman turning up in time to pick up my used trash—"

Ransom's aura split the air, and he closed the distance, his fist in Eric's shirt.

I noticed security move from the edges of the room. I reacted before thinking, slipping past Dusk and closing my grip around Ransom's arm.

"Ransom," I whispered.

It wasn't because I didn't want to see Eric hurt, but I could feel Ransom waver on the edge of that madness. The one I'd pulled him from in the first place.

My mates were not worth him tumbling back over that ledge.

With what looked like painful difficulty, Ransom released Eric's shirt. He didn't back off, though, his massive aura still shivering in the air.

Eric looked far too unperturbed. Perhaps he didn't think Ransom would attack him in public. Perhaps he wanted him to.

Everyone was watching, security hovering but not yet intervening.

And then Eric went absolutely still, his aura flickering in the space for a second as his gaze snapped to me.

Unwavering.

There was utter shock in his eyes.

It was the moment—I knew—he caught my scent.

My heart slammed against my ribs, nails digging into Ransom's arm to steady my breathing.

Endless seconds passed as we stared at one another, as if he couldn't understand what he was seeing. His face had drained of all its remaining colour.

But he knew.

He knew at that moment, his gaze locked on me.

It was no longer a secret.

"What?" Gareth's voice drew my attention as he stepped up to Eric, and then Flynn was there too.

In an instant, both of their eyes were fixed on me, arrogance falling away from Flynn's expression, the smile vanishing from Gareth's.

This… this was a mistake.

They were so close. Their scents were here, just like they had been.

Flynn's teeth threatened a dark bond. Gareth was filming me. Eric's weight pinned me to the bed as he took his time searching for another place to sink his teeth.

Panic rose its ugly head, but then Ransom's arm was around my waist. Their scents were here.

I was here with my pack.

My family.

My best friend.

I had claimed everything I had come here for, and I had done it without them.

"No." Flynn's growl was low and furious, and in his expression was more rage than I had imagined.

He looked sick with it.

I shrank back. Ransom's arm dropped, but immediately, I felt Dusk there, pulling me a step away.

"She's ours." There was something truly hateful in Flynn's eyes. It was more than hateful. It was… it was desperate. There was madness in that gaze as it darted from me up to Dusk. A chill skittered down my spine at his words.

"She's *our* omega," Ransom growled. "You will not touch her."

"She's our mate!"

"You hurt me." My whisper was harsh as my mind went numb. "You… you left me with scars and told me no one would ever want me again." My voice shook, my eyes burning, but I blinked the tears away.

I hadn't cried in front of them then, and I wouldn't now.

"We didn't *know* you were gold pack," Gareth hissed. "You hid your eyes."

Hiding my golden eyes was illegal, but the dark bond on my neck neutralised the penalties for that.

"What is that supposed to mean?" Roxy demanded. I glanced at her, grateful she was at my side right now.

Eric had a nasty look on his face, but Flynn spoke before he could. "We'll take her back." His voice was icy as he looked at Ransom. "What's your price?"

My lips parted in shock.

Flynn wasn't looking at me, though, as he adjusted his cuff, his dark eyes fixed on my alpha, as if I didn't exist.

"Price?" Ransom asked, sounding as stunned as I felt.

"What do you want us to say?" Flynn asked. "Well played. You won."

"Won?" Ransom asked.

On pure instinct, I stepped closer to him, heart racing like a hummingbird in my chest as I stared between my mates.

Flynn looked at Dusk. "You knew she was ours, and you hid her from us. When she tried to escape, and we didn't save her, you bonded her."

I frowned. *Save me?* But then I remembered what I'd overheard Jasmine saying. That she believed the Kingsman pack had been toying with me.

"Now you're dangling a scent match in our faces." Flynn's voice was stiff, as if he was trying to sound more casual than he was. "Well played. We lost. Is that what you want to hear?"

I felt Dusk's low growl vibrate against my chest as his hand slipped around my neck, cupping his bite as he drew me against him. Midnight opium quelled the rising panic attack as I watched my mates bargain for me like I was a trinket at a market stall.

"We'll take her off your hands," Flynn said. "Name the price."

"There is no price." Ransom's voice was strained with fury. "She's ours."

Eric looked between Dusk and Ransom, as if searching for the joke. Gareth laughed. "You can't be serious about wanting to keep her."

I watched Eric's eyes slide to me, lingering on the bites on my chest, his gaze slipping from amused to hungry for a moment.

Dusk drew me tighter against him. I could feel him through the bond, steadfast. A bastion I could cling to.

"She belongs to my pack." Dusk's voice was perfectly even. "Any marks she wears are mine."

Eric's eyes snapped to him, and I saw a flicker of a snarl pull on his lips before he caught it. "We claimed her. She is worthless to—"

Dusk cut him off, each word slow and vicious. "You *attacked* your own scent match. Those marks might prove your foulness, but they don't touch her worth."

I shrank against Dusk and felt him draw me closer. My shaking fingers were tangled with Roxy's, and she squeezed them tight.

Eric took a step forward, but Ransom cut him off, his aura—which was still a smothering force in the air—flaring. "You bit her in that video, didn't you? The one you wanted everyone to see. Too stupid to recognise your own mate, you called her a stalker." His voice dropped. "But you didn't claim her."

I felt Dusk waver in the bond just the slightest bit. Not with fear, but uncertainty.

I got that.

I didn't understand any of this. Even if I was their scent match, the only way to transfer the dark bond to them was through a princess bond.

The bond between mates.

But that was the opposite to the dark bond; it handed power to the omega. I thought I'd heard them discussing one all those months ago, but I'd written it off as imagination. The Lincoln alphas weren't ones who wanted to offer a princess bond to an omega.

"There is no price," Ransom said.

"There has to be a—" Flynn cut off at Ransom's growl. Until now, I'd never noticed quite how tall he was, rounding on them with ease.

"Take one more step closer to my omega, and I will put you all the way through the wall this time."

"This is *insane*," Flynn snarled, eyes darting to me. I felt a flutter of terror. There was a wild undercurrent of madness dancing in his eyes before Gareth grabbed him, dragging him back a step.

"Let's go," Gareth growled.

Flynn tore his gaze from me to Ransom, who was all but coiled to pounce—as were the security guards. Finally, he stepped back.

I watched them storm through the huge front door of the ballroom, my heart in my throat until they were out of sight.

"Do you want to leave—?"

"No." I cut Roxy short.

Not now. Not straight away.

They were out there, and I… I didn't want to run.

They were the ones running

"Are you sure, Little Reaper?" Ransom had turned to me, his aura vanishing in an instant.

I glanced around. I had to stay, even if half of me wanted to cling to Dusk and bury my face in his shoulder and let him carry me out of here.

But I couldn't.

They had fled, not returning to the seats they'd so dearly wanted.

I would return to mine.

Of course, every eye in the room was on us. Even the music had stopped.

"I want to stay. Even just a bit longer. If that's…" I swallowed. "If that's okay."

When we reached our seats, Dusk drew me onto his lap again. I'd made a step for my own, but I'd felt a flicker of discomfort from him through the bond, as if he didn't want me even that far.

"Something is wrong." His voice was low in my ear as he drew me close.

"That was…" Roxy trailed off, having taken the seat I'd occupied before. "That wasn't what I expected."

"What, uh… what *were* we expecting?" I asked.

I was shaking. It was obvious as I looked down, seeing the rich, dark skin of Dusk's hands contrasting the rippling goosebumps on my arms.

"I don't know, but Flynn was…" Roxy paused. "He looked insane. I mean, I get it, scent matches are a whole thing, but they didn't strike me as the kind of pack that cared that much."

I couldn't shake the look on Flynn's face.

"How long do you want to stay?" Ransom asked.

I glanced around. The music had started up again, and everyone was returning to their dance or chatter.

"Not long." My voice was weak. "I just don't want to run from them."

CHAPTER 41

Umbra

"Decebal." My growl was desperate as I turned.

We needed to warn Shatter not to reveal her scent, but there was no reception in here. "If they find out she's their scent match—"

"I'm going." He was already backing up. "You get more information," he told me, before vanishing.

"All of this is about aura sickness?" I asked, turning back to Vandle.

"Fascinating sickness," he said. "Really, not that devastating until ego is involved. Tell an alpha he won't be an alpha anymore? He'll burn the world down to change that. And you know what they say about it, that it's as random as a lightning strike? Yet, it's funny how, if you look, and I mean *really* look, lightning seems to strike cruel packs—though Dr. Wren thought there was more to it than that."

He rolled his shoulders, a grin on his face.

"More, like what?" I didn't know what I was seeking anymore; I would take anything he would share. I didn't know what was useful.

"The thing about mother nature," Vandle breathed. "She doesn't break. She is vengeful, and, more than anything in the world, she protects her children."

"What do you mean?"

"Aura sickness," Vandle said. "That's what Dr. Wren used to say. Nature's way of biting back." He dropped his voice. "Vengeance for the pain of gold packs. But it's not so simple to track crime from punishment. He didn't think it distinguished alpha from pack. Its target could be any of them—and in that, I suppose, it is like a lightning strike."

I rubbed my face, trying to work through everything he'd said so far. "Do you know what they did to me—why we're sick?" I asked.

Vandle's oddly coloured eyes were calculating as he took me in. "You're 66, aren't you? I think I remember. Became a success the moment your pack mate died."

My blood turned to ice.

He remembered?

It was the greatest enigma—our survival, when there were only two of us left in the bond. "How did the pack survive?"

"I think, because the bond registered a third member, even an unconventional one."

"What does that mean?"

"Your pack was born of theirs."

"It was… *what?*"

"They used your blood and a twisted binding. Not like usual bonds between alphas. But even then, as unnatural as it was, you still had to accept it. Do you remember the moment you connected? A moment of desperation to save your pack when there was nothing else?"

"I…" I trailed off, memories clawing their way back violently.

I had always known there was something wrong with that moment.

The bullet shredded more than just flesh. As 31's heart stopped, each one tore through our pack bond. Enough, by all laws of the universe, to destroy it.

No…

If the pack broke, I couldn't protect Dusk.

We wouldn't be of use to them anymore.

I flared my aura, reaching out desperately in the dark. Somehow, I found something to hold on to. Intangible and impossible, the energy was an anchor enough that I could hold on, even though it scorched me to the soul, unnatural and agonising.

I shuddered, cracks rippling through the very essence that made me an alpha; wounds that didn't feel as if they would ever heal.

"I… did this?" I asked, ripping myself from the vision before it pulled me from reality completely.

But… I had been right all this time.

This *was* my fault.

"You could not conceive of the power you handed to them when you did that," Vandle said. "The relationship was not symbiotic by design."

"Not… what?"

"They're feeding on you, 66. On you and 68. On your auras. A parasite draining you dry. A slow poison to wither you to nothing as you rot behind the bars of a cage."

A parasite?

"Once they knew you were going to succeed, he just had to take three injections of a serum with your blood, and the bond was sealed."

"That's what was in the briefcase?"

That's what this was? This sickness creeping in, devouring me.

The Lincoln pack… What they'd stolen, they were *still* stealing.

"They needed powerful auras to handle the demand of that bond, and even then, only the strongest alphas survived the process."

"Is that why… When Dusk touched one of them—" I cut off as Vandle's eyes went wide.

"You *what?*" he asked. "Dr. Wren had theories about what might happen if contact was made."

"We… we nearly died. Our omega… she saved us."

Vandle nodded slowly. "And nothing happened to them?"

I felt the hatred twist my face. "No."

Decebal had checked the bugs. Nothing.

"It's designed to be one way. Aura energy displacement won't cross the bond. It will just… reflect it back at you."

"What the fuck does that mean?"

"You cannot touch him or hurt him. Any damage you inflict will only reflect onto your own aura. It was a fail-safe, since the lab rats were never supposed to get out…" He laughed. "To hunt him down and… and…" He cocked his head. "And what? What are you going to do?"

I was still trying to keep up. "Why do you keep saying… *him*?"

Vandle considered me. "You and 68 are only bonded to one—and his pack only by proxy. To bind to more than one alpha… well, not even Dr. Wren's experiments could manage that."

Flynn…

Did that mean I could touch the others?

"We have an omega, another pack mate, are they—"

"No. Just you and 68. It cannot go beyond that."

Okay. I nodded. Shatter and Ransom were't going to be dragged into this fucked-up bond.

"What do we do?"

"Do?" Vandle asked.

"If we kill them—"

"If he dies, you die."

"If…" I trailed off, those words sinking in like a nightmare. "What?"

"It wasn't built for you. It wasn't built for *fairness.* You were never human to them."

"So, that's it? There's no way out?"

"Of course there is."

"What?"

"The bond was built for him, which meant there is a way out. But it will only break if he chooses to release it."

A growl loosed from my throat. I was sick to my stomach, every piece of hatred I'd ever tried to bury surfacing at once. To free ourselves of this, Dusk and I were at the mercy of Flynn *fucking* Lincoln?

"You said you bonded an omega?" Vandle asked, ignoring my outburst entirely.

"Yes."

Vandle peered down at the handkerchief. "This omega?"

"Why… why is it getting worse?" I asked, needing answers to that. "Since we bonded with her, the sickness has got worse."

It didn't make sense.

"It shouldn't be. She fixed us—"

"That *is* why it's making you sicker," Vandle said, a slight frown on his face. "She is balancing you—healing you. But the bond you have is parasitical. It cannot tolerate you being whole. In healing you, she's trying to sever the parasite. It cannot tolerate that."

Despite his words, a wild relief flooded my system. It had nothing to do with Shatter. There was nothing wrong with her at all. She was right… *too* right for us.

"What if she did manage to heal the bond?"

"Impossible," Vandle said. "Immovable object. Unstoppable force. There is no good outcome."

"So, what is going to happen?"

"Your omega will continue balancing you, and, out of self-preservation, the parasite will devour you whole."

I grit my teeth, trying to shove down more fury. If that happened, Dusk would die, too. He was a part of this. "How do you know?"

"You were a rarity, 66. How many failures did Dr. Wren see—did *I* see—before successes began? You think he didn't introduce a bonded omega to stabilise the connection? They always angered it. And the deaths always came sooner when it was a scent match."

I frowned. "She's… their scent match. Not ours."

"The survivor?" Vandle asked, peering at me curiously. "You think she scent-matched a parasite?" He held up the handkerchief. "*This* omega?"

"She did."

His eyes darted between mine for a moment, as if searching for a lie, then his face split in a grin. "I don't believe it."

"Why?"

"I can't imagine what that would be like. Alphas like you and I, we can appreciate this." He lifted his fist. "But they aren't like us. I think… well, it might drive them insane, being bound to an omega with a scent like that…"

"I don't understand."

He cocked his head, looking at me curiously. "It's called a *scent match*," he laughed. "You smell like blood, and hers is laced with poison."

A harrowing silence passed between us, filled by the mad howls all around.

"You're saying… she's…?" I swallowed, my mouth dry.

I saw the faintest flicker of sorrow on Vandle's face as he read my expression. "It would make sense she defaulted to match the dominant pack if she met them first…"

The world around me, the constant mad howls, the scent of damp metal and stone, it all faded at those words.

We knew the Lincoln pack had walked out of that facility with something. We'd known they'd stolen from us.

"They stole… our scent match?"

Shatter.

Shatter was… she was so perfect. I'd known from the moment I met her. Dusk had known. She'd brought Ransom back.

I felt something crack deep within me, opening a void, and this time, as it split, I knew it would never close

It wasn't just me, or Dusk.

My omega.

Who'd fought her way to this academy for a dream that was never real. For mates that weren't supposed to be hers because they'd stolen from her, just like they'd stolen from us.

All of this—all the suffering she'd gone through with the Lincoln pack, believing she was broken because she wasn't enough for them… For mates who had never been capable of seeing her for what she was.

And every scar she now carried.

It was because… it was because of me.

"Nothing is yours," Vandle whispered. "Everything yours is theirs. Even if she should be, she isn't. She's their mate."

There was a long, long silence as his words sank in.

"You love her?" he asked.

My voice was rough. "Of course I love her."

He cocked his head. "Then a bond was a cruel gift."

"The bond?" I asked.

No. It was the only thing we had been able to give her.

"I do wonder what your parasite thought when the cure continued after the facility shut down. He must be waiting for the miracle he gambled on to vanish. I can imagine he and his pack are searching for other solutions. Solutions like her."

"Never."

"Tell me. Does she love you?"

"Yes."

"And what happens if you dark bond another pack's mate?"

I frowned. "They… they can negotiate. The scent matches can make an offer to trade for the bond. But it's *our* choice if we hand it over—"

Vandal cut me off. "It's a princess bond… which means she *also* has a say—"

"She hates them."

"And yet, they have the most powerful bargaining chip in existence."

I stared at him, the realisation dawning on me before he even said it.

"They hold the keys to your salvation."

"We would… still have to give up the bond." It would be our choice before hers. That was how it worked.

It was why the dark bond Dusk had given her offered her safety. Our bite meant she couldn't be bitten by another.

Mates were the one exception. They could offer the princess bond, but it wasn't just that she had to accept. *We* had to choose to give it up, too.

"I told you," Vandle breathed. "Nothing in this world is yours, 66, not your body, not your soul, not your aura. What makes you think you could claim an omega?"

My aura flared, fear blinding me as I seized him by the shirt. "She is not theirs."

"They can steal her from you. If that pack bites her, it will be like your bond doesn't exist," he hissed. "And the moment they learn who you are, they will know that too."

CHAPTER 42

Shatter

When I reached the apartment, I felt safe at last.

It was late in the evening now, and I'd survived the ball.

I'd faced my mates.

The whole world knew who I was—*what* I was—and that was okay. I had a pack who loved me at last, and neither my scent nor the colour of my eyes was something I ever had to hide again.

We said goodnight to Roxy, and Ransom wound his hands around my waist, drawing me close as Dusk tugged his keys from his pocket.

Ransom's voice was a breath in my ear. "We're going to ravish you in your nest, Little Reaper."

I shivered, desire sending shooting stars through my veins as I leaned back, biting my lip as I took him in. Dusk unlocked the door and then tapped his phone on. The light drew my attention.

I frowned at how his expression went tense.

"It's Decebal—*Shit.* Ten missed calls. You guys go ahead."

"All right." Ransom turned back to me. The kiss he pressed to my lips was so passionate that my worries faded, and once again, everything was perfect.

Ransom dragged me closer, letting me tangle my legs around him with ease as he picked me up. His hands were firm on my waist and back, and I could feel his need for me through the bond.

I nipped his neck, impatience rising in my chest as he opened the door himself, and Dusk's muted voice sounded behind us.

Ransom chuckled, and as we stepped in, he pressed me against the living room wall, dragging rough kisses down my neck to my chest.

I moaned as his teeth found my nipple through my silk dress.

I think I was okay with Ransom claiming me right here, heels and all.

He could claim me anywhere he wanted to.

I was his.

There was a possessive growl in his throat. "I'm so proud of you, Little Reaper."

My fingers tangled in his hair as I drew him back, finding his eyes in the dim living room. "I faced them," I whispered.

And somehow, I'd—

Thoughts died as my eyes slid to the room behind him.

My blood ran cold.

Ransom, feeling me stiffen, turned, pupils constricting. A feral, guttural growl rose in his chest. It was the most frightening thing I'd ever heard, every one of my hairs standing on end.

The room was destroyed, furniture torn, and contents of the kitchen shattered everywhere. And the scent in here was wrong.

Traces of my mates, fading fast.

They had been here.

In my home.

Dusk

I heard Shatter's whine of terror from the hall.

My heart was in my throat as Decebal's voice in my ear faded in and out.

The words he'd spoken turned the world upside down.

"They can't discover she's their scent match, Dusk. Once they know, they'll never give up."

Too late.

But I drew up as I realised what Shatter's fear was for.

The apartment was in ruins, the fading scent of the Lincoln pack lingering in the air.

In *my* territory.

My aura split the air, and I felt Ransom slip into madness for a flicker, hackles up, every instinct dialled to a hundred. He was holding Shatter against him, scanning every inch of the room.

My shoes crunched on smashed plates and bowls as I stepped in.

"Get her out," I growled.

Their scents were fading, but it didn't mean they weren't still here.

"No…" Shatter's voice broke. Then she was trying to throw herself from Ransom's arms. To the hallway… To…

Fuck.

Her breathing was ragged. "Let me…" she cried, almost wild. "Dusk!"

"I'll go first," I said.

I reached her nest to find the door off its hinges.

My heart tripped over itself as I saw what was inside.

The destruction of the rest of the house was nothing compared to what remained of Shatter's nest. There was almost nothing within that was recognizable. The bed was the only thing that stood within the wreckage.

The faded scents were of an alpha's fury.

"What?" That was Decebal down the line. "What happened?"

"They broke in."

I spun as I felt something. Nails digging into my arms. Shatter was there, her eyes wide as she reached the nest.

"Wait—" I tried to stop her, but I was too late.

Her sob rose in the air, the most broken sound I'd ever heard as she saw what was within. It shattered me. Ransom drew her back, wrapping his arms around her.

"How did they get in?" he demanded. "The door was locked."

"Fuck…" My blood chilled, and then I was stepping back, turning and striding across the hallway to my room. The door was open, and I stopped at the doorway.

"Listen to me," Decebal sounded urgent on the phone. "We know what they did. If the Lincoln alphas bite Shatter, they *will* steal the bond from you."

Steal the bond?

I'd bitten her. No matter how it had destroyed me, her safety was the only gift that had never brought me an ounce of regret.

Decebal's voice was faint, the phone at my side. "You have to make sure they cannot find out who you are."

I looked around.

The room was ruined, and one of my windows was smashed in.

If they'd got in this way…?

"No…"

The world spun as I reached my closet door, tearing it open—

Before me was a huge, jagged hole across the drywall, as if something had been ripped clean out.

My heart turned to stone.

The safe—the place I'd kept all the information, every truth about our pack.

The safe was gone.

The end of part two…

To Olivia, Melissa, my husband, and my amazing team of alpha readers that helped me get this book done, even when it was being stubborn.
It wouldn't be here without you.

Marie Mackay

CHAPTER 1

Umbra

Madness stirred like a light breeze disturbing dust down an old, forgotten alley.

It was the middle of the night, and I'd just returned. The ruins of my omega's nest lay about me: splintered wood from pieces of bookshelves and shredded leaves of textbooks strewn across the floor. The air was cool from the broken window across the hall in Dusk's room.

The Lincoln pack—alphas I now knew held territory even within the bounds of my pack and family—had broken into our home to take more.

All of what was under my protection, destroyed.

What should be hers, gone.

More taken from me, just like it had been taken before…

Carnage lurked around every corner, the white walls of the old facility now a canvas of crimson. Alphas executed in cages like mutts that had used up their value.

We were next.

I was weak, leaning on Dusk to stay up. With every step, congealing blood glued my feet to the floor. He was mine to save.

My pack…

More gunshots sounded in the distance.

In Shatter's nest, the covers and sheets upon the bed were torn, their fluffy, white insides spread across the room. Pens and pencils were snapped and scattered around.

Her desk was broken, splintered in two, and there were deep gouges across the walls.

It was everything important to her. My precious omega's perfect world.

"Nothing you have is yours…" Vandle's voice echoed in my head.

I hadn't protected her—we *couldn't*, not even with the one thing that should be ours to offer. The greatest gift an alpha was born with. Yet, her sanctuary, the safety we'd promised, was poisoned. Just like the bond upon her neck—the ultimate claim and commitment we had to offer.

It was turned to dust before our eyes.

Cracked walls of hallway after hallway looked the same. Footsteps echoed down the next, every sound bouncing dully off of concrete.

In seconds, we were met with guns and two men clad in suits, wearing masks.

My aura flared, just for a moment, then shuttered out. I was too weak. The only body I had in this life stripped to the bone from test after test.

They were going to take him from me…

We were dead.

A low growl shuddered in my chest as Dusk stepped in front of me, his aura flaring. Stronger than mine now.

It would do no good.

When the gunshots sounded, I tensed, desperate to die before I saw his body like the rest.

Only, it wasn't Dusk who fell.

Our executioners crumpled, gunshots ringing in my ears, but we were caught by only the splintering dust and debris from where a bullet exploded into the old concrete at our left.

Behind them was another. An alpha that did not look like he should be here at all. His auburn hair was in a messy bun, and he wore a dress shirt, vest, and jeans, like he was ready for a night out in the city. His pure white sneakers were smeared with splatters of red.

A gun trembled in his grip, but he lowered it, his piercing green eyes widening as he saw us.

"Umbra."

At Dusk's voice, the vision died, and I glanced toward the door of Shatter's nest. He was leaning against the doorframe, and I wondered how long he had been there. The faint scent of midnight opium, dark vanilla with sharp ambers, was grounding and familiar.

And… I blinked… How long had my aura been out?

…Not yours…

I shoved away that thought.

"Why aren't you with her?" My voice was a barely audible rasp.

The thought shook me from my daze, and I went tense, about to go to her. She was in Roxy's apartment tonight.

"Ransom can keep her safe," Dusk said quietly.

The unspoken other half of that sentence was like a cruel taunt in the silence.

Better than either of us…

A simple touch from Flynn, and that might be the end for me. We were, I realised, perhaps the only alphas in the world who were completely debilitated when it came to protecting her from the Lincoln pack.

"You should be with her too," he said as he entered. I caught the shift in his scent, the bitter edges of midnight opium becoming sharp as he stepped over torn paper and wreckage.

I didn't answer as he sat on the bed at my side.

"I checked out," I said, voice quiet. "I let this happen."

"You didn't check out," he replied, and I opened my mouth, but he got there first. "You needed to heal—"

"I—"

"Or I wouldn't have had anyone left." His words shook with something beyond irritation. That was fear I felt from him in the bond.

I clenched my jaw, taking another deep breath. "Well. I'm out of time."

For *healing…*? Is that what I had done, anyway? As I'd slowly carved a painting across my body, one scar at a time?

A painting that was, after all of this, useless.

I had become weak, and maybe it hadn't mattered before, but now Ransom was back. *Now we had her…*

My little Nightshade, gentle and sweet.

She didn't deserve this… not the person I had turned into. A person who should never have been allowed to exist. Pushed by Dusk to change—when this nightmare had been going on the whole time.

When had I become fool enough to believe I deserved any of this?

Shatter needed better.

And I knew Dusk wasn't ready to do what had to be done if it came to it—to protect her, like we had so far failed to do.

He *couldn't.*

He wasn't the one at the epicentre.

Not like I was.

He would stop me if it meant losing me, but I didn't know that we could afford that anymore. We were cursed, and he wasn't ready to face the truth.

That there might come a day when there was only one option if we wanted her freedom.

And maybe—*just* maybe—if I did it, then she would be enough to save what remained of him…

"Umbra." Dusk's voice was cold as he felt me through the bond.

My claim swept in, a fist closing around his place in the pack.

When Dusk had taken pack lead from me, I had been so broken, I hadn't cared if I lived or died. The only thing keeping me here was him, and he had told me I needed to let it go.

My aura was stronger, though.

Strong enough to stabilise another alpha's aura sickness… Strong enough to take pack lead back.

I had been too late last time. Too late to protect what was mine. It might have been from another life, beyond memory, but that scar remained, a disruption across my soul that would never fade.

I could never be too late again. Not with her. There would be no coming back from that. The world would burn, and I would turn to ashes with it.

"Don't make it a fight." My voice was rough.

We could skip this part.

He could hand it over.

I tilted my head, gaze sliding to him.

His jaw was clenched, lips drawn in the faintest snarl, his whole body coiled as if anticipating a strike.

"Why?"

A storm was coming, and what was going to happen next? It wasn't possible she wouldn't be a part of this; she was tangled too deep.

"I will do what needs to be done," I said quietly. I would protect her without hesitation or remorse, even if it meant she hated me.

But I could already feel his conviction. Dusk wouldn't give it up.

"I won't lose you while saving her." He sounded so sure. So… Dusk.

Stubborn and impossible.

And for years, his words created the realities I existed in. Unquestioning. Too broken to push back.

But backing down wasn't an option for me.

For *her.*

I got to my feet, my aura crackling in the air. It felt strange to me now I knew why it was so fragmented.

Dusk still hadn't loosed his aura.

I turned to him. He hadn't moved, a vicious expression frozen on his face. His rich skin was ashen and fists balled at his lap.

It wouldn't last.

He *would* fight. His side of the bond was wide open. That conviction of his swallowed him whole.

Fine.

This was how it was going to be. I could end it fast, and he would recover quickly enough.

I could feel the person I'd become over years of sickness now falling away, a weakness drowning in what lay beneath.

And beneath was darkness.

That was the person Shatter needed now.

But before I moved, the air changed, the scent of poisoned petals sweeping in like a tide, and my gaze snapped to the door.

"Shatter?"

My omega.

My… my stolen mate.

Why was she here?

In nothing but an oversized black T-shirt and socks that revealed the smooth tawny skin of her bare legs. She must have walked like that from Roxy's apartment—ran, if the heaving of her chest was an indicator. Her honey hair was up in a messy bun, the redness of her eyes visible even in the dim light from the hallway. Distress from what had happened, from the ruin of this very room.

"What's happening?" Her voice was quiet, but I heard the quake in it. Her golden eyes flickered between us.

She was as bright as the day I'd first met her, a blinding star.

My shadows waned, and I tensed, trying, for a moment, to claw them back.

"Nothing," I told her.

She had to go back to Ransom, where she was safe.

Well… not dressed like that. Absolutely not.

"What are you doing?" she pushed.

"It's… between me and Dusk."

"I don't…" She swallowed, brows bunching. "I don't think it is." I saw the way she bit her lip to try and stop it from trembling.

No, no.

This was wrong.

She had been hurt enough tonight.

I couldn't do this in front of her, could I? I tried to conjure all the conviction back, but she took a step, then paused, the sole of her foot in nothing but socks touching the nest floor. I saw the shiver pass through her, like she was treading into a nightmare, but she barely hesitated.

Oh—"Wait!" I crossed to meet her. There were splinters of wood still scattered everywhere, and she would hurt her delicate little feet.

My mind wavered, tugged from darkness to light and back again, and I barely noticed that, by the time I'd drawn her up into my arms, my aura had vanished completely.

She cupped my cheeks, a frown still shadowing her face. "Tell me."

My gaze found Dusk. He was watching me carefully, as if he didn't know what I was going to do.

I shut my eyes for a moment, inhaling her scent, and the calm that flooded in was like a drug. I stepped back to the bed and sank down onto it, holding her against me tightly, the tension in my body uncoiling.

CHAPTER 2

Shatter

My nest was gone.

That alone had left me with aftershocks that hadn't faded.

Somewhere in my panic, when Dusk and Umbra were trying to settle me, I'd lost the necklace too. The golden necklace with their crest that meant they'd claimed me. It was in the rubble of my nest that the Lincoln pack had left behind. I don't know why I noticed that, the bare skin on my neck making me feel hollow, but I couldn't shake it somehow.

That wasn't the worst of it.

The shock of hearing the truth of what Umbra had discovered… I didn't know if that would ever fade. The Kingsman pack were *my* mates…?

Last night, when Ransom carried me to Roxy's door, I was still a mess.

She'd made me peppermint tea and set up one of her rooms for me, which was enough to calm my nerves. I needed to be away from the home that had been stolen—the reflection of what I now knew was my own failure.

The conversation with Umbra and Decebal on the phone still lingered in my head.

"The Lincoln pack are… connected to us?" I'd asked, still not processing what he was saying. "Like, they're the same pack?"

"More like their pack is connected to yours," Decebal said. "But they have all the control. It means if they bite you, the bond can pass without us needing to hand it to them. They can steal it."

That part still sent flutters of fear straight to my heart.

"Do you mean they might try to dark bond Shatter if they open the safe and figure out who we are?" Dusk asked.

"No—they could. But Flynn wants a sure fix to his aura sickness. A princess bond is the only promised cure for that."

"It still needs Shatter's acceptance, though. They will never have a princess bond without her saying yes."

Yet, the truth had lingered between us all. Because the only way for my alphas to be free of the Lincoln pack—for this sickness that was getting worse by the day—was for Flynn Lincoln to give up that connection by choice.

That was what they were afraid of. Not a dark bond at all. The Lincoln pack's offer of a princess bond if they could give my mates salvation.

Would I take that trade?

Enter a bond with the pack of my nightmares, if it meant Dusk and Umbra would be free?

I knew the answer as well as they did.

If it came to it…

Still, everything we'd learned left me terrified. All this time, my mates had been hidden from me, and I hadn't known… *How could I have not known?*

Was that something other omegas would have noticed? Something my twisted instincts hadn't been in tune with?

All night, Ransom and Dusk had held me close in a bed that smelled faintly of fir trees. Umbra hadn't returned yet. And I'd withdrawn from the bond, closing my eyes and slowing my breathing until they believed I was asleep.

Ransom tumbled into dreams with his arms around me, but Dusk never settled. He stayed, sitting beside me in bed in absolute silence, fingers tangled in mine, thumb stroking my wrist. He was the only one left in the bond. Umbra was awake, but he had vanished a long time ago.

I was glad Dusk stayed in the bond, even when the rest of us were gone. His presence helped me feel not so alone.

But *he* was alone.

If I came out, he would know I was awake. He would know the shame that was growing like a vicious beast within me.

After what felt like hours had passed, I finally felt the flicker of something down the bond. Umbra surfaced.

It was like nothing I'd ever felt from him before—a twisted darkness that went beyond fury or pain. Dusk tensed at my side, the slow movement of his thumb along my wrist halting.

Then, Umbra was gone.

Dusk slipped from the bed in a moment, and I opened my eyes, watching him vanish from the room as quietly as he could.

What was going on?

Whatever that had been, I didn't like it.

I shifted beneath Ransom's grip, not wanting to wake him. *One* of us should sleep tonight. It took a while, and I scent marked my pillow, so he wouldn't miss me.

I'd be back with him soon, but my instincts told me this was important.

When I was barely out of bed, I felt something shift in the bond. An unsettling upheaval, and with it came another flicker from Umbra.

I paused, examining it with a frown.

It felt like… like a giant, slowly lifting its rooted feet after a long slumber… The shift was quiet, slow, but… now that I focused on it, it was almost dizzying in its power.

My breath caught, and forgetting even my dressing gown, I crossed the room in a rush. I didn't know where they were, but only one place made sense.

Our apartment door had been left open a crack and I tried not to look at the upturned home.

My home. Stolen…

Instead, I made for my nest, knowing they would be there.

When I reached the door, I halted. My heart clenched as I saw it again, my breath catching like a void opening in my throat and making it impossible to even swallow.

My nest…

I shoved it down. That wasn't why I was here.

Umbra was standing amidst the wreckage, tense and still fully dressed, as if he'd just got in. His gaze fixed on Dusk, who was sitting on the edge of my bed, frozen, yellow eyes narrowed. He looked strangely vulnerable, with a drawn expression, wearing a T-shirt, sweats, and socks amidst the chaos of my nest. Through the bond, I felt his worry and fear.

Something *was* wrong. I couldn't put my finger on what, because I didn't yet know the distinctions of this bond enough to understand.

"Shatter?" Umbra's sandstorm eyes snapped to me. My scent must have drifted in; behind me, Dusk's bedroom door was open, and a breeze cooled my back from the broken window.

"What's happening?" I asked, working to steady my voice.

"Nothing." Umbra's voice was strained.

"What are you doing?"

"It's between me and Dusk."

No… "I don't…" I swallowed. I didn't know what I was feeling, but this *was* important. "I don't think it is."

Was Umbra *lying* to me? That wasn't like him. I warred with burning tears, my heart so fragile already.

But that didn't matter. *They* came first, and something was wrong.

It took every ounce of my strength to step into the nest.

The dead nest.

The one stolen.

My chest tightened, but I pushed myself on, treading across the debris of what had been—

No.

Don't think about it.

"Wait!" The tension in the room broke as Umbra crossed toward me, sudden worry in his eyes as he scanned the floor that was covered in shards of glass and splintered wood. Then he picked me up and drew me into his arms.

That strange *thing* in the bond vanished in an instant, and I felt a breath of relief escape me. I cupped his cheeks, needing him to look at me. His beautiful sandstorm eyes were darker than usual, their spark gone.

That wasn't right. "Tell me," I demanded.

He exhaled, then stepped toward the bed, sitting down beside Dusk. His yellow eyes fixed on the two of us, but his jaw had unclenched, and he looked as relieved as I felt.

"I have to know what was going on," I said.

Umbra had paled, and his eyes were still dark. "I need you to be safe," he whispered. "That's all."

"I am safe. I'm with you."

I could see the pain etched in his expression. That answer wasn't enough.

And maybe it wasn't…

Dusk had told me what they knew. That the bond left both Umbra and Dusk vulnerable to Flynn…

The calm of my mind wobbled again.

Worse than that—it wasn't secure. It didn't protect me from the Lincoln pack's bite. The alphas who had broken my nest, who wanted to claim me to fix themselves.

Who *knew* I was gold pack…

Fear rose in my chest like a wail, igniting panic in my veins, but I shoved it down.

No.

This fear—it was Umbra's too. And it was the poison that was changing him.

I couldn't let it.

They'd stolen my scent match, broken my nest. Would I let them take more?

Umbra drew me closer, something so sad in his eyes. "I haven't been what you need," he breathed. "Not like this."

"What does that mean?" I asked.

"I have to protect you—"

"But I don't want you to change." My voice broke, eyes brimming with tears.

Umbra looked so broken. "They've taken everything, and I wasn't enough to—"

"No. Th-they haven't."

And I realised in that moment that there was more to lose. *So* much more…

In fact, I'd fought this battle before and survived.

Dusk had shown me the truth.

They hadn't taken what mattered most, because *those* things—they couldn't take unless I gave them up.

And I'd been about to, with the fear they'd forced upon us.

"They haven't taken anything."

"Shatter—"

"Dusk promised me nothing changed," I whispered. Umbra frowned, glancing to Dusk, but I took his hand and lifted it to my chest, pressing his fingers to the scars over my collarbones. I knew he could feel them beneath the thin fabric of the top. "They tried to… to ruin my body, but Dusk said they didn't steal my value."

The words felt heavy in my throat, hard to say, as if they might burn me, but I made them come out. I clung to them, needing them to be the truth, both for me and for my pack.

"Of course they didn't, Nightshade." Umbra's voice was gruff, as if it hurt him even thinking I'd ever believed that. "They can never take that."

"Then they can't steal you. I d-don't want them to."

I watched his jaw clench, and his eyes drifted from mine, like he struggled with that.

He had to understand.

I *had* to make him understand.

I slipped from his arms, standing, and trying to keep my breathing calm as I looked around the nest. A place as scarred and broken as my body.

My gaze fell, at last, on Dusk. He was watching me intently, head cocked, something curious flickering in his eyes.

A few seconds passed, and then the faintest trace of a smile curved his lips.

He stood, turning, and lifting a large piece of splintered bookshelf from the torn duvet. Then the next, and the next, while Umbra and I watched. Finally, with the bed adequately clear, he stepped onto it, almost falling as a bottom corner gave out with a groan. He had to grab Umbra by the hair to steady himself, but then he was stepping through scattered pens and loose pieces of paper to the pillows at the top. There, he pulled back the blankets and settled in beneath them.

The last weight of the night lifted, freeing my chest and lungs as I climbed onto the bed after him and curled up in his arms.

It was a long time before Umbra moved, but he stood at last, surfacing in the bond as he tugged off his boots and shirt.

He wasn't better, not completely, but he was still him.

I smiled as he joined us and placed one possessive arm around my waist as he held me close. "Please don't leave me," I breathed.

I felt his sorrow at that, and his lips pressed to my forehead. "I love you, Little Nightshade. I'm not going anywhere."

"I chose to be yours," I replied. "They can never take that away."

A purr rumbled to life in his chest just as Ransom turned up at the door, rubbing his eyes and staring at us in confusion. He didn't question a thing, though, yawning as he climbed into the bed behind Dusk, shifting around until he found an angle where he could easily hold my hand.

I smiled as I realised their scents were enough to smother everything else, and the nest was mine once more.

This was the first gift my mates had given me, and no one could take that away.

And the necklace I'd lost? It was the same. I *had* their claim, Dusk's bite on my neck, and that was what truly mattered.

I closed my eyes and slept at last, warm and safe in the arms of my pack, despite the cool air and light breeze ruffling torn pages amongst broken splinters and ruin.

CHAPTER 3

Dusk

I woke to the sound of a low growl. Lily of the valley was a sudden and overpowering mist of outrage in the air around me.

I blinked bleary eyes open, trying to get my bearings and determine the source of the growl. I was first met by the sight of the ruined nest, shredded textbooks, and splinters of wood littering the floor—remnants of what used to be Shatter's desk and bookshelves. My attention was diverted by Ransom, however, who was sitting up in bed in the dim light, his lips drawn back in a snarl, his hands clutching his cheek.

"What happened?" I whispered, yawning.

"He *punched* me," he hissed, voice low and furious.

"Who?" I blinked.

"Umbra."

I tried to sit up, but as soon as I moved, I almost toppled to the floor.

How had I ended up on this end of the bed? I'd gone to sleep *next* to Shatter, with Ransom at my back.

Had he…?

I straightened. Had the little shit shoved me away while we were sleeping?

Oh. He deserved a punch.

"I'm pack lead." I kept my hiss low. "I get to sleep next to our omega." On the first night we'd all been with her, at least—or what the hell was this all for?

"*Neither* of us do," he hissed back.

I realised, with a grin, that there was a deep purple bruise swelling around his eye.

"He got you good," I said, peering over his shoulder. "What did you do?"

"I just wanted to cuddle her."

I grinned as I peered over to see Shatter curled up in Umbra's arms. She looked so tiny, engulfed in his huge frame, and he had both arms wrapped around her possessively as he held her close. Her eyes were closed, half her face obscured by curls that were still glossy from the ball the night before.

Honestly, violence or not, I'd take it. It had been a long time since I'd seen that side of Umbra, and he deserved a peaceful morning.

Ransom, however, did not look ready to drop it. He was pouting, and he shuffled closer carefully, reaching for her.

I *didn't* warn Ransom that violence while sleeping was not a new phenomenon for Umbra, and he certainly shouldn't try. He'd stolen my place next to Shatter, so it was fair fucking game.

Umbra shifted in his sleep, his arms tightening around her, a faint growl rattling in the air with a deep inhale. Ransom drew back, a bitter look on his face.

And that was when I caught Shatter inch one eye open the slightest bit, a flash of gold glinting in the dim light filtering from the bathroom.

Her gaze found Ransom, then mine, before she snapped it shut again.

I *swear* she wriggled against Umbra, the ghost of a *very* smug smile edging her lips as his sleepy growl cut off for a deep purr.

Shatter

Wolfsbane and blood vibrated in the air with Umbra's purr.

I was warm and cosy right now. There had only been one second this morning when I'd felt fear creeping in; a flicker when reality had crashed in and everything that happened last night came to haunt me.

And then, as if he could sense it—which he might have from my scent—Umbra had drawn me tight into his arms as he slept and drowned all my fears away.

My alpha.

He had gone to a dark place last night, and I needed to bring him back. That was my job—because I was theirs, no matter what anyone said about bonds and evil fucking parasites.

I knew it was hard for him. I knew how much it had devastated all of them, seeing the ruin of our home.

I was determined, though, that I wouldn't let it be enough to destroy us.

The real issue though, was that I *think* some of my worry had like… rubbed off on him on a hormonal level, because he just landed a lumbering, sleepy punch right into Ransom's face for trying to cuddle me.

It wasn't a good thing.

Not at all.

And I was definitely a really, *really* bad omega if it made me all warm and fuzzy inside that two of my favourite alphas were fighting over me.

Oh, and Dusk knew it too. He was awake, and he had just caught me peeking.

We needed to be serious this morning. We probably had a lot to talk about and plan.

But Ransom's hand trailed down my arm, and his scent was still furious. There was another low warning growl from Umbra that vibrated up my spine.

I snuggled desperately under his arm so Dusk wouldn't spot me smiling. I'd definitely be in trouble for that.

How did Umbra know what Ransom was doing? Was it just instinct, or was he awake, like me?

Ransom's cool forest lily of the valley spiked with downright indignance, and I dared to peek again to see him scowling.

Absolutely unable to help myself, I pressed back against Umbra, shifting against his huge, warm body. He drew me closer, his growl shifting to a purr for the briefest moment.

Wrong move.

Ransom let out his own growl, fingers closing around Umbra's wrist, ready to tug me free.

One beat passed, in which Umbra went absolutely still—perhaps waking up. Then he rolled just enough to tuck me beneath him, and his aura split the air as he launched over me completely, sandstorm eyes vicious as he reached for Ransom.

Oh…

Okay.

Well… *shit.*

Ransom's aura flared in response, but it faltered against Umbra's overwhelming force. In a swift, predatory movement, Umbra locked his grip around Ransom's throat as he pinned him against the mattress beneath the sheer mass of his body.

I was left by myself, deposited on my front, and I pushed myself up frantically, sweeping my hair out of my face to see what was happening.

"*Fuck…* you!" Ransom's voice sounded choked, and his fingers gripped Umbra's forearm to no avail. "You don't get to hog her!" In a surge of fury, he jerked his head forward, smashing his forehead into Umbra's nose. With what looked like every bit of his strength, Ransom twisted, using Umbra's disorientation to his advantage, and threw his full weight against him. To my utter shock, they both went tumbling over the bed's far edge, bodies tangled amidst limbs, and debris and furious snarls cut through the air.

Oh… dear.

They *were* actually fighting.

I met Dusk's startled yellow eyes for half a beat, then scrambled over the mess of bedding to see them both wrestling across the mess-strewn floor.

This was very bad.

So bad.

Mostly because I could feel the heat crawling up my neck as I watched them crash over debris with wide eyes.

Control your excitement, you horrible omega. What if they got scratched by all the splinters?

It would be my fault.

But why was it so hot?

Neither of them were upset through the bond, though. Not actually upset. In fact, what I was getting from them wasn't negative at all. Both seemed caught in a thrill that buried the undercurrent of darkness lurking in the pack bond since the moment we had seen the apartment last night.

"You aren't even trying to settle them, are you?" Dusk's voice, a soft murmur against my ear, startled me, sending a shiver down my spine. I attempted to whirl to face him, only for his grip to catch a hold of my hair and crush my cheek against the sheets.

"I *was,*" I lied. "I swear." He must be wondering why his omega was so immature that she was focused on her alphas fighting instead of sorting out the issues from—

My thoughts cut off as Dusk easily tugged my panties down and pressed a finger into me.

Oh.

Okay. Maybe not.

Heat shot through my veins, and I saw the scrap halt from the corner of my now limited vision.

"You're soaked, Gem," he breathed. "Does it make you wet, seeing them fight over you?"

I bit my lip, groaning again as he pressed in a second finger.

"Tell me." His command grabbed me as I felt him move behind me.

"Yes," I said with a desperate sound. He adjusted again, and then I felt his tip at my entrance. He drove into me without warning, his other hand on my hip so he could control his pace.

Umbra and Ransom froze mid-struggle, pupils blown, all attention fixed on me.

They both lurched toward us at the same moment. Umbra attempted to shove Ransom out of his way to be met with a defiant growl and a retaliatory body check that sent him staggering to the floor—pretty impressive, given Umbra's size. But Umbra managed to grab Ransom by the ankle and send him sprawling before he could reach us.

"Fight as hard as you can to get to them," Dusk breathed in my ear.

I blinked, one wild second passing as I processed the demand, then I threw my weight away from him with all of my strength.

Dusk's grip became punishing, and he released my hair, instead grabbing my hips in both hands and driving into me, hard.

I moaned, grabbing at the sheets, low panting coming from my chest. I fell into the command easily, struggling against him with all my might, blood scorching my veins as he slammed in again and another strangled whine rose in my chest.

The hormones in the air shifted palpably from frantic to downright primal in a split second.

Ransom let out a snarl from where he was pinned by Umbra—who had frozen, too, eyes back on me. I heard Dusk's breath of a laugh behind me as he dragged me and the sheets I had seized backward as he impaled me on his cock again.

The sounds I was making were frantic, blood pounded in my ears, and the pheromones in the room sent me barrelling toward the most intense orgasm of my life.

In a fluid motion, Dusk repositioned us both, so he was lying back against a stack of pillows. He dragged me back over his length with ease, leaving me facing the others while I straddled him. I grabbed at his wrists, fighting him, right as Umbra managed to shove himself free of Ransom's hold and finally came crashing onto the bed before us.

Dusk's grip tightened at my waist as Umbra drew up before us. His eyes were so inky with lust there was barely a fleck of sandstorm left in them—he was made of nothing but pure and feral alpha.

His touch clamped around my waist possessively, gaze roaming my body as if trying to work out what he was seeing. Dusk rocked into me, his knot teasing my entrance. I bit my lip, one hand releasing his wrists and reaching for Umbra. I whined as my fingers tangled in his hair, asking for… I didn't know what. I just needed him.

The room was a swamp of primal lust as Ransom barrelled onto the bed at Umbra's side, eyes darting between me, Dusk, and Umbra, and the hold they had on me. The auras had vanished at some point down the line.

Umbra tried to pry Dusk's hands away, but Dusk growled, and I moaned as I felt his knot press against me again, and my grip became vicious in Umbra's hair as I stared at him in need.

I needed him. I needed all of them.

I let out another breathless sound, trying to drag him closer, my teeth grazing the scars along his chest.

"You want us, Gem?"

I could barely form a comprehensible word as I nodded. I needed them claiming me here, right now.

I shivered on the edge of an orgasm, but Dusk hadn't moved enough to push me over the edge.

The drag of my teeth against Umbra's skin flipped a switch, and next thing I knew, he'd released my waist, pinning Dusk against the bed by his neck.

I thought he would try to pull me away again, but he didn't. He lifted my T-shirt, tugging it off and pausing only a moment to stare across my body. Dusk adjusted below me, settling deep into my core, holding me firm against him. Ransom shifted, hooking my arms behind my back and dragging me down. Between Dusk's grip that remained on my hips and Ransom, I was arched back, trapped over Dusk's cock while exposed fully to Umbra.

I whined again as I fought them, sanity draining in the face of a fierce and heady lust.

"Alpha…"

What were they doing? *I needed them.*

All of them.

Umbra shifted, using one hand to free his cock as he continued pinning Dusk by his neck with the other. Then I felt his fingers at my clit, but they didn't linger there, moving further down. I let out a breath of surprise as I felt him press his fingers into my core alongside Dusk's length. I tensed, eyes wide as he entered with ease through my slick, stretching me almost as much as a knot might.

The world faded for a second, edging with blackness as ecstasy tried to rip me away.

"Can you take us both at once, Gem?" Dusk's low voice grounded me, and I struggled against their hold as I looked between Ransom and Umbra. I whined again, far past words.

That, it seemed, was all Umbra needed to dare him on. With a low, rumbling growl, he released Dusk, caging us in completely as he adjusted himself. I couldn't move or see what he was doing. Before me were the huge, rippling tan muscles of his torso lined with his scars. I could just see Ransom above me somewhere, still trapping my arms as he watched my expression with a wild look in his forest green eyes.

Then I felt Umbra's tip at my entrance.

"Fuck…" My curse was desperate as he pressed slowly into the space already taken by Dusk. I sank back further against him, letting Umbra in. Blackness swept in again, and I lost a few moments to pure intensity. I was breathing hard, each exhale laced with desperation as my body adjusted to him. I could feel every shift and every movement of him stretching me to accommodate his girth. It was a collision of pain and pleasure that left my body shuddering and limp, completely theirs.

When my world reformed, Umbra was fucking me with long, hard strokes. The orgasm I'd been close to was gone, goalposts shifting further away as bliss swept through my whole body. His hands circled my waist, those primal, inky eyes full of intensity and fixed on mine as he drank in every moment of my ruin.

This was everything—*almost* everything.

"Ransom…" In a daze, I found him above me, auburn hair wild and loose around his shoulders from the fight, an expression just as intent as Umbra's. He was still pinning my hands behind my back, but he released me, replacing his grip in my hair. Then he forced my neck back so he could position himself on his knees at my side as Umbra picked up his pace.

"Mhmm…" I was giddy with lust as Ransom pressed his tip to my lips, and I pressed my tongue out, letting him slide in all the way easily. I was still shaking, overwhelmed with sensation as Umbra's pace slowed, each movement deliberate and deep.

"Relax for him, beautiful," Dusk breathed, and the command unwound every muscle in my body. Ransom groaned as one of Dusk's hands released my hips, wandering up my body until he caught my nipple between his fingers and twisted.

I shuddered as Dusk's grip tightened at my waist, shifting his knot the slightest bit into me as Umbra continued to drive into my core. "You're ours, Gem. Look how beautiful you are, letting us all claim your sweet body at once."

They were everywhere.

My safety.

My pack.

My purr sent vibrations through my body, my eyes rolling back as Ransom began a steady pace. Heat was boiling in my core, a million little bolts of electricity with every shift.

Ransom drove all the way into my throat, holding there for a long moment as Umbra continued.

"Fuuuuck." The word was a half snarl from Umbra as his pace picked up, while Ransom kept me suspended without air for another few seconds.

"Good girl." Dusk's breath tickled my ear, his hand dropping to my clit, circling it. I tensed, low sounds building in my chest as Ransom withdrew and thrust back in. Umbra let out a growl, and his strokes became slower and deeper.

Ransom picked up his pace right as Umbra groaned, he and Dusk reaching their peak at the same time, and I felt the deep warmth in my core as they finished inside me. My eyes rolled back as my body shook with my orgasm. There were low whines in my chest with every breath, another cresting my spent body as Dusk's touch on my clit became relentless.

I was shaking and lost to bliss as Ransom's strokes slowed, each thrust deep until his grip on my hair became punishing and he finished down my throat.

CHAPTER 4

Ransom

After Shatter came down from the high of her orgasm, Umbra pulled her straight under his arm. She was so fucking cute, curled up next to him, a bush of half-messy, half-glossy curls tumbling down around her. By the little smile on her face, she was clearly very pleased with herself.

It also hadn't gone over my head that she had definitely not been upset at the fight. I swear, when I had glanced up to see her staring at us from the foot of the bed, her eyes twinkled with delight, and down the bond, she'd been a ball of thrill.

And the *outcome*? Well, that was worth fighting Umbra a hundred times over, even if I had scrapes down my back from rolling in the nest's devastation. And I'd lost; I wasn't too proud to admit that. My aura was pretty impressive, but Umbra was a beast.

Shatter was, hands down, the hottest creature on the planet. The siren sounds she'd made, golden eyes heady with lust as she took Umbra and Dusk like that… Then she'd reached for me like it wasn't enough. Like she needed me for it to be complete…

Fuck…

Umbra stood, carrying her shaking frame (which was now wrapped around him with her face buried in his neck) to the bathroom.

I stared after them before looking back at Dusk.

He had tugged his sweatpants on and was also staring at the bathroom door, as if unsure what to do with himself. His eyes slid to mine, and I didn't think I'd ever seen Dusk quite as stunned as he was right then. He glanced back around the room—the nest that was in pieces—with the faintest frown.

I understood. I didn't understand how she could be so *Shatter*, even in the midst of this nightmare. After everything Umbra and Decebal had told her last night.

But that was how beautiful she was. The Lincoln pack thought they had stolen everything from us, but our omega could make a kingdom from rubble and dust. One I would happily live in if it meant nights and mornings like we'd just had. Even Umbra was back to being himself again. I'd woken in Roxy's apartment in time to feel the tail end of that darkness from him in the bond.

I closed my eyes. The real world would catch up with us at some point. It had to, even if Shatter had suspended us in this little bubble of happiness.

Hearing a low whine from the bathroom, my back straightened, my sombre thoughts evaporating. Was Umbra trying to sneak Shatter time without us?

I hurried in to find them beneath the steaming water of the shower. The lust woven into her cool, nightshade scent hadn't faded at all. Actually, the hot water was just lifting it into the air. Umbra held her hips at shoulder height, pinning her against the wall with her legs over his shoulders. I cocked my head, blood rushing to my cock again as I watched him press two fingers into her.

Well. That bubble hadn't popped quite yet.

"Umbra!" Shatter was breathless as he dragged her closer. She tried to steady herself, eyes wide. "Hold up—Dusk finished in me too!" Her voice was made of half a giggle.

"Uh-huh?" Umbra asked, dipping his fingers into her again before pressing his mouth to her centre. She moaned, teeth catching her lip.

Damn.

How likely was Umbra to punch me out again if I tried to get involved…?

Did I care?

Hmm… There wasn't much room in the shower, though. Her legs tangled around his neck as she panted, a wild smile on her face as she met my eyes, her fingers laced in his hair with a death grip.

I could live with watching.

She was letting out cute little mewls by the time she came apart again, needing Umbra to help support her as he set her down and helped her wash her hair.

When they were done, he set her onto the counter like she was a doll and towelled her off, humming to himself, which got me grinning. I headed into her walk-in and found her a nightgown and a pair of slippers, since the mess outside was a walking hazard.

She looked dazed and happy as she hopped from the counter and pressed a kiss to my lips. I drew her close. "You are the most incredible omega in the world," I told her, a low growl in my chest.

Her eyes shone as she drew back, blinking at me like she wasn't sure how to respond. Then her grin became cheeky. "I think you almost put me into heat again."

Well, fuck. I felt the smile spread on my face. "Don't make it a challenge, Little Reaper."

Then her eyes drifted back to the room behind me. I turned, seeing Dusk straightening from where he'd been shifting aside a few of the larger pieces of debris.

She crossed to him next, going for an embrace, but he caught her chin, drawing her into a kiss. I heard her purr from here as he ran his fingers through her hair, circling her waist and pulling her closer.

I don't think I would ever get tired of watching her with my pack. Umbra and Shatter—they flitted between cute and hot in the blink of an eye, but Dusk had a way with her that was captivating.

He was more in love with her than I thought it possible for someone to be. He was an alpha with sharp edges, and I'd never seen anything else from him before I'd become sick. But now… I don't know if she'd noticed yet, but his scent shifted when she entered the room, the richer coffee side to his scent peeking just the slightest bit. Possessive and attentive, as if he couldn't exist in a space she was in without being aware of her.

He'd die for me or Umbra. I'd always known that. But for Shatter? He'd burn the whole world to the ground—and that was a real concern when it came to a man like him.

Dusk Varis might be the only alpha in the world arrogant enough to claim his mate before the universe had even caught up.

"We have to talk about all of this, don't we?" Shatter asked, drawing back from the kiss.

"Only when you're ready, Gem."

"Well…" She peered around at the room. "I think we should. Should we maybe sort out the nest a bit first?"

"Like… clean up?" Dusk asked.

"No." She frowned, wringing her hands together, like she was nervous to admit something. "Well, not quite…"

As it turned out, the accurate omega translation of *sort it out* meant building a massive pillow fort.

Dusk and I ended up as pillow suppliers, while Umbra—taking to the task far too easily—hurried out to the kitchen to make her tea just the way she liked it. When he finished (and the rest of the apartment had been thoroughly stripped of every pillow, cushion, and blanket), he followed us around as we built the stacks, ensuring every addition was angled differently.

It wasn't until Shatter had finished perfecting the last of the stacks, and we were all huddled in a dim—admittedly cosy—fort that carried scents from each one of our rooms, that she nodded, satisfied with the work. Her nightshade scent hinted at surprised delight as she burrowed herself beneath the duvets inside before poking her head out, picking up her cup of tea.

While Umbra adjusted the tray on his lap, I clambered over to her as she poured a second cup and handed it to Dusk. To my relief, he seemed to enjoy her green tea. I watched Umbra eye her cautiously, but she seemed appreciative enough that Dusk had taken his serving that we appeared free from tea-drinking obligations.

I was riveted by the contentment radiating from her through the bond. Her eyes darted up the chaotic walls of pillows, then to Umbra, before sliding up to me. She smiled, hugging her mug close and edging further under my arm.

Her fear was still present; it was a quiet undercurrent in the bond, but it didn't hold the power it should—as if Dusk, Umbra, and I, and this madhouse we called a home, were truly enough to make her whole.

I wanted to know how she did it. I *needed* to know.

I'd been wrong in my assessment before—she hadn't just survived what the Lincoln pack had done to her.

She'd taken it and become more.

"So," she said, clearly bracing, her determined gaze falling at last upon Dusk. "We need to make a plan."

CHAPTER 5

Dusk

"All right," I said, looking around at the others. Shatter was tucked between Ransom and Umbra, and I could feel her worry as we finally settled into the conversation none of us wanted to have. "They took the safe and they're gone. We need to decide what we're doing next."

I was still reeling from what we'd learned last night, and the options before us were far from clear cut.

"There's no way we can find the safe?" Ransom asked.

"It's tracked," I replied. "But it was offline by the time Decebal knew it was gone."

Ransom frowned. "You think they found the tracker?"

"Or they took it somewhere the signal can't reach," I replied. "It happened quickly, too. The last ping came from the academy. I don't think they're smart enough to know how to block it or disable it, so either it was a fluke, or they may have hired someone."

"And if they get into it, they'll know that they can…" Umbra trailed off for a moment, eyes darkening. "They'll know they can bite Shatter out of our bond."

"You said it's rigged to destroy its contents the moment it's opened by force?" Ransom asked. "That's a start."

"If they have hired someone, then we can't rely on that," I replied. "There are ways to bypass the safeguards."

"I vote we leave," Umbra said. "Go up to the cabin. No one has found it. We would be safe."

"We can't," Shatter whispered. "Our baseline isn't stable."

"Baseline?" Umbra asked.

"You and Dusk are getting worse," she said. Her eyes darted between us, and I felt the weight of her fear through the bond. I hadn't been able to find a way to prioritise the danger me and Umbra were in—not now that I knew how much danger *she* was in. Yet her fear, *her* concern for us—it wasn't something I could ignore. The power she held in our pack bond was growing with every day that passed.

Umbra released a breath, as if he were fighting that fact just as much as I was. "I'm much more worried about—"

"We all need to survive this," Ransom cut in. "*All* of us."

Shatter glanced up at Ransom appreciatively and she nodded. "They'll come back. They have to. If they don't, we're in trouble. They just don't know that we need them as much as they need us."

"And I don't intend for them to," I said. The burden Umbra and I carried could not pass on to her.

I hadn't had time to process the full truth—Umbra and I weren't just sick. We were on the receiving end of a bond that might leave us dead. My priority was containing it—to just me and Umbra, if I had to, but as pack lead, if I could shoulder that burden myself, I would. For Umbra, especially, who had paid enough for my protection. I needed them all to walk away from this.

"So, we wait here?" Umbra asked. "Leave all of this in their hands? They can return at any time—could open the safe and learn the truth at any time. We don't know when they're going to come or how they're going to move forward."

"We have to assume it's protected," Ransom said. "If they get inside, it changes everything, but we can't make plans around that."

"So, we just stay at the academy and wait for them to show up?" Umbra asked. "When we know they're after—"

"I'm not saying we let our guard down," Ransom put in. "We won't leave Shatter on her own. But honestly, we don't have another option. And Decebal isn't far away, either. If something happens, he can be here with backup quickly."

"It sounds risky."

"We don't have a choice," Shatter said. "We need them to come back. Both of you"—she looked between me and Umbra—"might die if we don't fix this. We're in a race against the clock. The only way we know to cure it right now is for Flynn to decide to release the bond, which he can only do if he knows what's going on."

Umbra scowled. "But they could figure this all out without us, since the safe is a wildcard and they could get into it at any moment."

"It all comes down to the same thing," she pressed. "The only way for Dusk and Umbra to be free of their sickness is for Flynn to give it up—"

"The only way we *know* of," I cut her off.

"We *have* to talk about this," she said.

My blood chilled at the determination in her eyes. "I won't."

"If we want Flynn to give up the bond, he has to learn who you are. There's no other way to ask for him to do it. But giving it up means giving up the only thing keeping his aura sickness at bay. Outside of that, the only thing left that might cure him is a—"

"Enough." I didn't mean to use the dark bond, but she cut off in an instant, eyes wide. Her fists balled in the sheets as she looked from me to Ransom, and then Umbra. Both were stiff, all coming to the same conclusion she'd just tried to spell out.

A princess bond—and she was the only omega in the world that could offer him that. It was the only thing Flynn would want, without a doubt.

It was a truth I wouldn't discuss.

Shatter's lips drew back in a snarl like I'd never seen, and I felt a shot of pain from her through the bond. *"Dusk."* Her voice shook as she fought my command fiercely, and I let it go in an instant.

"Never."

If we went to the negotiation table and asked Flynn to give up this bond, we would be asking him to give up the cure that had worked for years.

And the bargaining chip?

It was her.

The only clear thing left to offer for such a thing. I *couldn't* hear her argue for this. I couldn't hear her suggest offering herself in exchange.

The scent-matched omega. The thing that would cure Flynn absolutely.

And I knew that was exactly what she'd been about to do by the storm of terror on her end of the bond. A terror that outmatched anything she'd felt yet. Fear at the idea of a bond with that pack. And it was something she would suggest, anyway.

Never.

And yet, I couldn't be sure we could keep her safe, regardless. The moment they understood who we were, they may realise that we held no power to stop them from biting her.

Of all the ways I'd imagined this coming to a head, this was an ending so... mundane.

Negotiations with monsters?

Her voice shook when she spoke. "We could set it up. Trick them—"

"I *won't* risk it." The only way to ensure they didn't take her from us, if they ever learned the truth, would be hiding her away so they couldn't find her.

She couldn't be near this.

"We stay to buy time," Ransom said. "Stall them with the expectation of negotiations while we work on other solutions. Even by staying for a discussion, they'll think a trade for Shatter is on the table and they just haven't come up with a good enough offer yet."

"What if they... they bit me, and then you..." She swallowed. "Then you..." Her lip trembled for a moment as she wrung the sheet between her fists.

And then we killed them?

I would—in a heartbeat. If any alpha in that pack ever put a tooth on her again, he wouldn't walk away.

I shook my head.

"Why?" she asked. "It's not—"

"Negotiations aren't that cut and dry," Ransom replied. "They'll know that's a risk—we made it clear at the ball that we care about you. There's no way they'll agree to any of it until they have better control over the situation. If they take you, you're not going to be more than a cure to them. People with their kind of money… there's a million places in this country they could hide an omega where she'd never be found. Not unless they wanted it."

There was a long, uncomfortable silence before I broke it. "That's the plan for now, then." I hated it, but Shatter was right. If we left, the clock might run out on me and Umbra. "When they come back, we make them believe negotiations are on the table. In the meantime, we figure out another way."

"I don't fucking like it," Umbra growled.

"We're gonna fix it," Shatter said, looking at me. "You want another way. This whole bond between Flynn and the pack—I think it's a new type of aura contract."

"Aura contract?" Umbra asked. "That's an Arkology thing, right?"

"Yes. An aura contract is the predictable response of auras in forming a connection when presented with consistent equations developed—"

"It's pack bonds, right?" Ransom asked, cutting her off, looking confused at her answer.

She nodded. "Alpha to alpha, alpha to omega, that kind of thing."

"If there's another way around this, you think it'll have to do with that?" I asked.

"I think so," Shatter said. "I'm going to need new textbooks. And anything Decebal has on studies about aura contracts."

I nodded. "Okay."

Ransom rose first from the pillow fort, giving Shatter a quick kiss before he left. "Guess I'll get textbooks," he said when he let her go.

Would he even know what books to get? The man had been feral for years.

Shatter caught his wrist before he could leave. "Do you want me to make a list?" she asked. "I need *specific* ones."

Ransom looked confused. "There's like a list for the classes? It can't be that complicated."

Shatter frantically shook her head, her beautiful curls bouncing back and forth. "I need the *right* editions."

"Why don't you tell him, and he can make a list?" Dusk said.

Ransom grinned, pulling out his phone as Shatter began rattling off her books, occasionally shooting dark looks at the ripped pieces of textbooks across her nest floor.

When we were done, Umbra had left to begin the kitchen cleanup, and I was left alone with her.

She was still upset, I could see that, but I didn't know if there was a way that we would see eye to eye on this.

I sank to my knees before her and tugged her to the edge of the bed. She chewed on her lip but didn't meet my eyes.

"I won't put you in danger to save us," I whispered. I reached up, cupping her chin, and she swallowed, seeming to struggle not to meet my eyes. "I can't."

That I couldn't be sorry for.

"I love you, Shatter."

She hunched, chin quivering, and finally, those beautiful golden eyes met mine. She was so unsure.

"Since the first time I saw you," I said. "I *swore* you would not be collateral, no matter who I thought you were scent matched to."

That's what Umbra had thought at first—when I'd claimed our enemies' scent match. But that was before he'd met her. Before he'd realised how important she was.

"I will find a way to fix this without giving you up. Do you understand?"

Another impossible. But that was what this pack did.

This time, I had a feeling that this one might cost me. I wasn't alone. It was exactly what had pushed Umbra to the edge last night. We both felt it: this impossible wasn't coming for free.

But that cost would never be Shatter.

She was gazing at me as if she could feel it too. She was too smart. I couldn't keep anything from her.

"Shatter," I whispered. "*Tell* me you understand."

She'd become lodged in this bond far too fast, and I realised the safe wasn't the true wild card.

She was the piece we could never have planned for.

Finally, she pursed her lips and nodded. "Yes." The word was quiet. "We will find another way."

CHAPTER 6

Shatter

It was Thursday, and I found myself standing at the door of my Omega Studies classroom. The week had slipped by without a whisper of the Lincoln pack.

Decebal was monitoring everything he had access to; the Lincoln pack finances, known houses, vehicles—even the Dean's emails, to see if they'd given a reason for leaving—but came up empty on clues. We didn't have tabs on everything, though. They'd apparently never found the trail of money that had been funnelled into the experiments. Whatever they'd used for that, it seemed they were using again.

I was making a huge effort to figure out my phone, as it allowed me to contact Decebal for access to research without going through Dusk every time. At first, I thought it was broken, until Ransom explained that, apparently, it needed to be charged *nightly* to keep it going, which seemed wildly inconvenient.

On Monday, we had returned to classes. It made me feel better, taking that step, as if it was another thing they hadn't managed to steal from me. Every night after, I had dived headfirst into the studies Decebal sent us, trying to unearth anything I could about this bond they had.

Roxy came over in the evenings to help us tidy up, and the apartment was almost back to normal. Aside from her initial question about the Lincoln pack break-in, she didn't push further, as if she knew there were things we couldn't explain. She had no idea how much I appreciated her for that.

The window had been replaced, as well as furniture. My nest was the last on the list for cleanup. I'd insisted the rest of the house was more important, since the nest was already everything I needed it to be.

Until now, I'd been with my whole pack wherever I went. Dusk, Umbra, and Ransom stayed by my side. But Umbra had walked me here, and I was ready to face my class with Roxy.

With a deep breath, I opened the door to my first Omega Studies class since… well, everything. I stifled my nerves as I stepped into the familiar classroom. I was instantly met by the sweet and floral scents of the omegas within.

The whispers that followed me were more intense than they had been before. It was like a replay of the moment I'd entered the ball. How long had I spent dreaming of walking into this classroom without being followed by judgement or laughter?

There wasn't laughter anymore. Instead, the omegas looking my way were just shocked. But I knew now that I had come to this academy searching for all the wrong things. So, I forced my head high, settling at a desk at the back with Roxy. She claimed our usual desk, just before the back.

I ignored everyone else, instead carefully organising my pencil case and pens just perfectly and telling myself I would be fine. The few times I dared peek up, I saw the stares, but this time, a few of the omegas gave me anxious smiles before darting their gaze away.

I shifted closer to Roxy, trying to avoid tapping my fingers on the desk and drawing more attention.

"Most people think the Lincoln pack narrative is a bunch of shit now that it's come out you're their scent match."

That's what Roxy had told me. Maybe that was true. Was this what pity felt like? They'd seen the Lincoln pack reject me and the dark bond on my neck that I wasn't hiding. Even my scent was out today, and I was trying not to be self-conscious about that.

Oliver and Jasmine arrived, the two I most dreaded seeing. When Jasmine stepped in, she drew up, her gaze finding me instantly. She stopped at the front of the room, then looked away, a nasty sneer on her face as she walked by. They took a seat behind me, but when my eyes met Oliver's as he passed, he dropped his gaze, and his scent of ocean breeze had a murky, uncomfortable edge to it.

I hadn't realised how heavy everyone's stares would be. The weight of everyone knowing all these things about me. Some true, some not. And most of what they *knew* was exactly what I wanted them to believe.

My mates had humiliated me in front of everyone and convinced the world I was the stalker. Now, that had come out as a lie, and everyone thought I was a gold pack chasing her mates and fleeing a pack of monsters who were toying with me.

A battle it looked like I'd lost.

They thought my story was over. That I had been reduced to nothing.

"Are you okay?" Roxy whispered.

I nodded. This was good. It was just hard too.

I don't know if it was what they thought of me that hurt, or what they thought of my pack.

Dusk, Umbra, and Ransom had saved me, and even if this was the only way to do the same in return, I hated that they were villainized.

This was it, though. This was the battle, and I was going to manage it.

At least, I *thought* I was.

I settled my nerves by replaying the moment I'd pounced on Jasmine at the ball. The feeling of my teeth at her neck.

I glanced over at a small giggle from Roxy, and by the way she was side-eyeing me, she knew exactly what I was thinking. I found myself fighting my own smile.

Okay.

I *could* do this.

And I could also ignore the occasional snide comments from Jasmine behind me about gold packs and foolish omegas who get themselves into stupid situations.

It was the worst when we were left to work on a textbook exercise for twenty minutes. "At least it's finally obvious why they were so 'obsessed' with her," Jasmine said, and I could practically hear the air quotes in the word. "They knew they were going to have a little pack slave the whole—"

"Jasmine." Roxy spun in her chair. "Shut your foul mouth. Everyone knows you're bitter because the North Prince pack dropped you after Shatter made a fool out of you at the ball."

I bit my lip, eyes wide as I hunched in my chair.

Ohmygod.

"You just said that to Jasmine's face?" I hissed under my breath.

"You can't judge me. You almost *bit* Jasmine's face," she hissed back.

Okay. But *that* had been because of instincts far more than bravery. Actually, I'd basically blacked out.

I looked back down at the exercises we were given on pack communication and diplomacy and tried to focus.

"...Lincoln pack received my application. I've been told they're considering me."

I froze at the next words from behind me.

Considering?

They hadn't even been seen all week.

"You... applied to join the Lincoln pack?" Oliver actually sounded stunned.

"Why wouldn't I?" Jasmine asked behind me. "Because some gold pack freak wants to ruin their reputation?"

I heard a chair scrape, and by the sounds of it, she was picking up her paper to take to the front. Only, when she stepped by me, she let it slip from her fingers. Her paper dropped onto my desk, and with it, a few more loose sheets of paper.

"Oops. *Sorry.*" Jasmine swept the large piece of paper back up, but I was frozen. I blinked down at the small, black-and-white printed pictures staring back at me.

Ice seeped down my spine.

They were stills from the video I'd never seen, from an angle I'd never imagined of what was competing for the worst moment of my life.

A video that the school had all seen.

I was back in Eric's room. They were taunting me. I was on my knees and Eric was before me. Flynn was at my back. Staring down at the picture, it occurred to me that I'd never realised how much bigger than me he was. How easy it had been for him to hold me still for Eric.

I don't know how many seconds passed. Maybe not even one. It wouldn't have mattered.

The photos were gone as Roxy tore them away, yet they were burned into my mind.

A low growl sounded from my side and a chair scraped.

"You *bitch*, Jasmine—" I didn't hear the end of Roxy's words. The world spun as I staggered to my feet.

"…Those are her fucking mates…" That was Oliver's voice. "They rejected her, you don't…" Someone was dragging Jasmine away from my seat.

I could hear her mocking laugh, but the world spun as I got to my feet. My boots took desperate steps against the hardwood, and then I was outside, hand clutching my throat as I tried to take deep breaths.

"Shatter!"

Roxy's scent of orange and fir tree was there, and she was pulling me into her arms.

"I'm so sorry, babe." I held onto her, trying to calm my breathing, but it was hard. "You're safe, Shatter," she whispered, hand at my back. "I promise, you're safe."

CHAPTER 7

Dusk

Shatter was in Omega Studies while I was stuck with Umbra and Ransom in a class neither of them wanted to be in. They were on their fourth game of tic-tac-toe in their notebook (in which both refused to take notes on a subject that might actually be of fucking use).

I jumped as my phone vibrated. I opened it, seeing a text.

Decebal: Bad news. Didn't take them long.

I stared at my phone, shoving away my irritation at Umbra and Ransom, but the call dropped before I could pick it up.

Decebal: Get somewhere you can talk.

Decebal: Lincoln pack showed up in their apartment this morning.

Decebal: Call me now.

Shit.

I ducked out of class, but by the time I arrived in the corridors beyond, Decebal had sent another few texts and a voice recording.

Decebal: They came back with another alpha. He's registered with the school as a prospective pack member, but he's not enrolling in any program.

What?

Why would the Lincoln pack be looking at adding an alpha to the pack? There was a risk of losing the scent match if they did—but I was already calling Decebal's number.

"What is going on?" I asked the moment he picked up. "If they get a pack member, there's a risk they'll lose the scent match—"

"This guy is not going to join their pack. It's a front."

"What the fuck does that mean?"

"His name is Mord Sato, and he's not an alpha you want to fuck with, if you can help it. I've crossed him once or twice back in the Gritch. He's bad fucking news."

"Hold up," I said, mind racing. The Gritch District was the significantly less well-off part of town that saw much higher crime rates than anywhere else. "They *hired* him? Like… protection?"

"Best money can buy—and that's not all he's doing. Listen to the audio. It's from the bugs in their apartment this morning."

I tapped out of the call screen to listen to what he sent. It had transcripts over the top, which was good because the volume was faint. I squinted at the sound of the door opening and footsteps.

Then I heard Flynn Lincoln's voice.

"You can have the room at the end of the hall, probably still smells like orange—"

"*Shut* up." A low, rough voice that I didn't recognise cut Flynn off.

There was a pause. "Excuse me?" Flynn sounded affronted. "I'm not paying you to speak to us like—"

"I said—" The second voice was sharp this time. "—*Shut.* Up."

To my surprise, Flynn listened.

The audio ended, but it was followed by another text from Decebal that read: *"this is a few minutes later."* Then I heard some loud rustling, a high-pitched noise, and the static on the feed cut off into silence.

I put the phone back to my ear, mind racing. "He found the bug?"

"Not just one," Decebal said. "He disconnected all three in the first ten minutes of arriving."

"Shit…" That meant the Lincoln pack now knew we'd been listening. That wasn't information we wanted them to have.

"Yup."

"Where did they find this guy?" I asked. "Can we pay him out?"

"Not a chance. I've never seen him flip on a client."

"A *client…*?" This was fucking madness. "He's what? A mercenary?"

"Yeh, and fuck me if I know where he got so good. Ex-military—that's my best guess? He wasn't anywhere near the Harpy's, that's for sure, but I don't know a single one who'll cross him if they can help it."

I knew Decebal had ties to the Harpy gang growing up; he and his pack mate were well-versed on the underbelly of New Oxford. If Decebal thought this guy was trouble…

Fuck.

"Tell me about him."

"He's efficient. Gets jobs done quick and clean, and he covers his tracks. The Lincoln pack must have offered him a lot for… well, whatever the fuck they told him this was. That, or it was their connections. They aren't exactly known for staying on the straight and narrow, so maybe they called in a favour."

"What do you think? Did they hire him for protection?"

"Would be a waste of good money to hire a guy like Sato and only use him for that. And finding the bugs?"

"Yeh. That was wishful thinking." I rubbed my face. "What the fuck do you think they told him this was?"

"I don't know. But my advice—I'd carry from now on. I don't care if it's to the cafeteria. And don't let her out of your sight."

Ah. "Shit."

"What?"

"She's in Omega Studies right now."

We'd thought she would be safe with Roxy for one class, but I was already backing into the classroom to grab Ransom and Umbra.

"Pull her out. I'll text you with anything else."

CHAPTER 8

Shatter

The Lincoln pack was coming back, and I *had* to be stronger than this.

I stared at my reflection in the bathroom mirror, at my eyes that were swollen from tears, my hair that had returned to its usual thick mane after a brief reprieve at the ball. Roxy had tried to insist on coming, but I'd begged her not to.

I needed to be alone in a stall and cry a bit. She had already seen me cry over this. How many more times before I became a burden?

I had to sort myself out.

My heart ached for the way I was feeling.

I tried to hold my head high and walk back to the classroom, but I had to take a break along the way, stopping and pressing a palm against cool brick walls.

"Roxy's going to have thrown away all the pictures. So, it'll be fine. You won't have to see them ever again."

Oh.

Oh no.

I stopped, then turned around, fists balled at the roots of my hair, hoping the pain would help me fight the tears.

Wrong train of thought. Now all I was doing was thinking about the pictures—

"No. No, no, no. You'll be fine. You can do this. You can face them all." I took a shaky breath, trying to fight the quiver of my lips and the burning tears. "You can't be gold pack *and* have a dark bond *and* go back in there, crying. It's too much. It's stupid."

With one final, painful squeeze of my hair, I dropped my hands. When I spun on my heel, ready to try, I crashed straight into what felt like a solid wall.

I staggered back with a squeak, catching myself on the worn stone wall so I didn't land on my backside.

I blinked up, registering a form-fitting suit as I tried to get my bearings. "Sorry, I didn't—"

"Shatter Kingsman?" The voice was low and rough, and when I looked up at him, I did a double take. I hadn't seen him before, and I definitely would have remembered if I had.

He was an intimidatingly tall alpha, perhaps in his late twenties or early thirties. Despite being dressed in a suit, like faculty members often were, his black hair was shaggy, tumbling into dark, hooded eyes. His skin was pale, and his face was lean with high, sharp cheekbones. There was a deep scar cascading down the left half of his face, cutting into his brow and reaching almost to his chin.

"You're…?" I asked, unsure. I looked down to see a folder in his hand.

"Mr. Sato, new assistant to the Dean. I was coming to fetch you from class. I have a few questions about your admissions papers."

"Admissions papers?" I asked, my mouth going dry. "They're, uh… sorted."

Dusk had sworn they were.

"If you don't mind, we can discuss this in my office."

I frowned, eyes darting down the hallway to where my Omega Studies class waited. "I'm really not supposed to…"

"What?" he asked, having half turned from me, but he glanced back, one scarred eyebrow cocked.

I noticed his subtle scent, clearly muted with dampeners. I caught the edges of… I cocked my head, unsure what was in the air. A dark wood… ebony? Maybe, but there was something else with it—something burned or charred that I couldn't identify.

That was strange. I could usually identify scents. Most omegas and alphas could, even without being told. It was like… instinct or something. But I already knew my instincts were very odd.

"My pack doesn't like me going anywhere alone," I told him.

"Not to meet with faculty?"

"I've never seen you before," I said.

He reached into his pocket and pulled out an ID that read "Mord Sato. Assistant to the Dean." It did look like the ones I'd seen from the teachers.

"There's an empty classroom here." He nodded to a nearby door. "If that makes you more comfortable."

I glanced between him and the door. Something unsettled in my stomach. "I think I should make an appointment. Then my pack can—"

"This isn't about *their* admissions," he said coolly.

"They helped me with it." I cupped the back of my neck, glancing again at my Omega Studies class. What was it, maybe… twenty steps away?

That mattered, all of a sudden, even if I couldn't place why.

"I'm not good with the online—" I cut off. I'd taken half a step back in the middle of my words, and the alpha tensed. For just the briefest second, his aura flared in the air.

It was overpowering and frightening, an invisible energy that smothered me.

As strong as Umbra's.

A threat.

My heart jumped to my throat, and goosebumps rose on my skin, but then the aura was gone as quickly as it had come.

I stared up at him, knowing I must be pale.

No faculty would let their auras out around a student like that. He hadn't moved, not even a flinch, and he hadn't said anything, either.

He didn't have to.

With the smallest movement, he nodded his head toward the room he'd pointed out. His eyes were lightless and unblinking as they fixed on me.

I weighed my options carefully.

This had to have something to do with the Lincoln pack.

But if he really wanted to talk in a classroom, how bad could it be?

And did I really have a choice?

There was no way I could get two steps without him catching me. Even without his aura, he was made of solid muscle beneath the suit.

I clasped my fingers, stepping past him into the empty room, trying to keep my cool. My scent was muted, like his was, but it wasn't gone, and he'd sense if I was scared. But that ship might have sailed. I'd left the bathroom on edge. If this had to do with the Lincoln pack, I shouldn't give anything away. The less I gave away, the more cards I had to play later.

The door latched shut behind me, and I balled my fists in my skirt. Just answer whatever questions he had, and then I could go straight to Dusk. But I heard the lock click, and I spun instantly, my gaze darting from the door, then back to him. His expression was frighteningly impassive, yet his eyes were drinking in every single one of my movements.

Again, I tried to stifle my fear. He knew how scared I was. From my expression to my scent. But last time I'd heard a lock click like that, I'd been in Eric's room.

Nothing like that was going to happen.

Besides, if I was gone too long, Roxy would think something was up… Right? Would she come looking for me? Or get Dusk?

I was only a few classrooms down…

"Sit," he said.

"I'm okay like this," I said, forcing my voice steady.

His hand closed on my shoulder, and I glanced about shakily, caving and sitting down.

I needed my pack.

What was going on? And what was in that folder? Did it have to do with what was in the safe?

"What do you want?" I asked.

He opened the folder as he sat on the desk before me, now far too close for comfort. Despite the natural burned wood edge to his scent, it was like a blanket of calm.

That, however, only set me on edge more. He wasn't worried about having me in here—not even a little—but I was sure he knew I had a pack.

He shifted slightly, his blazer moving with him, and I saw the flash of silver at his belt.

A gun?

Why did he have a gun?

What if Dusk, Umbra, or Ransom came in here? Might they get hurt?

"I'm new around campus, a prospective member of the Lincoln pack," he was saying. My eyes snapped to him, blood going cold as I fought to keep my expression straight as he watched me for a reaction.

"You're… joining them?" I asked, voice dry.

"There's a lot of politics to catch up on, and I always think it's easier to get it from the source." A strange smile flashed on his lips.

"Me?"

"They're rather set on turning that bond from black to… something more pleasant," he went on. "I'd be biting in after—no need to risk the scent match. But I'd say it's very much in my interest to get clarity about the full picture."

"I want to go back to class. Just tell me what you want, so I can go."

He didn't answer for a long time, peering down at the papers he held. "Your scent is very curious," he said, his eyes far too scrutinising as they lifted to me.

I didn't answer.

"Poison," he went on. "But not the natural kind. I thought they were lying." He set the sheet down. "But it's rather fitting, considering the bind you have your mates in."

I glanced down at the piece of paper he'd added to the stack. "Uh…" I reached out, tilting the top piece just a bit toward me as I read it.

Shit.

It was all the details of my enrolment at Rookwood Academy. With a flood of relief, I realised it wasn't from Dusk's safe. I'd memorised every page, back to front. That one had outdated information—before he'd given me the Kingsman name. Not like this one. "What do you mean?" I asked, looking up at him, finally able to breathe now that I knew this paper wasn't a threat.

"I never truly expected an omega's scent to match a weapon of war." He reached down and straightened the paper on the stack.

I chewed on my lip, still so tense with nerves. "You, uh… know what it is?" I asked, tearing my eyes back to him and trying to ignore that stack.

That top piece, though. It was my proof they hadn't got into the vault.

It was really important.

"The Atropa abomination?" he asked. I tried to focus on him, but it was hard. "I've seen it tear packs apart. One alpha—that's all it takes. One pack mate falls, and there are no survivors. Not even the last one standing. The one who wins?" He snorted, then lifted his hand and mimed shooting himself in the head. "Is that you, Omega?"

"What?" I asked, blinking up at him. I was still trying to keep my nerves in check. *What had he said?* I was inching my fingers toward the stack as I ran back over his words.

Kill entire packs?

Right.

I knew that about the poison. I mean, kind of. Vandle had been alive, and he'd been the one to kill his pack mates—but then, Umbra had said something about him being forced not to kill himself… I *think.*

Finally, my fingers brushed the paper, and I nudged it out of place from the others, nerves cooling.

Right.

Everything was right, again.

Except… Mord had replied, I realised, though his eyes had slid from me to the page I'd just adjusted. His lips drew into a line.

What had he just said about me?

"Devastation?" I asked him. Me? "No, I'm just—"

"Dark bonded?"

I frowned, swallowing at the weight he put into those words, as if they meant something different to him.

"What's your scent?" I asked, hoping to throw him off whatever trail he thought he was on. "I can't... I can't pin it down." It was true.

I saw a stiff curve to the edge of his lips. "What do *you* think it is?"

"Ebony wood. But I don't, um... know what the other part is."

Just... hold it together. It was just a test. Like an exam. I had to stay calm. I reached out for the stack again, but he got there first, placing another piece of paper onto it, keeping it perfectly straight.

My admissions page was hidden. Stuck in the stack... It was proof they hadn't opened the safe...

What if I'd imagined it?

"Why did they dark bond you?" he asked.

I stared at him, unsure of how to answer.

Why did he want to know that?

I didn't know what the Lincoln pack was doing or what their play was. Any answer I gave might destroy a position I needed to claim later.

Did I play the victim...? Or act like I was in on it all the time...? Was I in love with Dusk, Umbra, and Ransom—or did I hate them?

"I'm..." My voice was weak. "I can't talk about the..." I shut my eyes. "The bond."

"They've commanded you not to speak about it?"

I nodded desperately, even if it was a lie.

"Do you *want* their bond?" he asked. I gritted my teeth, eyes falling on the stack of paper. I reached for it again, but this time, Mord caught me by the wrist. "Do you want that bond?"

"They, uh..." My voice shook. Feigning this fear wasn't hard at all. "The Lincoln pack rejected me, and no alpha was ever going to want me after that. But they... they did."

Was that enough to walk the line? To let him conclude what he wanted? I shut my eyes, tugging my wrist from his grip.

"It doesn't matter now—" I began, but he cut me off.

"It matters a great deal if your mates want to bargain for a princess bond."

My eyes snapped up to him.

"What is interesting to me," he added. "Is that the Lincoln pack swore the feud evolved over time, yet it seems your pack had you marked for a dark bond from the moment they met you."

I frowned. "Why do you say that?"

"You were an honorary member from the beginning of term, Shatter *Kingsman.*" He lingered on my last name with far too much meaning.

"Dusk added Ransom's last name because I didn't have one and the Dean was suspicious."

Mord finally reacted with something more than indifference. One scarred eyebrow shot up, and the faintest grin slid onto his face. "You don't know?"

Uh.

This wasn't the way I'd anticipated the interrogation going.

"I don't know what?"

I tried to grab at the paper he had in his hand but jumped violently at the sound of my name being called from the hallway outside. "Shatter?"

That was Ransom, and he sounded urgent.

My eyes darted to Mord's hip, where his gun was, and then up to him. He didn't look phased in the slightest as he glanced at the door. He got to his feet, returning the stack of papers to the folder, and straightening his suit.

"That," he said. "Is even more curious." He was looking me up and down.

"What is?"

"Does a dark bond give an alpha the ability to geo-track their bonded omega?" he asked. My lips parted in shock for a second before there was a loud banging on the door.

"Nice to meet you, Mrs. Kingsman," he said quietly, then crossed toward the door that led out to the gardens. I was on my feet as he reached it, backing toward the door I could hear Ransom behind.

I felt an aura flare and then the door crashed open in an instant, but Mord was already gone.

CHAPTER 9

Shatter

"What did he want?" Dusk asked.

"He had a lot of questions," I said. "About the bond and my pack. He wanted to know if I wanted to be in the bond—"

"What did you tell him?"

"I didn't say anything. Not directly. I let him come to his own conclusions."

Dusk relaxed—well, as much as he could after what had happened. No alpha in this room was comfortable that I'd been taken in broad daylight.

We were back in the apartment, and I was sitting on Umbra's lap on the couch. I knew he was the most unstable right now. His arms were wound around my waist, discomfort stark from him through the bond. Dusk and Ransom were mirrors of that. I could see they were shaken.

"I need you to go over every question he asked."

"Okay. I can write it all down." It was easier to remember details when I pretended I was studying or doing homework.

"For now, Shatter never leaves our sight," Dusk was saying. "Not even for one class."

"The Lincoln pack wants to meet with me," Ransom said, looking up from his phone. "Got a text from… Flynn, it looks like."

"He just wants to see you?" I asked.

What did that mean?

Ransom wrinkled his nose in disgust. "Probably wants to know if there's a…"

"Rich prick connection?" Dusk supplied.

"I can go," he said. "They likely want to see if there's any way I can get them a trade for Shatter, but it could give information about where they're at—what they've figured out."

"You sure?"

"I haven't done anything else to help yet, have I? And this was the plan. Stall them until we have a better option."

"All right." Dusk looked like he was processing. "You go, we need to know where they're at. But give away as little as possible."

"I'll tell them early next week. That will give us time to put together a list of shit I can try to get out of them if I play my cards right."

Dusk nodded. "And I'm getting everything Decebal has on Mord. Until then, we play it safe. Shatter sticks with us everywhere."

"What about school rules?" I asked. We weren't allowed weapons on campus. Mord had only gotten away with it because he wasn't caught.

"They don't give a shit about school rules, so neither do I. But I need to know you're on board with this too. I thought we were being careful enough before, but if Decebal says Mord is bad news, I'm not risking anything."

I hugged myself, sinking against Umbra. "Yeh." I didn't like how afraid I was of the Lincoln pack, and to be honest, I felt much stronger when my guys were with me, anyway.

But there was one issue with how fast this was escalating. There was one place I had in mind for answers about the bond Umbra and Dusk had with the Lincoln pack, and if I sought it out, I knew I needed to do it alone.

True to their word, I went to bed that night among all three of my alphas. Dusk hugged me close, with Ransom on the other side, and Umbra behind him.

There was now officially a sleep schedule on the fridge, since my alphas were at risk of knocking each other out in the fight to cuddle me without it. I loved them so much. Mord and the Lincoln pack were a problem, but until anything else happened, I needed to do my job of balancing them.

Their attraction to me certainly felt relevant to that. Even in Omega Studies, there was a huge focus on making sure your alphas were obsessed. There hadn't, however, been a single chapter on early morning fights and fridge sleeping schedules.

I think they needed to update their curriculum.

I smiled at the thought, wriggling against Dusk contentedly and inhaling the soothing scent of midnight opium.

One more day of school—with all of them in Arkology classes—and then it was the weekend. They would protect me, and I would protect them. We were going to survive. I had to convince myself of that.

There *was* one thing I couldn't shake—something that nagged as I closed my eyes.

Mord's words, right before he'd left, stuck like a barnacle. I'd been too scared to process them fully at the time, but now they were irritants. Puzzle pieces that wouldn't fit anywhere right.

I think I'd figured out the first.

Geo-tracking a bonded omega wasn't an Arkological function of bonds. Alphas couldn't locate the omega they'd bitten, nor the other way around. But Arkological methods weren't the only thing Dusk had access to.

Dusk had bugged me.

That's how they knew where I was today.

It also answered a faint question that had been nagging me since he'd found me at the library. There was no reason at all he should have known I was there, but I'd been too caught up in the emotional aftermath of hearing what Eric had said about me to Roxy that day.

I wondered again if I was being paranoid, then almost snorted out loud. I wouldn't put it past Dusk for a second.

Really, I should have guessed. It was a very Dusk thing to do.

I'd thought back to everything I had on me that day. It had been easy enough to search my bag and pencil case this evening with them around, but I'd come up blank. Clothing wouldn't be reliable, which left one option.

But searching my boots wasn't easily done while they were all in the living room.

I lay in bed awake for a long time, waiting until Dusk's breathing was slow and his arms had slackened around me.

Then, with the utmost care, I managed to slip from his arms and off the bed. Pillows that smelled like me would do for a short while. I slipped through my bedroom door and down the hall.

This shouldn't take long. Then I'd be back, and Dusk would never know.

I kneeled beside the front door and picked up my boots. Carefully, I examined every side, crack, and crevice. Finally, my fingers hit a bump.

I tugged the leather inside out to peer at what I'd found.

"Ha!" I declared. "Sneaky fucking alphas."

The little black piece was latched on securely, placed in the upper lip near the laces, and where I'd never feel it.

He *was* tracking me.

I left it. I wasn't offended that Dusk wanted to know where I was, but if I took it off now, he'd know I knew.

Then I wouldn't be able to get around it when I needed to.

Emboldened by my success, I set my boots back and stood, now reconsidering the other thing that had surprised Mord today.

The conversation with him had gotten me this far.

He'd mentioned my admissions papers and documentation, and some of those were in the safe we no longer had. I crossed to the kitchen and opened the third drawer on the island where Dusk kept other documents—the less serious stuff.

Within, there were the pack's admissions papers, folders with copies of identity documents of the pack, including me. But then…

I frowned, seeing my name on one tucked at the back. It was alone, as if Dusk didn't want it paired with the others.

My chest was tight as I retrieved it, concern scratching at the back of my mind. But when I scanned the document, my mouth fell open in shock.

I read it over again, and again.

It was official documentation, as far as I could tell—even if it was definitely, *definitely*, forged.

My name was on it.

Shatter Kingsman.

And, suddenly, I understood Mord's surprise when I hadn't grasped the meaning of that title. Dusk had told me he'd changed my name, and… well.

He… *had.*

"Motherfucker…"

He hadn't *told* me?

Why hadn't he fucking told me?

My heart crashed against my ribcage, drowning everything else out, and my chest swelled with equal parts fury and elation.

"Shatter?"

I jumped violently, looking up to see Dusk taking the last few steps into the living room.

For a long moment, I just stared at him. He wore sweatpants and socks, but he was topless, and the scars across his chest that matched mine were pale beside rippling dark muscle. He was breathtaking in the moonlight that filtered in through the living room window. I couldn't take my eyes off him, half my brain seized by feral omega instincts, the other half tumbling into pure rage.

It took me a moment to find my voice, and by his expression, he'd gathered exactly what was in my hand.

"What the *hell* is this?" I asked, voice weak.

I knew, of course. I'd read the words a dozen times already, and I was equal parts elated and… well, fucking furious."Ah." Dusk cleared his throat, palming the back of his neck. "Well… a, uh… technicality."

I blinked.

The leaf of paper slid from my fingers and onto the island with a *swoosh.*

The world bled crimson, elation snuffed out in the blink of an eye.

What had he just said?

"A *technicality*?"

Dusk opened his mouth, then closed again, and his face, at least, had the decency to drain of colour.

"I… shit. I didn't mean it like that."

CHAPTER 10

Umbra

"What the hell is going on?" Ransom's voice was groggy as he kicked the duvet away. We'd been woken sharply from sleep by a loud clanging and shattering from down the hall, and a spike of emotion in the bond.

"Fuck," Ransom groaned. "We *just* cleaned everything up."

It took me two bleary seconds to realise that neither Shatter nor Dusk were in the bed. It took another to realise I was feeling a spike of what could only be described as nerves from Dusk in the bond.

I sat up straight, on high alert.

Anything that made Dusk worry was worth worrying about. That was before the other half hit me in full force.

Ransom was wide-eyed at my side as he tucked messy strands of auburn hair behind his ear. "What on *earth* is that?"

"That," I said, staggering out of bed with perhaps a little too much anticipation and sliding on my slippers, "is a really, *really* pissed off omega."

She must be pissed if Dusk was *sheepish* in the bond—I hadn't even known that was a feeling in his arsenal.

What the *hell* had he done?

Sure enough, when Ransom and I reached the living room, it was to find chaos. Shatter was climbing cupboards while sailors' curses flew from her lips. She was, it seemed, searching for weapons to launch at Dusk, who was standing halfway across the room, hands up defensively. Half the cupboard of glasses had been first, if the glass across the kitchen floor was anything to go by.

"Shatter, we can talk about this—"

"Shit!" I cut him off, diving for the kitchen. Those cupboards definitely weren't built to take the weight of a full—*Yup!*

The hinges screeched, breaking, and I caught her in my arms just in time. I set her down, extracting her from the door that had almost killed her, but she was unperturbed, already launching herself toward Dusk.

"What's going on?" Ransom asked, looking dumbstruck.

"Talk?" Shatter demanded of Dusk, completely ignoring the question. "*Fuck* you—" she began, but yelped when I caught her by the waist again, the cupboard door barely set down.

The floor…

Shit.

I lifted her, my slippers immune to the glass currently scattering the kitchen tiles. Shatter, on the other hand, with a nightdress and bare feet… I grabbed a knife along the way and dumped her over the back of the couch, where she'd be fully safe from cupboard doors and shards of glass cutting her precious skin to pieces.

Expectedly, she turned on me, a snarl on her face, hatred in her eyes. It drained away as I flipped the kitchen knife in my grip and held it out to her—a peace offering.

She took it and spun back on Dusk, her whole petite body tense with rage.

Better, I thought with a sigh.

Much better.

"He picked the couch," I murmured.

Just trying to be helpful.

With Dusk dodging out of reach, Shatter dug the kitchen knife into the couch with a fury that made me goddamned proud.

"Oh, for fuck's sake!" Dusk groaned. "Could you get a—?" His words cut off as a half shredded couch cushion launched square in his face, fluff exploding all over the living room.

"You *liar*!" Shatter was hissing. "You said you 'changed my name'!"

Dusk winced. "I did, technic—"

"Say that word again!" she snarled.

Dusk raised his hands defensively. "It never came up."

"Never came up?" she demanded. "Never—" She cut off, stabbing another cushion with outrage.

Nice. I nodded appreciatively. I didn't know omegas could hit that octave. She was in our bond now, and her trembling omega fury was like a volcano—one that, with the last words, erupted.

At my side, Ransom was picking his way through the mess, eyes darting about, as if trying to understand what was happening, since neither of them seemed interested in telling us.

What was the rush? It'd come out. I was much more interested in them.

"How would it *come up*?" she demanded.

"I just mean"—Dusk caught another flying cushion before dropping it—"there was a lot of shit going on, and I wanted to tell you when it was right. But the longer it went on, the more difficult it got."

"All this time?!" She had paused her onslaught to seize handfuls of her hair, and I reached out to tug the knife back, since it was dangerously close to her face. She flinched away, pulling it from my reach, eyes still fixed on Dusk. "Since the start of term?"

I dared to poke at her curiously through the bond but stopped immediately when her blazing eyes snapped to me. She was kind of scary. Plus, better not piss her off. Shatter being mad at Dusk always ended in the best of things for me.

I mean—it was terrible. Really, *really* terrible, whatever was getting her this upset.

But, uh… would she ever consider fucking me when she was like this?

That would be so hot.

"Oh my God…" Ransom's voice ripped me from the show. He was at the kitchen island, a piece of paper in hand.

"What?" I asked.

"Oh. My. God."

Dramatic prick. "Tell me!" I crossed over and ripped it from him, but I froze as I saw the words on the page.

Wait…

What?

It was a formal document stating that… I blinked.

A… marriage certificate?

Shatter was my…

My *wife*?

Our wife?

The word "wife" was like a sexy lynx wrapping itself around my brain and letting out a little purr.

"Why?" Ransom was asking.

"He said it was a *technicality*," Shatter hissed. Her voice… her beautiful scent… her *everything* was intoxicating. I just stared, every alpha instinct misfiring like a wagonful of fireworks someone had just tossed a match into.

I was lightheaded. *No, no, no.* Fainting would be really embarrassing right now. I mean, I couldn't faint… I was her *hu…* Oh shit.

Her *hu…*

Nope.

The word was gonna blow up my brain.

"I shouldn't have said that," Dusk was saying. "And I never would have done it if I didn't also want to be your hus—" He cut off as, with a shriek, the knife finally flew from Shatter's fist across the room at him. His aura split the air for a second, so he could properly dodge it.

Husband.

Fucking. *Husband.*

I gripped the counter, my world spinning violently.

Me?

Hers?

Was that fair?

She was out of ammunition, it seemed, but I couldn't take my eyes from her. Wild honey hair, lips drawn back in a feral snarl, all that power bundled into her perfect little fairy omega frame. The most beautiful person on the planet.

Oh, fuck me—I wasn't husband material.

I tried to steady myself as Dusk carried on digging his hole—*grave*—and realised *I* would bury him if she didn't.

"I needed to be sure that, if the Lincoln pack bit you and went the proper route of registering the bond, they'd meet a boatload of legal obstacles—and then I'd know about it too."

"That," Shatter snarled, "is the stupidest reason for a marriage I've ever heard!"

"*You* were getting all conflicted about fucking us because you said it was like cheating on them. So, I figured this would fix it."

"But then you didn't tell her?" Ransom asked.

"You got overwhelmed by the registration card; I thought it might be a bit much."

"Hold on," Shatter said. "*Fixed* it?" She still gripped her hair furiously—which was really cute, which reminded me my wife was that cute, which made the world spin worse. "That would have just meant I was cheating on *both* of you! *How* is that better for me?"

"Uh, well," Dusk said. "It wasn't supposed to be. It was supposed to be better for us."

Ransom groaned as I scanned the paper wildly again, as if it might offer me sanity. I hung onto every detail. My eyes landed on location and dates, and I was momentarily distracted. "A *winter* wedding?"

Okay.

I nodded with distant appreciation.

That was nice, I supposed.

She'd have had those little white fur rings on the cuffs of her sleeves and hood. Maybe I'd worn a ushanka.

I didn't realise I'd spoken out loud until Shatter's strangled sound of fury rang out. "I wanted a *beach* wedding!"

Every alpha in the room went still. My eyes snapped from the paper to her. Dusk straightened in shock, leaving him open to an airborne spoon, which caught him in the corner of the eye (I was wrong about the ammunition). He didn't even flinch.

"You… do?" he asked, dumbfounded.

We were all staring.

"NOT WITH YOU!"

But Dusk was already reaching into his pocket and pulling out his phone.

"What are you doing?" Shatter demanded, finally drawing up fully from her onslaught as Dusk started tapping furiously on his screen.

"Asking Decebal for a divorce."

"What?"

"You want a beach wedding—"

"NO!" Shatter launched herself across the couch, flying into Dusk like a rocket. He staggered a step back, and then they were a tangle of limbs as she tried to wrestle the phone from him. "Don't. You. *DARE*!"

"You don't—want—a—beach wedding?" His words were punctuated with grunts as he tried to detangle her.

"I don't want a divorce!" she wailed.

Finally, she actually managed to win the fight by sinking her teeth into Dusk's arm and making him yelp. Then she scrambled away, his phone clutched in her hand. I stepped forward to catch her before she backed into the island at high speed.

She spun on me, eyes wide and phone hugged to her chest like I was going to steal it. Then she relaxed as she took me in.

We just stared at each other for a long moment. "You're… uh…" *My wife.* I couldn't seem to form the words.

She nodded, a little squeak in her chest.

For a split second, as she took me in, there was a beam on her face, but when I reached to hug her, she burst into tears.

That was fine. Really normal reaction, actually, considering.

I drew her into my arms. Good plan, since she couldn't see my face that way, and it had decided it didn't care if it wasn't the moment for a stupid grin.

But Shatter was my wife. *All* of our wife… wives? Wife? I narrowed my eyes. Wasn't sure, actually.

Oh shit…

With a moment of panic, I realised I needed to get on Dusk's level of cooking—she'd certainly be refusing his food after this. And Ransom was worse than me *or* her.

Oh dear.

She was my wife now. I couldn't let her starve.

With watery eyes, she hugged Ransom next, letting out a vicious growl when Dusk tried to get his phone.

I had already opened mine and was bookmarking dozens of breakfast tutorials.

Did they have a culinary program at this academy?

CHAPTER 11

Ransom

My *wife*, it turned out, could hold one hell of a grudge, which made me wildly proud. She was taking the marriage thing in her stride, celebrating her new status and her husbands—all except Dusk, whom she was entirely ignoring.

And I couldn't begrudge her that, not when it had taken Umbra and I so off guard.

I was someone who always tried to avoid giving my upbringing too much thought. From the moment my life had collided with Umbra and Dusk, everything changed. Not just because of my illness, which made me wonder if I would ever have a normal life again, but because my pack brothers were so different from everything I'd ever known.

But I'd been raised in a home that assumed any pack I joined or omega I chose would be for political gain or alliance. A world in which things like scent matches were the enemy for how erratic and unpredictable they were.

And because of that, I had always hated the idea of partnerships like marriage or betrothals.

At least, I *thought* I had until I saw the papers naming Shatter as my wife. Nothing had changed, and yet, everything had.

No matter where she was in the room, I couldn't take my eyes off her. Whether she was napping in my arms on the couch or peering into a bowl of dough Umbra was mixing, with flour dusting her nose and honey brown locks.

Surviving this with our pack intact suddenly felt… possible. I couldn't explain it. It wasn't a want—it was a need, as if the life waiting for us on the other end of this nightmare had skipped the queue and found us already.

It was something I knew every member of this pack was anxious about because there wasn't a single one of us who believed we were destined for good. For something like a complete family, wife, and… future.

And yet, good had found us amidst all of this, and that was an unavoidable truth. Now, it was tangible. In reach.

On Saturday afternoon, Roxy came over to visit. She helped me get one of my hair masks properly through all of Shatter's thick curls, and they spent the next few hours letting Umbra show them how to play his favourite aura boxing video game.

Dusk left for the afternoon, and I thought I knew exactly why. Sure enough, he sent a slew of texts throughout the day, all with pictures attached.

Dusk: Do you think these are close?

Dusk: I'm getting an idea of the options.

Dusk: Or if you want to come, too, I can wait.

I hid my phone from Shatter as I scrolled through the photos of rings he was looking at.

Dusk: I can't find any that seem right. Trying another shop.

It wasn't for another hour that I got a text with a photo of the perfect ring.

Dusk: This is the one. I can even get the placement of the diamonds changed.

Dusk: I'm worried. It's not as expensive as the others, but they can do it in a pack set, so I can get it in three parts.

Me: It's perfect.

I don't think Shatter cared about the price at all. She deserved the *right* ring.

And besides, I knew Dusk and Umbra had never quite settled into that reality of my family wealth: money didn't matter. I grew up with so much that expensive gifts lost meaning. Dusk could buy her the most expensive ring in the shop, and that number didn't make a dent in our bank account.

Umbra: Agree. Last one.

Umbra: I think you should be the one to give it to her.

Me: Yup.

Dusk: I'm not rushing it. She deserves everything to be perfect.

Somehow, despite the circumstances, we found a semblance of normalcy.

We stayed in for the weekend, and Shatter continued to refuse to acknowledge Dusk. The alterations on the ring would take a little while.

To my amusement, her resentment included refusing to eat anything Dusk made—which was, apparently, a whole thing. Umbra, in light of that, was trying more and more extravagant cooking, which I would appreciate more if I weren't worried it might kill us.

One thing Umbra didn't stand a chance against was Dusk's homemade scones, and he actually made them on Sunday morning, possibly to bribe Shatter into claiming one. But Shatter had appeared in the kitchen to find two plates of scones to choose from. One that looked pristine, with a sprinkling of herbs, and the second, which somewhat resembled a pile of dense pale rocks in odd shapes.

Boldly, she took one of Umbra's rock scones, biting into it with a worrying crack as she sank to his lap on the couch while Dusk ate his breakfast.

And the rest of the day… well, it was glorious.

The afternoon was spent sorting the new (new) couch, and then we'd watched movies all evening. Shatter had taken it in turns between my lap and Umbra's, and apparently now, for Shatter, sitting on our laps also included bonuses.

In the cutest display of Shatter-dominance I'd ever seen, she'd curled her hand around Umbra's neck, tugged open his zipper and then sank right over his length until she'd knotted her sweet little cunt and was locked in tight. Then she proceeded to purr contentedly as the movie ran.

When it released her, she moved on to me.

"You can use me like this whenever you want, Little Reaper," I growled as she settled over me for the second time in the night.

It almost came to blows at one point, when Dusk had shifted where he was sitting and reached out to her. Umbra had caught his wrist without taking his eyes off the apocalypse movie we were watching.

"Touch her," Umbra growled, "and I'll break your fingers."

Dusk's lips had drawn back in a snarl, but Shatter, a ball of delight in the bond, had rewarded Umbra with a nip on the neck, then ground over him until he finished with his lip caught in his teeth and his grip circling her waist.

She was very, very smug as she curled back up against his chest, her golden gaze fixed on Dusk. He had withdrawn, watching her every movement with something deadly in his eyes. If Dusk was looking at me like that, I would take it much more seriously than she seemed to.

The omega power, I thought, was going to her head, even if I had no problem with that. At all.

I wasn't looking forward to the upcoming week. I had a meeting with the Lincoln pack on Tuesday evening, and I was surprised they thought they had a chance with me, but maybe it spoke to their desperation—hiring Mord Sato was desperation.

On the bright side, Monday morning brought with it some unforgettable entertainment. As we were getting ready for class, Shatter appeared with a sheer scarf around her neck, perfectly covering Dusk's bite. She was still ignoring him, and while he was showing more restraint than I'd expected, he did pause when he spotted her scarf.

"Shatter." His voice was deadly, and bright yellow eyes narrowed. "Take it off."

It wasn't a dark bond command, which seemed deliberate.

Shatter glared at him, folding her arms and doing nothing.

"Be mad at me all you want, but you will *not* hide my claim," he growled.

Her eyes flickered to him for the briefest second, something haughty in them, but still, she didn't move.

"Couch." His voice was low and deadly.

She spun on him from her seat. "What?"

"Don't make me ask again."

She looked about to argue but slipped from the bar stool and stalked over to the new couch. I raised my eyebrow as she pressed herself over the arm without a word. I wondered, for a second, if this was exactly *why* Dusk was so careful about picking out those couches. He wanted one with an arm high enough that she'd fit over it, just like she was right now.

I met Umbra's gaze. He'd frozen in the middle of mixing batter for pancakes, edging across the kitchen and looking completely ridiculous in his flour-dusted apron and slippers as he watched Shatter with undeniable interest.

This was one hell of a start to a Monday.

I grabbed my plate and joined Shatter on the couch, crossing my legs and getting ready for the show. She narrowed her eyes at me, but I'd missed far too many Shatter punishments to skip another second.

Besides, she was mad enough at Dusk, she wouldn't even remember my excitement.

What Umbra had said back in the cabin was right. The two of them had something… different. Special, and when I watched them together, I always learned something new about them both.

Dusk didn't stand from where he was finishing his piece of toast. "How many?" he asked, and he might as well have been reading a newspaper for his casual indifference.

There was a long silence as Shatter met my eyes for half a second. She pouted, but I felt that spike of lust from her in the bond. Angry, she might be, but this dance she had going on with Dusk turned her on. More, I thought, when we were watching.

"Shatter." Dusk's voice was a warning.

She made an angry little sound. "Seven."

I saw the twitch of a smile on Dusk's lips as he dropped his crust on his plate and got to his feet.

"Hand or belt?"

Dusk took his time pouring himself a drink of water.

Shatter's cheeks were burning, and I heard a little growl of irritation from her.

Finally, he stepped up behind her, his hand caressing her hip as he waited, lifting her skirt to show the rich skin of her perfect ass to the whole living room and kitchen.

"Belt," she whispered.

"What?" Dusk asked, hand lingering on her exposed ass, and she shivered at his touch.

"Belt," she said again, louder.

Dusk waited, his grip on her ass becoming punishing. Shatter wriggled, pressing her cheek to the couch and fixing her gaze on the TV.

"Belt, *Alpha*," she said.

"Better."

Dusk stepped first to the coffee table, where he opened a drawer and pulled out his bottle of massage oil. When he returned behind her, he unclasped his belt and removed it. I saw Shatter shift, trying to get a glimpse of him.

Her nightshade was heavy in the air, and her cheeks were bright pink. I might not swing that way, but I got it. Dusk looked deadly: dark button-up half untucked in black pants as he coiled the belt clasp around his palm, taking his sweet time. His yellow eyes traced her shivering body, bent over the couch as she waited for him.

The longer he took, the more she shifted impatiently, brows bunching in irritation. Her nightshade rose in the room to dangerous levels, and I had to readjust how I was sitting to give my own cock some breathing room.

I refrained from looking to the kitchen, rather preferring *not* to have the image of batter-stirring-Umbra in an apron and sporting a raging hard-on burned into my brain for life.

Dusk brushed Shatter's ass with his knuckle, and she jumped, the tiniest squeak escaping her before she realised it was just his hand.

"Are you being a brat because you're mad at me, or because you like what happens when you are?" He trailed his touch to where the slip of lace hugged her flesh. He pressed splayed fingers over her skin.

"I'm mad at—" She cut off with a breath as his middle finger dipped lower, then he pressed it into her without warning. "I'm mad at you," she whined.

I snorted at how pitiful it sounded, and her golden eyes snapped up to me with a glare. For half a second, anyway, before Dusk added a second finger and her lips parted.

He drew his hand back, letting go. "Are you ready, Gem?"

"Mm-hmm," she said, clearly losing her fight in the face of overwhelming lust.

Her whine was so hot as the first belt strike cracked against her skin. She balled her fists, her breathing heavy as Dusk picked up the oil from the counter and rubbed it on her sore flesh.

By the second and third, she was panting, a needy whine rising in her chest as Dusk massaged the oil in.

Fuck me.

I cracked, meeting Umbra's eyes (only). His batter stirring had come to a complete halt. I knew by the look we shared that we *were* both getting far too wound up for a Monday morning.

Could we just call it on class and fuck?

Another strike, and she wasn't even hiding her needy moans as Dusk squeezed her ass, stepping right up to her, so he could grind his hard-on against her cunt.

She was breathing hard, pressing back against him shamelessly.

Another strike, and another, and I swear she arched that perfect little body further with each, like she was presenting for him.

On the seventh strike, she was shivering. When Dusk stepped closer to squeeze her ass where he'd struck, she let out a little moan, wriggling back against him and—

"Shatter!" Dusk let go of her instantly, so startled, he didn't find his command before she let out a whine, body trembling with what was definitely an orgasm.

Umbra barked a laugh as I snorted.

"What?" she asked, breathless, failing epically at playing innocent as she pushed herself up and stared at him with pink cheeks. But nightshade had gone off like a bomb in the room, making me want to drag her over and bury my knot deep into her.

Dusk raised an eyebrow as she turned to him, and we all felt the flare of defiance from her in the bond.

Boy, was she playing with fire.

Dusk sidestepped her and took a seat on the couch. "Knees," he said coldly.

She tugged her skirt down and sank between his splayed legs, a dangerously smug look on her face.

"Unzip me," Dusk said.

She reached up, voice oh-so-bratty. "When I said seven, I didn't know you were going to—" She cut off with a whine as Dusk pulled her lips to his cock and pressed it halfway into her mouth.

"Gem," he purred, dragging her the rest of the way until her fists balled on his legs and his shaft was choking her completely. He held her there, and her wide golden eyes were fixed on him. "This is because you got cocky."

He waited a good few seconds before releasing her, and when she drew back, she took gasping breaths.

"Be mad all you want, but hide my claim, and I'll remind you who these holes belong to." He dragged her over his length again, and I watched the way her nails dug into his thighs. "And that they're mine to use whenever I want."

"Now. You do the rest," he told her, a command in the words. "And fuck that sweet throat worse for every bratty plan you've come up with in the last few days. I'll let you decide how they deserve punishment; if you think they were fair, you can go easy."

"W-wait—" Her eyes were wide in shock, even as she was forced to draw her lips back to his tip. "Dusk," she whimpered. "I wasn't going to *do* any of them."

He gathered her hair in his fist, a cruel smile on his lips. "And keep your eyes on me, Gem."

Dusk leaned back on the couch, a pleased expression on his face as he rested his head back, letting out a groan of pleasure as Shatter began what became the most brutal self-imposed face-fuck I'd ever even been able to conceive of.

The command was airtight, and there was clearly no shortage of vindictive ideas for her to punish herself over because she kept pressing those plush lips all the way to his swollen knot, eyes blazing with fury as she grappled with the order.

Dusk kept pausing her as he collected himself, and he made it last a good fifteen minutes.

She was panting by the time she finished, tears pouring down her cheeks, her cheeks bright pink, and sweat beading on her forehead. Through the bond, the empire of brattiness she'd been building over the weekend was swept away for submission.

"Good girl," Dusk growled as he finally finished, his fist returning to her hair as he held her over his length and emptied down her throat.

"Take off the neck covering," he said. "Tie up your hair and get on my lap."

She tugged it off as she got to shaky feet and fought with her hair to get it in a bun. It was a bit lopsided but outrageously cute as she slid onto his lap.

She folded her arms, eyes fixed on me defiantly as Dusk drew her close and sank his teeth into her neck again, renewing the dark bite he'd left.

Her lips opened in shock.

When he drew back, a trickle of blood glistened upon her skin. She reached for it, but he caught her wrist.

"You won't touch it," he hissed.

Her chest heaved, but her look of outrage was offset by how blown her pupils were—and her scent, which was still heavy in the space.

The problem was, this show was far too hot for a Monday morning, and I wasn't the only one who agreed. We were just exiting the apartment when Shatter halted. "Oh, just, um… give me a second. I forgot my water bottle."

"Since when do you have a water bottle?" I asked.

"Omega Studies said I should stay hydrated," she muttered. "Just, uh… don't come in—" she added, shoving Umbra back as he made to step back in with her.

"There's a couple of bottles in the cupboard over the sink," he told her. She nodded, then vanished, leaving the door a crack open.

We all waited in the hallway in silence, hearing the tap turn on. I took the time to adjust myself, trying to think of anything to rid me off this hard-on.

The water only ran for a few moments before it shut off. Then there was the undeniable crunch and scraping sound of someone scooping ice from the ice bin in the fridge, followed by the clatter that I guessed was the ice tumbling into a plastic bottle.

There was a pause, then the clatter of ice sounded again. Then again. Another pause, and then one more time. I raised an eyebrow, catching Umbra's eye. That, I thought, was a *lot* of ice, considering we were heading quickly for winter.

I glanced at Dusk, who was doing a shit job at keeping his expression neutral. The edge of his lips quirked mischievously as he folded his arms and leaned against the wall, not meeting our eyes.

As much as I took Shatter's side on the marriage thing, I couldn't help but admire Dusk. He worked well as pack lead. He waited, watched, and learned the best way. With me, he was patient. A rigid, cruel upbringing had left me sensitive to strict rules, but with Umbra, who he knew better than he knew even himself, he could be brutal. With Shatter, he'd found a perfect balance between rules and freedom.

He'd taken pack lead because he believed he'd had to, but he deserved it. I knew Umbra had tried to take it back, and Shatter had intervened, but I think that was a testament to how fast she'd come to understand this pack.

We finally heard the sound of the fridge closing and plastic on plastic as she screwed the top on the bottle.

Another brief pause, an indiscernible and furious mutter from Shatter, then the fridge opened again. At another sound of the scoop of ice, I caught Umbra grinning. I was battling my own at this point.

"The Arkology program won't allow another absence," I warned Dusk, adjusting my bag on my shoulder.

He glanced at me briefly. "I know."

"If she goes into heat…"

"I will, uh…" Dusk cleared his throat. "Take it easy."

Shatter finally appeared in the doorway, stuffing a water bottle (crammed to the brim with ice) into her bag.

"Okay. I'm, um… I'm good now," she said quickly, slipping past us, hand hovering over the fresh bite and drying blood on her neck that Dusk had commanded her not to mess with.

I noticed she kept as much distance from him as possible, but I had a strong feeling Shatter was going to be mad at Dusk for as long as she could possibly manage.

CHAPTER 12

Shatter

"Who gets Shatter?" Umbra asked as we settled into the booths in class. People were finding their seats on the benches below, bringing with them the usual scent of caffeine for the first class of the day.

"Gets me?" I asked, glancing up from where I was lining up my notebook and pens.

"I want cuddles, Little Reaper. You've got me addicted."

"It's *class.*"

"How about a coin toss?" Umbra asked, ignoring me completely and glancing at Ransom.

Wait… coin toss? *That* got my attention.

Out of the corner of my eye, I saw Dusk smirk, though it was all *his* fault that Umbra and Ransom were both so wound up they couldn't focus on classes. They really needed to. They were falling so far behind.

"Sure," Ransom replied, straightening.

But I couldn't deny I *was* curious. I'd been thinking long and hard about Umbra's tricks—and how Dusk had warned me away from playing his games when I'd first met them. I'd picked tails and lost, Ransom had picked tails and lost, and Umbra was always so sure about it. I *think* I knew what was going on.

"Heads or tails?" Umbra asked.

"Choose heads," I hissed at Ransom. "You'll win."

Umbra raised an eyebrow, a smirk on his face that gutted my confidence.

"Heads," Ransom said, glancing from me to Umbra.

Umbra rummaged in his pocket and took out what I knew had to be a trick coin. I couldn't contain the smile on my face as he flipped it. He caught it, hand over palm, and peered at me.

"You sure?" Ransom asked me.

"Yes." I folded my arms, eyes narrowed, suddenly unsure as I caught the twinkle of delight in Umbra's sandstorm eyes.

My grin vanished as he lifted his hand, and I saw the coin was tails up.

"What?" I asked.

"Fuck." Ransom wound his arms around my waist. "But I *want* her."

Umbra grinned, crossing his arms and looking to me.

"But I thought…" I pouted.

Well, fuck.

I kissed Ransom on the cheek and unwound his arms. "Later," I promised him. "All the cuddles."

"It *might* be prudent," Dusk murmured, not looking up from the textbook chapter he was examining. "To make him take the coin out of his pocket *before* you pick a side."

I paused, staring between them before it clicked.

"You have *two*?" I demanded as Umbra happily tugged me onto his lap.

Of *course* he had two.

"Okay. It's a mega important class today," I said. Kind of. Not like… solve-my-pack's-problems important (I'd scoured the textbooks repeatedly, so I was just hoping for new angles from the professors, at this point). But there was a guest speaker I really wanted to listen to. "You're not allowed to distract me."

"But that's the point." Umbra chuckled. "You're too smart. If I don't distract you, no one else stands a chance."

"It's school, not a competition."

"Everything's a competition," he said.

At first, it wasn't too bad. Umbra's muted wolfsbane and blood scent was always a little distracting, but once Professor Audrey began talking about her study on the recent discoveries on the difference between male and female alpha auras, I was really settled in. Actually, it was quite nice having the warmth of Umbra's arms around me.

I got a lot of stares nowadays, and I was getting better at ignoring them. The Lincoln pack was in this class, too, but the gentle brush of Umbra's thumb at my waist was grounding. It helped me forget the others in the room and focus on the lecture.

That was, until he leaned forward and whispered a command in my ear.

My cheeks blazed with heat.

"I can't do that," I whined. But my body was already betraying me as I shifted on his lap, readjusting my legs on either side of him. I jumped as I felt his hand against the small of my back. "Lean forward, Nightshade."

Oh… *bother.*

"You can't make it obvious," I hissed.

He chuckled. "It won't be if you don't keep saying things like that."

I shivered as I felt his touch beneath my skirt, tugging my panties out of the way. Then he adjusted himself.

"You can't *actually*—" I cut off with a barely contained whine as I felt his finger dip into me.

Dusk's and Ransom's eyes were fixed on me, and that was enough to make me curb my protests.

He shifted beneath me, and I knew what was coming before I felt his tip nudge my entrance.

"Come on, Little Nightshade," Umbra growled. "I want you down to my knot." I shut my eyes, burying my face in the textbook as the command took hold and I sank down over his cock, a little squeak of shock escaping me as he pressed up and into me, filling me completely.

Heat seeped into my core as he dragged me down further. "Wait, Umbra—"

Too late.

Ransom's eyebrows shot up. "Did he just…?"

"Fuck, Nightshade," Umbra growled, a low purr of satisfaction rumbling through him and making me giddy. His hands rested on my hips as he drew me back, and I bit back a whine of pleasure as he rocked into me.

He'd knotted me.

In fucking class.

"You're going to learn how to take my knot while you study," he breathed in my ear.

"Okay, but just… Why *in* class?"

"You're mine, Nightshade." He nipped my ear, sounding so fucking smug. "My wife. My omega. If I want you to keep me warm in class, you will."

Focusing now, with his knot and low purr to distract me, was impossible. The combination of both was absolutely the opposite of soothing, and my blood was heating rapidly, the pen in my hand shaky as I tried, and failed, to take notes.

I just about survived, shivering and fighting the rising heat, still managing to jot down the most important things—some of this was such new information, the textbooks didn't even have it, and Umbra was not going to ruin that for me.

That was, until I caught the faintest trace of coconut and plum, and I looked up to see Flynn Lincoln passing us. I froze, shrinking back against Umbra. I felt his low growl rumble in his chest, and his hand closed around my throat in an instant, dragging me back against him. Wolfsbane and blood soothed my flash of terror as, beneath the table, his finger found my clit and my breath caught as Umbra's knot pressed up further into me.

The look on my face made Flynn pause, as if he knew *exactly* what was happening.

"You will never belong to anyone else," Umbra breathed in my ear.

I had to drop my head, fingers clenched on the desk. My hair was up in a fucking bun, thanks to Dusk, so there were only a few wild strands that hid my expression as I had a literal orgasm in class right in front of Flynn.

"Should we be taunting them like that?" Ransom asked as I caught my breath.

"I don't give a shit," Umbra said, humming happily as he pulled me closer, entwined with me in the bond, tangling lust with safety. "They're not going to have you, Nightshade. Never."

CHAPTER 13

Shatter

It was Monday evening, and I was over at Roxy's, doing homework. My nest was mostly tidy, but I loved going to her apartment. Every time I arrived, there was something new. She was officially nesting, and Roxy, as it turned out, didn't just have a scent like Christmas—she loved Christmas decor too.

"Never tell my family," she said as I peered at the little village set up on a table along the wall.

"Everyone used to get me Christmas stuff for gifts—my birthday is in December too—and I hated it for so long. But once my hormones settled down…" She sat on her couch, a mug of hot chocolate in her hand. "My dad would never let me live it down."

"There's little people in there!" I crouched down, spotting a pack with a baby through one of the windows.

"I love the details," Roxy admitted. "It just makes me feel all warm and fuzzy."

"It's the same for me and the…" I frowned. "The bookshelves and having everything out of pattern." I didn't really know how to explain it. The chaotic hexagon bookshelves had been damaged in the trashing of my nest. Still, Ransom had told me this morning that he was going to sort them out.

We settled down to turn on the movie, but before it started, I turned to Roxy. "I… need a bit of help."

"With what?"

"Is there anything in Omega Studies about seducing alphas?"

"*You* need to seduce your alphas?" Roxy asked, an eyebrow rising sceptically.

"Well…" I tapped my finger on my mug of hot chocolate. "I'm feeling very seduced, rather than the other way around."

All the research I was doing to figure out how we might save them, well… all paths seem to be leading to the same thing.

Roxy grinned. "Shatter, you have those alphas wrapped around your little finger."

I felt the pout on my face as I thought of resorting to ice packs to survive class. Dusk hadn't even been trying. "I'm always the one being seduced." I needed to know how to flip the script.

Fucking Dusk and his fucking punishments. Heat crawled up my neck at the thought of it.

I tried to shove it away.

I had to be mad at him for a little longer. I can't *believe* he'd threatened a divorce. Instinct reared its ugly head at the mere thought of it, and I had to stamp it down so my nightshade didn't ruin Roxy's beautiful winter wonderland.

But how *dare* he—that pack was *mine.*

"Okay," Roxy was saying, "you have everything you need. You just have to know how to use it."

"How do I do that?"

"Do you want something specific from them?" she asked, giving me a sly look.

"Kind of." I crossed my arms. "Just a few asks that I don't want them thinking too hard about."

Not that I wanted to trick them, but this was important.

Roxy gave me a grin. "I know a couple of good pack romances that will show you what I'm talking about," she said, nodding at the TV.

"Yes!" I was so down for another movie night.

"So. Jasmine officially became the Lincoln pack omega," Roxy said, eyeing me as she typed the title of a movie into the TV.

"I heard." I chewed on my lip. "Guess they had to choose someone."

"Shit reputation or not, there is more than one omega in this school who would go for money, no matter what."

"You think they, uh… picked her on purpose?" I asked. "To… upset me?" It wasn't like people didn't know Jasmine and I didn't like each other.

"I think they're fighting to stay relevant. They're big on their own image. They looked too out of control after the ball. This makes them seem more… calculated? I suppose. Going for the only omega who challenged their own scent match." Roxy clicked on the movie but hit pause when it started. "Is there anything going on between you and them still?" she asked. "They wanted your bond at the ball, then they vanished. Have they asked for further negotiations?"

I considered that. I couldn't tell Roxy everything, but there were some parts that were obvious from the outside. "They're… trying."

"I hope Dusk's having none of it."

"Nope."

"Bit awkward for Jasmine if that gets out, though," Roxy said. "I doubt they told her that."

I nodded, wishing I could tell her more, but I didn't want to put my pack or Roxy in danger, and what was between the Lincoln pack and mine was far beyond school gossip.

"No omega will go near Jasmine, if that makes you feel better."

I hugged my pillow closer to my chest, fighting a small smile. "It does."

Those photos she'd dropped on my desk still haunted me, turning my stomach at the thought of them. "A bit." Maybe more than a bit.

I wouldn't be able to attend Omega Studies, since Mord was here, though Roxy was joining me in the shared Arkology classes we had together, and we spent some evenings studying too. Which this was supposed to be, but Omega Studies was also… school, right? So, watching the movie was like homework.

Though, if I was being honest, I was starting to realise my interest in Omega Studies had been much more about the fascination of being around other omegas. The curriculum itself didn't seem all that solid.

"Plus, she's in for a shock," Roxy added.

"What do you mean?"

"Honestly?" A cheeky smile played on Roxy's face. "Worst sex of my life with that pack. Eric tried to gaslight me into thinking he's a good fuck without actually making an effort."

There was a strange silence between us before I found the courage to ask. "But, uh… he wasn't?"

Roxy grinned. "God, no. Gareth's a minute man, and Flynn's awkward as shit in bed—and not in a cute way."

I giggled.

"They're terrible fucks and their scents are lame as fuck."

I grinned, my attention turning to the TV with a warm feeling in my chest as she pressed play.

* * *

"Okay, so…" I considered the movie we'd just watched as the credits rolled.

It was the third one of the night, and it was getting late. "I wanna make sure I'm not missing something…" I looked down at my list. "It looks like I'm sorted for a lot of the stuff I wrote down already…" I'd been taking notes on all the things that had been established in the pack movies, when it came to seduction, and narrowed it down to a few key things.

Things that make seduction easier:

- Alphas are really into the omegas — scent match is best
- Alphas have given gifts like nests or other things
- Alphas show desire to protect omega
- Alphas want a bond

I looked at the last part. "So… if I have all of this stuff, all I have to do next is… take off my clothes?"

That was the common denominator between all the movies.

"Uh…" Roxy giggled. "Yeh, that sounds about right."

"And then… what? I just ask for what I want?"

"Yup."

"Before or after the sex?"

"I don't think the order matters, at that point."

"No?"

"No, but best right after they finish."

"Okay." I nodded. "I can do that."

I was sceptical. This seemed a little silly.

Roxy was peering at my notes. "That's solid." She read through my list. "Scent match… receive gifts or nest… play damsel, dangle sex, remove clothes and… yup. That's it. Do that, and you can ask for anything in the world. Especially the damsel thing. There's nothing that melts an alpha's brain more than an omega in need of protection."

But then another question popped into my mind. "Do you think it would work if, uh… if I didn't have sex with them?"

Roxy considered that. "Honestly. It's just about getting them thinking about sex, then their brain has melted, anyway."

CHAPTER 14

Ransom

Maybe I shouldn't have done this alone.

I cocked my head to the side. If I tilted my head a little, the wood was level. Level enough.

Right?

It was Tuesday afternoon. There was a free block, and I'd been in the academy workshop late into last night and all afternoon today.

With paint, the angle would be less obvious… I think. I glanced at the tins of white paint waiting on the scuffed-up workshop floor. Well, they weren't pure white. Off cream… bridal colours, I'd been told when I'd turned up at the hardware store with beach wedding pictures.

Our wedding pictures could live on this bookshelf forever, beside all the Arkology books she was so particular about. I imagined she would be just as particular about the wedding photos when we had them.

I'd even bought the frames, all hexagons and pentagons—all supposed to look perfect on this shelf.

I frowned as I tilted my head the opposite way. Could paint really fix this?

Shit.

The others in the workshop gave me and my bookcase a wide berth. I'd thought it was because I was Ransom Kingsman… but now I was starting to wonder if it was because I was Ransom Kingsman with a monstrosity of a project no one wanted to have to comment on.

"Damn," I hissed, rubbing my brow with fingers raw from sanding. If I spent another few hours sanding the edges, could I maybe make that stupid level bubble lie to me? "No way I can give her this."

Would it even hold books? And what if it fell apart and she got hurt?

In my head, this had gone better. Every step, every agonising hour of figuring out how to use the tools in here, and I had been confident it was going to be perfect.

A gift beyond money, and more precious for it.

But in hindsight, that was pretty fucking stupid. Who did I think I was, making a bookshelf?

With only one step left, it still looked like it had been made by a toddler with a hammer.

Some marriage gift.

But, I couldn't give her *nothing*.

She was my wife, and my wedding gift to Shatter wouldn't be something I bought with the click of a button or a swipe of a card. No. My omega deserved a thought-out gift that was made just for her.

Something I made for her with my own two hands.

And I'd made… this.

A bookshelf that made unsettling groans when nudged. Maybe I should just scrap the whole—

"You *build*?"

Dusk's voice had me whirling where I stood.

He was crossing the workshop, looking around curiously with his oxfords clipping the paint stains and sawdust across the floor.

"How did you find me?" I demanded, stepping between him and the bookshelf, so he couldn't see the tragedy I'd made.

Dusk cocked an eyebrow at me, half a grin on his face. "I was wondering what the paint purchases were all about."

My cheeks flashed hot. "You're watching my *purchases*?"

"Like there isn't anything that could possibly stand out more on Kingsman bank statements than purchases from a hardware store." He tugged up the sleeves of his black button-up, grinning. "Need help?"

"No." I narrowed my eyes at him. I doubted he'd be any better than me.

Plus, it was his fault we were in this mess.

He drew up slightly, his eyes falling on the paint can. "Oh." I saw the comprehension in his eyes. "This is…"

"A wedding gift," I said. "For the woman you married into the pack without telling us."

I put my hand on the shelf protectively, which was a mistake, because it wobbled rather dangerously.

Ah. Shit.

"Doesn't matter, anyway. I can't give it to her."

Nope. No way could I give it to her. I'd give her something else for now—we'd have to buy more bookshelves from the store. I would practise making bookcases a hundred more times and *then* I would give her one from me.

But…

But what if she got attached to the one from the furniture store? What if she liked it enough that she wanted to put our *wedding photos* on it?

I fought back a growl, my jaw going tight.

This could be the only window I ever had to make a shelf she'd want.

"She's going to love it," Dusk said.

I blinked. "She'll… *what*?"

"Love it."

"It's not very sturdy. Or upright."

"What colour were you thinking?" he asked, ignoring me.

"I got a few bridal creams…"

"Have you considered varnish?"

I frowned. "Why?"

"She likes darks and wood textures."

"Did she tell you that?"

"No. But she hurries any lighter colour plates and bowls out of the nest quicker, and she keeps the darks longer—especially trays, and there's a mahogany one stashed under her bed."

"Oh." Was there?

Damn. I'd spent a lot of time on creams… But now I was thinking about it, he was right. All that time picking out this perfect… *Cloud White*—I think it was called—wasted.

"Varnish, then?" I asked, then frowned. I shouldn't ask. This was my project.

"I think if this gift had a good varnish, she'd probably try to stash it under her bed."

I felt a smile tug at my lips, and I was already tugging my phone out, going back through the Benjamin Moore website.

"I didn't come for that, though," he said.

I glanced up at him from the phone, frowning.

"I'm sorry. I should have told you. And her and Umbra. It's a big deal. At the time, I was just thinking about—" He cut off, palming the back of his neck. "Doesn't matter. Shouldn't have happened like this for you or her."

I hesitated. Dusk had never been one for apologies. If he'd tracked me down to give me one, he meant it.

I nodded.

"I think she's…" I couldn't stop my smile. "I think she's thrilled. Even if she is mad at you." Which did have its merits. "Kinda wild in the bond," I added. Like a fiery tornado of possessive omega in there.

Dusk nodded, clearly biting back a grin. He cleared his throat. "You ready for Flynn today?"

I nodded. That was tonight. I probably needed to finish here and change, actually. "Think so. Find out if they know anything. Try to give them enough hope for a deal over Shatter that they back off a bit."

"Not as easy as it sounds, sitting with those pricks with a poker face."

"I can handle it," I said firmly.

Only reason he knew that was because he'd had to do it while I was feral.

No.

I was far past my turn.

CHAPTER 15

Ransom

Just like I'd hoped, it was only Flynn waiting for me at the bar. He wanted a conversation from rich kid to rich kid, and that was exactly what I was going to give him.

I slid into the booth he was waiting in, noticing he'd already ordered himself a drink. Between his dapper clothes and carefully styled dark hair, he looked like the kind of guy who spent way too much time in front of the mirror. It was work not to wrinkle my nose at his coconut and plum scent. Everything about this pack set my nerves on edge.

"Kingsman," he said with a smile. "I'm glad you came."

"Flynn." I nodded, then ordered a drink when the waitress appeared.

Flynn waited until she'd gone before fixing me with an all-business look. Seemed he wasn't wasting time. "Things have become far too messy. I thought a proper talk was in order, but I hope this can stay between you and me," he said. "We're the same. Both in packs with alphas who didn't grow up in our calibre."

I met his eyes, nodding slowly and watching as he relaxed a bit when I didn't argue.

"You had me worried at the ball. Dusk… well, he seems to have a vendetta, but you… surprised me. I didn't think you would agree with him."

I raised my eyebrows. "I do not like assumptions made of me," I said, hearing my father in my words.

Distasteful, but he knew how to spin a conversation to get what he wanted from it. And what I wanted from Flynn was to give him the impression there was a possibility of an alliance with me. It would cool down the urgency to open the safe or villainize Shatter.

Flynn nodded, swallowing before taking a sip of his drink.

"We were taken aback. I hope you understand. You haven't been here, though we don't know why…" He trailed off.

"I was recovering from an illness."

Flynn's eyebrows shot up, and I could see a flash of relief in his eyes. "That's why you weren't here at the start of term?"

I nodded. There was one issue I had to tackle. When Shatter was with them, I'd turned up at their apartment and almost put one of them through a wall. "I wasn't made aware that she was your mate."

Flynn shifted, eyes calculating. "None of them told you?"

I shook my head as the waitress returned with my drink.

"What about the bond?" he asked when she was gone.

"Again. I had just got back the night I showed up at yours. I knew very little."

"Dusk bit her," Flynn said, eyeing me. "Did he speak to you before that?"

"No."

Flynn's eyebrows rose, and I saw a glimmer of hope in them. "Your pack has gone rogue, Kingsman. I'm sure your parents warned you about being selective with pack mates."

"Incessantly," I said, forcing bitterness into my voice.

Flynn grinned, relaxing considerably as he took a sip of his drink. "I get it, you know? Why do you think I'm with Eric and Gareth? They were well off *enough*, but nothing like us. I needed a change—my own control."

I let out a breath, making myself smile. "Yeh. It was… something like that."

Flynn was nodding almost to himself. "You know, maybe our parents were onto something. I can't imagine, if I was… indisposed, Eric and Gareth would… well. Not to say I don't *trust* them, but this kind of money and power… how easily it could go to their heads…" He looked at me, and I realised he was waiting for me to confirm it.

"I think you're exactly right."

"People see our power, and it drives them mad. They want in, but they'll never have it, not truly. Real power, you're born with it. Eric and Gareth could take pack lead, could throw my money around, but they'd never truly hold the power *I* was raised for."

I nodded, despite the irony. Flynn wasn't anywhere close to my family's league. He was still of the wealth level that wanted to show it off. Even my father, horrible as he was, had done everything he could to remain as quiet to the public face as possible.

Flynn went on, clearly entranced by the sound of his own voice. "You were sick, and he was in control. Then he discovered she was our match—*somehow*, and I don't know how. He must have got it from her. And he realised he could do it again, just like he did to you. Perhaps it's a game, something to make him feel worth more than us."

I nodded quietly. This was the direction I needed the conversation to go, and Flynn seemed happy to lead us there.

"It's a complicated situation," I added. "Dusk is pack lead, and he…" I trailed off, like I was contemplating sharing. "He took more than pack lead when I was sick."

"He has control over the estate, doesn't he?" Flynn said, his eager tone hushed. "Sato did some digging."

"Like I said, this situation is complicated."

"I'm still surprised at your stance at the ball—the party, even. I can't possibly imagine why you want to keep her?"

"I walked into this situation late—to Dusk telling me she'd been taken by your pack. Then she was dark bonded without my consent. I have a responsibility to ensure this situation is dealt with properly."

This was getting easier with the drink, and as much as I'd despised my upbringing, this sort of diplomacy was something I'd been trained for.

Flynn nodded, considering that. "How does she…?" He narrowed his eyes, as if unsure how to phrase it. "How is she with your pack?"

I took a while to consider that. "She's… fragile," I said carefully. "She escaped Dusk to be rejected by you." I held his eyes, wondering what he'd have to say to that. "She is afraid of a lot of things," I said, gauging his reaction. "Especially after what you did."

"Afraid?" Flynn wrinkled his nose in distaste. "Well, I don't trust her to be rational, but none of those things would have happened if she hadn't been hiding from us. She's a fool if she doesn't understand the position she put us in. We're alphas."

I blinked, trying to contain my reaction to that. They were *blaming* Shatter for how they'd attacked her?

"Men like us, we're run by instinct at the worst of times, and she was… well, she was taunting us." Flynn clapped me on the shoulder, and that, plus the lie he was spinning, was almost enough to break my composure.

But I'd known, if I was to play this card tonight, I would be faced with something vile. That was the thing I'd learned about evil people. Very rarely did they view themselves as the villain. That had been one of the most disturbing things I'd learned from my father. I had returned to confront him—before I'd become completely feral. Back when Dusk and Umbra had begun their own hunts in retribution for the alphas that had died in those experiments

My father had no idea the security systems were down. That he was on the brink of his own reckoning. I'd sat before him in his office and given him one last chance.

And what had he told me?

"There was nothing inhumane about it, son. Those alphas were pulled from the Cimmerian Vaults; violent and insane, left to rot behind bars. They aren't like us. This was the only opportunity they'd ever have to better the world."

In a way, I supposed he was right.

If my father had never pulled them from the vaults, Dusk would never have hunted him across his own mansion and ended him that night.

The world *was* better after that.

"Are you protective of her?" Flynn asked, a goading smile on his lips as he took me in. "*My* scent match?"

I straightened my expression, which I realised had stiffened considerably. "She's…" I trailed off, not finding a word that wouldn't give too much away.

"Gold packs." Flynn waved a hand, saving me from having to come up with an answer. "Nature's sirens. I don't blame you for being a bit attached, but it's nothing more than biology."

"I…" I swirled my glass. "She isn't what I expected."

"Be honest, you *must* want me to take her off your hands. You are the last of your line—and she complicates that."

"What about yours?" I asked, surprised by that take.

Shatter was a gold pack. Any alpha children she had would be rogues—alphas capable of breaking the Institute's laws that were designed to keep society safe. Flynn was right; legally, she could never have children.

Of course, that would mean nothing to Flynn, who saw Shatter as a cure for his aura sickness, but I wondered how he would mask that lie.

"We could work something out," he said easily, waving a hand again. "An arrangement out of pack, or, well… I mean…" He paused, as if toying with an idea. "With what the world's dealt me so far, a part of me perhaps enjoys the idea of…" He glanced around briefly, voice lowering. "Tripping the system." He grinned. "With enough money, you can get around almost anything. And *rogue* alphas… I do like the idea of handing more power to my children. She can, at least, offer me that."

Goosebumps rippled my skin as I processed those words, and it took everything I had to keep a hold on my aura.

His take was clear, though.

He was trying to play her off as worthless to me, while an asset to himself—but not so much so that he wasn't doing me a favour by offering to take her.

"You're a bigger risk taker than I am," I said quietly, swirling my drink to calm the boiling fury in the pit of my stomach.

At the lack of condemnation, Flynn downed the rest of his drink before setting it down with a scowl. "She is a gold pack caught between two families so far out of her calibre that it's embarrassing we're here, discussing her. The least she can do is give me some power back to my lineage." He snorted. "And she'll be in a fucking princess bond. I better get something back after having to offer it."

"I understand, but I'm still curious why you're pushing so hard for it."

"I wouldn't be claiming her if it wasn't for the match—I think my parents would tell me not to, but… well, it goes against my principles. She *is* ours."

I worked very hard to loosen my grip on my cup as he spoke those words. I took a breath, letting go as Flynn went on.

"It's only right we should take her. I didn't really imagine you'd have interest, with how much you are a representative of your family now. Not with the kind of work that will have to go into making her even remotely presentable. I mean, her show at the ball—pretty enough, if cheap. I couldn't take her to see my parents. Don't get me started on the eyes." He sighed. "I do wish we'd gone to the Valentine's Division sooner, found a decent match. Oh! Speaking of—" He tugged in his pocket and pulled out a business card. I frowned, catching a number of sweet scents tangled upon it. "I have a friend who works at the Valentine Division, you know. They're so regulated, but she can get around a few of their… rules. Make sure the omega scents you're exposed to are reputable. You might not be able to scent match after that dark bond, but it doesn't mean you can't find a good fit."

Ah.

This was his play?

He handed me a card covered in the scents of a dozen unbonded omegas, in hopes that… what? I would be drawn to one of them?

I took it without flinching, knowing I was going to have to burn it (and likely my entire hand) if I didn't want Shatter to start digging me a grave beside Dusk's tonight.

"Not a bad idea," I said.

"It would get their minds off of her—and this foolish vendetta. Think about it. Dusk strikes me as the primal kind. Get him another omega, and he'll forget all about her and this stupid… competition." He eyed me. "Claim a little dignity back."

"Dignity?" I asked, eyebrows shooting up.

He cleared his throat. "It might be hard to swallow, but everyone can see it, Kingsman. Those alphas claimed my scent match and ran rampant with your money. Time to leash them."

My blood flashed with rage for the briefest second.

The image of the first time I'd ever seen Dusk and Umbra. Gaunt and beaten down. Starved, white outfits stained in blood. Violated over and over by experiment after experiment. Nothing more than animals to those who ran the facility.

"If you take the power back, then we can come to a proper arrangement. I can see you want this nightmare over just as much as I do. I must say, learning that your pack forged marriage papers…" Flynn's jaw clenched. "You understand. She is ours. That *is* an insult."

I got to my feet with a nod, knowing I would get nothing more from this conversation, but that every moment I stayed, I risked cracking and snapping him in two.

"I understand," I told him. "I'll speak to Dusk and do what I can. But in the meantime, no violence. There's been quite enough. I would like to facilitate this arrangement, so she goes to you the right way. I might be late to this, but that's my pack's bite on her neck. It didn't sit well when your hired thug tried to… intervene."

I hoped that would make him think twice about sending Mord. My job, after all, was to buy us time. Flynn's jaw was clenched, but he nodded.

"Oh—Kingsman," Flynn said as I was turning away.

"Yeh?"

He was frowning. "She will *accept* the princess bond, won't she?"

I could almost see the pain on his face at being forced to ask such a humiliating question—whether a gold pack omega would be willing to accept the most valuable bite he could possibly offer. And finally, after all of this conversation, he'd circled back around to it, if only because it was his last and final obstacle. What a terrible inconvenience, Shatter's autonomy was, to an alpha like Flynn Lincoln.

"That," I said with perhaps my only honest smile of the night, "is a good question. But I'm afraid I can predict her behaviour about as well as I can predict Dusk's."

CHAPTER 16

Ransom

I wandered back to the apartments with a nasty taste in my mouth. Worth it, though. I'd done my job—a job I owed my pack after how far Dusk and Umbra had brought us while I was sick.

Flynn was appeased. He believed he had a mole working for him, and we could only hope that would slow him down.

But I'd also seen the other side of him. The arrogant monster who saw Shatter—who saw *my wife*—as nothing more than a means to an end.

As his property.

A notification popped up on my phone, and rage dissolved for surprise. "Shatter Kingsman tagged you in a post." I tapped on it, frowning.

Last I checked, she could barely make her phone function, let alone figure out social media posts. Not that it mattered; she only had Dusk, Umbra, Decebal, Roxy, and me added, and her profile was set to private.

"Ransom. Can you come to my nest tonight, please?"

I read it a few times, frowning as a comment popped up on it.

"Just you," she added.

Ah.

I think my sweet omega thought this was the group chat.

Grinning, I tapped out a reply. *"Yes, ma'am,"* just as a crying emoji popped up from Umbra on the *"just you"* comment. As I watched, a laughing emoji joined it with Decebal's name attached. My phone buzzed, and I saw the old group chat we had with Decebal that didn't involve Shatter.

Dusk: mute her, prick

Decebal: Nah.

Decebal: This is hilarious.

Decebal: watching your omega cock block you in real time

Snorting, I shut my phone off, hurrying up the stairs to the apartment. I loved how just knowing she wanted me around could shift my mood.

When I entered the nest, it was to find the lights dimmed and Shatter waiting on her bed, legs crossed as she picked through a textbook by the warm light.

"It worked." Her eyes were bright as she looked up at me. "I'm getting the hang of the group chat thing."

"Uhh…" Right. I opened my mouth to explain it to her, but she was barrelling on, a smile on her face.

"I thought we could have some *us* time."

"I would like that," I said, sitting down beside her as she closed the textbook and shifted to place it on her bedside table.

I froze, all intentions of group chat discussions vanishing from my brain as I got a flash of lace beneath her gown as she shifted closer.

"Ransom," she whispered.

"Yes."

"You're going to tell me everything he said, right?" she asked.

"He?" I asked, a little dazed.

"Flynn."

"Oh…" Shit. "Little Reaper, I can promise you don't want all the details…" I trailed off as she shrugged the silken robe from her shoulders and settled at my side, her wild hair framing pretty golden eyes that blinked up at me expectantly.

"I know you want to protect me," she said. "But I can handle it. I promise. I need to know everything."

I sighed, my mind trying to fully process the request as she fiddled with her gown. It kept flashing open, giving me glimpses of that beautiful body beneath. I saw the way black lace pressed against her breasts, and how her nightshade scent spiked with lust in the air around her was sinful.

"I could…" I suppose. I knew she was strong. "After? I want to enjoy an evening with my wife first," I said.

She beamed, eyes bright as she straddled me, drawing her lips to mine as the silk parted for me completely.

"God, I love you, Shatter," I breathed.

She was my angel, turning darkness to light in the blink of an eye. Her delicate hands wove around my waist as she kissed down my neck, to my chest, something insistent in the way she tugged on my belt.

But then she went absolutely still in my arms. Through the bond, terror spiked, and all my instincts went on full alert.

"What?" I growled.

"Ransom!" Her voice was weak.

"*What*, Shatter?"

She gripped me, face ashen, but her hand was still at my waist, she was tugging—

Her sharp whine of shock sent my aura flaring, and she was in my arms in a second as I jumped to my feet, holding her close, eyes sweeping the room.

"What is it?"

She clutched me like a koala, eyes wide and fixed on the bed. My blood pounded in my ears as I stepped back.

Holy hell, *what was it?*

"What's happening?" Umbra asked as he and Dusk piled in at the doorway. Shatter was shaking, crumpling against me with a wail.

Then I saw it.

"Oh."

Shit.

"No, no. It was Flynn—" I made for the little card that was lying on the covers—a business card marked with a dozen scents of unbonded omegas, but Shatter's nails dug in and her wail of distress rose in the air.

I'd brought it into her nest.

Into her fucking nest—totally blinded by the idea that she wanted me in here alone.

"I need it *gone*!" I'd never heard her more panicked. "Get rid of it."

"What?" Dusk sounded urgent as he stared at the bed, but it was Umbra who caught on quickest.

"Don't worry, Nightshade, I've got it." He was tugging off his shirt and edging toward the blankets. Shatter wailed again, clutching me tighter.

As if he was going for a spider, Umbra dove for it, scooping it up in his shirt and hurrying it from the room without another word.

Dusk cleared his throat, blinking and clearly trying to conjure the level of seriousness Umbra had just managed. "I will, uh… burn the sheets," he said. "You should probably—"

We all jumped at a loud *bang!* Again, instincts flared at the gunshot from the hallway.

Wait.

Had Umbra just—?

With a groan, Dusk buried his head in his hands. Shatter, on the other hand, relaxed instantly, clambering down from where I held her, her breathing easing like the threat had passed.

"Thank God for Umbra," she muttered, nodding to herself, now looking extremely pleased.

Dusk stared at her in a moment of incredulity, then fixed his face. "*I* will deal with the people about to appear at our door, asking why we discharged a firearm in student apartments." He glared at me. "*You* go shower."

He grabbed the bedding with unnecessary aggression and stalked from the nest.

"Shower…?" Shatter repeated it like a question. "Yes. Yes." She was already shoving me desperately toward the bathroom.

Fifteen minutes, I was instructed to stand beneath scalding water, until Shatter nodded approvingly and allowed me out. I wrapped a towel around myself as my clothing was now gone—likely in the same bonfire Dusk was setting for the blankets.

"I'm so sorry," I breathed, drawing her close.

She sank against me, now in only lace, since the silk she'd been wearing over the top had been contaminated.

"It's okay. I know you only had it because you were out with Flynn." She nodded. "You were protecting me." She drew me into a kiss. "I know you didn't mean it."

"You're going to have to, uh… get Umbra in here. He was the heroic one and all—"

"I can see Umbra tomorrow," she said. "I want a night with you."

"O-okay."

She was so fucking beautiful and mesmerising…

I set us back down on the bed (Dusk had replaced the sheets) and drew her close. She did seem to have moved past it.

"And, uh… do you think you can do something else for me?" she asked. "But you can't tell Dusk."

I dragged my gaze back up to her eyes. "What's that?"

"I need new clothes."

"New clothes?" I asked.

"Dusk got me all of mine." She pouted. "I want some from you."

I grinned, my grip digging into her hips and teeth drawing along her neck to the sexiest little moan. "Are you asking me to help you be more of a brat?"

Her golden eyes flashed in the dim light as she peered up at me through thick lashes. "If I was?"

I snorted. "If it gets me shows like the other morning, I'll help you be the biggest brat in the world."

Her touch was enough to unwind all the stress that had been pulled tight in the last few hours. I let out a low, possessive growl at the feeling of her soft lips against my skin.

If she wanted clothes, I'd buy her an entire store.

"And, Ransom?" she asked.

"Yes, Little Reaper?" Her hand was trailing lower, easily finding how hard I was beneath the covers.

"A new pair of shoes?" she said.

"Shoes?"

"Mm-hmm."

"Is there a particular shoe type you want?"

"No. But I do like the boots. They're comfy."

"All right. I'll get you boots," I growled. "Anything my sweet wife wants." I flipped us, so I was over her, already dreaming of all the ways I was about to claim her as a delighted purr rumbled to life in her chest.

CHAPTER 17

Shatter

It had worked.

I had my list, and it had totally worked. Ransom was getting me new boots. And after bringing me tea first thing this morning, he'd told me everything Flynn had said.

And I'd had a whole beautiful, amazing, sexy night with him. We'd fucked way too late for a school night, and I'd fallen asleep knotted to one of my favourite alphas in the whole world.

I loved him so much, and now I got to protect him and fuck him all at once. It wasn't that I enjoyed not being totally honest (actually, that made me a bit nervous), but this was life and death. Plus, the orgasms had been honest.

Umbra was in the kitchen, cooking breakfast, when Ransom carried me in like a princess.

He set me down, and I wound my arms around Umbra's waist, delighted at his low purr as he flipped a pancake. "You recover?" he asked.

"Mm-hmm," I replied. "You saved the day."

"Were they pissed?" Ransom was asking Dusk as Umbra poured me a cup of orange juice.

"Three fines from the board," Dusk said mildly.

"Three?" Ransom asked.

"For the discharge of a weapon and setting a bonfire on the school grounds."

"That's two."

Dusk grinned. "Third was a bonus for receiving two in one night. *'Blatant disregard for school rules and wasting faculty time.'*"

"But the card is dead, right?" I whispered to Umbra—I still wasn't talking to Dusk—as I clutched my orange juice close.

"Smithereens," he said, humming happily as he served up the pancakes and removed his apron.

CHAPTER 18

Umbra

Shatter had fallen asleep, her arms on the kitchen counter. Ransom was snoring on the couch.

She hadn't stopped studying at all. Not since everything we'd discovered, and she was still burning the candle at both ends to find a solution for our pack.

Our perfect omega.

Ever so gently, I picked her up in my arms, holding her head against my chest. She stirred, but a low purr rumbled to life in my chest and she curled up tighter, a low, contented sound slipping from her.

She'd said she wanted to spend the night with me, so I carried her to my room instead of the nest. I was okay with sleepy omega cuddles; that was more than enough for me.

She woke when I set her gently on the bed. "Oh…" She blinked up at me, then glanced around. "I didn't mean to fall asleep."

"I don't mind."

"No, no, actually, I found you something."

"You did?"

"Yes. There was this thing that popped up on my phone… a cooking class, but it's videos online."

I perked up. "Was there?"

"Here…" She pulled out her phone. "I left it on the page because I didn't know how to save it." Checking the time, she said, "It's not that late. We could watch it together."

I smiled, finding an old laptop and pulling up the page she'd found, then I drew her against me as the cooking program began to play. It was hard to ignore that her nightgown had slipped open, and I was rewarded with a lovely view of black lace and rich tan skin beneath.

The cooking video she'd chosen was called *Mastering Beef Wellington: A Step-by-Step Guide.*

Good.

I'd like to be a beef Wellington master (whatever a Wellington was).

"Thank you for dealing with those horrible omega scents," she whispered as the tutorial began.

"Of course, Little Nightshade," I said, humming happily as she clung to me tighter.

Definitely worth the fine of discharging a firearm.

The video rolled and I paid close attention.

We were just at the part where the chef was showing exactly how fine I needed to chop the chestnut mushrooms and shallots. In a hot pan, they said to—

I jumped.

Shatter was hugging my arm, and her teeth had grazed my skin. My cock jumped to attention, as it should, at the feel of her teeth on my flesh.

"It's okay, you can keep watching," she said, something strange in her voice, as if she were keeping something from me.

I eyed her curiously as she lowered herself between my legs, easily freeing my length and grasping it in her dainty hands. I could watch that all day. I was totally torn between the tutorial and the way she drew her tongue up my shaft, perfect and slow.

Fuck.

Video.

I blinked back at it as they discussed wrapping the beef.

The moment my eyes drifted from her, I felt her lips press to the tip of my cock, taking me in.

I looked back to her. "Are you trying to school me in how difficult it is to study while someone's being distracting?"

She drew her lips from the tip, an indignant expression on her face as she narrowed her eyes at me. "So what if I was?"

"Well"—I brushed my thumb along her cheek, and the low, earthy note of her nightshade scent became frenzied with lust—"I'd say I need a really solid education to get where you're coming from."

Fuck, it was hot, seeing her fist close around my cock like that.

Her lips returned to the tip, and I groaned as she took my length in her mouth. She was way too good at this, and her golden eyes were molten with feverish lust.

"… around the beef, twisting the ends of the cling film to secure. Chill this in the fridge to ensure it holds its shape…"

Right.

Uh. I did need to be paying attention to how that wrapping looked. I glanced between her and the screen. She didn't deserve anything less than a Wellington master.

This *was* a test.

Hmm.

I nudged the laptop closer to my legs so I could see them both easier, then felt a little spike of heat in my veins as her expression flashed with derision.

"Keep going, Nightshade," I told her as she looked around to stop. "I want to see you fuck your tight little throat like you do for Dusk."

She'd told me she liked it when I used the bond, anyway. Plus, she did say I needed a proper lesson.

How could I argue with that?

The hand not closed tightly around my swelling knot dug into my thigh as she took me all the way. I did love how submissive she was. Her expression mixed brattiness and lust as she was forced to keep taking me down, and I heard the low growl in her chest as my eyes flicked between her and the laptop screen.

"This is a good lesson," I told her, my hand tangling in her hair as I felt myself reaching my limit.

Nah.

Not yet, I wasn't ready.

I halted her movement, my fist in her hair. "I want to see you impale yourself on my cock, Nightshade."

She drew back, releasing my shaft with her fist, then crawled forward, adjusting the lace of her panties so she could take me.

"Slow, beautiful."

I wanted to watch every moment of it.

She didn't disappoint, biting her lip with the cutest frown as she sank over me, a cute mewl in her chest as she settled right above my knot.

"Good girl." I dragged her back into an arch and leaned forward, easily nudging her lacy bra out of the way and catching her nipple in my teeth. She moaned, clutching me desperately. "I want you to fuck me real good and slow," I told her, releasing her hair and leaning back.

She adjusted her position for maximum control and started to slide up and down over me so beautifully. I could see the slick glistening on my length from how turned on she was.

"A little faster."

The video was now discussing the oven temperature. I think I was taking it in, even as she was making the hottest little noises every time she sank to the base of my cock.

Yup.

I was in heaven as her dark nightshade scent flooded my room, enough to linger in here all week.

Then I heard something on the tutorial and frowned.

"Wait—why do I have to chill it again?" I asked. "Didn't it just chill?" I wish they would explain shit like that.

I reached for the laptop to rewind it, but Shatter, it seemed, didn't agree with my concern. She let out a hiss of fury, and the next thing I knew, my laptop was slammed shut before it sailed across the room, exploding against my wall.

Heh.

Of course, I'd seen something like that coming a mile off. I'd dug out a very old laptop that was on its last legs, anyway, but she didn't need to know that.

Shatter fixed her gaze on me as she continued, this time a lot more aggressively than before, and she was clenching down on me so goddamned tight.

There it was.

I'd wanted to be angry-fucked since the moment I'd seen her climbing the walls with rage when she'd found out about the marriage.

Shatter was delivering, her nails digging into my pecs as she dragged her tight little cunt over my length until her own eyes rolled back.

"Knot yourself," I told her. "Go slow."

It was so hot, watching her slowly lower herself over my knot, shaking with the orgasm still in her veins.

When she was locked onto me at last, I took her hips, rutting her good until she finished again as I spilled my seed deep into her.

"I love you, Little Nightshade," I breathed. With her still locked over my knot, I drew Shatter close, letting her nuzzle close as my happy purr rumbled to life in my chest. When we were like this, it was almost possible to forget everything else.

And besides, I could become a beef Wellington master another day.

CHAPTER 19

Shatter

"Shatter."

I spun, jumping out of my skin at the sound of Roxy's voice. I was in the parking lot, and Roxy was hurrying toward me, wearing a cream winter coat with a bag slung over her shoulder.

"Hi!" I said.

"Where are you going?" she asked, surprised.

"Nowhere."

Roxy frowned, eyes narrowing. "You're lying."

"I'm not." My voice was far too high pitched.

Dammit.

It was Saturday morning, and I was sneaking out. It was the culmination of all of my plans. And (partly) the reason I'd been banging my alphas every night this week. Except Dusk, who was banned from my nest for the time being. But if they weren't so worn out, there would be no way for me to have snuck out with the new boots Ransom had gifted me last night.

"Where are your alphas?" she asked.

"I got new shoes, and I was going to try them out…" I trailed off pathetically.

"Well. I'm coming. There's a really nice coffee shop that just opened—"

"You can't," I said quickly, edging back. "But I'll be back to study later."

Roxy's eyes narrowed even further, then she was tucking her phone into her bag and striding after me.

"Oh. No, really. You can't." *Shit.* I glanced around. I was sure I didn't have much time to get away before one of them noticed I was gone. "I mean. You won't have fun."

"I don't care."

Oh bother. How could I get rid of her?

"It involves… bussing. And a lot of walking," I said. Not a lie.

I'd mapped out my entire route before my phone had broken again.

"You're leaving campus?" she asked, but I covered her mouth instantly.

"Shh!" There was no way I was getting rid of her. I could see it in her eyes. "You can't tell anyone."

"Your pack doesn't know?" she asked when I finally removed my hand.

"It's top secret," I whispered.

"But the Lincoln alphas are after you—you said Dusk was worried it wasn't safe."

"If you come, you have to keep everything secret."

"My lips are sealed," she said.

"And you have to turn off your phone." I'd looked it up on the internet, and apparently, if they were switched off, it was harder to track them.

Roxy was already tugging out her phone. "Done. But we aren't bussing anywhere. I *have* a car."

I chewed on my lip, considering that. "Well…" That did sound better.

"Do you know the address?" she asked, dragging me to where she was parked.

"Yes. It was going to take about four hours on transit, but it shouldn't be as long to drive."

"I'm surprised you got away at all. They're like barnacles," Roxy said as I climbed into the passenger seat of her little blue car. I smiled as I spotted a Christmas tree dangling from the rear-view mirror.

"Oh. It was a lot of work. I had to make them *really* tired—and I still almost woke Umbra."

Roxy snorted as she turned on the engine. "Make them really tired?" she asked, giving me a side-eye. "Is that why you haven't been available for studying evenings this week?"

"Maybe."

Well, that, and I'd been collecting all I needed to know for this trip. I had a folder in my bag with everything important. I tugged out the paper with the address and handed it to her.

"I did a great job," I said smugly as Roxy copied it into the GPS.

"And you're sure Dusk doesn't have some crazy way of tracking you?" she asked.

"Boots!" I declared, showing her my fresh new ones. "But I got Ransom to buy me new ones. The seduction thing is really…"

I trailed off at the look on Roxy's face.

Oh.

I think she'd been joking.

She snorted. "I suppose I really shouldn't be surprised."

This trip ended up being a lot more fun than I'd expected, thanks to Roxy. Otherwise, I'd have been a big ball of worry for the entire bus ride.

"Why a bus and not a taxi?" Roxy asked me as we turned onto a country road that marked the last stretch. "It's not like the pack doesn't have the money."

"Buses are safer, I think," I said. "Once, a taxi driver kicked me out in the middle of nowhere because of my scent…" My blockers had worn off accidentally. "I had to walk for a really long time to find a bus."

Roxy frowned. "That's… horrible."

After I'd left the estate, I'd been alone for months. It had probably been the loneliest time of my whole life, waiting for the start of term, when I knew I'd reach my mates.

Shoving back the thought, I shrugged stiffly. "I just stuck with public transit after. It's always a bit easier to lie low in crowds…" Plus, the pretty beta I'd stolen the suitcase from had also had a city-wide transit pass.

I realised Roxy had given me a side-eye the way she often did when I brought up stuff like that.

"It's better now. The bite balanced my scent," I said reassuringly.

I'd spent most of that time hiding out and scouting Rookwood Academy. I'd avoided interacting with people, but sometimes, I'd bus back and forth on my favourite routes when I was lonely. Those were always the quiet residential routes, with fewer passengers who were mostly elderly. Elderly people often didn't have as sharp a sense of smell, and they weren't as quick, so even if I did have a blocker mishap, I would be much more likely to be safe.

Plus, there had been one lady I'd seen a few times, and she always offered me bran cookies. I would take them back to the little attic I was hiding in at the time and make them last all week, pretending I had a grandma who'd baked them just for me.

My nerves grew as the GPS told us we were nearing our destination. But it wasn't until Roxy pulled up the long gravel driveway of the great estate that my anxiety really hit.

The gates were open, though that wasn't uncommon. This place was shielded by its isolation from the rest of the world more than anything.

"What is this place?" she asked, peering out at the sprawling gardens and perfectly trimmed lawns. It was late fall, and autumn leaves covered glistening grass, leaving many of the beautiful trees bare.

"It's where I used to live," I said quietly. It was the place that might offer me answers.

We got out of Roxy's car, heading up the stone steps to the huge brickwork arch, framing a large, dark wood door. Taking a deep breath, I lifted the heavy knocker.

The man who answered was everything I remembered. He wore the burgundy suit I'd seen so often, right down to the patch on the breast I'd watched Aunty Lauren sew on one day while we watched a movie together. His hair was more salt than pepper, but otherwise, he was the same.

"Shatter?" His eyes went wide as he took me in. "You're…" He gathered himself. "What are you doing here?"

"Uncle." I took a breath, hugging my bag close to my chest. This was it. The last shot I had at answers—answers no one else could give. "I need your help."

CHAPTER 20

Umbra

A note.

A fucking note was all she'd left.

A note and her goddamned boots with the tracker Dusk had set up.

Without the note, I think I would have lost my mind. Shatter had been planning way too well for this, though, because Decebal couldn't trace her phone, either, which meant it was switched off.

Instead, I scoured the campus until I got Mord in my sights at least once, and that was the only thing that settled my nerves. That, and the solution I knew I needed to commit to today.

Dusk was planning protection from the Lincoln pack and Mord, and Ransom was helping to keep them at bay. Shatter had studied her books, trying to come up with any answers to free us of the Lincoln pack.

But I knew there was another answer, and when we got her back today, I wouldn't risk losing her again.

I didn't need to plan or study. I wasn't foolish enough to think I'd ever catch up on Arkology enough to be useful in that. I could join Dusk and Ransom on the layers and layers of plans, but I didn't have to.

My answer was clear as day.

Shatter was so incredible. I believed in her—I truly did. With time, she would come up with the most amazing solution. Something to save us all. But the truth was, I don't think she had the time we hoped for, because I could feel this sickness worsening, faster and faster with every day. Jaws slowly closing shut.

I sat on the side of my bed, opening my drawer and pulling out the knife, setting it on the side table. Then, for luck, I added the other things from within.

It was a strange assortment of things that made up who I was, and I couldn't remember the origins of two of the three.

Two double-sided coins. Double heads and double tails.

A trick deck.

My knife.

The knife, strangely enough, was the most personal because I knew why it was here. I remembered the first time I'd picked it up, drawing it across flesh to discover a source of relief. The only one I'd ever found until Shatter.

I pictured her sitting beside me. In my head, she curled her cute, delicate fingers around my wrist, holding me steady as I picked up my knife from the bedside table.

Carefully, I turned it in my hand as I reached out within my pack bond. This time, not toward my brothers or even Shatter.

Instead, I reached in a different direction. In the darkness, I brushed up against something. Something I shouldn't be able to touch. It was deadly, and upon my contact, I felt it tug at me, drawing me in like a black hole.

My fingers gripped the knife like a safety, my stomach churning violently. It shook in my grip as I lifted it, ready to use it if I needed to return.

"Umbra," Shatter whispered.

She was here, *remember*?

She wasn't, but she was. She *would* be if I asked, and because of that, I could imagine just what she'd say. She'd tug me to face her with those golden eyes holding mine, her nightshade scent stilling my fear. *"Come back to me."*

My omega.

My wife.

I lowered the knife, holding those beautiful eyes in my mind's eye, and let her be the lantern that led me back. With her, I managed to withdraw, already feeling the edges of my aura and sanity unravelling just from proximity. I had the confirmation I needed, but if I ever did this again, she couldn't be there.

There would be no lantern. No turning back.

I took a breath, steadying myself as I set the knife back down on the side table.

I hadn't needed it. Just her.

I *would* protect her.

No matter what happened, she would be safe. Dusk was the first line of defence, but I was the last.

Shatter

"What is it I can help you with?"

Uncle sat behind his desk in a formal posture with fingers clasped, as calm as ever, yet there was a look on his face that hadn't gone away since the first moment he'd laid eyes on me.

I was sure he'd believed I was dead.

I was still reeling from returning to this place, a thousand memories flooding back. Memories that weren't memories, but instead, an unidentifiable smudge of time.

A nightmare.

And everything in this place was the same.

From the pristine cream foyer, marble floor, and giant crystal chandelier hanging overhead, to the spiral staircase that led up to his office. In here, it still smelled faintly of his autumn scent. The bookshelves were the same, and I sat on one of his comfy, oversized reclining chairs that were so familiar to me.

The smell of a wood-burning fire permeated the room, his hearth alight.

Roxy was waiting downstairs in the foyer, being the best friend in the world and never asking a question—not even at the shock on Uncle's face as he'd caught sight of the dark bond on my neck.

"I need to know what happened in the facility I came from before the Institute took over."

"That wasn't anything I was involved with," he said, his face paling ever so slightly.

"You must know something about it."

He took his time replying to that, considering me. "If I *did* know anything, I would be wise to keep quiet about it. The people involved with those sorts of—"

"My mates." I took a breath, daring myself on and praying I wasn't making a huge mistake. "My mates were in those trials."

Uncle froze, eyes widening. "You claimed your mates were—"

"The Lincoln pack. I… I thought they were. I need your help, and for that, I'm going to tell you some things." I anxiously drew out the papers I'd brought. I could memorise lines like this easily, but when I was nervous… well, it was better to have it here. "You can't tell *anyone* else—and you have to swear you won't or I'll… I'll tell the Institute that you lied to them about me. I saw my files," I pushed on, not daring to look up at him. "You told them that I died in your care."

It was something that had surprised me in the file that Dusk had been given by Decebal, the one about me—though I'd dared not bring that particular piece.

"I rather thought you might be grateful," Uncle said. "The Institute is relentless. There was no other way to truly guarantee your freedom."

I swallowed, fingers holding the files tight.

It wasn't the only thing he had done. I'd known before I left, something I'd been told by Aunty Lauren, but scouring his letters to the Institute had confirmed it.

He'd never once given them my chosen name.

To them, I was Subject One, and I had never been anything else.

And he was right. Now, I was going to use that against him, but I didn't have a choice.

"If they find out you lied about that, you'll be in huge trouble. I-I looked it up." I lifted the file I was holding, trying to keep my voice steady. "They classified me as a… Phantom Anomaly." I worked to stop my words from tripping over themselves. "It says, 'Impeding the Institute's efforts in the surveillance, apprehension, or detention of entities of a Phantom Anomaly classification or higher is considered a national security threat, punishable by…'" I cleared my throat, pushing on. "'By indefinite confinement in a secure facility, as per Article 42, Subsection 3C of the Civic Safety and Unknown Arkologic Entities Act, enforced by the Containment and Supervision of Biohazardous Entities branch of the GPRE.'"

I finished in a rush, and there was a long silence as I set the paper down, daring to look back up at him.

He was fixing me with an unreadable expression that made my skin crawl. "Punishable by indefinite confinement in a secure facility… sounds… really… really bad," I said weakly.

"Yet, to report me, you will undo the safeties I put in place for *you*."

"My… my pack is in trouble," I whispered. "If I don't help them, they could die."

"Your *pack*?" he asked. "Are you referring to the alphas who dark bonded you?"

I straightened, holding his gaze furiously. "I *asked* for the bond." My voice was hoarse. "I love them, and I won't leave without your help."

He leaned back in his seat, considering that, and he was a lot less surprised than I'd imagined he would be. I think, perhaps, something even softened in his eyes. I rarely saw that for anyone other than Aunty Lauren.

More seconds ticked by, and I nervously shifted the stack of papers, trying not to break his eye contact.

"I was worried that when she saw that bite, she would… she would… well, she would never forgive me. She already doesn't."

"Aunty?" I asked, voice hoarse. "She's here?"

"She's away for the weekend. But I hope that she will be able to see you again, perhaps when this matter is dealt with. Especially if there's a chance that the bond on your neck isn't as dire as it looks. I don't think… Well, she was so very worried when you left. The thought of you becoming bonded against your will gave her nightmares. Both…" He cleared his throat. "Both of us."

I frowned, somewhat taken aback by that admission.

"I rather thought you were here for sanctuary," he added.

"From… *them*?" I asked, fingers touching Dusk's bite.

"Yes."

I blinked at that. Mostly because, even believing that, he'd let me in. I'd run from him after he'd taken me in. He'd risked a lot to protect me, and still, he was prepared to help if it were a pack of alphas who had put an unwanted bond on my neck.

"She loves you, Shatter. I hope you know that. I… I have been far from perfect, but I do want to see you find happiness."

"My pack," I said, seizing that. "I need to protect them. It's the reason I'm here, and I don't think anyone else has answers."

He nodded.

"Well. I admit a reasonable amount of curiosity. I don't know a great deal about what happened at the facility before, but in the community, breakthroughs do have a way of spreading—no matter how much the Institute wished they didn't."

"Do you know what they were trying to do?"

"Not explicitly, though one can draw some conclusions with the right puzzle pieces."

"What puzzle pieces?" I asked.

I knew Umbra and Dusk had tried to overturn every stone for those answers about what the experiments were trying to accomplish.

"I've been in this line of work for a long time. The Arkologists they arrested were old colleagues, some of whom I'd even studied with. I knew their drives—their obsessions. And only *obsession* could push one of our own to go to such… unethical lengths for answers."

I nodded. "The Lincoln pack was part of it."

His eyebrows rose. "The pack I sponsored—the alphas you claimed were your mates—were a part of those trials?" he asked.

I nodded. "Clients helping fund the… the studies."

"Now that," he murmured, "is rather disturbing. I assume one or more of them—"

"Flynn," I said. "Flynn has aura sickness."

He nodded, considering that. "That explains their interest in Arkology. Did they think they could, perhaps, contribute to the solution themselves? Rather arrogant, but then that isn't so uncommon in this field… I heard rumours, but tell me, did they find a cure?"

I considered that. This information was dangerous to give away. If it got around, more Arkologists may pick it up and ruin more lives.

Yet, I didn't think Uncle was like that.

The man before me, Dr. Eugene Howard, was the most ideal candidate for the research they'd been attempting with me, which was focused on reversing gold pack status. He'd fielded many studies on gold pack omegas. Not only that, it was one of the most well-funded research projects ever undertaken.

But he'd left.

"Why did you quit the research project I was in?" I asked.

He frowned. "The first strike was the incident with you. But the investigation that followed also revealed some unfortunate truths about the subjects we were to research. I learned that not all of them were gold pack when they arrived. Some were held for months and denied the injection—*forced* to become gold pack. It seems there were a few involved that were tracking data of their own and wished to know if the outcome of the experiments would be affected by whether an omega chose golden eyes or had the decision taken from them."

"Do… you think it would have?" I asked, curious about that.

Uncle shrugged. "An omega's choice is never insignificant, but I do not think the answer to that was worth tainting the research with ethical issues—not an answer any true Arkologist knows, anyway."

"What does that mean?" I asked.

"There are no loopholes in Arkology," he said. "Everything comes around with bites and bonds."

I was silent for a moment, thinking. "So, you left the study because of the ethics?"

"I'm not perfect, Shatter. You know that. Lauren does, too, but when it comes to my work, I want a legacy I can die peacefully with."

I nodded, circling back to his original question: Were the studies successful?

"They found a… fix in those trials," I said. "But not a cure."

A cure *wasn't* what Umbra was to Flynn. The tainted bond between their pack had temporarily halted the effects of Flynn's aura sickness, but that was all.

"A fix?" Uncle asked. "Of what nature?"

"Aura contracting—as far as I can understand."

"Pack bonds?" he asked curiously. Aura contracts were known as one of the more powerful energies in Arkology, but they were also the most rigid and almost impossible to influence outside of their natural course.

They were, in essence, contracts between alpha and omega, alpha and pack, or pack and pack—essentially, the forces behind binding us together.

The formation of alpha-centric packs—such as Dusk, Umbra, and Ransom being in a bond—was a form of aura contracting. It was a phenomenon that occurred when alphas took Syvex, the bonding drug, and accepted a pack with one another. Another was when an omega accepted a bite into a pack. Even the bond on my neck was a form of aura contracting, even though dark bonds weren't natural.

Most importantly, all aura contracts followed similar laws, and the connection between my pack and the Lincoln pack was the same. Or so I believed.

"Yes," I said. "But not any aura contract I've ever seen or heard of."

He tilted his head. "How does that work?"

"From what I can tell, they tried to manufacture alpha-to-alpha contracting in a similar way to how dark bonds work."

Uncle froze, eyes widening. "That is a dangerous game…"

He was right. It wasn't only a volatile energy source to work with—evidenced by the many alphas who had died in that facility—but it was one of the most heinous crimes within Arkology. "To mess with a force as restricted as dark bonds… And… it worked?" He looked concerned.

"In a way."

"How?"

"The pack with aura sickness connected to the other—my pack."

"Like a dark bond?"

"Not exactly." I'd thought about this. "It did require consent from the pack lead, unlike a dark bond. But the nature of the connection between pack and pack is… parasitical."

"So, they used the auras from one pack in order to stabilise the other?"

"Yes," I said. "We think they needed alphas with extremely powerful auras, and the bond is now slowly devouring the host. It's not stable."

"I very much doubt it is," he murmured, scratching his chin. "What's extraordinary—and extremely dangerous—is that they've done something I haven't heard of in a long time. In fact, tampering with what the Institute calls *established Arkologic forces,* which include all known aura contracts, is one of the greatest crimes you can commit—it can result in the death penalty. The last time we tampered with those forces, we were left with an abomination we've never rid ourselves of." His eyes slid, for a moment, to the bond on my neck. It was a grim piece of ancient Arkological history.

Dark bonds weren't natural, and they had never been intended, either. Arkologists had intended to form the princess bond in order to further incentivise alpha and omega packs. In the end, they were successful.

But nature balanced out; with the stable formation of the princess bond came its equal and opposite, and dark bonds had joined the ranks of nature's law.

"Still," Uncle went on, "it doesn't seem they've found success on a level that will change the foundation of pack bonds. It does explain why it was kept so quiet. Disturbing these energies may violate international law, but that hasn't stopped governments and terrorist groups over the centuries. Mother nature isn't just vengeful—she's stubborn. Most attempts result in failure and death, and continued experimentation of this kind will often see a massive decline in alpha-omega populations. Even the most desperate countries don't try it. They're too afraid that their own populations will dwindle if they do."

"But this parasitical bond they created—"

"Does not sound near stable enough to even begin to seep into natural Arkologic forces. But that—while good news for the world—does not mean good news for you."

"If it's unstable, then might there be a way to break it?"

"Not that I would risk," he said. "An unstable aura contract is more likely to result in self-destruction. When tampered with, auras can turn on their own hosts."

My blood ran cold. "That's… what is happening to them."

"If I were to make my best guess, the connection was created by the sick aura. A waning aura is energy breaking down, and until it dies, it seeks healing. That, most likely, is where they found an opening."

"You're saying the contract was built around the sickness?"

"Most likely."

"If that was the case, then if the aura was healed… would that sever the connection?"

I think I knew the answer he would give, yet I had to ask.

Uncle considered me carefully but, to my relief, didn't address the elephant in the room. That the only true known cure to aura sickness was a princess bond with a scent match.

Instead, he nodded. "If the connection was established via the sickness, then curing it would sever the connection."

I looked back down at the papers in my hand.

"You said you were their scent match," Uncle said quietly. "I didn't think it was possible after studying your aura. Yet, if you were to cross a pack who had, *somehow*, seen their own share of… unusual experimentation…"

I glanced back up at him, a lump caught in my throat.

"And *if* those alphas were in an impossible bond with another pack…" He trailed off, a frown on his face.

"You… believe me?" I asked, voice small.

"I should have believed you at the start," he replied. "I have seen enough years in this field to know I don't know everything. It was arrogant of me to dismiss you. I'm… I'm sorry I did."

There was a long pause, and I warred with my tears, adjusting the papers on the desk so I could remember where we'd been.

"What of the flip side?" Uncle asked. "How did the victimised pack become a part of this contract?"

I thought back to what Umbra had said. "The pack lead's bond mate died, and the pack should have fragmented. Instead, he says he found something to hold on to, to keep it together."

"So, the pack lead accepted the bond?"

"It sounded like it," I said, then added, "though he didn't know he was accepting it at the time."

"The problem remains that, if the bond required acceptance, and that acceptance was given, that leaves it more stable than if it was forced."

"So, we're back to square one?"

"In a way. If it's stable, that means it's predictable. But it also means you may be beholden to the laws that already exist in order to rid them of it. In this case…"

"They have to give it up…" I swallowed. Flynn had to give up the bond for Umbra and Dusk to be free. "That's… that's unfair."

"Not all contracts are fair."

"What about cleaving? Could the packs separate somehow?"

"Even if I could imagine how to adapt cleaving to such circumstances, I wouldn't recommend it. Playing with the unknown when it comes to these packs and bonds can result in painful deaths. Auras can become untethered or devour their hosts whole."

"So… you're saying… there's no other way."

"I'm sorry, Shatter. I wish I had a better answer for you. But if your pack wishes to rid itself of this bond, the parasite must either give it up, or…" He trailed off, not meeting my eyes.

"Or I have to heal the aura sickness," I said.

The Lincoln pack would never let that bond go—not if it risked their auras. And to heal them, I would have to accept their offer of a princess bond.

I'd come all this way, and still, all paths led to the same place.

CHAPTER 21

Dusk

It wasn't until late in the afternoon that there was a light knock on the door. I dived toward it in an instant, Ransom on my heels.

My heart skipped a beat as I wrenched it open, afraid it wouldn't be her, but—

"Shatter!"

It *was* her.

Relief almost closed my throat as I found guilty golden eyes peering up at me from a mess of honey brown locks. I couldn't move, frozen in absolute silence as she slipped in and let me close the door behind her.

Ransom barrelled past me, grabbing her and drawing her into a hug.

"Fuck, Shatter." His voice was choked.

"I know…" She clutched him, voice rough. "I didn't mean for you to worry."

I didn't take my eyes from her. "Where did you go?"

"Ummm…" She swallowed, extracting herself from Ransom and taking in my expression. She rapped her knuckles anxiously, hunching her shoulders, eyes darting about. "I can't say."

"You…" I trailed off, indignance replacing relief. "You can't say?"

She straightened her back, holding my eyes with shaky defiance. "I *won't* say."

"Shatter." My voice was dangerous as I stepped up to her, catching her chin between my fingers. "You were gone all day. The Lincoln pack is watching us. They want you."

"I… I was with Roxy. I was safe."

Roxy?

Fuck. I knew it. Decebal had tried to get a ping on her phone and got nothing, but it wasn't a guarantee with her devices, so we hadn't been sure.

"You tricked Ransom into slipping out of my tracker—with Mord Sato on your heels like a hound."

"Yes," she said.

"And you won't tell me where you went?"

I could command her to, but there was a stubbornness in her eyes that told me she didn't care how much pain the dark bond would put her through.

In fact, she stepped back, tugging from my grip. She hurried to the table and carefully set her bag down, then crossed to the couch.

My eyebrows shot up as she straightened her skirt, and with about as much dignity as the motion allowed, lowered her torso over the arm of the couch, pressing her cheek to the cushion, back arched.

I pinched the bridge of my nose while Ransom let out a breath that might have been amused.

When I crossed toward her, my gaze fighting the gravitational pull of her sweet ass as she presented like an omega in heat, it was to find one defiant golden eye fixed on me.

Fuck.

I knew to my bones that whatever she'd done today was not something she planned on letting come from her mouth. I was equal parts annoyed and impressed. Or turned on. I wasn't sure.

"Why?" I asked as I stepped up behind her, feeling her shiver as I ran my knuckle along her bare flesh.

"I'm…" She trailed off. "I'm your omega. It's my job to protect my pack, no matter what that means."

I saw Ransom frown.

Where the *hell* had she gone? I'd already realised today that I'd underestimated her. By a lot. I wouldn't do so again.

"And in this case, that means not telling your pack lead?" I asked.

"Y-yes."

"And I suppose Roxy won't be spilling."

"I made her pinky swear."

"And whatever you did today, might it put you in danger?"

She went still, clearly considering that. "N-not more danger than I'm already in."

I frowned. I didn't believe her. If that was the truth, then she wouldn't have snuck away, and she wouldn't be refusing to tell us.

But I wasn't willing to hurt her, not when I didn't think she would cave to a dark bond command, anyway.

It would be fine. I had my own plans with Decebal. Whatever it was she thought she was doing, she wouldn't get there

I would fix this before she could.

And if she thought this was all I'd be doing to discover where she'd been today, she was sorely wrong.

So instead, I stepped back and sank onto the couch. "Come here."

She pushed herself up, and I almost laughed at the little flash of disappointment in her eyes as Ransom dropped down at my side. His face was still drained of colour, and he looked about as shell-shocked as I felt.

Shatter circled the arm of the couch and sank down on my lap, her pretty eyes holding mine. I just tugged her against my chest. She might be the reason my heart was racing in the first place, but she was also the only thing that would slow it. I drew my jaw along her temple because… well, because scent marking her seemed like the natural thing to do right now. "Don't ever do that again," I whispered.

She didn't reply, just squeezed me tighter.

She hadn't even said *sorry*, which meant she was truly committed to whatever it was she'd done.

That was worrying.

"I'm still mad at you," she whispered.

"Does that mean I'm going to keep finding scent marked *gifts* under my pillow in the evenings?" I asked. I'd found the third last night.

She leaned close, her voice a breath in my ear. "It was *your* command," she said. "You told me every time I scent marked something in our home, I was to bring it right into your bedroom."

Ah.

I *had* said that.

"And all the things you feel the need to scent mark these days are knives?" I asked.

"When I've been threatened with divorce, it is where my instincts take me."

I was starting to think that the duration of her vendetta might be solely driven by my divorce comment.

She drew back, clambering over to Ransom so she could give him a hug.

"You tricked me with the new boots," he murmured.

"I'm sorry I wasn't honest about that," she said, and I saw the first sign of true guilt in her eyes.

"Is that what that night was—"

Ransom cut off as she pressed a finger to his lips with a small shake of her head, and she leaned up, pressing her lips to his briefly before pulling him into an even tighter hug. "Only like… ten percent," she whispered.

Ransom shut his eyes, wrapping his arms around her.

The damned boots.

I'd almost lost it when I'd learned Ransom had got her new ones, but he hadn't known, and he didn't need to feel worse.

I heard a low purr in his chest as he drew her close.

I felt my own little flash of jealousy, which was followed by a wave of smugness from her in the bond. Ransom gave her a nip on the neck and flashed his canines at me.

Back to normal, then. "You and Umbra are enjoying this a bit too much," I murmured.

"Where *is* Umbra?" Shatter asked as she drew back from Ransom, frowning.

Uh. Shit. I'd just assumed he'd feel our relief through the bond and come out. "He's up in his room. Spent the morning looking for Mord. When we spotted him, we came back here."

And felt fucking useless all day while our omega was gone. It would be a while before I recovered from today.

"There's…" Her brows knitted together as she cocked her head. "There's something wrong."

"What do you mean?"

She was already getting to her feet, a frown on her face. "With Umbra…"

I stood, unsure, but she held up a hand, staring up at his room.

"I think… I need to go see him myself."

CHAPTER 22

Shatter

I found Umbra in his room, seated on his bed.

On the bedside table were two coins and a knife. His eyes flickered to me as I opened the door, but he didn't move.

There was something wrong. He was hiding in the bond, but something surrounded him, a numbness I'd never felt.

As I crossed toward him, his eyes followed me, and I reached out and took his hand in mine. He flinched, sandstorm eyes hard—more than I'd ever seen. Even his scent was different, blood so much sharper than the cooler tones of wolfsbane.

"Where…" He shut his eyes, jaw clenched. "Where were you?"

I took a breath, hating saying it now more than I had with Dusk. But they couldn't know. If they found out, they would likely guess the truth I'd learned, and we couldn't afford hopelessness. Not now.

Not when there was one more thing I needed to discover. One more piece of the puzzle beyond even Uncle.

And I needed to find it before the Lincoln pack opened the safe.

"I can't tell you," I whispered. My eyes burned. I hated lying to them. I hated tricking Ransom.

I hated that it was the Lincoln pack doing this to us.

Umbra tugged his hand from my grip, gazing up at me, and I saw what I'd been feeling at last. That quiet numbness.

He reached up, cupping my cheek in his hand. "I love you, Shatter."

"I know."

"I can't lose you."

I frowned. "Umbra—"

"Tell me where you went." His voice was low, his aura sweeping into the air like a frigid autumn wind.

Shock hit my system as I felt the command lock into place. A demand for truth fuelled by the bite on my neck. Fuelled by the massive weight of his alpha aura.

I opened my mouth, words forming on my tongue, before panic gripped me and I shoved him out with every ounce of strength I had.

I shut my mouth, and my breath caught, pain tearing through my body, a thousand needles driving into my skin as I warred with the bond on my neck. The command was a harsh whisper in my head, demanding I succumb. That I make this pain go away.

Umbra was on his feet, still cupping my chin, and I clutched his arm as I shook, tears filling my eyes as he stood, gaze locked on me.

"Shatter." His aura flared as the command grew to a scream.

I gritted my teeth, drawing a sharp breath, and shook my head. "No."

"Umbra!" The door behind me slammed open.

The command dropped, and I took a breath.

"What the hell are you doing?" Dusk demanded, reaching us. Ransom was on my other side, his hand on my back.

I still gripped Umbra, my nerves frayed. I couldn't take my eyes off him. Everything was wrong…

"Stop me again, and I'll take pack lead," Umbra snarled at Dusk.

Stop him?

I was catching up slowly, my mind foggy from the pain. The command had dropped because Dusk had dropped it. He had the final say on my commands.

"You will *not* hurt her—" Dusk began, but Umbra cut him off, letting go of me and seizing him.

"I will not survive the day when she is gone because I was too weak to face this now!"

Dusk sounded unnerved. "Umbra—"

"Leave." I was shocked at how steady my voice was as I turned to Dusk.

"Shatter—"

I shoved between them, turning on Ransom in fury when he tried to pull me back. "Leave us!"

Something changed in the room. I don't know what it was, which meant it was probably me. Umbra's aura was gone and Dusk stepped back, yellow eyes wide as he glanced between the two of us. I looked at Ransom, who was staring at me in shock.

I didn't know anything in that moment but pure instinct. I grabbed Umbra and shoved him back toward the bed. "Sit. Down."

He just stared at me for a moment, unsure, but my hand snapped up and closed around his neck. "I said, *sit*."

He did almost instantly, and I sank against him, my breaths settling only when I felt his hands rest at my waist. My fingers tangled in his sandy blond hair and I tugged his head back. His grip on me tightened as I sank my teeth into his neck.

A temporary bond between us flared and my pulse settled.

Until I heard one of the others shift behind me.

A vicious growl rose in my chest, and my grip on Umbra's hair was unfairly tight until the door shut and their scents were gone. I shut my eyes, releasing him and winding my arms around his chest.

Then I did something I'd never done in my life.

I sought out my first memory.

The flashing ERROR.

The rising scent of death around me.

But more than that, the bone-shaking agony that had torn through my body for endless second after endless second.

Umbra's grip tightened, but I didn't let it go, sinking so far into those memories that I became them. Letting him feel them through the two-way bond.

I needed him to know it wasn't just agony I'd endured. It was agony I'd been *born* into.

Pain wasn't what I feared.

It was what had happened after that… the months and months that slipped away in silence at the Estate. Becoming nothing… losing who I was.

That was worse.

The place he had been when I'd walked into his room moments ago.

I don't know how long had passed.

When I opened my eyes at last, we were lying on his bed. He was holding me tight, an unsettled purr in his chest.

Looking up at him, I cupped his cheek, and I could see the relief in his sandstorm eyes.

"I'm..." He scrunched up his nose, his voice thick. "I'm sorry."

"You aren't allowed to leave me," I whispered. "Not like that. Not again. You mean too much to me."

"You can't give yourself up for us."

"You're my alpha and husband, and I'm yours," I replied. "We have to protect each other."

He winced, not meeting my eyes. "There's nothing..." His voice shook. "Shatter, I'm already..." He trailed off, shaking his head. "I'm not..."

I cupped his cheeks, making him look at me, and I found the thing at the centre of all he was. With my bite between us, our souls were entwined closer than they had ever been.

When I reached out to him in the bond, he turned to smoke. Wind blowing him away like he was never there.

I heard at last the words he couldn't say. The truth that trapped him. And I realised it had nothing to do with trials or the experiments he'd endured for Dusk over and over. Those didn't haunt him. They weren't even pain. They were relief—salve on a burn.

From the burden he'd carried before any of it.

The core of what made him what he was and the reason his aura was like it was—perhaps the reason he had been in the Cimmerian Vaults in the first place, when he'd broken enough to become too dangerous to be left free.

And I heard the words that were carved into his very soul, his truth that meant pain where there should be happiness. Guilt where there should be love.

I'm not supposed to be here.

A scar deeper than any left across his skin, festering with every day that passed, with every moment of happiness he couldn't bear.

Of surviving.

Tears leaked from my eyes.

"I don't know how to..." He took a breath. "I don't know how to face what you want me to face. I don't know how to be more for you."

"I'm your mate," I whispered. "I've always been your mate, and I will not give up on you."

He held me tight, fingers lacing through my hair as he arched my neck. Relief shocked my system as I felt the brush of his teeth on my skin.

Aside from Dusk's, their bites weren't needed for the bond, but I wanted them, anyway. All of them.

I shifted, dragging his teeth lower until they were on my breast, over the place Eric had left a mark.

A low whine escaped my chest as I felt his mark upon my flesh, a claim that bound us together.

A claim that meant I would never leave him behind.

CHAPTER 23

Ransom

The whir of the drill made me anxious as Umbra secured my bookshelf to the wall.

Those screws meant this was real. Shatter was over at Roxy's for movies, but she'd be back before long, since it was Sunday evening, and we had to be up early for school tomorrow.

Umbra was surprisingly efficient with the power tools I'd borrowed from the workshop, and right now, I was holding the bookshelf in place while he worked.

I peered at him and got an eye roll as he felt me prodding through the bond again. I wasn't sure what had happened between Umbra and Shatter after we'd left yesterday. It had been a rather unnerving hurricane of hormones when we'd come into Umbra's room. When she told us to leave, it was like she had us all by the throat and she owned the dark bond.

Rather impressive.

It wasn't long until I'd felt them both through our connection, Umbra somehow sheepishly relieved.

"You, uh… all right?" I asked him as we both stepped back to take a look at it.

We hadn't spoken much, despite working on the shelves. He'd seen me hauling in the bookshelf through the front door and wordlessly hummed to himself while he helped me bring it in.

Umbra side-eyed me and grunted.

Man of few words today.

He tilted his head, staring at the shelves. Now that they were affixed to the wall, I was less worried. We could fix them a little more, to be safe. One of the shelves had fallen off during the journey from the workshop to the apartment.

I handed Umbra another screw.

Finally, after a few more, Umbra set down the drill, took a step back, and regarded the bookshelf from a distance. Then he nodded to himself and clapped me on the shoulder. Hesitantly, I reached out to push lightly against the side of the shelf.

No movement.

Not even a shiver of a wobble.

It was sturdy.

My racing pulse slowed, and I gave it one more shove. It didn't move.

Thank fuck.

If she wanted to move it, we could. It just might take a while. But I'd move it wherever she wanted.

"Thanks for helping," I muttered. "Now to pray she likes it." I swallowed. It might be safely fixed to the wall, but that didn't make it quite as pretty as I had envisioned.

I'd wanted perfect hexagons, not wonky shelf after wonky shelf. I don't really know how I'd managed it, actually.

Fuck.

I wrung my fingers. She'd be back soon…

Dusk had been right about the varnish. The deep mahogany matched the room, and I had found that tray stashed under her bed, along with a dark wood jewellery box that was empty, but smelled suspiciously like orange and fir tree, and lastly, three acorns.

Shit.

You know. This was a mistake.

Was there time to take it down?

I stepped forward, only for Umbra to catch me by the collar and drag me back.

"I think…" I stared at it.

The more I looked at my creation, the more I convinced myself…

Lopsided.

And the varnish job was patchy. I don't even know how.

No. It definitely had to come down. I turned on Umbra, grabbing him by the wrist, but he cuffed me on the cheek with a grin. I growled, tugging my hair from my face.

"You're overthinking it," Umbra said, ignoring my growl and shoving me away from the shelf.

"Oh, he speaks."

"You fucking idiot. She loves you. She's going to love it."

"I don't know if she loves me enough for this—"

"She loved you when you couldn't talk and we kept you chained to the wall in a dark room," he said with a grin. "I don't think you could fuck a shelf up bad enough to match that."

"I know she loves me," I muttered. "It's more about what she deserves."

More than me.

They all deserved more than me, but especially Shatter. All I brought to the table was money and connections. No skills. No sense half the time—I knew that. My father had been quick to let me know. I'd trusted him, and Umbra and Dusk had paid the price.

The more often I reminded myself of that, the less I felt like I deserved our omega. I would never let her go, because I was selfish, and she needed all the protection she could get, but I wanted to prove myself.

"Our *wife* deserves to have what she wants," Umbra said. "And she wants you."

I thought back to how she'd reacted when Dusk had suggested a divorce. It had sent a shock of discomfort through me to think about splitting from her in any capacity, and she hadn't wanted to split from us, either.

Shatter Kingsman.

She had my last name, and that's how she wanted it to stay…

I met Umbra's eyes properly. He did seem different. More light, somehow.

"Prod the bond one more time, Ransom, and I'll deck you."

I grinned for half a second before I heard a voice from the hallway.

"Ransom?"

Oh. Shit. Panic rose in my chest, and I choked instead of responding to her.

This was it.

"Dusk said you had a surprise for…" She trailed off as she reached the door, peering in, then caught sight of us, eyes wide.

Umbra clapped me on the shoulder before striding out and leaving me stuck like a deer in headlights.

Fuck. I couldn't fucking move. Or breathe.

Her dark nightshade scent washed over me, and I stared at the delicate flush to her cheeks. The chaotic waves of her hair that were more shiny now we were doing masks. Then her golden eyes slid from me to the empty shelf on the wall.

And she *froze.*

Oh dear.

What had I been thinking? This was her nest.

The book stacks were perfect. She didn't need a fucking bookshelf.

Slowly, she stepped in, eyes fixed on it.

"It's…" I swallowed. "Your wedding gift. From me." I stumbled over the statement. "A bookshelf. I was thinking you could use it for your textbooks and maybe some photos of us? I know it's not, uh, perfect. But I made it…" I trailed off. "For you."

She reached it, her hand trailing the surface. She was seeing how wrong it was.

"I'm not the best at stuff like this, but I made it from scratch. I promise, Little Reaper, but I think I jumped the gun. The next one won't be as…well…" I winced. "I'll figure out what went wrong with the varnish. I…" I cursed internally. I never should have done this. Furniture stores existed for a reason.

It was me.

I was the reason.

"I just wanted to make you something…"

"It's…" Her voice was soft, and my stomach dropped as she turned to me.

No.

Oh *shit.*

Those were tears.

I'd fucked up so bad.

CHAPTER 24

Shatter

The second my eyes welled with tears, Ransom panicked.

Well. Panicked more. He'd *started* to panic way before that, but it got worse when I cried. His tan skin went ashen, and he took a step toward me before immediately retreating again.

He thought I didn't like it, but he'd *made* me a gift? No one had ever *made* me anything like this before.

I choked out a sob and threw myself into his arms, burying my face at his neck. His arms came around me and he held me tight.

"Fuck, Little Reaper. I'm so sorry. I'll get you something else. A million of them."

He rumbled with a purr, a desperate attempt to soothe me—but that was all wrong.

"N-no, I… I love it," I choked out.

Ransom's purr stuttered. "Um… can you… could you say that again?"

I drew back, my lip quivering embarrassingly. "It's so perfect," I said, staring up into his pretty jade eyes.

A *wedding* gift?

I couldn't even… I blinked back more tears. Sometimes I had to shove away the thought of the marriage. Even a fake wedding, in winter, that never happened was… well, it was so much more than I thought I'd ever get.

I was gold pack. Broken. A pack was too good to be true, let alone a wedding.

And now Ransom was making me a wedding gift?

"You… don't want it gone?" He was half-bewildered.

I growled on instinct, shifting to the side until I was standing between my mate and my gift. That shelf could *never* leave this room. Ever. Well, until my nest moved.

"It's *mine*," I said adamantly, hackles raising, like I might have to fight. "You already… You already gave it to me, so you can't take it back."

That's how it worked, right?

Ransom's sad panic faded from his eyes as I pout-glared at him. His lips twitched into a smile as he stared at me in awe.

"I love you so fucking much." He kissed my forehead, then my nose. "No one has ever…" He paused, throat bobbing. "You're just… perfect Shatter."

I turned back to the bookshelf. I didn't understand why he was anxious.

Maybe because he'd been bringing something into my nest without me knowing. But it had been destroyed, so I was in a transition period, anyway.

But the gift was so far beyond perfect. A bookshelf for all my textbooks that was crafted all… not straight, exactly how I liked it. Not a tangent line in sight.

My teeth sank into my bottom lip.

He must have worked so hard on it, too. Ransom was rich and smart and good at stuff, so it must have taken a lot of effort for him to make it all *not* straight for me.

His grip on me tightened, and suddenly, I couldn't ignore how close he was, and my scent started to rise, slick gathering in my core.

"When I went feral, Shatter, I barely had anything. No family, except Umbra and Dusk, and I didn't know if I'd wake up, or if I did, whether they'd even still be there. They shouldn't have been, you know? I owe those two so fucking much, but the best thing they've ever done is find you."

I whined, reaching up to wind my arms around his neck.

"Waking from hell to find you was more than I ever deserved. You're my omega, Shatter Kingsman. My beautiful wife."

Before he could move, I surged up and crashed my mouth against his. His scent spiked around me, cool rain in a forest, lily of the valley drowning me.

I *needed* him.

Our tongues tangled, and I moaned against his lips while spinning us and walking him backward until his back hit our wedding bookshelf.

Ransom

Shatter deftly got my pants undone.

"Shatter—wait, you don't—*shit*, I wanted to be the one to show you how much—"

My wife cut me off with her lips on mine. She was up on her toes to reach, her fist squeezing my cock roughly and getting another groan from me.

Nightshade was heavy in the air, and my growl made her shiver. I wove my fingers through her hair and tugged her head back, exposing the delicate curve of her throat, kissing along the soft skin and the bite Dusk had left.

Her grip on my cock faltered as she grew distracted, but with a disgruntled little whine, she focused on it again. She glared at me when I flashed her a grin.

"I want you to claim me right here," she whispered, breathless, her grip on my cock bordering on a threat.

The hold I had on her hair was useful to push her down—and she didn't resist. Shatter dropped to her knees, immediately kissing the side of my length. I groaned but didn't let her engulf my length with her hot mouth yet.

"Tongue, Little Reaper." I hadn't intended to use the bond, but I'd gotten caught up in the moment. She was just so goddamn sexy. I felt a rush of lust from her and decided not to drop the command like I'd been about to.

Her golden eyes glittered as she looked up from her knees, waiting for my cock.

She was my angel, and I was in fucking heaven.

I could stare at her like that forever, but she let out a little whine, reminding me that the dark bond far from meant I was in charge.

I'd also seen her take a punishment from Dusk enough to know that she did not want me being nice about it. I dragged her lips to my tip.

"Choke yourself," I growled. Dusk was playing with fire when he used *that* as a command. So, I didn't go quite that far, but my head fell back against the shelf and I gritted my teeth with pleasure as she drew my cock into her mouth.

Shatter's instincts were riding her harder than I'd thought because she didn't waste a fucking second.

She whined as I gripped her hair, and I was already so close. I held on, letting out a growl, a rush of pleasure sending reverberations down my spine.

This was fast. Way too fucking fast.

There was a moment when she gagged, and I almost pulled back, but she forced me deeper on her own. Her nails dug into my thighs through the jeans, and I couldn't have gotten my cock out of her mouth if I tried.

Not that I was going to.

She could swallow me down like this every minute of the day if she wanted to.

I wanted to hold out, to avoid coming so I could savour this, but she wasn't having any of that.

With a glint of determination in her eyes, Shatter took me deeper and deeper until she was swallowing around my tip, eyes watering.

For the love of—

She whined deep in her chest as she took me deeper, like she was trying to take my knot into her mouth too.

That was it for me.

My grip tightened in her hair and my vision flashed white as my orgasm overtook me and my seed spilled down her throat. *Too rough,* I thought, as each shallow thrust pushed my knot against her lips.

CHAPTER 25

Dusk

It was quiet in the library where Shatter and I were working.

It was Tuesday evening, and she'd wanted to do a deep dive into some set of studies or another. She was so far ahead in the Arkology curriculum, I could never tell what she was looking for. Umbra and Ransom had basically checked out of Arkology class entirely, so it was me and her in the library, as I had homework I could work on.

She was trying, and epically failing, to not keep shooting me glances as I ran my thumb along her skin where my hand rested at her waist.

I smirked the next time she glanced over, which made her cheeks go pink. It was late, and the rustling of paper could be heard in here with us, but no one was in sight.

I leaned over, letting my teeth graze her ear. "Am I distracting you?"

Shatter shivered but gave me a haughty look. "No."

"Lying to me?" I asked. *"Come here, Gem."*

"I'm not—" She cut off with a pout as the command gripped her and she shuffled closer.

"Not enough," I told her. "I want you on your knees for me."

"Here?" she asked, voice weak.

I nudged her chin up, my blood already hot for what I was about to claim. "It's been too long," I said, my voice a breath in her ear. "I only have so much patience when it comes to that sweet body of yours. Especially when you keep flaunting it in front of me." I leaned back. "Now. On your knees, and get me ready to fuck that bratty mouth of yours."

Her chest heaved, eyes furious, but the dark bond meant she was already setting her book down and slipping down beneath the desk.

She didn't have anything more to say as her fingers fumbled for my zipper, though the fury in her eyes was beautifully clear.

"Good girl," I purred as she freed my cock. She was positioned so perfectly for me to claim her, knees spread, snarl on her pretty lips only an inch from my tip. "Tongue out."

Her cheeks burned red as she did as she was told, and I felt a shot of lust from her down the bond. "You're so pretty when you're angry," I murmured, my fist closing around her hair as I pressed my shaft all the way down her throat.

Beautiful golden eyes held mine in fury, but I grinned, drawing her back and pumping in a few times. She was so tight, her throat squeezing my tip so good.

"Fuck…"

I wouldn't last long if I wasn't careful.

She couldn't be mad at me forever, but when she was, she was a storm of conflict. I hadn't fucked her yet, not since the fight. Only because I could swear she was getting hotter for me every day I didn't. And every day she got brattier, like she was daring me to claim her while she was pissed.

I'd also discovered that both Ransom and Umbra were both so compliant when she wanted to use my pack to taunt me that it almost bordered outright glee. Fucking traitors.

I fucked her mouth roughly, each stroke trapping her lips against my swelling knot and cutting off her airway.

Her eyes were sparkling with tears as I neared my climax, my fist still balled in her hair as I used her, controlling everything, down to her breaths.

When I came, a low whine sounded in her chest, nails biting down on my legs as I forced her to swallow every drop.

I let her go, leaning back and catching my breath as I did up my pants. She was everything. "Lap," I said. I wasn't done with her. I needed her close.

I wound my arms around her waist, holding her tight when she slunk onto my lap, then leaned down and brushed my teeth over my bite, making her shiver. "I bet you're so wet, forced to let me use your little holes like that," I breathed.

I was watching her in the bond, feeling the rush of lust and submission sweep her away for a moment.

Only… I froze, spotting the slightest movement out of the corner of my eye. Incrementally, I noticed the slightest shifts of shadows, along with a faint rustle. With effort, I kept my eyes fixed on the textbook before me.

"You know," I breathed in her ear. "I think we have a stalker." She went still, trying to look up at me, but I held her against my chest. "Curl up just like this until the others come. I don't want anyone watching to know you're all hot and bothered."

They could keep guessing at the nature of our relationship, and it was a rather convenient show they'd just walked in on.

"I'm *not*," she hissed, sounding so cute and bratty.

"I'll have to punish you later for lying to me again, Gem," I replied for only her to hear.

She didn't say anything, but I felt her fingers dig into my shirt, another shiver running through her. It was official.

I loved her grudges.

I shot a text to Umbra and Ransom, then set my phone down, stroking my thumb along her waist on the underside of her shirt again. I halted as the beginnings of a purr rose in her chest before she caught it and passed it off as a cough.

Stifling my smile, I leaned close. "Are you upset that we might have been seen?" There was a long pause, then she shook her head incrementally. "That's my sweet omega," I murmured.

I turned a page of the textbook absently, one hand always on her waist possessively. If there was someone watching, I would show them she belonged to me.

It could be random, but I didn't have room to believe in chance.

Either it was a member of the Lincoln pack, or it was Mord Sato. Well, that, or I was jumping at shadows. But I didn't have room to doubt, not when those pricks could get into the safe at any moment.

It took ten minutes for Ransom and Umbra to show up, though they waited just beyond the bookcase, giving us space like I'd asked. Umbra was eyeing me curiously, but Shatter would catch them up.

I straightened, turning on the bench so she'd be able to leave.

"Kiss me goodbye, Gem," I said before she drew away.

Her eyes flashed, and I didn't think I was out of the doghouse quite enough to think she was *just* acting for our stalker. She took my face in her hands and drew me close, her plush lips pressed into a bratty frown the whole time.

"Lace tonight," I said. "And I want you in my bed when I get back."

Her expression went dark, clearly furious with my request, but she didn't argue. "Shall I wait up?" she asked coldly.

I grinned, squeezing her ass and drawing my teeth along her neck hard enough that she let out a little whine.

God, I loved her.

"I don't care if you're awake or asleep when I punish those tight little holes of yours."

That I said loud enough that whoever was back there definitely heard.

When she stood and stepped back, she was wringing her hands, eyes darting around the space like she was trying to find a way out. All the while, I felt nothing but a thrill of anticipation down the bond.

"Is that everything?" she asked, voice wobbly.

"Yes."

With that, she grabbed her books and backed up, hurrying toward Ransom and Umbra, glancing back at me anxiously once.

I stifled my smile. Pissed at me or not, she knew how to act. I hadn't seen nervousness like that from her since I'd first met her. And no matter what, there was one command still between us. The one in which I'd instructed her to tell me if I ever told her to do something that made her uncomfortable.

When they were gone, I closed the textbook and leaned back, waiting a minute before speaking. "Enjoy the show?"

Would they come out?

If there was some random coward behind that bookshelf who tried to run, we'd be paying off another pack to shut their mouths about a hospital visit.

I doubted it, though.

A long few seconds passed before I heard a few quiet footfalls, and Mord Sato appeared around the corner of the shelf. He stepped past the table and dropped onto the bench opposite.

He considered me for a long moment, dark eyebrows cocked.

"You know," he said mildly. "She seems just the temperament the Lincoln pack is looking for. Obedient. Quiet. Ready to please."

A little flare of rage stirred my touchy alpha instinct as I took him in. His scent was strange, ebony and something unreadable. He had a jagged scar down the left side of his face, dark eyes that seemed to see everything, and long black hair, tied up loosely. The alpha who'd just watched something that belonged to me.

Would it be helpful to just… put a bullet in his skull right now?

Middle of a library might be pushing it, even for me. But I'd killed more dangerous men than Mord Sato in the name of my pack's safety.

Or purely for vengeance.

I stamped it all down, knowing that any reaction I gave was information. I didn't want him believing there was more to my relationship with Shatter.

As I cooled my thoughts off, I realised I didn't buy what he claimed.

"That's why you're skulking in libraries? To check my omega's temperament?" Not a chance in hell. "What a waste of talent."

"And what is it you think of my talent?" he asked, something humorous glinting in his eyes.

"I know it's below your paygrade to be hired by rich cowards to fight their battles."

"Want to know a secret?" Mord asked, absently fixing the stack of books on the table a previous student had left.

I raised an eyebrow, waiting.

"I had no intention of taking this case before I read up on you and your so-called brother. Far too many holes to make sense—and the more I poked, the less my clients' claims seemed like paranoia."

"That doesn't change the nature of the job," I replied. "A fall from grace for the man who put Riot in the sights of the GPRE."

Mord snorted, a flash of genuine delight in his eyes. "I truly love that rumour."

"It's not true?" I don't know why he wouldn't want it. Lie or not, Riot was one of New Oxford's most notorious criminals. He hadn't been caught by the GPRE, but Mord's involvement had brought it down to the wire, according to Decebal.

Mord considered that. "I suppose it *is*, more or less."

"And now you're cleaning up frat boy messes?"

"I enjoy difficult puzzles. Call it professional curiosity."

"Professional curiosity?" I wasn't buying it.

"I'll tell you, if you'd like to hear."

"Tell me what?"

"Why I took the case."

I cocked my head, waiting, unsure if I should expect a lie.

"Your pack's hidden paper trail has a Harpy signature. Don't worry too much—you can't hide in plain sight without a trail of some kind. It's… let's say Harpy, but…" He nodded his head in a so-so motion. "Not quite. Ex-member, non-drug related—which rounds it down to one guy in the city."

I frowned. He wasn't far off. Both Decebal and his pack mate, Kai, were from the Harpy Gang in the Gritch District. They'd got out, which didn't happen often, but it was Kai who was responsible for all of our forged documents.

"The arrogant leader of the Mandela pack might get involved with distasteful operations to boost his fragile ego, but that only makes the fact that his pack mate, Kai Ekkon, can't be *bought* all the more stark. He's one of the best and notoriously ethical, which begs the question, what have you—with your dark-bonded omega—done to convince him to help?" Mord asked.

"You're interested because I have ties to the Mandela pack?" If that was it, I was going to give Decebal an earful.

"Nah," Mord said. "I'm far more interested in what was buried, why Ekkon doesn't believe it's a problem, and…" Mord paused, as if considering whether he should say the next part. "If it has anything to do with your very curious scents."

Our *scents*?

That's what he was fucking interested in? I wondered, for a moment, what that meant. It had never been confirmed, but we were sure our poison scents were a result of experimentation.

"If I told you, would you fuck off?" I asked. I *wouldn't* tell him, but I wanted to poke at his mask.

Mord leaned back, the echo of a smile on his face, as if he didn't believe it at all. "The safe and that omega of yours are a far more interesting challenge."

It took every ounce of my self-control not to react at the mention of Shatter. Instead, I took a breath, mulling over the rest as I tapped my finger on my jeans. First off, the safe, it seemed, was still locked. Not that Mord would be here at all if it wasn't.

Second, I *was* surprised he was willing to say as much as he had, but his curiosity lined up with what I knew of him. He was calculated, patient, deadly—but even so, mostly tied up in work that didn't have a bad ending. Well, not as bad as it *could* get in the underbelly of New Oxford. Maybe I could push on that one. "You said Kai's work is ethical. You don't consider yours the same?"

"I consider my work selfish. I prefer tasteful jobs, but nothing kills business faster than flipping on clients."

At least we weren't pretending about the obscene lie that he was considering joining the Lincoln pack. The conclusion was clear. His interest in what was hidden about our pack was worth the risk of taking a job that might end up distasteful.

So, buying him out wasn't an option.

Fucking great. We'd left blood in the water, and the sharks had come. *Not* a complication I needed.

Except, I had learned something just by his presence.

"So." I tilted my head, pushing the facade Shatter and I had already put up. "Did they ask you to watch their scent match getting throat fucked by another alpha, or are you just lonely?"

Mord lifted his shoulders in a half shrug, his eyes fixed on me without flinching. "Lonely," he said. "It was a good show."

I snorted.

He wasn't giving up anything else. Every word he chose seemed calculated, hosting a potential for double meaning. Even the word *show* seemed designed to leave open whether he thought it was an act.

But he'd picked the wrong moment to watch if he wanted confirmation that Shatter was in love with our pack. I was, at least, confident about one thing—something I'd known just by catching him here.

I got to my feet, sure I'd got everything I could get out of this conversation.

"I'm asking the same questions you think I am," he said mildly, crossing his legs as I picked up my textbook. I glanced at him, eyebrow cocked. "Is the Lincoln pack playing me, trying to take something they shouldn't?" he supplied. "Or are you playing them?" There was a pause, and I thought I saw his eyes flash. "Or perhaps that pretty little golden-eyed thing is playing all of you."

I measured my expression as he outlined what he already knew I'd gathered from catching him here. He was looking for over defensiveness, something to give away that Shatter meant more to me than a dark-bonded prize—especially at the mention that he was watching her.

But that last option? That was what I needed to avoid.

She *wouldn't* be caught in the middle of this

I found a smile without too much difficulty. Playing a part had always been easy, and I knew it was a piece from my missing past. Had I been a performer once upon a time? Theatre had a good ring to it, but I would never find out if we didn't get free of this curse.

I clapped him on the shoulder as I passed. "Have a good evening with your new roommates. I have an omega to enjoy."

CHAPTER 26

Dusk

"Shhh shh, sleep, Gem," I growled, the weight of the dark bond and my alpha bark behind it as I settled onto the bed beside her.

Just like I had asked, she was waiting for me in my room. I wasn't sure what to expect from the command to put her back to sleep, but her breathing instantly slowed, her eyes drooping back shut.

Well. That was…

Fuck me.

I was going to ruin her.

She was in loungewear, with black sweatpants that were easy to tug off. Beneath was a pretty lace thong that I left for now. She was wearing a black silk nightgown, and all I had to do was free the belt, like unwrapping a present, and it pooled around her, revealing golden skin beneath. Perfect round breasts cupped by a bra that matched her thong.

Now, I could take my time.

I tugged the lace aside and gently slipped my finger into her cunt, pumping in slowly to feel the warmth of her slick pool.

Fuck, she was soaked for me.

She let out the cutest little moan, back arching, toes curling in the sheets as I began to work her, my palm pressing against her clit as I did.

I would start slow, but she would be trembling for me by the time she woke. Her teeth caught her lip as I added another finger, stretching her tight walls out for me.

"Good girl," I breathed, keeping my fingers in place before I lowered myself between her thighs.

She was shaking by the time I drew back, her fists balled in the sheets as she squeezed me tight. She was panting, her low moans rising beautifully in the air as I kept working her, curling my fingers into the spot that made her see stars. But she wouldn't. Not yet.

Finally, when her chest was heaving, goosebumps rippling across her whole body, I drew out.

Her fists uncurled, a little frown on her face as the stimulation stopped.

I freed my cock, using my fingers to coat it with her slick before I adjusted her.

So very carefully, I nudged the tip into her entrance. I took my time, sliding in and watching how her lips parted. Her knees were up, feet planted on the sheets, and I curled my hands around her waist, watching the way my cock stretched her open as I buried myself into her slow enough that she didn't wake.

I shut my eyes for a moment as my knot reached her entrance; her fists balled, back arching to try and take me.

Fuck, that felt good.

"You're so fucking perfect," I breathed, pleased when she let out another cute moan. As slow as I'd entered her, I drew out, feeling her pussy clench around me tightly, as if she didn't want to let me go.

She was made for me—for us. My scent match, omega, and wife.

We'd claimed her in every way there was. I bowed over her, pressing my lips to the bite I'd left, my thumb tracing the scars I'd matched across my skin as I slid into her now. The second time was easier for the amount of slick she'd produced.

"I love you," I breathed, rocking my knot against her. This time, when I pulled back, she let out a little growl, one hand reaching up, nails dragging along my side.

I grinned.

Had her dreams lined up with what I was doing to her?

I rocked against her again, enjoying the way she clenched over me, her nails digging in harder. I could already see the goosebumps lifting on her skin that told me she was closing in on an orgasm.

"Not yet, Gem," I breathed, not changing the pace.

As I hit her core again, her breath caught, breasts pressing against her bra, and the low whimper she loosed as she was denied caught me off guard. I climaxed without warning, groaning as I rocked into her, filling her with my seed as she clutched me, still shivering with denial.

I grinned, kissing her neck again as I finished, then drew back, replacing my cock with two fingers, pressing my cum into her and feeling it leak from her cunt.

I'd push her to the edge a few more times, preparing to wake her to an orgasm that would wipe her mind blank.

So gently, I removed my fingers and turned her on her side. I swept her slowly to her front, my arm around her waist as I held her up. *"Present for me."*

She let out a sigh, hands finding purchase on the sheets lazily as I slipped my fingers back into her core, pumping in and getting her to arch for me.

"You're so fucking hot, little omega," I told her, and she let out a little mewl. My grip closed around her outer thighs as I sank down between her legs.

The sounds she made as I played with her, using my tongue and occasionally sinking my thumb into her, were enough to get me hard again. I think she almost woke when I swirled my tongue around her back door. Her breaths picked up, and I had to tell her not to come again.

It wasn't long before I lined my cock back up with her needy cunt and sank back in. She was so turned on, I didn't have to go so slowly this time.

"You're taking me so good," I growled, scooping slick from around where my cock was seated fully inside her and placing my thumb over her back door. I pressed down gently, watching as she tensed, brows furrowing as she felt me there.

"Relax, Gem, let me use your perfect holes while you sleep."

She listened, back arching further as she released a breath. With the movement, my thumb stretched her tight opening a little. Shatter's whine was so fucking cute, and I pressed in a little more, watching as the glistening star swallowed the tip.

Fuck.

I rocked my knot into her cunt as I pressed my thumb in deeper, and she whined again, the sound breathy and unsure. Her body was shivering, and I got the impression she wasn't sure if she wanted more or not.

Holding her steady by the hips, I kept her suspended on the edge of my knot as I began to pump my thumb into her tight little ass. Fuck, I was close to finishing again just from seeing her take me like this. She wriggled a bit, cheeks pink, frowning as she adjusted to the intrusion.

I kept this up for a while until her whines shifted to something more desperate. There it was. She was getting close to finishing from a very different kind of orgasm. I kept it up until she was right on the edge. *"Don't come yet,"* I said, speeding up, biting back my own climax as she whimpered, her body shuddering with denial as I forced her to the edge of an orgasm she couldn't claim.

I cupped her cunt with my other hand, circling her clit while I left my thumb in place. *"One more,"* I told her.

She was breathing heavily now, pushed to the edge of multiple orgasms.

I released the command for her to sleep as I freed her fingers from the sheets and placed them between her thighs. Then I grabbed her hair with my free hand, drew back, and slammed into her cunt. She woke with a jolt, the golden eye I could see wide with shock.

"Play with yourself, Gem," I growled. "Take my knot."

"Dusk…" Her voice was breathy. "I haven't… *ugh!*" She let out a groan as I switched my thumb to two fingers. At the intrusion, she gasped, still trying to follow my command to back her tight cunt over my knot.

I bowed over her until my breath tickled her neck, careful not to shift my cock any further in. "Fight me all you want, Gem, but I'm claiming that tight little ass of yours."

Fuck, she was tight.

I tilted her head just a little more, so her cheek was pressed into the mattress, and I could see the precious expression cross her face.

"You're so pretty when you're helpless to stop me from taking you whenever I want."

"Dusk…"

She was breathless; a queen arched beneath, and through the bond, she was as bright as a beacon. A blaze of lust, submission, and reluctant anticipation, as if she was clinging desperately to still being mad at me.

I still hadn't released the command that she couldn't come, and she was already shaking.

Each of her breaths were punctuated with a whine as I drove my fingers into her back door brutally.

"Dusk!" She looked wild.

"Beg me, Gem."

She didn't even pause. "Please!" She was almost sobbing, her voice half a whine. "Alpha, please."

I released the command, one hand gripping her hips as I rocked into her, two fingers still stretching out her tight little back door.

"Come," I commanded with every ounce of alpha and pack lead power I had.

She cried out, her body seizing over me violently as the waves of three different kinds of orgasm crashed into her all at once.

When she'd made it past the waves of pleasure, I removed my hand, circling her waist as I dragged her body against me. "You're going to come again."

"I can't," she gasped. She was a shivering wreck.

"Tell me you're sorry for being a brat all week," I told her. "I might go easy."

Her one visible eye darted up to me for a moment, wide with nerves. "I won't."

I breathed a laugh. My perfect, stubborn omega.

I gripped my cock, which was glistening with her slick, and pressed it against her tight little bud. "Are you sure, Gem?" I asked.

"Fuck you," she hissed, then let out a squeak as I slid the tip past her quivering hole that was still trying so hard to reject me. She bared her teeth in a snarl, scrabbling at the sheets, another whine slipping out, then froze again as her struggles seated me further into her sweet ass.

"I'm going to make you scream my name before I allow you to come," I told her, sliding in slowly now until I was buried to the knot. I paused, letting her body adjust to me.

Her pants were more shallow, her eye still burning with fury. But the noises she was making gave her away. Indignance, sure, but those low whines were more than pain.

"How is every part of your body so perfect, Shatter?" I asked. "How is it there isn't a single inch of you not worth worshipping?"

I felt the effect of my words, felt the way her body relaxed around me.

I drew out of her, and her breath caught in shock, but she was completely aroused, and slick coated every movement now, making it easy. "Even this hole is soaked for me, little omega."

"It's *not* for you."

I almost laughed at how ridiculous that was, pausing for a moment, almost completely out of her but for my tip. She tried to wriggle away, but I caught her hips.

"Stay still for me, Gem," I told her, pressing my palms on either side of her. *"Keep presenting that perfect body."*

Her back arched, breathing short and sharp as I remained bowed over her. "You know that was such a bad lie, that's almost not worth punishing," I growled in her ear, giving it a nip and feeling her shiver as she was trapped beneath me, forced still by my command. "Almost."

I drove back into her, and she let out a whine but didn't fight. "It's my words, turning you on." I buried my cock into her once more and then began at a steady pace, loving the sweet sounds she made with each thrust. "I'm the one claiming your tight little ass, Shatter. No one else."

Even now, with a snarl on her face, her body was giving in to me, her chest heaving as I fucked her. I leaned closer still, letting my teeth graze her neck as was becoming our ritual. "You're ours, Gem. Our omega. Our wife."

Her body jolted in shock as her orgasm hit too fast. I leaned back, grasping her hips and fucking her brutally. Her low, shuddering moan broke free as I dragged her orgasm out, stimulating her over and over until she was a limp puddle.

And then I dragged her up against my chest by her neck, taking my turn, enjoying each whimper and shudder as I filled her hole with my hot seed.

"My perfect wife," I said again. My pack might be pissed at me, but they had no idea how long I'd been waiting to say those words. I drew her close as I purred at her back. "You took me so fucking well."

It took a while for her to catch her breath. Through the bond, she was a collision of shock and dreamy peace.

"I'm still… still mad at you," she whispered at last. There wasn't much effort in it.

"I like when you're mad at me." I pressed a kiss to her neck again. "Makes claiming your holes so much better."

She shivered, a reaction she couldn't control.

"I love you," I whispered. "So fucking much. Pissed at me or not."

We lay in peace, and she was content with me holding her close, purring at her back. She turned when she was free, her beautiful golden gaze finding mine, still a little dazed.

"I love you," she said quietly. Her lip quivered. "So much. I just wish you'd told me."

I shut my eyes. "I *am* sorry."

"I'm just scared that if you wait to tell me something because you think I'm fragile, you might…" She swallowed. "You might never get to tell me at all."

I nodded, cupping her cheek. "I won't do it ever again."

Only, as I made that promise, I realised I was holding out on something else.

Shit.

This, I realised, was the time. I couldn't wait. "Get dressed," I told her, sitting up. Umbra and Ransom had been bugging me to do it all today and yesterday, telling me it was the time, but now I knew for sure it was right.

"What?" Her eyebrows raised.

I grinned. "Get dressed. We're going out."

"But it's late. And Tuesday."

"I don't care."

CHAPTER 27

Shatter

"Truce?" he asked me as we pulled up to an empty gravel parking lot. We were on the side of a mountain, a decent drive from the city.

It was cold outside, but the heat was turned on, and I peered out the windshield to look up at the clear night sky above. Every star was clear in the night, clearer than in the city.

I'd been quiet the whole way, just existing in his scent of midnight opium and the undercurrent of nerves from him in the bond. I'd never felt that before, and it was strangely comforting.

I pouted, glancing back at him. "You think you can just fuck me real good, and I won't be mad at you anymore?"

"I was hoping it was a start."

My lips quivered with a smile. "I'll allow a truce."

He grinned.

I watched as he hopped out of the front seat, tugging open the trunk and grabbing a coat, which he handed me. I tugged it on, peering around. The light from the SUV was the only one in the whole space.

"It's really fucking cold, and I didn't think this through," he said. "I just wanted to be somewhere other than the academy. Decebal said this place was great for being under the stars."

It was possible to see right down and across the whole of New Oxford at night, right to where the city met the sea, and the world turned to blackness but for a few ship lights. "It's really pretty," I whispered, hugging my coat tight around me as I glanced up to see the constellations above again. "I don't mind a bit of—"

I cut off, everything wiped from my brain as I turned back to Dusk, finding him down on one knee. Wait—

"W-what are you doing?" I stammered.

He took a black velvet box from his pocket, and my pulse went haywire.

What *was* he doing?

I glanced around the midnight field, as though it might give me answers. "D-Dusk…"

This was crazy.

No matter what a piece of paper had said, I was… I was gold pack.

Broken.

All wrong.

Dreams stayed dreams for a reason.

"Will you claim me as your husband, Shatter Kingsman?" he asked as he cracked the box and showed me what was inside.

I tried desperately to blink away tears that sprung up in my eyes. Glinting in the dim light of the SUV was a ring.

The most beautiful ring I'd ever seen. It was made of three thin bands that fit together—one for each of them—and the diamonds upon it… They were…

Not only were the diamonds large, but in clusters of hexagons across the top, scattered in a haphazard way perfectly imperfect. Perfectly imbalanced.

ERROR

ERROR

ERROR

Flashed in my head. Bright lights swimming in my vision.

I was broken.

A poison—

"I'm sorry it's so backwards," he said.

Oh… *bother…*

I had just been standing here for an age, my mouth hanging open. "It's, um… it's okay." I was choked as I tried to shove back haunting memories, glad I could find my voice. "This pack is all backwards and upside down…"

He was still holding the ring out, still on his knees.

It must be cold.

I was making him wait.

I was supposed to… to answer or something. But I was mesmerised by the patterns across the ring. It was so beautiful. Something he'd chosen for me. But I was both mesmerised *and* terrified.

How could something as beautiful as that be for me?

I didn't understand.

I reached out and took it, trying to grasp what I was looking at. He'd bought this for me.

"I just… I need a moment."

Dusk

So.

That hadn't gone quite as I'd imagined it would.

Her eyes had gone wide as she'd stared at the three-part ring—*normal.* She'd teared up—*normal.* Then she'd taken a step back, like she was going to run—possibly… normal?

Then she'd re-engaged constricted omega pupils on the ring, let out a little whine, snatched it, and fled.

Definitely not normal.

Well. No. That wasn't true.

It was very Shatter.

I found her in the back of the SUV, buried under the spare blankets I'd packed for the drive.

When I ducked under to join her, it was to find her curled up with the glow of her phone as she cupped my ring in her hands, staring at it.

When she'd snatched the ring, she'd vanished in the bond. I don't even think she'd closed it. I think she'd just… gotten lost. She was nothing but a buzzing tangle of instincts and hormones.

She glanced up at me as I joined her, then returned her gaze to the ring she was cupping so carefully it was as though she thought that, if she moved too suddenly, it might burn her.

I think the little hexagon diamond design might have done her in. This was some Lord of the Rings level shit.

"Are you… okay?"

"Uh huh…" Her lip trembled, though, the same quivering smile that I'd seen the day she'd found her registration card.

"I don't believe you, Gem." I needed to bench my nerves. This was a gift I wanted to give her, no matter how she received it. It wouldn't be worth much if its value changed for how she responded.

"Well…" She swallowed. "I'm just focusing really hard." She returned her gaze to the ring with intensity.

"On what?"

"Not crying."

I smiled. "You can cry however much you want."

"Really?" she asked, glancing at me. "It's not… s-stupid?"

"No."

"Promise?"

"Promise."

"Oh, thank God." She burst into tears, hugging the ring close. "Because it's the most… m-most beautiful thing I've ever seen."

"So they're… good tears?"

She dragged her arm across her eyes, fixing me with a wide-eyed stare, and sniffled. "Y-yes."

Okay.

Relief flooded my system. I don't think I'd been this nervous in… well, ever.

She tugged the blanket back from over our heads and snuggled closer. I kept spotting her glance at the ring before ripping her eyes wildly away, as if she didn't know how to look at it.

Fresh tears tracked her cheeks with that sweet smile.

"It's… well, it's from all of us. But I know Ransom wanted to do the shelves, and Umbra said it wouldn't be proper if you didn't get it all at once and that I had some…" I scratched my head. "Some making up to do."

She giggled.

"Can I put it on?" I asked.

She frowned, peering up at me. "*You* want to wear it?"

I snorted, taking her hand and sliding the ring onto her ring finger. Her expression went from a smile to pure terror, but it fit perfectly.

I stared at the diamonds glinting beside the beautiful rich tan of her skin. A claim so far beyond the necklaces the academy provided.

"It's…" Her breath caught, then she looked up at the ceiling again, her expression crumpling. "It's, uh… it's perfect. Like a little n-nest that goes with me everywhere."

I couldn't contain my smile at that as I tugged her closer. "I'm sorry I didn't make it special the first time," I breathed, holding her close. To be honest, I didn't even think this was good enough. I'd just dragged her to a cold field in the middle of the night, thinking it might be romantic.

She leaned up, and I felt her teeth pierce my neck, blowing our connection open wider than it was in the regular bond.

"What was that for?" I asked, though I wasn't complaining. I could feel everything from her. Her joy soaring high above, and her insecurities, worry and fear pulling her down. I drew her closer, never wanting her to feel she wasn't enough.

"You asked if I would claim you as my… my husband," she whispered. "I did."

I growled, pulling her into a kiss. When I drew away, her eyes were dancing. "I love you, my perfect wife."

CHAPTER 28

Shatter

We were extremely late for class the next morning. My fault, as I went back and forth for ages over whether I should wear my ring. My husbands had sworn they wouldn't mind if I wanted to keep it on the down-low for now—and a part of me wanted to keep it for just… me.

Me and my pack.

I switched between wearing it around my neck on a necklace, to leaving it in my drawer, to slipping it onto my finger.

Finally, I decided to be bold. It wouldn't ruin any narrative we were trying to spin. Quite the contrary. Just like everything else the Kingsman pack did, it would look, to everyone else, like a bid for control.

I did, however, have to wear the ring upside down because I was prone to bursting into tears every time I saw the cute little hexagons placed haphazardly across the silver.

It almost happened six times in the Neuro and Behavioural Patterns Arkology class, but luckily, that wasn't the one I cared about right now. I'd made it to lunch, and I'd dared to flip it hexagon-diamond side up for now as I headed to the water fountain with my cup.

I was feeling more hopeful than I had in so long, closing in on what I needed. I'd had Dusk make Decebal get me website after website of all the kinds of studies I needed to scour, to be sure.

The last puzzle piece. And I was getting near the truth I needed for my plan.

Even if it was… well, it was scary. It was all for our future. The future that felt a thousand times more real now there was a ring on my finger.

I turned, a cup of water from the drink fountain in my hand, and almost walked straight into Jasmine Lynn. She sneered at me, taking a step back, but I gritted my teeth, side-stepping her and reminding myself of the time I'd sunk my teeth into her neck.

I didn't have to care what she thought. Plus, Roxy said she was an outcast now. Of course, not *outside* of Omega Studies, since all she'd been doing was tailing the Lincoln pack like a puppy, but it still made me feel a little better.

She had a bitter look on her face as she pushed past, but halted as her eyes found the ring on my finger. "They did propose, then?" Her voice was snide, and a grin was spreading across her face. "Someone said the ring was pathetic, but I had to see for myself."

I felt the blood drain from my face as I took a step back.

"A pack that rich, and you get a ring that can barely catch the sunlight."

"*I* love it," I said, heat rising in my blood.

"You're gold pack." She laughed. "You'd cry with joy if they bought you a ring made of plastic."

Passersby were staring, but I gritted my teeth.

This wasn't worth my time.

"You're just jealous because you joined a pack that doesn't want you." Roxy was at my side in a moment, and I saw Jasmine's eyes flash with disgust.

"You're far from top nowadays, Roxy. A packless fucking loner."

"Funny, because the alphas who rejected you have been leaving flowers at my doorstep for days now."

Roxy's hand was on my arm, already tugging me away.

"Wait—are they?" I asked.

Roxy grinned. "Not just flowers," she said smugly. "The North Prince pack and the Valaren pack seem to be in a bit of a war."

"Are you going to say yes to any of them?" I asked.

"No. But I will keep my mouth shut long enough to see how far the courting gifts go. And to be honest, I don't have any plans for my next heat." She shrugged. "Anyway." She waved away the conversation. "For the record, Shatter, I know for a fact that Dusk had that custom-designed." She eyed my ring.

"He *did?*" I asked.

"I'm pretty sure everyone in his contact list got unending pictures. I suggested an adjustment for"—she pointed to one of the hexagons in the piece—"this one. It was just a little too organised, I think."

I grinned as we sat back down with the others, and I hugged the ring close.

"Everything all right?" Ransom asked, looking at me curiously.

"Jasmine was just being a jealous bitch," Roxy said with a shrug. "I think she's realised that the Lincoln pack isn't as obsessed with her as she'd hoped."

I stared down at the ring, second-guessing and hating that Jasmine got that kind of reaction from me. Did that mean the Lincoln pack was going to find out? I mean… of course, they would. I'd known that when I'd chosen to wear it. It was probably better if they found out through Jasmine, anyway. Then I wouldn't have to live through it.

"I'm glad you wore it, Nightshade," Umbra said to me as we made our way back to the apartments after classes. "We should celebrate with a movie night."

I perked up. "In the nest?" I asked. That way, I could get cuddles, do my research, and watch movies all at once.

"Yeah, why don't you guys get started on the homework, and I'll grab some food for the evening."

I busied myself adjusting the pillows in the bed just perfectly while Ransom flicked through his textbook, grumbling at the work set and complaining that he wasn't going to pass the class, anyway, so what was the point?

I grinned as Dusk got to his feet. "I'll be right back. Decebal's just out front," he said, tucking his phone in his pocket.

"What does he want?" Ransom asked.

"Just dropping something off."

I peered up at him, noting that Dusk had just vanished from the bond.

"Oh, he called earlier," he added, catching my expression. "He said to tell you to look into case study 632 he sent. Said it seemed to match what you're looking for. Something about, uh, cleaving—no, uh, bond transfer. Unusual case, alpha… died part way through? Something like that."

If he was watching me carefully to catch my reaction, he got it. I dove for my laptop, flipping it open in seconds.

"All right. I'll be back in a moment. Ransom better have picked the movie."

The case studies were blurring on the screen as I scrolled, searching for the one he'd referenced. What he'd described sounded exactly like what I needed.

"What do you think Umbra's getting?" Ransom asked, flicking through the channels. The start of a movie sounded before he hit pause. "Won't be ruined by some popcorn, will it?"

I was barely listening as I reached the study.

He chuckled and kissed me on the temple, and I realised he'd said something else. I hadn't heard.

"I'll get you all the options," he said, leaving the room.

The little circle was loading on the screen as I clicked the study. Not fast enough.

This could be it, the answer I'd been searching for.

A Hail Mary.

Finally, the page loaded and my eyes scanned it, reading through.

Sure enough, it was a dark bond transfer. The pack lead had died part way through the negotiations.

But *how* had he died?

That's what I needed to know.

Ransom had returned in the doorway already, but I didn't look, instead reading line after line, skimming to get to the answer.

"One second," I said vaguely, glancing up, and then I froze, my blood turning to ice.

The alpha in my doorway wasn't one of my mates.

Mord Sato was standing in the doorway, watching me curiously.

But… this was my home.

My *nest*.

He wasn't supposed to be here. He *couldn't* be here—not when I was so close. My heart hammered in my chest as I glanced down at the computer screen, just in reach, yet…

Mord took a step forward, and I shifted back, a low whine in my chest, eyes fixed on his one boot that was in my territory.

"Your mates," he said quietly, "are out of patience."

CHAPTER 29

Ransom

I saw him from the kitchen.

An intruder.

An alpha who should not be here, taking a step into her nest.

My omega's nest—my *wife's* nest.

And I was the only one here to protect her.

"No." The flip was instant as I watched the tail of his trench coat almost vanish. My aura split the air, and he took a step back, his dark eyes sliding to me as I made for him.

A flash of the gun I'd left in the second drawer down flickered in my mind.

The rational choice.

It vanished as soon as it came, drowned by an old demon raising its head, finding no place for a weapon like that. Even when Mord lifted his gun, the barrel raised at me, it didn't matter. I was almost on him, the world around me fading into fury. Not in my home.

This alpha had a foot in her nest.

A low growl rose in my throat. I was almost on him, but not for a moment did I believe a bullet would be enough. A dark beast seized me, and Mord's aura flared as he flipped the gun in his grip in the last second, using it instead to strike at me as he tried to duck out of my way.

"Run!" I growled, my command ripping from the core of fury that drove everything I was right now, as sanity began to fade. I felt it seize Shatter as I caught the faintest glimpse of her through the door, on her feet, eyes wide beside the bed. Then pain exploded across my skull as Mord managed to smash me against the wall.

He grabbed the door and slammed it shut, trapping her inside.

No.

He grunted as my elbow caught him. Briefly, I realised he was too well trained. He could fight far better than me. I snarled, my aura flaring as I flung my weight against him, wild sounds ripping from my chest as the beast became frenzied.

"Fuck!" Mord grunted. My grip on his shoulder dug in, my whole weight thrown against him.

I heard a crack. Pain was a distant howl.

I threw my weight against him again, trying to go for anything that would stop him.

His grip loosened, and I lunged again, teeth closing around nothing before another pain, closer this time, became suddenly overwhelming. Heat trickled down my cheek.

The world was fading to red.

No…

A faint whine sounded in the air.

Mine…? I thought.

Or hers?

No…

Mord was stepping back, fading fast as the world spun. With another crash of pain, the world went black, his last words swimming through my foggy mind.

He almost sounded like he was amused.

"...More than I expected for a rich prick..."

This was too soon.

I shook from shock, replaying the fight between Ransom and Mord.

He's going to be okay, I told myself desperately.

He was alive.

I'd found the courage to open the door a crack, right as Mord had knocked him out. Before that, he'd been a raging ball of... I shivered, of *something* else. That hadn't been Ransom.

Not *my* Ransom...

Even his command that I run had been... a flash of power. Then nothing, as if he couldn't hold it. I shoved my tears back. Mord hadn't hurt him too badly. He could have, but he didn't.

Mord had straightened his coat and rolled his neck. Then he turned as I watched through the crack in the door. Dark eyes met mine, cold and deadly.

When he spoke, his voice was far too calm—completely different from the taunt I'd just heard from him as Ransom had fallen. "Are you going to run?"

Shakily, I pushed my nest door open, unable to bear the idea of him stepping into it again. There was a gun in his hand, and my alpha was unconscious on the floor at his feet. There wasn't a choice, not really. Even if at my back was a laptop with the last piece of the puzzle.

A piece I knew I would now never have in time.

We reached the door to the apartment, and he nudged my pair of new boots toward me.

"Bring them."

I picked them up shakily, my mind reeling as Mord tugged a spray can from one of the pockets of his huge trench coat and doused me in a mist before I could react. A scent blocker, I realised as I blinked through it.

Then he dragged me from the apartment and into a closet down the hallway before shutting us in. I was still shaking, scrambling for the right words. He was so calm, like this was a job to him—a normal day.

He peered at his phone again, and this time, I saw it was a video feed on the academy parking lot. As I watched, it jumped to a different feed.

"Put your boots on. A barefoot omega will draw too much attention."

As I struggled to get my boots on with shaky hands, he tugged something rectangular from his pocket. It was a device of some kind with a small antenna. He held it down at hip level, and I watched as Mord flipped a switch on it. I heard a small click, then nothing.

"Wh-what was that?" I asked.

"If he was tracking you, he's not anymore," Mord murmured, tucking the device back into his pocket. I jumped as he clamped a hand over my mouth, barely even looking at me as he waited. He was huge, and even without his aura out, frightening. The glint of his gun in his other hand was hard to ignore.

My pulse was racing out of control, and it wasn't long before I heard the sound of thundering footsteps.

Dusk…

Tears beaded my eyes, but I didn't dare make a sound.

Mord didn't hesitate, pulling me out moments later. I'd had to fight my whine of desperation as I caught the scent of midnight opium lingering in the air, and tangled with it was Decebal's roses and cranberries scent.

They'd *just* been here…

I squeezed my eyes shut, trying to conjure up the words on the webpage I had just been on. Not enough…

But this was it, whether I had my answer or not. The Lincoln pack was done waiting. And that meant I needed to keep the lie I'd let Mord believe the first time I met him.

"Where are we going?" I managed to ask as he dragged me out to the academy parking lot.

He'd tucked away his gun now. I could fight him, make a scene to the passing students, some of whom were throwing me frowns, but even if I did, it might get me nowhere. That seemed like the natural response. Try to run. To get away. But I couldn't.

He didn't answer as he shoved me into the back seat of a black car.

"Don't make me regret not tying you up," he said as he slammed the door and locked it.

My lip trembled. "Deep breaths," I whispered, my fists balling in my skirt as he circled the car to the driver's side. "You can do this, Shatter."

I clenched my teeth, fighting my tears. He was taking me to the Lincoln pack, and I had to be ready.

I wasn't, but I had to be.

"They could call the police," I said as he shifted the gearstick and pulled out of the academy parking lot.

"They won't."

"How do you know?"

"I've looked over quite a few of their activities over the last few years. Seems they haven't involved the authorities for anything. Not even when the wellbeing of their own pack mate is at stake. I can only imagine that the authorities pose a greater threat than anything I might."

We drove for a while, though it was hard for me to see where we were going with the blacked-out windows, and I didn't know the city well enough to keep track. Finally, I heard gravel below us as the vehicle slowed.

Where were we?

Then the door at my back was opened, and he tugged me out with ease. I only had a second to glance around at a massive industrial-looking building, closed off with tall fences, before he was tugging me toward a huge metal door.

Inside, he led me through winding corridors, all with concrete walls and peeling paint and not a sign of life in sight, and we finally stopped before another metal door.

Mord unlocked it, and I saw a few rooms within that were host to not much beyond a few old seats and a dented wooden table. It almost looked like a… makeshift home. Not that this sort of building seemed like a home at all…

I shrank, unsure what to expect.

At my side, Mord crouched down to undo his shoelaces. He was so unnervingly… casual, no matter the situation. I hadn't seen him as anything but neutral, besides the moment when he'd won against Ransom.

I watched as he tugged his shoes off and placed them neatly at the door, then he stood carefully, dusting off his coat before stepping in.

I frowned, still clutching my own fingers together as I looked within, my instincts filling in the gaps for me.

He had brought me here to stay for a while? The walls might be bare, and the air damp, but I think this *was* a home, by the ebony and mystery scent in the air.

Not wanting to upset him, I crouched down and fumbled with my own boots, removing them before entering. When I looked up, Mord was watching me with a half-cocked eyebrow as I hurried in, my gaze dropping to my socks with the first mild amusement I'd seen.

Okay.

Seeing him amused just made me more scared, but I think that meant I was right…

He shrugged off his coat as he stepped into the first room through an open door, then tossed it over the back of a chair. Then he sat down, reclining back and crossing his ankles on the table. I watched as he pulled a pack of cigarettes and lighter from the draped trench coat pocket.

I clasped my fingers, looking around. "Will my mates come?" I asked, anxiously taking the other chair, watching him closely.

He nodded, lighting one of the cigarettes.

Okay…

I had to sort myself out. Had they opened the safe? Is that why he'd brought me?

To bite me…

I swallowed.

"Did… did you, um… open the safe?"

Mord grimaced, taking a drag. "The… pale one… idiot with the stupid posh accent—"

"Eric?" I asked.

"Had a tantrum earlier. Thought he could get in faster than I could."

"Oh…" I trailed off. "What does that mean?"

Mord blew out a plume through his nostrils. "Blew up, didn't it? Burned everything inside."

Right. So, they didn't know they could claim me at any moment?

Maybe I had time.

The study…

If I could just… "Can I use your phone?" I asked hopefully.

He blinked, pausing halfway through a drag, but said nothing. The silence stretched, and I clasped my fingers, looking away.

That, I thought, was Mord speak for no.

Okay. I needed to compose myself. The bond was shut down on all ends but Dusk's. I hadn't explored it to feel how worried he was. I already knew. My alphas were about to burn the world down to protect me, and I had to be as strong as they were.

Because there was no one else left to protect them.

CHAPTER 30

Umbra

I came crashing into the apartment to find Ransom on the couch with Dusk and Decebal. Dusk was almost out of his mind, arguing.

Ransom was out cold.

Not dead. I had to remind myself of that.

My heart was pounding, their words barely making sense. Shatter was gone. Really, truly gone this time. Mord had taken her.

Did that mean they knew they could bite her? And if not, how long until they realised they had a bargaining chip that would get their agreement?

"We can't do anything without a location." Dusk was snarling.

"Kai's on it. Been pissed since the moment you mentioned Sato called him out. I think he'll find him."

"Can he?"

"Said Sato gave himself away too. Limited ways he could have dug up as much as he did on your pack, and they can't be hidden, either—not completely. Involves getting into Institute databases. He pulled the rest of the data he's collected on Sato over the years. Might get him close."

"If we do, we could get a location?"

"There's a chance."

"How long?" Dusk demanded.

"He's working as fast as he can."

It wasn't enough. How long until she vanished from the bond with us? My throat almost closed entirely at that thought. This was it. The ending I'd known was coming, and I wasn't going to let the others pay the price.

What Shatter had taught me last weekend was that she was so much stronger than I'd ever imagined. I'd felt what she'd suffered, what she'd survived. Despite her fear, she was strong enough to survive the Lincoln pack's cruelty so she could save us.

And I couldn't let her do that.

Because if she was gone, and Ransom was like this, would we lose him too? I knew the answer. It was the same answer that made me convinced that, if I didn't do something, Dusk would make himself a martyr.

For her. For Ransom. For me.

I could see it in his eyes as he held Ransom close. I could feel it through the bond. His terror was everything we'd claimed back over the last few weeks. The happiness. The joy. Now, it was all being ripped away.

I had to get to the Lincoln pack before Decebal could lead Dusk to his own demise.

I realised I might have a way to do that. I'd lingered at the kitchen island, which was why I had caught the faintest trace of oranges and the others hadn't.

A hint of Christmas. And the door was open a crack.

I waited, not closing the door or even looking in its direction, not until the conversation had died down.

"I'm checking their apartment," I said.

"What?" Dusk asked.

"The Lincoln pack. Gonna see if they left anything they shouldn't have."

Dusk stared at me like he was trying to process what I was saying, then nodded.

I slipped out, peering down the hallway to find no one there. But instead of going downstairs, I knocked on Roxy's door.

It opened almost instantly, as if she'd been waiting.

Her face was pale, eyes wide as she looked up at me.

"How much do you know?" I asked.

"She's in trouble," Roxy whispered. "I didn't… I didn't understand anything else. I just called her, but she won't pick up. She doesn't have her phone most of the time, anyway, but—"

"Do you want to help get her back?" I asked.

"Yes." She swallowed. "It's the Lincoln pack, isn't it? They've taken her?"

I nodded.

"But they can't… they can't bite her if you don't give up the bond…" She trailed off, eyes glittering. Roxy was smart enough to know that if it were that simple, we wouldn't be reacting like we were.

"What do you need?" she asked, voice hoarse.

A unique in. One only she had. "The Lincoln pack. Do you think you can get one of them to come to you, alone?"

She chewed on her lip, eyes darting between mine as she thought.

"They took her," I said quietly. "It will have to be good."

"Yes. Eric. I think… He's desperate. I had to block his number yesterday. He heard I, uh… I was talking about my heat to other packs." She opened her phone, scrolling through texts. "He was pissed, saying… here, uh…" She wrinkled her nose, reading out one of the texts. *"You're a filthy whore… No pack will pay a dime for your heat after you were ours."*

"You said desperate—"

"That is as desperate as it gets." She scrolled back through some texts. "If I tell him I'm in preheat and no one wants me…"

"You sure?" I asked.

"Oh, he'll come." She nodded. "You're going to kill him, right? After what he did to her…"

I coughed, scratching my head. "Right."

I didn't think I was supposed to say that out loud.

It was the truth, though.

Eric Harrington *was* going to die, but only *after* he gave up the location of my omega.

CHAPTER 31

Shatter

The Lincoln pack arrived not long after we did.

I was grateful all of a sudden for the scent-blocking spray, because there was no way I would be able to mask my fear when they stepped in. I dropped my eyes, not ready to see them yet.

Flynn took one look at me and waved a hand. "All right. I need a fucking drink. Bring her in five," he said, waving at Mord, then stepping by us and down the grimy hall to another room. He paused, and I could feel his gaze on me. "Why is she in socks?"

"Good news." Mord shrugged. "Your omega has manners."

Flynn rolled his eyes, vanishing, and Gareth followed, muttering something about staying in a shithole.

Eric lingered, though. "Come here," he said, and I dared glance up at him to see him watching me with dark eyes.

I swallowed, unable to stop myself from glancing at Mord. His cigarette was long out, but the stub remained between his lips. He watched me carefully as I got to my feet and forced myself to cross out and into the hallway, where Eric waited.

"Why do you look so scared?" Eric asked. "Aren't you supposed to be happy you're saved?"

I glanced up at him, then back down to the floor. "H-he's got a gun," I whispered.

Eric snorted.

"Hands."

"What?"

"Show me your hands."

I lifted my hands before catching myself. I realised, as I stared down at my palms, what he was asking for. A low growl rose in his throat as his grip closed around my left wrist and he lifted it.

My ring…

It was still there, glinting in the dim sunlight that filtered through a few grimy windows. The diamonds and hexagons facing the wrong way. Now, those diamonds danced through tears as I braced, already knowing what was about to happen.

When he ripped it from my finger, he might as well have ripped my heart from my chest. The world blurred, but I tried so hard not to cry.

"Done with that fucking pack taking shots," he muttered, his aura flaring as he crushed it in his fist. He looked ready to throw it, chest heaving, but then he shoved it in his pocket instead.

My pulse was thready, and I jumped violently as he grabbed me by the chin.

"Tell me why you're crying over them if you're ours," he snarled.

I clutched his arm, my whole body shaking as pain radiated from his grip. His aura was out and my instincts screamed danger. I couldn't speak, low whines of terror slipping from me with every breath.

"What the hell are you doing?"

His grip was gone, and Eric's furious green eyes focused behind me, where Mord's growl had come from.

"Eric!" Flynn's voice was sharp from the other direction. "What's going on?"

"Tryna kill your fucking omega," Mord snapped.

Eric shoved me out of the way. "We didn't pay you to—"

"*You* didn't pay him at all!" Flynn caught Eric before he could launch at Mord. "Enough." Flynn shoved Eric toward the room he'd just come from. He turned to Mord. "Give us a fucking minute."

The door slammed, but I heard raised voices through the walls.

I was shivering, breaths tight, terror still shooting through my veins. I flinched at the rustle of Mord's movement. He was leaning against the doorframe, eyes fixed down the hall in the direction of the Lincoln pack.

I blinked away more tears, pain shooting through my jaw as I swallowed, the ghost of Eric's grip impossible to shake. This was harder than I'd thought it would be. A *lot* harder. Eric was terrifying. But… I'd already known that.

What if… if everything went wrong?

What if the study wasn't what I needed it to be?

What if they bargained for Dusk's and Umbra's freedom, and it was my only choice?

Everything could still go wrong…

"It'll be okay…"

I blinked, realising I'd whispered that out loud. I didn't look at Mord, my arms waving awkwardly as I fought the urge to hug myself. I don't even know why I didn't want him to see.

Dusk and Umbra.

Saving them from this pack mattered first. Everything else… it was up to the universe.

I glanced at Mord, but he hadn't moved.

Finally, there was a bang on the door ahead, which I think meant they were ready for me.

I didn't move.

I tried to, but I couldn't. Oddly, I didn't want to be in that room without Mord, which seemed… unreasonable.

To my relief, at my inaction, he stepped toward me and hauled me into the room that was full of the Lincoln pack's scents. When he let me go, giving me a shove toward my mates, I met his eyes for a moment, knowing how desperate I probably looked.

He still looked empty inside, but those dark eyes met mine, and he leaned against the doorframe, crossing his arms and staring past me at the pack behind.

Okay.

Okay. I clasped my fingers. I could… I could do this.

I turned, seeing Flynn, Gareth and Eric waiting. Gareth was lounging on another of the clinical-looking metal chairs, Flynn was perched on the edge of the table, cracked beer in his fist, and Eric was leaning against the wall, arms crossed, watching me darkly.

Their scents were all in here—passion fruit, sesame seeds and sunflower, and coconut and plum. It was hard to put a dam on the memories that tried to surge back at those scents.

I watched Flynn's gaze drop from my eyes to my chin and neck, and a shadow crossed his face.

Bruising, maybe?

Gareth was staring, too, before shooting Eric a glare.

Flynn cleared his throat. "As I'm sure you know, we intend to make you an offer you don't deserve," he said. "But only if you help us."

"Help you?" My voice cracked. I tried to find the balance. I couldn't fall into their arms too quickly, not if I wanted this to be believable. Some of my hatred and fear of them, I think I needed that. "You… hurt me. You forced me to… to…" I trailed off, unable to say it, not looking toward Eric. Trying to shove away the memories of their teeth on my flesh, on the way Flynn had held me still while—

"Forced you to what?" Eric asked, raising an eyebrow. "You blame *us* for our response when you *hid* the scent match all this time?" He leaned forward. "When you told us you were stalking us, then tried to pretend you didn't want—"

"Th-that's not—" I swallowed, my hand jumping to my collarbone. To the canvas of scars they'd left on my skin.

"We were pushed to the edge of insanity," Eric snarled. "We didn't *hurt* you, we claimed you. How could we not? You *tricked* us, lying about the scent match and driving us mad. What did you think was going to happen?" he asked. "What alpha would have done differently, knowing you'd just spent a heat with *them*? Not knowing why it was twisting us up."

I stared between them, trying to ground myself, to find a plan amidst my panic.

Flynn was the one who went on. "We're willing to take you back, even after you've been *defiled* by other alphas—yet it seems you're nothing but ungrateful."

I recoiled, my heart thundering in my ears as I stared at him with wide eyes. I opened my mouth, ready for… for what, I didn't know. Venom rose in my chest, hatred like I'd never felt.

Ungrateful?

The pause, the blinding fury at what he'd just said. It was the only thing that saved me. I froze, suddenly dragging every ounce of hatred to a screeching halt as my mind scrambled with that.

No… I took a breath. Now I was here, now they were talking, I could hear echoes of these words in what Ransom had told me they'd said.

I knew this part.

They still believed that I was trapped in the middle of this, caught between a dark bond and mates who'd rejected me. They still believed everything that I'd wanted them to believe the day I'd put on that dress that revealed all of my scars.

I squeezed my eyes shut, trying to find my voice.

"You still… you still want me?" My voice was weak.

"That's why we brought you here, but you will first understand how much you have to make up for. A princess bond is no small offer—not to an omega like you."

"Why… why would you do that?" I asked.

"We are not the kind of alphas who would leave behind a scent match," Flynn said.

That was a lie.

They would leave me a thousand times over, if they didn't need this bond. But they didn't know I knew that.

"You haven't made this easy," Flynn went on. "Your lies have left us humiliated, and even when we bit you, you asked for *him*—when you could have just told us about the scent match."

"I… I was going to." My mind raced, still dizzy with this card I was trying to play. "I *was*—that's why I needed Roxy to help me figure it out b-because she was your omega and she would know if you would still want me when you found out I was gold pack… But Dusk knew I was—he had a picture, and he told me I could never tell you, so I had to be sure."

Flynn's jaw was clenched. "We were *right* there—"

"I thought you were going to dark bond me, and Gareth s-said… that you would never want me after I spent my heat with them…"

"Because you *lied* about the match," Gareth snapped. "And then you ran straight back to him."

"You don't understand…" My voice shook. "He *knew* I was gold pack, and he claimed me, anyway. I thought—maybe even with the bites… And no one else was ever going to want me again." My breath caught. "I didn't realise he was going to…" I swallowed, my chest heaving. "To…"

"You didn't know he was going to dark bond you?" Eric asked, incredulous. "After you came back to him like that?"

"He said he loved me." My voice was small.

"How the fuck did we get matched with such a stupid bitch?" Eric snorted, glancing at the others. "This is insane." He looked back at me. "You could have just told us, and none of this would have happened. Do you know how much money this has cost us? And they still might not give up the fucking bond."

"I thought that when you saw my eyes—"

"You didn't give us a *chance*," Flynn snapped. "You drove us mad instead, didn't you? And now we're forced to offer a princess bond if we want to save our mate."

"I w-was scared…"

"That pack has fucked with her head," Gareth said. "You're acting scared now, but you don't seem to hate them in public—"

"It's Dusk," I said quickly, shrinking down. "He gets upset if I act out. He wants me to be grateful for the dark bond. He's big on punishment."

Gareth snorted. "Seems the type."

"At least we know you can tolerate being put in your place," Eric mused. "That won't be over when we save you. You have a lot to make up for."

"I-I understand."

"You've almost single-handedly ruined us," Gareth added. "*I* need something to prove your gratitude today."

Proof?

"Like what?"

"What do you think?" Gareth asked, something nasty in his eyes.

"I c-can't," I stammered, far too quickly. My mind raced to come up with a reason. "He's jealous. The commands—p-please don't… He's told me I can't with any alpha out of the pack…"

Gareth grinned, straightening. "You're saying if we fuck you, that dark bond you walked right into is going to hurt?" he asked. "Sounds like the least you owe us. It's a good start."

Fuck me?

"Gareth—" Flynn began, but Eric interrupted.

"No. I'm with him. She was in tears when I took their ring. I want proof."

I knew the risks of playing this card, but it was moving faster than I'd planned. My mind was going cold, memories of Eric's room creeping in, tightening my chest.

Gareth got to his feet, eyes glinting.

I cracked, backing up. I wasn't strong enough for this.

Only, I crashed straight into a wall of solid muscle. The faintest trace of ebony assaulting my senses.

As useless as it was, I scrambled behind Mord, my nails digging into his arm, as if he wasn't paid by them.

Gareth was grinning, something manic in his eyes.

I tried to calm my breathing, not daring to look up at Mord's expression, afraid of how cold it would be.

"The bond is…" I swallowed. "I can't."

"Either you come back here," Gareth breathed. "Or I'll have him hold you still."

I bit down a whimper of fear, my eyes darting around, knowing there was no escape.

But I *couldn't* do this.

"No." Flynn's voice was low. I looked at him, relief almost dizzying. "As foolish as our scent match might be, we are *courting* her. We will do it with dignity, no matter how little dignity *she* cares for."

My breath escaped my chest at last as Gareth scowled, but he sank back into his seat.

Stranger still, I swear Mord's muscles uncoiled beneath my grip. He was so statuesque, I hadn't noticed he was tense in the first place. I glanced up at him, unsure for the first time, but his expression was as impassive as ever, and I wondered if I'd imagined it.

With all the courage I could find, I stepped back around Mord so I wasn't cowering behind him anymore.

"When's your next heat?" Eric asked. I forced back another wave of nausea. With how sickened they made me, with them, it would be never. "It *was* a heat you had with them, right?"

I nodded with a wince, knowing that wasn't something I could lie about.

"A month or two?" Gareth asked. "You'll be making it up to us then."

The more I seemed to agree, the more they relaxed. I hadn't realised, until now, how much they believed the picture we'd painted. This pack believed Dusk was the ultimate villain, and I was nothing to them but the prize, so desperate that I would do anything for the chance to escape.

Eric crossed the room toward me, and I saw Flynn stiffen, as if concerned.

"You will not walk into this bond thinking you've won," Eric hissed. "What we're offering—what we're going to do to free you from the *foolish* position you've put yourself in—is far more than you deserve. Do you understand?"

I nodded, fighting to control my breathing.

"Say it."

"Yes." My whisper wasn't enough to distract from the overwhelming horror that had been building.

I clenched my jaw, eyes suddenly burning, but I couldn't burst into tears right now. I was so close, though. Not because I was afraid, but because of the vile truth that *they* were who I had come to this academy in search of. Because I was pushing every emotion I had to its limit in order to pretend for them. And I had been so close to ending up here.

Dusk, Umbra, and Ransom had been the only ones in the way of that.

"I still don't like the fact they had her heat," Gareth murmured, not looking at me anymore. "We're taking their leftovers."

I shut my eyes, trying to calm my breathing. I wasn't going to make it. I was so scared. So scared and fucking pathetic.

"We don't have much of a choice if we wish to honour the scent match," Eric said coolly. "But I want fucking atonement."

I blinked at him. He stepped toward me, adjusting his cuffs with a sickened expression on his face.

I forced myself to nod, hoping that would be enough for him. "Of course. Yes. I c-can do that."

His phone buzzed in his pocket, and as I stepped back, he glanced down at it. He did a double take, eyes scanning the screen, eyebrows shooting up.

"Were they any good?" Gareth asked. I looked back to find his gaze was fixed on me.

"Gareth," Flynn snorted. "Come on."

"No. I want to know. When they fucked our omega through heat, did she want them to? I want to know if our omega was begging for other alphas' knots."

"Since she's in a dark bond, I can't imagine—" Flynn cut off as my breath caught.

I cracked, tears finally flooding my cheeks.

Stupid.

But Gareth was grinning, apparently satisfied.

Right… I took a breath, wiping my eyes. They thought I was crying at the thought of heat with the Kingsman pack?

That was the best I could hope for.

Eric had tucked his phone away, his sneer levelled at me. They were convinced, but he'd been the one who'd seen me cry over the ring. So, I did the most insane thing I'd ever forced myself to do, and I flung my arms around him. "Th-thank you."

He was rigid for a long moment, and then I felt his hand at my back. Not moving, but firm.

I hated him.

I hated him with more fire than I had ever hated anyone. Bile burned my throat as a thousand horrible moments all teemed in my head. So, I clung to him harder and let his horrible passion fruit scent shift to something disgustingly satisfied.

"All right. I think that's enough." Flynn's voice was clipped.

"I agree." Eric had a cold smile on his lips when I looked up at him. "If we're done for the evening, I'm going out."

"Where?" Gareth asked.

"Bit of fresh air. Process the corner we've been forced into." I didn't like the look in his eyes. "I won't go far."

"Mord." Flynn waved dismissively. "Take her?"

I peered from Eric's shirt to see Flynn getting to his feet, straightening his button-up with an oddly cold look on his face.

"Is that everything? Are you sure we can't—?" Gareth began.

"That's everything." Flynn's voice was still stiff. Gareth opened his mouth, but Flynn cut him off. "As pack lead, I say we're done here."

I processed that, trying to understand the way his scent wavered, and I thought Flynn's scent of coconut and plum might be bitter. His eyes were fixed on me.

Was he…? Could he be…?

Oh.

He was jealous. I let go of Eric and stepped back, surprised when his hand became firmer, as if he didn't want me to leave.

I took a step toward Flynn, though, determined to figure out if I was right. "You're… really going to save me from them?"

He frowned, though I saw the spark of pleasure in his eyes. "If you don't make any more stupid mistakes."

Following instincts that I truly wished I wasn't having, I fell into his arms next, finding him far faster to place his hands around me.

But over the last few weeks, I'd learned with distinct clarity exactly what it was that drove Dusk, Umbra, and Ransom crazy, and I just had to hope it would be enough for the Lincoln pack too.

"Thank you," I said again. "I can't believe you still… still want me."

"Like I said. The word *mate* means something to us. I expect you to take it seriously too."

"I swear." I looked at him with wide eyes, the next words that came up as sour as vomit. "If you save me from Dusk, I'll be anything for you."

I watched his pupils blow, and his fingers dug into my waist. I tried really, really hard not to feel the arousal I'd just given him.

When I stepped away, I noticed Gareth remained seated, his frame tense, eyes narrowed. The last of their pack's scent in the room, sunflower and sesame seeds, wilted with bitterness as I looked back up to Flynn, not making a move toward him.

"Right. We're done," Flynn said. "Go with him. I have arrangements to make so we can get out of this shithole."

I turned, forcing myself to smile in the face of Mord's cold scowl. If I was going to play this card, I had to commit, and the bitter edge of Gareth's scent was still in the air. I think, just like Flynn, Gareth was jealous. And jealous alphas were never rational.

I needed *them* irrational, while they believed I was stupid, desperate, and terrified.

So, I hurried toward Mord and grabbed him in a huge hug, too, despite feeling the hard edge of the gun that was tucked into his belt. "I know it was dangerous for you."

He froze in surprise, but I looked up at him with wide eyes. "And you said you might join the pack?" I asked, to which he gave a non-committal grunt. "Your scent is *very* dark, but I really like it—kind of matches mine—so I think that should be okay…" I nodded, glancing back at the other three, who were staring at me in utter shock.

I reached up, cupping Mord's cheek and dropping my voice just for him. "Thank you for bringing me to them." His eyes were narrowed as he watched me, as if he wasn't sure *what* he thought. He was much more scrutinising than the others, so I just had to pray I did a good enough job.

CHAPTER 32

Dusk

The bond was empty, except for me.

Again, I remained, needing to be an anchor for them. Needing to feel her in this bond somewhere.

First Shatter had been taken from us, now Ransom was out cold on the couch, and before he'd vanished in the bond, I'd felt the feral sickness taking hold. But now *Umbra* had vanished too?

"What's he thinking?" I asked Decebal.

I knew the answer, though. It was something I'd been frightened of since I'd found Umbra waiting in Shatter's nest, ready to fight me for pack lead.

"She's still in the bond." Decebal was working hard to keep us calm, though it wasn't working. "That means they haven't bitten her—"

"It doesn't mean they haven't opened the safe. It could mean she's the one holding out on the princess bond," I spat. My blood chilled at the thought. "Would we know?" I asked. "If they offer her that bond—will we feel the offer, even if she hasn't accepted it yet?"

"I…" Decebal frowned. "I'm not sure."

I clenched my jaw, shoving away what that might mean for Shatter right now.

I needed to think.

I'd been halfway through an argument with Decebal in the parking lot when I'd felt her fear. An argument over what he'd brought for me. "I need it. Now," I growled, continuing that argument where we'd left it off. "I'm out of time."

"Dusk—" Decebal's voice was a warning, his jaw clenched.

"You know what he did for me," I hissed. "You know I need this on the table."

"It's not a good idea."

"It's the *only* idea."

"I'll give it to you on one condition—" He cut off as I stood and grabbed him by the shirt.

"Don't play with me, Decebal. She's gone. Umbra's gone. Ransom's—"

"And then what? You'll be next?" Decebal demanded. "I'm not spending this many years of my life watching you drag this pack from the fucking edge, so you can throw it all away in a day—"

"They took her!"

"And if this kills you—what then? Ransom is unstable, Umbra needs—"

"Her. I'm not stupid. I've been watching. This pack has everything it needs without me."

At last.

Saying those words was like the final weight lifted from my chest.

It was, I realised, the truth.

And that was, for the first time, a good thing.

There was a long silence between us. I'd never seen Decebal like this before. "There is no pack without you, Dusk. I don't know if you noticed, but you're out of alphas, and if you kill Flynn—"

"They can start a new pack with her in the centre."

Three alphas were required to form an alpha-centric pack, but if they bit in with the omega in the middle, that was different. The rules changed. Ransom and Umbra would stabilise.

"Give it to me!"

Decebal said nothing, his pale jaw ticking.

"I paid you for this," I hissed.

His lips drew in a snarl. He hated when I brought money into this.

"She's gone, and I can't protect her, not without them. And if I can't protect her, what's the point?" There was a long silence. "I won't use it unless I have to. But don't take away my shot at fixing all of this."

Finally, he released a breath. Then he dug in his pocket and shoved a small black box against my chest. I let go of him, taking a step back as I took it, relief searing my veins right as Decebal's phone blew up.

He glanced down, scanning the screen. "Kai's got something."

"A location?"

"Near enough. Narrowed it down to a block—"

"A block?" I asked. That was too fucking broad. I tugged my phone from my pocket as I heard it buzz. I froze as I saw a text from Roxy.

Roxy: I think I fucked up.

"What?" Decebal asked, clearly catching my expression, but I was already tapping on her number.

"What happened?" I asked.

"He said he was going to save her…" Roxy's voice was choked through the phone.

"Umbra." I knew already.

"I got him to take me to Eric. I thought he told you where we were going, but he didn't. He's going to get hurt. I don't know if he's in his right mind—he seemed really off."

"Where are you?"

"There's this massive old building, a facility, somewhere near…" She trailed off.

"I have it," Decebal said almost instantly. "Abandoned alpha penitentiary. Trust Sato—likes his old buildings, dramatic prick."

"I'm on the way," I said to Roxy. "Are you inside?"

"No. In the car. He went in and told me to stay away. I'm sorry, Dusk. I was so worried about her, I didn't think—"

"I'm on my way. They're going to be fine, all right?" That had to be true. "Just don't go in."

The last thing we needed was another omega in the mix. Decebal stepped after me as I made for the door, but I turned to him. "You have to stay with him." I glanced at Ransom.

"You aren't going by yourself—"

"They don't know I'm coming." I'd have the advantage. "But if he wakes"—I jabbed a finger at Ransom—"you have to keep him here, and you're going to fucking lie to him. Tell him she's safe."

If Ransom got near this, slipped any further into that void, we'd lose him…

"Fuck, Dusk, this is—"

"Once backup's here, then come. But I'm *not* losing him."

If something went wrong… I didn't want to think about it, but if we lost Shatter from this bond, Ransom could be on the brink of becoming feral again.

CHAPTER 33

Umbra

The hallways around us were cold and dark. I was in an abandoned penitentiary that hadn't seen life in a long time.

Eric had appeared outside its walls, just beyond the door I was dragging him to right now. My aura was out as I hauled him into the room, my hand clamped over his mouth. His aura was pathetic compared to mine, and it wasn't a struggle.

If Shatter was in this building, I would be better off getting the answer out of Eric instead of trying to hunt her down. Eric *would* tell me, and the size of the place meant no one would hear his screams.

Or perhaps they were close and they'd come for me. I welcomed that.

I shoved him to the ground, aiming a kick into his stomach that sent him crashing against the wall. He groaned, clearly winded, as I reached for the bent metal chair that was toppled over in the corner.

Setting it down before him, I took a seat, letting him catch his breath as I glanced around. The walls were concrete with scratches through worn-down paint. The corners of the room had gathered years of dust, and there was a long window across one wall, reinforced by metal, that showed another room beyond. It looked like a viewing window, one built strong enough to keep alphas out—or in.

It was dim in here, the only lights leaking from hallway windows beyond.

It was a surprisingly poetic location, reminiscent of my earliest memories. Of the place Eric had known me last. But even in the dim light, I could see that his pale face had completely drained of what colour it usually had.

"Where is she?" I asked, turning back to Eric.

She was safe enough for now. Through the bond, she would occasionally surface, her terror making it impossible to keep her out, but I knew they hadn't bitten her.

Not yet.

I would get to her before anything happened.

Not Flynn, not even Mord Sato, would be enough to stop me.

"You've gone mad," Eric spat. He tried to pick himself up, but I made to stand, and he froze. He wasn't chained or tied up. I didn't have a weapon. But Eric was a coward, and he knew the threats my aura held.

"You took her," I said quietly.

"She's… she's our scent match—"

"No." My voice was cold. "You stole my scent match."

Eric went still, eyes wide as he took me in. "You're… insane," he spluttered.

But he was taking me in now, truly taking me in. Dusk was the one for the dramatics, but today, I'd tumbled into my void, compulsions leading me.

I was seated on the old metal chair, watching as his green eyes scanned me again and again. Brows slowly creasing, uncertainty deepening in his expression.

What was he seeing?

The alpha he'd known through the flickering video, tortured and suffering?

I needed that alpha. The one I'd once been. *He* had paid. Had known no joy, had existed before Shatter, and I needed him to remind the universe of what I'd given so that she could walk away free.

So Dusk could survive.

More payments ached, more than I'd ever done before in one sitting. It was as if I could feel the blood seeping from those wounds.

"Tell me who I am." My voice was low and rough, dead compared to the voice I used around her. I had to claw back everything I'd once been.

"This is some kind of joke," Eric stammered.

"It was," I said. "*I* was. To you, to your brothers. A number. A bet."

Eric dragged himself to his feet, his gaze sliding to the door, before looking back to me, equal parts confused and afraid. He didn't take one step before I got to my feet. I saw the movement of the swallow down his neck as he considered me.

"Tell me who I am." I spoke each word slowly this time.

It took him a while.

I underestimated the satisfaction I would get from watching the dawning recognition in his eyes. I wanted to see his fear as he finally realised who we were.

"I d-don't know what you want me to say."

"Fuck with me, Eric, and I will break every finger, just to hear the sound of them snapping."

It was a promise I wasn't far from.

His lips drew back in a snarl, and his aura split the air. He made for the door in an instant, but I mirrored his movement, my aura smothering his with ease. I slammed him against the wall, not caring how hard his head hit it.

"You're m-mad," he said.

"And why is that?" My grip tightened at his neck, and blood trickled down the side of his head. His lips were still drawn back, but he looked more terrified than arrogant now. *"Tell. Me."*

"You're…" His voice was choked as he stared at me. "You're 66."

CHAPTER 34

Shatter

I'd wanted to wait, but I could feel Dusk's panic through the bond when I pried into it. I tried not to surface, knowing my fear would make things worse, but I could tell from his desperation that things were bad.

I didn't have time to wait.

So, I slipped back down the hallway to the room I knew they were in.

"Has Jasmine been blowing up your phone?" Flynn asked. "She's getting irritating."

"Yeah." Gareth snorted. "You think that's where Eric went?"

"If he did, why is she still texting us? And he shouldn't have left. Directly against what Sato said."

"Stupid that we have to wait in here," Gareth grumbled.

I finally dared poke my head around to see him on the metal chair, and Flynn still leaning on the table, which now hosted a box of pizza.

"They're on the last checks. I'm happy to lie low, if it means not waking up to those pricks at my doorstep."

"You think this is going to work?" Gareth asked. "Take her and hope they give it up?"

"They'll have to, eventually. Or they'll get bored when there's no bragging rights. This is a pissing match for them, anyway. But for now—" Flynn cut off as he spotted me in the doorway. "What?"

"Can I speak to you?" I asked, glancing between them.

"You're supposed to be waiting with Sato."

"It's, um… important."

Flynn raised his eyebrow, waiting.

"Do you think it's okay if I speak to you…" I swallowed. "Alone?"

"Why?" Flynn asked as Gareth went tense.

"Oh…" I wrung my fingers together, frowning. "I'm not used to things being like this."

"What does that mean?" Flynn asked.

"With the K—with the other pack, they take pack lead so seriously," I said. "But if here, it's more relaxed—"

"No." Flynn straightened his shirt, lifting his hand to stop me. "Gareth, give us a minute."

"You're joking?" he snorted.

"We're biting in an omega," Flynn replied. "Things will be different. We need to adhere to standards we didn't before." Gareth opened his mouth to argue, but Flynn got there first. "I won't have any news until we find out if *my* mansion upstate is clear."

When Gareth reached me, I dropped my eyes, still clasping my hands nervously. He stopped before me, his stupid sesame seed scent displeased.

He didn't say anything, but when I didn't lift my eyes to him, he relaxed a little. "Forgive me." I found my voice at last. "I didn't mean to cause any problems."

There was a long silence, and then he leaned close, his knuckle brushing my cheek. "I'll forgive you if you bring *this* attitude to me in bed after I bite you."

I nodded, stomach turning.

Again, his scent shifted, irritation fading for lust, and it made me want to throw up. He stepped past me without another word.

I crossed toward Flynn, who was taking the seat Gareth had vacated. I knew I needed to make an impression, so I settled on my knees before him.

"What is it?" he asked.

I swallowed, my fists balling in my lap. "I'm… scared. I thought I could talk to you about it."

"Scared of what?"

"I'm worried, if things don't work out, and I end up—"

"You won't." He cut me off. "No matter what, you won't be returning to them. We have a plan. Everything moved forward a little faster than we expected, but we won't be here long."

I almost glanced up at him but controlled myself. They planned on taking me away, regardless of the negotiations to come. I bit back my fear. That was one possible outcome of many, and I had to focus on my job.

"Okay." I clasped my hands together anxiously.

"Was there something specific you want?"

"I don't…" I swallowed. "I don't want anyone to die because of this."

There was a long pause. "You've come to me to ask for mercy?" he asked. "For alphas who dark bonded you?"

"This whole mess was my fault," I whispered.

"It is." Flynn snorted. "But can I be sure this isn't a lingering command from them?"

I shook my head. "No, it's nothing like that."

Again, there was another silence. "Ah…" From my periphery, I saw him lean back in his seat. "I think I understand." He held a hand out to me, and I looked up at him. "Let us talk frankly."

What did that mean?

I took it, a shiver brushing my spine as my skin touched his. He helped me to my feet, his gaze curious as he watched closely.

"You're afraid that, if we fail and you end up back there, they'll be angry that you turned on them."

"I…" That… wasn't what I'd meant. My mind scrambled, trying to keep up as I looked at him. I saw something intense in Flynn's eyes, a kindled flame of a spark I'd seen earlier.

I nodded, heart in my throat as I prayed that I was reading into it right.

"Please save me." My voice trembled as violently as I gripped him. "I can't go back."

My fear, at least, was real. It was a rising tide in my chest, and I let it in, feeling a terrified purr rising in my throat.

Flynn reacted instantly, drawing me close until I was in his arms, and I let him read it as comfort, not the sickness of being in the arms of an alpha so vile.

"Don't worry." One hand lingered on my hair as he held me against him. "We will protect you." He held me close for a long time.

This was good. Of all of them, I think Flynn was my best chance. He had the most to lose and the most to prove.

"What will your commands allow for?" he asked at last.

My eyes widened and I looked up at him. We were so close, our noses brushed. I held steady, though, my gaze holding his.

"You… want me?" I asked. Another purr stumbled out, and his lips curved up at the edges.

"I do understand it now, I think. Your presentation is very… hard to appreciate." His hands tightened around my waist. "But I see the scent match now."

My fists closed in his shirt.

"What about a kiss?" he asked.

I tensed, shutting my eyes for a long moment before forcing them open.

"I…" My breath caught at the thought of his lips on mine. Something romantic. Sweet. Something reserved for my pack. Never for him. "I think…" I swallowed. I had to commit to the plan. My pack's lives depended on it. "If it would convince you, it would be worth a little pain."

"No." His smile faded. "I see you've had enough pain." His eyes lingered on my jaw, where I knew there was bruising from Eric. My eyes widened in real surprise as I stared at him.

Not what I had expected.

My mind raced. I'd thought he would go for the offer of physicality, but if he didn't… What did that mean?

I was still so new to this—to the omega things I really should know, but I needed to understand. My palms brushed his cheeks, sensing that I may be able to tug on this thread with safety. As foul as he was, I think he would play the honourable one if it made him the saviour. He wanted to protect me—to be the alpha I'd painted him as.

"Are you sure?" I asked. His breath touched my lips, and his pupils were dilated. "I would pay in pain to feel your protection." I paused, letting those words sink in. "Alpha."

A low growl rumbled in his chest, and his grip became painful at my waist. I thought, for a second, he would do it.

I braced.

But he held back. "I would be no better than those you're running from."

Flynn Lincoln was repainting a picture of himself in my eyes, and that, to him, was worth more than a kiss. I found a smile, something true in it at the spark of victory. He drew me back against him, seeming content to just have me close.

I had to swallow back more bile.

Cuddles were *Umbra's.*

A tear tracked my cheek before I could stop it, and I let him wipe it away. "What makes you sad about this?" he asked.

"I'm not sad," I told him. "I just… I've been dreaming of you for so long. After the party, I thought you would hate me forever. I thought I wouldn't be worth saving."

I understood it at last: the power of an omega, and not just from the lists I'd made watching movies with Roxy. I had learned it from the push and pull between me and my pack—only, they cared for me and for who I was.

Flynn Lincoln might not care about me, but he *did* care that I made him feel powerful. And right now, I was the broken omega he could save.

"I'm here, now." His touch caressed my waist, as if he wanted to know my body more.

I clung to my conviction.

To my plan.

I clung to that as I drowned in the coconut and plum scent that haunted my nightmares. As his body pressed to mine. As he tried to claim an omega from the pack he'd almost destroyed.

My pack.

So, I held tight to the knowledge that Flynn Lincoln was going to pay as his fingers dipped under the hem of my shirt.

I tensed, letting out a breath of shock.

"Is that…?" He trailed off but didn't draw back. "Triggering the command?"

"I don't want that command to mean you're…" I swallowed. "You're disappointed in me. I can push through—"

"No." He withdrew his hand at last, but I didn't miss that he didn't do it until I'd spoken.

I was still putting all the pieces together, figuring out how he worked.

I knew, now, that the idea of me was more than the reality of claiming me. He was willing to wait if the trade was the power I made him feel—if he thought I was becoming desperate to please him.

His knuckles drew along my cheek. "It will be all the better after I've freed you."

I wound my fingers around his wrist, holding his touch on my cheek as I stared up at him. "You truly want me?"

"Claiming you is all I can think about."

I smiled, my heart aching at this act, but he was the catalyst to everything, so I spoke the words that would seal his fate.

"I don't care what the others say," I breathed. "I want you to keep pack lead after the negotiations."

CHAPTER 35

Umbra

Hearing those words from Eric was a breath of cool relief, and years of wound-up fury seeped from me in an instant.

He knew who I was.

I shut my eyes, feeling it fall away. In its wake were hatred and madness. In its wake was the person who would do anything to protect her.

"Y-you should be dead," Eric stammered.

"If I were dead, wouldn't sickness have consumed your precious pack lead by now?"

"We thought…" He trailed off, a spark of uncertainty in his eyes, as if he didn't think he should say what he had been about to.

"What?" I asked. "What did you think?"

"That, maybe when you died, it cured him."

I sneered. So willing to believe what was convenient for them.

"What do you want from me?" Eric asked.

"I want you to tell me where she is."

His eyes darted to the door, and I realised my mistake. He was terrified of what would happen if he gave me what I wanted. "Look, we can figure this out. If this is about making fools of us—?"

"Making *fools* of you? You think that's what we care about?" My voice was hateful as I slammed him against the wall again.

"Hold up," he said. "This is about Flynn, n-not me. He's the one with the sickness. He's the one that needed the trials. I swear, I had nothing to do with it—"

"*You* hurt her more than any of them, Eric."

It was my darkest secret, the thing I had never admitted to her. The thing I should never have done. But this monster lurking, slowly stirring and lifting its head, had won.

Then and now.

"I don't k-know what you mean," he stammered.

"I know every mark you gave her."

She'd let me in. Let me see those scars, even when she had been hurt by them. It was a betrayal of her, but I'd spent so long examining them, fingers tracing her skin as she lay curled in my arms. And as if it was burned into my twisted, alpha instincts, I recognized the difference between each. She was mine to protect. "I know which bites were yours," I breathed, clamping my hand over his mouth. He fought me, his aura flaring, but nothing happened. "I knew you decided bites weren't enough to make her suffer. You decided you wanted more. But she's mine. She was never yours, and any teeth that touch her flesh, those are mine too."

My thumb pressed against his teeth, and his growl turned into a low whimper of pain. I pressed harder, and there was a sneer on my face as I cracked his perfect smile. As I dislodged a tooth and he let out a whine of agony.

Her scars weren't all I'd seen. I'd betrayed her. The video they'd sent out to the whole school, I hadn't been strong enough not to watch—not like Dusk and Ransom—that vicious part of me needing to know what it was I would punish.

What he'd taken from us. From Dusk. From her. I needed him to know the fear he'd given her.

I pressed my palm over his mouth, my lips drawn in a snarl.

"Swallow it."

His eyes widened, and I could feel the hot blood sliding between my fingers as he tried to spit it out. I crushed him harder against the wall as he fought.

"I said, swallow it."

I smothered his mouth and nose, relishing the strangled sounds coming from his chest, the terror in his eyes as he fought me and got nowhere. As his air began to run out.

I waited until his struggles became more desperate, but still, his strength was nothing compared to mine.

I knew when he had done it because he almost choked. I waited another few seconds to make sure, and when I let him go, he buckled, blood still pouring from his mouth.

"Now," I said again. *"Tell me where she is."*

CHAPTER 36

Shatter

"Pack lead?" Flynn had frozen. "What does that mean?"

I shrank down. "I don't... I thought you knew."

"Knew what?"

I'd read the logs Decebal had given Dusk. I'd heard what Gareth and Eric thought, that Flynn had negotiated pack lead with his money, and I was hoping that it was something he was anxious about.

"Outside, before you stopped him, Eric said that… I don't know, um… you negotiated pack lead, but when I was bitten in, then that didn't hold up anymore."

Flynn didn't know I was aware of his aura sickness—and that did nothing but aid my case.

"He said that?"

I nodded.

"That traitorous *fuck*... Is Gareth in on it too?" He straightened, as if he was going to stand.

"No, wait…" I tried to make him look at me. "I just got here. I can't screw this up already—"

"Telling me was the right thing to do," he said firmly.

"Please don't tell him I said anything. I know Eric hates me already. Flynn, please," I whispered. "An alpha like you *should* be pack lead."

He frowned at me, pausing.

"After I'm bitten in, I will back your claim. I'll refuse them anything if they go against it. I don't trust anyone else to keep me safe," I said, brushing my chin where Eric had grabbed me.

"You're the best of them…" I swallowed. "I thought I would never be loved again. And they're angry, and they have every right to be, but you, Flynn. You've never been like that—you knew, always, that I was your mate. *You* came to find me at their doorstep… Your instincts were right."

He was staring at me, muscles unwinding.

He nodded, jaw clenched. "I always knew there was something different about you," he said quietly.

"Of all of them, *your* instincts were the sharpest. You *are* pack lead, Flynn, and you know their strengths and weaknesses." I pressed my palms to his chest. "I will be theirs, but yours first. I want to change their minds about me, but I can't do it without you."

He was nodding slowly, arrogance etched into his features.

"We can't afford to fight now," I said. "Show them you're worthy of pack lead by claiming your scent match."

There was a long pause. "Yes…" He nodded. "I'm glad you told me, but you're right. We need to wait."

I let out a breath of relief. "Thank you."

I think I had done what I needed to do. The next part of the plan was risky without the confirmation I was seeking in that study.

Flynn went still, eyes wide, cutting me from my thoughts.

"What?" I asked.

"It's… Eric. He's… *fuck*."

Gareth was in the doorway, eyes wide. "They have him."

There was a snarl on Flynn's face as he took a step toward the door before turning back to me. "You'll wait here. Negotiations might be sooner than we think if they've got Eric."

Ransom

I'd woken when Decebal's backup had arrived.

Now, he was gone, leaving me with an alpha I hadn't met before.

I was in the parking lot before an old building, and I was seated, deadly still in the back of a car that was locked. The alpha in the front was watching me in the rear-view with a furious, ice-blue gaze.

I took a deep breath, steadying myself.

I could feel the walls closing in, narrowing my vision until there was only one thing left.

Her.

I needed to get out—*had* to reach her. But I was on the brink of collapse, one flare of my aura away from losing it.

If I lost myself now, I wouldn't be able to save her—and I knew she must be in the building up ahead.

She was still vacant in the bond.

What kind of fear was she hiding?

I couldn't think about it.

Another breath.

Only one alpha.

I could take one.

There was supposed to be two, but Kai—Decebal's red-eyed pack mate—had ducked out without warning, slipping a gun into his belt and sprinting for the building ahead before anyone could stop him. The alpha in the front seat had cursed, darting from the car, shouting after him, but he was too late.

Another breath.

The alpha in the front spoke. "So much better things I could be doing with a Friday evening than babysitting while they get all the fun," he muttered.

I didn't like him one bit, not down to his pretentious-ass whiskey and chocolate scent. It was calming, focusing on that and not her.

Anything but her.

Another breath.

I shut my eyes.

Another.

I love you, Shatter.

I had to hold on to that love. It was the thing that had brought me back.

I love you so fucking much.

"What are you doing?" whiskey and chocolate growled from the front.

I didn't open my eyes. My aura flared, loose and fucking huge.

He swore, but I'd already thrown myself at the door. It buckled like a tin can, and I was out in the air.

I was met by the alpha, who'd stumbled out of the front seat, cocking his gun as he did. Dirty blond hair, ice-blue eyes, and—well, fuck. I *knew* him. Kind of. Rich circles ran small. He was a friend of the cousin who'd sent me to Decebal, and a prick with a reputation about as shit as my dad's had been.

"Back in the car," he snarled.

One chance. One, because he was Decebal's pack.

"Move," I growled.

I paused as he levelled the gun at me. "*Back* in the car."

He thought a *gun* was enough?

I was already waning, madness lurking and trying to rip me into its depths.

I held on for now. For her.

"You know." Logan Mandela sneered. "You give alphas a bad name, letting an omega leave you this *weak*—"

He didn't finish.

My lips drew into a snarl, and my aura flared viciously. I noted the way tanned skin lost its colour as he realised what he'd felt from my aura was the smallest spark of a bonfire.

Then I lunged for him faster than he could react to. Faster than the trigger.

The gun hit the ground as I grabbed him, slamming him into the car hard enough for it to dent.

My chest was tight, crimson seeping into my vision as I crushed his throat. He made a choking sound, his expression twisted, eyes wide with shock.

Not the enemy.

Find her.

I loosened my grip on his neck, but he threw his weight against me, his own aura pale beside mine. I reacted like lightning, smashing my forehead into his and feeling him go limp in an instant. I didn't bother lowering him to the ground, instead satisfied with the dull thump his body made as he hit the ground.

I turned to the huge building, every instinct flaring with my aura as it threatened, again, to swallow me, but with it came a thousand sounds. The wind rattling against the fence behind me, distant sounds of cars on nearby streets, the creak of a door somewhere deep within the building.

Shatter…

I'm coming.

CHAPTER 37

Dusk

Cleaving: the act of an alpha leaving their pack. This process is volatile, carrying the risk of leaving the alpha unable to forge new bonds or, in extreme cases, can result in death. Traditionally, cleaving involves the application of a uniquely designed brand to the alpha's skin on three separate occasions.

The scene I walked in on made my heart trip.

Umbra was standing over Eric, who was shaking on the ground, blood pooling from his mouth. He cocked his head when I entered, barely turning as he fixed his sandstorm eyes on me. He looked like a fragment of our past. A distant memory I thought we'd left behind.

The iron tang of blood was thick in the air, Eric's mingling with Umbra's wolfsbane. There was very little human left in my brother.

We stared at each other for a long moment.

"You weren't supposed to come." His voice was rough.

"Do you know where she is?" I asked. That's all that mattered.

He took a moment, then nodded.

Okay.

If we got to her, this would be over and Shatter would pull him back from that ledge, just like she had before.

She could do it, even when I could not.

But then Umbra's lips drew into a snarl as he looked past me to the door. He stepped toward me in a moment, tugging me back, but I was already pulling out my gun.

I turned to find myself facing Flynn and Gareth in the doorway, and Gareth had a gun trained on us right back.

Flynn's eyes darted to where Eric lay, then back to me and Umbra.

"What the hell?" Flynn hissed.

"They're…" Eric's voice was weak as he tried to pick himself up. "Flynn… it's… 66."

Flynn's eyes bugged out as he looked back at us, and he shook his head. "Not possible."

"Where is she?" I asked.

"This isn't about her," Gareth hissed back, staring between us, as if he wasn't sure who to aim it at.

"This is *only* about her," Umbra snarled, aura flaring. His scent was an iron tang in the air as his fury rose.

"Then drop the gun," Flynn said. "Mord has orders to snap her in two if anything happens to us."

Did he think that would be enough to make me drop it?

I felt Umbra's eyes shift to me, wondering what I'd do. But I knew Flynn wouldn't risk harming her. He needed her. He was, however, more of a threat than even he knew, both to me and Umbra. One touch, and he could destroy us, and there was no telling if, this time, it wouldn't end in our death.

I turned the gun, letting go of the trigger. Not because I believed their threat, but because I needed them with their guards down.

Flynn looked pleased as I lowered the gun to the floor.

"You should be dead…" Flynn said, words faint, as if he couldn't quite believe it. But I could see, at last, the flicker of recognition in his eyes, as if he were finally matching us with the malnourished, broken alphas he'd once placed bets on through a video stream.

The alpha in me was howling at the restraint I needed to maintain, at the fact that I couldn't lunge for them with my aura out.

But I couldn't. I couldn't go near him.

Not like this, anyway.

As I stood, my other hand slipped into my pocket as I slowly drew out the small vial Decebal had given me. One sharp prick and the drug would be in my system.

And then, I would be able to touch him.

After that, I didn't know.

Cleaving took three strokes of an iron, but this was a vile drug, one with unpredictable outcomes, banned from public use, that emulated the first two.

It would sever me from the pack enough that Flynn shouldn't be untouchable. But I wouldn't be cleaved entirely. It would give the pack a chance to escape and make a plan, even if the worst happened. Because Decebal had been worried about the effects it would have on my body, but Umbra had survived worse.

Now it was my turn.

"What's going on?" I asked.

Something was wrong—even in the bond.

Mord had me by the arm and was dragging me down a dim, grimy hallway. He didn't answer, checking around the next corner, gun in his hand before he tugged me with him.

"Why did you come back for me?" I asked. "I thought you were splitting up and looking for Eric."

"I don't trust they aren't waiting for me to leave you," he said.

The bond felt empty. Too quiet. Even Dusk was gone, like we were all afraid of going into it and revealing what was happening. Sometimes I felt a flash from one of them, disturbing moments that were making me begin to panic.

I shook it away, gathering myself. This was all going wrong, and I was losing what little control I'd gained.

Mord was cautious as he tugged me forward. One step, then another down the hall. I could hear nothing but silence around us.

And then I caught it. The faintest trace of a cool forest, of raindrops in the early morning.

Lily of the valley.

An aura exploded into the hallway, an invisible energy that was thick in the air as Ransom moved faster than I had ever seen.

Mord managed, just, to trigger his aura before he was rammed into the concrete wall with a crack.

I staggered back, eyes wide, seeing Mord's gun clatter to the floor on the other side of them.

"R-Ransom."

No…

There was something wrong. His eyes were wild, pupils constricted, lips drawn in a snarl.

Mord tried to grapple free but failed, leaving Ransom open to close a fist around his neck. Mord was huge, but Ransom was…

"No!" I dared a step closer before he turned on me, a warning growl in his throat. The movement gave Mord the opening he needed to slip from Ransom's grip. And I saw his eyes again.

There was almost no one left in there.

My chest was tight, terror choking me as I was forced back another step.

He *couldn't* be.

Would I be able to pull him back?

The fight was much closer this time—now Ransom teetered on the edge of going feral once more.

Ransom

Mord slipped from my grip too fast, always seeming able to use my momentum against me. For an alpha his size, he was able to play defence too well.

I tried again to seize him, knowing all I needed was a good hold and my aura would be enough, but he ducked my fist. Next thing I knew, my arm was behind my back, and I was pinned to the wall. The leverage was too much, even with the strength difference.

No.

It was happening again.

Mord's low growl sounded at my back as I struggled against his grip. But I couldn't let him win this time. I couldn't fail her.

Yet, I was never enough. Always a burden. To Dusk and Umbra, for years—and now a failure. My omega had been taken from me, slipping through my fingers like water.

I could feel her fear at last. She'd opened her side of the bond and it had lit among us like a beacon, terror and desperation.

I didn't dare look. Last I'd seen, she'd stumbled back, hitting the floor and scrambling out of the way.

I would never let her get hurt, though.

Not after I'd given up everything.

No…

Not everything.

Not yet.

I plunged deeper, knowing I may never surface again, and the world around me changed. Sounds echoed from all over, deafening and dull all at once.

I was made of nothing but roiling instincts, fury and rage driving me on, and the sound I made was nothing but feral as I flared my aura again, and the weight at my back was gone.

Moments ago, it had been a trap… *a cage…*

I turned, vision swimming, sharp knives slicing my mind as I forced the world into focus.

He was there in the centre of the bleeding crimson swamp at the edges of my vision, a huge alpha picking himself up, staggering, hand on his head. Dark hair, scar down his left cheek.

The one who'd taken her.

My prey, with a scent of ebony burning deep in a void.

A low growl rolled through my chest until I heard a cry. Something that blistered, dragging me up for a moment, up toward a surface still so far above.

I looked around wildly, trying to understand.

And I saw her.

She was picking herself up from the floor. The centre of the whole world, with eyes of molten gold that were fixed on me, wide with terror.

She was speaking—no. Shouting. I didn't understand. The words scored my ear-drums, while made of mist, all at the same time. Tears streamed down her face as she reached for me, staggering forward.

Then she stopped, eyes darting to the side, breath catching.

That was all it took.

I flinched, snapping my gaze to the other alpha, who was reaching for a gun only feet away.

My mind broke.

I lunged for him.

I was lost, but he would never have her.

We crashed to the floor, and my hands were at his throat.

Shatter…

My vision drowned in red, an ocean of nothingness coming to sweep me away.

I love you.

The alpha fought, but he didn't stand a chance. Not when the price was her. Peace was a cold shock to my system.

She would be safe.

My Reaper.

Then, before the alpha broke beneath my fists, sickness ripped through the pack bond like a plague. A sickness that wasn't mine.

Something had happened.

My… brother…

I heard her scream behind me as I watched my fingers slip. The alpha shoved me off, coughing for breath, his fist in my hair as he slammed my head to the ground.

The world went black.

Umbra

Untethering: when an alpha with a critically damaged aura chooses to release it. The aura begins to draw energy directly from the alpha's body, enabling them to wield their power without restriction. However, once the existing energy is exhausted, the aura dies, and the alpha with it.

"We don't need you." Flynn was almost laughing. "All of this, to come and show us you're worthless to us?"

In my peripheral, I could see two things.

First, Eric edged along the wall to his pack mates. And second, Dusk stood statuesque as he waited for the injection of the cleaving drug to take effect.

It never would.

He'd injected nothing but saline. I'd long guessed he would plan something like this. Long known he would believe it was on him to protect me.

But our pack had always needed him more. I was spent and broken, as worthless as a trick coin.

He was still waiting as I straightened, closing my eyes for just a moment, picturing a golden goddess.

My Nightshade.

A shooting star I had never been meant to catch—not even if I scarred my skin until there was nothing left of it.

They knew they could take her, which meant he couldn't leave.

I felt the faintest flash of worry from Dusk in the bond. He'd taken his injection, but his plan wasn't working.

He didn't know why.

That was okay.

I reached out, just for a moment, to touch him on the shoulder. I wanted to meet his eyes, even for a second. Wanted him to know it was going to be okay.

I couldn't, though.

I wasn't strong enough.

So, without taking my eyes from the alpha ahead, the alpha who'd stolen my life, I did the thing I shouldn't be able to. Something only alphas who'd lost their packs could do.

But I'd been burned alive, torn to shreds by drug after drug, ripped apart and put back together, and left to cling to an alpha who saw me as nothing, just so my bones didn't turn to dust before my eyes.

Just so I didn't lose everything.

Again.

It felt like the most natural thing in the world, that I could un-tether my aura. That I could step into the void and let it have the last thing it had been hunting all this time.

The power leached into the room like a fog, heavy and unnatural, and I faced it differently this time. Different to when Shatter had been there to save me the day Dusk had touched Flynn, and my own aura had tried to burn me alive.

She had been there, and everything since was extra. A gift she had given me, far beyond what I deserved.

It could have me now, but first, I would use it to break the monsters that had begun this.

They were the last left to kill, and finally, I was out of time.

I stepped across the threshold, giving myself to the void, hoping she would forgive me, and maybe, one day, I would see her again.

CHAPTER 38

Dusk

Everyone in the room felt it the moment Umbra's aura untethered.

The Lincoln pack had tried to run.

Umbra, moving faster than should be possible, shoved me back so hard the world spun.

That wasn't what broke my world into pieces. It was feeling him detach, as if with every flare of his aura, he was being ripped free of it entirely.

A gunshot fired, but when I pushed myself up, no one seemed to be hit. Umbra had Gareth by the neck and was dragging him back into the room before slamming the door.

My head was ringing, panic choking my lungs and making it hard to breathe.

How long before he was gone?

Before he was dead?

With every burst in which he used his strength, he was ripping energy from himself. And when that fire burned out…

"No!" My word came out half growl, half groan of agony.

He wasn't just destroying himself; he was ripping a wound across our whole pack. One that would fall to pieces when he was gone.

If he felt that same pain, he didn't show it as he held Gareth. I heard the bone crack in Gareth's arm as he flung him against the wall and his scream rent the air.

Eric cowered in the corner, and their gun—or what remained of it—was an almost crumpled ball of metal.

Umbra had as much power as he wanted, but the more he used, the faster he would die.

He turned from Gareth, going instead for Flynn. Flynn held his hands up, eyes wide with terror. "W-wait! We can—"

Umbra seized him.

Flynn's aura was like a wisp in the air, nothing next to Umbra's.

Eric used the opportunity to scramble for the door.

Trying to find purpose or direction, I threw myself toward him, a growl rising in my throat.

They would die tonight.

And my brother would die with them…

I shoved the thought away, flaring my aura before I was caught by another wave of agony, blistering and white hot.

I recognized it. The exact same thing I'd felt when I'd touched Flynn only weeks ago.

The floor came up to meet me, and I struggled to stay conscious.

Umbra… was… I tried to make my mind focus.

He was pinning Flynn to the wall by his neck. I felt the pain of that touch as if it were mine, but his eyes burned with hatred, not seeming to feel the agony, only the power surging through his veins.

I tried again to stagger to my feet.

The only reason Flynn wasn't dead was because Umbra didn't want him dead yet.

"You took everything." Umbra's voice was guttural. There was nothing left of him—of that man who'd saved me over and over.

A memory flashed behind my eyes.

Fists bled for how I pounded them against the metal door to our cell. I screamed until my throat burned.

They'd taken him again, and again, and again.

I could do nothing to stop it.

I threw myself against the door until I collapsed. The panic had faded to a selfish despair. It went beyond helplessness.

I needed him.

I couldn't be in this room alone—I wasn't strong enough to do this without him. He was my compass.

And they'd taken him from me.

Now they were taking him again.

My chest heaved, each breath agony. Flynn was shouting, but I couldn't make the world right or the words make sense. I *had* to, even if it was over.

When I'd dragged Umbra from those experiments, I'd become what he'd been to me. Years and years would never be enough, but one thing had never changed.

I still wasn't strong enough to do this without him.

"No…"

I pushed myself up, begging my aura to be enough to fight this. My palm pressed against a cracked concrete wall.

Then I heard the slam of a door and a sound that made my heart trip.

Her whimper of terror was enough to draw me up, and my worst nightmare swam into my vision. Shatter was pinned to Mord's chest, his hand over her mouth, gun to her temple.

He didn't have to say anything.

Umbra's aura vanished in an instant, and he sagged, dropping Flynn and crashing out of the high. I staggered toward him, catching him just in time, every instinct alight with fear, eyes fixed on her. Her cheeks were tear-tracked, her whole body shaking, and her glistening eyes saw nothing but Umbra.

She was here, just like I was, desperately reaching for us across a torn-up bond that survived like the last dying embers in a storm. She was a touch of life that nearly broke me, even without a word.

"Against the wall," Mord said quietly.

Lost in a way I'd never been, knowing I could lose them both in seconds, I drew Umbra back a step.

"Get his gun!" Flynn snarled at Eric.

Eric, who looked shell-shocked, stumbled forward, grabbing my gun that had hit the floor and passing it to Flynn.

"We're going," Flynn spat at Mord. "We don't need them. Not for any of this. We never have. Give her to me."

I jolted with fury as Flynn jammed his gun into Shatter's side, his fist closing in her hair. Mord's gun moved in a flash, though, pointing not at me, but at Umbra. At my side, he was shaking, barely able to stay upright.

Had he burned through too much already?

Not that fast… *surely* not that fast?

But… he shouldn't be able to touch Flynn. What if that connection had drained him faster?

"Lock the door," Flynn added. "It's made to keep in alphas."

Mord cocked an eyebrow, not taking his eyes from us. "I don't think it's built for alphas like this—"

"If he comes through"—Flynn cut him off—"shoot him in the fucking head."

Mord's cold eyes were fixed on us, and there was a strange curiosity in them. I heard Flynn's words before the door slammed shut.

"He's dead, anyway. What's the fucking difference?"

CHAPTER 39

Shatter

I couldn't look through the glass to the other room. Couldn't see them as this happened.

The metal of the table against my hip bones was jarring as Flynn crushed me against it. I shut my eyes as his fingers closed in my hair, and pain surged through me as he dragged my neck to the side.

"I'm going to make the offer and you are going to accept it."

"You'll let them go?" I asked. It was just me and the Lincoln alphas in here. Mord was outside, and my mates… they were trapped on the other side, watching everything.

"What does it matter?"

"I d-don't want anyone to die," I stammered. "You won't need them anymore."

"He deserves to fucking pay," Eric snarled. He was almost unrecognisable, with drying blood coating his chin and neck. "You're going to accept the bond."

"I need to know you'll do it."

Flynn's growl was low. Then the weight at my back was gone. I took a breath, sending a thousand prayers into the universe.

I shuddered as he returned, and I felt the cool hardness of a gun at my back.

"You're going to accept the fucking bond, you little cunt. Do you understand me?" He was different from how he'd been earlier, now thrown into a frenzy from the fight.

I took a breath.

One steady inhale as the world spun.

Terror washed over me as I opened my mouth, the broken answer a whisper. "Y-yes."

When I felt the offer of the princess bond light up between us, it came with a sickening wrench in my chest. The dark bond on my neck burned and goosebumps rippled across my skin.

He didn't have to do anything for this part—he just had to make the offer. The bite, and my acceptance, came next.

"Please," I whispered. "Please free them."

"Don't fucking play with us," Gareth snarled.

The gun was a persistent pressure, and tears spilled down my face. I tried to focus on that, on the offer made, on the gun that was pressed against my skin.

I took a breath, my chest tight, and accepted a princess bond with the Lincoln pack.

CHAPTER 40

Shatter

Flynn barely hesitated.

His teeth at my neck were everything my nightmares were made of. Only, this time, he wasn't threatening a dark bond. There was a slam on the window, as if the weight of a body was being thrown against it, and I heard a faint shout, raw and desperate.

Ransom was gone.

Umbra was gone.

Dusk's terror was the last thing I felt.

The gun vanished and Flynn grabbed my arm, turning me and slamming me back against the table as he dragged my neck into an arch and sank his teeth into my flesh. A whine escaped my chest as I felt the pain of his vicious mark precisely over Dusk's bond.

One bond replaced another as he took my mates from me.

I shuddered, my throat closing up as Dusk's presence in my mind turned to smoke.

Tears flooded my face as I was ripped from one pack to another. It was a strange and uncomfortable sensation. The place I left was home, and this new one… it was cold and empty.

I squeezed my eyes shut, fingers digging into the table.

"That's it, then?" Gareth's voice was low. "It's healed?"

"Is it instant?" Flynn asked. "Should be, right?"

Flynn's grip fell away, but I didn't dare open my eyes, not yet. "I'll consider freeing them when we're far out of range. They're fucking insane, and I don't trust them to not do something stupid."

"I want my bite now," Gareth growled. I jumped violently at his touch as he lifted me roughly so I was sitting on the table, closer to his height. Sesame seed and sunflower made me want to gag.

My breathing was ragged, and my eyes were still closed as my memories flashed back to the day I'd visited Uncle.

"Shatter," Uncle said, catching me before I left.

I turned to him, clutching my bag to my chest, trying so hard not to feel defeated.

"There's something else," he said.

I waited, and he looked uncomfortable. "Your death wasn't the only thing I lied about." His lips were drawn in a flat line.

"What?" I asked.

"You shouldn't have survived that injection. The consequences were far more... unpredictable than we ever imagined. There was... one other thing. I never told the Institute because I knew, if I did, they would never let you remain here. They would have taken you and locked you up forever."

My blood chilled. "What do you mean?"

It was a truth I should have known since the moment I'd woken.

From the blinking ERROR sign, when I'd seen the kaleidoscope of colours in clinical, white lights above.

In the hours it had taken before they'd freed me from the bindings that strapped me to the table, agony had torn through my body over and over.

When my breathing had dissolved to wails and I'd realised the truth I couldn't see—not with my head bound in place. Not when all that had been in my vision was the blinking sign and the broken glass upon one of the monitors that had been dragged on its side, tilted against the wall.

And I'd wondered, endlessly, why was it like that?

Why was it broken—as if someone had grabbed it violently?

Why had it taken them so long to get me out?

Something had gone wrong.

I'd been given something I shouldn't have. I may have no past, but *that* I knew. When I was finally rescued, it was by figures in white suits with their faces masked.

And, by then, I'd known why it had taken so long.

That I'd already begun to beg to be freed over and over, as I realised that around me were bodies, still and lifeless.

I was left there long enough that their smell of decomposition began to rise in the air. The Institute had wanted to keep me for more than just the fact that I was broken.

They had wanted to keep me because they believed I was dangerous.

A trickle of blood rolled slowly down my neck from Flynn's bite, hot against each goosebump it trailed.

Please...

"I've been dreaming of biting you since the last time." Gareth's breath was hot against my neck. His scent smothered me, vicious and possessive. Doubt turned my stomach, panic lurking at each second that passed.

What would I see if I opened my eyes?

Was it enough—

His teeth sank in, making me jump, the bite so much more painful than Dusk's had been.

"The full and final effects of the experimentation came when that alpha tried to form a bond with you—a bond you didn't want."

I frowned at my uncle, thinking back to the alpha with a goatee, the bond he had tried to make. "But I tried to say yes."

"Did you truly want it, Shatter?" uncle asked. "Or were you just afraid?"

I stared at him, unsure how to answer that.

"The want—the true want of an omega matters greatly," he went on. "Some packs think they can get by with a dark bond simply because a seer will confirm it was accepted. But if it was blackmail, coercion—if it was never truly wanted, there will be sickness in that connection. Those packs wither. They turn on one another, cursed and decaying.

"Those of us who study this field for a long time know that truth, even if it is hard to quantify. We might have manufactured the dark and princess bonds, but there is no tricking nature."

"What does that mean?"

"When he tried to bite you into a connection you didn't want, he became sick."

"Sick?"

"Atropa's poison—the modified substance designed to drive alphas to kill, believing if they don't, they will die themselves. The same poison you were accidentally injected with. That unwanted bite he gave you sent him into a frenzy."

"I don't understand."

"Your blood," he said. "It poisoned him."

A click echoed in the room. The sound of a gun cocking.

I heard a low rumbling growl behind Gareth.

"What the fuck do you think you're doing?" Eric sounded shocked.

Three auras flared, and Gareth's hands released me as a gunshot split the air.

"But... but I've been bitten before," I said, staring at uncle, confused.

"I believe the full effects of the poison were only an issue when the bite was intended as a bonding mark—but, more importantly, when it was unwanted."

"If the institute knew—"

"They don't."

"That's what you lied about?"

He leaned back, his expression suddenly cool. "If they had discovered your blood became poisonous in defence against unwanted bonds, they would have taken you, without a doubt. Perhaps, for the safety of society, but more likely to discover how to reverse engineer such a thing. Alphas and omegas with poisonous blood? I think I've seen quite enough experimentation in my lifetime not to contribute more to that."

"D-did he live?" I asked.

"Barely. We managed to contain him before he hurt anyone. You had fled to the gardens, thankfully. Lauren didn't want you to know. She believed you had suffered enough."

My mind raced with that information, processing it all, filing it away, trying to find something of use in it for my pack.

Blood was sharp in the air, and I tried to pretend it was tangled with wolfsbane. The world was still pitch black, my eyes squeezed shut as my nails dug into the table.

Another gunshot echoed, making me jump violently.

A savage snarl tore through the air.

The poison was taking hold. Poison Umbra and Dusk had already survived for their willingness to die for each other. Poison the Lincoln pack would not live through.

I couldn't look, not until I heard the violent pounding on the window. It was the only thing that gave me the strength to open my eyes. Their absence was a void in my chest, and I needed them.

The world spun as I looked around, unable to avoid the fight before me.

"Fuck!" Flynn was clutching his side, holding himself up against the wall. Gareth had Eric pinned to the ground by his neck. Eric's eyes were wide as he fought, and for one strange moment, they met mine.

I saw his terror and confusion, but all I felt was dread.

Gareth looked mad, his pupils constricted as poison tore through his veins while he strangled his own pack mate, succumbing to the very drug he'd watched given to others all those years ago.

Eric's face was ruddy, and he struggled between reaching for the gun and throwing Gareth off. I tried, again, to drag my eyes from the way Eric's movements became weaker with each second.

I took a breath, chin quivering.

Dusk was right there.

Why couldn't I look at him?

Tears wet my cheeks, my pulse thready in my veins.

"This…" I whispered, trying to drag my eyes away from the fighting alphas. They were dying, and I hadn't… I swallowed. I had never wanted anyone to die.

In my periphery, I saw movement stop, the choked gurgles cutting off at a dull *crack* that shook me to the core.

I felt the loss of one of the alphas in this vile bond with me like a knife to the heart.

Eric was gone.

That was… that as forever. Unchangeable. I shook.

"This is a lot, you know?" I released the desk, fingers tangling together tightly enough that the pain distracted me for just the briefest of seconds.

I had to look up.

To look away from what was before me.

To see who I was protecting.

It would help… right?

"Uncle?" I asked. "I have one more question. It's about aura contracting. There are a few times when one alpha or pack is obliged to surrender a bond for it to pass from one pack to the next."

"Like when a pack negotiates for their scent match from a dark bond?" he asked.

I nodded. Just like that. It wasn't what I was asking about, but it was the closest thing I'd heard of that mirrored what Flynn had over the Kingsman pack: the bond he had to surrender in order to free Umbra and Dusk.

"If those negotiations began, and the pack with the dark bond destroyed themselves before a resolution, would that constitute a surrender?" I asked.

I needed to know how the principle worked.

Uncle narrowed his eyes, considering. "I… I think so, yes. But I'm not sure. I've never heard of that happening."

I nodded, knowing now what I needed to find.

Proof that it worked. A case study in which a pack had died before the negotiations completed. Or even better, that a pack had destroyed themselves before that moment.

The last piece of the puzzle I needed to know beyond doubt, and the answer—that study Mord had pulled me from—I'd never been able to read it.

Everything that happened from here was unknown.

My soul shook as I watched. There was blood everywhere. Flynn's aura, healed from the princess bond I'd accepted, was strong in the air as he fought with Gareth.

"Shatter!"

I heard my name. Faint through the thick glass, but it was enough, even in this nightmare, to drag my gaze away. Yellow eyes fixed on mine, and I felt my lungs unlock.

The sounds in this room were horrible, enough for years of nightmares, but I could see Dusk.

He was an alpha made of vengeful fury, and yet, right now, as his enemies died before him, he wasn't looking at them. His palm was on the glass, eyes fixed on me as he spoke furiously, and I could see the words upon his lips.

"Look at me!"

At a strangled, desperate whine from my left, I almost glanced back, my frame tense, tears burning my eyes, but I didn't.

Even when I felt the death of another alpha in this bond with me.

The bright yellow of Dusk's gaze was enough. I reached my hand toward his, placing it on the glass, trembling to the bone as the sounds of fighting in the room died down at last.

My heart raced.

Only ragged breaths remained.

One alpha.

Flynn or Gareth?

I had to wait. I heard the scrape of metal upon the concrete floor and the click of a gun. I didn't look back, but for the briefest of seconds, Dusk faded and the reflection of the room came into focus.

Flynn was there.

The gun was in his hand, pointed, not at me, but to his own temple.

One. Alpha. Left.

"Shatter!"

Bright yellow returned, fixed on me, my hand to his and my whole body jolted with the ear splitting *bang!*

And with that, my mates' bond flooded back.

My breath caught, tears blurring away the most beautiful eyes in the world as I felt them.

And not just any bond…

Something… new.

Something more powerful than it had ever been. Flynn Lincoln had taken everything from Umbra and Dusk, had stolen from body, to soul, to the scent match that should have been theirs. But the twisted bond he had offered me now became a gift to the alphas he'd tried to destroy.

My breathing was short and sharp, the scent of blood strong in the room. Too strong.

Blood and death, caused by me…

All of this…

My palm remained on the glass, Dusk's eyes holding mine for… I don't know how long. Then blood tangled with wolfsbane.

"Nightshade…" Umbra's voice was low as his touch soothed my terror, and I was drawn away from the glass as huge arms enveloped me. He pulled me against his chest, and I clutched him, trembling violently, relief shattering my fear at last, and blackness seeped in.

He was back.

My alpha was back.

Tethered to me by the strongest bond in the world. To a princess bond that made my pack whole at last.

CHAPTER 41

Dusk

I clutched Shatter to my chest as I carried her to the cabin.

Decebal had driven, but she'd been between Umbra and Ransom. None of them were awake, but Ransom had laced his fingers with hers.

Ransom was vacant, the fury of his feral spiral having died to catatonia.

Umbra had collapsed after he'd pulled Shatter into his arms in that room.

Both would survive because of her.

I was still in shock.

She'd succeeded where we'd failed. The omega who had made my pack whole. She hadn't just saved us—she'd found a miracle within an ocean of darkness.

Because the princess bond had defaulted back to us when the Lincoln pack had died.

The most powerful bond in the world.

An anchor like no other, tethering Umbra and healing Ransom. She was more than I'd ever dared dream. More than I could have conceived of the day I'd first seen her. And she'd found a way to accomplish what I'd been fighting for ever since we'd escaped that facility.

I reached the spare room and sat on the bed, holding her close, unable to imagine letting her go again.

Her terror was impossible to shake.

The moment Flynn had died, I'd felt her through the bond. She'd broken, teeth clenched, tears tracking her face. And that made what she'd done so much more powerful. Born of fury and violence, to me, vengeance was a gift.

For her, I realised, it was a nightmare.

And she'd done it, anyway.

I lay her down in bed and tucked her in before helping Decebal bring in Ransom. He was half with it, taking a few tired steps, but he curled up next to her in a moment, clutching her close. Thankfully, we had Decebal's massive pack mate, Bane, to help haul Umbra into the cabin. Kai had stayed behind to clean up the mess we'd left.

I sank down onto the couch so I could see them all, still in shock.

"He'll be all right?" I asked.

The pack had all but disintegrated beneath us, and Ransom had needed this bond to become stable in the first place. "I think so," Decebal said as we tucked Ransom in beside Shatter. "The pack is whole. He'll be okay with some rest."

Umbra sat beside the bed, holding her hand, his usually rich skin, ashen. I was still in shock, not something I was used to. Experiments had scorched my being from most human responses to fear or challenge. But this—being so close to losing the only good thing we'd ever found—had torn back a thousand charred layers.

It was another reminder of her beauty.

She made me human.

Decebal set a beer on the table to my right before cracking his own and sitting on the couch beside me.

"Roxy's on the way."

"She is?" I asked.

"Blew up every pack number she has, so I told her the location. She sounded on the edge of a breakdown."

I nodded. That was good. Shatter needed all the support she could get when she woke up.

"What about the police?"

"We wiped everything from that room but the Lincoln pack. Removed all evidence of you or her. Kai made sure it looked like a bad trip. Contaminated drugs have been an issue recently. He laced some with the poison and left it at the scene."

"And Mord?" He knew we'd been there. "How much did he see?"

"Pretty much everything. We found you just in time for the Lincoln pack to fire the last bullet."

"Did he give you trouble?"

"The opposite." Decebal snorted. "When we realised what had happened, he seemed to find it funny. Said he'd got his pay and vanished. Gone before we got your door unlocked." He shrugged. "Sato's not in the habit of running his mouth to the cops. Not worth picking a fight over, if you ask me."

I nodded, rubbing my face, still trying to catch up on everything.

"I'm sorry, mate," Decebal said quietly. "All of this—years, just to bail on you at the end."

"Nah," I grunted. The building was massive; it had been pure luck who'd run into who. "Anyway, you were there."

That was worth the world, getting that door open so one of us could be there for her.

I'd never been frozen a day in my life, but holding her eyes through the glass, I hadn't been able to move. Even when she'd been shaking. It had been Umbra, weak as he was, who'd staggered past Decebal and Kai to get to her.

She'd sunk into his arms, clutching him like her life depended on it, and I'd felt the drive in him through the bond.

He'd been on the brink of collapse, pushed to the edge and ripped back.

But he'd *had* to be there for her.

"Nothing stronger than a princess bond, Dusk. They're both going to be fine."

"I know."

There was a pause.

"The injection didn't work."

And despite that, it had all worked out—somehow. Shatter, I realised now, had been holding on to her plan the whole time. One that cost her everything. And yet, if I'd managed what I'd tried for—partially cleaving from the pack so I could save them all from Flynn... If Ransom had lost himself, and Umbra had untethered... Well, I don't know. It was possible the pack would have fallen apart before she could have saved us.

"That was Kai," Decebal said, something a little sour in his voice. "Umbra contacted him. Told him he knew you'd be trying something stupid. That weasel swapped out the vials on me."

"All so Umbra could try something stupider?" I scowled. "He could have died."

"Same goes for you," Decebal said quietly.

I turned on him, furious. "Umbra *would* have died without her—no two ways about it."

"Fuck off, mate." Decebal snorted. "It was *all* precautionary. I could have dealt with Flynn if it came to it, but you all had to go off, half-cocked, didn't you? Fucking idiots—but you can't deny, with Umbra's plan, he *would* have killed them without a doubt. *You* could have taken that shot and dropped dead that second. Since you were both insisting on suicide, Kai figured Umbra's was a better bet, and I don't like it, but he wasn't completely wrong."

Fucking red-eyed prick.

And *fuck* Decebal too.

I opened my mouth, then shut it, scowling as I eyed the alpha at my side. I don't think I'd ever heard Decebal say so many words in one breath.

"Plus. Then she'd have had to anchor Umbra, heal Ransom, and drag her stupid-ass pack lead back from a half-finished cleaving."

I clenched my jaw, turning back to my pack, trying to quell the panic of what could have been.

"You have no idea how…" Decebal trailed off, and I glanced at him. His jaw ticked, his whole body tense as he stared at the three of them curled up on the bed. "I'm glad you all made it."

I nodded, looking back at Shatter, who was resting between Ransom and Umbra, looking peaceful right now.

Again, I took a breath.

They were all alive.

We were a pack still, somehow—more a pack than we'd ever been.

"Your files are all on the kitchen table for when you want them," Decebal said.

"Files?"

"History." I saw a glint of delight in his eyes.

Shit…

Oh… *shit.*

My history? The person I'd been before all of this. Before the Cimmerian Vaults. It had been a pillar to chase, towering in the distance, always out of reach. My heart crashed irrationally hard against my ribs now that it was real.

Until this moment, I hadn't realised how little I'd believed we would ever see the end of this.

Was I ready for that?

Did I want it?

"I'm not going to lie, there've been times I wondered if I'd ever get to give it to you." Decebal's jaw was tight as he glanced over at the bed. "She's special," he added. "Way too perfect for you."

"You're next, you know that?" I asked, shoving away my nerves and looking back at him. "And I hope whoever the universe gifts you for a scent match is a pain in your fucking ass."

Decebal snorted before taking another sip. "I hope that's not too far off."

I glanced at him, frowning at the strain in his voice.

He grimaced. "Thought it was insensitive to bring up before, given the... situation. But it's…" He scratched his jaw. "It's Angel."

"What about him?" I knew Angel was the fifth member of Decebal's pack, though I'd never met him.

"Aura sickness."

I frowned, working through that. "Shit."

"We'll, uh… we'll figure it out." He didn't look convinced as he took a swig of his beer.

"Where's Logan?" I asked. I swear it had been Logan that Decebal had told me was coming, not Bane.

Decebal snorted. "Pissed, that's what. I'm sure Angel won't thank us for leaving him to tend to Logan's wounds all night."

"Wounds?" I asked.

Decebal sounded amused. "The ego sort. Ransom knocked him out and dented his Mercedes. I don't know if he'll survive."

I got to my feet, finding a smile at that.

"I'm grabbing a quick shower. No need for all of us to reek of Lincoln pack blood when she wakes up." I turned as I reached the door. "And, Decebal?"

"Yeah?" he asked, meeting my eyes.

"You're fired."

As I turned, I saw him raising his drink, a broad grin on his face. His mutter followed me out the door. "About fucking time."

CHAPTER 42

Shatter

I woke in a calm room with my pack's scents in the air. It took a long moment for me to process where I was, the peace of the space a contrast against the shadow lurking over my mind like a storm cloud.

I blinked bleary eyes open, the wooden panels across the ceiling coming slowly into focus.

My consciousness had swum in and out a number of times, and each time, I'd checked for them in the bond and their scents in the air before I'd passed back out.

Once or twice, beside the warmth of my alphas at my side, I'd felt dainty arms wound around my waist. They weren't here right now, though, which was sad…

And then, at last, reality hit, dread and relief crashing into me with equal force.

The Lincoln pack…

Flynn with a gun to his head…

Ransom. He'd been sick, and—

"Umbra…?" My voice was choked as panic blitzed through my system. My whine rose in the air as I tried to control my breathing.

"Shatter!" That was Ransom's voice, but I could barely hear it.

He'd… he'd *untethered.*

A sure death, except—

The room finally came into focus, a low growl sounding at my side. Warm arms closed around me, dragging me near. Wolfsbane and blood filled my senses.

But...

"How?"

What happened at the end was blurry. When I tried to remember back to it, all I could see were the yellow of Dusk's eyes fading for the reflection of Flynn.

Ransom's expression cracked with a smile, the likes of which I'd never seen from him. His hand cupped my cheek as he pressed his lips to my forehead.

"You crazy, brilliant omega," he whispered, drawing me close.

"The bond…?"

I reached up, feeling the bite on my neck, as if it might tell me. I didn't need to, though. I could feel it.

"I got…" Tears blurred my vision as he drew back, tilting my chin up.

"Shatter, you saved us all and got a princess bond."

Right… I… I could feel it.

The thing that was different as I met bright green eyes from the safety of Umbra's arms. "You saved him, Shatter," Ransom told me. "You tethered him with a—"

"A princess bond?"

That couldn't be true…

But I could feel it. The shift. Darkness to light. Dusk's bite, and Umbra's… they were both alive, but different. *No* bond with them would be worthless—not when I'd wanted it from the beginning—but the connection was different, as if the threads that held us together were made of golden light.

I burst into tears.

Ransom's hand stroked my hair.

"And you're… you're okay?" I whispered.

"I just woke up a few minutes ago. Umbra's still sleeping, even if he's, uh…" Ransom glanced past me to where Umbra was holding me tight. "Clearly possessive, and Dusk's getting food. Everyone is safe."

I nodded, though it wasn't sinking in.

"Shatter. You saved us."

Before I could respond, the door opened and Dusk backed in, tray of food in hand.

"How long have I been out?"

"About a day."

"What about all the others?"

"Decebal and pack are fine; stayed a bit, but left earlier this morning. Roxy's okay now. I think… She was so upset, her sister apparently almost took her to the ER, but Decebal gave her our address, and she got here last night. She didn't stabilise until she saw you."

"Is she still here?"

"Yup. She is…" Dusk trailed off, scratching his head. "I knew omegas were possessive. I didn't know that carried so… seriously to best friends too."

"What does—" I cut off as Roxy appeared around the corner, a half-open box of what looked like Christmas tinsel in her hands.

"Would it be okay if I used one more—" The box tumbled to the floor as she caught sight of me. "Shatter!"

She shoved past Dusk, blue eyes wide, her usually sleek hair up in the messiest bun I'd ever seen her wear. Next thing I knew, Ransom was being shoved aside for a very tricky hug, since Umbra was still holding me against his chest.

She broke the hug, drawing back and checking me over like I might fall apart. "Are you okay?"

"I… think so…" I frowned. "What is the… tinsel about?" I asked curiously.

Roxy chewed on her lip. "Well, I hope this is okay—Dusk said you wouldn't mind. I couldn't sleep."

"Mind what?" I asked, peering past her to the tinsel she'd dropped on the floor.

"She's been… comfort decorating," Dusk supplied.

"What?"

"The cabin is well ahead of schedule for Christmas," Ransom clarified.

Roxy looked nervous. "I tried to take it easy and keep it just to what helped with my anxiety…"

Dusk did a very poor job of masking a snort with a cough, but I was grinning. I pulled her back into a hug, my eyes brimming with tears.

Everyone I had ever loved was here and safe, and somehow, I had a princess bond with alphas I loved more than anything else in the world.

CHAPTER 43

Umbra

I awoke with my omega in my arms and my pack at my side.

For such a long time, she lay in my arms while I tried to ground myself. When I still couldn't speak, she led me to the shower.

Even as hot water streamed over my skin, her calming nightshade scent filling the air, and the gentle touch of a cloth washed away the blood crusted across my skin, I couldn't settle.

My mind was far off, drifting and unable to find firm ground.

She didn't complain once, my perfect omega. When I was dressed and she'd brushed my hair, she forced me to the couch so she could slide onto my lap and take my face in her hands.

At last, she came into focus.

More beautiful than I could compute, and I could feel her in the bond—my shooting star, as bright as a sun and bound to us by gold as brilliant as her eyes.

She had a princess bond.

Everything she deserved.

It was over…

She was my anchor, but I couldn't… I squeezed my eyes shut. I couldn't hold on to her properly. Not yet.

So, I pressed my lips to her forehead and stood, setting her on her feet and making my way to the car.

I knew what I needed to do.

By the time I returned from my shopping trip, I was clearer in the head. Clear enough, anyway.

I set my bag down on the counter, glancing up to see Shatter quietly shutting the door of one of the spare bedrooms.

"She's wiped." Her voice was hushed, a smile on her face as she looked from Dusk to Ransom, who were waiting for her.

"No shit." Ransom scoffed.

She?

I frowned, then clocked into the orange and fir tree scent, which was light in the air. It didn't bother me. Shatter was ours, and Roxy was hers, so she was welcome here.

The whole living room was decorated like it was Christmas. Lights sparkled across the walls and around a Christmas tree. A cute little glowing village with electronically animated ice skaters was scattered across side tables and the TV stand. Tinsel hung from paintings and fixtures, while fake snow sat upon window ledges.

I nodded approvingly. Quite tasteful, actually. We'd never really been into Christmas as a pack. Decebal would come over with gifts, but it had felt sort of… depressing, with just me and Dusk, and Ransom still sick, so we'd tried to pretend it wasn't happening.

"You're back," Shatter said, hurrying over to me and peering at what I had in the bag. "What are you making?"

I found my voice at last, peace settling over me as I pulled out the ingredients.

Ice cream, chocolate and strawberry toppings, sprinkles, whipped cream, cherries, and four bananas.

"Banana splits."

She looked up at me, eyes sparkling. "Sounds amazing."

I prepared in a peaceful quiet as Dusk got the bowls lined up for me.

I'd spent a lot of time memorising banana split instructions. I could recite them in my sleep because banana splits were what you ate when a family was put back together. That's what... someone had said once.

I thought maybe it meant the payments were paid.

The debts were finally clear.

And I'd been waiting a long time for my Ransom banana split.

"Heh." That sounded wrong. Shatter shot me a funny look as she drizzled an obscene amount of chocolate over one of them.

This was perfect. Better than perfect. I had a family to take care of. A pack that was mine.

So, I settled down, passing one to Ransom, Dusk, Shatter, and keeping the last for myself.

But I took my first bite, only to realise I'd definitely never had a banana split before in my life.

Well… *shit.*

That didn't…

I frowned. That couldn't be right.

Right?

I blinked, shadows lurking from distant memories. They were blurry and faceless. Always smaller. Always needing to be cared for.

My heart tripped, a fist closing around my throat, and for a moment, I reached out, trying to make them focus, but a chasm opened beneath me and I reeled back.

No… I think… I would break.

I already had once, for this.

And now I had Dusk, and Ransom, and Shatter—they had faces. And it also seemed right that, when I died, I would see everyone's faces. And then… I swallowed…

And they would tell me,

They were happy I didn't break

Over memories

When I was the one

With more to make.

I cocked my head, the faintest smile fighting my frown.

Yup…

I nodded slowly, squeezing Shatter's hand that had somehow found its way into mine. That sounded good.

It was an absolute truth already lodging deep into everything I knew to be right in the world. I dug my spoon into my banana split and took another bite. (Turns out, I didn't like bananas, either, which seemed like a stupid thing not to have figured out by now.)

CHAPTER 44

Ransom

"I… failed my classes?" Shatter's voice was weak. "I've never failed a class in my life."

"How do you know that?" I asked curiously, placing my arm around her as I sat at her side.

"I…" She swallowed, and—shit, she was fighting back tears. "I just do."

We were sitting around the fireplace outside on the cabin deck as the sun set over the trees. Dusk had just got the fireplace going, and Umbra was finishing making us hot chocolates.

The dancing fire was enough to keep away the cold, though not enough that Shatter wasn't huddled in a fluffy Snuggie that she'd unwrapped as a gift from Roxy. The decorating had, apparently, included Christmas gifts. Umbra, Dusk, and I were all wearing ugly Christmas sweaters at Shatter's behest—even though Roxy had left. It was Tuesday, and she would miss too much class if she didn't return to the academy.

Shatter, unfortunately, didn't have the same concern.

"I'm sorry, Little Reaper." I tugged her close under my arm. "You missed one class too many, and even my title isn't enough for the Dean this time."

"We've already submitted the application for next semester," Dusk said. "And… we secured you a sponsor."

"A new pack sponsor?" she asked.

"No. Actually. He's sponsoring you as an individual. The Dean allowed it, though it took a few days for them to figure out how it fit in the system. They're set up for pack applications."

Shatter was frowning.

"Turns out Professor Eugene Howard made an inquiry about your class scores."

"Uncle?" she asked, eyes wide.

"Given the PR disaster of his last choice, he wrote to the Arkology board, and I quote, *I need a home run to redeem my reputation. I've never seen a student with more potential.* The Dean couldn't argue, so you're enrolled for next term."

"Really?" Shatter asked.

"Yup. And he's made the request for you to be moved to second semester, anyway, since your scores speak for themselves and he doesn't want to waste any time."

"So… I didn't actually fail?"

"Well. You missed too many classes to pass, but you did so well that it doesn't matter."

She pouted. "I suppose that's a bit better."

"There is one condition, though," Dusk said.

"What?"

"I told the Dean there was no way in hell you were doing classes by yourself, so he has to accelerate me too. He said he'd allow it if you caught me up."

She brightened. "I can do that. You'll be much easier to teach than Ransom."

I straightened. "Excuse me?"

She blinked up at me. "You never cared about Arkology."

I let out a huff. "Not particularly, no."

"I *knew* it."

"I did like what studying with you entailed, though," I said, pulling her onto my lap and drawing her close.

"So, are we ready?" Umbra was stepping through the doorway with a tray of mugs.

"I'm ready," Dusk said, straightening and picking up the huge envelope at his side.

"Still going to risk it?" Umbra asked as he handed out the hot chocolate.

"I can't believe you're not," I said.

"I think… I might too," Shatter said. "If I had mine, I mean."

"Actually…" Dusk said, scratching his chin. "About that."

Shatter's whole body went rigid. "What?"

"Last few puzzle pieces came out. Decebal was in contact with your uncle for more details and… well. He found something. A history. He's pretty sure it's you."

"Pretty sure?" she asked, voice weak.

"He wouldn't have given it to me unless it was indisputable. There's just very little hard evidence because the Institute covered their tracks well."

"I can find out where I came from?" I felt her through the bond, ever so vulnerable all of a sudden.

"Only if that's what you want." Dusk handed Shatter her own envelope.

Her hands shook as she took it. "Is this… real?"

"It is."

"You okay, Nightshade?" Umbra asked as he sat beside Dusk, his gaze fixed on her.

She nodded, drawing the envelope against her chest.

"You think you want to open it?" I asked, leaning closer and tucking her hair behind her ear.

"I'm not sure. Maybe… you guys go first?"

"Dusk goes first," Umbra said, turning his file in his hand. "Since he might be the only one."

Dusk caught my eye, shaking his head. Neither of us believed Umbra was seriously going to chuck his past into the flames. Dusk tapped his envelope for a moment, looking around at us. I don't think I'd ever seen him this nervous.

"I mean, we could just all—" Umbra leaned forward, about to drop his in the fire. Dusk grabbed his hand with a growl.

"Just. Wait. I'm going to look."

Umbra scoffed. "Why does that matter for me?"

"What if I find something… good and then you want to, as well?" I asked.

Umbra cocked an eyebrow but shrugged. "Go on, then."

With a breath, and not wasting another second, Dusk tugged out the paper from within his envelope

We were all silent, Shatter clutching hers to her chest with eyes wide as Dusk scanned the page.

I watched as his brows furrowed, jaw clenching.

"What… what does it say?" Shatter whispered.

"Uh…" Dusk seemed lost.

Umbra peeked over his shoulder, reading over the words.

His eyebrows rose.

"Tell us," Shatter begged.

"Looks like…" Umbra scanned a bit longer. "Grew up in New Oxford. He was a… street kid pickpocket turned con artist…" Umbra read on. "…Ejected from the Harpy gang after an unexplained seizure ruined a heist operation. Aura triggered upon rejection from the community. Admitted to Cimmerian Vaults due to chronic IAVD… It says the Doctors theorise illness is connected to the seizures, which are also… idiopathic in nature or…" He frowned. "Something like that?"

"What… does that mean?" I asked.

"Chronic idiopathic aura volatility disorder," Shatter supplied. "AVD. It's when an alpha goes into violent rages they can't control. It's really rare, but happens mostly when someone's aura emerges for the first time because of extreme trauma. Only… that type of AVD is often temporary or curable. Chronic idiopathic AVD, though, that means… Well…" She trailed off awkwardly. "Well, it means they don't know why it happens, and it won't stop."

There was a strange silence, and Shatter slipped from my lap, tugging the papers from Dusk's grip and peering over them.

He let her take them, looking a little shell-shocked.

He cocked his head. "I was put in one of the most secure facilities for dangerous alphas on the continent, and they don't even know why?" he asked, stunned.

"Oh—but, look," Shatter said. "Decebal connected it all—he knew all the time, right? He thinks after you got the Atropa's poison, most of the AVD symptoms vanished. Even your seizures became much more intermittent. That's…" She frowned. "Well, that's fascinating. You haven't had any seizures in ages, right? Decebal said a few when you first got out, but that's it?"

"The trials…" Umbra had to cover his spluttered laugh with a cough. "Cured you?"

Dusk tugged the paper back. "This all has to be wrong."

Umbra snorted. "What did you want it to say?"

"I don't know. Not this. Something… dramatic, like I went crazy and lost control of my aura while protecting my baby siblings from a bad guy or something? Like… heroic."

"You *were* heroic." Umbra scoffed. "Apparently, you got five high-ranking members of the Harpy gang apprehended because you elbowed the fire alarm when you went down."

"Decebal got the wrong file."

"What about family?" I asked curiously. "Do you have siblings?"

"No," Shatter said, scanning the document again.

"So… you were a spoiled Harpy-runner only child."

"I'm not Harpy," Dusk snapped.

"No, you're not," Umbra said. "Says here they didn't want you after that, anyway."

Dusk picked up his hot chocolate, as if wanting to find something to do with his hands as he glared into the fire. "That was lame as fuck," he grumbled at last.

"Exactly why I'm burning mine," Umbra said with a grin.

"What if there's someone out there looking for you?" I asked.

Umbra's frown was stiff for a moment as he looked down at the paper. "There isn't." He looked at Shatter. "What about you, Nightshade?"

"I…" She chewed on her lip. "What do you think? Maybe… could someone read it and tell me if I should?"

I shook my head. "I don't think that's a good idea."

"Why not?" she asked.

"Because if we know, and it's not good… I don't know. You'll always wonder. And besides, Decebal has seen them. If there was anyone looking for you, he would…" I frowned, realising what I was about to say.

"So… there's no one," she whispered.

My throat was dry, but she steeled herself, always so much stronger than I gave her credit for. She swallowed, glancing between us, and looking sure as she crossed back to me and settled into my lap.

"What are you thinking, Little Reaper?" I asked.

Shatter

Are you sure? a little voice asked as I held the envelope over the flame.

This was it, and somehow, it felt final.

But seeing Dusk read his had changed my mind in a way I didn't expect.

His was *wrong*.

Nothing I'd read on that paper had anything to do with the alpha I knew. He'd changed so much since the experiments, been forged into something so different, that I'd lost all faith in anything these strokes of ink on paper could mean.

There *was* a person on this paper. A girl turned omega with a past and a life.

Maybe it was good.

Maybe it wasn't.

But she wasn't me.

And good or bad… Would it haunt me? Or might it change things?

I met Umbra's sandstorm eyes, the curve of a smile on my lips as I dropped mine first. He grinned, matching me, and we both stared as the corners of the paper curled to black in the flickering flames and turned to ash before our very eyes.

No.

This pack was my family—more than I could ever have dreamed when I'd stepped up to those academy doors, a broken omega in search of my mates. Now I knew I wouldn't change anything. Not one second, not for the whole world.

EPILOGUE ONE

Dusk

The sand was hot against my bare feet.

I had never been on a beach vacation before, or any, actually, but today the sun, the sand, and the sound of the ocean crashing behind me made it the most nerve-racking thing in the entire world.

"Why is *this* the scariest thing we've ever done?" I asked as Ransom fixed my cufflink. "I mean, we've done some wild shit."

My heart was slamming against my ribs and had been for the last hour.

Ransom grinned. "I think it's the first time I've been the least worried out of all of us."

Umbra was on one of the fold-out seats in a neat suit, fingers clasped, eyes shut like he was saying a prayer.

We'd told Shatter we were going to Disneyland, and the lie had stuck unexpectedly well, since she had no idea that Disneyland wasn't on a tropical island. Or that, usually, your best friends weren't flown in for a weekend of your vacation.

"She said beach wedding, right?" I asked. "It was definitely a—"

"It was a beach wedding," Ransom confirmed with a grin.

"What if this wasn't what she had in mind—?"

"Dusk." Ransom nudged me lightly. "It's everything she wanted. Get a grip."

"What about the ring?" I asked. "There are all these traditions. I don't think we're supposed to just use the one we already—"

"It's perfect, and it's the one we're giving her," he said. "Like any of this is traditional, anyway."

Umbra chuckled. "She literally can't wear it face up. It's the *one*."

And, oddly enough, a parting gift from Mord, who had, before he vanished, told Decebal which pocket Eric had tucked it away in.

"Right, but—"

"I do not owe Mord Sato a favor just for you to get cold feet on the fucking ring." Decebal's voice came floating from up the steps. I glanced to see him approaching, dressed in a white button-up and shorts. Upon his head was the most offensive and ridiculous straw hat I'd ever seen. Probably good, since he was pale as death and might burn to a crisp in five seconds flat otherwise.

"I was going to ask if you were nervous, but I think it's rather obvious." Decebal chuckled.

I'd been having trouble taking a full breath since I'd woken up this morning. She was not far off, in a room somewhere, getting ready with Roxy, unknowingly preparing to walk down the aisle to us.

"Do you think maybe the surprise has gone a bit far?" I asked. "What if she runs?"

She *had* fled with the ring.

Ransom snorted. "I am pretty fucking sure she'd stress more than you if she knew what was coming."

"What if she's upset it isn't Disneyland?"

"Already got it covered," Umbra said, straightening his button-up. "Backup tickets booked, in case that's an issue."

"We're… going to Disneyland for real after this?" I asked.

Umbra shrugged. "If she wants to."

"Wait," I said, a bit offended. "*I* want to."

"Well, then, guess we're going."

"I can't do it."

"Yes, you can, girl."

"N-no, you don't understand. I really don't—" I cut off as Roxy seized me. I couldn't walk down the aisle—*aisle*, as in a wedding. A wedding—because I'd finally figured it out.

On a beach.

Oh no.

I was going to throw up.

"Shatter. Look at me. You're going to be fine."

"Roxy," I hissed. "Help me. I'm going to cry the whole time."

"You're allowed to cry the whole time."

"No, I'm not—"

"It's your wedding. You can do whatever you want."

I turned at a knock on the door, and it cracked open. I panicked for a moment; if it was one of my pack, they weren't supposed to see!

But instead, I saw a familiar face, and my mouth popped open in shock.

"Aunty…?" My voice was weak, my heart suddenly in my throat.

Aunty Lauren?

She wore a neat skirt and button-up with a small brown purse held tight to her chest. She was everything I remembered, down to the gentle look in her kind eyes.

"Little One…" She seemed lost for words.

My hand was over my mouth as Aunty Lauren crossed the room in a strange, stunned silence and pulled me into a hug that smelled like fresh linen. So familiar and comforting. Then she drew back, examining my face, her eyes glistening with tears.

"I never thought… our sweet Shatter? Getting married? And…" Her eyes fell on the bond on my neck. It was glittering and silver right now. The bite Dusk had left turned from dark to light, drowning out the other marks around it from Flynn and Gareth.

She stared at it for a long moment, and then her whole expression crumpled and she burst into tears.

"Eugene told me… oh, what you must have done, Little One."

Right, Uncle had all the pieces.

"You must love these alphas."

"So much," I whispered.

Her lips turned up in a smile, and she nudged a few of her tears away. "Shatter, I'm sorry we didn't believe you. This is everything you deserve and more."

Before I knew it, I'd grabbed her into a hug again, shaking with... well, I didn't know what.

Love?

She'd come.

Like my mother might... Like family.

"I don't know how I'm going to do this," I whispered, wringing my hands. "They're waiting out there for me, and I have to go out there and... and do things. And say things."

The little piece of paper was in Roxy's hand.

On the flight over, Roxy had helped me write out a little line about why I loved all of my alphas so fucking much.

Vows.

It all made sense now.

But I had to say them out loud and not break.

"Nonsense," Aunty said. "You are going to be just fine. I've seen you fight through much harder things."

"There *are* no harder things," I wailed.

"Shatter, look at me." Roxy's voice, and her orange and Christmas scent, swept over me. "Take a breath. We'll be here the whole time."

Umbra

The moment Shatter stepped from between the trees just up the beach, everything else in the whole world faded away. Her golden eyes were wide and her grip was like a vice on Roxy's arm as she approached, her lips parted in shock.

Music had started, but I couldn't really hear it. None of my senses were working right.

Shatter wore the most beautiful cream-white dress, loose and free enough to match the beach we were on. It billowed in the wind as tears streaked her face. Her feet were bare, and delicate golden jewellery adorned her wrists and ankles, along with the beautiful shimmer of gold Roxy had painted upon her at the ball, emphasising every bite upon her skin. In her hands was a bouquet of tropical flowers, and her hair was loose, with petals woven through it, glossy honey brown waves rustling in the wind.

It took a lifetime for her to reach us, and during that time, I saw her first tear fall. Roxy helped her find the right place to stand before stepping back, taking the bouquet with her.

The turnout was small, just my pack, Roxy, Shatter's Aunty Lauren, and Decebal.

Our perfect little world, all here.

We didn't need any more.

The officiant began to speak, but I couldn't take my eyes off her, barely registering the words he was saying. My omega was trembling, and whenever she dared peek up, I saw the glittering tears that were flooding her cheeks.

The officiant seemed a little concerned, but no one else understood.

When it was her turn to speak, Roxy handed her a folded piece of paper, then had to help her open it since her fingers were shaking so badly.

This part, they could see, with her quivering lip and glassy eyes, but it was only a small piece of what she was. The other half, the part of her spirit that lit the bond, that part was a thousand times more than what the world would ever know. She was so bright and full of joy that I wasn't surprised she was shaking. I don't think there was any physical manifestation in the world that could truly reflect who she was right now.

But that was okay, because *we* knew.

Tears still tumbled from her cheeks, smudging the ink on the piece of paper as she tried, again and again, to speak her side of the vows. And finally, when she was finished, I plucked the handkerchief from my breast pocket and handed it to her, and she wiped away her tears before I stepped forward.

"Oh—I, uh…" The officiant seemed thrown.

I didn't know why.

This was perfect.

Everything was as it should be.

It was then that I realised that, despite all of her attempts, Shatter hadn't managed to speak a single word. Yet everything she'd meant to say had come through the bond already. I took Shatter's hand in mine, finding the ring from my pocket.

The first piece of three.

A thousand demons I'd faced in my life, and every battle was worth it to get to this moment, yet never had *my* hand trembled as much as it did right now.

Oh. Well, fuck, we couldn't both be shaking.

Her delicate fingers blurred in my vision, and the ring wouldn't stay steady. I tried to take a breath.

This was important.

She needed me to pull myself together.

Her other hand took mine, steadying it somehow, despite her own nerves, and I looked back into golden eyes that glittered with a thousand joyful tears in the setting sun.

My chest unwound, my breath came again, and finally, my head steadied. I slipped the ring onto her finger, suddenly captivated by the way it looked. The first part of the hexagon pattern, unfinished and waiting for completion.

Waiting for my brothers.

I felt a broad smile on my face as I lifted her, drawing her into a kiss.

The officiant was saying something, but I didn't hear much, just a rushed, *"You may kiss…"*

The words vanished as my lips met hers.

Her fingers wound through my hair.

When I leaned back, she was clutching me desperately, eyes bright and tears finally clearing.

"I love you, too, Little Nightshade."

Ransom

I don't know if I'd been able to take a full breath of air since the moment I'd seen her in that white dress. It was beautiful, cream white, and thin enough to flow in the light wind, with two thin straps that left all her bites revealed—bites she'd embraced with pride.

Even from here, I could see Dusk's; a mark that was once black, now pearly white and glittering in the sun.

I hadn't seen anything in the world with such beauty as when I stared down the aisle at my bride.

After Umbra had kissed her, Dusk stepped forward, pulling out his third of the ring. I'd never felt him more anxious as he slipped it onto her finger, where it slotted right into place beside Umbra's.

He cupped her cheek and she leaned into that touch.

"You are our missing piece, Shatter," he breathed. "You fought for us when we couldn't, and you became the one who made us whole."

Her smile was breathtaking as Dusk leaned down, and with more tenderness than I'd ever seen, he pressed his lips to hers.

I was last.

I stepped forward, drawing her into my arms, feeling her shaking.

"I can't wait to spend the rest of my life with you," I whispered. A life that, without her, I wouldn't have. "You saved me, Little Reaper."

My lips brushed hers, and every shift of my skin on hers was like static. When I drew back, she shifted, tilting her head to the side just a little. I reacted on pure instinct, my teeth brushing her neck over the shimmering silver, then I bit down, offering her the final bite she would ever need

My bond.

My bite.

My wife.

And, of course, because the wedding couldn't possibly end any other way, upon our connection, her scent detonated in the air like a blast of confetti. She drew back, eyes wild, pupils blown wide as she stared at me.

"Oh…" In her dazed eyes, I could almost see the heat haze taking hold. "Oh, *bother.*"

EPILOGUE TWO

Shatter

My amazing husbands swept me to our honeymoon home in one hell of a hurry. Luckily, it wasn't far away. We were staying in a bungalow over pristine blue water, but I would have to take a better look at that later because, right now, I was happy when the doors had closed.

I didn't know who was holding me until I caught the scent of lily of the valley.

"Ransom." My voice was a low whine.

"I got you, Little Reaper," he told me, and then there was soft bedding beneath me.

I felt firm hands at my dress, but I let out a whine of impatience, an ache growing in my stomach.

"Now." My voice was demanding, and there was a ripping sound. Good. The dress was so nice, but it all had to go.

I *needed* them.

I could barely think straight, heat boiling in my veins, needing relief until—

I groaned, my fingers tangling in Umbra's hair as he tugged my knees apart, panties aside, and entered me without hesitation. My eyes rolled back to find wooden panels above.

"Mmm…"

Dusk settled beside me, pulling off the rest of my clothes as Ransom's lips brushed the burning skin of my neck, then down to my breast as he caught my nipple in his teeth.

Fuck yes.

Umbra drew me close, turning us so he was below and I was on top. He gripped my hips, dragging me over his length, and I let out a whimper of pleasure as he drove deep into my core. I moaned, bowing over him as his huge length gave me the relief I needed.

The room came into focus as Dusk's fingers curled in my hair, dragging me up. Around me was the white canopy of a pack-sized bed that faced a broad window overlooking the ocean. My vision swam as Umbra gripped my hips tighter, slamming up and into me again, and I grabbed at Dusk's wrist, the sound I made purely feral.

"You're so fucking perfect, Shatter," Dusk growled. "Going into heat on our wedding day."

The praise heated my blood.

"I want you," I whined, my eyes wide as I stared up into bright yellow eyes. "I want you all."

I bit my lip as Ransom settled in behind me. The room was full of natural woods and tropical decor, but if it had a scent, I didn't know it. All I knew was theirs: midnight opium, wolfsbane and blood, and lily of the valley.

My pack.

Ransom's hand found my clit, making me see stars.

The first orgasm came fast, and Umbra took my chin, making sure I was looking into his sandstorm eyes as I let out a gasp, my whole body shaking as he dragged me over his knot. It was bliss, the rush of heat cooling as he filled me.

I couldn't take my eyes from his as my nails dug into his chest, feeling all the little lines and scars, ones that would, at last, never change from what they were right now.

"You want us all, Gem?" Dusk's voice was a low growl.

I let out a needy sound, adjusting over Umbra's knot, my eyes crossing with how good it felt.

Ransom moved closer behind me, his finger still working my clit as I felt pressure at my back door. "Relax, Little Reaper," he breathed, his teeth grazing my ear.

The burn felt good as he stretched me out, going slow enough that I wiggled back against Umbra to no success, trapped as I was.

Dusk grinned, and Ransom let out a groan of pleasure as he filled me completely. My hormones surged, and my fingers fumbled for Dusk's zipper, wild with lust.

It wasn't enough. *All* of them. I needed to be claimed by all of them.

"Tongue out." Dusk didn't have a dark bond anymore, but I obeyed him without question. He guided his cock down my throat as Ransom drew out and began fucking me with long strokes.

Beneath me, I could feel Umbra release a breath of pleasure, and he pinched one of my nipples in one hand, the other taking over at my clit as Ransom settled his grip on my hips so he could speed up his pace.

Another blissful sound rose in my chest, half a purr stuttering to life as they claimed me like this.

The raging heat died to a warm buzz in my tummy.

My eyes were fixed on Dusk as he pressed his length all the way into my throat and Ransom stretched me out on his knot just a little, as if getting a feel for if I could take him.

Fuck...

Another orgasm swept through me at just the idea of it, my eyes crossing as Dusk began pumping into my mouth, his hand in my hair giving him absolute control.

"You're so beautiful, Gem," Dusk growled. "Trapped and taking us all like this. Our omega, with every perfect hole claimed."

I moaned as he held his length deep within me, and my lips pressed to his knot and Ransom stretched out my back door again, his knot pressing in once more. I was shaking with sensation.

Umbra squeezed my breast, speeding up on my clit. My veins were alight with pleasure, as if the orgasm was ongoing, waves crashing into me over and over as I stared up at my pack lead, his dark skin a canvas that mirrored my own, a reverent look in his eyes and pupils blown wide.

"You're ours, Shatter," Ransom growled from behind me as Dusk drew out and let me catch my breath for only a second longer. "Forever."

Their bites glittered on my skin, their ring on my finger, and now they were claiming me through my heat.

Totally and utterly.

The heat burned on throughout the night, and there was never a moment when one of my alphas wasn't claiming me.

Even when Dusk dipped out to grab us energy drinks and snacks, they didn't stop. Not even as I shivered with more orgasms than I should be able to manage. Umbra held my arms behind my back as Ransom kneeled before me, his fingers dropping between my legs.

"Little Reaper," he growled, his teeth grazing the sensitive part of my inner thigh and making me shiver, "I don't want you losing a drop." I moaned as I felt him use two fingers, pressing the cum that had leaked from my cunt back in.

His other hand squeezed my breast as he played with me like that for a while, two fingers pumping their seed back into me as I arched against him, the stimulation too much and not enough at the same time.

By the time Dusk returned, I'd begged for Ransom's knot, and he was rutting me gently, hands roaming my body as his knot locked the seed he had spilled into me. Umbra kept my arms behind my back, kissing me long and deep as I shuddered with another orgasm.

At some point, I passed out, exhausted and locked onto Dusk's knot, only to wake to a burning ache in my stomach. Dusk wasn't locked against me anymore, but Umbra was there. He had tucked me in his arms, his scent of wolfsbane and blood filling my senses, turning me desperate in a moment.

He blinked bleary eyes open beside me, seeming to pick up on my distress in an instant. He lifted me over him so that I had to catch myself on the headboard as he dragged his tongue up along my clit and buried his fingers into my cunt, a low purr in his chest as I sighed, the ache dying down at his touch.

Ransom blinked, waking slowly, but lily of the valley spiked with lust the second he saw me, and the next thing I knew, he was up on his knees and I was reaching out for him, desperately needy. His tip pressed between my lips as Umbra pumped his fingers into me faster, and I moaned in sleepy bliss.

The first wave of heat hadn't passed yet, though, and I don't think I've ever had one this intense.

I felt so loved as they took care of me, never leaving me long enough that the ache in my core grew too much. The time blurred together.

…I was locked over Dusk's knot as Ransom held my arms behind my back and Umbra took me from behind…

…Dusk held my shivering body in the warm stream of the shower, pressing kisses across every inch of me as he buried his knot into me beneath the water. I was so dazed I didn't know how we'd got there, only that I was begging for him…

…Sweat glistened across Umbra's rich tan skin as he caged me in, driving into me from behind, each thrust choking me on Ransom's length…

I passed out again but woke completely claimed, a vicious orgasm tearing through my blood that made me shake with bliss and moans that were trapped in my chest.

There was a cock buried to the edge of a knot in my core and one pressing down my throat as I felt another pressure behind me. Not in my ass, this time.

"Good girl," Dusk growled. "Relax. Let Umbra claim that throat while Ransom and I take this sweet cunt together."

"Mmm…" My body all but melted beneath them, and Umbra's fist in my hair was all that held me up as he slid into my mouth, slow and gentle. I shivered as I felt that pressure again, and Dusk stretched me out more than I had been since the last time they both claimed me there.

I was still shivering from the overwhelming lust at being woken like this, but I whined desperately, overwhelmed as Dusk fucked me with long strokes beside Ransom's cock, and Umbra dragged me over his length, claiming my throat.

The feral growls from Ransom sent me over the edge, and the orgasm that found me wiped my mind completely blank.

Dusk

Waking Shatter to an orgasm that intense was enough to break her heat.

And break *her*, apparently.

I thought everything had been going great. Sure, this heat felt like running a marathon and we were barely keeping up, but it was worth it. She was a golden-eyed lynx, absolutely desperate for us, sexy and fucking demanding in the best way.

She was so fucking beautiful right now, having been pulled into Umbra's arms. She was glowing with her heat. She might not be wearing a scrap of clothing, but her long waves tumbled over her body, giving me occasional peeks at the tanned flesh of her breasts as she shifted. A few of the thin golden chains had survived, delicately resting around her wrists and ankles, and the ring we'd given her glinted on her finger in the moonlight.

A true goddess.

But… something had gone wrong. She'd trembled with an orgasm that had lit the bond like nothing else I'd ever felt, and then devolved into a shivering mess.

At first, I thought she was crying, but now…

Umbra looked at us, confused, as she shook with silent tears of…

Well…

Those were tears of laughter.

"I'm…" She tried to take a breath. "I'm sorry…"

Ransom shot me a concerned look. "Did we do something… funny?"

"I don't… I don't know," she gasped. "I just can't—" She cut off with a splutter. "I can't stop." Another uncontrollable giggle escaped her, and she grabbed Umbra by the arm to bury her face against him, clutching him harder as she shook. Umbra was peering at her like she was a curious puzzle.

"I—I'm *serious,*" she choked out, giggles seizing her once more, making her words jittery. "I can't stop. I—I don't know why." Her expression was caught between mirth and bafflement. "Help me!" she squeaked.

Umbra grabbed his phone from the side table and typed something into it, but I could feel the curve of a smile on my lips.

"Is it a bad thing?" I asked.

As cute as it was, listening to the sound of her giggles muffled in Umbra's chest, it *sounded* kind of bad.

"No…" Shatter shook her head, wide, teary eyes finding me. "No—it was great. I'm great." That was all she could get out before she burst into another round of laughter.

"Ha." Umbra said, looking up as he set his phone down.

"What?"

"Endorphin rush." He looked smug.

"It… it was," Shatter choked out. "I mean, you both…" She spluttered into another round of giggles as she glanced between me and Ransom. "*How* do you both fit?"

Umbra barked a laugh this time and swept her tighter into his arms, holding her close.

"So, it's a good thing?" I asked, a little worried.

"Looks like…" Ransom had grabbed the phone, skimming the page. When he looked up, there was a very smug expression on his face. "We fucked her too good."

Shatter

The whole strange laughing orgasm broke my heat, which was good, because while I had the intention of banging my alphas plenty more, there were beach things to be done.

Well.

In the morning.

Right now, I'd woken in the middle of the night, chugging enough electrolyte drinks to get me through six heats as I considered the strange realisation I'd woken with. Heat, I think, meant being in touch with my omega side, and I think I had an answer to a question that had been nagging at me.

I dug out my phone, finding the text feature (the real one this time), and pulled up Decebal's contact.

Me: This is Shatter.

Me: Do you talk to Mord?

I stared at the phone, and to my delight, he replied.

Decebal: Not if I can help it.

Me: Can you give me his number? I know what the other half of his scent is.

Decebal: I'm not giving you Mord Sato's number. Dusk would strangle me with his bare hands.

Decebal: But what's his scent? I've never been able to tell.

Me: Promise you'll tell him.

Decebal: Fine.

Me: Okay. Don't make fun of me. I know it sounds crazy. I just woke up, and I knew.

Decebal: Now I'm really curious

Me: Ebony and moon dust.

Decebal: How the fuck do you know what moon dust smells like?

Me: Don't question my instincts. I saved everyone.

Me: You promised me you'd tell him. You have to.

Me: And tell him I don't think he's nearly as mean as he wants people to think.

Decebal: There is no chance in hell that I'm texting New Oxford's most dangerous mercenary at 2 in the morning to tell him the crazy weapon-of-war omega thinks he smells like moon dust.

I scowled.

Me: Okay. Morning is acceptable.

Me: Also. Dusk told me about your pack mate and the aura sickness. I'm really sorry.

Decebal: Thanks. It's been rough.

Me: How's the pack doing?

Decebal: Honestly, not great. Everything's absolute havoc right now, especially the bond. We weren't exactly stable before.

Me: You definitely need an omega.

Decebal: No luck yet.

Me: You will.

Me: I trust.

Me: You're going to get your scent match and a princess bond, just like you always wanted. Angel will be better in no time.

I shut off my phone and lay back down, climbing in between Dusk, Umbra, and Ransom and passing back out with ease.

By morning, I was completely refreshed and ready for the honeymoon. We had the rest of our vacation to try out the local food, go shell hunting on the beach, and snorkel in the ocean off the edge of our bungalow—which sounded great until I spotted a shark. No amount of convincing from my alphas could make me dip a toe in after that. I was, however, happy to watch them risk it from a deck chair with an iced drink.

Umbra was happy to swim until he turned into a prune, and I wondered if he was reconsidering his dislike for marine biology. He had enrolled in a culinary program and woodworking, alongside Ransom, for next term, so he would have room in his schedule.

It was going to be amazing. I would be in classes with Dusk and Roxy, and I would be living on campus with my pack, threat-free at last, with all the studying in the world to do.

That evening, we curled up on the bed with the view of the stars through the ceiling window, and I brushed my finger along my ring. Three layers of uneven diamonds.

Perfection.

My purr rumbled to life as my chest uncoiled, and I took my first true breath with the realisation that *this* was it. The start of my happily ever after with my alphas.

At the start of this all, I'd set out to find my mates with the belief that I would never be worthy of love—that I would have to beg them to take me.

Instead, I had found so much more than that.

The end.

CHAPTER 15

Summary

The Lincoln pack hold the FMC in their room. They film the interaction, and also bite her a number of times (non-bonding marks).

Roxy comes to the door, but Eric doesn't let her in. They use a Sharpie to write on her, then remove her from the apartment.

The FMC realizes during the scene that they seem to be changing, shifting from competition with other alphas to obsessive about her. The FMC is worried that they might realize the scent match, so she uses Dusk (telling them she wants him) in order to keep them in their competitive mindset, which she believes will keep her safest. She escapes without them discovering the scent match.

Before she leaves, Eric empties her pencil case onto the floor and tells her she won't be wanted by alphas ever again. The FMC runs, leaving her registration card behind.

You can continue reading from Chapter 16, in which there is a brief threat of SA that goes nowhere and is swiftly dealt with.

Made in the USA
Monee, IL
11 April 2025

7cbf4151-fb46-435b-9948-24c942949754R01